CAMBRIA

CAMBRIAN PICTURES

OR

EVERY ONE HAS ERRORS

ANN OF SWANSEA

With an introduction by Elizabeth Edwards

WELSH WOMEN'S CLASSICS

First published in 1810 by E. Kerry, London;
reissued in 1813 by the Minerva Press, London
First published by Honno in 2021, from the Minerva Press edition.
'Ailsa Craig', Heol y Cawl, Dinas Powys, Wales. CF64 4AH

ISBN: 978-1-912905-29-4 paperback
ISBN: 978-1-912905-29-4 ebook

Printed with the financial support of the Books Council of Wales

Cover image: I. Havell, Singing to the Harp and Dancing, 1814
Cover design: Graham Preston
Text design: Elaine Sharples
Printed by 4edge Limited

INTRODUCTION

ELIZABETH EDWARDS

i. 'God knows who she is!': introducing Ann of Swansea

> 'Ann of Swansea,' was unquestionably a great genius, and Swansea has reason to be proud of the name she assumed. Had she lived 100 years later, judging from the numerous successful publications now-a-days, she would have met with a very different reward.[1]

'Ann of Swansea', the pen-name of Ann Julia Hatton (1764-1838), published poetry and fiction from the 1780s to the 1830s. Had she indeed lived and written a century later, she would have been the contemporary of novelists previously re-published by Honno Classics, such as Allen Raine (Anne Adaliza Puddicombe; 1836-1908), Amy Dillwyn (1845-1935), and Hilda Vaughan (1892-1985). In later historical and commercial contexts, her novels might have been bestsellers, as Raine's were. Or her compelling biography and Swansea connections might have produced the sort of interest that Dillwyn now inspires. This introduction to Hatton's now little-known first novel, *Cambrian Pictures; or, Every One Has Errors* (1810), both places her back in her early nineteenth-century moment, and outlines her relevance for our own. This reprint also contributes to a longer sense of continuity in Welsh women's writing, reaching beyond Victorian figures like Dillwyn and Raine to include an earlier era of fiction.

Hatton was not always obscure. Sometimes noted in the late-nineteenth century as a Swansea luminary, in her own lifetime the influential critic Leigh Hunt grouped her with novelists who remain household names today: Frances Burney, Ann Radcliffe, Maria Edgeworth, Charles Maturin and Walter Scott, among others. Hatton was the only Welsh-identified author on Hunt's list, which dates from 1833. But her Welsh status, and particularly the Swansea aspect of her writing life, is significant for several reasons, not least her reception history. As a young journalist in 1932, Dylan Thomas, for example, described Hatton as 'the first local writer of anything approaching importance', in one of the lines of connection through time that defines her as a writer who matters.[2]

For Leigh Hunt a century earlier, Hatton's Swansea identity was in fact her only one, or so he claimed in print. Although Hatton was a notorious figure for biographical reasons (outlined below), her real name and her pseudonyms – she tried out several before settling on 'Ann of Swansea' – were not necessarily interchangeable. In a comment as vicious as it is flattering, Leigh Hunt suggests that the women novelists on his list

> sometimes write as if they had not learnt the first rudiments of grammar; yet with surprising acuteness, liberality of sentiment, and insight into men and manners; of which our beloved Anne [sic] of Swansea (God knows who she is!) is an instance.[3]

No fan of Hatton's style – '[s]he writes … like an inspired lady's maid' – Hunt nonetheless praises her liberal perspective and searching plotlines. It seems significant that he made these comments in the radical 1830s newspaper *The True Sun*:

Hatton's novels, which are shaped by themes of power, wealth, class, moral decency, self-determination and equality, evidently appealed to him despite his dismissive tone.

So who was Hatton, and why where these her themes? Her biography is a dramatic one, but as a chronicle of disadvantage and dispossession it also suggests reasons for her sympathy with marginalised figures, and longstanding concern for fairness and personal freedom. She was born at Worcester in April 1764 to Sarah Ward and Roger Kemble, part of an Anglo-Irish family of itinerant actors. By the early 1780s, Hatton's eldest sister, Sarah Siddons, was becoming a celebrity on the London stage; her brothers John Philip Kemble and Charles Kemble would also become well-known actors. From childhood, Hatton's prospects had looked more limited than those of her siblings: she suffered from a physical disability (a form of lameness) that apparently prevented her from joining the theatre business. Details of her early life are scant, but she began writing seriously at a young age, publishing her first poetry collection, *Poems on Miscellaneous Subjects*, in 1784. The preface to this text, however, alludes to the 'Difficulties' she had already faced in her short life.

The collection was published under her married name, Ann Curtis, though it also prominently advertised her status as Siddons's sister on the title page. Her marriage at the age of sixteen to the otherwise unknown Curtis, an actor, was a personal disaster: he turned out to be a bigamist and the marriage was annulled. What Hatton delicately terms 'Difficulties' in her *Poems* also included working for the controversial electro-sexual therapist Dr James Graham from 1780, attempting suicide in Westminster Abbey in 1783, and later, in 1789, an episode in which she was the victim of a shooting at Covent Garden (perhaps while working as a prostitute). All of these events were dragged through the London press, but Hatton fought back, soliciting the help of her now-famous actor siblings via newspaper advertisements. The scandals combined with the press coverage must have had some effect: Siddons and John Kemble offered Hatton an annuity of £90 on condition that she lived at least 150 miles from London. Rejection from her family in this way was a painful experience – she later wrote that 'the errors and indiscretions of a girl of sixteen did not deserve so long a life of abandonment' – but the annuity enabled her to marry William Hatton, a London violin maker, in 1792.[4]

The couple emigrated to New York later that year, in a move that invigorated Hatton's writing. Her new life in America coincided with the ongoing political consequences of the French Revolution, and she lost no time in writing poetry in support of democracy and republicanism. By March 1794, Hatton had written the libretto for *Tammany, or the Indian Chief*, an opera depicting (and denouncing) the extreme corruption and violence of white colonisers.[5] Forced to leave New York after an outbreak of yellow fever, the Hattons returned to Britain via Nova Scotia, settling in Swansea in 1799, where they leased the town's bathing house. On William Hatton's death in 1806, Hatton gave up the bathing house and moved to Kidwelly, where she briefly ran a school for young ladies. By 1809, she was back in Swansea, where she lived and wrote until her death in 1838.

Hatton's Swansea writing life includes at least fourteen novels published between 1810 and 1831. It is very likely, however, that she had been writing consistently throughout the events outlined above. In 1811 she published her second poetry collection, *Poetic Trifles*, under the name 'Ann of Swansea', which she had used for *Cambrian Pictures* the previous year. The sheer size of *Poetic Trifles*, at nearly 400 pages long, is evidence that she wrote the collection over many years, while authorial notes within the text also state that particular individual pieces were written long before they were published. Yet Hatton is not always easy to find in literary and historical archives on account of the various names she lived by and published under: Ann Kemble, Ann Curtis and Ann Hatton are just the start. Tracing her writing after 1800 involves several new and similar-sounding names, especially in relation to her newspaper poetry, which appeared mainly in the Swansea paper *The Cambrian*. Between 1800 and 1810, she published at various points as Ann of Kidwelly, Julia of Kidwelly and Julia of Swansea, in addition to Ann of Swansea.

None of these names are particularly recognisable today. But the 'Ann of Swansea' pen-name is one of the most striking aspects of Hatton's writing career as whole. As Jane Aaron explains, 'Ann's recreation of herself as Welsh, an unusual move in any epoch, was in the first decade of the nineteenth century virtually unprecedented.'[6] By using the name she chose to appear on her work after 1810, the title page of this edition therefore follows the original style of *Cambrian Pictures* and almost all of the novels that followed it. It also emphasises the Welsh aspect of her identity, a key element in her career as a novelist in general and in *Cambrian Pictures* in particular.

ii. Introducing *Cambrian Pictures*

Hatton's first novel centres on Wales and Welshness from the title and authorial pseudonym onwards. Signposting location in this way is a fair reflection of the novel that follows, which is mainly if not exclusively set in Wales (Devon, Cumberland and Italy also feature as important sites in terms of the plot). Featuring a huge cast of characters and a complicated, fast-moving narrative played out over three volumes, *Cambrian Pictures* is at its simplest the intertwining story of two friends, Henry Mortimer and Horatio Delamere. The novel opens with a prefatory masquerade scene and a debate on the pros and cons of marriage. The presence at the event of the mysterious figure of Delamere – handsome, wealthy but unaccountably single – prompts the unknown narrator to delve into Delamere's backstory, which, he reasons, will help him to settle the debate. The novel that follows reveals that story.

The plot begins in north Wales with Henry Mortimer as a baby, born to the son of peer who has been cut off by his family for marrying the daughter of a poor vicar. Henry is quickly orphaned, leaving him to be raised at Dolgelly Castle near Caernarfon by friends of his parents, Sir Owen and Lady Llewellyn, whose daughter Adeline becomes his adopted younger sister. The Welsh setting of the novel deepens via depictions of local life, which draw further characters into the world of the Llewellyns; Adeline's lively best friend Eliza Tudor and her family, for example, open up several subplots throughout the novel. Towards the end of the first volume, Henry, now aged twenty, is abducted by a much-older dowager duchess, whom he has refused to marry (in defiance of his grandfather's wishes). Hoping to coerce Henry into changing his mind, the duchess imprisons him at her castle in Cumberland, from which he is eventually rescued by Horatio Delamere.

Back in Wales, Henry falls increasingly in love with Adeline; meanwhile the Montgomerys, an East Indian nabob and his family, arrive on the north Wales scene. In contrast to the thoughtful and refined Adeline, the women of the Montgomery family are the source of much comedy on account of their vulgar diction and manners, and outsize ambitions for social advancement. In a parallel strand of the plot that hints at an unreliable moral compass, Delamere travels to Italy where he embarks on an affair with a married aristocrat, with disastrous consequences. Back in Wales, Adeline reluctantly marries Henry, for whom she feels only sisterly affection, while a further family consisting of the Percivals and Jenkinses enters the narrative. Gentle but attractive, the young Rosa Percival mirrors Henry Mortimer in several ways: she is also the product of an unequal marriage (between a rakish baronet, Sir Edward Percival, and a Welsh girl); she has also been brought up by a surrogate parent, her uncle, Gabriel Jenkins, having lost her mother in babyhood and subsequently been abandoned by her father; and she is abducted and imprisoned by a wealthy lord when she refuses to marry him (it transpires that her father has effectively sold her in order to pay off his huge gambling debts). She escapes and, once again helped by Delamere, she returns safely to her home where she makes a happy marriage with the virtuous Hugh Montgomery. In the final volume of the novel, Delamere visits Henry and Adeline at Dolgelly Castle, where Delamere and Adeline fall instantly and ruinously in love. By the end of the novel, a much-chastened Horatio Delamere is left to raise Henry and Adeline's young son, Owen, alone.

This bare outline does not, however, do justice to Hatton's vibrant characters, often sparkling dialogue, and a narrative range that seems to shift effortlessly between comedy, Gothic shock, action scenes, lyrical landscape description and sentimental set-pieces. As the opening debate in the preface suggests, marriage, especially as it relates to power and/or coercion, runs as a motif through the novel. The novel's main title – *Cambrian Pictures* – similarly gestures towards its status as essentially a Welsh-set domestic drama. As a theatre of manners and morals, its subtitle – *Every One Has Errors* – is important too: each character in the novel possesses a fatal flaw, from greed to lust, pride, impetuosity, naivety, cowardice or timidity, that animates the plot. Through these cross-cutting lines of tension, and often incompatible desires or motives, themes of obsessive love, toxic masculinity and the pressures within families and friendships weave through the novel. Hatton's subtitle also, however, enables her to be perhaps surprisingly even-handed in her treatment of her cast of characters. Virtually no single villainous action or individual seems, in the end, responsible for the story's outcome.

The novel's commitment to Wales, however, matters in several ways. Setting her work in Wales, Hatton may have been trading on contemporary trends for domestic travel, which presented the north (rather than Hatton's own home of Swansea in the south) as a fashionable tourist destination. Her depiction of Dolgelly Castle as on the coastal edge of Snowdonia enables, for example, a picturesque aesthetic that she exploits to the full:

> DOLGELLY CASTLE stood delightfully elevated on a bold eminence, near the sea shore; on one side were hanging woods, through which the predecessors of Sir Owen Llewellyn had cut a road to the ancient and romantic town of Carnarvon. Situated at the distance of six miles behind it were mountains of stupendous height, and the other side

> presented rich meadows, and land in a state of the highest cultivation. The winter had been long and severe: the mountains were covered with snow, and the woods exhibited a fantastic appearance, their leafless branches being decorated with frost-work, which the keenness of the air had condensed into a variety of forms. The weather had been for many days dark and gloomy, and the little party at the castle had in vain wished to see the yellow rays of the sun illumine the gothic windows of the library, near which Adeline sat finishing a moonlight view of a ruined watchtower, that nodded in proud desolation on an adjacent mountain. (p. 34)

Yet Hatton is nothing if not versatile. Chapter 3 of the first volume features a comic-Gothic section exploring the cultural differences enabled by the novel's Welsh context. A minor character from the military, Captain Maitland, plots to seduce Gwinthlean, dairymaid to the Tudor family, arranging to meet her in the reputedly haunted 'red barn' after dark. Women are frequently in jeopardy in *Cambrian Pictures*, but this episode inverts the threat, in what Jane Aaron calls 'a rough introduction to the terrors of wild Wales'.[7] Gwinthlean's fiancé Hoel hides in the barn disguised as the devil – 'a huge terrific black figure, with cloven feet, fiery eyes, and tremendous horns' – in order to serve Maitland a form of community justice:

> [the figure] seized him in its strong grip, pinioned his arms behind him with an iron chain, threw him on his face, fastened his legs together in the same way, then swinging him across his shoulders, flew with him to the stables behind Tudor Hall, and stuck him up to his neck in a dunghill. (p. 56-7)

Ridiculed by all around him, not least his fellow officers, Maitland is forced to transfer to another regiment, abruptly exiting the novel.

One of the tensions running through the novel concerns a longstanding moral opposition between Wales and England, and between rural innocence and the corruptions of urban or metropolitan life.[8] 'Bless me … Rosa, I have heard that great people in London are nothing in the world but bags of deceit', Gabriel Jenkins observes to his niece (p. 382). Some of the novel's most powerful social comments emerge from the drama surrounding Rosa Percival, and her father Sir Edward's attempt to marry her (for money) to the dissolute Lord Clavering. When Rosa resists, her uncle Gabriel, who would rather be speaking Welsh than English ('I would speak Welsh to you, but I suppose you are not learned enough for that – it is a pity you do not understand Welsh, for I am more at home in that than English', p. 386), interprets her rejection of Clavering's proposal as a sign of her innate and specifically Welsh qualities of honour and independence.'I long', he says, 'to let them see a bit of Cambrian blood, pure and honest, neither ashamed nor afraid to refuse the gingerbread gilding of a title, when the heart does not approve the man' (p. 384).

Echoing Mary Wollstonecraft's *A Vindication of the Rights of Woman* (1792), Hatton then goes further, drawing her 1790s criticisms of slavery and colonialism into a view of the condition of women in her novel. In the words of Gabriel, Rosa is – for her father and Clavering at least – a piece of property, to be exchanged at will:

> your father would have sold you without pity, just as if you had been timber on his estate, to this Lord Clavering, and

> this noble lord would have bought you: very decent proceedings truly, just as bad to the full as if you had been a negro slave in a West-India plantation. (p. 384)

Rosa's refusal to be swayed by money or rank marks her out as the opposite of Lucretia Montgomery, daughter of a Welsh nabob and a former servant in India 'whose sole attraction was a pretty face, for the sake of which [Mr Montgomery] had elevated her from a state of servitude to that of a Nabobess' (p. 207). Determined to raise herself socially, the wealthy Lucretia is deceived into marrying cash-strapped Sir Edward, though only after she has failed to attract the attention of Henry Mortimer.

Character-specific dialogue is a key means of illustrating character throughout the novel. The vain and ambitious Mrs Montgomery, for example, is constantly portrayed in terms of her servant class origins, which Hatton explores via offbeam modish diction: Mrs Montgomery's frequent use of 'perdigious' (prodigious) and 'fortin' (fortune), along with neologisms like 'terrificatious', imply her lack of education and coarse manners. Dialogue describes gender, class and nation elsewhere in the novel, too. The sailors involved in Henry's abduction speak the language of seafaring: 'Hawl in a reef or two of your questions; lower your jib and back your mainsail' (p. 95), the captain warns, when Henry tries to find out what is happening to him. The 'red barn' incident includes Gwinthlean's own voice, notable for its strong north Wales accent – 'Got pless hur, hur cout not come before, and was afrait to come at all, for the peoples sait that the tefil haunted the parn' (p. 56). And Hatton introduces a Scottish brogue when Eliza Tudor disguises herself as a man in order to fight a duel with an unwanted suitor, a London accountant who navigates all situations via the language of money and business. '[K]eeping separate accounts will I am certain be found most profitable to us both', Eliza informs him when she turns down his proposal (p. 140).

Aside from the spirited Eliza, women often lack agency in this novel. Things happen *to* them; they are repeatedly misled, seduced and overruled. This trope is upended in the case of Henry Mortimer's abduction, but that aside it is possible to map national politics onto gender conflicts within the novel. The romance plots of *Cambrian Pictures* do not strictly add up to a national tale, a form emerging in this period that typically figures marriage as union or reconciliation between contrasting or opposing nations. But Hatton's themes of dependence and dispossession, allied to her hostile depictions of English characters – rapacious, cruel, villainous – suggest that national narratives are being considered in this text.

Vulnerable femininity and/or vulnerable Welshness meets some resistance, however, in the figure of Hatton herself, whose self-fashioning in this novel does not end with her pseudonym. One of her many subplots tells the story of a Welsh girl, Jessy Jones, seduced and abandoned by Lord Clavering on one of his previous visits to Wales. Jessy dies giving birth to their son, who is brought up by her blind poet father, Herbert Jones. Working in a defence of patronage along the way ('the rich and great who ought to support and encourage talent are too much engrossed by frivolous and unworthy pursuits to become the patrons of merit', pp. 474-5), Hatton puts her own poems into the hands of Herbert. The first of these, 'Hoel's Harp', is a medievalist tale examining 'the relationship between society's privileged elite and their subordinates'.[9] Fitting neatly within the class-oriented aspect of the novel, the poem reappears the following year in *Poetic Trifles* – Hatton had effectively given her novel-reading audience a preview of her new poetry.

Each chapter in the novel is also headed by a poetic epigraph, sometimes two or more. These epigraphs come from a range of contemporary and earlier writers, from Ann Yearsley and Walter Scott to Milton and Dante. Of the novel's twenty-six chapters, at least ten are prefaced with quotations from Shakespeare, including *Othello*, *Macbeth*, *Romeo and Juliet* and *The Merchant of Venice*. It is possible that Hatton's early experience of the acting world fed into her brilliant command of dialogue. Her knowledge of the theatre would also explain her canny use of Shakespeare in her fiction – a passage on *Hamlet*'s Gertrude, for example, to head the chapter on Henry's abduction by the lust-filled duchess. But here too, Hatton attempted some self-promotion: at least seven epigraphs are attributed to 'AJK' or 'AJH' – surely 'Ann of Swansea' herself, for those in the know.

Are these epigraphs performances for initiated readers, or was Hatton making more significant claims for her writing (particularly her poetry)? If so, then this would be at odds with the standard view of her fiction, which has long been seen as belonging to a body of fiction dismissed as popular or 'potboiler'. But here, too, critical opinion is shifting. Hatton was a prolific novelist, undoubtedly writing for money, and *Cambrian Pictures* appears to have been her entry point to the period's main publisher of popular fiction, the Minerva Press. First published in 1810 in London by E. Kerby, it was reissued in 1813 by Minerva, who subsequently published a novel a year for Hatton between 1814 and 1819. Minerva Press novels have typically been seen as formulaic and derivative, providing stock for circulating libraries but not of significant literary value in their own right. But with the emergence of national tale-oriented critical approaches, alongside ever-more nuanced understandings of the Gothic, popular or middlebrow fiction working across these modes has found its moment. As Elizabeth Neiman has recently argued, restoring the fiction of the Minerva Press to the wider ecology of Romantic-period literature challenges 'the dominant aesthetic associated with canonical Romanticism: the poet's turn inwards, as if free from the market, politics and all conventional social constraints'.[10] These novels, she continues, 'expand what we see about authorship, then and now'.[11]

Cambrian Pictures and its Minerva Press stablemates open up new territory for Welsh women's writing, too. Hatton's models clearly include eighteenth-century British ones, such as Samuel Richardson's accounts of pursuit and abduction in *Pamela; or, Virtue Rewarded* (1740), *Clarissa; or, The History of a Young Lady* (1748-9) and *The History of Sir Charles Grandison* (1753-4), a novel that Hatton directly references in the third volume of *Cambrian Pictures* ('to be run away with like poor Miss Byron, in Sir Charles Grandison', p. 417). Her direct contemporaries are not Raine or Dillwyn but writers like Edgeworth, Scott and also Jane Austen, a much more minor figure in her own time than she is now, whose romance plots have much in common with Hatton's. 'I am certain you will have to combat [your grandfather's] pride and his prejudices; he will at least try to make you the tool of his ambitious schemes' (p. 73), Delamere warns Henry, early in the novel. *Cambrian Pictures* is not exactly a cross between *Pamela* and *Pride and Prejudice*, set in a Gothic and sociable Snowdonia, but it is not a million miles away from it either.

Notes

---

[1] *The Cambrian*, 13 April 1888.
[2] Walford Davies (ed.), *Dylan Thomas: Early Prose Writings* (London: J. M. Dent, 1971), p. 100.
[3] Leigh Hunt, 'True Sun Daily Review', 14 September 1833, in Robert Morrison (ed.), *Selected Writings of Leigh Hunt: Volume Three* (London: Pickering and Chatto, 2003), p. 231.
[4] The fullest account of Hatton's life to date can be found in Jim Henderson, 'Ann of Swansea: a life on the edge', *National Library of Wales Journal*, 34:1 (2006), 1-47.
[5] For a further discussion of *Tammany*, see Jane Aaron,'The Rise and Fall of the "Noble Savage" in Ann of Swansea's Welsh Fictions', *Romantic Textualities: Literature and Print Culture, 1780–1840*, 22 (Spring 2017), http://www.romtext.org.uk/articles/rt22_n06/.
[6] Ibid.
[7] Jane Aaron, *Welsh Gothic* (Cardiff: University of Wales Press, 2013), 13.
[8] For the development of this trope in eighteenth-century fictions of Wales, see Jane Aaron and Sarah Prescott, *Welsh Writing in English, 1536-1914* (Oxford: Oxford University Press, 2020), 118-21.
[9] Catherine Brennan, *Angers, Fantasies and Ghostly Fears: Nineteenth-century Women from Wales and English-language Poetry* (Cardiff: University of Wales Press, 2003), 49.
[10] Elizabeth Neiman, *Minerva's Gothics: The Politics and Poetics of Romantic Exchange, 1780-1820* (Cardiff: University of Wales Press, 2020), xvii.
[11] Ibid., xviii.

Note on the Text

The aim of this edition is to present a readable text that reproduces the original published source as far as possible. With this balance in mind, inconsistent spellings in the original have been silently corrected, as have archaic spellings that may confuse (e.g. staid/stayed) or feel unnatural to modern readers (e.g. 'color', 'honor'). Grateful thanks to the National Library of Wales for supplying the source text on which this edition is based, as well as the cover image, and to Jane Aaron, Eurwen Booth and Wini Davies for help with preparing the final version. Any remaining errors are my own.

CAMBRIAN PICTURES;

OR,

EVERY ONE HAS ERRORS

IN THREE VOLUMES

An age of pain does not atone for a moment of guilt.

T. Corneille

If that adversity which arises from loss of fortune fix our attachment stronger towards the friend that suffers, and force us to new efforts to assist him, the loss of innocence, when it happens from no habitual depravity, forms a much stronger motive to exertion, when those who have fallen struggle to raise themselves up.

Sethos, Book 8

VOLUME I

PREFACE

"Reader, forgive me if the page is dull –
I sit down to create a tale of imaginary sorrows,
in order to beguile real ones."

IT was I think on the seventeenth of January, a most bitter cold and freezing night, that after having spent some hours very stupidly at the Marchioness of Austerville's masquerade, being heartily tired, I was preparing to depart and had actually reached the hall door with this intention, when Lady Delwin and her beautiful daughters (who had been at a rout in the neighbourhood) entreated the use of my carriage to convey them home, their own having by some accident got entangled with another, and had a wheel torn off. I handed them into my chariot: with pleasure I wrapped my domino round me, and was proceeding to walk to Portland Square; but a heavy shower of rain that instant falling, I was glad to retreat again to the scene of gaiety I had just quitted, not only with fatigue, but absolute disgust.

I had scarcely entered the ballroom, when my attention was arrested by two gentlemen in black dominos, who were loudly disputing on the subject of matrimony. I was myself in love, "steeped to the very lips," and at that very moment weighing and debating the point in my own mind, "whether to be, or not to be" a husband. Thus situated, their conversation was highly interesting, and I attended with the most serious attention to their arguments for and against the wedded state. The one recommended matrimony in the most florid and energetic language, spoke of it as the only sublunary situation in which felicity could possibly be expected, and man appear in the proper dignified and useful character which nature had designed him to support. His antagonist strenuously opposed these opinions, which he called fallacious, visionary, and romantic, spoke in acrimonious terms of women, their caprices, their follies, their inconstancy, the impossibility of attaching them to any one object, however deserving – and adduced in favour and support of his own arguments several recent instances of female frailty and infidelity, and obstinately persisted that in freedom, unshackled and unrestrained, man could alone find happiness. His opponent was neither convinced nor silenced, but continued with increasing energy to reprobate and condemn his illiberal and profligate ideas, to extol and recommend the wedded state, to represent woman in the most amiable light, and as man's greatest blessing.

"Woman," said he, pursuing the subject with fervour, "woman is the loveliest object in the creation."

"So she is! By heaven!" said a mask, suddenly interrupting him, who was then passing with a large party; "I adore the whole charming sex; go on, I wait with impatient pleasure to hear their praises."

"Hear him, hear him, hear him!" said several voices together, and instantly a large circle was formed round the two speakers.

"Pshaw! ridiculous!" said the anti-matrimonialist, "he is endeavouring to persuade me to become a husband, to resign all the bewitching delights of variety, wishing to convince me that the bitter draught of matrimony is a most delicious cordial."

"He might as well try to persuade us, Frank," said a young buck, taking the arm of the domino, and drawing him into the circle, "that this nipping, freezing, hyperborean night, is as delightful as a soft balmy moonlight evening in Italy. D – m it, for all the crowd, I am as cold as a winter in Lapland, and yet no doubt he would be hoaxing us with the idea of the boisterous wind being vastly salubrious, though I am sure if I go to bed alone, I shall be found congealed to an icicle before twelve o'clock tomorrow."

A loud laugh followed this elegant and curious speech. The advocate for matrimony had stood irresolute and embarrassed, but on the cry of hear him, hear him, hear him, being loudly and universally repeated, he bowed gracefully, and after a moment's hesitation, said:

"It certainly was not my intention to obtrude my opinions on the public ear; but thus conspicuously placed, thus publicly called upon, I shall not decline delivering my sentiments on what my feelings induce me to consider a subject of the utmost importance to society in general. At this particular crisis, when dissipated manners, and licentious principles have gained so alarming an ascendancy, and if my arguments, or representations, shall have the good effect of reclaiming the libertine, of removing illiberal prejudice – if my rhetoric shall have power to raise degraded woman to the rank heaven designed her to hold in the mind and heart of man, I shall for ever bless the occasion that presented me with an opportunity of becoming her advocate and champion."

"Bravo! bravissimo!" and, "hear him, hear him!" resounded from every quarter of the room, which was now crowded. An interesting pause succeeded, when the most profound silence being observed, the speaker resumed his discourse.

"Let not my fashionable friends and associates be surprised or disgusted, if, in order to make my own ideas more impressive, and add weight to my arguments, I call to my assistance a text from a book, which, though but seldom read, and still less attended to, nevertheless abounds with truth and beauty: and which, boasting the resistless charm of novelty, will doubtless claim their attention. I mean the Bible."

A loud laugh from part of the auditors now drowned the voice of the speaker, many of the company exclaiming: "Make way, let us go! D – m it, he is going to preach a sermon. What a queer quiz! the fellow is a methodist parson! How the devil did he get admittance here?"

Many of the company bustled away, while other masks, attracted by the noise and crowd, again formed a circle round the orator, and on "go on, go on," being vehemently vociferated, he proceeded to say:

"Though my intended discourse is not exactly a sermon, I trust that it will not be considered profanation, if I borrow from the fourth chapter of Ecclesiastes, and the eleventh verse, a text suitable as well to the bitterness of the night, as to my purpose of promoting matrimony.

"If two lie together, then they have heat:
but how can one be warm alone?"

"Solomon, that wise and potent monarch, to whose eyes the depths of philosophy were unveiled, and from whose penetration the most abstruse truths were not hidden, confessed after minute and deliberate investigation, that it was not good for man to be alone. In this absolute conviction, no doubt it was he wrote the text, from which I hope to prove the inestimable blessing bestowed on man in the creation of woman: thus says the enlightened and inspired preacher:

"If two lie together, then they have heat:
but how can one be warm alone?"

Doubtless when the divine power had formed and fashioned man, and placed him amid the unfading bowers of Paradise, he knew that though he had shaped him in the most perfect mould, in his own express image, had united in his form grace and proportion, flexibility and strength, had embellished his mind with every noble and excellent faculty, with every sense and exquisite feeling, proper and necessary to enjoy and appreciate the value of the innumerable delights that every where surrounded him; yet love, the vivifying principle, the primary cause of all that attracts or repulses, the light of his existence, was still unawakened. This was still wanting to call forth the energies of his nature, to kindle the dormant warmth of his soul, to complete his felicity. '*It was not good for man to be alone.*' Though encompassed with angelic guards, residing in the blissful and aromatic groves of Eden, reposing on the soft mossy banks of rivers, that rolled their broad pellucid waves over beds of golden sand; though inhaling the breath of flowers that every where shed their odorous balms around, his eye unconsciously wandered over their various beauties; no object interested him; there was an uneasy vacuity in his mind; he felt a listless void, a cheerless apathy – *he was alone!*

It is evident from scripture that Adam was created at least a day or two before Eve; and here we cannot sufficiently admire the wisdom of the Almighty, who by making Adam sensible of the want of a companion, certainly intended to impress upon all his senses the value and importance of the gift he designed to bestow upon him; for in this short interval man was sensible that he had within him an ungratified desire, a longing after a good unknown and unpossessed: his night or nights passed heavily, cheerless, and cold. '*For how can one be warm alone?*' His heart panted for some undiscovered bliss: he spoke, but no gentle voice replied: echo alone repeated the mournful, solitary, word *alone*. He stretched out his arms to clasp he knew not what; his agitated bosom heaved with deep sighs, but no sympathetic bosom heaved responsive to his undefinable emotions.

"He was alone!"

"The rising sun beheld him lord of the creation; the stately and majestic lion crouched at his feet: he beheld the fierce Leopard fawn and lick his hand, but with these he could not associate, on them he could not exhaust the dissolving tenderness that swam in his eyes, that ran in thrilling currents through his veins: he was restless and agitated: lost in wonder, he saw that the beasts and birds had mates: he beheld with indescribable emotion the dove expand her downy wings to receive her glossy partner, and softly nestle his little head among her silky plumage.

"But he, alas! was alone!"

"The beasts sunk down in fond embrace, and were warm;
"For when two lie together, then they have heat:
but how can one be warm alone?"

"The all bountiful and omnipotent creator saw that it was not *good for man to be alone*, and he created woman, lovely, charming, resistless woman: the Almighty gave her glowing in beauty to the arms of man, to be the sharer in his delights, the companion of his pleasures, his last but chief blessing, the supreme crown of his felicity.

"Adam received her with rapturous gratitude: his expanded arms embraced her with hallowed transport; his eyes wandered over the soft and feminine graces of her person with tumultuous delight, while his reason, his faculties bowed before her, and confessed her the sovereign ruler of his passions and his affections.

"Inspired as with a new soul, all nature appeared to his enraptured sight to wear a brighter and more captivating aspect. Ten thousand new beauties burst on his astonished view; the golden beams of the refulgent orb of day, the rich and cloudless azure of the sky, the perfume breathing flowers, the song of the birds, the murmuring of the streams, were now beheld and listened to with delight. His eyes sparkled with ineffable joy, his gestures were animated, his step elastic, and his tongue uttered the tender and impassioned language of hope and love.

"But when evening came, when the gorgeous sun had finished his diurnal course, when the dewy star of twilight called home the feathered people to their nests, when he drew his new-gained treasure to the nuptial bower, when reclined on a bed, formed of the fragrant and silken leaves of roses; when folded in each others arms, he found *if two lie together, then they have heat*. It was then, even at that moment of superlative rapture, that man devoutly praised his magnificent creator, and acknowledged with overflowing gratitude the magnitude of the inexpressible blessing bestowed upon him.

"Let not the licentious or profane presume to suppose that the inspired writer designed by this text to encourage the voluptuary in sensual gratifications, or intended to inflame the senses by saying

"If two lie together, then they have heat."

"The pious and contemplative mind will here search for the true and pure meaning of the text, which it will instantly and entirely divest of sexual meaning. The heat to be understood is not the effervescence of a riotous imagination, nor the feverish impulse of desire: but that delicious sympathy of soul which exists between two persons joined together by the holy and mystical band of marriage; the warm interest they take in all that concerns or affects each other; the ardent solicitude which prompts them to avert as far as human capability can accomplish all that may afflict, or can injure their spiritual or temporal happiness;

"For how can one be warm alone?"

"Though nature has undoubtedly planted in our bosoms a certain portion of self-love, necessary for our existence and preservation, yet few experience for self that exquisitely warm affection that throbs in every pulse of the heart for the partner of our hopes and wishes. Centered in ourselves, it is only a lukewarm feeling: but when participated, it kindles with celestial flame, expands in mutual acts of kindness and affection, warming not only our own bosoms, but extending with melting tenderness to our offspring, and glowing with zeal and charity for all the human race.

"Assuredly the wise Solomon, in writing the text, meant forcibly to recommend matrimony, not only as productive of extreme delight to two persons mutually attached, but also as a powerful means of extending and strengthening the links of society, affording to man an opportunity of softening the ruggedness and asperity of his nature, and of populating the world.

"The nature of man is not solitary, for he is pensive and unhappy when alone, he experiences the privation of those tendernesses, those enchanting attentions, which woman from the natural softness of her disposition, the elegant refinement, the exquisite delicacy of her mind, best knows how to dispense.

"Woman is in reality every thing to man; she arranges all that peculiarly belongs to his person: she regulates with systematic exactness the economy of his domestic concerns, decorates his table by the graceful ease of her deportment, and affability of her conversation, increases his comforts, and adds to the number of his friends. In the hour of affliction her tender consolations sooth his troubles, in sickness her voice animates and cheers him, her hand gently smooths his uneasy pillow, and with patient and watchful tenderness she administers to all his ailments.

"Feeling and knowing that woman is really the *cordial drop* thrown by heaven into life's cup of bitters, how is it possible that man can exist alone? Matrimony is a sacred and honourable state, and where two persons of congenial mind resolve to promote and contribute to each other's felicity, it is "a consummation devoutedly to be wished." O, ye who have never known the holy delights of wedded love, no longer deprive yourselves of a happiness which the Almighty himself ordained, and the wisest of men recommended, both by precept and example. No longer shiver through the cold and cheerless night, but be convinced that *one cannot be warm alone*.

"Solomon, the greatest monarch that ever reigned: Solomon, the wisest of the sons of men most certainly intended to promote matrimony, not only as a laudable, but absolutely necessary institution; and who will be hardy enough to question the wisdom of Solomon? To him who has experienced the felicity of connubial love, it will be surely unnecessary to enforce the words of the preacher. He will not want to have it pointed out to him how much delight he loses by a solitary life, of how many days of comfort, and nights of blissful repose, he deprives himself: it surely will not be necessary to say to him, attend to the words of the inspired preacher, for thus hath the wise Solomon written, in the fourth chapter of Ecclesiastes, and the eleventh verse,

"If two lie together, then they have heat:
but how can one be warm alone?"

The orator ceased, bowed profoundly, and complaining of fatigue, the circle divided, he darted forward, and was out of sight in an instant, while some warmly applauded his discourse, and others declared his intellects were deranged, and that he was much fitter for a dark garret, and a straight waistcoat, than the polished entertainments of elegance and fashion. The crowd which this singular occurrence had attracted now dispersing, I perceived my old and particular friend Lord Elphinstone, with a gentleman, who being without a mask, discovered the handsomest and most intelligent countenance I ever beheld, but clouded with so deep a shade of melancholy, that the most superficial observer might discover his mind partook not of the festivity of the surrounding scene. As I approached, Lord Elphinstone started from the pillar against which he was leaning, and came forward to meet me, and after having exchanged a few mutual compliments and inquiries, introduced me to the Honourable Mr. Delamere. Our conversation turned on the sermon we had just heard. Mr. Delamere praised the orator's delivery, which certainly was animated, elegant, and accurate; he also spoke in terms of general approbation on the subject of his discourse, and added that his opinion perfectly coincided with the speaker's respecting the happiness of the married state, where it was a union of hearts, and not a mere compact of interest. Lord Elphinstone gaily replied:

"Well then, Horatio, as you thus publicly allow that you consider wedlock a desirable and eligible state, I trust you will very shortly select a fair one for your bride from among the very many who are displaying all their graces, and putting on all their charms, in order to warm your icy heart, with the delightful hope of being distinguished by the desirable appellation of the Honourable Mrs. Delamere."

Mr. Delamere attempted to smile, but it was a fruitless effort: a sigh in spite of his endeavours would have way. He shook Elphinstone by the hand, politely bowed to me, and wishing us good morning, walking away.

"If personal beauty," said I, gazing after him, "can attract and attach, surely no man has higher pretensions to female favour than Mr. Delamere, and no man is more courted or more admired by the ladies than he is: his person is uncommonly fine."

"And his mind is equal if not superior to his exterior,"

replied Elphinstone. "I am hurt to the soul to perceive that I have incautiously touched a chord whose slightest vibration gives him pain, I know that he will never marry: poor fellow! his affections are buried never to revive. I see I have excited your curiosity, and as I know I can rely upon your secrecy and honour, I will in the course of the day send you a history of the particular incidents which he in the fever of romance considers sufficient to condemn him to perpetual celibacy."

The company had now nearly deserted the magnificent apartments of the marchioness. Lord Elphinstone and myself left the mansion at the same moment; and as he ascended his carriages which drew up before mine, I repeatedly bade him remember the promised history. My own disposition being enthusiastic and romantic, I expected to find in the narrative of Mr. Delamere sentiments and feelings exactly in unison with my own. I already felt inclined to love, to pity, and respect him, and most impatiently longed for the development of his character, that I might ascertain to how large a portion of my esteem he had a claim. Having reached home, I hastily undressed and threw myself into bed, in a state of mind not easily defined; one moment my heart, yielding itself up to confidence and tenderness, resolved upon soliciting an immediate union with the beautiful object of my affections, so much did I accord with the sentiments, and approve the picture the young orator at the masquerade had drawn of woman; the next the pale and interesting countenance of Delamere presented itself to my imagination, and I resolved that his story should either determine me to marry immediately or to break off my attachment by a violent effort at once, and go abroad. Agitated with hopes and fears, with doubts and resolves, it was long before I slept, and late in the day before I awoke: my first inquiry was for the wished for and expected packet; it was not arrived. I remained all day at home, no packet came. I sat down to a solitary dinner, reconciling my mind with all the old rules which the sages of antiquity wrote, to prove that disappointment is the natural inheritance of man. After I had drank a few glasses of wine, I prepared to visit my fair enslaver. I had taken up my hat, when a servant entered with the packet.

"No," said I, laying it on a table beside me; "no, my lovely Caroline, I will not visit thee till I am acquainted with the sorrows of Delamere."

I sat down and wrote her a billet; my heart smote me for wording it so coldly. I hesitated whether I should not burn it, and write her another. I held it over the flame of the candle.

"Hang it," exclaimed I, "let it go: should Delamere's history determine me not to marry, why she will have less to accuse me of on the score of profession."

I dispatched my billet, and tore open the envelope of the packet. What a piece of work is man, how noble in faculties, how infinite in reason, and yet with this infinite reason, these noble faculties, I trembled like a weak woman, as the first words of Delamere's narrative met my eyes: "*Thou shalt not commit adultery*."

"I will never marry," said I, laying down the packet, and throwing up the sash: the window looked into the square, I watched the groups that passed: many of them no doubt were married, some of them perhaps happily, but to be dishonoured. It was an agonizing thought. I looked up to the sky; the moon was struggling through a dark cloud.

"Just so," exclaimed I, mentally, "man is fated to buffet with adversity, and were it not for hope, whose bright beams irradiate his gloomy path, life would not be worth preserving."

I continued to muse on the chance of attaching the heart of a woman, on the means of securing her affections, when the servant entered with an answer to the billet I had sent to Caroline: she expressed some solicitude respecting my health, supposing that I walked home when I put her mother, herself, and sister, into my carriage the preceding night and requested my company to supper.

"I shall not go," said I, throwing her note disdainfully from me; "she is too easily won; in order to secure her conquest, she should be cold and repulsive. She knows the poverty of her house, and wishes to secure to herself an affluent alliance. She deceives herself; I come not to her lure; I will never marry."

I threw myself on the sofa, and for a moment fancied my heart was free; but as my eye glanced upon her note, which lay upon the carpet, fancy presented her as she really is, modest, beautiful, and gentle, a blush on her cheek, and a tear in her eye. I snatched up her note, read it again; it was delicate and proper; my conscience reproached me. I pressed the note to my lips, thrust it into my bosom.

"I will sup with thee, my lovely Caroline."

I caught up my hat, pushed Delamere's papers into a cabinet, resolved to defer their perusal to the next day, when my senses would be more calm, and my mind less prejudiced, when the voice of Caroline should have soothed my perturbed spirits, and her beautiful person and correct behaviour again persuaded me to believe that women are angels.

CHAPTER I

"— What's the vain boast
Of sensibility, but to be wretched?
In her best transports lives a latent sting,
Which wounds as they expire."

Anne Yearsley

AUGUSTUS MORTIMER was the second son of Lord Dungarvon, a nobleman as remarkable for his unbounded pride as his ridiculous and unconquerable partiality for genealogy. All the branches of his house for time immemorial had on every side made honourable and dignified alliances, and when Augustus reached the age of manhood, his family were thrown into the utmost consternation, rage, and astonishment, by his peremptorily refusing to offer his hand to Lady Lavinia Montalban, the niece of the Duke of Aluster, merely because his romantic mind felt no predilection in her favour. Pomp, rank, aggrandizement, were the ruling passions of the ostentatious Mortimers, and they had not entertained the most distant notion that a descendant of theirs would disgrace and sully the noble and ancient armorial bearings of their honourable and illustrious house, with quartering upon it any arms less dignified than nobility. Augustus was young, ardent, and romantic. Having an elder brother, who was his mother's doting boy, the early part of his life had been spent with an aunt, who having unfortunately conceived a passion for a man of inferior rank, had voluntarily devoted herself to celibacy, rather than disgrace her noble house, by introducing into it a person whose family were engaged in commerce. From Mrs. Gertrude Mortimer Augustus imbibed sensibility, and elevated sentiment, but she failed to inspire him with pride, to which she had sacrificed the happiness of her existence. Mrs. Gertrude Mortimer had certainly designed to make Augustus the heir of her fortunes, but dying suddenly, and without a will, he became entirely dependent on his father, Lord Dungarvon, who perceiving, with no small degree of resentment, how little worship rank obtained from Augustus, bestowed on him but a small portion of the affection he lavished on his son Richard, who in person and mind was the exact counterpart of himself. Ostentatious pomp was not the idol of Augustus; he paid no adoration to rank – his young heart resigned itself, with all its hopes and wishes, all its tender and impassioned impulses, to the daughter of the Vicar of Lyston, to which living he had been presented by Lord Dungarvon. In the morning of life the mind is sanguine; whatever it wishes it believes possible. It had never entered the imagination of Augustus, from the marked indifference with which he had ever been treated, that his parents would think him of consequence enough to oppose his inclination, as they had repeatedly declared, they looked up to his brother Richard as the support and guardian of their ancient and future dignities; he could not conceive that Lord Dungarvon, when he should be acquainted with the state of his heart, and the bounded extent of his wishes, would deny his assent to an union on which his peace and happiness depended, or refuse to bestow on him the means to support the lovely object of his affections, in retired and elegant sufficiency.

Louisa Berresford's virtues, beauty, and attainments, were

undeniable; but all these are nothing, when the grand essentials, rank and fortune, are wanting. Augustus's avowal was received by his relations with rage and contempt; he was bade, on peril of their everlasting displeasure, to think no more of so disgraceful an alliance. The innocent Louisa was accused of art, and her father, the most liberal, just, and upright of men, of encouraging her ambitious designs – of wishing to mix his plebeian blood with the rich, uncontaminated stream of the noble and illustrious Mortimers.

At these violent, gross, and unfounded accusations, the generous spirit of Augustus took fire; he vindicated the injured characters of Louisa and her father with manly and becoming warmth; protested that Mr. Berresford was absolutely ignorant of his affection for his daughter, nor knew that he had professed himself her lover. Lord Dungarvon commanded him to be silent, and rising haughtily from his seat, bade him prepare to attend him the next morning to the Duke of Aluster's.

"Resolve, sir," said he, sternly, "to become the husband of Lady Lavinia, who honours you with her esteem, and is willing to bestow herself and her immense fortune on you, unworthy as you are."

"I confess myself unworthy," said Augustus; "I have nothing to offer in return for this excessive generosity, except cold respect."

"That is quite sufficient," rejoined Lady Dungarvon: "People of rank leave to the commonality the vulgar and fulsome nonsense of love."

"He is in possession of my sentiments," replied Lord Dungarvon; "let him accede to my wishes, or he is no longer my son."

Saying this, he stalked from the saloon, followed by her ladyship and Richard Mortimer, leaving Augustus to reconcile his mind to splendid misery, or inevitable poverty. He chose the latter – his mind understood the duties of a son, but he felt those duties might he carried too far, when they demanded the sacrifice of his dearest hopes, his tenderest affections. He reverenced his parents, but he was not a blind and submissive slave to their ambitious schemes and imperious mandates; he was convinced that the gentle artless Louisa loved and confided in him: and after a few struggles between duty and affection, he determined to fulfil his engagement to her immediately, and to trust to time and nature to reconcile him to his family. He was setting off on a visit to the vicarage when, he was summoned to his mother's dressing room.

"Augustus," said she, taking his hand as he entered, "I grieve to think how much you have irritated your father, who has set his heart upon an alliance with the Aluster family, on account of their great ministerial interest: but I trust a few moments' consideration has convinced you of the folly of opposing the united desires of your relations: having heard our just and proper representations, you no doubt entirely relinquish the ridiculous and degrading intentions of introducing into a family of our rank and consequence the mean and indigent daughter of an obscure country parson."

"Speak of Louisa Berresford, madam," said he sternly, "as she is – as the virtuous, elegant, and accomplished daughter of the most enlightened, the best, and noblest of mankind. The *best*, because he suffers no worldly passions, no ambitious wishes to actuate his actions; the *noblest*, because he scorns to degrade with contemptible malice innocence and worth, let destiny have allotted them a rank in society ever so humble."

Lady Dungarvon felt the justice of his reproof; her colour heightened: "I was in hopes, sir, to convince you of the impropriety of your conduct. I was inclined to treat your ridiculous passion as a mere boyish attachment to a girl whom chance had provided with a few favourable opportunities of shewing you kindness; but I perceive it would be mere waste of words to attempt to reason with a person who wilfully shuts his eyes against conviction. But take heed, infatuated boy," continued she, swelling with passion: "your obstinate spirit may be taught to yield, or if it perversely persists in disobedience, your contumacy may be visited on the head of the syren who seduces you from your duty. It will be strange, indeed, if a man of Lord Dungarvon's consequence cannot find means to punish and remove the obstacles to his wishes."

Augustus was about to speak – Lady Dungarvon interrupted him. "No reply, sir: I have fulfilled my duty as a mother, in pointing out yours as a son: you may retire, sir."

Augustus bowed and left the dressing room. Her ladyship's menace filled him with apprehensions: he knew that the noble-minded Berresford would never consent to his daughter's entering into his family by a clandestine marriage; he also knew that the worthy vicar considered himself under obligations to Lord Dungarvon, and he feared that his family might influence him to remove Louisa from the country. To prevent the possibility of this, he determined to persuade her to elope with him that very night. Having arranged all matters necessary for a journey to Scotland, with a faithful servant whom he ordered to wait with a post-chaise and four horses in a lane near the high road, he set off for the vicarage.

Louisa Berresford was just turned of seventeen – Augustus Mortimer was little more than twenty-one: the very age when passion, full of fiery impetuosity, derides and overwhelms the cold lessons of caution and prudence. He was handsome, ardent, and eloquent; she was tender, gentle, and susceptible; – he vowed, argued, and persuaded – she loved, believed, and consented. She left the Vicarage with her eyes swimming in tears, exclaiming, "My father, my dear father!"

Augustus placed her in the chaise, followed her himself, ordered the postillions to proceed, and by taking a circuitous route, evaded the messengers Lord Dungarvon had dispatched to overtake and bring back the fugitives. They arrived without impediment or interruption in Scotland, were married, and as expeditiously as possible returned to the Vicarage. But what was the remorse and agony of Louisa, when she found the house shut up, and her father lying ill at a neighbouring cottage! The feelings of Mr. Berresford had been severely wounded by the inconsiderate elopement of Louisa; but he remembered that he had himself been young, been in love, and imprudent, and he forgave her, though he too truly foresaw the train of evils that would inevitably follow this ill-advised marriage. The third day after their elopement he received a note from Lord Dungarvon, containing the bitterest reproaches, accusing him of the basest ingratitude, and hinting that it was expected he would resign the living bestowed on him at a time when his lordship supposed him incapable of seducing his son from his duty, and of bringing eternal disgrace on an illustrious house. Berresford, though mild and peaceable, had yet a touch of human nature; his feelings were hurt, his pride was wounded: – he resigned the living, and when Louisa threw herself at his feet and implored forgiveness, he was struggling with the double anguish of present pain, and the dread of future poverty. The sight of his Louisa was, however, his most powerful restorative – he blessed and pardoned her. Augustus, who dreaded that the influence of his family would be exerted to separate him from his wife, immediately procured a licence, and was again married to her in the presence of a few witnesses at a neighbouring church. He then applied to his particular friend, Sir Owen Llewellyn, who having lately married, had retired from the tumultuous scenes of high life, to enjoy nature in her sublime and beautiful character, among the romantic mountains of North Wales. Sir Owen Llewellyn's friendship evinced itself in actions, not professions; he presented Mr. Berresford with a living, which though not equal in value to that of Lyston, was yet sufficient to afford him those comforts and conveniences he had been accustomed to: and what was of the utmost consequence to his present frame of mind, it enabled him to quit for ever a spot where he had received undeserved outrage, and unmerited insult. To the care of Sir Owen Llewellyn and his amiable wife Augustus committed his Louisa while he attempted a reconciliation with his relations: his endeavours to procure an interview with any branch of the family were entirely unsuccessful – the domestics were strictly forbidden to admit him within the gates of Mortimer Abbey. Finding it impossible to gain an audience, he tried to soften the obdurate hearts of his parents by letters: here he was also disappointed, for all, except the first, were returned unopened. Yet still Augustus hoped, that when time had softened their resentment affection would return, and that they would yet do justice to the merits of his Louisa, and receive her as their daughter. He repaired to Dolgelly Castle, and in the soothings of friendship, and the endearments of love, forgot for a short time the anguish occasioned by the inflexibility of his parents. But from this transient dream of happiness he was soon roused by the receipt of a packet sealed with the Dungarvon arms, which on opening he found contained a captain's commission in a regiment raising for the West Indies, and a draught for two thousand pounds. In the envelope was written, "Augustus Mortimer has no longer father, mother, brother, or relations – by his disgraceful marriage he has dissolved all ties of consanguinity: but to prevent further infamy from attaching to the illustrious family of which he was once a member, they enclose him the means of providing bread for the woman be has made his wife, and of seeking for himself an honourable grave. If he accedes to the wishes of Lord Dungarvon and goes abroad it will be well – if not, his lordship desires that he may never again hear from or be troubled on his account."

This was too much for the sensitive mind of Augustus: he fell senseless into the arms of Sir Owen Llewellyn; a fever seized his brain, and he lay many weeks at Dolgelly Castle in a state of derangement. The mournful intelligence of his illness reached Mortimer Abbey; it was talked of and deeply lamented by the domestics, by whom he was much beloved. It reached the ears of Lord and Lady Dungarvon, but it made no impression on their hearts; he had disappointed their ambitious views, and stifling every natural emotion, they only expressed a wish that he might expiate by his death the wound that his rebellious conduct had given to their family pride. Contrary to the predictions of the faculty, Augustus, after having tottered as it were on the very verge of eternity, began slowly to recover; but as his health returned that of the delicate Louisa began to decline: his illness had banished all the hopes her sanguine imagination had cherished – she saw that she had crushed for ever the fortunes of the man she idolized; she felt that she had drawn down upon him the malediction of his parents. With unutterable anguish she beheld herself the insuperable bar to his future greatness; her mind was acutely agonized, and though the attentions and adoration of Augustus knew no abatement, yet every cloud that passed across his fine countenance struck upon her heart as a reproach – every sigh he heaved gave an additional pang to her bosom. With the advice of Mr. Berresford and Sir Owen Llewellyn it was agreed that he should accept the commission and join the regiment, part of which was already embarked for Barbados.

Louisa was now far advanced in pregnancy, and it was with much difficulty on her part, who wanted to accompany her husband abroad, concluded that she should remain at Dolgelly Castle, under the protection of Sir Owen and Lady Llewellyn, till after her *accouchement*, when herself and the child were to follow the destination of Augustus. Fifteen hundred pounds Augustus vested in the funds for the use of his wife, from whom he parted with agonies almost too great for human nature to sustain.

"We shall never meet again in this world," said Louisa throwing herself into the arms of her father, as the chaise which conveyed away her husband was hid by the woods that surrounded Dolgelly Castle, and she spoke prophetically. The winds were favourable – no storm impeded their passage. Augustus arrived with the troops safely at Barbados – he distinguished himself on many occasions; was promoted to the rank of major; his prospects began to brighten. His constitution had withstood the unwholesome climate – hope had again arisen in his heart, his Louisa was to come out to him in the spring; an insurrection had taken place among the blacks; his regiment was ordered out. Augustus was considered the post of danger, the post of honour; he received a wound in his side from a poisoned spear, the blacks were reduced, and Augustus found an honourable grave. He was interred with military honours, and his brother officers, to whom his story was known, shed upon the earth that covered his remains the mingled tears of respect and pity.

Louisa had given birth to a son, who was named after her father and her husband, Henry Augustus. She employed herself busily in making preparations for her intended voyage, while her father and her friends saw that consumption with rapid strides was hurrying her to "that bourn from which no traveller returns." While animated with the transporting hope of joining her husband, Louisa neither felt nor complained of illness: but her altered figure reduced to shadowy thinness, the frequent hectic flushings of her cheek, the progress of her disorder, spoke too plainly to the apprehensive heart of her father. She bore the news of her husband's death with uncommon fortitude: after reading the letter that brought the fatal intelligence she turned with a faint smile to Lady Llewellyn, and said,

"I shall not long survive him; he is gone a short time before me to that world where goodness and virtue only obtain pre-eminence. I said but too truly that we should meet no more in this world; but oh! my Augustus, my adored! thou whose image never for one moment since our cruel separation has left my mind. I shall shortly be with thee to part no more."

In a few moments she sunk into a gentle sleep, in which she continued for some time: a faint colour settled on her cheeks; a smile played on her lips and when she awoke her eyes shone with uncommon lustre. She was supported to a Venetian window that opened on the lawn.

The moon had risen, and the clear blue vault of heaven was thickly studded with stars. It was the middle of summer: she complained of heat – the window was thrown open, and a servant at that instant entering with candles, at her desire retired with them again.

"This soft tender light," said Louisa, "I am particularly pleased with. I remember, O, hour of bliss! I remember it was at the tranquil hour of twilight that my sainted Augustus first confessed his love – that love" continued she, deeply sighing, "which blighted all his budding honours; that love which has fatally terminated his existence! I have often pleased myself with the idea that my beloved mother, who died when I was quite a child, witnessed and approved my actions. Tell me, dear Lady Llewellyn, what is your opinion – do you think the immortal spirit, after death, is admitted to a knowledge of the transactions of this world?"

Lady Llewellyn tenderly took her hand and replied, "My dear Louisa, this is a subject on which no person can presume to speak with any degree of certainty; but surely there is something pleasing in the idea of our departed friends watching over and approving our conduct; but whether it is really so or not there is certainly nothing wrong in encouraging the idea, because it may be a means of suppressing evil propensities, and inciting us to goodness and virtue, while we believe that those we most loved and valued in this life are, though invisible to us, spectators of our most secret transactions."

"I thank you," said Louisa, "and am delighted to find that your opinion on this subject does not materially differ from my own."

Her father now entered the apartment and seated himself on one side of her. She requested to have her child brought;

she took him up in her arms, pressed him to her bosom, and raising her beautiful eyes to heaven said, "Not long shall I remain in this world: may it please the Almighty Disposer of Events that thy father and myself may be permitted to watch over my babe!"

"Louisa!" said Mr. Berresford mournfully.

"Oh my dear father," continued she, "I have occasioned you much trouble and sorrow; my imprudence has poisoned the peace of two hearts dearer to me by far than my own. My ill-advised marriage has been a source of perpetual grief to you, and eventually it has murdered my Augustus! but I beseech you pardon me: I feel I am going to him, and I trust that Lord Dungarvon's resentment will be buried in the grave of her who has unfortunately caused him so much inquietude. Thy father," said she pressing the soft check of the sleeping infant, "thy father is in heaven! May Lord Dungarvon extend to thee that affection and kindness he denied to his son."

She grew faint – the child was taken from her; she sunk on the shoulder of her father, and the moonbeams falling on her pale face gave her the appearance of something super-human. In a few moments she recovered: Sir Owen Llewellyn had now entered the room, and had taken the child from its nurse. A medicine was administered to Louisa, who observed it was very bitter; "But what," continued she, "is the bitterness of this compared with the agonizing reflection that I must leave that helpless babe a destitute orphan fatherless, motherless!"

"Not so," replied Sir Owen; "speak not thus despondingly; the child of Augustus Mortimer becomes mine not only by adoption, but by the remembrance of that friendship so sincerely felt, so sacredly observed by his father and myself; here is its mother."

Lady Llewellyn received the infant on her bosom, and in a voice drowned in tears assured Louisa that she would ever consider him as her own – that she would, in every sense of the word, be a mother to him. Mr. Berresford's feelings rendered him nearly inarticulate, and it was with great difficulty he could express, that while he lived he would not fail to watch over him with the fondest solicitude and tenderest care.

The strength of Louisa was unequal to this affecting scene: she endeavoured to express her gratitude to Sir Owen and Lady Llewellyn; she tried to console her father. She kissed and blessed her child, and after continuing silent for some time, said, "I could have wished that my mortal part might rest with my Augustus; that as our hearts were firmly united, our ashes might have formed at last one undistinguished heap; but it matters not. The ocean now rolls its broad waves between us, but our souls will shortly be joined in those realms of happiness where calamity can persecute no more. My father, I see you not; once more bless your Louisa."

"Bless thee! bless thee, my child!" said the weeping Berresford, who with clasped hands was bending over the end of the sofa on which she reclined.

"Tomorrow," said Louisa, as if suddenly recollecting herself, "for tomorrow I shall be nineteen – I shall not see tomorrow! – my course is soon finished! Oh! ambition, how many victims dost thou immolate on thy insatiable altar! Augustus, I am thine for ever – Heaven, be merciful –"

Her eyes closed, her lips moved for a moment, but they uttered no sound; her frame underwent a slight convulsion, her pulse stopped, her heart ceased to beat; the breath that animated the pale but beautiful form was fled for ever. Louisa

Mortimer was buried under a plain marble slab, in Dolgelly church, simply inscribed with her age; but though the marble bore no testimony of the loveliness of her person, and the virtues of her mind, in the hearts of her father and her friends the remembrance was recorded: and it was long, very long before they ceased to lament, that so much loveliness and worth was at so early a period consigned to the oblivious darkness of the grave. Louisa had been buried many weeks before Mr. Berresford was sufficiently recovered to look over her papers, among which he found a note to himself, inclosing a letter to Lord Dungarvon, in which she particularly requested, that as soon as she was dead, her letter might be forwarded to Mortimer Abbey: he immediately inclosed it in a few lines from himself.

To the Right Hon. Lord Dungarvon.
My Lord – the writer of the letter I have the honour of transmitting to you has nothing now to hope or fear from the house of Mortimer, she sleeps peacefully in an humble grave, prepared for her by hard-hearted pride and inflexible ambition. I hold the wishes of the dying sacred: but had not my now beatified Louisa made it her particular request that her letter should be delivered to your lordship, you never would have been troubled with a remembrance of any sort from

HENRY BERRESFORD.

To the Right Hon. Lord Dungarvon.
At the moment when my heart has overcome all its resentments, subdued all its passions, save only one which is wove into my existence, and will only expire with its last throb, my unconquerable love for Augustus Mortimer, I

presume to address your lordship in favour of his child. – Remember his father is no more: perhaps you will say he might still have lived but for me – might have been great and happy – spare me I beseech you: a few, a very few days will terminate the existence of her, so hated, so despised – but my child, the child of Augustus Mortimer, the grandson of Lord Dungarvon – will you visit on his innocent head the crime of his parents, must he be reprobated and abandoned: surely you must have more justice, more humanity – receive him, protect him: his duty, his obedience, shall expiate the offences of his parents: perhaps he may be fated to perpetuate the name of Mortimer: condemn him not to obscurity: let him not be brought up on the bounty of strangers, who may hereafter say the heir of Dungarvon owed his very existence to their charity: but now, when the remains of the ill-fated Augustus Mortimer moulder in a foreign clime, when the wretched heartbroken Louisa sinks into the grave, receive their offspring, and by your protection of him, prove that resentment is not carried beyond the tomb, so may your latter days be blest with tranquillity, so may your last moments be soothed with the consoling thought, that you have effaced the injuries you heaped upon Augustus Mortimer, with kindness to his son. May heaven so prosper you, as you fulfil the last request of

LOUISA MORTIMER.

Lord Dungarvon, after reading the letter, snatched up a pen, and addressed Mr. Berresford in the following terms:

"Sir, I return you the letter you inclosed me from your daughter, of the legality of whose marriage with the late

Major Augustus Mortimer I am, I must confess, not exactly satisfied: it is now, however, a matter of no kind of consequence – My son, the honourable Mr. Mortimer, will in a few days unite himself to a lady of high birth and exalted rank, which marriage I trust will raise an heir to the illustrious house of Mortimer, whose claims will be clear and indisputable: in the mean time I beg leave to signify, that I do not consider myself at all bound to provide for the future support or establishment of the offspring of guilt and disobedience.

DUNGARVON."

"Proud and unfeeling man," said Berresford as he read the letter, "the hour may arrive when your heart may be sensible of the sorrows of mine – you may yet be childless as I am – and this poor orphan boy, whom your inveterate malice would ever stigmatize with illegitimacy, you may yet be obliged to look up to, to perpetuate that name and those honours of which you are now so proudly vain."

Mr. Berresford lived to see Henry Mortimer five years old, the darling of Sir Owen and Lady Llewellyn, who shared between him and their own daughter, who was born three years after the decease of Mrs. Mortimer, their warmest affections. Adeline Llewellyn was a lovely interesting child, mild, timid, and gentle – Harry was bold and spirited, full of frolic and mischief, but fond to excess of Adeline, whose smile would recompense him for any difficulty he encountered, and whose voice would allure him from his young companions, and his most favourite sports. They studied, walked, and rode together. Adeline regarded Henry with the temperate affection of a sister, while he felt for her a sentiment more tender, more ardent, more impassioned than that of a brother. Henry had just attained his eighteenth, and Adeline her fifteenth year, when Lady Llewellyn after a short illness died, lamented by all that had the happiness of knowing her. Sir Owen's excessive grief for her loss had nearly proved fatal to him, when the recollection of the unprotected situation of his daughter recalled the wish for life; he now exerted himself to sooth her sorrows, and reconcile her mind to a misfortune which was irremediable: he again attended to her studies, and busied himself in preparing Henry for the finishing of his education at Cambridge. In these occupations his mind felt great relief, and Adeline too discovered that employment took much from the keen edge of sorrow. At length the time arrived for Henry's departure. Sir Owen allotted him a liberal stipend for college expenses: he was now entering into life; and as Sir Owen had lived in the gay world, and knew the dangers and temptations to which a young man of acute sensibility and warm passions was likely to be exposed, he gave him such advice as he considered appropriate to the occasion.

"I do not expect you to be absolutely faultless, my dear Henry," said he: I hope I have sufficient liberality of mind to make allowances for accidental errors, and unpremeditated weaknesses; but I trust the lessons of goodness, the precepts of virtue you have so often received from that angel who is now no more, will never be effaced from your heart; that the remembrance of them will deter you from the commission of any act that would disgrace my friendship, or degrade the name of Mortimer. Return to me again the same open hearted generous fellow that you depart; bring back to me my son, and to Adeline her brother."

Henry was affected, his eyes filled with tears, while he promised never to forget the advice of his more than father.

He folded Adeline to his bosom, kissed away the tear that was straying down her cheek, and several times entreated her not to forget to write to him.

After the departure of Henry, Dolgelly Castle became dull: and as it was winter, and the ground covered with snow, Adeline felt in her confinement to the house the loss of his society, which was scarcely compensated by the company of her favourite friend Eliza Tudor, the daughter of Sir Griffith Tudor, who resided at the distance of two short miles from the castle. Eliza Tudor was a little lively animated brunette, with glossy raven tresses, and sparkling black eyes. Adeline Llewellyn was tall and graceful, with the airy lightness of a sylph; her eyes were a lucid melting blue, her skin was transparently fair, and her hair a light auburn, which, falling into natural ringlets, strayed over her ivory forehead, and wantoned upon her fine turned neck: her rosy mouth was adorned with dimples, and her teeth might without exaggeration have been compared to pearls: added to this extreme loveliness of person, Adeline was highly accomplished – she danced elegantly, was a perfect mistress of music: the harp was her favourite instrument, and she accompanied its entrancing notes with a voice of plaintive sweetness, that "took the prisoned soul and lapped it in Elysium." She drew and painted in a style so exquisite, that her landscapes appeared as if genius had guided the pencil of fancy – her disposition was mild and generous, her sensibility acute, her imagination warm, and her perceptions accurate. There never existed a more striking contrast than was exhibited in the persons and characters of Adeline Llewellyn and Eliza Tudor; yet they were both open hearted, liberal minded, and amiable; and though Eliza had neither the talents nor perseverance of

Adeline, yet she danced with animation, and sung many of the popular songs of her country with taste and spirit: and notwithstanding her accomplishments were for the most part merely superficial, she frequently attracted more admiration than Adeline, whose timid and retiring character made her shrink from observation, and induced her to remain in the back ground; while her more vivacious friend commanded the attention of the beaux at the neighbouring assemblies, by the unrestrained playfulness of her manner, and her eternal *gaieté de cœur*.

CHAPTER II

— It was a moment big with peril,
But the bold deed gave to the fair one life,
And in return for what she term'd my valour,
She gave the matchless treasure of her heart.
A. J. K.

DOLGELLY CASTLE stood delightfully elevated on a bold eminence, near the sea shore; on one side were hanging woods, through which the predecessors of Sir Owen Llewellyn had cut a road to the ancient and romantic town of Carnarvon. Situated at the distance of six miles behind it were mountains of stupendous height, and the other side presented rich meadows, and land in a state of the highest cultivation. The winter had been long and severe: the mountains were covered with snow, and the woods exhibited a fantastic appearance, their leafless branches being decorated with frost-work, which the keenness of the air had condensed into a variety of forms. The weather had been for many days dark and gloomy, and the little party at the castle had in vain wished to see the yellow rays of the sun illumine the gothic windows of the library, near which Adeline sat finishing a moon-light view of a ruined watchtower, that nodded in proud desolation on an adjacent mountain. While Eliza, with one arm hanging over the back of her chair, sat reading to herself a romance, suddenly she burst into a loud laugh, in which she indulged for some time; at length composing her features, she turned to Adeline, and with affected gravity said, "Pray, my dear, were you ever in love?"

"No," said Adeline, smiling at the question, "why do you ask?"

"Because," replied Eliza, "I wish to know whether this description of the passion is true. You shall hear." She then applied to the book, and read the following passage –

"When imperious love takes possession of the heart, all its gaiety departs; to nights of calm repose and dreams of happiness, succeed visions of terror and despair; the bosom, once the mansion of peace and tranquillity, is tortured with an agonizing train of doubts, fears, and jealousies – restless and dissatisfied, the mind busies itself with hopes that can never be realized, or in conjuring up misfortunes it may never encounter. – Time ever passes too swift or too slow. The meridian sun is dark and gloomy as the noon of night in the absence of the adored one."

"No more, for heaven's sake," said Adeline; "shut the book, Eliza, the picture is absolutely terrific."

"Nonsense," replied Eliza, laughing, "the author of this book knew nothing of human nature. – Now do I most heartily wish, that fortune would send some dear delightful, bewitching, handsome fellow, straying over our mountains; I would assuredly fall in love, on purpose to convince you that the picture is too highly coloured, a mere daub, with which reality has nothing to do. Love, my dear, is a frolicsome urchin, dressed in smiles, and wreathed with roses; you should see I would laugh all day, dance half the night, and sleep soundly the other half; and if I had dreams, they should be sportive visions, in which that leaden headed fellow Morpheus should act as master of the ceremonies, and introduce whim and caprice to dance a reel with me."

"Perhaps you may be mistaken," said Adeline. "Love may yet occasion you uneasy days and sleepless nights; you may yet be fated to meet the man who may change all your smiles into tears."

"Never," said Eliza rising, and tossing the book upon the table: – "What! sigh for a man, dim these bright luminaries with tears? No truly. Believe me, my child, I am too fond of admiration, to spoil the beauty of my face with grief, and the dismals; besides, to let you into a trifling secret, I have already been about a dozen times in love; but in the very height of the fit I never ate an ounce less, or got up an hour later in the morning."

"Surprising," said Adeline laughing, "but pray who were the objects of your tender regard?"

"You shall hear," resumed Eliza: "the first person who inspired me with the soft passion was Sir Hugh Meredith."

"Sir Hugh Meredith!" said Adeline, pursuing her drawing, "why he is old enough to be your grandfather."

"No matter for that," replied Eliza, "he is asthmatical, and six months in the year he is confined with the gout: but he is immensely rich; mercy on me, his money would have enabled me to shine here and rattle there. I could have bought oceans of frippery and nick nacs, that I could have found no possible use for, and I could have made myself the astonishment and admiration of all the natives here, not to say a word about the delight I would have had in treading on Sir Hugh's gouty toe, or in mistake taking hold of the hand bound up in flannel, and giving it a hearty shake, with a good night, or a good morning, Sir Hugh: but all my seductions would not do, though I smiled and simpered, shook up the sofa pillows for his gouty legs, poured out his madeira with my own fair hand, and played the

"Noble Race of Shenkin" to him till my fingers were numbed, the silly obstinate old fellow denied me the pleasure of spending his money, and breaking his heart."

"What a mad creature!" said Adeline.

"Then," resumed Eliza, "I became desperately enamoured of Sir Watkin ap Rice's elegant carriage and iron greys. Do you know Sir Watkin, Adeline?"

"No," said Adeline, "I have not the honour."

"If you did," rejoined Eliza, "you would not wonder at my infatuation. You have read Don Quixotte. His visage exactly resembles the description of the knights of the woeful countenance; his person is remarkably tall and meagre, and when habited *en militaire* with his helmet on, he looks like a rush-light crowned with an extinguisher."

Adeline laughed heartily.... "But mum," said Eliza, laying her fingers on her lips, "I hear Sir Owen, you shall have the conclusion another time."

Sir Owen came to tell them that he had just received an invitation from the officers of the Scotch Greys quartered at Carnarvon, who, after a general review, proposed giving the ladies of the town and vicinity a ball.

"Charming fellows," said Eliza, capering about the room, "I dote on a red coat."

"And you, Adeline," said Sir Owen, turning to his daughter.

"I have no particular partiality for a red coat, sir," replied Adeline, "but I love dancing you know."

"We shall accept the invitation then..." said Sir Owen. "Adeline, the effect of the moonlight on that turret is very fine," observed Sir Owen, looking over her drawing. "You have been busily employed this morning. Eliza, my dear, have you nothing to shew me; what have you been doing?"

"Me, sir, me! – I have been doing – nothing at all, sir," –

"Well, really," said Sir Owen, "that is surprising. What, not engaged in mischief?"

"I wish my brother Henry was here to go with us," said Adeline. "I shall feel so awkward at a ball without him; but when, sir, is it to take place?"

"Next Wednesday," replied Sir Owen.

"Bless me," said Eliza, springing up, "next Wednesday! why, I shall never have any thing in readiness. – I have ten thousand orders for my milliner and mantua-maker… Adeline, my dear, what will you wear?"

"Really my dress has never yet entered my imagination: it will be quite time enough to think of that tomorrow." –

"For my part I shall think of nothing else," rejoined Eliza.

"Well, ladies," said Sir Owen, "I suppose you will not make me one of the cabinet council in this important affair, so I shall leave you to settle it between yourselves, and take the opportunity of visiting Sir Griffith Tudor. Eliza, my dear, have you any commission to honour me with?"

"Only my affectionate duty, sir; and you will be good enough to mention the ball."

Sir Owen rode off, and Eliza obliged Adeline to lay aside the drawing, and proceed with her to the dressing-room, where, having approved and again rejected various articles of ornament, she still remained undecided as to the dress in which she designed to take by storm the hearts of the officers at the ball. Adeline's patience was almost exhausted, when her maid appeared to say that Sir Owen was returned, and had brought with him two officers, who were to stay dinner. Away flew Eliza to her toilette, where having at length adorned her person to her satisfaction, she descended with Adeline to the library, where Sir Owen shortly after presented to them Colonel Effingham and Captain Seymour; they were both handsome men, but Colonel Effingham had a serious air, a sort of thinking gravity, which did not exactly accord with the lively taste of Eliza, while Captain Seymour's gay manners, brilliant bon mots, and lively repartees, riveted her attention and won her approbation: they were a pair that heaven seemed to have made on purpose for each other – all whim, frolic, and caprice; and before they parted in the evening she had promised him her hand for the two first sets at the ensuing balls.

Lady Tudor, the mother of Eliza, whose handsome though masculine person and florid complexion seemed an eternal contradiction to that ill health and delicacy of nerves she declared she possessed, affected a softness of manners and tenderness of disposition which often displayed itself in faintings and hysterics. Sir Griffith Tudor was a little man, about four feet five inches high, with an intelligent countenance and sparkling black eyes: he was boisterous in his behaviour, passionate in his temper, with the lungs of Stentor, which he exercised to the extreme discomposure of her ladyship's delicate nerves, and the terror and annoyance of the servants whenever an opposition to his sentiments, or a demur to his commands was offered. He loved nothing in nature but his hounds, his horses, and Eliza, whom he suffered to play all the mischievous tricks her sportive nature could invent unrestricted and uncontrolled: he was very rich; she was his only child (three sons having died in their infancy) and being said to resemble him in person he never allowed her to be opposed or contradicted in any of her frolics. Happily for those about her, her heart was good, and if her wild disposition inflicted wounds, her feeling and generosity led her to make instant reparation: in this too she resembled her father, who though rash and pertinacious when under the influence of passion, was in his temperate moments liberal and feeling towards those who came recommended by misfortune to his notice and his pity. For his lady's fanciful complaints he had no sort of compassion, and to tease and throw her into hysterics was one of his highest enjoyments.

On Wednesday morning Lady Tudor in her carriage, and Sir Griffith on horseback, arrived at Dolgelly Castle, where her ladyship expressed much displeasure at her daughter's refusing to accompany her.

"No, please fate," said Eliza, "I will not be stoved up in a close carriage such a fine morning as this. Papa, I ride: what say you, Adeline?"

"It certainly was my intention to go on horseback," replied Adeline; "but if Lady Tudor wishes it I will with much pleasure accompany her."

"You have done finely for yourself now," whispered Eliza; "why mamma will have all the glasses up, and you will neither have the pleasure of seeing nor being seen."

"Miss Llewellyn is all goodness," said Lady Tudor, "and if I thought it would not be repugnant to her wishes –"

"Pshaw! damn your fine speeches, Winefred," said Sir Griffith interrupting her, "you may take your oath the girl has no wish to be stuffed into your carriage and poisoned with hartshorn and valerian water. Plague confound it, do recollect that you was once young yourself."

"I am very unwell this morning, Sir Griffith: I had a very bad night."

"Why the devil did not you stay in bed then, and make it out this morning?" replied Sir Griffith.

"I entreat, Sir Griffith –"

"And I beseech you, Lady Tudor," said he raising his voice, "to remember that Adeline Llewellyn has committed no crime for which she deserves the penance of listening to your doleful history of brain fevers, sleepless nights, palpitations of heart, spasmodic affections, and the devil himself knows what beside."

"But, Sir Griffith, if Miss Llewellyn desires –"

"Don't provoke me, Lady Tudor; you know I am by nature the most peaceable creature that can be, but I hate contradiction. Damnation! I say it is unnatural to suppose that a young girl can prefer the company of an old woman, with a long rigmarole of weak nerves and dismal complaints to the conversation and admiration of a parcel of fine athletic young fellows."

Adeline felt uneasy at this dispute, and to end it would gladly at once have slipped into her ladyship's carriage, so much did she dread the violence of Sir Griffith's temper, though at all times she preferred riding on horseback, and particularly at this time, when she expected so much pleasure in witnessing a variety of military manoeuvres. Eliza, who was accustomed to these scenes of altercation, sat anxiously waiting for the moment when her father's impatient temper should be sufficiently wound up to insist on Adeline mounting her horse – and to this crisis it approached the next instant, when Lady Tudor, turning to Adeline, said she thought it was time for them to set off. He swore she might set off to the devil as soon as she liked, but that Adeline should by no means accompany her. Lady Tudor took out her smelling bottle.

"Aye, aye, sniff away, my lady," said Sir Griffith, "sniff away – recover your spirits, for damn me if Miss Llewellyn goes with you."

"Sir Griffith, you are –"

"I know I am, my dear," said he, "I know I am determined to have my way for once."

"For once, Sir Griffith!"

"Yes, for once I am determined to carry my point, so you may have a fit as soon as you like, but I will be damned if I don't have my way. Your ladyship is not prepared for an hysteric I perceive; shall I have the honour to hand you to your carriage?"

"I am not disposed to go yet, sir."

"O, you are waiting for me!" said the incorrigible Sir Griffith. "I beg a thousand pardons for my inattention; your hand, Lady Tudor."

Her ladyship snatched away her hand, and sunk back in her chair. Adeline approached and said she would go with her ladyship. Eliza began to be ashamed of the scene, and said they would both go in the carriage.

"I will be damned if you do though," said Sir Griffith, "and my horse too." He rung the bell violently, and on the appearance of the servant ordered Lady Tudor's carriage.

Sir Owen, who during the dispute had been absent, now entered the room, and perceiving from all their countenances that something was amiss, inquired what was the matter.

"Only the old matter," sobbed Lady Tudor, "only the old matter, Sir Owen! my weak and gentle disposition is imposed upon, my poor spirits flurried, and my weak nerves shattered."

"Come along, my tender, meek gentle dove – no grumbling. Remember, my sweet essence of asafœtida, that you took me for better, for worse! love, honour, and obey, you know. As for love, whew! (here he whistled) that flew God knows where, the Lord knows how long ago; and as for honouring,

Fal de ral tit; (here he sang) but as for obeying, damn me, I'll make you do that."

He then clapped her arm under his, and in less than two minutes, in spite of the united remonstrances of Sir Owen, Adeline, and Eliza, Sir Griffith whisked Lady Tudor into her carriage, and told her she was at liberty to have an hysteric as soon as she pleased.

Her ladyship, highly provoked and vexed, was too much out of temper to proceed to Carnavon: she ordered the carriage home, lamenting her evil destiny in having a husband who contradicted all her wishes, and a daughter who disobeyed all her commands. The rest of the party proceeded to the review on horseback. The ground allotted for the display of military science and skill was a large plain situated between two hills, upon which Carnarvon and its neighbourhood had poured out its populace to witness a spectacle of unusual grandeur. On one side of the plain was a road leading to the town, and on the other a narrow winding path cut over rocks and precipices that led directly to the sea. Adeline and Eliza had received the compliments of all the officers introduced by Colonel Effingham and Captain Seymour, and had been pressed by them to enter a large tent on an eminence, which had been pitched for the accommodation of the ladies, and from whence they could command a view of the whole field: but this they declined, and preferred remaining on horseback. The soldiers went through their several evolutions to the entire satisfaction of their commanding officer, and the gratification of the spectators. A sham fight succeeded – the discharge of cannon, the beat of drums, and sound of trumpets, made a glorious confusion: but a standard taken in the heat of battle from the foe, waving too near the eyes of Eliza's horse, the animal suddenly took fright, and, regardless of the rein, flew with the velocity of lightning along the narrow path among the rocks. The tide was full in, and every moment the distracted Sir Griffith expected to see his daughter plunged in the waves.

Captain Seymour from a distance beheld the confusion, and saw a horse flying with a lady over the dangerous precipice: he instantly took a circuitous path, and at the very instant the terrified animal was in the act of plunging into the sea he turned an angle of the rock, and caught him by the bridle. Eliza had firmly kept her seat, though fear had deprived her of recollection, and she recovered to see herself supported in the arms of Adeline, while her father was loudly blessing and shaking Captain Seymour by the hand, swearing he was a damned brave fellow, and that he would give him the best horse in his stud. When Captain Seymour had set off with the idea of stopping the horse, he did not know that it was Miss Tudor to whom he intended so essential a service: and it was with additional pleasure that he had preserved the life of a person who had already made for herself no small interest in his heart.

Eliza soon recovered her spirits, and having expressed her gratitude in the warmest terms to Captain Seymour, with her accustomed gaiety assured him that the fright she had received would not prevent her fulfilling her engagement with him at night. Adeline felt really ill; she had been greatly terrified, and it was with extreme difficulty she kept herself from fainting: she rejoiced when Sir Griffith proposed going home.

"You will not mount that animal again?" said she to Eliza.

"Most certainly," replied Miss Tudor, springing on his back. "Poor Rolla had no intention of breaking my neck or dashing me into the sea; it would be hard to punish him for an accidental fault – besides I believe he has suffered even more than I have."

Sir Griffith called her a good girl – patted the neck of the horse, said he was a fine fellow, but swore if ever he played such another prank he would blow his damned brains out. As they rode along, "It is well," said he, "that your mother was not present; we should have had rare work with her fits and vagaries – all the smelling bottles in Carnarvon would not have set her nerves to rights. Eliza, mind, mum's the word, or her ladyship will for ever upbraid me for having prevented your going in the carriage with her. Damn it, if she knew, she would crow over me finely: I should be absolutely stunned with a string of accidents, probable and improbable, that might have taken place, such as fractured skulls, broken arms, dislocated elbows, and the Lord knows what besides; and then her own brain fever, hysteric affections, spasmodic contractions, shattered nerves, and sleepless nights would be dinned in my ears to eternity: so damn it, Eliza, mind my girl, not a word."

At night, as gay as if nothing had happened, Eliza appeared at the ball in a white sarsenet dress, covered with blue crape formed into draperies, with chains of small silver roses; her hair was confined with a diamond crescent, and her arms and neck were encircled with the same costly ornaments. Adeline wore a silver net over a dress of white satin; her beautiful hair was braided with wreaths of pearl, and strings of the same ornamented her arms and hung upon her ivory bosom. Among the many gentlemen who crowded round Eliza to congratulate her on her providential escape the Honourable Captain Maitland was most profuse in his compliments:

"'Pon my reputation," said he, "if your horse had taken to the sea it would have been a very serious affair."

"Very true," said Eliza, "for I should not only have spoiled my new habit but lost my life into the bargain."

"Shocking!" replied the gallant captain, "'pon my reputation the beaux would have been *tout desespoir*: and for me I could not have survived the horrifying catastrophe; I should have been so miserable that – Ha! Montrose, 'pon my reputation you smell worse than a civit cat – never use any thing but *esprit de rose* myself; your lavender is too much for my faculties."

He bowed to the ladies, and passed on to another group, Montrose requested the honour of Adeline's hand, but she was already engaged to Colonel Effingham, who that instant led her out. Eliza and her gay partner footed it away merrily, and were so pleased and entertained with each other that they mutually regretted when the customary etiquette obliged them to change partners; they however settled to dance together again when the next change took place. Colonel Effingham was a young man of great good sense and excellent education. The modesty and gentleness of Adeline had even more captivation for him than her beautiful person; and while he touched her soft hand, and led her through the mazes of the dance, he wished that it was possible to interest her heart in his favour. He admired the vivacity of Eliza; he was charmed while his eye followed her sportive steps and saw her animated gestures: but when he turned to Adeline he beheld in her a graceful modesty, a retiring sweetness, a blushing loveliness, that while it commanded respect inspired love.

Adeline lamented to Eliza the absence of Henry, while Eliza laughingly asked if Colonel Effingham did not make love to her satisfaction as she wished for a substitute. At a moment when they were taking refreshments the Honourable Captain Maitland again joined them, and asked Adeline if she did not feel fatigued: on her answering in the negative he expressed great surprise.

"'Pon my reputation," said he, "it is marvellous to me how people can undergo the fatigue of dancing."

"A Scotchman," replied Eliza, "and consider dancing a fatigue! why I always understood that they were as proverbial for their love of that amusement as the natives of our country."

"Shocking, 'pon my reputation," replied the Honourable Captain Maitland. "Only consider how it heats the blood: much of so violent an exercise is enough to throw a person of robust constitution into a fever. I never dance," continued he yawning, "it is far too fatiguing."

"O fie!" replied Eliza, "a soldier and talk of fatigue! suppose the duties of your profession were to call you into action, sure the fatigue of dancing would be nothing compared to long marches and harassing campaigns!"

"The child would fall sick," said old Major Fergus, "and so escape both the fatigue and the danger!"

"And the glory too," replied Adeline.

"On my soul," continued Major Fergus, "I dinne ken what the deel such Jemmy finical fellows do in the army, unless it is to entitle them to wear a red coat, which I have often heard is very attractive with the ladies; it would have been a far better present if the noble lord your uncle had presented you with a rod instead of a commission."

The Honourable Captain Maitland affected to laugh, and in reply said, "'Pon my reputation, major, you are too severe."

"The deel of any reputation will you ever have but that of being the greatest coxcomb between this and the Hebrides," said the major; "and if your head is not strong enough to bear the roar of cannon, and you are too indolent to dance, you have no business to disgrace the coat of a soldier, or stand in the way like a post in a ball-room."

"Give me the man," said Eliza, "who will caper all night for his amusement, and fight all day for glory and his country: such a character can never fail of being a favourite with the ladies."

The Honourable Captain Maitland affected not to hear these speeches, but turned to Adeline, and wished her much amusement in the cotillion set she was preparing to join with Captain Seymour, who had requested her hand when he had resigned Eliza's, and sauntered away to another part of the room where a group of ladies were complaining of the scarcity of gentlemen: to several of these he addressed himself, and declared upon his reputation he was extremely concerned to see them without partners, wished for their sakes that he was able to divide himself, but that not being in the chapter of possibilities he would not dance at all, being fearful of giving offence to the rest should he select any one in particular – that he adored them all, and *enverité* he wished to continue in all their good graces. He then displayed his cambric handkerchief, declared 'pon his reputation the room was enough to suffocate him, made a sliding bow, and passed on.

Lady Tudor, notwithstanding her illness and disappointment in the morning, had recovered sufficient temper and spirits to be at the ball at night: she perfectly agreed with the Honourable Captain Maitland in the idea of dancing being too robust an exercise for persons of delicate nerves. Cards had been prepared in an adjoining apartment, and her ladyship was on the point of winning the third rubber at whist, when a lady observed that Miss Tudor looked uncommonly well after her morning's accident. In vain Sir Griffith coughed and winked; the person without observing him had answered all her ladyship's inquiries, who having heard the recital of her daughter's danger gave a loud shriek, and fell back in her chair in strong hysterics. In a moment all was confusion – the card table was thrown down, a candle fell into Lady Tudor's lap, and set fire to the end of a long veil that hung over her shoulder: Sir Griffith snatched a large goblet of water from the hand of a gentleman and threw it souse into her ladyship's face. The fire was extinguished, but before she could recover from the shock this sudden action occasioned, while she was gasping for breath he caught up an old lady's snuff box, and taking a large pinch between his fingers, crammed it up her ladyship's nostrils, saying, "Sniff, my lady, no hartshorn to be had." This was too much to bear: Lady Tudor, forgetting that she was in fits, started in agony from her chair, sneezing violently, her eyes streaming from the effect of the snuff which lay in a large dab on her cheek, and her garments drenched with the water Sir Griffith had thrown upon her.

"Inhuman, barbarous wretch!" shrieked the gasping Lady Tudor.

"Sniff, sniff away, my lady," said Sir Griffith pursuing her round the room; "the snuff I see is more effective than hartshorn or burnt feathers."

"Barbarian! you have almost drowned me: I shall catch my death of cold."

"Well, well, my lady, you must impute it all to my excessive affection; there was you kicking in fits, and your head all in a blaze – on water, out fire, you know. Here do, my dear, take a little more snuff: it is a grand restorative, better by half than Solomon's Balsam of Gilead. Take another sniff, my lady," said Sir Griffith offering her the box: "it will wonderfully relieve your nerves."

Her ladyship pushed his hand from her face; the box fell to the ground, but the snuff flew up in a cloud, and almost blinded him. Smarting with agony he stamped and swore like a madman: her ladyship forgot her own sufferings and joined the general laugh at the grotesque figure of Sir Griffith, who was jumping about the room like a parched pea. It was long before the tumult subsided, when Lady Tudor ordering her carriage, protested it should be the last time that ever she would subject herself to such outrageous treatment by coming into public company with a man who paid no regard to the delicacy of her feelings, or the weakness of her nerves.

"Damn your delicate feelings; damn your weak nerves," vociferated Sir Griffith. "I wish with all my soul you were performing an hysteric at the bottom of the sea: may I be poisoned with asafœtida, and suffocated with burnt feathers, if ever I come abroad with you again."

A gentleman handed Lady Tudor to her carriage. Sir Griffith hastily stooped down, and grappling up the snuff that had fallen on the floor, flew after her ladyship, who was just seated in her carriage; he threw the snuff into her face, and desired her to sniff away, for as she had found so much benefit from it already, it would surely keep her from hysterics on the road home.

The news of this rupture did not reach the ball-room till after the departure of Lady Tudor. At a late, or rather early hour, the company broke up: before they parted Captain Seymour had prevailed on Eliza to allow him to visit her in the character of a lover. Colonel Effingham had also resolved to address Adeline, but her very retiring behaviour had prevented his entering on so particular a subject, though his attentions had been sufficiently marked to convince Eliza that the colonel was deeply smitten, though the unconscious Adeline had not vanity enough to suppose that she had made the slightest impression on his heart.

CHAPTER III

Ah, fear! ah, frantic fear!
I see, I see thee near;
And lest thou meet my blasted view,
Hold each strange tale devoutly true.

Collins

"Go to the war, my hero. I will not tarnish
The lustre of thy laurels with a tear."

SIR OWEN LLEWELLYN doted on his daughter, but it was not a blind or a partial fondness that resulted from her being his only child, and the heiress of his fortune – it was an affection that had for its basis the knowledge that her mind abounded with all the amiable virtues and estimable qualities that adorn human nature – and while he gazed with tears of tenderness upon her beautiful exterior, his heart exulted in the proud conviction that her person was only the lovely casket that contained a still more exquisitely lovely mind. When Colonel Effingham modestly expressed his hopes and wishes respecting Adeline to her father, the worthy baronet at once referred him to herself, saying "That he had the firmest reliance on her prudence, and should entirely leave it to herself, to determine a matter of such importance as that on which the happiness of her future life must depend." Adeline acknowledged herself flattered, and obliged by Colonel Effingham's preference, but declined accepting his addresses, at the same time assuring her father that her heart owned no sort of predilection for any man in existence, himself and her brother Henry excepted, and it was the darling wish of her heart to pass the remainder of her days with him in a single state. Sir Owen smiled as he kissed the glowing cheek of his daughter, and mentally exclaimed, – "Sweet innocent! thy time is not yet arrived." To Colonel Effingham he politely expressed the pleasure he should have experienced in the hope of calling him his son, and though Adeline had declared herself averse to accepting him as a lover, he should be proud at all times to receive him as a friend. Colonel Effingham's heart acknowledged the candour of Adeline's behaviour; he admired in her that superiority of mind which was above encouraging attentions she could not approve; and he sighed with deep and sincere regret to think that he had been unable to interest her in his favour, the only woman he had ever felt a real passion for. Eliza in her lively way had affected to condole with Colonel Effingham on his rejection.

After having mimicked his dejected air and pensive looks, she bade him cheer up, and cast away despair, for if Adeline at all resembled her, she could not possibly be sure of her own mind for a day together: and that it was not only possible, but highly probable, that what she disliked tonight she might warmly approve in the morning.

"And now," continued Eliza laughing, "I have a most lucky thought – only bribe me handsomely, and I promise to let no opportunity slip of abusing you to my friend."

"Of abusing me!" said the astonished colonel.

"Most certainly," replied Eliza, "I will represent you as a wild, profligate, inconstant rake; accuse you of ten thousand faults that you never committed, and most likely never thought of. Believe me, my doleful colonel, this is the only method to make her mind give you credit for virtues, and perfections you never possessed: women generally act by the rule of contrary: if you can prevail on Sir Owen to join in the plot, and forbid his daughter to encourage your addresses, my life upon it her own inclination, aided by my persuasions, will make her downright in love with you in a month."

Colonel Effingham incredulously shook his head; he was convinced that Adeline's mind was differently organized to that of her lively friend, and having once refused his love, she would at no future period accede to it – all that remained for him was the hope that time, and the duties of his profession, might weaken his attachment, and restore him again to ease and happy indifference.

Eliza rallied Adeline unmercifully on her rejection of the colonel, told her that whether she had approved him or not, she was silly not to retain him in her suit –

"There is no pleasure equal to having a string of adoring swains," said Eliza, "to see them seriously and earnestly contending for the immense honour of picking up your glove, or handing you to your carriage: besides the exquisite pleasure of making them jealous, setting them together by the ears, and standing the chance of having a duel fought on your account."

"You and I, my dear Eliza, think very differently on these matters," replied Adeline, "I should never pardon myself were I for a moment to encourage hopes I never intended to realize; and surely there cannot be a greater cruelty than that of keeping a mind in suspense, when you have it in your power to restore it to comparative ease, by placing it in a state of certainty. And as to the duel, I would not endanger the lives of my fellow creatures for the universe… No, Heaven forbid!"

Eliza laughed heartily, "I believe in my conscience," said she, "you intend to die an old maid, and be canonized for saint; however, allow me, as you seem to be quite a novice in the ways of men, to set your innocence right in a small matter or two, which you appear to place in a wrong point of view. Be assured, my dear, men make love as much for the gratification of vanity as any other motive; very few of them have sensibility enough to be happy or miserable, whether they are received or rejected, further than as it affects their pride, their self-consequence, or their interest… And if they fight duels, it is more for the sake of notoriety and the fame of bravery than any acute feelings of love or jealousy."

Adeline blushed, "Nay, my dear Adeline," resumed Eliza, observing her heightened colour, "do not imagine that I think Colonel Effingham is in love with you."

"If he is not, he must be the greatest hypocrite in nature, and can indeed have neither eyes, ears, heart, nor understanding."

"Now, I actually believe, that he is really, truly, and veritably suffering the malady of disappointed hope. – But I have made man my chief study, and I find the generality of them of dispositions similar to his own: my vanity is pleased when I am admired; I delight in being courted, followed and flattered: but as to love, *pardonnai moi*, that is *une autre chose*."

Captain Seymour almost lived at Tudor Hall; he was Sir Griffith's inseparable companion; he hunted, sung, and played at cribbage with him, and was in fact so great a favourite, that there did not appear a bar in the way of his union with Eliza, by whom he had been received as a favoured lover. Lady Tudor, indeed, favoured the wishes of the honourable Captain Maitland, whose delicate sentiments, and soft gentle manners, exactly accorded with her ladyship's notion of elegance and refinement. She entirely disapproved of the noisy romping mirth of Captain Seymour, and felt chagrined and angry when Sir Griffith ridiculed the soft white lusty-like hands and rose-scented cambric handkerchiefs of the honourable Captain Maitland. Eliza flirted, laughed at, and despised him, but this his vanity would by no means allow him to see. He knew his pretensions were favoured by Lady Tudor, and as he was the presumptive heir to a title, he flattered himself with the hope of gaining Miss Tudor, whose large fortune appeared vastly convenient to redeem some pretty deep mortgages, with which the extravagances of noble relatives had encumbered the estates annexed to the title; but of becoming his wife Eliza had not entertained the remotest idea: her heart was really Seymour's, though she would have made no scruple to encourage the adoration of a score of admirers.

Sir Griffith Tudor had a very handsome dairy-maid, on whom the honourable Captain Maitland in his walks about the grounds had cast his eyes, and whose virtue he had assailed with all the united artillery of vows, promises, and flattery. Gwinthlean had for a long time resisted his overtures, and endeavoured to avoid him; but at length her virtue began to give way, and she made an appointment to meet him at a barn, within sight of Tudor Hall. The hour was nine, and a clear full moon lighted the amorous captain to the place of assignation. He waited more than half an hour, and the keenness of the air had not a little contributed to cool his passion, when Gwinthlean came running towards him – he complained of the cold, and having waited so long, protested 'pon his reputation that he should have a sore throat, which he began defending with his cambric handkerchief.

Gwinthlean said, "Got pless hur, hur cout not come before, and was afrait to come at all, for the peoples sait that the tefil haunted the parn."

The captain, to whom the sight of Gwinthlean had given warmth and spirits, used many arguments to quiet her apprehensions, and win her to his purpose; Gwinthlean resisted, and declared, "she was afrait to consent for fear he would not keep his promise of making her a fine laty."

The honourable captain swore 'pon his reputation that he would do much more for her than she wished, or he had promised: he threw his arms about her. Gwinthlean avoided his embrace – "But my mother," said she, "always tells me if I don't take care of my virtue the tefil will fly away with me; and only think," said she, shuddering, "if I was to see him, with eyes like saucers, and horns like pitchforks –"

"'Pon my word," said the captain, you are enough to horrify one; come, come, we lose time that might be employed much better: let us go into the barn. I shall go to Carnarvon in the morning, I have something particular to say to you."

Gwinthlean reluctantly suffered him to draw her into the barn, after much rustling; at the very moment the captain supposed himself on the verge of accomplishing his wishes, she burst from his arms with a loud shriek, and flew out of the barn. The honourable Captain Maitland, astonished at this action, would have flown after her: but between him and the door stood a huge terrific black figure, with cloven feet, fiery eyes, and tremendous horns, which seized him in its strong grip, pinioned his hands behind him with an iron chain, threw him on his face, fastened his legs together in the same way, then swinging him across his shoulders, flew with him to the stables behind Tudor Hall, and stuck him up to his neck in a dunghill. He had not remained in this lamentable situation long, before Sir Griffith Tudor and Captain Seymour, who had been to fetch Eliza from Dolgelly Castle, rode past. The groans of the poor wretch, who had struggled to extricate himself till he was nearly exhausted, and almost suffocated with filth, attracted their attention: they turned back, and inquiring who was there, discovered the deplorable situation of the Honourable Captain Maitland, whose head alone was visible on the top of the dunghill.

Sir Griffith laughed immoderately – "What, my noble captain," said he, "sunk in a morass? all owing to the war, hey! – why damn it you have got a soft bed! But what the devil stuck you up to your chin in that filthy hole?"

"Hush, hush," said Maitland, rolling his eyes wildly, his teeth chattering in his head; "it was the devil himself in proper person that fixed me here; but for the love of heaven help me out."

Eliza, scarcely able to sit her horse for laughing, rode to the house to summon assistance; the servants dragged him through the dunghill while Sir Griffith and Seymour stood convulsed with laughter. His new regimentals, in which he fancied himself irresistible, and in which he had hoped to triumph over the simplicity of Gwinthlean, were completely spoilt, and the disappointed captain exhibited a most deplorable spectacle of mud and terror.

They led him to the servants' hall, where he was stripped and cleaned: after having been washed and scrubbed, Sir Griffith begged to know by what accident he came in the situation in which they found him? The captain looked wildly, and protested seriously that the devil had caught him up and flew a long way with him in the air, and then stuck him in the dunghill. The servants whom this strange occurrence had gathered together, and who stood with their mouths wide open gaping to catch the marvellous story, actually believed that Satan had paid him a visit, and they expected that Sir Griffith's turn would come next, who laughed at and ridiculed the fear-stricken wretch so unmercifully.

"But come," said Sir Griffith, "you don't tell us the particulars of this strange affair – what was you at? where were you when the devil clapt his claw upon you?"

The Honourable Captain Maitland was silent. Seymour repeated the question, "Where were you?"

He groaned out, "At the *red barn*."

"Why damn it," said Sir Griffith, "all my servants say the devil has appeared in that barn ever since poor Hugh Jones hung himself there. Pooh damn it, I need not ask what you were at – you had got a girl there I will lay my life – you plead guilty, do you? What, and so his infernal majesty spoiled sport, did he?"

The Honourable Captain Maitland begged to be spared any farther question, declaring, 'pon his reputation that he should never get over the shock he had sustained, and that his nerves were so shattered that they would never recover their proper tone. Sir Griffith sent to Lady Tudor's dressing room for cordials and essences to sweeten the captain, who vowed that the smell of horse-dung and brimstone quite overcame him. When the restoratives arrived he took a little of Lady Tudor's cordial, and requested some rose-water to bathe his hands and face. Sir Griffith officiously offered his assistance, slyly exchanged the bottle, and the unfortunate disappointed captain had his hair, hands, and face sluiced with asafœtida, which, added to his former uneasy sensations, threw him into such agonies that he actually fainted away. In this state Sir Griffith would have had him carried under the pump, swearing that there was nothing equal to cold water for removing its smell, and restoring animation, except snuff, with which unfortunately he was unprovided.

Lady Tudor, who to her other weaknesses added superstition in a most superlative degree, swallowed the marvellous story of the Honourable Captain Mainland's being flown away with by the devil and stuck up to his neck in the dunghill with the greatest avidity, and was expressing her wonder to Eliza how the captain came to go to the red barn at that time of night, when Sir Griffith burst into the room and addressed his daughter with –

"Here's a pretty damned scoundrel of an honourable captain; comes to my house with the pretence of making love to you, Eliza, and all the while is unlawfully poaching after the maids – that's his delicacy and propriety and be damned to him; but I think he has got a surfeit for some time of curds and whey and butter milk."

"What do you mean, Sir Griffith?" inquired Lady Tudor; "what do you mean?"

"Why I mean that your favourite milk-sop, your man of delicacy and refinement, that walking bottle of essence, that compound of frippery, foppery, and foolery, the Honourable Captain Maitland, has been dishonourable enough to try to seduce my dairy-maid Gwinny."

Lady Tudor drew herself up, and protested she could not credit it.

"Then you may do the other thing and be damned," replied Sir Griffith, "but it's nevertheless true whether you believe it or not; and if I did not think he has already suffered sufficient punishment from fright, I would make the damned rascal hop over my horsewhip all the way to his quarters."

"But did he really see the devil, Sir Griffith?" asked my lady.

"Aye, did he, and feel him too," rejoined Sir Griffith; "his new regimentals are burnt in twenty places by the fire from his nostrils, and his shoulders and sides bear testimony of the iron grip of the fiend – has your ladyship any thing proper to apply to his bruises?"

Lady Tudor turned up her eyes and prayed that herself and family might be defended from such a dreadful visitant, while Eliza laughed at the representations her father made of the poor captain's lamentable situation, who had insisted that two men should watch by his bedside all night, for fear of the devil paying him another visit. The Honourable Captain Maitland was several days before he was sufficiently recovered to quit his room, during which time he had been visited and unmercifully ridiculed by his brother officers, who had at length brought him to entertain some doubts whether it was really the devil in proper person who had handled him so roughly, or some sweetheart of Gwinthlean's, who had, instigated by her, thought proper to punish him for his licentious designs. Ashamed and mortified he was about to quit Tudor Hall, when Eliza and Sir Griffith insisted that he should stay and assist at a wedding that was to take place the next morning. With, much reluctance he passed the day amidst the reproofs and advice of Lady Tudor, who felt greatly scandalized that at the very moment he had engaged her good offices, and obtained her promise of befriending his suit with Miss Tudor, that he should have been led astray from decorum by a blowze of a dairy-maid. Sir Griffith swore he deserved picketing, and

Eliza and Seymour laughed and rallied. The morning was fine; Sir Griffith, Eliza, and Adeline, who had arrived for the occasion, with Captain Seymour and Maitland, set off for the village church, where Captain Maitland was told he was to officiate as father, and Eliza and Miss Llewellyn as bridemaids. The bride contrived to conceal her face until the ceremony had begun, and he felt no small share of vexation and confusion when he discovered he was to give away the rosy Gwinthlean to a tall athletic fellow whom he had no doubt was the person who had performed the part of the devil at the red barn.

When the ceremony was over Sir Griffith set the example of saluting the bride; the Honourable Captain Maitland hung back, but the bridegroom advancing, said, "Captain, you may have a kiss *now* and welcome; but take care how you offer to make a fine lady of my wife, or persuade her to meet you again at the red barn for fear I should be there and play the devil; for if I am compelled to wear horns, depend upon it worse will follow than sticking you up to your neck in a dunghill."

The company laughed, and the Honourable Captain Maitland looked even more silly than ever; he took courage however to assure Hoel Watkin that his wife's chastity might rest in perfect security from any future attempts of his: but he begged him to allow her to accept five guineas, which he presented as a reward for her having resisted his temptations.

"There was no temptation in the case, look you," said Gwinthlean, "for I had no regard for you at all, and I love my own dear Hoel in my heart, and so I told him all about the fine offers you had made; and poor Hoel, look you, was quite jealous, and said if I wished to convince him that I did not care about you, that I must promise to meet you at the red barn; and that he would wrap himself up in the hide of an ox, and cure you of trying to ruin innocent country girls: inteed when I saw him I thought it was the tefil, and I ran home as fast as I could."

After this explanation the poor crestfallen captain affected to cough – he shook the bridegroom by the hand, kissed the bride, and wished them joy, though he secretly felt much chagrin to think his person had been despised and maltreated for the sake of a vulgar bumpkin, and he pitied the depraved taste of the girl who had preferred a gigantic corn thresher to a man of his elegance and graces He was however necessitated to smother his mortification, and what was still worse, to leave Tudor Hall without the smallest hope of making an impression on the heart of Eliza, whom he evidently discovered gave a preference to Captain Seymour; – for though she had listened to his professions of tender regard, she had on all occasions exercised her lively temper upon him, and made his conversation, his dress, and manners constant subjects of ridicule; yet still his vanity induced him to believe that he should, aided by Lady Tudor, who encouraged his hopes, carry his prize: but since his adventure at the red barn, and his designs upon Gwinthlean had become public, Sir Griffith had treated him with such pointed rudeness, and Lady Tudor with such haughty reserve, that he entirely relinquished the expectation of liquidating his family debts, through the means of an alliance with Miss Tudor.

The unfortunate story of the devil and the dunghill pursued him to the parade and the mess-room, till at last the Honourable Captain Maitland found it necessary, for the preservation of his reputation, to exchange into another regiment, the officers of the Scotch Greys holding him in such contempt that they avoided as far as possible having any acquaintance or communication with him. Captain Seymour was not exactly to the taste of Lady Tudor, but Sir Griffith happening to approve him, her opinion was not considered of much consequence. Eliza frequently declared there was no pleasure in a love affair without opposition, and wished that her father and Seymour would fall out, that he might be forbade the house, and herself confined to her chamber.

"Then," said she, "we should have glorious confusion; Sir Griffith would storm, swear, and threaten – Lady Tudor would preach duty and obedience, and I should laugh at them both. Seymour would lament, entreat, and propose an elopement – I should talk of prudence and discretion, and at last consent. The plan would be this: twelve o'clock, the night dark as the grove – a rope ladder to descend from my window into the arms of my lover – a chaise and four foaming horses – the north road – off we drive."

"Eliza, Eliza," said Adeline, "my dear girl, you are certainly mad."

"That is your mistake, child," replied she. "Sir Griffith indeed would be stark mad when he discovered what a trick I had played him."

"And would you really elope, Eliza, if any thing was to happen to effect a change in your father's sentiments with respect to Captain Seymour?"

"As sure as I live," replied she; "and indeed, Adeline, to be married with papa and mamma's consent is but a humdrum sort of a business; no, no, a runaway match for me – a jump from a two pair of stairs window, and a journey to Gretna Green – off we go, helter skelter. Would not you accompany me in my expedition, Adeline?"

"No," replied Miss Llewellyn, "because my conscience would not allow me to encourage an act of disobedience. I know, my dear Eliza, you do not mean what you say: I am sure you would not marry in opposition to the wishes of Sir Griffith and Lady Tudor."

"Ah! Adeline," rejoined Eliza, "you judge me by yourself; you I know would pine yourself into a consumption rather than disobey your father, but I shall never arrive at your perfection. I love my father too, but he has encouraged me from my earliest recollection to contradict even him; and I fear in so essential a point as matrimony I should be wicked enough to feel a double satisfaction in acting contrary to his commands."

Sir Griffith had many times expressed a wish that Seymour would quit the army, but these hints he had affected not to understand, as added to his predilection for the service he felt it would be dishonourable to resign his commission at a moment when his country was engaged in war, and it was expected that the regiment he belonged to would be ordered abroad. He had obtained the consent of Sir Griffith to his hopes, and Eliza had confirmed them, when suddenly, as he had foreseen, the Scotch Greys were commanded to embark for Holland. It was now Sir Griffith spoke his wishes in plain terms, and proposed to Seymour his quitting the army at once.

"No, sir," replied the spirited young man, "it is impossible: I should for ever brand my character with infamy. I am sorry to refuse a request which I am persuaded proceeds from your regard for me; my country wants my service – I will not, like a coward, desert her. I cannot, will not disgrace the name of Seymour; I will either live without reproach, or die with honour."

Eliza's bright eyes glistened; she held out her hand to him with a smile of approbation; he pressed it to his lips.

"You may as well spare your kisses," said Sir Griffith, "or if you go to Holland, you shall never be my son-in-law."

"And if he does not," replied Eliza, "he shall never be my husband. What, sir, do you suppose that I would unite my destiny with a paltroon who struts about in a red coat while security is the word, and meanly pulls it off at the approach of danger. No, sir, I love his honour, and will never wish to tarnish it. Go, my dear Seymour, meet the foes of your country – the prayers of your Eliza shall follow you to the battle!"

"If he does," roared Sir Griffith, "I'll be damned if ever you are his, Eliza."

"Then," replied she, "I will never be any other man's."

"Go to your chamber, madam," said Sir Griffith; "I admire your heroics, but I will be damned if I don't find a way to lower you a peg or two yet. If I don't watch you I suppose you will be for disguising yourself and fighting by his side – you for love, and he for glory."

Seymour would have reasoned and expostulated, but in vain; the storm was up. Sir Griffith would hear nothing, but swore that he should that moment decide either to quit the army, or renounce his daughter; for whom he added he could have no violent affection, or he would not hesitate which way to determine. Seymour ardently loved Eliza, but his reputation, his honour was at stake; before he could reply she advanced to him, and said,

"If you are despicable enough to resign your commission we never meet again: no force shall compel me to unite myself to a man at whose dastardly principles the finger of scorn must continually point. Go in the firm assurance of my faith – I have given you my firm promise to be yours, and I will fulfil it should it please heaven to return you to me safe, or I will never marry at all."

"Then I will be damn'd if you don't die an old maid," vociferated Sir Griffith: "and now, madam, after having so nobly put your father to defiance, you may depart; but for you, sir," turning to the distressed Seymour, "the sooner you quit Tudor Hall the better. Go, you obstinate slut, leave the room this instant; I shall take good care you lay no plans for corresponding. Troop to your chamber this moment; you little, damned, perverse —"

Eliza threw herself into Seymour's arms, and in spite of the ravings and oaths of her father, again encouraged him in his duty, and renewed her vow of constancy. Sir Griffith never gave up a point; once set upon a thing opposition only provoked him to madness without altering his determination: and deaf to the entreaties, reasonings, and arguments of Seymour, he saw him depart, wishing that his courage might get cooled, and swearing that he would sooner give his daughter to a coal-heaver, than suffer her to marry a puppy who preferred the "bubble reputation," and sought it "even in the cannon's mouth," to the more solid enjoyments of ease and his friendship.

CHAPTER IV

I have no spur
To prick the sides of my intent, but only
Vaulting ambition, which o'erleaps itself,
And falls on the other side.

Shakespeare

Ah! what's more dangerous than this fond affiance?
Seems he a dove? his feathers are but borrow'd;
For he's dispos'd as the hateful raven,
Who cannot steal a shape that means deceit.

Ibid.

HENRY MORTIMER, now in his twentieth year, joined to a most graceful person a mind rich in intellectual endowment, and an understanding which education had improved to the highest degree of excellence. At college he had contracted a strict friendship with the Honourable Horatio Delamere, by whom he was invited to spend their next vacation at the seat of his father, Lord Narbeth, in Devonshire. Sir Owen Llewellyn knew that Lord Dungarvon and Lord Narbeth were upon visiting terms, and he secretly indulged the hope that chance might introduce his grandson to his notice. At a moment when his passions, calm and unprejudiced, would suffer nature to assert her rights; and that he would bestow on the son of the unfortunate Augustus Mortimer that affection he had so cruelly denied his ill-fated parent.

It happened, at the time of Henry's visit at Narbeth Lodge, that the dowager Dutchess of Inglesfield was at Mortimer Abbey and in her rides about the country with Lady Dungarvon had frequently met the young friends, Delamere and Mortimer. The person of Henry had attracted the fancy of the dutchess, now in her fiftieth year, who to a set of uncommonly long and sharp features added a tall meagre figure, extremely crooked and ill shaped. However, though her person held out no temptations, her high rank, great interest, and large possessions had procured her two husbands, who having been removed to their ancestors, she felt inclined to venture a third time into the blissful state of matrimony, so much was she fascinated with the personal graces of Henry Mortimer. Lord Dungarvon had been apprized of his grandson's visit at Narbeth Lodge, and had studiously avoided, both in his walks and rides, all places where he thought it probable he might encounter him: and with this disposition of mind he had not failed to acquaint Lord Narbeth, who kindly forbore to inform Henry of the rancour that still pervaded the heart of his unrelenting relation: but when Lord Dungarvon heard the extravagant praises of the Dutchess of Inglesfield, who affirmed that Henry was the most finished workmanship of heaven, the most charming creature she had ever seen, his mind instantly underwent a revolution; his ambition was again awakened – he began to conceive the project of bringing about a marriage between them; of wiping away the blot the father had cast upon the family escutcheon, by the aggrandisement of the son.

Miss Lonsdale, the niece of Lord Narbeth, a lively young woman, whose person, tolerably good, and exquisitely fine voice attracted much of Henry's attention, seemed in Lord

Dungarvon's eyes a terrible bar in the way of his scheme. He considered her as a grand impediment to his wishes, though he hoped that the knowledge Henry must certainly have of the misfortunes and distresses his father had brought upon himself by an imprudent marriage, would deter him from forming an engagement with Miss Lonsdale, entirely dependent on her uncle, himself not rich. Henry's heart as yet was perfectly free from the "witcheries of love;" if he felt a preference for any of the lovely sex, it was for his sister Adeline Llewellyn, who, when his mind drew a comparison, constantly bore away the palm from all her fair competitors.

Lord Narbeth was surprised one evening by a note from Mortimer Abbey, in which Lord Dungarvon invited himself and family to spend the next day at Narbeth Lodge, for the sole purpose of meeting and receiving to his warm affection his grandson. Lord Narbeth felt suspicious of his neighbour's motives, when he reflected how very short a time had elapsed since Lord Dungarvon had declared he would as soon encounter a rattle snake as the son of Louisa Berresford. Still he was inclined to hope that Henry's virtues, joined to his elegant person and captivating manners, would ultimately secure him the affection of his grandfather; and he felt it the duty of humanity to assist to bring about so desirable an event.

Henry had been prepared by Lord Narbeth and his friend Horatio to meet Lord Dungarvon, for whose person and character he entertained no very high veneration, when he remembered the sufferings of his mother, whom Sir Owen Llewellyn had often described to him as the most lovely and amiable of women: and when the banishment and fate of his father rose upon his mind, his heart swelled with indignation, and he felt it would be impossible for him ever to love or respect the being whose cruelty had sunk both his parents to a premature grave.

At the appointed hour Lord and Lady Dungarvon, accompanied by the Dutchess of Inglesfield, drawn forth in all the gay adornments of youth, arrived at Narbeth Lodge. Lord Dungarvon changed colour when Lord Narbeth presented Henry Augustus Mortimer; he thought of past events, and felt a pang of remorse – it was but momentary, for pride, ambition, and avarice, had steeled his heart against nature and feeling. Lady Dungarvon could not stifle the mother – she beheld in Henry her son, the buried Augustus Mortimer, and she sunk nearly fainting into the arms of Lady Narbeth:

"You perceive, sir," said Lord Dungarvon, addressing himself to Henry, "how much the recollection of past disagreeable circumstances, and the painful memory of your father's disobedience, affects Lady Dungarvon; may we in you, whom we are inclined to receive with parental affection, meet a recompense for all the disappointments and mortifications his imprudence inflicted."

Henry's cheek glowed, and his bosom swelled with indignant sensations, but he suppressed them, and only answered the unfeeling and haughty Lord Dungarvon with a bow, which his self-importance construed into acquiescence and submission. He was now introduced by his grandfather to the Dutchess of Inglesfield, who played off a thousand girlish airs and youthful graces, to the infinite diversion of Miss Lonsdale and Horatio Delamere, and the absolute disgust of Henry, whom they were designed to captivate. He had, to his extreme chagrin, been placed next to her at dinner, and during the whole day was unavoidably constrained to remain by her side. Miss Lonsdale sang and played with peculiar taste and elegance: Horatio Delamere was an adept in music, and Henry performed on the flute with grace and expression. He heard the proposal for retiring to the music-room with pleasure, as he expected to find there a cessation of the unceasing volubility of the Dutchess, whose affected sprightliness and nonsensical conversation had become wearying and trouble-some, and who had so entirely engrossed his attentions that he had been scarcely able to exchange a single syllable with any other person. The Dutchess declared music was her darling passion; she beat time, and made so many remarks on modulation and harmony, that Miss Lonsdale evidently dis-covered she wished to be asked to display her musical abilities. Having concluded a song, she rose from the in-strument and entreated the Dutchess to take her seat, who, after many excuses and grimaces, suffered herself to be prevailed on, but declined Miss Lonsdale's music, saying she would give them an old, but very favourite air of hers: she then played the song introduced into Shakespeare's Twelfth Night, "How imperfect is Expression!"

Chance had placed Henry at her elbow, and she evidently directed the song to him, endeavouring to throw into her coun-tenance confusion and tender meaning, while her large glaring eyes were fixed on his face in a way that made him blush, and disconcerted him so much that he would gladly have retired from her side, had he not feared his removal while she sung would be construed into unpoliteness. Her squeaking and squalling afforded the highest entertainment to Miss Lonsdale and Horatio Delamere; and notwithstanding Henry's unpleas-ant situation, his risible faculties were so powerfully excited, that it was with the utmost difficulty he kept himself from laughing in her face. Before the party broke up Lord

Dungarvon told him he should expect to see him with the earliest convenience. Henry promised to pay his duty at Mortimer Abbey the next morning; he found himself constrained to hand the Dutchess to her carriage, who bestowed on him so many soft sighs and tender adieus, that when he returned to the drawing-room Miss Lonsdale, imitating the voice and manner of the Dutchess, said, "Parting is such sweet sorrow, I could say good night 'till it were tomorrow."

"I rejoice we have parted at last, however," said Henry; "for of all others I think her the most disagreeable woman I have ever seen."

"But then her rank and fortune – only take them into consideration," said Miss Lonsdale.

"With all their glitter they cannot restore youth, or give her beauty," replied Henry.

"Heaven help you," said Miss Lonsdale; "you are quite a simpleton: when you are a few years older, and have gained a little experience in the ways of the world, you, like the rest of your mercenary sex, will consider wealth an equivalent for youth, elegance, and loveliness. Money will give understanding to an idiot, and the bloom of Hebe to age and ugliness."

"Never in my estimation," replied Henry; "I have no ambition to be great, therefore shall never outrage my feelings to obtain those proud distinctions, which in my opinion would be dearly purchased with my mind's content and the loss of self-esteem."

"You are certainly not the grandson of Lord Dungarvon," said Horatio Delamere; "such sentiments as these, expressed in his hearing, would lose you his favour for ever."

"As I have never yet enjoyed it," rejoined Henry, "I shall

have nothing to lament – brought up by the noblest, worthiest of men, I trust I shall never disgrace the principles he has been at such pains to inculcate. I have been taught to estimate wealth only as it enables its possessor to be more benevolent; to worship, to admire, and covet honour, humanity, and virtue: and in my opinion the poorest labourer on the Mortimer estate, enriched with these, is a greater man than Lord Dungarvon."

"Degrade rank and splendour as you think proper," replied Horatio, "I am persuaded Lord Dungarvon will endeavour to exalt them in your estimation. I am certain you will have to combat his pride and his prejudices: he will at least try to make you the tool of his ambitious schemes."

"He will meet a disappointment then," rejoined Henry: "Lord Dungarvon has been pleased to pass me over to these years as undeserving his notice or regard: he can scarcely expect me to renounce my settled opinions, to sacrifice the smallest of my comforts to his pride, or to be at all subservient to his ambitious views."

"Suppose he was to propose a union with the Dutchess of Inglesfield," said Miss Lonsdale, "sure you would not have the cruelty, the temerity to refuse."

Henry burst into a fit of laughter: "Good heaven! how could so ridiculous an idea enter your imagination?"

"My life upon it," said Horatio, "it does not strike his lordship as a ludicrous scheme: her interest is favourable to his ministerial engagements – her rank would add dignity even to the ancient and illustrious house of Mortimer, and her immense wealth purchase all the proud distinctions, the ostentatious trappings he is so dotingly fond of."

"They shall never purchase me," replied Henry; "what, tie

myself to a woman old enough to be my grandmother, with the additional disagreeables of ugliness and deformity! My dear friends, change the subject, I beseech you."

Horatio Delamere rode the next morning with his friend to Mortimer Abbey, but left him at the gates, supposing that family occurrences would be talked over, at which the presence of a stranger might well be dispensed with. Lord and Lady Dungarvon received Henry with the utmost cordiality and show of affection; they spoke of his father and mother, and expatiated with much apparent feeling on the disappointment and distress their imprudent marriage had occasioned the family: they reverted to their son Richard, who had lately buried two promising sons, praised him as the most dutiful of human beings, who in all that concerned the dignity and honour of the family had never appeared to consider his own wishes. They mentioned that he was then in the deepest affliction, dreading to lose his only surviving child, who, far gone in a consumption, was ordered to Lisbon for the recovery of his health. Henry thought he now perceived the motive of their kindness to him, in the dread of the noble house of Mortimer being without an heir, a circumstance his unfortunate mother had predicted in her letter to Lord Dungarvon. But this notion had never yet floated in his lordship's brain; the Honourable Richard Mortimer was yet in the prime of life, and his wife, some years younger than himself, was then pregnant. After having spent some time in the library, he was conducted over the superb mansion, which was decorated with every ornament that wealth could purchase, or luxury invent; but no place so much delighted the taste, or interested the feelings of Henry as the gallery, the walls of which were hung with family portraits: among the most conspicuous for beauty was a picture of Mrs. Gertrude Mortimer binding up the white wing of a wounded pigeon, which was held by a boy of most engaging figure, in whose animated countenance commiseration and gratitude were finely depicted.

"It was done for your father," said Lord Dungarvon, observing Henry's eyes fixed on the painting; "when he was about eight years old he bought the pigeon of a boy who had shot, and was going to kill it. His aunt undertook the cure of the wounded wing; the bird lived many years, and was a great favourite with both: but there," said his lordship, "is a likeness that was taken when he was about your age."

The face of the portrait hung next the wall – Henry turned it; Lord Dungarvon's eyes glanced over it – an expression resembling sorrow rose in his face, but like a passing cloud, it was gone in a moment. "It might be taken for you," said he, "the likeness is so striking."

He strode to an open window, and entered into conversation with some person below. Henry stood mournfully contemplating the picture of his father; all the melancholy circumstances of his banishment from his family, the parting from his wife, his voyage to the West Indies, his death and that of his mother, all rose to his imagination, and the mingled tears of affection and regret trembled in his eye: as he gazed upon the portrait he fancied it smiled upon him, and yielding to the momentary delusion, he was ready to sink on his knees and implore a father's blessing.

He was roused by Lord Dungarvon, who led him from the gallery to the Dutchess's dressing-room: she had just concluded the mysteries of the toilet. Her glass had flattered her into a belief that her rouge had all the appearance of nature, and that her rich dishabille hid the deformity of her person. In perfect good humour with herself she received Henry with smiles of affability and delight, told him that he had been the subject of all her waking thoughts, and the magician who had created her dreams.

Henry blushed, and declared she did him too much honour.

"Why I protest," said the Dutchess, "you blush like a miss just led forth from the nunnery, and exposed for the first time to the rude gaze of man – you must discard this silly practice. A blushing girl is a subject for ridicule in fashionable circles; but a blushing man, mercy on me! he would be the jest of enlightened society."

Henry laughed and apologized for his *mauvais honte*, said he had but just escaped from the mountains of Wales, and that as yet he had not got his feelings in subjection.

"O then you have feelings!" said the Dutchess looking languishingly in his face.

"Yes," said Henry blushing still deeper, "and I trust they will never be blunted by an intercourse with fashionable manners; though I wish the time may arrive," added he gaily, "when I may be able to rule my sensations, and command my countenance so far as not to let it betray me upon every occasion."

Lord Dungarvon, excusing himself on the plea of particular business, left them together.

The Dutchess invited Henry to take a seat by her on the sofa; he was far from being pleased at being shut up with, and condemned to pass his morning with her, yet still his natural politeness induced him to make an effort to entertain her: he talked of the country, of the beautiful rides and walks about the abbey, of books, of drawing, and music. Her grace's reading had been very confined: she knew but little of books

– for drawing she had no taste, and her knowledge of music was equally circumscribed; but she thought Henry talked like an angel, and if he spoke so well on indifferent subjects, how eloquent must he be when love was his theme! Her eyes and ears were fascinated, and before dinner was announced she felt she must be miserable if Henry Mortimer overlooked her partiality, and declined her alliance. The rest of the day passed tolerably pleasant.

Lord Dungarvon was a man of sense and education, and when not occupied in schemes of grandeur, or influenced by pride, was an extremely agreeable companion. Having an end to accomplish, he behaved to Henry with the utmost kindness and condescension; at the same moment impressing him with an high opinion of his extensive knowledge, and admiration of his cultivated talents. The dutchess simpered and languished, and made such pointed advances, that if Henry had not been the most diffident young man in nature, he would have seen that her attentions were designed to say in unequivocal language that her heart and hand were his whenever he could assume sufficient courage to solicit them.

Henry returned to Narbeth Lodge pleased with every thing he had met at Mortimer Abbey, except the dutchess, for whom his disgust seemed hourly to increase. Before he retired to rest he sat down to give Owen Llewellyn an account of his introduction to his grandfather, and his reception at Mortimer Abbey: he concluded with saying he hoped Lord Dungarvon expected no submission or obedience from him but what would accord with his principles, as he determined never in any instance to deviate from the precepts of honour inculcated by his more than father, and to which he would ever pay a religious reverence.

Henry had seemed to gain ground every hour in the good graces of his grandfather, who had made him several valuable presents, and Lady Dungarvon treated him with such tenderness that his heart began to resign itself to the delightful idea that he should be happy in the sincere affection of his family, whose endearments he now believed were influenced by no sinister views. Horatio Delamere and Miss Lonsdale still adhered to their opinion that Lord Dungarvon had secret ends to accomplish, and that the present halcyon days would end in tumult and storm. Henry received a letter from Sir Owen Llewellyn congratulating him on his brightening prospects, but exhorting him never to lose sight of honour and rectitude – never to sacrifice his peace of mind for the attainment of rank or the possession of wealth, but always to remember that he had in him a father, in Adeline a sister, and a home in Dolgelly Castle, should any unforeseen circumstance hurl him from the pinnacle on which hope and Lord Dungarvon's favour had placed him. A portion of every day Henry passed at Mortimer Abbey, and every day seemed to draw him nearer to Lord Dungarvon's heart. The dutchess had ogled, flattered, and made advances to him which his modesty and insensibility let pass utterly unregarded till she began to grow impatient and out of temper, at what she termed his stupidity, and his grandfather thought that his project was ripe for disclosing.

Having one morning requested Henry to accompany him in a walk to a plantation at a short distance from the abbey, after some little embarrassment and hesitation he began expatiating on the misery he had experienced in having his proudest, fondest hopes crushed and blighted by the disgraceful and imprudent marriage of his father, and the heart-rending affliction he had afterwards endured at his death.

"To you, my dear Henry," said he, "I now look up to make me a recompense for those mortifications, those disappointments with which your father so barbarously lacerated my heart."

Henry was silent; he felt an unpleasant presage that some request was about to be made with which he should be unable to comply, and which would for ever destroy the plans of felicity his sanguine hopes had formed, and force him from the happiness he had began to enjoy in the bosom of his family. Lord Dungarvon had waited for Henry's reply, but perceiving him absorbed in thought, proceeded to state that he had not intended by the mention of his parents to raise melancholy remembrances, that the past could not be recalled, and retrospections were useless and unavailing: therefore he would not wound his sensibility with the recapitulation of their errors.

"No, my dear Henry, I only wish to know, to ask, whether you are willing to gild the evening of my days, to render my declining years happy; to compensate by your obedience to my request for the sorrows your unhappy, ill-advised father occasioned me."

Henry shuddered and stood irresolute, but being again urged by his grandfather, he desired to know by what act of duty he was to prove his wish of conducing to his happiness.

"By an act," continued Lord Dungarvon, "which will elevate, enrich, and aggrandize yourself, and add splendour and dignity to our noble house. I have fixed my hopes, and set my heart on the accomplishment of this darling wish: promise me, Henry, on your word of honour, that I shall not be disappointed."

"Pardon me, my lord," said Henry; "even in the most trivial matters I have been taught to hold a promise sacred: I dare not pledge my word to fulfil a measure which neither my honour nor my wishes can approve. Speak your wishes plainly, and be assured that nothing short of a violation of those principles I cannot infringe will induce me to refuse obedience to a request you may think proper to make."

"The Dutchess of Inglesfield," replied Lord Dungarvon, "regards you with partial eyes."

"I am sorry she is so ridiculous my lord," said Henry.

Lord Dungarvon frowned: "Have you then," said he, in a voice scarcely articulate from passion; "have you also engaged yourself to some offspring of a dunghill, some low-born wretch?"

"Hold, my lord," said Henry, "spare yourself and me these painful interrogatories; my heart is free. I am under no engagements – bound by no promises."

"Why then not accept the honourable alliance that is offered? An alliance," continued Lord Dungarvon, "which for high rank and unbounded wealth is not to be surpassed if equalled in the kingdom. What objection can you possibly make."

"A most natural one, I think," answered Henry; "the disparity of our ages, not to say a word about the disagreeableness of person."

Lord Dungarvon smiled contemptuously.

"No, my lord," continued Henry, "my principles, the honour I worship, will not allow me even to think of binding myself to a woman, the folly of whose deportment renders her in every discerning eye an object of contempt and ridicule; whom I could neither love nor respect. I would indeed do much to retain your lordship's favour, but if you demand the sacrifice of my whole life's happiness, I confess you rate it too highly."

"What plebeian notions!" replied Lord Dungarvon; "silly boy, it is not likely that any great portion of your happiness would be sacrificed, as you term it: the dutchess is far from young, and her health..."

"And you would persuade me," interrupted Henry, "meanly to marry a woman who is my aversion, merely to enrich myself by her death? Are these the real sentiments of Lord Dungarvon? Do such pitiful, such sordid notions disgrace the illustrious Mortimers? What would the scrutinizing world say of wealth so acquired?"

"The world, sir," replied the enraged Lord Dungarvon, "is too well bred to search with much exactitude into the affairs of their superiors. It bows with submissive homage to wealth and splendour, and is never troublesome in its inquiries."

"But my conscience would, my lord," said Henry; "I have hitherto, thank heaven, escaped its reproaches; my days have been calm, and my nights blest with repose. I am neither ambitious, nor mercenary enough to exchange my bosom's peace for wealth which must be acquired at the expense of truth and honour. How could I promise to love a woman whose person is disgustful, and whose age would make the match unnatural?"

"Degenerate offspring of a degenerate father, I have no more to say; I have expressed my wishes; you have thought proper to disappoint them. Go, sir, return to the mountains where you have hitherto vegetated; hide in the shades of obscurity those notions which in the great world, among enlightened people, would be laughed at and despised. I would have made you a great and distinguished character, but I see in you the dirty, ungrateful puddle of the Berresfords, predominates over the noble blood of the Mortimers. Hence from my sight thou serpent; too much resembling her who in return for the benefits I had heaped upon her father seduced from his duty a son, who but for her arts might have still lived an honour to the illustrious family from which he sprung."

This attack upon his sainted mother, the most artless of human beings, roused all the indignant feelings of Henry's nature; the fire flashed from his eyes while surveying Lord Dungarvon with a countenance expressive of the utmost contempt: he replied, "Yes, I will bear from your sight a form that must indeed be a perpetual reproach to you, because it must for ever accuse your lordship of meanness and barbarity. I go to enjoy upon the mountains and among the shades the bliss of tranquillity; I leave to your lordship rank and splendid misery. The character of her you have stigmatized with such unrelenting malevolence, by the lustre of her virtues reflected dignity on her humble house. You, by insatiable ambition, by inordinate avarice so disgrace the name of Mortimer, that I would gladly exchange it for the untitled one of Berresford."

Lord Dungarvon stayed to hear no more: he turned towards the abbey, and left Henry to the indulgence of his own thoughts, which were not indeed of the most pleasant nature: "So then," said he, "all Lord Dungarvon's kindness and affection were but traps in which he hoped to catch my inexperience. Not content with immolating my parents on the altar of his insatiable ambition, he would elevate me to a life of wretchedness, merely to add a few more swelling titles to his family, and increase those riches of which he has already too large a share."

Henry returned not to the abbey – he wished not again to encounter Lord Dungarvon, whose recent conversation had entirely destroyed the respect he was inclined to award him, and obliterated from his heart the affection consanguinity might have claimed. He proceeded on foot to Narbeth Lodge, where he disclosed to Horatio Delamere the breach with Lord Dungarvon.

"Did I not tell you," said he, "that the dutchess had cast on you the tender glance of love? What an insensible piece of frost-work you must be, to behold such attraction ready to sink into your arms! Why your heart is harder than adamant; it is not calculable what you have lost by refusing her: she would have procured you a peerage, and then her wealth, it would have purchased you…"

"Every thing but felicity," said Henry; "I would not bind myself to that shrivelled old wanton if she could present me with a diadem. Why she has already buried two husbands!"

Horatio laughed; "Aye, and has not the least objection to marrying two more."

"What extreme indelicacy," rejoined Henry; "there are some circumstances that might furnish a woman with an excuse for taking a second husband, but when it comes to a third I acknowledge my sentiments are not very favourable; and for the dutchess, I hold her in the utmost contempt and abhorrence. I am told she has three daughters marriageable, and so much wealth that it leaves her not a desire ungratified."

"Save that of taking to her embraces a young husband," rejoined Horatio; "and so determined is she to have another, that she confines her daughters, one of them near thirty years old, to the nunnery, because they shall not make her look old."

"Are the daughters handsome?" inquired Henry.

"You have no objection to marry one of them, perhaps?" said Horatio, "but I cannot reply to your question; I have never seen them – all that I know of them you shall hear. My cousin, Captain Lonsdale, was vastly enamoured of the youngest, Lady Isabella Belville, a fine girl of about nineteen, whom he met with her nurse somewhere near Raven-hill Castle, a seat of her grace's in Cumberland, where it seems she immures her daughters, suffering them to mix with no society, or walk beyond certain boundaries. Unfortunately, before Edward could carry off the young lady, which it seems was his intention, the dutchess made a discovery; she chose to disapprove, and confined her daughter, who I have heard is now in a state of derangement."

"But why did the dutchess disapprove," said Henry; "and what was her objection?"

"Want of title was the objection," replied Horatio, "but the true one I believe is the dread of being made a grandmother. Odious, ridiculous woman! A braver, nobler fellow does not exist than Edward Lonsdale: but being of an untitled family, her grace upbraided him with effrontery in presuming to look up to the daughter of the Earl of Lucan. I fear some unwarrantable means have been used to reduce this young lady to the state she is described to languish in."

Lord Narbeth joining them the subject was dropped; he expressed no surprise at the account Henry gave of his grandfather's requisition, but said he had always feared and suspected, that some extraordinary sacrifice would be demanded as the price of his lordship's condescension and apparent fondness.

"It is well," said Horatio, "that you are not dependent on him – if you were your fate would be pitiable."

"Ah, my poor father," sighed Henry, "now I am more fully sensible of what you suffered! Inexorable, unfeeling Lord Dungarvon, surely your heart is quite callous, or the remembrance of his disastrous fate would for ever deter you from wishing to influence the affections of your family. I go no more to Mortimer Abbey, for having explained my sentiments, and expressed my determination, I shall not choose to enter into any further altercation with Lord Dungarvon on so hateful a subject, for if the price of his esteem must be the loss of my own, I cannot consent to enjoy his favour by for ever relinquishing that first of blessings, an approving conscience."

"Tomorrow, my dear Horatio, with Lord Narbeth's permission, we set off towards Cambridge."

Lord Narbeth replied, "No, not tomorrow: perhaps Lord Dungarvon may repent – may wish to be reconciled; he may on mature consideration forbear to urge a matter he sees you so repugnant to. Give him a few days to get rid of these new formed wishes; he may hold out the olive-branch and recall you to Mortimer Abbey." Henry replied, "He would in all his best obey him." Lord Narbeth settled their departure for the beginning of the following week.

The young friends proceeded to the drawing-room, where Lady Narbeth and her niece rallied Henry severely on his cruelty to a lady who was absolutely dying for him. Miss Lonsdale called him an actual simpleton for not marrying the dutchess who could not live many years to plague him, and then master of immense wealth, he might select the girl of his heart.

"I once remember," said Lady Narbeth, "a match of this sort, where the ambitious family of a worthy but weak young man persuaded him to marry a woman more than thirty years older than himself, with the hope that she would die and leave him to enjoy her fortune; however their views were frustrated – the old lady by her whims and caprices threw her young husband into a decline, and his disappointed relations followed him to the grave, and saw that wealth they had been so eager to obtain flow in a channel remote from their wishes."

"I pity the fate of the poor young man," said Horatio Delamere.

"My aunt said he was weak," replied Miss Lonsdale, "and the sequel of his history proves him so. O, that some rich old fellow with ten thousand caprices and whims would offer me his hand!"

"You would not accept him?" rejoined Henry.

"You are mistaken, my friend, in that point," replied she; "I would marry him, and then for the trial: I will engage I would out whim him and out caprice him too. If he talked loud I would be louder still – if he was sulky so would I; no doubt in one year I should be able to tire his patience and break his heart, and then for a dash upon the world with all the glitter of wealth, and the charms of widowhood."

Henry and Horatio laughed; Lady Narbeth shook her head.

"If I were not assured, my dear Emily," said her ladyship, "that what you have just uttered proceeds from unthinking vivacity, and is not the sentiment of your heart, I should be inclined to pass a very severe censure upon you; but I know that you are an amiable, though a giddy girl, and in reality think differently to what you have expressed on the subject of matrimony. No person, in my opinion, should enter that sacred state except those whose ages and dispositions assimilate, and who have seriously determined to make the happiness of each other their first consideration. So assorted wedlock is a state of felicity; but

> "When souls that should agree to will the same,
> To have one common object for their wishes,
> Look diff'rent ways regardless of each other,
> Love shall be banish'd from their genial bed,
> And ev'ry day shall be a day of cares."

CHAPTER V

Whither do you lead me –
To death or prison glooms? Yet think betime
There is an eye can pierce the dungeon's depths;
There is an ear that listens to the captive's
Moan; heaven sleeps not while you do these deeds.

A. J. H.

DISAPPOINTED and irritated almost to madness by Henry's opposition to his wishes, Lord Dungarvon made no inquiries after him, and at the appointed time he left Narbeth Lodge with Horatio Delamere and their servants. They intended to sleep at Axminster the first night, but left the post road for the purpose of visiting a friend who lived a few miles across the country; with this friend they dined, and remained until rather a late hour: in order to gain the right road they had to traverse a wood. The evening was cloudy, the moon had not risen, and it was with much difficulty they traced their way. When they had proceeded about four miles, and were in the middle of the wood they heard a whistle.

"We shall be robbed," said Henry.

"I have no such idea," replied Horatio; "in a road so little travelled it is not likely; the whistle proceeded from some labourer or wood-cutter, who perhaps has a dog that has strayed away, and whom he wishes to be his companion home."

Henry was behind Horatio, in a path too narrow to admit

two horses a-breast, and so rugged that they were obliged to proceed with the utmost caution – the servants were far behind.

Suddenly Henry's bridle was seized by two men who darted from behind a tree; four others gagged and blindfolded him. After travelling some miles in this way, through rough paths and down declivities, during which no sound met his ear, the bandage was removed from his eyes, and the gag from his mouth. The moon had risen – he saw the sea at a distance, and several small vessels at anchor. Henry now asked where they were hurrying him, and for what purpose? One of the men who appeared to be the leader of the gang replied, "As to where you be going, my young master, that is more than I can tell, cause why, I don't know."

"By whose order do you act?" enquired the astonished Henry.

"You will be in the secret all in good time, my young master," said the man; "but as to whose orders we act by, why we can't tell what we don't know ourselves."

"Not know!" exclaimed Henry.

"No, all we knows about the affair is, that we shall touch the shiners for putting you safe aboard yonders little sloop; there our care ends: and that is all we knows of the business, my young master."

"Where is my friend, the gentleman that was with me, and our servants?" inquired Henry.

"O never fear for them: they are safe enough – on their road home, my young master."

"Then you had no orders respecting them?"

"No, no, my young master, only to take care they did not watch which way you went."

"Thank heaven," ejaculated Henry silently; "Delamere will never rest until he discovers the fate of his friend. – and what may that fate be. Lord Dungarvon, to what miseries have you destined the son of Augustus Mortimer?"

He addressed the man who rode by his side again: "Answer me, I entreat you: am I to be sent abroad?"

"Lord knows, my young master; I am as ignorant as the man in the moon what is to become of you after I parts from you – but I am sure I hopes no harm, because you be as fine a person, and as handsome a gentleman as one would wish to clap eyes on in a long summer's day: I should be sorry to my heart…"

"If you would be sorry," said Henry interrupting him, "that any harm should happen to me, why not prevent the possibility by allowing me to escape?"

"O no, no, my young master, I can't do that; I have tooked the money, and I can't be such a big rogue as to break my word. Times are very hard, my young master; I have a sick wife and nine little children – I could hardly get bread for them: I was glad to earn money to buy the poor things meat."

"How vile, how debased must the man be, who takes advantage of the necessitous – who compels the needy wretch to those acts which but for imperious poverty his nature would revolt at. But if," said Henry, again addressing the man, "a larger sum should be secured to you for allowing me to escape…"

They had now reached the edge of the water where a boat waited, and before the man had time to reply four sailors jumped on shore, and surrounded Henry. In an instant he was dismounted from his horse, and in the next found himself rowed from shore. The clouds had dispersed, and a clear full moon shone on the waves. At any other moment such a tranquil lovely scene would have been delightful to Henry, but now his mind was too much occupied with reflections on what might be his future destiny to attend to the charms of nature. He attempted to converse with the men, to draw from them to whom they belonged, and what was their destination. All he could learn was, that their captain's name was Lawson; that his vessel was called the Ceres; that they belonged to Plymouth, but as to where they were bound they could not say, but they believed to Plymouth strait.

Henry finding he could obtain nothing satisfactory from the sailors continued silent, endeavouring to fortify his mind, and prepare it to sustain the afflictions he foresaw were preparing for him. Sometimes he supposed Lord Dungarvon, in whose power he conceived himself to be, had contrived to send him abroad – to sell him to slavery. At other moments he imagined he was to be immured in some seclusion from whence his complaints would never reach the pitying ears of his friends. While these and a thousand other painful ideas passed in rapid succession through the mind of Henry, the sailors unheeding him were gaily singing a merry ditty, to the chorus of which their oars kept time. They soon made the sloop, on board which they no sooner entered than Henry was conducted below, to what they called the cabin, a little dirty hole about eight feet square, so full of tobacco smoke that he could scarcely discern two men, the captain and his mate, who sat at a table enjoying themselves over a can of flip. The captain, a little squab old man with squinting grey eyes, a turn-up nose glowing with carbuncles, and long yellow teeth, habited in a greasy tattered blue jacket and canvas trowsers saluted Henry with, "You are welcome, my hearty – though by the soul of my aunt Nell you have been a devil of a while coming; thought I should have lost the tide, which as I suppose you are a scholard, you knows waits for no man."

Then moving a little scuttle over his head he bawled out, "Weigh anchor, you lubbers." Then pushing the flip towards Henry, he said, "Take a swig, my hearty." The mate, on the command for weighing anchor being given, went upon deck. He was a tall hard featured man with a wooden leg; and as he passed by Henry stared him full in the face, and muttered an oath between his teeth. The captain appeared to be intoxicated; and as it is said that liquor opens the heart, and makes men communicative, Henry hoped to know from him where he was going, and how he was to be disposed of. He sat down, and being thirsty, drank of the flip offered by the commander of the Ceres, who shook him by the hand and exclaimed, "That is right, my hearty; pull away, we will have another when this is out – we have plenty to last our voyage."

"Will it be a long one?" inquired Henry.

"No, no, not long, all inland."

"Where are you bound to, captain?" said Henry.

"Bound, my hearty; why I am bound to Plymouth, but I steer another course, take a contrary tack or two to oblige an old acquaintance."

"But where do you land me?" said Henry.

"O, by the soul of my aunt Nell that won't do, my hearty; mum's the word with Anthony Lawson – my mouth's stopped, do you see (cramming into it a large quid of tobacco). There is your bed," continued the captain, "and a nice, snug, warm berth it is; you may turn in as soon as you like." At the same time opening a little cupboard in the side of the cabin, "I must go upon deck and see what them there lubbers are at." Saying this he extinguished the lamps that hung over the table, and left Henry to his meditations. The smell of tar, the noise of getting in the anchor, united with the motion of the vessel now under weigh, affected the whole frame of Henry so much that for a moment he felt inclined to throw himself upon the bed, and endeavour to sleep away the horrible sickness that assailed him; but remembering that when he cast his eyes into the hole, where he had been told he might turn in, it had appeared dirty and wretched, he determined to grope his way upon deck, and try the effect of fresh air. He had no sooner gained the deck than he was accosted by the captain, whose head was defended by a striped woollen nightcap:

"What my hearty, not turned in – you had better stay below; we shall have dirty weather – there is a squall brewing in the north-east."

"No matter, captain," replied Henry; "I am too sick to bear the confinement of the cabin: I shall die if I stay below."

"Die! no no; when you have emptied your bread-basket you will be as tough as an oak plank. Ned Ratlin, keep a sharp look out that we don't run aboard any of them there little craft."

Henry sunk upon a hencoop, and complained of extreme sickness:

"Aye, aye, my hearty, you fair weather sparks that don't know larboard from starboard, or stem from stern, are always yawish when you first put to sea; you will be used to it by and bye, and be able to take your allowance with the best of us."

Henry lifted up his head; "by and bye," thought he. "How long do you suppose we shall be at sea?"

"How long, my hearty, if the wind comes round, we may be at the end of our cruise by this time to-morrow: but if it holds as it is now, by the soul of my aunt Nell we may be beating about on this tack and t'other tack for this three weeks."

"I hope not," said Henry.

"I hope so, too, my hearty," replied the captain; "for if I be kept long in this here latitude I shall be for tumbling you overboard like another Jonas. Shiver my mizzen," continued he, "but I want to be at Plymouth, and if it was not that I am to be devilish well paid for this here trip I would have seen you make a bait for a shark, my hearty, before I would have steered out of my course on your account."

"I am infinitely obliged to you," said Henry.

"Whether you are obliged to me or not is as it may be; and don't argufy nothing," replied the captain; "here you are, and I must fulfil my agreement."

"What was your agreement?" inquired Henry.

"Hey! why you must understand, my hearty… luff, luff, you lubber," said the captain stalking up to the man at the helm.

Henry thought he had brought him to the point he wished, and unwilling to lose the opportunity he followed him, and again repeated the question, "What was your agreement?"

The captain crammed another quid of tobacco into his mouth, and drawing Henry to the binnacle, asked him if he could box the compass.

"I don't understand you?" said Henry.

"Can you do a day's work?"

"Of what sort?" said Henry.

"Of what sort, you land-lubber? Will you undertake to carry this here vessel safe to Greenland?"

"No," said Henry.

"And yet," said the captain, "you have all your jawing

tackle on board, and will undertake to steer round me, and understand my course. Hawl in a reef or two of your questions; lower your jib and back your mainsail. By the soul of my aunt Nell, you may as well strike your inquiries, for you will get nothing out of Anthony Lawson. Will you turn in?"

Henry preferred remaining upon deck.

"Then I shall take the inner birth," said the captain. "Ned Ratlin, keep a sharp look out."

"Aye, boy," growled the man with the wooden leg, as the captain descended the companion ladder.

The fresh breeze had recovered Henry: he sat musing on his strange fortune: he thought of Sir Owen Llewellyn, of Adeline, of Horatio Delamere, all of whom he knew would exert every nerve to discover him: one moment he indulged the consoling hope that he should soon be rescued from Lord Dungarvon's power, the next, yielding to melancholy, he believed himself fated to be the victim on whom his relentless grandfather had intended to revenge all his mortifications and disappointments; and he shuddered to think how little able he was to withstand his vengeance now so completely in his power.

The squall the captain had foretold now came on; the wind rose, and rattled in the sails, which were all taken in by the order of Ned Ratlin: the sea swelled mountains high, and tossed the little sloop with such violence that she one moment appeared to be mounting to the clouds, and the next sinking to the bottom of the fathomless deep – a wave broke over the lea side, and run along the gunnel. Ned Ratlin seeing Henry with difficulty keep himself upon the hen-coop, advised him to go below, as it was going to rain. Henry thanked him for his attention, but declined his advice.

Ned Ratlin limped away, and returned in a moment with a large watch coat.

"Here, messmate," said he, "haul this coat about you, it has seen a good deal of service – shiver my limbs but it has weathered many a tough gale."

This man, thought Henry, has a heart formed of tenderer materials than his rough exterior promised.

"I am strong and well, my good fellow," said he, "you are an invalid, and want the comfort of your coat in this tempestuous night."

"I never wear it, messmate," said Ned; "I have another below, that now and then serves me to lay my head upon when I sleep on deck, so you may as well haul it about you."

Henry was glad to avail himself of Ned's kindness, for the next moment the rain fell in torrents, and the vessel was so agitated by the wind and waves, that he began to believe he should escape the malevolence of his grandfather, expecting every moment that the sloop, unable to buffet the storm, would go to the bottom. Ned Ratlin told him that there was no danger, that she was a tight little vessel, and would live through a thousand such squalls as that. Henry addressed himself to heaven, and leaned his head against the creaking mast. In a short time the wind subsided, the dark clouds dispersed, the rain ceased, and the moon again shone in radiant beauty. – The man at the helm began a doleful ballad; Ned Ratlin stumped backward and forward; Henry left the hencoop, and leaning over the side of the vessel, stood pensively watching her keel divide the sparkling waves.

A voice at his ear whispered, "Mr. Mortimer;" he started, and beheld Ned Ratlin.

"Do you know me?" said Henry.

"Yes, I should have known you, if I had not heard the captain say you were Lord Dungarvon's grandson, by your likeness to your father, with whom I sailed in the same ship to the West Indies. Aye, messmate, I was then merry, young, and hearty: I had not lost my precious limb, nor," said Ned, drawing his hand across his eyes, "I had not lost my tight pretty Sue, nor little Ben; but they are all gone. I was then in his majesty's service; could hand, reef, and steer with any Jack on board: but, Lord help me, I was persuaded to go a privateering to make my fortune. Well, I lost my leg, and now – but no matter. Do you know, messmate, where you are bound?"

"No!' replied Henry.

"Into Cumberland," said Ned; "your port is Raven-hill Castle."

"So, so," said Henry, remembering this was the Dutchess of Inglesfield's seat, that Horatio Delamere had spoken of; "and what is to become of me there?"

"I can say nothing to that question, messmate," said Ned; "I know the captain is to receive a good sum for steering you there. But tell me, can I be of any service to you? Your father, the honourable Captain Mortimer, saved my life when I fell overboard, and I feel in duty bound to serve you if I can; for I see, messmate, that you have been run down; you are not here by your own free will."

"No," replied Henry, "I am forced away from my friends, brought here without my consent, and what I am yet to suffer heaven alone can tell."

"But can you think of no way in which I may be useful to you, messmate?" replied Ned.

"Yes, by giving my friends notice where I am conveyed," replied Henry.

"I would gladly do this, messmate," said Ned, "but more is my mishap, I am no scholar – I never had no learning: I can neither read nor write; and you may see with your own eyes," continued he, pointing to his wooden leg, "that I am but badly built for travelling."

"We can manage this matter very well," said Henry. "I will take the opportunity while the captain is on deck of writing a few lines, which you can put in the post-office at the first port you touch at."

"That will be Plymouth," replied Ned; "but avast, messmate, where will you get paper? for I doubt whether such an article is to be found aboard, excepting with the captain." Henry had a letter about him; he could use the cover of that. A few words would be sufficient to apprize his friends of his situation.

"But then, splice my mizzen, you can't write with salt water," said Ned; "what will you do for pen and ink? are you supplied with these articles too? for I guess they will be hard to come by."

This was the worst part of the affair: Henry had indeed a pencil, with which he might have run the chance of writing a few lines; but how was he to direct? The pencil-mark would surely rub out.

He explained this dilemma to Ned, who promised to take good care it was not rubbed out while on board, and that as soon as he set foot on shore he would get a friend to trace over the direction with ink. This affair being arranged, the mind of Henry became calmer: he questioned Ned Ratlin respecting his knowledge of his father.

"He was as fine a man," said Ned, "as ever stepped between stem and stern; he would stand for hours together as you do now, looking so mournful, leaning on the side of the vessel with his eyes turned towards England, and fetch deep sighs, just as if all his thoughts were left behind him, for he never seemed to mind what was going on with the other officers, who were full of mirth and fun; and at night when it was my watch I always found him on deck: for my part I think he never turned into his hammock at all. Then he had a little small something, about the size of a crown piece, tied to a black ribband round his neck; I have often seen him kiss it. I suppose it was some love-token he had taken from his wife when they parted."

"It was her picture," said Henry.

"Likely, messmate, likely," replied Ned; "but be what it will, poor gentleman, he seemed to prize it highly. The last time I parted from my Susan she gave me this sixpence with a hole in it; I have kept it ever since. Poor girl, she died of the fright she got at seeing me stump into the house with this piece of timber spliced to my knee: she had not lain in of Ben above a week. Well, well, we must all die sometime, but it was hard to lose my leg, my wife and child, and all in the short space of a year."

Ned wiped his eyes, and opening his check shirt took from his bosom the sixpence; he gazed upon it – his tears gushed out: "This," said he, "goes with me to the grave; and when Sue and I meet in the other world I will tell her I never forgot her or little Ben, nor parted with her love-token."

Henry was affected; he looked on the sixpence suspended from the neck of the sailor, and in his eyes it appeared a rich and holy relic, embalmed with the tears of a most sincere affection.

"I suppose," said Ned, "I should be called a watery-headed

lubber for this, but never mind, I have seen the time when I scorned snivelling as much as any man, and would not have skulked in the hold from the enemy's fire; but now my hull is leaky, and my timbers are shattered, it is time I was laid up in safe moorings, for I am not fit for service: but at the time I fell overboard I was a strong stout fellow, able to grapple with half a dozen Frenchmen. I should have been stowed in Davy Jones's locker though if it had not been for your father, messmate; he jumped in after me, and towed me safe to the ship; and shall I ever forget that kindness to me? No, may I be sent to sea in a leaky boat, without provisions or compass, if ever I do."

Henry shook him affectionately by the hand.

The morning was clear and fine. At an early hour the captain came upon deck – "Well, my hearty, what you have kept watch all night? Will you have a spell below now? I have warmed your berth for you. Are you ready for your allowance? Here, you Tom Hawser, bring the pork and biscuit, I shall breakfast upon deck."

Henry had but little appetite for the dirty fat pork which the captain and his mate devoured with the highest relish, and swilled down with grog.

"Come, my hearty," said the captain, "it argufies nothing to be sulky; what must be must, you know; worse luck now the better another time: so drink and drown sorrow. The wind is in the right quarter – hoist the scudding sails: we shall just nick the evening tide."

Henry wished to be alone that he might prepare the letter for Ned Ratlin. As soon as their repast was finished he went below, and wrote with his pencil to Horatio Delamere: –

"After our strange separation no doubt my dear Horatio is anxious to be acquainted with the fate of his friend: I am now on the coast of Cumberland, in a vessel scarce bigger than a cockle-shell; all that I know of my future destination is that I am to be conveyed to Raven-hill Castle, but whether as the prisoner of Lord Dungarvon or the Dutchess of Inglesfield I am yet to learn. You will inform Sir Owen Llewellyn of my situation, who I have no doubt will lose no time in procuring my liberty. You will perceive that I write under dread of a discovery; but as providence has raised me a friend who promises to convey this to the post-office, I trust it will reach you in safety, for on this alone rests the hopes of

HENRY AUGUSTUS MORTIMER."

Having finished his letter he was at a loss to seal it, but in this exigence also he determined to rely on honest Ned. He was fatigued, his spirits were exhausted, his eyes were heavy, and he felt inclined to accept the captain's proposal of turning in: but casting his eyes into what he had termed his warm, snug berth, it even appeared more filthy and deplorable by day than at night, and he turned in disgust from the idea of sleeping in so wretched a hole. He stretched himself upon the floor; in a few moments his eyes closed, and forgetting the strangeness of his situation, and the hardness of his bed, he sunk into a profound sleep, and enjoyed for several hours that sweet and refreshing repose which never visits the weary eyelids of guilt. It was evening when he awoke; he felt hungry, and went upon deck, where he found the captain at his constant avocation, smoking.

"What, my hearty," said he, "by the soul of my aunt Nell,

but the little Ceres has nicked you as snugly as if you had laid in your mammy's cradle; you have had a rare long spell. Well, is your stomach come to? Can you peg your allowance now? You land lubbers are for the most part cursed dainty, but after a spanking breeze you are brought to. Can you eat lob-scouse?"

Henry answered he believed he was hungry enough to eat any thing.

"The fin of a shark, hey, my hearty, or any other such delicate morsel. Here, you greasy chops," speaking to a boy that was picking oakum, "hoist sail, and make the lob-scouse hot: mayhap Ned Ratlin may be able to take some grub now. Go below, and see how he is."

Henry listened in dismay to this last order.

"Is he ill?"

"Aye, my hearty, poor Ned dropped down by my side in a fit this morning, as dead as a herring," replied the captain. "Him and I have rode out many a rough gale together. As good a seaman as ever doubled the Cape; but he will soon be a log upon the water: his sand is almost run – his watch is nearly out."

"Good God, how unfortunate!" said Henry, reverting to his own fear of not having his letter forwarded.

"Aye, unfortunate enough for me, my hearty: I shall have a sore loss in him. By the soul of my aunt Nell, he is as good a seaman as ever flung a log-line, or stood at a helm. I remember him twenty years ago, a fine strong fellow, when we engaged the Dutch in the Mediterranean; we fought yard arm and yard arm for nine glasses. It was hot work, my hearty, every man to his gun; well, Ned got a shot in his shoulder; the captain would have sent him down to the cockpit for the surgeon to dress his wounded fin. – 'Avast there,' said Ned, 'though my left arm is disabled, I have still the right able to fight for my king and country; and if they were both blown away, while my props would support my hull, Ned Ratlin would stand here, and encourage his shipmates to do their duty, and not suffer Mynheer Vanswagger to hoist his *dirty rag* over a *British Jack*. Huzza! England for ever!' We gave three cheers; Ned helped to take the Dutchman: but what signifies all this? Death has benumbed him at last; his sails will soon be furled up."

Henry's feelings did justice to Ned's valour. He wished to see him: he was interested about him from a double motive – he considered him as a brave and honest fellow, whose heart was an honour to human nature, and he hoped most sincerely that the captain exaggerated his danger, for he saw that with him must perish the hope of letting his friends know his situation.

When he had ate the mess set before him, he descended with the captain to the hold. Poor Ned was stretched on a miserable hammock in a hole to which neither light nor air had access. "Good heaven," said Henry, as he just distinguished the form before him, "must the man who has nobly fought the battles of his country die in such a hole as this without help, without comfort?"

"Avast there, messmate," said Ned, opening his languid eyes, "all on board are ready to help me; a sailor's comfort is a glass of grog, I can have that too; and as for dying in such a hole as this, what matter where a man dies? – the grave is a darker locker than this, and so long as no sins burden my conscience, why I can die happy any where."

"Don't talk of sheering off, Ned," said the captain, "we shall drink many a can of flip together yet."

"I trust," said Henry, "you will recover."

"Never in this world, messmate," replied Ned; "my death-warrant is signed, I shall soon be under hatches – I shall soon be with Sue and little Ben."

Henry was nearly suffocated; Ned's wits began to ramble; he talked incoherently; Henry gladly accompanied the captain upon deck; he saw it was impossible Ned should live, and his own hopes seemed expiring with him.

The wind had filled the sails of the Ceres, their course had been pursued without interruption, and early in the evening the towers of a castle were visible in the horizon; and as the breeze was still favourable, they soon had a full view of the ancient edifice. Such a scene under any other circumstances would have gratified the taste of Henry, which ever delighted in the grand and sublime. In a short time the captain told Henry that he was to land him at that castle. –

"And for what purpose?" inquired Henry. –

"That, my hearty," said the captain, "I never troubled myself about – it is no *business* of mine you know; and by the soul of my aunt Nell, I have plenty of my own to *mind*, without stirring other men's porridge."

Henry turned from him, and surveyed the surrounding objects: the sea washed the rocky base of a majestic mountain, round which wreaths of mist were curling in fantastic clouds, which as they ascended assumed a variety of forms. A forest of dark pine and oak bounded the view on one side; on the other, cultivated lands and pastures, enriched with reposing cattle, met the eye, while in the distance rose, in dark and proud magnificence, the pointed turrets and ivy-covered battlements of Raven-hill Castle, which, sportively silvered by the clear moon-beams, presented a grand specimen of gothic architecture. Henry gazed and sighed deeply, as his agitated mind endeavoured to pierce the thick-woven veil that enveloped futurity. He thought of the dear happy domestic circle at Dolgelly Castle – of his friend Horatio Delamere, whom he was perhaps fated to behold no more. He heard the captain order out the boat with sensations of horror such as he had never before experienced. Soon after he told the men to lie to; then addressing Henry, "Come my hearty," said he, "the boat is ready, your cruise is nearly over."

Henry was sensible that resistance was of no avail; his eye again glanced over the dark towers of Raven-hill Castle, and he felt the agonizing assurance that he was devoted to suffering – the unhappy offspring of most unhappy parents, doomed to encounter more wretchedness, worse misery, than they had endured.

As he descended the sloop's side he inquired after Ned Ratlin.

"He floats yet," said the captain, "but death grapples him; he will soon have him under hatches." –

"Peace be with him," said Henry; "he will escape the thousand ills that flesh is heir to."

"I don't know that he was heir to any thing excepting sorrow," said the captain; "and by the soul of my aunt Nell, he had always a full allowance of that, my hearty."

The boat cut swiftly through the waves; the captain began smoking, and the men that rowed the boat laughed and talked of their friends and families at Plymouth. One said his mother had received news of his death, and how she would rejoice to see him come "capering on shore;" another spoke of a friend, and a third of a sweetheart. "Alas!" thought Henry, "all are in expectation of happiness – all rejoice in the transporting idea of meeting friends and relatives, except me, and I am torn from every dear connection, every valued friend, to encounter I know not what evils, to meet a fate terrible to imagination, because unknown."

In less than an hour they made the castle. A low arched door belonging to one of the towers stood half open: two men, apparently in waiting, stood ready to receive them; the captain hailed them, and was instantly answered. One of the men approached to the edge of the water, and said, "Why, Lawson, we thought you would never come; we have waited for you till our patience is nearly worn out."

"Well, my hearty, we are here at last," said the captain, "as quick as wind and tide would let us; and by the soul of my aunt Nell, I hope you have got something good in the fort to wet our jackets with. Shiver my mizzen, my throat is as dry as a piece of old junk."

He jumped on shore; Henry followed, and addressing himself to him who appeared to be the superior, inquired by whose orders he was brought contrary to his inclination to that remote place, and for what purpose.

The man eyed him with a malicious grin, and turning to his companion, said, "A good likely well-grown fellow!"

"Aye, aye, let the old one alone," replied the other.

Henry repeated his questions.

"As to by who and for what you are brought here," said the man, "you will find out in time if you have any luck; and bad as you may fancy your case is, it is far better than what is worse." The man laughed at his own wit, and proceeded to state that the breeze was sharp, and that he was numbed with waiting so long in the cold.

Henry looked round, but no possibility of escape presented

itself: he was encompassed round by men who seemed resolute to execute the orders they had received, and he was obliged to submit to circumstances that were irremediable. One of the men roughly seized his arm, and dragged him under the gateway, the iron door of which was closed after them with a noise which made Henry shudder. "Now then," said he, "I am completely in the power of my enemies, secluded for ever from friends and liberty."

"Cheer up, my hearty," said the captain, puffing a cloud of tobacco smoke in his face; "life's like a ship on the troubled ocean; just now to be sure you sail against wind and tide, with the enemy close at your stern; but you may yet slip the cable of ill-fortune; and by the soul of my aunt Nell, though your anchor is lost, and your mast torn by the board, you may weather the storm, and ride safe into port, for all the underwriters have given you up for lost; so cheer up, my hearty."

CHAPTER VI

An act
That blurs the grace and blush of modesty,
Calls virtue hypocrite, takes off the rose
From the fair forehead of an innocent love,
And sets a blister there. O! such a deed,
As from the body of contraction plucks
The very soul; and sweet religion makes
A rhapsody of words. Rebellious heat,
If thou canst mutiny in a matron's bones,
To flaming youth let virtue be as wax,
And melt in her own fire: proclaim no shame
When the compulsive ardor gives the charge,
Since frost itself as actively doth burn,
And reason ponders well.

Shakespeare

THEY now entered the extensive court of the castle, on the high and ponderous walls of which, at equal distances, were placed ravens sculptored in black marble, supporting the arms of the Belville family. A long and magnificent flight of marble steps led to the grand entrance, up which Henry was desired by his conductor to ascend, while he perceived the rest of the party disappear through a passage leading to the servants' offices.

Having crossed a splendid hall, and many apartments and highly decorated galleries, they passed through a long arched passage that led them to another court, apparently situated at the back of the castle: here they found two men loaded with hampers. He had not as yet exchanged a single syllable with his guide, expecting that every door he passed through would usher him to the prison he was fated to occupy; but seeing the men in waiting, he had an idea that the articles they carried were for his use, and that he was to linger out his being in some remote dungeon, far from human aid and human pity.

Some conversation took place between the men, but it passed in too low a tone for him to distinguish what was its purport: he leaned against the massy wall, and remained lost in agonizing conjecture, till the unlocking of a door close by him roused him to observation. A dark passage presented itself; Henry drew back, but the men having deposited their load, he was compelled to enter with them. He heard the door lock behind him, and in spite of remonstrance he was hurried forward.

He perceived they did not go straight on, but made several turnings: at length one of the men said, "Sure we have passed the stairs."

"No, you fool," replied another, "we are not come to them; here they are on your right hand."

"Yes, yes," said another voice, "here they are sure enough, the devil has not moved them. I remember these same stairs well enough, and so do you, Tom. You can't forget the time you helped to carry my lady dutchess's…"

"Curse on your prating," said another voice; "keep moving, I want to get back to the inhabited part of the castle; I hate this place."

"And not without a cause," replied another voice; "and for the matter of that I have no particular reason to like it."

"You are a couple of cowardly scoundrels," rejoined the

first speaker, "and would be afraid of your own shadows were you to see them on the wall."

The dim light of the moon streaming through a narrow window placed high in the wall discovered to Henry that they were traversing a long matted gallery.

"Go forward, Frank," said the leader of the party, "to the last room on the left hand, and strike a light."

"May I be hanged if I go alone to that room," said Frank.

"And hanged you will be one day or other, if you have your deserts," said he who appeared to have most authority among them; "strike a light here, you shallow-brained oaf; you have a devilish deal more reason to fear the living than the dead."

A light was struck, and they entered the apartment on the left hand. Henry recoiled as he beheld its desolate appearance: a broken chair, a worm-eaten table, and a low couch were all its furniture: the men opened the hampers; they contained some slight covering for the couch, a few logs of wood, and provisions.

"And is this place," said Henry, casting his eyes round the apartment, "allotted for me?"

"We are so instructed," replied one of the men who was placing some food on the table.

They kindled a fire, arranged his couch, and lighted a lamp. One of them then advancing to Henry, said, "Having provided for your necessities, our commission for the present ends; to-morrow we shall visit you again."

They then quitted the room; Henry heard the door locked and bolted, and listened to their retreating steps as they sounded along the lofty gallery. Until that moment hope had supported his spirits; but when he found himself indeed a prisoner, shut from society, far from the knowledge of those beings he most loved and valued, immured where his sufferings would never reach their ears, he sank in despondency upon the couch, and gave himself up to all the bitterness of grief.

A few moments served to convince him of the weakness of his conduct, of the folly of yielding to despair; the morrow might present some favourable turn; he might by seeking for opportunities, by perseverance, escape.

No sooner had this idea struck him than he started from the couch, and with scrutinizing eye searched his apartment: it was matted like the gallery; he shook the door, but it was cased with iron, and too strong to yield to his efforts. He next examined the window, but it was too high in the wall for him to reach, and the table and chair appeared too crazy to sustain his weight. He was hungry, thirsty, and exhausted: he ate of the food, and drank plentifully of the water, the only beverage that had been left him; and though unused to such humble fare, he felt satisfied and refreshed. He next examined the couch, which though coarse was clean, and he threw himself upon it, ruminating on the folly of man, who plunges into guilt, encounters peril, ventures on hardships and fatigue, to procure the luxuries that ultimately destroy his health and peace, while modest nature is satisfied with plain simple viands and the running stream:

> "Man wants but little here below,
> Nor wants that little long."

"If Lord Dungarvon were only sensible of this truth," thought Henry, "his mind would escape the tortures of remorse, nor should I be the imprisoned victim of his pride and his ambition."

Henry passed the night in sweet and undisturbed repose; and with the first beam of morning sprang from his lowly couch, again to examine his prison, in the hope that he might find some means of escape. He placed the table against the wall under the window, and springing upon it, found, contrary to his opinion, that it would bear his weight; but he was yet too low to reach the casement. – In descending to the ground his hand struck against something in the wall, which he found to be the fastening to a recess, so nicely matted that it appeared a part of the wall. He unclosed it, and was agreeably surprised to find it contained books.

On opening one, a parcel of letters fell to the ground, and under the last volume he found several sheets of manuscript poetry.

The books were Zimmerman on Solitude, Plato on the Immortality of the Soul, and the poetic works of Savage and Chatterton. – "A melancholy collection," said Henry, as he looked over the title page of each volume, "and most probably belonged to some such unfortunate being as myself – one perhaps whom the strong arm of power had secluded from the blessings of society, to whom these hooks were a real acquisition." He looked on the superscription of the letters; they were addressed in a female hand to Horace Nevil, Esq. The contents of one ran thus:

> "Yes, dearest Nevil, I admit the truth of your reasoning; but while my judgment is convinced, my heart, unable to relinquish the transport of loving you, shrinks from the idea of separation, and clings to the hope of overcoming your scruples, of thawing your frigidity, of triumphing over that philosophy which, while it proclaims the calmness of your

feelings, agonizes mine. Why did you ever say that Julia was dear to you, if you can coldly resign her, at the moment when she is ready for thy sake to sacrifice family and fortune, when she would fly to thy arms, and, renouncing the pride of birth and the splendour of affluence, would gladly share thy cottage, happier, prouder to be called thy wife, than the daughter of the Earl of Lucan? I know you will speak of your poverty, will tell me you are untitled: but have you not a mind rich in elevated sentiment, in exalted worth? Before these, the adventitious advantages of rank and wealth, in my estimation, sink to nothing. Nevil, I am greatly thy inferior; I seek thy alliance to ennoble myself. Come at midnight to the pavilion; but hope not, beloved of my soul, to persuade me to forget thee: no, "while reason holds a place in this distracted globe," so long will that reason worship thee; so long as this heart shall throb, its hopes, its wishes will all be thine. Lady Lucan may menace, but my affrighted soul still flies to the bosom of Nevil."

The rest was torn off. "This," said Henry, "was love. Oh! will the heart of any gentle being ever throb for me – ever cherish sentiments like these?" He opened the next:

"I send you the manuscripts, and I know I need not tell you to lose no time in their correction. You know not with what pleasure I write, while I believe that the talent with which it has pleased heaven to gift me will assist to provide for the exigencies of life. There are many persons in the world who get their bread by the efforts of their pen; and with such an instructor as Horace Nevil to correct and embellish my productions, I feel assured of success. Look over the little tale I send with this, and give me your opinion of it. The Earl and Lady Lucan are much displeased at my scribbling passion, degrading they say to a woman of fashion. What have I to do with fashion, I who am devoted to love and the muses?

The earl disapproves of books in general, and says a female of rank is sufficiently learned, if she can read and write a visiting-ticket. What a revolution in his lordship's opinions! He has not always thought thus, or why were you introduced at Raven-hill Castle? – why authorized to direct and superintend my studies? Oh! it was powerful destiny that led thee hither – that decreed thee the sovereign ruler of Julia's heart. Yes, it was almighty destiny that led me to find in thee a congenial spirit, a kindred soul.

I cannot come at the usual hour to the pavilion. I know not whether our meetings are suspected, but the gate is locked, and the key is I understand in the possession of Lord Lucan. The iron door leading to the chapel was I observed today unclosed; by that road you can reach the west tower, and from thence to my dressing-room. Do you remember when we were last at chapel we returned that way? Shall I ever forget that hour? no, never! – when the voice of Nevil whispered in the delighted ear of Julia, "I love thee." At midnight all will be retired, and most likely every one's eyes closed in sleep, except those of thy devoted and expecting

JULIA."

Henry remembered to have heard that the Dutchess of Inglesfield's first husband was the Earl of Lucan; this Julia then was their daughter – Ah! how unlike her mother! he proceeded to the next letter:

"Am I indeed thine, my Nevil? – Has the sacred ceremony past that has indissolubly bound our fates together? – It seems like a blissful vision – Can it be reality? – Yes, I perceive on my finger the magic circle, the little golden amulet. I press it to my lips, to my heart, and that heart's quickened pulses assure me I am the wife of Horace Nevil.

Lord Lucan is giving orders for the travelling carriages to be ready at early hour on Wednesday morning, to set off for London. Nevil, beloved of my soul, before then we shall be on our way to thy cottage, to Julia's Eden. Do not come before twelve tonight. Hitherto I have met thee with dread, I have trembled with apprehension: but now all these uneasy sensations are lost in floods of dissolving tenderness – thou art mine! – the worshipped of my heart is my husband, and only death can divide us. Jane has asked my permission to go to her sister, who is ill. I was rejoiced at the opportunity of getting rid of her: she is to remain all night. We shall meet without interruption. Nevil, how does thy heart feel? – mine beats with sensations never known before. Am I indeed thy wife? – Am I no longer Julia Belville? Come and receive my sighs of happiness – come and hide my blushes in thy bosom."

Henry was replacing the letters, when he heard the sound of footsteps in the gallery, and had just time to descend from the table, when the bolts of the door were withdrawn, and one of the men who had attended him the night before entered with a fresh supply of provisions and fuel.

He saluted Henry with much respect, and hoped he had rested well.

"Perfectly well," said Henry; "I have, I thank heaven, no

remorse of conscience to prevent my sleeping: I am far more "sinned against than sinning;" and most likely have enjoyed on this mean pallet more sweet and undisturbed repose than those who have condemned me to this prison, though stretched on beds of down."

"I wish it was in my power, sir, to alter your condition, I would most willingly. I have seen a good deal of sorrow in this chamber."

"Who last inhabited it?" said Henry.

"A gentleman," replied the man, "who suffered much hardship: he was said to be married to one of our ladies. Poor thing, she is quite out of her wits."

"Was the gentleman's name Nevil?" said Henry.

The man stared. – "Did you know him, sir?"

"No," replied Henry, "only by name."

"Poor gentleman, he got from this chamber, and nobody knows how nor which way. He was it seems a great scholar, and some of our servants say he raised the devil, and that he helped him to escape; however, sir, get away he did, some how, by hook or by crook; but for my part, I believe Lady Lucan, who is now Dutchess of –."

The man stopped suddenly.

"Proceed," said Henry; but the man looked confused and continued silent.

"At once to relieve your mind," said Henry, "I will satisfy you that I know where I am: this edifice is Raven-hill Castle, and belongs to the Dutchess of Inglesfield. Was not her daughter, Lady Julia Belville, married to Mr. Nevil?"

"Yes, certainly, more is the pity; but do you know that they were surprised together on their wedding-night; that he was dragged from the arms of his wife, and confined in this chamber, where he pined for more than a year, and that his wife lost her senses?"

"No," said Henry, with a deep sigh, "I did not know this."

"She is quite mad still," continued the man, "and wanders about the apartments of the west-tower, holding conversations with her husband, whom she fancies she sees. It is now ten years since her marriage, and during that time her mother has never visited her but once, for she is afraid of her, though, poor lady, she is perfectly harmless, and spends her time in making verses, so mournful, and singing such doleful songs, your heart, sir, would bleed to hear her."

"But respecting Mr. Nevil's escape," said Henry.

"I can give you no account how or which way he went, but there are those in the castle who could tell if they chose," replied the man. "At the farther end of the gallery through which you passed last night is a private staircase that leads to the vaults belonging to the chapel; I suspect that his body was conveyed that way."

"His body!" repeated Henry.

"Yes, sir, to be hid underground," rejoined the man; "but I shall be wanted, and the steward, Mr. Barnet, by whose orders I came, will reprimand me for staying so long."

He made up the fire and departed, fastening the door after him.

"To be hid underground!" repeated Henry, groaning; "wretched, ill-fated Nevil! but still more unhappy Julia! – his miseries are terminated; his heart has forgot its sorrows – she still exists to suffer. And may not my own fate resemble his? May I not be destined to languish out a miserable existence in this desolate apartment – to die among strangers, and have my hapless remains hid underground, unlamented by the heart of friendship, unwept by those who loved me; no sacred rite performed, no consecrated earth laid over me!"

Several days past in which Henry was so occupied with mournful reflections on the fate of Nevil, and the lamentable insanity of Lady Julia, in commiserating their divided loves, and deploring their disastrous fortunes, that he almost forgot his own sorrows. He was attended during this time by the same man, who one morning in addition to his usual humble fare brought some fruit, which as he was but scantily supplied with plates, he laid on the table on a newspaper.

"Perhaps, sir," said the man, "it will give you some pleasure, to know what is going forward in the world. I stole this paper from the steward's room; he talks of visiting you himself tomorrow; you will take care to destroy the paper, for should he discover that I have even brought you this little indulgence, I should be exchanged for somebody else, who may not be as well inclined towards you."

Henry thanked the man, and promised to observe his caution. He took up the newspaper: the first thing that struck his eye was an advertisement offering immense rewards for his discovery, describing at large the manner of his being seized and conveyed away.

"I am not forgotten," said Henry, his eyes swimming in tears, as he pressed to his lips and his heart the names of Sir Owen Llewellyn, of Lord Narbeth, and Horatio Delamere.

"My father, my friends, shall I ever again behold you," exclaimed Henry, "will Adeline ever again fly to meet, and embrace her brother?"

Again his eye wandered over the paper; one column was entirely filled with his adventure, and severe strictures on the conduct of Lord Dungarvon, who was strongly suspected of having entered into a plot against his grandson. The Dutchess of Inglesfield was ridiculed, and condemned; it also announced the decease of Selwyn Mortimer, the only remaining son of the Hon. Richard Mortimer, who died while preparations were making for his voyage to Lisbon.

"So pass away," said Henry, "all the proud aspiring hopes of Lord Dungarvon, the sickly pampered offspring of his favourite, all moulder in the sumptuous mausoleum of their ancestors, while the neglected son of Augustus Mortimer, in spite of oppressive tyranny, still enjoys Heaven's first great blessing, health."

Again he read the paper, and again the cherished hope of escape possessed him. Suddenly he thought he might stand upon the door of the recess, and from thence reach the window. He knew he should not be visited before morning: the moon was yet too young to light him, but at all hazards he resolved to attempt an escape. The day appeared unusually long, and he hailed the approach of night with transport; he placed the letters and manuscript of the unfortunate lady Julia in his bosom, and it being nearly dark he ascended from the table to the door of the recess: and after much toil he succeeded in reaching the window, the stone work of which being decayed it yielded to his touch and fell out with a splashing noise, that convinced Henry the sea ran beneath: after many unsuccessful attempts he at last stood on the sill of the window. The night was calm, the stars shone with unclouded brilliancy: he contemplated the thickly studded arch of heaven with religious rapture, and recommending himself to the protection of the Being who taught the planetary system to roll its splendid course, he dropped from the window to the battlement that ran round the tower, and perceived that the sea encircled all that side of the castle: from the battlement was no retreat except along a narrow ridge indented in the wall, from which one false step would precipitate him from an immeasurable height into the "world of waters." He saw there was only a few crumbling stones between him and eternity; but he resolved to proceed, though his situation, full of peril, threatened him every moment with destruction, climbing over decayed parts of the edifice, that shook beneath his weight, while many a heavy moss-covered stone loosened by the touch of his foot, or his hand, fell with appalling noise into the waves beneath. Almost exhausted, his clothes torn, his hands bruised and lacerated, he gained a wall about seven feet high, against which he perceived the tide was flowing, and he determined to wait till it should recede: he sat down on the wall, and heard a clock strike twelve.

"Good God!" said Henry, "how many hours have elapsed since I began my perilous journey – how little does Sir Owen or his gentle daughter think of the dangers that encompass their unhappy wanderer. Sweet and peaceful be their slumbers! soon, very soon I trust, I shall press them to my bosom, shall hear the honest indignation of Sir Owen, shall see the tear of soft compassion tremble in the mild and expressive eyes of Adeline."

Many an anxious look Henry cast on the swelling tide, many a wish escaped him that it would retreat. At length it began to ebb, and with inconceivable joy he beheld it recede from the wall. – Henry uninjured felt his feet touch the sands; he walked with a quick pace, and soon lost sight of the frowning turrets of Raven-hill Castle. The sun had scarcely risen when he found himself opposite a farm house, into which he immediately entered, requested some refreshment, and inquired if he could be supplied with a horse and guide to the nearest town. Henry's coat was torn in many places: his linen was soiled, and his hands and face were scratched and bloody, for he had wounded them in scrambling over the sharp stones and flinty walls of the castle. The man to whom he addressed himself stood for some moments with his mouth open staring at him; at last he inquired where he came from, and in such a miserable plight. Henry briefly related his adventure, and promised the man a handsome reward, if he would assist him to the next town, declaring himself too weary to proceed on foot.

"Pretty work, indeed," said the farmer, "to carry a man away by force, and shut him up, as a body may say, without leave or licence: why for what I know this may turn out to be a hanging matter. Yes, yes, young gentleman, I will do my best to help you, but you must indeed be very tired, so my dame shall give you a bowl of new milk, and shew you to a bed, where you had better take an hour or two's rest: my horses are all out at plough at present, and it will be some time before they can be fetched here. Dame, why don't you come in?"

Presently a clean elderly woman made her appearance, to whom the farmer repeated Henry's story, which she every now and then interrupted with exclamations of anger and pity. Henry made a delicious breakfast on bread and new milk, and was soon after shewn by the good woman to a clean comfortable bed: for some time he could scarcely persuade himself that he was awake, or that he had in reality escaped from the confinement of the castle. As his thoughts became more calm, he anticipated the delight of surprising his friends by his unexpected presence, of receiving their congratulations, and recounting to them his perilous adventures. Fatigue at length weighed down his eyelids: he had not slept long before he was roused from his repose by some person roughly shaking his arm; he started up, and found the farmer's wife by his bed side:

"Get up, young gentleman," said she, "get up and begone. You have ran away from one danger to fall into a worse. My cross husband is brother to the steward of Raven-hill Castle, and is just set off to give notice that you are here: make haste and begone."

She left him, and Henry hastily throwing on his clothes, was down stairs in an instant after her. He would have pressed some money upon her, but she steadily refused, and bade him keep it to help him on his way, for that would be a friend when none other was near. She directed him a bye road across a moor to the next town. Henry blest and thanked her, and turning into the fields according to the good woman's direction, pursued his way for some miles without impediment or molestation. The evening was now closing in; it was gloomy, and the wind swept in long and chilling blasts over the heads of the shrubs that were thinly scattered on the moor upon which he had entered. So many paths now presented themselves that he stood perplexed and irresolute which to pursue. Providence, thought Henry, must be my guide. He struck into a track, along which was visible the impression of wagon wheels, and followed it, till at last it led him to a low white gate, a few yards beyond which stood a neat thatched cottage. Henry quickened his pace, and seeing a decent looking woman, resolved to pass the night there if she could accommodate him. She told him that herself and son inhabited the cottage, that he was gone on particular business ever since before day to the steward at Raven-hill Castle, and that she was looking for him home every minute.

At the mention of Raven-hill Castle Henry determined on

proceeding: he feared to trust himself again in the power of persons who were in any way connected with that place. He started up, and inquiring the road to the nearest town, hastily departed, notwithstanding the lateness of the hour and the darkness of the night, dreading to encounter the young man on his return from the castle, lest, having heard his person described, he should know and be influenced to detain him.

Fatigued and unwell, in the agitation of his mind he pursued his way to the right instead of the left, which the good woman had directed, and before he had proceeded a mile his foot struck against something: he lost his equilibrium, and fell into a deep pit: here he lay stunned and motionless for some time; at length recovering his recollection he endeavoured to rise. He had received a violent contusion on his head, and both his ankles were sprained: he was unable to stand, his only alternative therefore was to wait till some charitable person should pass by, of whom he could implore assistance to leave the pit, which was deep and large. He now felicitated himself on still possessing his watch and his purse, as he feared he should be some time before he could reach his friends.

The appearance of the farmer at the castle with the intelligence of Henry's escape filled the steward with the utmost consternation: they flew to the matted chamber, and finding the window forced out, understood at once how he had liberated himself; but the door of the recess being closed, they were quite at a loss to comprehend how he had reached the window: a ladder being brought, their astonishment was increased as they viewed the outside, nor was it unmixed with shuddering sensations of terror, while they gazed on the narrow jutment, and loose hanging stones, over which he had pursued his desperate course.

"Thank Heaven he is safe however," said the steward.

"Aye," replied the farmer, "he is safe enough sure, taking a comfortable nap I warrant in dame's best bed – and rest he must want for certain after his toilsome journey. I would not take all my lady dutchess's money to scramble over those places as he did last night; why, man, if his foot had slipped, or one of these stones had given way, souse he would have fell into the sea, and I would not have given a broken horse shoe for his life; but what," continued he, "does my lady dutchess want of him, brother?"

"Want of him!" replied the steward, "why she wants to marry him."

"O Lord! is that all," said the astonished farmer. "Ecod! I wish my dame was under ground, and she would marry me; we would not have any prisonments, or scapes out at windows about that affair."

"You!" said the steward, laughing, "no, no, you are not young enough for her purpose. But come, I expect her hourly; let us begone, and bring back the runaway. Mercy upon me! should he not be forthcoming when she arrives, I would almost as soon be steward of the lower regions as governor of Raven-hill Castle."

The brothers were not long reaching the farm, where finding Henry had departed, they flew into the most violent rage, venting execrations in abundance upon the good woman, who in vain asserted that she was not able to detain him.

Emissaries were immediately dispatched in different directions, and large rewards promised to the neighbouring peasantry who would undertake to secure and deliver him safe at Raven-hill Castle.

Henry had passed the night in extreme pain; his limbs were

stiff and cold, and before the dawning of day his corporeal agonies, joined to his mental suffering, had brought on a fever, and he lay on the damp flinty bottom of the pit, unconscious of the wretchedness of his situation

It was a stone quarry into which he had been precipitated. Early in the morning a man came to his labour, and seeing Henry lying at the bottom of the pit, called out to him, "Halloo, master! you have picked out a rough sort of a bed for yourself there."

Henry opened his eyes, but unable to utter a word, closed them again. The man got down into the pit, and seeing his face bruised and covered with blood, compassionately tried to raise him up. He found he was unable to lift him out of the pit, and he ran home to his cottage at a short distance to call his wife and daughter.

They brought a rug, and with much difficulty raised the unconscious Henry from the pit, and carrying him between them, humanely laid him upon a bed. – The man bid the woman take care of the poor young fellow, and went to his work.

They washed the blood from his face and hands, but finding he was much bruised, and his legs dreadfully swelled, they were quite at a loss to know what to do for him.

In this exigence the daughter (a pretty looking young girl) ran off to a neighbouring public-house, where she told a lamentable story that a young gentleman had been robbed and almost murdered by some villains, who had thrown him into the quarry, and that her father had found him there almost lifeless, bruised from head to foot, and covered with blood.

During this recital a man on horseback, who was drinking at the door with Mr. Muggins, the landlord, listened attentively and bidding the girl shew him the way, galloped after her to where Henry was raving of Lord Dungarvon, and struggling to escape from the friendly woman, who was trying to hold him down, and soothing him with expressions of the utmost kindness.

The man had no sooner recognized the disfigured countenance of Henry, than he loaded the woman and her daughter with thanks, and putting a guinea into the mother's hand, bade her be careful of the young gentleman till his return, which would be as soon as he could procure a chaise. He rode off full gallop.

Mr. Muggins by this time had arrived at the cottage, and seeing the gold in the poor woman's hand, who was almost frantic with her good luck, busied himself in assisting to bathe Henry's bruises and his sprained ankles with warm vinegar. The woman cut off part of his fine hair, which was clotted together with the blood that had streamed from the wound in his head.

"I am afraid the poor dear creature will die," said the woman.

"I hope not," said the daughter: "only look at his fine white skin: it would be a thousand pities that such a handsome young man as he should die."

"Handsome or not handsome," said the landlord, "he must die when his time comes, as well as Hodge Nixon and I; and mayhap, though his skin may be finer than our's, I question if the worms will relish him a bit better, or make a daintier meal upon him than us."

"Don't talk so wicked, Mr. Muggins," replied the girl, "I am sure I should be main sorry if he was to die: it would be a pity for the worms to eat such a sweet young gentleman as him."

The landlord was displeased, and casting a look of contempt upon her, said, "And what do you know about him pray, that you should be sorry? – what is it to you whether he lives or dies? You are plaguy concerned all about a stranger; it would be as well for you if you was to mind which side your bread is buttered on, and pay some notice to other folk, who mayhap are as good to look on as him, though their skins are not so fine."

"You may as well be still, Mr. Muggins," answered the girl, "for I shall never like you, let your tongue wag as much as it will; and you ought to be ashamed, so you ought, to talk of this here fashion about dying and worms, when your own poor old wife have not been dead above a month. Poor soul! she can hardly be cold in her grave yet."

Mr. Muggins laughed till his fat sides shook. "I am willing," said he, "to let you take her place in the bar, and make you landlady of the Rising Sun; and as to the worms, they may feast on her as long as they like, though they will have but a sorry meal, for she had fretted all her flesh away, and left them nothing but bare bones to pick. But I suppose Will, the miller's man, is more to your liking."

"Mayhap he is," replied the girl, "and mayhap he is not; but whether he is or not, you might have found some other time to talk about such things, seeing the poor young man here in such torment."

"No time like the time present," said the landlord; "and as for Will, let him have a care of himself; it is odds but I get him sent aboard one of our frigates: it will better become him to be fighting the French than to be skulking here after the wenches."

During this altercation a chaise stopped at the door, and the same person who had been at the cottage before, attended by another, jumped out of it.

"Aye, confound his carcase," said the steward of Raven-hill Castle, as he looked upon Henry, "it is his unlucky phiz sure enough. A devilish pretty dance he has led us, but we have him now safe enough, and I think he won't escape from my clutches again in a hurry."

Mr. Muggins stood bowing and scraping, and explaining what he had done for the poor young gentleman: the steward only answered the landlord's politeness with curse him.

"I wish he had been at the devil before I saw him. A fine shaking and jumbling I have had of it, driving here, and galloping after him there; but I will answer for it he don't give me the slip again." The woman hoped his honour would do the young gentleman no harm, as they feared he had not long to live. "Then," said the steward, "he may die, and – "

"Oh, Lord! pray don't swear, sir, it is so wicked," said the young girl. The other man chucked her under the chin, swore she was a pretty wench, and asked if she would go with them.

"Come, Frank," said the steward, "we shall hardly reach home before dark."

Mr. Muggins hoped they would remember him for his trouble. The steward asked him how much vinegar he had used: he could not exactly say, perhaps a quart.

"No, nor half-a-pint," replied the girl: "why should you wish to impose on the gentleman?"

The steward gave him a shilling. Mr. Muggins eyed it with contempt. "If I had known how I should be rewarded for my pains," said he, "I would have seen his skin stript off like an eel's, fine as it is, before he would have had my vinegar or my help, if I had known how I was to be paid."

All this time Henry was perfectly quiet, and suffered himself to be placed unresistingly in the chaise. The steward gave the girl half-a-crown. Frank struggled to kiss her, and told her she should soon see him again.

"Don't trouble yourself," said the girl, "to come this way upon my account; I have no business with gentlemen that wear such fine clothes as you do; I get an honest living by my hard labour, and at present I am quite content and happy, but perhaps if I was to see you often, I should get proud and lazy, and wish for fine clothes too."

They sprang into a chaise, which drove off at a furious rate, while the landlord abused them for mean shabby scrubs, and told the girl that he should give up all thoughts of making her Mrs. Muggins, for he would not give a toss up of a brass farthing for a landlady at the Rising Sun, who would make any bones about scoring double. In the mean time the dutchess's courier arrived at the castle with intelligence that his grace would be there next day. All was bustle and confusion: the apartments that had not seen sun or moon for years were thrown open to receive light and air, and the long deserted corridors echoed with the placing of furniture, and the steps of domestics passing backwards and forwards.

The motion of the carriage had roused Henry from his quiescent state: his fever had arisen to an alarming height, and the men, who travelled in fear of their lives from his outrageous conduct, and who with difficulty kept him in the carriage, rejoiced when they found themselves in the spacious court of Raven-hill Castle, and the gates closed upon them. Henry was immediately stripped and put to bed; the housekeeper prepared a medicine, which was with much trouble forced down his throat, and she bathed his ankles and his bruises with an emollient of her own making.

The next day the dutchess arrived, palpitating with the ardent hope, the blissful idea, that Henry, tired of his confinement, would accede to her terms, and rather consent to become her husband than live a prisoner for life; but what was her terror, her disappointment, to find him delirious; her horror to hear him execrate Lord Dungarvon, and rave of her in terms of abhorrence and disgust. In her moments of compunction she had him removed to a sumptuous apartment, and sent off to the neighbouring town for a physician: he came, and pronounced that the patient could not live twenty-four hours: he examined his head, and declared that his skull was fractured, and the brain injured, and if he were to survive, which appeared utterly impossible, he would always be a lunatic.

The dutchess heard this account with the utmost dismay; her conscience had already a sufficient burthen to sustain, and she felt that the addition of his death, or his insanity, would be a weight too horrible for her nature, callous as it was, to support. Every moment her attendants were dispatched to his apartment, and when she was told of his unceasing ravings her sufferings more than equalled his, for his agonies were inflicted by the hand of Heaven, who sometimes sees it right to punish the innocent, while the wicked groan under the excruciating torments of remorse, more dreadful, because awakened conscience confesses to them the merited scourges of guilt.

CHAPTER VII

"Honour pricks me on:
But how, if honour prick me off when I come on,
How then? Can honour set a leg? No: Or an arm? No:
Or take away the grief of a wound? No: Honour hath no skill
In surgery then? No: What is honour? A word: What is that word?
Honour – Air; a trim reckoning. Who hath it? he who died o' Wednesday.
Doth he feel it? No. Doth he hear it? No. Is it insensible then? yea, to the dead.
But will it not live with the living? No. Why? Detraction will not suffer it;
Therefore I'll none of it. Honour is a mere scutcheon."

Shakespeare

SIR OWEN LLEWELLYN had been indefatigable in his search after Henry. Lord Narbeth and Horatio Delamere had in concert with him done all that wealth or interest could effect to find out the spot where he was immured; yet still he remained undiscovered, and his fate seemed involved in impenetrable mystery. Ardent is the cause of friendship: they had severally written to Lord Dungarvon on the subject, and had each received haughty replies, indicating that the young man had by his grovelling notions entirely convinced Lord Dungarvon that he was utterly unworthy his notice, and that he had in consequence abandoned him to the enjoyment of that mediocrity for which he seemed by nature, habit, and inclination fitted: that he wondered any person properly acquainted with the rank and consequence of Lord Dungarvon would venture to associate his character with that of a jailor, or presume to believe that he would convert any one of his mansions, consecrated by having once been the residence of an illustrious Mortimer, into a prison for the son of Louisa Berresford. These answers, though they by no means convinced, obliged the friends of Henry to resign the hope of obtaining satisfaction from their application to him, and to rest their reliance of discovering him from the large rewards they continued to offer through the medium of the public papers. But as yet no clue had been obtained, and Henry and his sufferings remained concealed from the anxious inquiries of his lamenting friends.

At Tudor Hall things wore an equally unpleasant aspect. Sir Griffith deeply felt that he had sustained a loss in Seymour's society which he could not supply: and this want of a companion to join in his mad freaks and projects served to keep alive his resentment, even at the very moment he could not help secretly admiring, and doing justice to the brave spirit that had disappointed his hopes and wishes.

Through the means of Gwinthlean, Eliza had contrived to correspond with her lover, whose letters breathed everlasting love, and inviolable constancy. At this period Lady Tudor's nephew, the son of an English merchant who from many years of successful commerce had accumulated an immensity of wealth, arrived at Tudor Hall. Mr. David Morgan, the heir to his father's extensive property, was a young man of Colossium stature, very plain face, and coarse manners. His father had wisely considered the time unprofitably wasted that was not employed in getting money, and at twenty-four years of age, David Morgan was ignorant of all rule, except the *rule* of *three*: he had seen but little beyond his father's counting-house in Milk-lane: but he felt all the consequence annexed to wealth, and was conceited and overbearing. The immense property to which he was to succeed gratified the pride of Lady Tudor, who found out perfections in his awkward person and illiterate mind undiscoverable to every other eye. She flattered her fancy with the hope that Miss Tudor, separated for ever from Seymour, would be sensible to the merits of her cousin, and that by forming an alliance with him, there would be wealth enough united in the fortunes of Tudor and Morgan to purchase a principality.

Sir Griffith seldom adopted or entered into any scheme of his lady's but this: contrary to her most distant expectation, he warmly and eagerly promoted it; he had bitterly sworn his daughter should never marry Seymour, against whom his anger still burnt fiercely, and he took every opportunity of recommending Mr. Morgan to Eliza's favour, not that he either liked or approved of him, but merely because he delighted in contradiction, and because he saw that her heart and thoughts dwelt on Seymour; and he obstinately determined that she should never marry a man who had dared to avow an opinion and follow a course he had disapproved. The spirits of Eliza were still animated: she breathed many a fond regretful sigh in secret, and put up many a prayer for Seymour, but her fate wore no trace of sorrow, and she mimicked and ridiculed her ungraceful cousin with a vivacity that her recent disappointment had neither power to check nor diminish.

The heart of Mr. Morgan was not entirely insensible to the charms of beauty: he had not overlooked the sprightly graces of his little wild cousin, whom he assailed with the refined rhetoric of city eloquence. He boasted of his riches, enumerated his expectations, repeated the names of the many ladies who were anxious to be noticed by him, related a long history of disputes that had taken place at the Crown and Anchor balls between Miss Alderman Congo and Miss Deputy Figgens, who had fallen into fits because he had taken out Miss Congo.

These narrations highly diverted Eliza; and being by nature a coquette, she was not displeased at having a new admirer, even though her eye disliked, and her judgment despised him.

Adeline Llewellyn, who had witnessed her flirtation, seriously remonstrated with her on the cruelty of raising hopes she had no intention of realizing, on the danger of entangling him in a hopeless passion, and hazarding the possibility of making him for ever miserable.

"Never fear, child," replied Eliza. "I will venture to prophecy that Mr. David Morgan's heart is not made of such penetrable stuff; no, he will never be miserable on account of any woman breathing; he feels his own importance too proudly, to suffer much from woman's wiles, or the witcheries of love."

Mr. David Morgan had been taught by his prudent father some good old adages, which had deeply impressed themselves not only on his memory, but on his judgment, and with the value of which he was perfectly acquainted: such as, "*Delays are dangerous*;" "*Never put off till tomorrow what may be done today*;" and several others of equal merit; therefore, having received from his cousin what he considered sufficient encouragement, he ventured one morning to suggest, that as time was extremely precious, and his presence much wanting in his father's business, he hoped that his worthy uncle, Sir Griffith, would take his situation into consideration, and have the great goodness, the extraordinary kindness, to influence Miss Tudor to name an early day for their wedding.

Sir Griffith shook him by the hand, and swore they should be married that day fortnight.

When Eliza was acquainted with her father's determination, she unhesitatingly put a negative upon Mr. Morgan's hopes, declaring that she considered six weeks (the period he had been at Tudor Hall) as far too short a time for her to decide upon his merits, or to determine whether he was the sort of man she should approve for a husband.

"The sort of man!" replied Sir Griffith: "confusion! madam, have not you eyes to see that he is more than six feet high and that – "

"Oh! my dear sir," rejoined Miss Tudor, "the man is quite tall enough I confess: but I am rather doubtful whether his understanding may be commensurate with his height: and whether nature, in one of her frolicsome moods, may not, in extending his figure, have contracted his understanding."

"So much the better if she has, madam," replied Sir Griffith, "so much the better for you: his want of understanding is all in your favour; for I will be d – d if any man with an ounce of brains would ever think of troubling himself with such a little unmanageable vixen. What the devil can you find to object to? His family on the female side is the same as your own: he has plenty of money to keep pace with your extravagance: and as to himself, he is a very good sort of a young man."

"Yes, sir," said Eliza, "I acknowledge that Mr. David Morgan is a very good sort of *good for nothing* kind of person.

I thank you, sir, for your offer; but I will never be the wife of this good young man."

"Perhaps," said Sir Griffith, "you flatter yourself with the notion of marrying that hot-headed fellow, Seymour: but if ever you do, I will be – "

"Pray don't swear, sir," interrupted Eliza; "I should be very sorry to be the occasion of your breaking an oath; but I have pledged my word, you know, either to be his, or remain 'in single blessedness;' and I have in the present instance neither inclination nor temptation to falsify my promise."

"Very fine! mighty well, madam!" roared Sir Griffith, "we shall see which will gain the day, you or me. I must do you the credit though to allow that you are a very sweet, pretty, d – d, obedient –"

"Obedient!" rejoined Eliza, "no one can question that. Did not you command me to love Captain Seymour, and did not I most dutifully obey you?"

"Now then, you perverse, little, d – d obstinate but I will not suffer my temper to be ruffled – I will not get in a passion. Remember, and let me see a proof of your obedience and duty – I bid you hate and detest him."

"But this, sir," rejoined Eliza, "is so unnatural a command, so extremely unreasonable, that really I fear it will be impossible for me to obey. Besides, sir, you forget that I am of the race of Tudor, a people famous, if tradition may be relied upon, from generation to generation, for contradiction; – you would not have me disgrace my family, cast a blot on the fair fame of my honoured mother, and bastardize myself?"

"Yes, and tradition might also have informed you, madam," replied Sir Griffith, foaming with passion, "that the males of the Tudor line never suffered themselves, right or wrong, to yield a point to a female: so prepare yourself, for you shall go to church this day fortnight with David Morgan: or I will be d – d to all intents and purposes if I don't drag you there; so prepare your lace, and your muslin, and your frippery, and gew-gaws; get your frills, and your flounces, and furbelows ready."

"Yes, sir," said Eliza, curtseying obediently.

"Yes, sir" said Sir Griffith, staring, "why, what the devil! – what do you mean?"

"I mean, sir," replied Eliza, "to avail myself of my aunt Rees's invitation to go to Monmouth for a short time, only till Mr. David Morgan shall have returned to his computations and calculations in his father's counting-house, and Sir Griffith Tudor to a recollection that there is a line of duty for parents to observe as well as children: I will then cheerfully return to Tudor Hall, in the hope of seeing those days restored, when Eliza was the darling of her father's heart – when he was her companion and friend, not her tyrant."

She was now quitting the room, but Sir Griffith caught her arm, and swinging her round, swore she did not get off so easily.

"No journey to Monmouth: no driving my horses here and there, and the devil knows where!" vociferated Sir Griffith; "no carrying complaints to that soft-headed, silly oaf, Lady Rees, who, if it was for no other reason in life than the pleasure of thwarting me, would aid and abet you in your wicked and unnatural rebellion against my authority; but here comes David, and you had better behave yourself with decency, or a dark garret and bread and water – you understand me."

Mr. David Morgan hoped he did not interrupt private business.

"No, David, no," said Sir Griffith, "the business we was upon will soon be public enough: it was your marriage we were talking of."

"I hope," said Mr. Morgan, "my cousin has no objections."

"Indeed but I have though," replied Eliza, "and a great many. In the first place, matrimony is too serious a matter to be entered upon without mature deliberation."

"Very true, cousin," said David.

"And in the next place," resumed Eliza, "I think I am yet too young to marry."

"That's a lie," said Sir Griffith, "a d – d barefaced lie: you have fancied yourself old enough ever since you entered your teens."

"And then," continued Eliza, unheeding her father's gross interruption, "our turn of mind is so very different."

"That makes little odds," said Mr. Morgan, "we shall you know live in the city"

"In the city!" echoed Eliza, contemptuously.

"Aye, cousin, in the city, to be certain," rejoined David Morgan; "and you will find plenty of wealthy and agreeable acquaintance to visit. – There is Alderman Sparable's family, Deputy Snakeroot, and Mr. Gammon, the common council man's lady and daughters, who were brought up at Chelsea boarding school, and can parle vouz as if they had been born in France, besides Miss Figgins and Miss Congo, and a hundred others, all ladies of large property and expectations; while I am busy in the counting-house with the clerks in a morning, you will find them all ready to gossip with you."

"I really feel highly indebted to Mr. Morgan," replied Eliza, "for his having fixed upon me in preference to so many deserving females, among whom I have no doubt but he might have selected one, whose heart and sentiments, more in unison with his own, would have rendered her more sensible than I am of the honour he confers in the offer of his hand."

"Why as to the matter of that there, cousin," replied Mr. Morgan, "I could certainly have found girls enough in the city, who would have jumped at the thought of being Mrs. Morgan, but my mother loves her own family better than any body else, and she wished that I should travel and see a bit of the world: so according to her advice, I came all the way from London, over the wild mountains of Wales, to pay my addresses to you, a great many long miles, and a great expense too, cousin, only for that there purpose, and I should not like to be made a fool of, and laughed at for my pains and trouble."

"Certainly not, David, certainly not," rejoined Sir Griffith; "no man likes to be made a fool of; and I shall take care that nothing of this nature happens to you, my boy."

"To prove to you," said Eliza, "that I have no intention of this sort, I beg leave to observe, that if your visiting Wales had a marriage with me for its object, you have no one but yourself to thank for having come upon a fool's errand. I, whose opinion was of most consequence in the affair, was never consulted, nor till now my opinion asked upon the occasion: if I had, I should at once have put a negative upon the business."

"Why look you, cousin," replied David, "you might, being sharp enough at most things, have guessed my meaning. Have not I attended you here and there and every where; and have not you accepted my services; and have not I, for all you talk in this here odd way, always made myself agreeable to you?"

"Not exactly," replied Eliza, "though I am willing to admit the goodness of your intention. Depend upon it, Mr. Morgan,

I am not calculated for a wife for you: our manners, our habits, our educations have been so very different."

"Very true, cousin," replied Morgan, "the hours that you have slept away in bed of a morning I have employed in getting money; and as for your classic and outlandish French and Greek books, I don't pretend to understand any such gibberish: but for book-keeping after the Italian manner, and Bonicastle, I believe I am as well acquainted with them as most folks."

He said this with a tone, of such proud exultation, and an air of such importance, that Eliza burst into a loud fit of laughter, which entirely disconcerted Mr. Morgan, and threw Sir Griffith into a fresh rage, who swore that if he were to have a hundred more daughters, not one of them should ever learn to read or write: for that all the good books had done for Eliza was to turn her brain, pervert her principles, and make her refractory and disobedient. He then insisted that she should treat her cousin with more respect.

"Undoubtedly," replied Eliza, "I shall ever respect Mr. Morgan as a man of figures, with this special observance, that he makes a trifling mistake in his arithmetic if he reckons upon having me for a wife. Cousin, cast up your account; you will find the sum total of your journey into Wales comes exactly to disappointment. As my mother's nephew, I am ready to shew you every proper attention: but if I were to consent to take you 'for better for worse,' we should then be 'a little more than kin, and much less than kind' so, my dainty Davy, keeping separate accounts will I am certain be found most profitable to us both."

Sir Griffith shook with rage. "You shall be his wife!" roared he, in a voice of thunder. David turned pale, and jumped from one side of the room to the other – "you shall be his wife this day fortnight, or I will turn you out of doors, and you may go and carry the knapsack after that fellow Seymour, who with his red coat has bewitched you to forget your duty. You will cut a d – d smart figure upon a baggage-waggon, or tramping on a broiling hot day along a dusty road, after a drum."

"You seem to forget, sir," replied Eliza, "that it was your own approbation that sanctioned my regard for Capt. Seymour, and that you once encouraged the pretensions and thought highly of the man of whom you are now pleased to speak so degradingly. My mind, however, admits of no alteration: he has my perfect and unchangeable regard; my word is pledged to him, and whatever may be my future destiny, rich or poor, I will be his, or the wife of no man breathing."

Eliza appeared agitated. Mr. Morgan approached, and attempted to take her hand, which she drew back. "Sure, cousin, you can't be in earnest in that there speech – you don't mean that I should take it for true."

"As the gospel," replied Eliza: "and knowing my engagement and the state of my heart, if you, Mr. Morgan, had either delicacy, honour, or humanity, you would at once decline a suit that you see occasions so much uneasiness."

But Eliza knew not that she was appealing to the feelings of a man who was at that very instant computing the expenses of his journey into Wales, and the possible extent of his losses in being so long absent from his desk in Milk-lane; and resolving to call Sir Griffith Tudor's wealth his, if it was by any means to be obtained.

Sir Griffith, however, spared her the trouble of a reply, by telling her she might as well reserve her speeches, for it was his determination to marry her to David Morgan. "Your hero," said he, "is fighting up to his knees in the trenches of Holland, all for renown; you are parrying, battling, and skirmishing with your father, mother, and David here, all for love: now, my little obstinate, we shall see which understands manoeuvering best; we will try which can carry on the war most successfully. D – n you, David," said he, striking him a blow on the back that made him reel again, "let multiplication and addition alone for the present, and I warrant we have the victory."

Eliza, finding she could not quit the room, sat down by the window, took up a book, and would have read, but Sir Griffith snatched the volume from her hand, and throwing it to the other end of the room, told her with all her learning she was d – d ignorant, and knew but little of good breeding, to attempt reading in company.

Mr. Morgan drew a chair to the window, and assured her when she was his wife she should be as happy as the day was long, that she should entirely command the servants and manage the children as she liked, and go where she pleased, and wear what she chose.

"Indeed," said Eliza, "you are wonderfully condescending."

"Yes, indeed, cousin, I am quite in earnest, I assure you, for I shall never attempt to concern with or meddle about them there matters."

"Then," replied Sir Griffith, "you will act like a d – d ass, David; giving women their way too much ruins them. What the devil and all his imps, suffer women to rule! I never allow any person to pretend to govern in my family, except myself, and you see – "

"Yes, sir," said David, "I see."

"What the devil do you see?" said Sir Griffith, pettishly.

"Only how well you govern the family, Sir Griffith," replied Mr. Morgan, rather confusedly.

"What," replied Sir Griffith, sneeringly, "I suppose you think that I shall suffer that little minx, that bit of perverseness, that epitome of all her sex's obstinacy to get the better of me? – No, no David, she may contradict, she may refuse, she may thwart, but she shall yield, she must obey at last. All her spirit is gasconade, mere flash in the pan: for, d – n me, if I don't make her thankful to submit, or say I am not the son of Griffith Glendower Tudor."

"And if ever I do submit to be the wife of David Morgan," said Eliza, springing out of the window, "say my sex have lost all their spirit, and that I am not the daughter of Griffith Tudor."

Mr. Morgan started from his seat in amazement.

Sir Griffith burst into a loud laugh. – "Look at her, David," said he; "is not she a beautiful little jade? – she runs like a deer: d – n me, there is not such another horse-woman in all Wales; leaps a gate or clears a hedge with as much ease as she did this window. Can any of your pale-faced city girls do as much?"

"Why no, Sir Griffith, I can't say I ever heard of their being over expert at them there kind of matters; but then they can dance nicely," said Mr. Morgan.

"Dance, David!" replied Sir Griffith, "show me one of them that will follow a fiddle with my girl; why she foots it like a fairy: and then for spirit – Oh! d – n it, she's a Tudor every inch of her."

"Yes, Sir Griffith, she a good deal resembles you," replied the young man, who thought a great portion of her spirit might very well have been dispensed with, and whose mind would by no means have reconciled itself to her electricity, but from the hope of enjoying the large estates to which he knew she was the indisputable heiress.

"Yes, yes," said the delighted Sir Griffith, "every body allows that she has my features, my temper, my spirit; not an atom of her mother's weak nerves, die-away airs, and fanciful vagaries. – D – n me, she's a wife for an emperor. When you get her, David, you will be the envy of all the city bucks."

"Nay for that matter, Sir Griffith," rejoined Mr. Morgan, "my cousin will be as much envied for having of me. I could have had Miss Figgins, or Miss Congo, both of them large fortunes, and were monstrously in love with me, but I preferred doing the will of my mother, who desired me not to mind them there girls, but to go into Wales, and court my cousin Eliza, and indeed, Sir Griffith, I had a tedious journey of it, jolting over hills and mountains: and now I shall be laughed at in the city, by all my acquaintance, if I go back as I came, without a wife."

"Cheer up, David," replied Sir Griffith, "you shall have her – have not I said it, and let me see who will offer to dispute my authority when I choose to exert it, you shall see she will come to as meek and gentle as a lamb."

Several days past in which Lady Tudor urged, Mr. Morgan courted, Sir Griffith swore, and Eliza remained inexorable, when being assembled in the library, in the midst of one of these altercations a letter was delivered to Mr. Morgan, which having read he turned as pale as ashes, and presented it to Sir Griffith, who no sooner glanced over it, than he turned to Eliza, his eyes flashing fire.

"Here is a d – d pretty kettle of fish," said he. "So madam, you have contrived to let Seymour's Scotch clan know all that passes at Tudor Hall."

"Not I, indeed sir," replied she, "and for the best of all possible reasons, I knew they were at too great a distance to render me any service."

"Then how the devil, you little witch, should his cousin know any thing of David Morgan?" Sir Griffith then read aloud.

"Mr. Lionel Seymour, first cousin to Captain Seymour, of the sixteenth regiment of Scotch Greys, expects that Mr. David Morgan will meet him on Rhudlan Downs this evening at seven o'clock, in order to give him satisfaction on the part of Captain Seymour, now absent on duty, for having made pretensions to Miss Tudor his affianced bride. Lionel Seymour leaves to Mr. Morgan the choice of weapons, but shall expect him with his second at the appointed place and hour, or will not fail to fix the epithet coward to his character publicly and privately."

Sir Griffith rang the bell. "Who the devil brought this letter?"

The servant replied, "A countryman, who said it required no answer."

"What is to be done, sir?" inquired the trembling Morgan.

"Done!" replied Sir Griffith, "why, you must meet and fight him, to be sure. Why d – n it, David, you are as white as Eliza's petticoat – you can draw a trigger can't you?"

"Indeed, sir, I know very little about pistols; I have never been used to meddle much with them there sort of articles," said Mr. Morgan.

"But you can fire a pistol, David: I saw you take aim at a robin the other day."

"Yes, Sir Griffith, yes, but shooting a bird and a man is quite and clean another guess sort of a thing; and then this here letter says I must bring a second: where can I find a man to go with me upon such a bloody business, I that am quite a stranger to every body in these here parts?"

"I shall be your second, David," said Sir Griffith, "and if Mr. Lionel Seymour kills you, I will be d – d if I don't shoot him through the head: let that content you, David."

"No, Sir Griffith, no, that will not content me, I did not come here with the wicked intention of duelling: besides I am but a very bad shot; and what will my poor mother say, and what will my father do without me, if I should be killed?"

Eliza, starting up, clasped her hands in agony, and laying hold of David, who shook like a leaf, entreated him not to think of exposing his life; that the Seymours were all famous marksmen, and that she should never forgive herself if she was the occasion of his death.

"He shall fight though," said Sir Griffith, "for all your snivelling. D – n me, if a person that pretends to the honour of belonging to my family shall sneak from the smell of gunpowder; I have a most excellent pair of pistols, so prepare yourself, David."

Eliza knelt, prayed, and entreated, but the more she opposed, the more determined and vehement Sir Griffith grew. In a few seconds the house was in an uproar, the servants informed Lady Tudor, who shrieked, fainted, and loudly insisted that Sir Owen Llewellyn should be applied to as a magistrate, to apprehend the bloodthirsty delinquent, who was defying the laws of his country, and planning to take away the life of her nephew.

Sir Owen Llewellyn was gone some miles across the country to visit a friend: the next magistrate was from home also, and Sir Griffith swore, and loaded his pistols, which he gave in charge to his groom, while Lady Tudor screamed in hysterics, and poor David Morgan, white as a sheet, stood silently looking on, the very statue of despair. Sir Griffith ordered Lady Tudor to be conveyed to her apartment, and swearing a terrible oath, told the almost lifeless David Morgan that if he were afraid to meet his challenger, he might go and be d – d, for a sneaking cowardly chicken-hearted puppy: for since Seymour's relation had shewn so much spirit, and thought his girl worth hazarding his life for, the conqueror should have her.

"As to that, Sir Griffith," replied the gasping Morgan, "perhaps I may have as much courage as another man, though to be sure, as to swords and guns, and firearms, and them there sort of things, I have never taken any particular account of them, because I had no notion that a peaceable disposed man like me would have occasion for their use: was the matter to be decided by fair boxing, it would not be of so much consequence: supposing as how one did come off second best, a black eye may come to its colour again, but the taking away a man's life who does not want to die, who has got plenty of money, and the good things of this life to enjoy, it is quite as one may say another sort of affair; it is not a bit better than downright murder: seeing you are not able to give back life when you have once taken it away, and seeing – "

"D – n me, but I see you are a devilish coward, David, with all your eloquence," said Sir Griffith: "one need not be much of a conjurer to see that – but mark my words, David Morgan, you may be Lady Tudor's nephew, and the son of an opulent merchant for any thing I know to the contrary, but if you don't meet and exchange shot with this Seymour, like a man, I will be d – d, and my horse too, if ever you are Sir Griffith Tudor's son-in-law. So you may as well make up your mind at once, either to use the pistols with spirit, or trot over the mountains back to England as fast as you can: but if I am not mistaken in my man, trot where you will, this mettlesome spark will overtake, even if you should seek shelter under the desk in Milk-lane."

In vain Eliza entreated. Sir Griffith became at last so frantic with passion, that she was obliged to give up the point, and retire to her apartment, there to wait with what patience she could assume the termination of an event that had put the whole house into confusion, and spread dismay and consternation among all its members, Sir Griffith excepted.

At the appointed hour, Sir Griffith Tudor led, or more properly speaking, dragged Mr. David Morgan to Rhudlan Downs, the field of action, where they were met by the two young gentlemen, the one so very small, that he did not appear taller than a boy of twelve years old. The elder of the two introduced him as Mr. Lionel Seymour. At the sight of this pigmy antagonist, David Morgan's courage revived for a moment – in stature himself a Goliath, and his opponent a David: but when he beheld the pistols in his hand, and recollected what he had heard of the unerring skill of the Seymours in shooting at a mark, he was seized with an ague fit; his teeth chattered in his head, and his knees actually knocked against each other.

"Why, hey day! what the devil," said Sir Griffith, "are you the Lionel Seymour that sent the challenge?"

"Aye, gude troth am I," replied the young gentleman in a broad Scotch accent, "what din ye ken in that, mon?"

"Why, d – n it, young gentleman," said Sir Griffith, "because you appear a mere child."

"Cheeld as I am," rejoined the little fellow tartly, "I have winged and prostrated as tall men as Mr. Morgan in my day: but time gangs awa while we are prating: I am eager for vengeance upon the mon who has usurped the rights of my cousin, Captain Seymour."

David Morgan, turning pale, stammered out, that he should think it a pity to hurt the young gentleman.

"Fire and fury, sir!" replied Mr. Lionel Seymour, "do you mean to insult me? – Pity yourself, and if you have any thing on your mind that in the hurry of this affair you may have forgot, be brief, and communicate it to your friend. Commend yourself to heaven – I never yet missed my mark; and your blood must atone for your presumption in addressing Miss Tudor, and presuming to rival a Seymour."

David Morgan in agony unutterable saw the ground measured; they then drew lots for the first fire: the chance was in favour of Mr. Lionel Seymour; he drew the fatal trigger, and Mr. Morgan fell to the earth.

At that instant Sir Owen Llewellyn appeared, with several of his own and Sir Griffith's servants, whom he directed to take Mr. Lionel Seymour and his second into custody, notwithstanding the loud oaths and remonstrances of Sir Griffith Tudor, who swore it was d – d hard he should not be allowed to keep his word with poor David, and shoot Mr. Lionel Seymour through the head, which he had faithfully promised he would do, in case Mr. Morgan fell.

As Tudor Hall was nearer than Dolgelly Castle, the two young gentlemen were guarded there, while the rest of the servants took charge of the body of the unfortunate David Morgan. They laid him pale and lifeless on a couch, his waistcoat and hands crimsoned with blood, supposed from a wound in his side. A neighbouring surgeon was called in; the body was stripped and examined, and he declared that the ball had penetrated no where, and that Mr. Morgan was terribly wounded with fear only; and that losing a little blood in reality, with the comfortable aid of a warm bed and a basin of white wine whey, would effectally remove all the ill consequences that might be expected to ensue from the shock his spirits had undergone.

CHAPTER VIII

"As for a woman's scorn, good lack! I shall
Survive it: only fools and madmen die
For love. When I consider my own proper
Person, I shall get over this, no fear.
I may be a coward as you say, for
I have no appetite for fighting; and
If ladies' favours are only to be won
By turning soldier, I shall no doubt
Remain a bachelor."

AT this declaration of the surgeon's it is difficult to say whether contempt, disappointment, or surprise was the predominant sentiment in the breast of Sir Griffith Tudor, and he stood almost without motion, while the crimson stains were washed from the hands and face of Mr. Morgan, who began to give signs of existence, and in a short time was sufficiently recovered to thank heaven that he was in the land of the living.

Sir Griffith, recovering also from his astonishment, laughed, whistled, and swore alternately, as he examined the pistols, which he found had been filled with blood and a few pease. He vowed vengeance upon the author of this trick: while Lady Tudor, having just got the better of an hysteric, told him he ought to thank heaven that it was a trick, and that murder had not in reality been committed: though she should not wonder if the continued alarms she was put into was to be the death of her at last.

"No, I will be d – d if any thing of the kind kills you," replied Sir Griffith: "you are as tough as old iron for all your weak nerves; no such luck for me; more is the pity. But," said he, turning to the pale, woe-begone, terrified David Morgan, "you may make your congee as soon as it is agreeable: you may return to your counting-house in Milk-lane as soon as you please, for Eliza shall never contaminate the noble blood of the Tudors by mixing it with that of a pitiful coward, who fell at the mere report of a pistol, and fainted at the very thought of being wounded."

Saying this, he left Lady Tudor to compose her spirits, apply restoratives, and console her nephew, while he in prodigious fury sallied to the apartment of his daughter, whom he strongly suspected of being at the bottom of this adventure, if not the absolute plotter and contriver of David Morgan's disgrace. – Eliza was no where to be found: she had not been seen since she quitted the library previous to the gentlemen going out. – Supposing she had set off to Dolgelly Castle, Sir Griffith was on the point of dispatching a messenger to order her home, when Sir Owen Llewellyn requested the favour of his presence at the examination of the young offenders in custody.

He turned hastily into the room, and addressing Mr. Lionel Seymour, said, "Well, my young spark, you have put a d – d pretty trick upon us."

"I dinna ken your meaning, sir," replied the young gentleman.

"But do you ken," said Sir Griffith, "that you have assaulted Mr. Morgan on the king's highway."

"Hoot awa, mon; nay, I ha din na sic thing; Rhudlan Downs I understand is your property, not the king's."

"Here is equivocation with a vengeance," said Sir Griffith:

"but far as you come north, you are not keen enough. – Do you ken that though you have not committed absolute murder, you have put him in bodily fear, which deserves the punishment you shall most certainly receive. I have ordered a bunch of nettles, and intend with my own hand bestowing the correction you merit."

Sir Owen Llewellyn laughed.

The little fellow cocked his hat, and strutting up to Sir Griffith, replied, "You munna think to frighten me with moonshine; you would as soon cram your hand into the fire as use it after the way you have mentioned. You dinna ken what you speer about, mon. – You would not dare to put your threats in execution."

"And how the devil did you dare, you young villain, to put such a trick upon us? A pretty joke it will be all over the country! But, pooh! what need I mention Wales? The jest will soon travel to England: it will reach London I warrant before David Morgan: the cowardly scoundrel will be sneered at in his counting-house by his own clerks, and laughed at upon 'Change – and what the devil and all his imps, you little mischievous rascal, you worse than all the plagues of Egypt, can you say in your own defence?"

Not a word was uttered by the young culprit, whom Sir Griffith continued to interrogate with a string of questions which he did not give him time to answer: at last, having raved himself out of breath, he concluded with – "Who set you upon this cursed plot? – Where did you spring from?"

The offender turned away and laughed heartily, which irritating the already frantic Sir Griffith, he insisted that Sir Owen Llewellyn should make out his mittimus, and commit him and his companion to prison, till they should by repentance be brought to render not only a proper account of themselves, but also of their abettors and employers.

"Well, Sir Griffith, for your satisfaction, that shall be done immediately: my own heart was my abettor, my own invention my only employer."

"Hell and the devil!....Hey! how! what!" said Sir Griffith, as the well known voice of his daughter struck on his ear. "Why, you little d – d hareum scareum mad devil, Eliza! Sure this is not one of your frolics?"

"Yes, indeed, but it is, papa," replied Eliza; "all stratagems you know are fair in love and war: you said we would try which could manoeuvre best, and I hope you will allow me some credit for my generalship."

Sir Griffith looked bewildered: he stood for some minutes in absolute astonishment. – "D – d odd I should be so taken in! Strange I should not know the little devil!" He turned her round and round to convince himself it was really her: while she bowed, and in the broad Scotch accent said, "Dinna you ken me, mon, when there is na sic a lassie in aw Wales?"

"No," said Sir Griffith, having satisfied himself as to her identity, "nor in all the world; I will be d – d, and my horse too, if there is. But pray, madam, or sir, have the politeness to introduce me to your companion."

"Oh! my companion," rejoined Eliza, "is the sister of my waiting gentlewoman, Jenny Jones, who being out of place, has been some time at Tudor Hall."

"Her time is out then," replied Sir Griffith; "but though I must do you the justice to say you have topped your parts to a miracle, not an hour longer does she remain under the roof of Tudor Hall. Troop, you d – d hussy, quit the house this instant, and at your peril let me ever see your ugly phiz within my doors again. This is 'eat my mutton, drink my wine, and then poke my eye out,' I will entertain no plotters, no schemers, no contrivers."

"Nay," said Eliza, "I beg I may not be deprived of the merit of the plot and contrivance, which was all my own. I assure you, sir, poor Jenny by my persuasions was only an humble assistant, instructed by me: and really, papa, I think you ought to rejoice that the denoument, without being tragical, has discovered the real character of the courageous David Morgan."

Sir Griffith's rage against Jenny was so extreme, that she was thankful when she was pushed out of the room from him, so much had his frantic gestures terrified her; and she gladly set off, at tired as she was, to Dolgelly Castle (at the instigation of Sir Owen Llewellyn), to avoid his fury, which now rose to an ungovernable pitch.

As he swore to Eliza that she should never again quit her apartment till she left it to go to church with her cousin David, who, sneaking, cowardly scoundrel as he was, should yet marry her if he would, and when she was his wife, he would be a d – d fool if he did not pay her off for all her tricks. Sir Owen Llewellyn interfered, and kindly entreated, seeing the confusion of the family, that Eliza might be permitted to spend a few days with her friend Adeline; but this Sir Griffith peremptorily refused, swearing she should remain in strict confinement till the day of her marriage with David Morgan.

"Say then," replied Eliza, "that I shall remain in confinement to the day of my death; for never, no, never, will I become the wife of that dastardly animal. What! sacrifice myself to ignorance and cowardice – give up the brave generous Seymour for that creature! no, never; I am content to suffer every hardship first."

"And if I don't make you suffer may I be d – d!" said Sir Griffith: "and to prevent any more of your devilish plots and cursed schemes, I shall take the liberty of escorting you to your chamber. Come, Mr. Lionel Seymour, I shall see if I can't turn the key upon you, my little volatile spark. I shall endeavour by confining you to put an end to your gambols and vagaries, before you do any more mischief: as it is, you have almost killed dainty Davy, and brought on all your mother's confounded string of hysterics, spasmodic affections, and the devil himself knows what besides."

Saying this, he caught her up in his arms, and in spite of her struggles, carried her into her chamber, and throwing her upon the bed, told her she might now compose herself, as no doubt the fatigues she had undergone would render rest necessary.

With this he locked the door upon her; adding, she might, if she could not sleep, set her wits to work, and get out of confinement if she could.

Sir Owen Llewellyn reasoned with his friend on the rashness of his behaviour, and would have been a mediator for Eliza: but Sir Griffith, alive only to rage and resentment, persisted in the determination of keeping her under lock and key, till she was sensible of the folly of contradicting and opposing his wishes.

Eliza had wrote to Sir Owen Llewellyn an account of her project, and requested his attendance; but having mentioned a later hour for the meeting on Rhudlan Downs than she designed it should take place (as she feared he would prevent her scheme), he did not arrive till after the rencontre, too late to prevent the cowardice of Morgan being exposed, of herself from experiencing the unpleasant consequences of her father's anger.

The next day Mr. Morgan, being partly recovered from the terrors of dissolution, and encouraged by the presence of Lady Tudor, who thought him extremely ill-treated, appeared at the dinner table, where Sir Griffith, having cooled a little, began to consider how unpleasant a circumstance it would be to embroil himself with his wife's family, behaved to him as if nothing had happened, and resolved if he refused Eliza (which he heartily wished he might), that it should be his own act and deed.

After the bottle had pretty freely circulated between them, Sir Griffith endeavoured to set Eliza's frolic in the most favourable light.

"Eliza's frolic," said Lady Tudor, drawing herself up.

"Aye d – n it, my lady," continued Sir Griffith, "did not I tell you before that it was Eliza who personated Lionel Seymour: and a devilish smart little fellow she looked, did not she, David?"

"As to the matter of that, Sir Griffith," replied Mr. Morgan, "I know very little about her smartness, seeing as how it was not light enough to distinguish: but I think Miss Tudor might have had more discretion than to act in that there out of the way fashion for a young lady."

"Well, well, David, say no more upon the subject," rejoined Sir Griffith, "Eliza is frolicsome, but she means no harm. D…n it, man, don't be sulky, but forget and forgive."

"As to forget and forgive," said Mr. Morgan, "that is clear another sort of matter, Sir Griffith, and much easier talked about than done, seeing as how I can never forget that I have been monstrously ill used, and I don't see how I can forgive such an affront as this here is."

"Pshaw, David, this is all idle talk; d….n it, when you are married – "

"Hold there a bit, Sir Griffith: I have no great appetite left for marrying. Miss Tudor is far too wild for me, who wants a prudent careful quiet wife. Lord help us! the city, big as it is, would not be wide enough for her to cut capers in; so she had better stay here among the mountains, where she will have range enough for them there frolics, and I shall go back to London with a little more wit instead of a wife, that is all, Sir Griffith."

Lady Tudor was incensed beyond measure when she was given to understand that it was Eliza who had committed such a bold indelicate action, as to put on male habiliments, an outrage against female modesty, which she protested she would never overlook nor pardon, more especially as it was certainly done with the abominable intention of putting an affront upon a member of her family, who was by no means to be despised or condemned for the weakness of his nerves, an affliction unfortunately hereditary in their family, as she unhappily was obliged to experience daily and hourly; nor did she know that courage was a quality so very requisite to gentlemen who were not designed for soldiers or sailors.

To this speech Sir Griffith replied with a sneer: "Heaven help Great Britain – she would be in a woeful way indeed if her armies and navies were composed of men with nerves like David Morgan's; but however, Eliza's nerves are like her father's, pretty well braced: and d – n it, David, you are not serious sure in giving her up – a girl of her spirit."

"There it is, Sir Griffith; she has far too much spirit for me," said Mr. Morgan. "I protest I have lost all inclination for matrimony, and will remain a few years longer a bachelor; and if ever I should enter the pale of wedlock, it shall be with a partner who makes no pretensions to that there spirit which you like so much, but which I must make so free as to say I think very ugly and disagreeable."

Sir Griffith's temper now took a different turn; and, notwithstanding what had happened, he considered himself affronted by Mr. Morgan's rejection of his daughter; and on Lady Tudor's saying she deserved to be confined for a month for her conduct, he flew instantly to her apartment, and led her to the parlour, in the hope that she would by fresh tricks and new mischief contrive to plague and mortify David, whom he now held in sovereign contempt: but Eliza had gained her end: she had broke off the intended alliance, and she suffered him to recover his spirits without attempting to conciliate his favour, or provoke him with further contrivances.

David Morgan pretended to be reconciled to his cousin, but his heart never cordially forgave her: he affected to treat her with neglect; and, in order as he supposed to mortify her, he attached himself to Miss Llewellyn, to whom on all occasions he paid all possible court; and, notwithstanding his recent declaration of remaining a bachelor, he soon after made her an offer of his heart and hand.

Adeline saw the motive, and felt all its indelicacy, but she pitied the ignorance of the man, and contented herself with rejecting his proposals, without betraying her contempt for his character.

Eliza was reinstated in her father's favour, but Lady Tudor maintained a haughty reserve: her darling scheme of blending the family fortunes had been frustrated, and she chose to keep up a resentment against her daughter, which, while it hurt the feelings of Eliza, who tenderly loved her mother, contributed to add to her detestation of David Morgan, who seeing all his matrimonial projects fail, departed from Tudor Hall in high dudgeon, declaring that if he had only supposed that he should have met such treatment in that there place, he would as soon have taken a journey to Jericho as to Tudor Hall – and as for marrying Eliza, he would every bit as soon tie himself to an outlandish creature from foreign parts; for she was wilder by half than the goats on her own mountains, and had more tricks than any monkey he had ever seen at Exeter Change, where they had exhibited them there mischievous beasts.

Eliza rejoiced from the very bottom of her heart when he was gone, for she dreaded lest some sudden whim, or new contradiction, might re-instate him in her father's good graces, and again expose her to his addresses.

Lady Tudor lamented the departure of her nephew, and expatiating on the ill treatment he had received in Wales, reproached Eliza for her conduct to him, which she assured her would not fail to be represented in England, where his relations would not forget to resent the affront she had put upon her cousin David with becoming spirit.

"And who the devil, Lady Tudor, values their resentment or their spirit," replied Sir Griffith, "Eliza Tudor wants no favours from them I suppose, and as to him, I am ashamed of the relationship. A poor, pitiful, sneaking, cowardly, ignorant blockhead: I am glad in my soul that the girl did try what mettle he possessed. I should have been d – d sorry to have had such a chicken-hearted puppy as that for a son-in-law – a fellow as big as the Philistian giant, and yet so destitute of courage as to be afraid to say boo to a goose. Did your sister nurse him at home? D – n him, I believe he is an impostor: he has not an ounce of Cambrian blood in his veins."

Lady Tudor would have defended her nephew from the

imputation of cowardice, and would have assigned physical reasons for the weakness of his nerves; but Sir Griffith ridiculed her explanations, and treated his character with so much irony, that her ladyship was obliged to give up the point, protesting that the strength of Hercules would be insufficient to combat with him, and Mr. David Morgan had really a lucky escape in not marrying Miss Tudor, who happening to have a robust constitution herself, would have had as little mercy on poor David's weak system as he had on hers.

"As to his weakness, Lady Tudor," replied Sir Griffith, "it chiefly lay in his head; but it is all owing to his education: if he had been a son of mine, I would have taught him. But d – n it, what is the use of talking to you. If I had suffered you to bring up Eliza after your fashion, she would have been screaming at the sight of a frog, and fainting if a wasp had buzzed in her ear. As it is, she has no affectation, and knows nothing of weak nerves, hates the smell of hartshorn and burnt feathers; never is troubled with low spirits and hysterics, but is full of health and animation."

"I wish she had less animation, and more delicacy," replied Lady Tudor.

"Delicacy! a fiddlestick!" rejoined Sir Griffith. "D – n delicacy, it makes a woman worse than a fool. I hate your die-away dolls that are forever swallowing slops, and sniffing essences, and fancying themselves ill if the wind blows upon them. I hate your hot-house plants, sickly, and drooping – my girl is a fine spirited, lively, mad little devil, and I love her because she can gallop after a fox all day, and dance after a fiddle all night: and d – n me, she does not mind the smell of gunpowder, and that is more than can be said of some of the family, who no sooner come within scent of it, than they faint away."

Mr. David Morgan returned to London, mortified and disappointed beyond measure. The great wealth to which it was known he was heir had rendered him an object of universal importance and attention among the young ladies of the city, who had not been niggardly in displaying all the attractions of dress, airs, and graces, to obtain the notice of Mr. David Morgan, in the contemplation of whose riches they had sunk the plainness of his person. It was true that Miss Congo and Miss Figgins had severally assailed his heart, and had even disputed the honour of being his partner at the city balls: but he had cruelly overlooked the tender advances of these ladies, and at the instigation of his mamma, had set off for North Wales, supposing that in those remote parts, a person coming immediately from London, the emporium of taste, elegance, and fashion, would be considered a demigod. His cousin Eliza, brought up in Wales, he had been taught to consider an absolute mountaineer, who could not fail to be attracted by his graces, and whose affections and consent would be obtained without the smallest difficulty; for how was it in the nature of possibilities to suppose that a girl whom he imagined had only been used to the rude society of Welch boors, could resist, or fail to be captivated by the various attractions that united in him, who, in order to accomplish himself for genteel company, had since he had arrived at man's estate taken a dozen private lessons from Signor Latoni, who undertakes to improve the gait, and teach grown gentlemen to dance; of him whose crop had been elegantly trimmed by the Prince of Wales's own hair dresser, whose coat had been made by the Duke of York's tailor, and whose hussar boots had been bought of Hoby.

So equipped for conquest, David Morgan, and David

Morgan's mamma, conceived him irresistible. What a disappointment! What a mortification! What a degradation! A little Welch romp had insolently refused him, had put a trick upon a man of his figure and consequence. Another mountaineer had also rejected him: he measured his way back in a far different frame of mind to that in which he undertook the journey. When seated at his desk in Milk-lane, he began to calculate and lament the money he had so unprofitably wasted, to curse his journey into Wales, and the natives, among whom he did not forget to include Adeline Llewellyn, and to prepare and fortify himself to sustain the sneers and airs of Miss Congo, and Miss Figgins, and the rest of his city acquaintance, who he knew would be glad of the opportunity of shewing off their wit at his expense.

His mamma vowed never to forgive the affront put upon her darling boy, while his father gravely observed that "A bird in the hand is worth two in the bush," and that if David had followed his advice, and taken "Time by the forelock," all would have been well, but it was a true saying, "Farther on fare worse;" that if he had wanted a wife he need not have gone from Dan to Bethsheba; there were enough to be had: plenty as mackarel in the city, without travelling so far to bring back nothing. However, he hoped he had bought a pennyworth of wit; and that he would understand in future that "A penny saved was a penny earned," and that it was not all "Gold that glittered."

Mrs. Morgan desired her husband to hold his tongue, and to think before he spoke. Davy was not at all to blame, he had acted, as he always did, like a dutiful son, and had followed her advice, which she had given to the very best of her judgment; and if it had not turned out as they wished, why they could not help it, and it was in vain to reflect upon them for the faults of other people.

Mr. Morgan told David that Miss Figgins's West India uncle was dead, and had left her a hundred thousand pounds: and now there was another chance for him.

Mrs. Morgan approved the idea, and advised David to deny altogether having gone into Wales to court his cousin, and to lose no time in offering himself to Miss Figgins, who would now be one of the greatest fortunes in the city.

David promised to obey, and his father told him to "Strike while the iron was hot;" that Miss Figgins had once expressed a great regard for him, and he hoped that she would not now tell him "He that will not when he may, when he will he shall have nay."

David said he was not afraid of that. Miss Figgins had often expressed herself plainly in his favour, and he had no doubt but he might have her whenever he liked.

The next day Mr. David Morgan, armed at all points for conquest, went into Gracechurch-street to visit Miss Figgins, and beheld before the door an elegant coroneted barouche, and half a dozen servants with their liveries covered with silver lace hovering about it.

Mr. and Mrs. Figgins received him with their usual kindness, but he was soon given to understand that Martha was on the point of marriage with Lord Delmore, a young nobleman, whose estate, a good deal out of elbows, had condescended to bestow his title on Miss Figgins in exchange for her wealth. While he was receiving this appalling intelligence, Miss Figgins entered the room, and scarcely bestowing a nod of recognition on poor David, told her mother that she was going with Lord Delmore to an auction.

David Morgan, vexed and disappointed, left the house in greater haste than he had entered it: but before he had reached the top of the street, he encountered an acquaintance, with whom he entered into a long conversation on some mercantile transaction, which detained him till the coroneted barouche, in which Lord Delmore, attended by his servants, was driving Miss Figgins, came dashing along: just as it got opposite to David, the wheels passing through the kennel splashed the unfortunate fellow all over.

Miss Figgins, delighted at seeing his face spattered with mud, laughed immoderately as she rolled triumphantly along, seated by the simpering peer, the envy and admiration of all her city friends.

Mrs. Morgan consoled her son, and wondered at Mr. Figgins allowing his daughter to throw her money away upon a spendthrift from the west end of the town, who, when they took wives from the city, always treated them with contempt, and made them sensible that their wealth was all their attraction.

"Aye, aye," replied Mr. Morgan, "'light come, light go.' Toby Figgins and Jonathan toiled late and early, and got their money by the sweat of their brows; now it will go like 'Chaff before the wind.' This lord will soon race it away upon the turf, or rattle it away at a gaming table, and then her ladyship, reduced to beggary, may wish she had been content to be plain Mrs. Morgan, the merchant's wife."

David, sore with disappointment, vowed that women were all jilts, that he would have nothing to do with them, but make up his mind to live and die a bachelor; for seeing as how that women were always changing their minds, a man would have nothing to do but study their tempers, and after all very likely not be able to please them – so for his part, as they had treated him after that there ungrateful fashion, he should give them up entirely.

Mr. Morgan senior laughed heartily at his son's determination, which he was sure he would break before a month was at end, and he was to remember that "Bad beginnings made good endings," and that "marriages were made in heaven," so that when his time came he would be sure of a wife, for "marrying and hanging went by destiny."

David listened, and was consoled: his father's wisely treasured sayings comforted him in the hour of affliction and mortification, for his sorrows were of a nature to be soothed.

Love was not to make either the felicity or misery of his life, and as long as commerce flourished, and money accumulated, his heart disdained to sigh for so capricious a toy as woman.

VOLUME II

CHAPTER I

And who is she, that gliding slow along,
Seems like the shadowy form of other worlds,
With bosom cold as monumental stone,
Whose face the pale moon beam illumes? – 'tis air,
And see the lovely vision melts away.

And she who thrill'd at music's magic flow
Was fancy's victim, passion's frantic child;
One who soft tears had shed for others' woe,
While at her own hard fate she sadly smil'd.

A. J. H.

AFTER an illness of more than two long tedious months, Henry's naturally fine constitution began to triumph over the ravages of disease. The harassing fever, which had long been intermitting, at last entirely left him: he slowly recovered strength and memory: his brain, in defiance of the physician's prediction, was uninjured; and with health a poignant recollection of the past recurred, with all its consequent regret: though could he have reconciled his feelings to his situation, he had nothing to complain of. The suit of rooms appropriated to his use were decorated with sumptuous and voluptuous elegance, his table was spread with luxurious delicacies, and he was allowed the indulgence of walking in a long gallery, into which his apartments opened. Here, as Henry viewed from the narrow pointed windows the surrounding country, its rich scenery and bold features recalled the sublime views that had so often charmed his eyes in North Wales, while he gazed on the hanging woods and stupendous mountains, or watched the sparkling blue waves dividing from the smooth expanded ocean, and rolling away in distant recollection, returned with more painful sensations, he sighed for freedom, for the delightful romantic walks round Dolgelly Castle, for the tender, magic smiles of Adeline, for the converse of those dear and valued friends, from whose society he believed himself torn for ever. Agonized with these reflections, regardless of returning health, he ungratefully wished that he had sunk to the peace of the grave, rather than survived to linger out an useless being, shut from the world, and all the blessings of life, a solitary prisoner. The dutchess had twice ventured into his presence during his delirium, but his ravings had so terrified and disconcerted her, that now, when her attendants brought the hope renewing, transporting account, of his recovered reason, she shrank in terror from the idea of encountering the freezing scorn of his expressive eye, from meeting the cutting severity of his reproaches; her mind was a chaos, in which reason was bewildered and lost, and she remained irresolute and undetermined how to act respecting him: one moment yielding to the reproving impulse of shame, and softened by remorse for the sufferings she had occasioned, she resolved to liberate him, to accelerate his return to his connections; the next, the tumults of her bosom, for as yet in her the "hey-day of the blood was not tame," the remembrance of his fine person swept away like an impetuous torrent all hopes, all wishes, but those of gratifying the desire he had excited; and burning with increased passion, which hourly gained ground from opposition, she concluded to retain him her prisoner, till weary with confinement, and thoroughly sensible of the blessings and advantages in her power to bestow, he should be brought to accept her hand. To beguile time of its tediousness, Henry had requested to have some books, but the key of the library (an apartment never visited by the dutchess) had rusted in the lock, and the door could not be opened; and day after day elapsed without the lock being taken off, as the steward had promised. Henry now recollected the manuscript poem he had brought from the matted chamber, and was much pleased on inquiry to find it safe. The inhabitants of the castle had long been retired to rest, while he full of melancholy reflections continued to pace the gallery: though weary, he did not feel inclined to sleep, and in order to banish uneasy thoughts he took up the poem, and seating himself in an arched recess, began to read.

EDA, OR THE BRIDAL NIGHT:

A LEGENDARY TALE

Hark, 'tis the raven hoarsely croaks;
 The white owl shrilly screams;
The wind groans through yon aged oaks;
 The stars shed sickly gleams.

Oh, would that morning's beam give light –
 I dread these falling glooms,
Have you not heard at dead of night
 How ghosts forsake their tombs?

What form is that which o'er the heath
Glides slowly as if on air –
God, 'tis as pale as ashy death,
And seems a shroud to wear.

'Tis Eda's spirit, at this hour
She from her grave doth rise,
And seeking Albert's bridal bower,
Appals his heart and eyes.

Albert to Eda often swore
He lov'd her more than light,
That every day he lov'd her more –
To her his faith did plight.

He vow'd if heaven would spare his life
That he with her would wed,
That she alone should be his wife;
She only share his bed.

A ring he gave, a ruby heart
Pierc'd with an arrow keen,
From which the blood did seem to start,
And lie in drops between.

"Let this upon thy finger stay,
A pledge of love most true;
May peace from me be far away,
When I prove false to you."

A tear-drop fell on Eda's cheek;
Her heart his words believ'd:
"Pray God," she cry'd, "who hears thee speak,
I ne'er may be deceiv'd;

For nought from death could Eda save,
If thou should'st from her fly,
And soon within the grass-bound grave,
Heartbroken she would lie."

Albert renew'd his vows of love,
He kiss'd her tears away,
And more his heart's firm faith to prove,
Thus fervently did pray:

"If I should break my vow of love,
And with another wed,
God grant thou may'st my chamber rove,
And share my nuptial bed.

And may this ring with ruby heart
Upon thy finger shine;
May drops of crimson from it start,
And stain this hand of mine."

Again he kiss'd, again he swore,
And cheer'd her doubting mind,
Yet not a week had gone before
False Albert's vows were wind.

Mabel, a rich and haughty dame,
On Albert fix'd her eyes,
And he with joy beheld a flame
That promis'd such a prize.

The timid beam of Eda's eye,
Like violets bright with dew,
Her blushing cheeks, vermilion dye;
Her bosom spotless hue.

All were forgot as Mabel glanc'd
At wealth and large estate,
As she her senses held entranc'd,
And vow'd to make him great.

No more of Eda now he thought,
His heart was swell'd with pride;
That faithless heart for gold was bought,
And Mabel was his bride.

And Albert from the church came gay;
His friends around him prest,
And he to grace his wedding day
Invited many a guest.

All gay the merry bells rang round,
All blithe the tabor play'd,
But strait before them on the ground
A grave was newly made.

"For who is this pray?" ask'd the bride:
'Tis Eda's grave they say
Albert then shuddering turn'd aside,
And musing went his way;

And soon he heard the funeral bell,
And saw the village move,
"Oh, God!" he cry'd, "it is the knell
Of her I swore to love."

The bride sat gaily at the feast,
In splendid robes array'd,
But chill and sad was Albert's breast,
His conscience sore dismay'd.

And when the midnight hour drew nigh,
When all retired to rest,
Mabel with bright expecting eye
Her bridal pillow press'd.

And Albert, full of thought and woe,
Prepar'd to join his bride;
When through the chamber pale and slow
Did Eda's spirit glide.

Henry found something in this poem which made him pause to lament that the genius of Lady Julia should now like "sweet bells jumbled and out of tune," only pour the incoherent rhapsodies of madness. Again he had resumed the manuscript; a deep sigh, seemingly breathed near him, drew his attention; he lifted up his eyes, the hour, the stillness of the night, the story he was reading, his own forlorn situation, might well excite melancholy ideas; but Henry was a stranger to the idle weakness of suspicion. Again he began to read, when an odd kind of rustling noise at the other end of the gallery again called his attention; be looked and saw a female figure gliding along, so light, so shadowy, that he was almost persuaded it was Eda's ghost: it advanced towards him, and laying a thin transparent white hand upon his arm, and at the same time throwing up a veil that hung over its pale face, fixed a pair of soft melting dark eyes upon him, and said in a tremulous hurried voice: –

"I have made you wait a tedious time, my Horace, Lord Lucan has detained me to remonstrate and menace, but nothing could prevent your Julia from coming to her appointment."

Henry beheld Lady Julia Nevil, the beauteous maniac, whose sorrows he had so much commiserated; he gazed on her still fine though faded person in speechless sorrow, while she continued: –

"Yes, yes, you are a philosopher; but, oh, God! philosophy cannot conquer love: thine is a frigid heart, it neither glows with nor understands the warmth of mine. You tell me to forget you; no, no – I cannot, will not forget you! it is impossible! I see you every where; your image pursues me in my retirement, if I read I find you in all my books; if my hand sweeps the chords of my harp, you mingle in its most melodious strains. Nevil, I have shed on thy account oceans of tears, but I can weep no more; no drop falls on my burning cheek, no shower relieves the pain that rankles here."

Her hands were pressed upon her bosom: for a moment she stood silent, then as if in reply suddenly exclaimed: –

"Well, never grieve: though Lord Lucan has forbade you the castle, he cannot banish you from the heart of his daughter; no, ever worshipped, for ever adored, that heart is all thine own."

Henry took her hand; it was cold as ice; he spoke to her, she appeared frightened, and snatching away her hand, retreated from him; in a few seconds she returned, and removing his hand from his forehead, said mournfully: –

"No, no – for ever, we are parted for ever." Again gazing earnestly in his face, she shook her head, and continued: "The eyes of Horace Nevil were not dark: his hair was brown, and his mouth – love played upon his lips, and recoiled in smiles about his mouth. But, fare thee well. I remember we were wedded – for a little hour he was mine and I was his. Once, only once his fond arms encircled Julia; once, only once, his breath mingled with mine; that was a moment of soul rapture. Oh, what have my moments since been! Yes, yes, come to my dressing-room tomorrow night; it will be the safest place. Escape with thee, most certainly beloved of my soul! what is the world to me – thou art Julia's world."

Her unconnected ramblings pierced Henry to the soul: he felt that reason, frighted from her throne, was fled for ever, and his mind, ever full of humanity and compassion, experienced an indescribable pang, as he surveyed the beautiful ruin before him, as he contemplated the overthrow of such a mind.

"Ah!" sighed he, "what avails the inspirations of genius, the bright emanations of talent, they only render sensibility more acute, they only barb the arrows of misfortune."

Lady Julia again laid her icy fingers on his, and with a look of unutterable woe said: –

"He sleeps peacefully! He knows not, feels not my sorrows!

But we shall meet again – I trust we shall; I will then tell him all I have endured: they would have married me, but Nevil, I am thine; could Julia fold another to the bosom on which thy head had rested. You must be gone, love, before day. Yes, yes, I have expected thee; day after day I have said he will come; I have felt the torture of suspense, the misery of procrastinated hope. Remember, how can I fail to remember, what is traced in burning characters upon my heart – we meet tomorrow night."

Again she let the veil conceal her features, and darting across the gallery, disappeared in an instant at the upper end. Henry flew after her, but in his haste he unfortunately extinguished the light; the moon indeed shone brightly through the windows at the end of the gallery where he had sat; but the upper part was obscured in darkness: he felt for the panel through which he knew she must have passed, but it was closed, nor could he discover any spring or secret method by which any part of what appeared to be solid wall could open. This incident, however, renewed the hope of escape: he had no doubt but Lady Julia would visit the gallery again, and he resolved not to let that opportunity pass without endeavouring to profit by it. With a mind filled by recent circumstances, melting with pity for the incurable malady of the hapless Lady Julia, and throbbing with renovated hope, Henry threw himself upon his bed, not to sleep, for he never felt less inclined that way; but to reflect, to wait for day-light, that he might again search for the opening through which the lovely maniac had vanished; but sleep, like death, "will come when it will come," and many hours of the morning had elapsed before he awoke from dreams of happiness and freedom, to the certainty of being a prisoner. His first thought was the gallery; he examined it with scrutinizing exactitude, but still without discovering the object of his search. A whole length picture of a warrior in armour engaged his attention; it shook beneath his hand. This was the panel through which Lady Julia had passed; but its fastening was on the other side. Pleased with having made the discovery, he taught his mind to wait with patience for the next visit of the fair wanderer, whose steps he determined to follow, trusting that they would lead to liberty: this point being settled, he sat down to finish the story of Eda.

Her chilly arms did him embrace,
"Albert, thou'rt mine," she cries;
"Dost thou not know thy Eda's face?
Come turn on me thine eyes.

Albert, false Albert, thou art mine,
Behold this ruby heart,
Heav'n lets it on my finger shine;
Bids blood-drops from it start."

And Albert's hands were spotted o'er;
The ring dropt blood and blaz'd;
He felt the grasp, beheld the gore;
His eyes with horror glaz'd.

"Just like this ring my heart has bled;
Keen anguish did it know,"
And now the spectre hollow said:
"Thy nights will all be woe

For soon as darkness veils the pole,
I from the grave shall glide.
When deep the midnight bell doth toll,
Expect thy buried bride,

Then every night in my embrace
Shalt fear and horror feel,
And every night upon thy face
The kiss of death I'll seal.

And thou shalt see the grave worm draw
Across my neck its trail,
And thou shalt see the black toad gnaw
My cheek so sunk and pale.

And every night I'll clasp thee round;
Thy ring shall bleed and shine,
And in thy ear my voice shall sound –
False Albert, thou art mine.

Sleep ne'er shall on thy eye-lids hang,
Or give thy horrors rest,
Till thou hast suffer'd every pang
That harrow'd Eda's breast.

Albert, false Albert, thou art mine;
Know'st thou not Eda's face?
Thy ring doth on my finger shine;
My arms do thee embrace."

And now the morning's trembling ray
Saw Eda's shade depart,
But Albert sunk, in anguish lay,
With horror at his heart.

Mabel, who'd nothing heard or seen,
Lay wondering till 'twas light,
And little did she joy I ween
In this her bridal night.

She thought indeed 'twas more than odd
That she a new made bride
Should have a dull and stupid clod
Lie lumpish by her side.

But every night 'tis just the same,
For Albert seems as dead,
And Mabel, though a wealthy dame,
Wishes she ne'er had wed,

And sunk is Albert's sparkling eye,
And blanch'd his rosy cheek,
Cold damps upon his forehead lie,
And fear his looks bespeak.

And he who late so gay was seen,
To every pleasure dead,
With measur'd step and mournful mien,
Now bends to earth his head.

Constant still upon the heath,
Wrap'd in a winding sheet,
That pale and icy form of death
At this lone hour you'll meet.

Albert, the wealth that won thy heart
By strangers shall be spent,
Childless from life shalt thou depart,
And none shall thee lament;

While still the hapless Eda's tomb
With willow shall be drest,
And maids shall weep her early doom.
And bid her spirit rest;

And many a rose impearl'd with dew,
By meek ey'd evening shed,
Shall tender pity's fingers strew,
Across thy turfy bed.

"And this," said Henry, laying down the manuscript, "is the production of her whose feeling mind sunk in intellectual gloom, glows no more with the divine inspirations of genius. Love only, like a solitary star, visible on the black curtain of night, elicits its bright sparkles to irradiate the midnight darkness. And Nevil, him so worshipped, whose adored image never fades from her remembrance, he, who amidst all her wanderings, reigns undivided sovereign of her distempered imagination – the magnet to which her trembling fancy, ever faithful to his beloved memory, invariably turns; he is at rest. – The strong arm of oppression can torture him no more, his heart has forgot to throb, and love and misfortune can afflict no longer. But her, whose callous soul, whose unfeeling pride, separated such hearts – whose shameless folly broke the links of a most dear and sacred affection, can her days pass peacefully away? Are her nights blest with repose? If so, eternal justice slumbers. Can such a guilty being boast of happiness? Can the glitter of wealth, the pageantry of rank, cast a veil over the appalling remembrance? Can it conceal the horror of having driven a daughter to madness, of having desolated a mind rich with the invaluable treasures of genius, taste, and sensibility?"

The longer Henry reflected on the derangement of Lady Julia, the more he thought of her talents, so lost, so destroyed, the higher his detestation arose of the Dutchess of Inglesfield, who, as he reviewed her conduct as a mother, appeared before the tribunal of his judgment a very fiend in human shape. And he was even led to doubt, though he shuddered at the idea, whether Nevil had not met a violent end. Another tedious week had now worn away, and Henry had almost lived in the gallery, but the fair maniac did not return. Constantly and anxiously his eyes were turned on the warrior, whose stern and forbidding countenance seemed to frown disappointment on his cherished wishes, and the first rays of light illumed the east every morning before he could prevail on himself to quit his station, or seek that repose his wearied frame and harassed feelings rendered so requisite. After having spent a day of more than usual melancholy, his spirits almost sunk in despair; hopeless, and almost lifeless, he beheld the evening set in dark and stormy – hollow gusts of wind rattled the gothic windows, and swept along the gallery – black and heavy clouds seemed to hover on the agitated bosom of the ocean, loud peals of thunder rolled heavily along the sky, and bright and jagged lightnings darted their blue fires through the windows. It was a scene in unison with Henry's feelings, and he sat mournfully listening to the tempest, and watching the vivid concuscations, when a low creaking noise struck his ear; he started from his seat, and springing across the gallery, saw the stern old warrior slide out of sight, and in his place appear the fair maniac; with a lamp in her hand. As she entered from the opening, her veil, and long dark hair, that hung in loose tresses on her bosom, floated in the wind, which rushed through the panel, and gave her the appearance of one of those cruel beings which fancy loves to embody. Her face was pale as death, but her eyes, her melting expressive eyes were more brilliant than ever; she had a transparent muslin robe wrapped loosely round her, and her thin form seemed even more shadowy, more light than when he had last seen her. As she entered, she looked round as if expecting some person: at length in a whispering voice she said: –

"Dearest Nevil, all is prepared, come." Henry advanced gently towards her: she held the lamp to his face, looked disappointed, sighed heavily, and waving her hand, said in a hurried tone: –

"Go, go –" He moved to a little distance from her; she advanced to the window, and exclaimed: –

"See, see the skiff will be lost! how the waves rise in mountains round her. Oh! she will sink, and with her will be lost all hopes of flying from this dismal castle."

Henry looked out, a vivid flash of lightening shewed him a vessel in the offing; but was any meaning to be attached to her words; were they any thing more than some of the wild ideas that continually chased each other across her imagination.

"All is in readiness, rny beloved," said Lady Julia; "but my greatest treasures I carry about my person: here," continued she, drawing a paper from her bosom; "Here are the scriptures of the loyal Leonitus; this is a talisman, I wear it on my heart. And here," said she in a voice of mournful melody, pointing to the finger on which was her wedding ring, "here is a momento of lost happiness. Oh, Nevil, Nevil – adored of my soul, lost, lost for ever. They forbid me to think of him – but who shall restrain the privilege of thought! The tyrants with inventive cruelty may forge manacles for the limbs; but where exists the gigantic power that can confine thought."

This was the second connected sentence that she had uttered that night, and Henry hailed them as the happy harbingers of returning reason. He approached her, and gently taking her hand inquired after her health.

"Health," echoed she, "it fled with Nevil – with my happiness. The wind blows cold," added she, wrapping her veil round her; "but my heart is warm, my brain is all flame, and I have dreams – oh, such dreams – so blissful, so agonizing; I see him in the deep gloom of night, and I hear his voice softer than the sighing of the summer's breeze – and that fascinating smile. I thought he loved me; he told me he did, or I would never – Hark! he calls me – worshipped of my soul, I come."

Henry had placed himself against the picture to prevent its closing, and as she darted through the aperture, he followed her into a little square closet, where opening a low door, she descended a flight of steps; a sudden gust of wind blew out her lamp. All was involved in darkness; he could not see his hand before him, nor could he distinguish the steps of his fair conductress – was she yet near him – in this perplexity, he determined to proceed, and groping by the wall, he reached the bottom of the stairs in safety. A long and heavy peal of thunder seemed to shake the castle to its foundation, and in the next instant, a vivid flash of lightning discovered to Henry a gallery similar to the one he had left above; he pursued his way cautiously along it. A light streamed through a door that stood ajar. Henry now paused; this might be the dutchess's apartment; if it were, he resolved to enter – to upbraid her with her conduct, to demand his liberty, to shame her, if she were not entirely dead to modesty, into compliance. Full of this idea, he pushed open the door; and saw her reclining on a sofa, reading a letter, with which she was so occupied that she did not hear him enter – not the Dutchess of Inglesfield, but a creature young, beautiful, and finely formed, fair as the fabled houri of Mahomet, her rich auburn hair playing in luxuriant ringlets over a forehead of ivory, and shading eyes whose colour seemed borrowed from the bright blue arch of heaven. Henry, in the utmost astonishment, was beginning an apology, when a faint shriek from the lovely object before him threw him into the greatest consternation: he feared he should repent his imprudence in entering the apartment, should he again be prevented from escape. He would have flown from her presence, but catching his arm, she told him he had nothing to apprehend, for her attendants were retired for the night, and not easily disturbed; she apologized for her scream, which was the sudden impulse of fear, and added: –

"My own folly was near frustrating all my hopes of future felicity. You bring me intelligence of Captain Lonsdale?"

Henry had listened in evident surprise to the beginning of her speech; but at the name of Captain Lonsdale he began to comprehend, and he hastened to undeceive her, by recounting to her as briefly as he could who he was, by what means brought to the castle, and how he came into her apartment: she attended to his recital with mingled amazement and regret, and in return for his confidence gave him the pleasing intelligence that the hour of escape was really near at hand. From her conversation, he learned that she was Lady Isabella Belville, the youngest daughter of the late Earl of Lucan, and coheiress with Lady Julia to his estates, unjustly withheld, she being now near three and twenty years of age. With many blushes, she confessed that having no prospect of softening her mother's heart in Captain Lonsdale's favour, nor of being released from the disagreeable restraint in which she lived; she had prevailed on one of the domestics to favour her correspondence with her lover, and that she expected him, and a near relation of his, the very next night to deliver her from worse than Egyptian bondage. "Not supposing," continued she, "that the Dutchess of Inglesfield had converted the castle into a prison for any other than her own family, I concluded you was the gentleman Captain Lonsdale proposed sending, not choosing, his own person being well known, to hazard a discovery by appearing about the castle himself." Lady Isabella was much affected at the shameless conduct of her mother, who, she informed Henry, was unwell, and that her indisposition by confining her to her apartment would give them a more favourable opportunity to escape; that the vessel he had seen in the offing was one prepared, and waiting to carry them to Italy, where they intended taking Lady Julia, in the hope that a warmer climate would at least restore her health; her senses she feared were fled for ever. Henry expressed his hope that her malady might yet be curable.

"I have no hope," replied Lady Isabella, "but my tender

affection for the dear sufferer would not allow me to leave her. I am the only person whom she regards, and while she lives, I will watch over her – I will as far as I am capable soften the calamity with which it has pleased heaven to afflict her."

As she spoke the tears fell from her lovely eyes; sacred, thought Henry, are the drops of pity shed for the woes of another, they sink not unregarded in the earth: no, angels collect them; they shine in heaven, the holy records of a feeling heart. Mutual explanations having taken place, and arrangements made for their departure, Henry perceiving day appear, left Lady Isabella to her repose: he regained the gallery, and sat down, till it was sufficiently light for him to see to fasten back the spring of the panel, which he dreaded to have closed again, lest in the hurry of their departure he should be forgot, and lose the only opportunity of escape that might ever offer.

CHAPTER II

Oh 'tis a fearful thing to die, to go we
Know not where; to leave the pomp and
Pageants of the world, to diet worms.

Shakespeare

Can storied urn or animated bust,
Back to its mansion call the fleeting breath,
Can honour's voice provoke the silent dust,
Or flattery sooth the dull cold ear of death?

Gray

In the deep unbroken silence of the
Grave, the wailing voice of sorrow is not
Heard – Love, Genius, Friendship all are mute.

A. J. H.

"THE poet was certainly right, when he gave to time the epithet of leaden footed," said Henry, as he walked with impatient steps through his apartments to the gallery, and from the gallery to his apartments again. "He experienced as I do all the anxious feelings of hope, all the tortures of suspense." Never had day been so wearisome, never had it appeared so uncommonly long; never was the lengthened shadows of evening hailed with so much joy; never half so welcome, as those which held forth the promise of a liberation from the gloomy confinement of Raven-hill Castle. Henry watched the last rays of the sun, sinking behind the mountains, with sensations of delight he had long been a stranger to; while the enchantress Hope suggested a far distant happier scene, when it should set on the morrow. He counted hour after hour, as the deep toned oracle of the east turret sent forth its loud and reverberating sound. It was near midnight, and Henry was on the point of descending to the apartment of Lady Isabella, when an unusual bustle in the gallery gave to his apprehensive and agitated mind the distracting idea that the enclosed panel had been discovered; and he was hastily leaving his chamber to ascertain the full extent of his misfortune, when he was encountered by the steward, who in accent of grief and terror told him that all concealment was now at an end; that the Dutchess of Inglesfield was dying, and had requested with solemn earnestness to see him. Henry felt an extreme reluctance to obey the summons – he apprehended some new contrivance – he wished to remain in the gallery. The expectation of liberty was infinitely more interesting to his heart than the expiring dutchess, for whom he felt but a small portion of compassion, and whom he thought might be spared from the world, where her violent passions and tyrannical dispositions had rendered her an object of universal hatred, and where she had only proved a scourge to those dependent on or unhappily connected with her. But on the steward saying her daughters were in her apartment, he no longer hesitated, but followed to the chamber of the dutchess; who, propped up by pillows, and gasping for breath, lay under a superb canopy of scarlet velvet, richly embroidered, and adorned with fringes and tassels of gold. Every article about her apartment was of the most costly and magnificent kind, and all its arrangements wore an air of voluptuous luxury; Henry contrasted the splendid adornments of her bed and chamber with her own emaciated form, cadaverous countenance, and hollow eyes; and thought how unavailing riches were in an hour like that, when death stood grinning over his prey, and the grave yawning to mingle her with her native earth.

When Henry was announced, she appeared greatly agitated, and attempted to speak; but unable to articulate, she sank back on the down that supported her; and the only words that could be distinguished were, pity, forgive. You are at liberty. – Henry forgot all she had made him suffer, as he viewed the ghastly form before him, as he contemplated the anguish depicted on her features, and heard the exclamations that told how unwilling she was to quit the world. Lady Isabella knelt weeping by the bed-side, and was vainly endeavouring to soothe her mother, and console her with the hope of eternal happiness; but awakened conscience was now reproaching her with duties neglected, with crimes committed; and deaf to consolation she was offering the physician seated near her immense sums to prolong her life only for a month, a week, a single day.

Lady Julia Nevil stood mournfully leaning against the chimney-piece, unnoticing any thing, till roused by the dutchess exclaiming: "I cannot, will not die" She slowly advanced to the bed, and leaning over her mother, said: –

"Where is Horace? where have you hid my beloved Nevil?" The dutchess shuddered, as she beheld her gaze fixed upon her; and as if to shut out so terrible an object, closed her eyes, while a deep groan burst from her.

"What!" said Lady Julia, "do you groan? I thought that was my exclusive privilege. Oh, I thought no one had occasion to groan but me. Well, well," continued she sighing heavily, "the time will arrive when we must all render up our accounts at the tribunal of heaven; the cause for groans will then be investigated."

The dutchess trembled; her countenance underwent a frightful change. – "Julia, my dearest Julia," said Lady Isabella, rising from her kneeling posture, and tenderly taking the arm of her sister, "let me lead you hence; our unhappy parent is dying."

"Aye," replied the fair maniac, "and my Nevil is already dead – he waits for me in heaven; but where will his murderer go?"

The dutchess gave a convulsive shriek, and the attendants endeavoured to remove Lady Julia, but avoiding them, she caught her mother's arm, and said, "Stay, stay, don't you go to my beloved Horace; the time will soon, yes, very soon arrive, when we shall sleep quietly in the grave together, but don't you come to disturb and separate us." The dutchess appeared in the greatest agonies: Lady Isabella aided by Henry would have led her sister from the apartment: but clinging to the drapery of the bed, she continued to question her mother respecting Nevil; and telling her that heaven never slept, but had witnessed all her miseries during her affecting ravings. The dutchess had appeared to suffer the most excruciating pangs of mind and body. In the midst of this distressing scene, an elegant young man was ushered into the room, who flying to Lady Isabella caught her in his arms, while she, half fainting, murmured, "Dearest Lonsdale!" Lady Julia had now sunk into a state of melancholy silence; and the dutchess, having had a medicine administered, beckoned them to her: they sank on their knees before her; she made an attempt to join their hands – but this effort, trifling as it was, proved too much for her exhausted frame – she just uttered the word bless, sunk back on her pillow, and fell into convulsions, in which she remained above an hour; and recovered only to reproach herself for past crimes, and then expired.

Henry shuddered at the fearful end of a woman who had lived only for herself, and the gratification of her own diabolical passions, who had left this world without hope of happiness in the next, quitted the apartment with Captain Lonsdale. The steward led them down the grand staircase, and threw open the door of a magnificently furnished saloon, where a gentleman was standing examining a picture; as they entered he turned round, and Henry had the unhoped felicity of beholding his dear friend, the Honourable Horatio Delamere. After the tumultuous feelings of surprise and joy their unexpected meeting occasioned had in some degree subsided, Henry narrated at large all the adventure that had occurred since their strange separation.

"And now, my friends," said he gaily, "I believe my romance is concluded; for, to wind up the catastrophe properly, the witch of the castle is dead, and I am released from durance vile."

Delamere and Captain Lonsdale had been listening to Henry's account of his confinement with silent astonishment, and now in turn congratulated him on his liberation, and commiserated the sufferings he had undergone; at the same time expressing their suspicion that the scheme had not been carried into effect without the approbation and connivance of Lord Dungarvon; but this opinion, which Henry had also inbibed, was shortly after entirely confuted by Lady Isabella, to whom the dutchess, being given over by her physician, and without any hope of recovery, had confessed the whole history of her passion for, and designs upon Henry, together with his being a prisoner in the castle, with which the Earl of Dungarvon was absolutely unacquainted, and which nefarious scheme had been planned and carried into execution through the contrivance of the prolific brain of her favourite woman, who was sister to Captain Lawson, the gallant commander of the Ceres; by whom the whole business of seizing Henry, and conveying him to Raven-hill Castle had been managed. Lady Isabella had also acquainted her mother with her intended elopement, now no longer necessary; and the dutchess requested to see Captain Lonsdale when he arrived, intending to bestow her consent, when it could no longer be of consequence, to an union which nothing but a strict adherence to duty on Lady Isabella's part had prevented taken place two years before. – A stranger even to the branches of her own family, without a female friend or companion; the situation of Lady Isabella, heiress to incalculable wealth, was extremely awkward; she had lived in such absolute seclusion, that she had not even an acquaintance that she could send for to remain with her – and now surrounded by death, and her lover an inmate of the castle, her situation was peculiarly distressing, without a friend on whom she could rely to superintend the funeral of her mother, or arrange her affairs. It became necessary to invest some person with power to act for her, in this distressing emergency. It was not in nature to suppose that her grief for the death of a woman, who had constantly denied her every indulgence her rank in life and large fortune authorised her to expect, could be very violent. But Lady Isabella was tender and amiable – she forgot her faults, and remembered only that she was her parent, to whose memory she wished to pay every proper respect: but she was absolutely alone; her sister in a state of confirmed derangement, and herself encompassed with difficulties, and called upon to act in a business with which she was utterly unacquainted, and totally unfit for; she was therefore necessitated to wave punctilios, and obliged to yield to the ardent and pressing solicitations of Captain Lonsdale, and the advice of his friends, to give herself a legal protector – it was therefore concluded, though with evident reluctance on her part, while her mother lay a corpse in the castle, that the next day, the second after the decease of the dutchess, should begin the felicity of Captain Lonsdale, by uniting him with the object of his tender affection, the amiable and beautiful Lady Isabella Belville.

Lady Julia Nevil, who had for many days appeared more calm, and had even given late the hope of recovering reason, on the night of the dutchess's death relapsed into greater gloom and deeper melancholy than ever: her insanity had taken a new turn; she no longer fancied her husband lived – no longer wandered to different parts of the castle to meet and converse with him; her imagination now only dwelt on the deceased Nevil; and she insisted on having robes of the deepest mourning. In her wildest fits, in her most frenzied hours, music had always acted upon her like a charm: in the moments when her malady hurried her into actions of violence, if her attendants placed her harp before her, she would sink into calmness; and sweeping its strings with tremulous fingers, would draw forth sounds of melancholy sweetness, to which she would sing the plaintive incoherences that floated in her distempered fancy, in tones so melting, so pathetic, that every eye except her own would be suffused with tears, while she "sat smiling at grief:" she would also listen in mute and raptured attention to the airs her sister played and sang; but now music had lost its attraction, she no longer listened…no longer was charmed by the "melody of sweet sounds," or attended to its soothing powers. But restless and agitated, she continued to wander from her own apartment to the chamber of her mother, now stripped of its magnificent adornments, and hung with black, where the Dutchess of Inglesfield, ghastly and disfigured, wrapped in the dreary habiliments of the grave, lay under a stately canopy of black velvet, on which was emblazoned the arms of the family in gold, surmounted with an enormous plume of feathers, which waving mournfully over, seemed to say: "fie, this is pageantry." For hours she would stand gazing on the corpse: twice she had taken the cold damp hand of her mother, and laid it on her bosom, saying: – "Only feel how it beats; you can never hope to still its throbbings, never expect my heart to be tranquil, though you have buried him."

At another time, after looking wistfully in the dutchess's face for some moments, she clasped her hands together, and in a tone of agony whispered: –

"Can you sleep, you who have banished repose from me – you who have murdered Nevil! Was she my mother? No, no – mothers are tender of their children! they do not destroy them."

To Henry's inquiries respecting Mr. Nevil Lady Isabella informed him that he was the son of a poor clergyman, a young man of elegant figure, and captivating address; a scholar and a gentleman: that he had for his extraordinary abilities been engaged by the Earl of Lucan, as preceptor to his son, who died before he had attained his eleventh year: that her sister having even in infancy discovered strong indications of genius, Mr. Nevil had been retained after the death of their brother, to superintend her studies. The romantic and susceptible Julia became but too sensible of the merits and graces of Mr. Nevil, she imbibed a passion for him ardent and unconquerable; the glowing effusions of her muse were addressed to him, and every word, and every look, told the warm attachment of her heart. Was it wonderful that a young man so flattered should feel an equal passion for her, whose person, sufficiently attractive, possessed the double charm of talent and of congenial mind. Lady Lucan was the first to discover their affection; Mr. Nevil was dismissed the castle, but Lady Julia and him contrived to meet; and his father, a needy and ambitious man, married them. In the night of their nuptials, a servant privy to the circumstance betrayed them to the enraged earl, who with the entire approbation and advice of Lady Lucan had him torn from the arms of his wife, and confined in the matted chamber. Mr. Nevil's father, dreading the consequences of having married an heiress to his son, abandoned the unfortunate young man to his fate; and went abroad, where he died. In struggling with the servants, who were forcibly dragging him up the stairs, Mr. Nevil's arm was broke: it was never properly set, and it brought on a fever that fixed on his nerves; and after languishing many months in hopeless despondency, his unhappy existence terminated: he was buried with all possible privacy at midnight in the vaults of the castle, without any rite or ceremony whatever. The miserable Julia lost her senses the night her husband was forced from her: and she had now for more than ten years dragged on a wretched life – lost to all enjoyment. The victim of pride and resentment sunk in cureless insanity.

Henry heard this tale with the sincerest emotions of pity; his heart felt the deepest commiseration for the unfortunate divided pair; but out of respect to Lady Isabella, he forbore making any comments on the inexorable being who had occasioned, and could behold the calamitous effects of her cruelty unmoved, who could witness the barbarous devastation she had made, nor endeavour to atone before too late. In her dying moments her self-reproaches had convinced him that she had kept alive the resentment of the Earl of Lucan; that she had loved Horace Nevil, and that jealousy had been the avenging fiend who had occasioned the death of him, and the distraction of Lady Julia.

The next morning the happy and enamoured Captain Lonsdale led the beautiful blushing Lady Isabella Belville, attended by the honourable Mr. Delamere, Henry, and a number of the male and female domestics, to the altar, where they plighted to each other those sacred vows dissoluble only by death: the ceremony was concluded, when Lady Julia Nevil, unobserved by any one, entered the chapel, and gliding up a remote aisle, reached the altar just as the benediction was pronounced: she sunk on her knees between her sister and Captain Lonsdale, and laying her white arms on the altar, said with solemn earnestness: –

"Here I vowed to love him to the last hour of my existence – here I renew that vow. Nevil, I was thine! am thine for ever."

Her eyes closed, and she fell into the extended arms of Captain Lonsdale. In a few moments she again beheld the light, but it was only to press her wedding ring to her lips, to say: – "Bury me with my adored Nevil." The agonized spirit then burst from its mansion, and the victim of romantic love was at peace; the heart that had throbbed with the truest, most ardent affection felt the excruciating pang of disappointment no more. Lady Isabella was carried fainting from the altar; and this event, though little to be lamented, because it released a sufferer from the worst of miseries, involved the castle in the deepest affliction: the dutchess had expired utterly unlamented by all, except those few whose interest was connected with her being; and whose situations were lost by her death. But the beautiful interesting maniac, the suffering Lady Julia Nevil, was beloved by all: her disastrous passion, her distressing malady, had for years furnished stories of lamentation among the domestics of the castle: and every heart and every eye paid a weeping tribute to her genius, her worth, and her sorrows. Henry, though extremely impatient to be at Dolgelly Castle, could not resist the entreaties of his friend Horatio, and the pressing solicitations of Captain Lonsdale and Lady Isabella, to remain with them till after the funerals of the Dutchess of Inglesfield and Lady Julia Nevil had taken place.

"I do not, cannot wonder, my dear sir," said Lady Isabella, "that you are anxious to remove from a scene where you have suffered so much injury, where you have worn away so many unhappy hours; but for the sake of her memory, out of respect to her who so much interested you, my beloved ever to be lamented Julia, I trust you will stay and see her remains deposited with her husband, unless you wish me to believe you have not yet forgiven my misguided mother, and that your resentment reaches to me."

Henry pressed the white extended hand of Lady Isabella respectfully to his lips, besought her to believe that he had no resentments, that all was forgiven, all consigned to oblivion, and that he would cheerfully and readily acquiesce with her wishes. He then retired to write to Sir Owen Llewellyn and

Adeline, to detail to them his adventures, and to appoint a time for his return to his now more than ever loved home, and the delightful intercourse of friendship. The bones of the unhappy Horace Nevil were taken up: a hole had been dug in the earth in one of the vaults near the chapel, and his body wrapped in a sheet thrown in. He was now laid in a superb coffin, and the same day saw the remains of the Dutchess of Inglesfield and the two victims of her cruelty committed to the earth, with equal ceremony and with equal state and magnificence.

The same grave received the unfortunate lovers, who though divided in life, in death were united; and their ashes permitted to mingle in the same earth: they were buried near the altar in the chapel, and an exquisitely wrought white marble cenotaph was erected near them expressive of their loves and their misfortunes. The health of Lady Isabella, always delicate, had received a severe shock in the late melancholy occurrences; and the physicians recommending a change of scene and climate, it was concluded that as soon as they could arrange their affair, they should spend the period of their mourning in Italy, upon which tour it had before been settled that Horatio Delamere should accompany them and he still preserved his intention of visiting the scenes celebrated by his favourite poets. The taste and elegance of Henry's mind led him to wish to be of their party, he would have been delighted to tread classic ground; to have visited the soil that had nourished so many men of genius; his fancy was enraptured with the idea of kneeling at the tomb of Virgil, of lingering under the shades where Petrarch had sighed his unhappy passion; where Tasso had waved in melodious verse the Christian banner, and Ariosto breathed the wild energies of frenzied love. But gratitude and duty called him to Dolgelly

Castle, where Sir Owen Llewellyn demanded his attention, and Adeline, the companion of his childhood, the sister of his heart, expected his presence.

The public papers having announced to the world the marriage of Captain Lonsdale to the heiress of Raven-hill Castle, and rejoicings having taken place in the vicinity, visitors continually poured in to see the lovely bride, and congratulate the happy pair on their nuptials. Miss Lonsdale having arrived, and consented to accompany her sister-in-law abroad, Henry conceived that his company could now be dispensed with, and resolved to return to North Wales; he took a most affectionate leave of Horatio Delamere, with whom he settled a plan of correspondence, and parted from the fair owner of the castle and her husband with mutual sentiments of respect, esteem, and regret; different now were his sensations, as the antique towers of Raven-hill and its frowning battlements receded from his view, to what they were when he fled from them. He was now at liberty, feared no pursuit, was journeying to meet those whom gratitude as well as affection gave the highest claims upon his heart; yet a feeling something like sorrow pervaded his bosom, as he reflected on the circle he was leaving, endeared to his mind as much by their virtues as by the remembrance of the kind attention and the friendship he had experienced from them.

At the first stage that Henry stopped, as he was stepping out of the chaise, he was accosted by a beggar, who in a gruff tone implored his charity, saying "For God's sake give a trifle to a disabled seaman, who fought many a battle for my king and country before I lost my precious limb." There was a tender chord in the heart of Henry, that always vibrated to the voice of misery; but these were tones that particularly struck him; they sounded familiar to his ear. He looked earnestly in the beggar's face, and beheld his old acquaintance Ned Ratlin, whom he thought he had left dying on board the Ceres. Henry shook him heartily by the hand, and was beginning to question him respecting his present situation, when perceiving a crowd gathering about them, he turned into the inn and bade Ned follow him.

The dress of poor Ned had seen better days; it was an old blue jacket and trousers, literally in rags, which, as the weather happened to be windy, blew about in all directions, and displayed his skin, not of the fairest hue, through many of the apertures. As he stumped after Henry, he waved his hat exultingly over his head, huzzaing with all his might – then turning to the crowd with a disdainful look, exclaimed, "Avast, you lubbers; weigh anchor and sheer off: none of you had bowels enough to throw a bone to a poor starved dog like me to pick, but see now the sweet little cherub that sits up aloft, takes care of poor Ned. Just as I was going to strike, and sink upon the shoals of mishap; who should come sailing along, but the grandson of a noble lord, yes, you lubbers, he is, and with no more pride than a foremast man, and says, Ned, how are you, shipmate, and shakes me by the fin, just for the world as if I was his equal. You know I have been beating about the Chops of the Channel here, and hoisting signals of distress for these three days, but none of you launched out a stiver to help me – why there is more charity among Turks; but splice my mizzen, I shall fetch all up now with a wet sail. The Mortimer for ever, huzza." Ned again waved his hat in the air, and gave three cheers, which were echoed by the mob, as flourishing his wooden leg he stumped into the Golden Eagle after Henry.

When he had satisfied the cravings of his stomach, which

had not known the comforts of a good meal for many days with some excellent roast beef, and washed it down with a sufficient quantity of grog, Henry gave him money, and sent him out to get new rigged, as he called it. This business was now accomplished to his entire satisfaction from head to foot, and before Henry had finished his dinner he presented himself before him, in a new bluejacket, striped waistcoat, and blue trowsers; his beard had been taken off, and he had got a new hat.

"Messmate," said he – "no, no, I beg pardon for my boldness – noble young gentleman," at the same time making a low bow, "my canvas, thanks to your bounty, does not shiver in the wind now, but I have not spent all the shot; here is a little left in the locker yet." He then drew out some silver that he had received in change after paying for his clothes; but Henry bade him put it in his pocket, and asked him if he would go with him into Wales, where he would provide for him the rest of his life.

"Any where," answered Ned, "through the wide world;" and bursting into tears, would have fallen at the feet of his benefactor if he had not prevented him. Henry respected the overflowings of a grateful heart; he pressed his hand cordially, and giving him a glass of wine, told him they would set off immediately. When Ned recovered speech, he said, "I was certainly born in cucumber time, for I am but a watery headed fool; for when my heart is full it always runs over at my eyes; though, man my foretop, I have had salt water enough in my time," added he dashing away his tears with his hand; "but it is enough to break a fellow's heart with joy, to meet such fair weather, and such an anchor to rest upon at last, after having been drove out to sea in such hard gales, and drifting as one may say upon a leashore all one's life."

During their journey, Henry was informed by his companion that when the Ceres arrived at Plymouth he had been put on shore, and that death not having a berth ready for him, he had been suffered to recover, notwithstanding two doctors had said his death warrant was signed for the other world; and that a little dirty French privateer had fallen in with the Ceres, and made a prize of her; and that Anthony Lawson, her gallant commander, was damning the soul of his aunt Nell in a prison, he feared without a whit of tobacco, or a can of flip to comfort him; "and as for me," continued Ned, "having lost my berth in the Ceres, I could not get a ship, this piece of timber," pointing to his wooden leg, "was such a stumbling block in my way; well, what was to be done: my money was all run out, my friends looked shy: I could not work, for I was brought up to no trade, I scorned to steal – all I had left for it, was to beg; and I thought having lost an understander, and found so many scars, I might presume to ask a morsel of bread from that country in whose service I had spent my youth, and spilt my blood: but hold there a bit, I was upon the wrong tack, no longer pipe no longer dance. Every body remembered the engagement in which I got this scar across my cheek; they had all heard the name of the gallant commander of the Agamemnon, but nobody had heard the name of Ned Ratlin. The newspapers mention the names of the officers, one by one, but the men are all stowed together in a lump, like ballast in the hold. I remember the chaplain of our ship used to bother a great deal about providence, to which I paid no heed, for Tom Capston and I used to laugh and say: 'sink o' swim, luck is au,' but I find the chaplain was no liar, for providence has taken me in tow at last."

Overcome with joy, affection, and gratitude, Henry sunk at

the feet of Sir Owen Llewellyn, whose emotions as he hugged him to his heart were scarce less acute than his own. The tender name of father and son issued from their lips, as each gazed upon the other, with eyes animated with delight, but when Adeline flew to his arms, when she in the tenderest accents deplored his sufferings; when she with smiles of pleasure welcomed him to his home, he felt that she was the arbitress of his fate, and that as she directed his future life would be happiness or misery.

She was even more beautiful than Lady Isabella Lonsdale; her smiles were fascination, and her eyes – but their expression was only to be felt, not described. Henry introduced Ned Ratlin to Sir Owen and Adeline, who were highly entertained with his rough manners and strange expressions, almost all unintelligible to Miss Llewellyn. Sir Owen applauded Henry's patronage of the weather-beaten sailor, and told him his home was now to be Dolgelly Castle; but when Adeline laid her soft white hand upon his, and told him that it should be her particular pleasure to attend to his comforts, and make him happy, the tears chased one another down his furrowed cheeks, and he sobbed out, "You are the cherub that Tom Hawser used to sing about, for I am sure nothing belonging to this life can be half so beautiful or good as you."

Ned soon became a general favourite at Dolgelly Castle; to the servants he told marvellous stories of mermaids, waterspouts, and tempests; with Sir Owen he made fishing nets and lines; and for Adeline and Henry, he steered the boat when they went by sea to Carnarvon.

The presence of Henry spread a general joy round the neighbourhood: at Tudor Hall a grand entertainment was given, and Eliza protested that she did not wonder the old dutchess had fallen in love with him, for that he was positively a divine fellow; "And as to that amphibious creature, Ned Ratlin," said she, "I think he will yet rival Seymour in my affections."

Henry had much to hear, as well as to relate, and he listened with no little entertainment to Eliza's history of her lovers, and the tricks she had been obliged to play to get rid of them. – When he had quitted Dolgelly Castle for Cambridge, Eliza Tudor was a pretty little romp – she was still the same, full of frolic, wild and mischievous; while Adeline, tall and graceful, had improved in loveliness and elegance, inclining to pensivenesss: she won upon the heart with irresistible sweetness – her manners were gentle, and her voice soft, touching, and melodious. To the children of want Eliza Tudor would give with cheerful liberality, but she would laugh even while she listened to a tale of sorrow, and find subjects for pleasantry even in the midst of scenes of calamity; while Adeline, like the angel of pity, a tear trembling in her eye, would not only relieve, but listen to the story of distress, and entering the meanest hovel, console and comfort the afflicted; thus eminently lovely in person, thus angelic in mind, her father lived but in her smiles; the domestics of the household, the peasantry round Dolgelly Castle idolized her, and Ned Ratlin, as her eyes beamed on him the radiance of compassion and kindness, swore that he would die for her, while Henry, the impassioned Henry, as his heart acknowledged the virtues of his disposition, and his senses felt the captivation of her beauty, sighingly confessed, there was nothing worth existing for, except the lovely Adeline Llewellyn.

CHAPTER III

True love declares itself by its respect.
Fearful it shuns itself, itself it loses.
A single smile, a look of the beloved,
Is happiness supreme; much it desires,
But little it presumes, and nothing dares.

Dante

He wore his endless noons alone,
Amid the autumnal wood;
Oft was he wont in hasty fit,
Abrupt the social board to quit,
And gaze with eager glance upon the trembling flood.

Warton's Suicide

The blissful evanescent hours of childhood are always regretted: the mind, disgusted with the depravities and ingratitude of mankind, or worn with sorrow and adversity, flies from present evils and disappointments to the melancholy solace of reviewing the days that are gone. Memory turns with delight to retrace the tranquil moments when passion slumbering left the unvitiated senses to the full enjoyment of nature, in her most beautiful and innocent forms; when all was harmony within – when the gay and elastic mind suffered no sorrow to press upon it, but buoyant with hope forgot the trifling vexations of the present in the rapturous contemplation of future happiness.

To such days the sick mind of Henry Mortimer continually reverted; he remembered with thrilling sensations of delight the times when he had carried Adeline in his arms across the streams that glittered over and intersected the paths in the neighbouring woods, when he had lifted her over gates and stiles or ran with her up the sides of the steep mountains, gathered shells and sea-weed with her on the sea-shore, or sat on the grass in the meadows, and twisted the cowslips, violets, and hedge roses into garlands, with which he decorated her hair, and fantastically adorned her cherub form; and received for his reward unnumbered kisses from her rosy mouth, while her little arms entwined his neck with innocent fondness. Henry recollected these days of happiness with sighs. Adeline was now grown a woman, and though her regard for him was still the same, it was regulated by reserve, by retiring delicacy: she no longer sat on his knee, her arm encircling his neck; she no longer offered him a kiss as a reward for any little service he performed – she no longer permitted him to hold her hand a willing prisoner in his; and while he remembered with regret the innocent freedoms in which but a few, a very few years before he had been indulged, he wished, ah! how sincerely wished, that they were children again. – Yet, though she was continually present to his imagination, though he was miserable in her absence, and saw none amiable, none lovely in an equal degree with herself, yet he dared not think, presumed not to confess even to himself, that he loved her beyond the calm, the temperate affection of a brother – the only child of Sir Owen Llewellyn might aspire to titled wealth; his mind deeply felt all he owed to the bounty, to the unabating friendship of her father, and he felt it would be a base return for unrequitable obligations; a violation of every grateful and honourable principle, to endeavour to gain the heart of Adeline. No, born to prouder hopes, to brighter prospects, he dared not even hope that she would cherish for him the tender sentiments of love, or bestow the rich treasure of her beauties on him, a dependant on her father's bounty.

Yet, though Henry had silenced every glowing throbbing hope with the stern voice of rigid honour, yet he was not philosopher enough to conquer his feelings. So fascinating an object continually before his eyes was too much for his susceptible heart; he lost his appetite and his sleep, while his sunk eye and pale cheek evidently declared all was not tranquil within. Adeline was the first to discover his altered looks, but to her tender inquiries he would answer with a melancholy smile that he was perfectly well.

Things were in this state at Dolgelly Castle, when a family of the name of Montgomery came on a visit to Sir Owen Llewellyn. Mr. Montgomery, of ancient Welch extraction, had made a large fortune in the East Indies, where he had married his lady, whose sole attraction was a pretty face, for the sake of which he had exalted her from a state of servitude to that of a Nabobess. Their family consisted of a son and daughter; the young man, Mr. Hugh Montgomery, well educated, and tolerably handsome in person; his sister, plain in face, ungainly in figure, superficial, vain, and conceited, but the doting child of her mother, who considered her as a model of perfection. The young lady had been but a few days at Dolgelly Castle, before she fancied herself violently in love with Henry Mortimer, in which she was encouraged by Eliza Tudor (who had contrived to ingratiate herself into her favour), while her brother had seriously become enamoured of Adeline. To avoid the importunities of Miss Montgomery, who was perpetually teasing him to sing, to play the flute, or provoking him to romp with her, Henry would stroll into the depth of the woods, or climb the rocky eminences, in the hope that whilst his eye beheld the grand and beautiful scenery of nature he should forget the passion that was preying on his heart, and banish the idea that Hugh Montgomery had rendered himself of importance to Adeline. He had marked the assiduous attentions of Mr. Montgomery, he had seen Adeline receive those attentions with smiles of affability – her smiles bestowed on others were poison to his peace. He wished to fly from remembrance, from her, from himself, but to the deep solitude of the woods her image pursued him. On the tall cliff he saw her radiant in beauty; and her smile, the smile she bestowed on the happy Montgomery, was perpetually present to his fevered imagination.

Mr. Montgomery was fond of fishing, and a very fine trout stream running across a neighbouring island, Commodore Ratlin was ordered to prepare the boat for an expedition to Terramawr, where Sir Owen had built a fishing house, and where he proposed spending the day. Mrs. Montgomery objected to going in the boat, declaring that she had for ever done with expecting pleasure in jaunts upon the water; she had met with a sickening of sea journeys in coming all the way from the East Indies. It was therefore agreed that Lady Tudor, who was to be of the party, and herself, should proceed in her carriage to the opposite side of the island, where the river being narrow, they could cross over in a few moments in a small boat.

"Aye, aye, that is right," said Sir Griffith, who had listened with much seeming satisfaction to Mrs. Montgomery's arrangement; "had you gone with us, my lady, you would have spoiled all my fun, for if the boat had heeled ever so little to one side you would have fancied yourself going full tilt into the other world, and then what a fuss we should all have been in – a fit or two of the hysterics would have been nothing to it – we should have had such gules of hartshorn, such fumes of assafœtida –"

"Well, if I ever heard the like of you," said Mrs. Montgomery, priming up her pretty face, and arranging an expensive lace veil: "Why, if Mr. Montgomery was to go on in the strange way you do, Sir Griffith, I would hate the sight of him."

"O, my dear madam," replied Lady Tudor, applying her salts to her nose, "Sir Griffith I fancy would be perfectly easy on that head; no man on earth troubles himself less about the preservation of tenderness and affection."

"It is all a parcel of ridiculous nonsense," said Sir Griffith; "fine bother to talk about tender affections, after having swung in a matrimonial noose for upwards of thirty years. Curse it, my lady, your affectation has worn out my affection; and as to your fine feelings, you talk indeed a great deal about them, but I believe, like your spasmodic affections, they are only found in your mouth. – Love, my lady, has but a squeamish delicate sort of stomach, and you have poisoned him with valerian and surfeit water; and as to his wings, poor devil, you have not left him a single feather, for you have plucked every quill to burn under your nose."

"And what, Sir Griffith, may I thank," replied her ladyship, "for having been obliged to have recourse to such odious medicines but your boisterous temper?"

"My temper!" rejoined Sir Griffith, "why every soul in the county knows that there is not in the universe a more peaceable temper than mine; but your whims and conceits, and fooleries, would provoke the patience of St. David himself: d – n it," continued he, raising his voice, "your dressing-room is a garden of physical herbs – your bed-chamber an apothecary's shop, and as to your stomach it has been a receptacle for more cathartics, carminatives, juleps, narcotics, draughts, pills, bolusses, and potions, than would set up all the quack doctors in Christendom."

"More is my misfortune," retorted Lady Tudor; "and you in particular ought to compassionate the maladies you have occasioned."

Sir Griffith burst into a hoarse laugh.

"Aye, Sir Griffith," resumed Lady Tudor, "you may unfeelingly triumph in the ravages you have made: when I married you I was allowed to be blooming and beautiful."

"Why to confess the truth," replied he, "you was fresh and fair; your person was not much amiss."

"Yes, Sir Griffith," continued Lady Tudor, bridling; "and besides beauty, which every body allowed I possessed, I had a fine constitution and excellent spirits; but you have destroyed the one and ruined the other. – My health is quite gone, and as to my unhappy nerves…."

"O d – n your nerves," said Sir Griffith, jumping up, "I am off: if once you get upon that everlasting topic, we may give up the idea of going to Terramawr, for I am sure we shall not reach there today." Saying this, he bounced out of the room, banging the door with such violence after him, that Mrs. Montgomery, who had been during this dialogue admiring her person in a mirror, started, and turning to Lady Tudor, protested that Sir Griffith was perdigiously vulgar, and so astonishingly boisterous, that he was almost as bad, if not quite, as a tornado in the East Indies. Lady Tudor apologized, and bewailed her cruel destiny, in being the wife of a man so void of feeling, one on whom the softness and weakness of women made no impression, but only excited derision, and provoked contempt.

They were just stepping into the carriage, when Sir Griffith flew up to Mrs. Montgomery, and pushing a large snuff box into her hand, told her it was true Irish blackguard – no sham, but the real thing.

"Bless me, Sir Griffith," replied Mrs. Montgomery. "What is this for? I don't take snuff."

"Perhaps not," replied the incorrigible Sir Griffith, "perhaps not – but Lady Tudor is fond of the blackguard."

"Me, sir! I beg – "

"Aye, Lady Tudor, and I beg," said he, interrupting her, "that you will not flurry your nerves. My dear madam," again addressing himself to Mrs. Montgomery, "you know she has been complaining of her nerves all the morning; now she may have a fit on the road. I have proved the efficacy of snuff in hysterical cases; you will have nothing to do but cram a good pinch up her nostrils; I warrant it will bring her to her recollection presently if you can but once get her to snuff it will do – it is the true Irish blackguard I assure you."

Mrs. Montgomery threw up her eyes. Lady Tudor, as red as a Turkey cock, ordered the coachman to proceed, and Sir Griffith bawled after Mrs. Montgomery not to spare the snuff. The rest of the party embarked with Commodore Ratlin. The day was remarkably fine – the sun in unclouded radiance beamed from a clear blue sky – the views round Dolgelly Castle were highly picturesque; and as they sailed over the unruffled ocean, the hanging and stupendous cliffs exhibited a variety of shades, whose rough and craggy sides the restless waves had worn into many grotesque excavations. Waving woods, the ruins of castles, magnificent even in desolation, and scattered villages, alternately met their view.

Adeline was pointing out to Mr. Hugh Montgomery, who sat next her, every object worth observance as they past along; the three elderly gentlemen were discussing a political subject; Eliza was listening to Ned Ratlin's sea phrases; and Miss Lucretia Montgomery unblushingly making love to Henry Mortimer, who, burning with jealousy, sat watching Adeline, totally inattentive to the fine speeches Miss Montgomery was addressing to him. After having asked him two or three questions, to which he had made no reply, in an angry and sharp tone she said, "Well, I suppose this is Welch politeness…. I never was so neglected, never treated with such rudeness before."

"Madam," said Henry, roused by her complaints from the reverie into which he had fallen, "of whom do you complain?"

"O Lord, sir," retorted she, "I complain of nobody not I, no indeed! complain, no truly. I shall not feed your vanity so much."

"My vanity! Miss Montgomery, sure you mistake."

"No, Mr. Mortimer, there is no sort of mistake," replied she, "it is plain enough to see that you suppose yourself somebody – but sure as you may think yourself of my affection –"

"Me, madam," said the astonished Henry, "I declare I never presumed –"

"Yes, sir, you have presumed," replied she, interrupting him " – have you not squeezed my hand, and have not you looked at me – Lord, sir, I am not such a fool as not to know when a gentleman is making love to me."

"I declare," rejoined Henry, "I never entertained such an idea."

"Well then," continued she bridling, "you might have had a worse idea. Miss Montgomery, with a fortune of fifty thousand pounds in cash, besides the worth of as many more thousands in diamonds, the only daughter of an East India nabob, might have been worth an idea; but I suppose I am not fair enough: to be sure I have lived under a hotter sun than Miss Llewellyn has, not but what my mamma took care that I should never be exposed even to the air without a veil; and if I am not as white as a wax candle, why there are as many brown beauties as there are fair ones."

Henry knew not what answer to make to this indelicate speech: he was really so destitute of vanity, that he felt no triumph, no pleasure, in the knowledge of Miss Montgomery's regard. It was evident she expected a reply, but he was so confounded that he was unable to answer her, and fortunately for him Ned Ratlin bawled out, "Heave a head there, we are going to cast anchor."

Henry had involuntarily placed himself by the side of Adeline, and was offering to assist her from the boat, when Mr. Montgomery told him that Miss Llewellyn was his care, and that no doubt Miss Tudor and his sister would be thankful for his attention.

"Is this your wish, Adeline," said Henry, turning his eyes upon her with a glance of impatience and vexation.

"O yes, most certainly," replied she, "I wish that you should take care of my friends."

"You shall be obeyed, madam," said he, coldly dropping her hand, and bowing to Mr. Montgomery. "I owe you an apology, sir, for having wished to usurp your rights."

Adeline blushed. Mr. Montgomery looked pleased; and Henry left them to offer his assistance to Eliza Tudor and Miss Montgomery. The boat was hauled within a yard of the shore, a plank was thrown across – Eliza Tudor stood on the edge of the boat, and jumped on land, but Miss Montgomery affecting fear, hung upon Henry, who was obliged to carry her in his arms to shore.

Adeline had accepted the arm of Mr. Montgomery, and they were the first who reached the fishing-house, where Lady Tudor and Mrs. Montgomery had arrived in a most pitiable condition: the small boat in which they had crossed being leaky, their petticoats were not only wet but so dirty, that Sir Griffith when he saw them advised that they should pull them off and wash them.

Mrs. Montgomery vowed that she never would go upon the water again to be made such a dirty figure – "Only see, Mr. Montgomery, what a pickle I am in – not fit for anybody to look at."

The nabob laughed, pitied, and consoled his lady, who vowed her Persian shawl was quite spoilt, for unfortunately the ends had dragged upon the bottom of the boat; and as to her silver muslin robe, she could never put it on her back again.

"La, mamma," said Miss Montgomery, "you bewail your clothes as if you had your wardrobe on your back; sure the loss is not of such great consequence to a person of your fortune."

"True, Lucretia, very true, my dear, but you know it is perdigiously disagreeable to be made in such an amazing figure."

"You should have provided against accidents," said Sir Griffith, "by dressing in things you did not care for."

"We need not expect consolation from you I am sure," replied Lady Tudor peevishly: "my feet are as wet as if I had walked through the river: I shall have a sore throat, and perhaps lose the use of my limbs."

"I wish you had lost the use of your tongue," rejoined Sir Griffith, "with all my soul; but one seldom hears of anything happening to disable that member."

"Lord, and what could a woman do without a tongue?" said Mrs. Montgomery. "I am sure such weak, delicate, defenceless creatures as we are, need have something to pertect us."

Hugh Montgomery, who always blushed when his mother attempted to speechify, endeavoured to turn the conversation by saying that Sir Owen Llewellyn and Ned Ratlin were already prepared for fishing.

"Aye, so they are," replied Sir Griffith. "Come, Montgomery, let you and I see if we can take a trout, the ladies no doubt will think them an addition to their dinner."

Montgomery would have excused himself, saying, "the ladies ought not to be left alone."

"O never fear; five women will not be as mute as fishes, I warrant," replied Sir Griffith; "they will find a way to entertain themselves no doubt."

"I love fishing of all things," said Eliza, springing from her seat. "I shall go and try whether I cannot hook a trout with the best of you. Come, Adeline, come, Miss Montgomery."

Miss Montgomery put her arm through Eliza's, but Adeline said she would remain with Lady Tudor and Mrs. Montgomery, unless they wished to be of the party.

"La yes," said Mrs. Montgomery; "I should be perdigiously pleased to make one, but only see my train, how it is drabbled; and only look at my shoes, what a colour the water has turned them; to be sure, I am not fit to be looked at by a Hottentot, I am such an amazing figure – and see how my hair hangs, all out of curl, like a pound of candles, just as strait as my finger."

"O d – n it," rejoined Sir Griffith, "settle it among yourselves; if I wait here till you are ready to start, I shall lose all the fun. Come along, Montgomery. What the devil you are not tied to your mother's apron-string are you?"

Montgomery would have stayed to attend the ladies, but Sir Griffith forcibly dragged him away with him. Mrs. Montgomery observed that Sir Griffith was perdigiously rude, and paid no regard to the ladies in the least.

"O no, madam," rejoined Eliza, "my papa is a disciple of the new school, and so far from being rude he is the very essence of good breeding. In your young days no doubt –"

"Young days!" echoed Mrs. Montgomery, "why dear me, Miss Tudor, I suppose you think then that I am as old as Mr. Mathuseler in the bible, but I assure you I was only sixteen when Hugh was born, and he was only one and twenty last birth-day."

"Pardon me, madam," said Miss Tudor, "I had no idea that you were even as old as you say you are. I only meant to observe, that some years ago I have heard it was fashionable to pay compliments, and be attentive to females; but in the present age of enlightened refinement, the gentlemen seem only to feel for themselves, without the least consideration for the ease or accommodation of the ladies, to whom it is I understand the very height of high breeding, and the true criterion of fashionable manners, to be as rude and inattentive as possible."

"Your father then," exclaimed Lady Tudor, "has reached the acme of perfection in modern tactics, but commend me to a disciple of the old school. I remember when a gentleman would have been ashamed to appear deficient in his attentions to the ladies; but heaven defend me, the world is quite altered within a very few years – no politeness, no observance; and as to Sir Griffith Tudor, but I need not mention him, for every body that knows him will acknowledge, that he is ruder than a Greenland bear."

"My father is under infinite obligations to your ladyship," said Eliza.

"O miss, you are your papa's own child," answered Lady Tudor, "modelled by himself, and from under the hands of such an artist you can be no other than a finished specimen of modern manners."

During this speech Lady Tudor had been tying on her bonnet and arranging her dress, and Mrs. Montgomery tucking up the train of her silver muslin, and wiping the ends of her elegant Persia shawl; these important matters being settled, though not to their satisfaction, the ladies set off for the trout stream, where they found all the gentlemen busily employed, except Henry, who was not with the party, and for whom Miss Montgomery anxiously inquired. They thought Henry had remained to escort them. – "As sure as I live," said Miss Montgomery, "he is in a fit of the sulks – we had a little tiff in the boat, and he is in his altitudes."

Hugh Montgomery looked at his sister, but unabashed she proceeded to say – "that she would find him if he had not drowned himself just to vex her; will you come, Miss Tudor?"

Eliza excused herself on the plea that when a reconciliation took place between parting lovers, it was better the tender scene should take place without witnesses. Miss Montgomery said she would seek him; her brother called after her. Mrs.

Montgomery laughed at what she termed "Lucretia's liveliness," and her father was too busily employed in fixing a hook to his line to notice her. Presently they heard her scream out, "There he is, I see him, stop, Mr. Mortimer." Hugh Montgomery seemed to feel the impropriety of his sister's conduct, and would have followed her, but his mother told him to let Lucretia alone, that she was every way capable of taking care of herself, and that it was perdigiously odd he should be so amazing busy in what no way concerned him; and that for her own part, she did not see no reason why people of fortin were not to please themselves, and not be tied down to mind rules, and prim behavior, just as if they had to work for their living, provided they did no harm; and if Lucretia liked Mr. Mortimer, and Mr. Mortimer was in love with her, why it was nothing so very wonderful. Mr. Mortimer was of a great family, and Lucretia was of a good family too, and would have money enough; and so what objection could there be to their marrying, if they fancied each other.

"None in nature that I know of," said Sir Owen emphatically, "if they do fancy each other."

"This is the first syllable that I have heard of it," said Mr. Montgomery.

Adeline looked with astonishment at her father. Hugh Montgomery was evidently hurt, and Eliza Tudor was obliged to bite her lips and cough, in order to stifle the laugh that struggled to have vent. Sir Griffith swore he was never better pleased than when he heard a wedding was in agitation. Eliza Tudor had caught several fish, and now protested that she was so hungry that she must go and hurry the preparations for dinner. She took the arm of Adeline, and as they walked away together, they perceived at a little distance Miss Montgomery and Henry Mortimer in earnest conversation.

"Well," said Adeline, "if this should really be a match, I shall consider it as wonderful."

Eliza laughed, and looking archly in her friend's face said, "You know it never will."

"I know!" replied Miss Llewellyn; "and pray, my dear Eliza, how long have I been gifted with prescience?"

Eliza laughingly told her she was either the greatest hypocrite or the most innocent creature in existence.

"Acquit me, I beseech you, of hypocrisy," said Adeline, "and let my innocence understand you."

"What!" replied Eliza, "will you pretend not to know that your brother Henry is desperately in love with his sister, Adeline?"

"Pshaw! this is downright nonsense," said Adeline.

"Very true, spoke like a sensible girl – love is all nonsense, and I wonder for my part how a clever young man like Henry Mortimer has fallen into this folly; but," continued Eliza, "I fancy Miss Montgomery's passion for him may find a cure by being directed to a more susceptible object, one upon whom her money, her diamonds, and expectations, may have some effect; for as to Henry Mortimer, if she had all the wealth of the Indies at her own command, I suspect he would prefer Adeline Llewellyn before her."

When the company met at dinner, which was spread under some large trees, near the fishing-house, Henry appeared unusually thoughtful, and complained of a violent headache, which he mentioned as an excuse for his apparent rudeness in absenting himself from the company. Miss Montgomery was evidently displeased. Sir Griffith threw out hints, which though meant at himself, Henry erroneously concluded were allusions to the intended marriage of Adeline and Hugh Montgomery, whom he envied, hated, execrated, and wished happy in the same moment, so strangely mingled are the feelings of the human heart, when agonized with love, inflamed by jealousy, and tortured with disappointment.

Sir Owen Llewellyn and the elder Montgomery were, aided by Sir Griffith, laying down plans for the improvement of an estate the nabob had purchased in the vicinity. Mrs. Montgomery was explaining at large to Lady Tudor the manner in which she designed to furnish her house, which was spacious and elegant, and every now and then referring to her dear Lucretia, who she said had a perdigious fine taste in fancying furniture and decorations.

Miss Montgomery was, however, too full of spleen to oblige her mother with any help on this occasion, who smiling said she supposed Lucretia had an intention to keep all her taste for ornamenting her own house, and did not wish to display it on hers. Miss Montgomery pettishly replied, that some folks did not know their own minds, and therefore other folks did not know when they might have a house of their own to decorate. "But you know, mamma, these sort of things are so natural to me, that they require very little if any consideration. I suppose Hugh may require some of my taste before I shall want it exerted for myself."

"I do not know on what occasion," replied her brother.

"Lord," said Lucretia, tossing her head, "I believe it is become quite fashionable for men to give themselves airs, and deny what their actions and looks have given proper reason to suppose; but I dare say if you, brother, think proper to follow other folks in their ways, Miss Llewellyn, no more than myself, won't break her heart."

Henry started up and flew from the table; Adeline blushed scarlet deep. – Hugh Montgomery was covered with confusion, while the inquiring eyes of Sir Owen Llewellyn, fixed on his daughter, seemed to ask an explanation of what he had just heard. The nabob, whose whole ideas were engrossed by the good things of this life, had paid attention to his bottle only; he had been indefatigable in getting money till he considered himself sufficiently rich (a point of wisdom few men arrive at), and further than indulging himself in the pleasures of the table, he seldom interfered, leaving it to his wife to bring up his daughter as she judged most proper. – His son had been educated by an uncle, whose estate he inherited; by him therefore Miss Lucretia's delicate speech had passed unnoticed entirely, had not Sir Griffith taken it up by slapping Hugh on the shoulder, and asking him whether he did not think marrying and hanging went by destiny.

Eliza Tudor felt for Adeline: she feared her father would say something that would hurt the feelings of her friend, she therefore asked if any body would run a race with her. Lady Tudor frowned, and said Eliza would always be a romp. Sir Griffith replied he loved romps, and asked who would accept her challenge. Glad of an occasion to depart, Hugh Montgomery started up, and said he would try to out-run Miss Tudor. In an instant they set off, and Eliza flying like the wind, soon outstripped Hugh Montgomery; but what was her surprise when she reached the large tree, their destined goal, to find Henry Mortimer stretched at its root, so utterly unconscious of external objects, that she had spoke to him twice before he was sensible of her presence: he rose from the earth in some embarrassment, complained of his head, and asked if they were thinking of returning home. The rest of the party had followed to see Eliza's triumph, who, turning to Hugh Montgomery, said: –

"You must not pretend to run with me: forsooth, see the vanity of men."

"I fear," replied he, in a whisper; "mine is fated to be humbled in more instances besides this."

Lady Tudor, seating herself on the root of the tree, declared that she was quite fatigued. Sir Griffith observed Eliza was as fleet as a greyhound, and would have outran the famous Atalanta herself.

"D – n it, my lady," said he, walking up to Lady Tudor, "what pretty animal is that you have got in your lap?"

Miss Montgomery shrieked out: – "O Lord! it is a nasty filthy frog." Lady Tudor and Mrs. Montgomery screamed in concert; while the poor little creature who had occasioned this alarm hopped away more frightened than themselves. Lady Tudor had an hysteric: Sir Griffith laughed immoderately, and stood looking on and enjoying the bustle, while all the party were busily employed in fetching water, applying smelling bottles, and chafing the hands and temples of Lady Tudor, who, when recovered, protested that her nerves had undergone such a shock that she should not be herself for a month.

"I hope it will confine you to your chamber," rejoined Sir Griffith, "for then I shall be released for four weeks from the doleful history of your complaints: now, who the devil, Lady Tudor, would look at your person, and your healthy looking face, and suppose you were such a cursed fool as to pretend to fall in fits at the sight of a poor harmless frog? Why d – n it you look able to assist Hercules in his labours – and to hear you talk about your weak nerves – upon my soul it is too ridiculous."

Lady Tudor, swelling with indignation, told Sir Griffith he was a brute, and she had no doubt but he put the frog in her lap on purpose to frighten her, because he knew her abhorrence of all reptiles.

"Yes, my lady, but a frog is not a reptile."

"I don't care whether it is or not," replied Lady Tudor; "you are – "

"D – n it, Winefred, I know I am the best humoured fellow in the world; if I was not, you would have laid me under the turf long ago. But I fancy we had better be off, for I see a storm brewing above, as well as this below."

"A storm," echoed Mrs Montgomery. "O, for heaven sake, Lady Tudor, let us go, I am so perdigiously alarmed at storms: you have no notion – la, I would not be on the water in that little boat if it should thunder for the world."

"We had better be gone then before the storm comes on" said Sir Owen.

And he went instantly to give orders for their departure. Mrs. Montgomery would have persuaded her daughter to have taken the third place in her chariot, but this she declined; it was then offered to Adeline and Miss Tudor, but they also preferred the boat. In a few moments Mrs. Montgomery and Lady Tudor were rowed across the narrow part of the river, and entering the carriage, were out of sight before the rest of the party embarked, who were not above a mile from the shore when the prognosticated storm came on. There was a small cabin, and to this the ladies hurried, for the lightning had frightened them from deck; here, however, the motion appeared more violent, and the closeness of the place had such an effect on Adeline, that she was obliged to venture again in the open air. Henry had stood watching the vivid coruscations, and listening to the thunder as it rolled awfully along the sky, now veiled in black and heavy clouds, and thinking of the night in Raven-hill Castle, when he had waited for the appearance of Lady Julia Nevil.

"Was I then miserable?" said he to himself; "did I think any thing was necessary to my happiness, except liberty? How vain are our thoughts, how wild our expectations: misery borrows all its pangs from comparison, happiness all its joys – is my heart more tranquil, more satisfied now?"

His thoughts were interrupted by the soft voice of Adeline, inquiring of Ned Ratlin if there was any danger.

"No, miss, no danger at all," replied he: "we have a tight boat and plenty of sea room; don't be frightened at this cap full of wind."

Henry now took the hand of Adeline, which trembled in his, and seating her beside him, threw his arm round her; while, in order to escape the sight of the lightning, her face reclined on his shoulder. Henry's heart beat tumultuously; his arm encircled the woman he adored; his cheek felt her balmy breath; it was a moment of feeling, when the soul, alive to all the finer emotions of spirit, forgets every thing but the object of its adoration. The storm, the agitated ocean, were no more recollected; Adeline was his world, and in her centred all his hopes and wishes.

"Henry, my dear, would to heaven we were safe at home," murmured Adeline, clinging closer to him, as a louder clash of thunder seemed to burst the clouds above their heads. Henry felt the quick palpitations of her heart: this was not a moment to investigate whether the motive of its throbbing was love or fear; her heart seemed to beat responsive to his: could Henry wish to be at home, to resign the exquisite pleasure of enfolding all he loved. O no, he blessed the storm; the thunder was to him the music of the spheres; the lightning that glanced along the foaming waves, the wind that rattled in the shrouds, were viewed and heard by him with sensations of rapture. His arm entwined the waist of Adeline; his hand held hers; it declined not his tender pressures; she averted not her cheek from his, while he whispered assurance of safety.

A large case bottle, which had been put in a locker contiguous to the cabin, unfortunately, not well secured, fell from its station to the floor, with so violent a crash, that supposing some dreadful disaster had happened, and that the boat was sinking, Eliza and Miss Montgomery rushed upon deck; Adeline alarmed also by the noise and screams of her friends started from the shoulder of Henry, and in a voice of terror inquired what was the matter. The gentlemen also crowded to the helm to learn the subject of alarm.

"Shiver my mizzen," said Ned, "I am sorry the brandy bottle has split; no splicing that together; gone to pieces at last, and lost all the cargo. Avast there to larboard don't you see how the boat heels; we shall be upset if we don't keep to quarters."

Henry again took the hand of Adeline, and seating her, resumed his former position.

"Yonder," said he, "are lights; they gleam from the windows of Dolgelly Castle; a short time will deprive me of the happiness I now enjoy; and I shall be obliged to resign you to Mr. Montgomery."

"And he," replied Miss Montgomery, who had contrived in the bustle to place herself next Henry, and had (both being tall) been mistaken by him for Adeline, "he will have no objection I am sure to my pleasing myself."

"Good God!" said Henry, dropping her hand, and moving his arm from her waist: "Miss Montgomery!"

"Yes, sir, Miss Montgomery; dear me you appear surprised."

"I am indeed," replied he; "after the explanation of this morning, I did not suppose – " Henry stopped.

"You may as well proceed," said she; "I understand you."

"Then it cannot be necessary for me to say any thing more," added Henry, walking away.

"You are an insensible creature," said she, "and have no heart at all."

"You are right," replied Henry, "I have no heart; but call me not insensible; I feel –"

"I would not give a fig for people to feel," rejoined Lucretia, "if they don't feel for me, and I am sure you are insensible, for I have told you plain enough."

"Spare me the pain, the misery of appearing ungrateful," said Henry; "may you be happy with some man who may be sensible of your generosity, who may be able to make you the return you wish: I confess it is not in my power."

"Lord bless me, my papa and mamma have often told me that money would purchase every thing," said Lucretia; "but they are not so wise as I thought them, for my money seems nothing in your eyes."

"And would you not despise the man," asked Henry, "to whom your money was an attraction?"

"Lord! no," said she: "if I liked him, what difference could it make to me whether he married me for the love of my person or my cash."

Henry made no reply, for Ned Ratlin had brought the boat close to shore, and told them they had better land there, than venture lower down where some ugly rocks shelved out into the water. In stepping from the boat, Adeline's foot slipped, and she would have fallen into the sea, but for Henry, who, standing to see her safe on shore, fortunately caught her in his arms: though thus providentially saved, she had not escaped unhurt; she had twisted her ankle, and was unable to walk. Sir Owen was for sending for the carriage, but Henry, taking her up in his arms, insisted upon carrying her home, urging the probability of her taking cold from waiting in the air for the carriage; besides, it was likely that the storm would end with rain. Mr, Hugh Montgomery offered to share the honour of carrying Miss Llewellyn with Henry, but this he declined, observing that he was used to the delightful office, having carried her many times.

"Yes, dear Henry, but I was not then so heavy." "Nor I so strong," replied he, proceeding with alacrity. Miss Tudor and Miss Montgomery each took an arm of Hugh Montgomery, who was no more pleased with Henry having the privilege of carrying Miss Llewellyn than his sister was with her being carried; and who believed she was not hurt bad, but only shammed a sprained ankle for the purpose of throwing herself into the arms of Henry Mortimer. Henry never halted till he had placed his lovely burden on a sofa in her dressing-room, at Dolgelly Castle; who to his tender inquiries confessed she was in great pain, but trusted that the next day she should be able to walk. Henry tenderly kissed her hand, and left her to the care of Eliza Tudor and the house-keeper, who was skilful in sprains and bruises, and who was besides the maker of an infallible embrocation.

CHAPTER IV

This life is but a chequered scene of
Disappointments.

It is not he that most deserves shall be
Most happy.

Ignorant wealth shall proudly sit in state,
While indigent merit, alas! too oft
Must humbly bend the knee, and doff the cap
To Fortune's silly favourites.

A. J. H.

DURING Adeline's confinement, which, contrary to her opinion, lasted for more than a week, Mr. Hugh Montgomery, with the entire approbation and concurrence of his parents, explained to Sir Owen Llewellyn the passion he entertained for his fair daughter, and requested his permission to address her as a lover, and respectfully solicited his influence in favour of his suit.

"On that point, my much esteemed young friend," said Sir Owen, "you must excuse me: you have my cheerful and most hearty assent in this affair, together with my warm and cordial wishes for your success; but I will never attempt to influence the inclinations of my daughter or use the authority of a parent in so momentous a business – woo her, my friend, and win her: if you are the object of her choice, be assured I shall feel most sincerely happy to call you son."

Availing himself of the worthy baronet's permission, the first day that Adeline left her apartment was the last of Hugh Montgomery's hopes: he declared the affection with which she had inspired him, in the tenderest and most respectful terms and was gently yet decidedly rejected. The mind of Hugh Montgomery was sensible and delicate; he forbore to urge a suit which he found was disagreeable, but he felt the disappointment of his hopes acutely, while his intrepid sister, undaunted by Henry's evident contempt, unrestrained by his coolness, unabashed by his repulses, declared unblushing to her mother that her affections were so deeply so unalterably fixed on Mr. Mortimer, that if she had not him for a husband, she would never, no, never, marry at all.

"What," said Mrs. Montgomery, "you, Lucretia, you die an old maid, you! why, child, this will be most perdigiously odd; why we never had a maid in the family yet – what, you sit behind hell gates to mend bachelors' breeches. Oh! dear, dear, this must never be, you die an old maid with your beauty and fortin!"

"What signifies beauty," cried Lucretia viewing herself in the glass, "or what signifies fortune if it won't buy what one wishes for; my fortune will soon be enjoyed by somebody more happy," added she affecting to weep, "for it is not likely that I shall long survive my cruel disappointment: no, no, my fond, my too susceptible heart is almost broken: my peace is destroyed, and my health is already beginning to fail."

Mrs. Montgomery's maternal feelings were shocked and alarmed at this pathetic speech of her daughter's, whom she fondly loved, and foolishly indulged: to the sobbing Lucretia she promised to spare no efforts towards facilitating her wishes, and procuring her happiness, and wondered that any man could be so amazingly stupid as to be blind and indifferent to her charms:

"However, dry your beautiful eyes, my lovely Lucretia," continued Mrs. Montgomery, "I will have a little talk with Mr. Mortimer upon this subject: I will endeavour to convince him how mad and out of the way he is, to neglect his own interest in such a foolish nonsensical manner, by not being proud and happy to think, that a nabob's daughter, a young lady of Miss Montgomery's beauty, accomplishments, and great fortin, is ready to bestow that and all her charms on him – dry your sweet eyes, my darling Lucretia; I dare say I shall bring him to his wits: I shall soon teach him to understand on which side his bread is buttered, I warrant you."

While this conversation was passing, Miss Montgomery saw Henry making towards a temple at the end of the pleasure-ground facing her dressing-room window.

"See there he goes, the charming, ungrateful insensible!" exclaimed Lucretia: "he shall, he must be my husband, or I shall die."

"God forbid," said her mother; "God forbid you should die for the sake of a man! I will see," continued she, snatching up her veil and throwing it over her head, "I will see what he is made of immediately: I will go after him, and do you, my darling, compose your spirits – do, my love, try to be easy; I will reason the matter, and argufy it with him, and no fear but my elerquence will convince him that a man may gape, and gape, and stretch his jaws many times afore fortin drops into his mouth."

Smiling at her own wit, she kissed Lucretia, bade her pray for good luck, and left her to watch from the window her steps to the temple, in hopes she would indeed convince Henry of the extreme folly of steeling his heart against the brilliant charms of fifty thousand pounds, and refusing a hand laden with the rich offerings of pearls and diamonds.

Mrs. Montgomery mounted the steps that led to the temple in great haste, having arranged to her own entire satisfaction a piece of unequalled oratory, with which she intended to subdue the obdurate heart and subjugate the feelings of Henry Mortimer.

Panting for breath, as well from the haste with which she had walked as the agitation of her spirits, she threw herself on the marble bench beside him, and seizing his hand, said, "Well, dear me, only see how fortinate I am to find you here all alone; I might have sought a hundred times for such another lucky opportunity, and have missed it."

"Have you any commands, madam, to honour me with?" said Henry rising and bowing, surprised at her hurried manner and strange address.

"Commands!" echoed Mrs. Montgomery, "no, no, my dearest Mr. Mortimer, not commands. I am comed here on purpose to persuade, to beseech, to represent, to advise, to lay before you, to reason, to convince, to demonstrate – "

"What in the name of heaven!" said Henry, losing patience and hastily cutting the thread of her eloquence.

"What indeed," replied Mrs. Montgomery; "but you male creatures are so perdigiously masculine, so robustous; but, dear Mr. Mortimer, pity, compassionate my deplorable situation. I am rich enough, not yet very old; and people say 1 am tolerably handsome; yes, yes, all the world, my dear sir, knows that I have every thing that fortin can buy – but yet, my dear Mr. Mortimer, there are indulgences, there are tender wants, sir, that do not so much depend on money, as on other people's inclinations."

Henry started; he doubted whether he heard aright: when bursting into tears she pressed his hand, and added, "Indeed, my dear sir, I am very unhappy, perdigiously miserable I do assure you."

Henry was embarrassed, and in a confused voice; stammered out "I am extremely sorry."

"Are you sorry indeed?" said Mrs. Montgomery, wiping her eyes with her lace veil; "well now that is amazingly civil and obliging; sit down then beside me, and I will tell you all my trouble."

Henry resumed his seat on the marble bench, while she drawing nearer to him, and laying her hand on his shoulder, continued, "Laws, now I always said you was a good-natured creature as ever lived, pertickerly to the fair sex; and if you are so sorry for me as you say, you will I am sure oblige, and make me happy by doing me the favour."

"Madam!" exclaimed Henry still more astonished.

"You must be sensible that a female must suffer a great deal before she can bring herself to speak her mind in downright plain terms; and a man of sense and feeling," continued Mrs. Montgomery, squeezing his hand, "a man of feeling will spare her blushes, when he knows how much her heart is inclined in his favour."

Mrs. Montgomery was still handsome; her eyes were yet brilliant, and her complexion fresh. Henry was young and sensitive; her arm rested on his shoulder, and her face was turned invitingly towards him: they were alone; her conversation had been sufficiently encouraging: his pulse beat quick – his blood rushed with velocity through his veins: for a moment yielding to the power of temptation, he was on the point of snatching her to his arms: but recollecting that she was the guest of Sir Owen Llewellyn, and a married woman, he blushed to think that he had even in idea yielded to temptation; and after a pause of a few minutes he attempted to speak:

"Do not interrupt me," resumed Mrs. Montgomery, "but let me tell you in plain English what I expect, and what I want."

Astonishing effrontery thought Henry.

"You must be very sensible, Mr. Mortimer, that my husband, the Nabob, regards you with an eye of the greatest kindness, that my son Mr. Hugh Montgomery has a most perdigious esteem, sir, for you; and oh! my dear, dear Mr. Mortimer, you have no kind of notion, no idea of the amazing regard I entertain for you."

"You do me too much honour, madam," said Henry, every instant more abashed, and astonished at what he considered her unprecedented assurance.

"Honour! fiddlestick," continued Mrs. Montgomery, "no honour at all: but sit down and answer me," for he was again rising: "sit still I say, and listen to me; what signifies or argufies all our regard for you, if you are resolved to slight and throw cold water upon the passion I come to offer you? if you are determined cruelly and barbarously to break my poor fond heart, to send me to the grave with grief and disappointment? Oh! Mr. Mortimer, consider, sir, reflect before it is too late, what an amazingly terrificatious thing it will be, to have my death lying like a great log upon your conscience."

"Good God!" thought Henry, "the woman is certainly possessed."

Again he attempted to rise with the intention of quitting the temple, but hanging upon him she began to weep, and represent the advantages that would necessarily accrue to him by obliging her.

"Is it so difficult," said she sobbing, "to comply with my desires? Cannot my tears move you to consent to my wishes?"

Henry was no more than man: honour and inclination were combatting in his bosom: – the conflict was fierce, but honour triumphed, and he replied, "I trust, madam, that no arguments, however eloquent, will have power to induce me to commit a dishonourable action; pray retire to the house and compose yourself, or suffer me to leave you."

"Not till I have softened your hard heart in my favour," answered Mrs. Montgomery: "if you knew how many nights thinking of you has kept me waking, how I have turned and tossed, and tumbled about my bed, while Mr. Montgomery has been comfortably snoring beside me, and never dreaming of my uneasiness – surely, surely you are not made of marble, you are not fixed in the cruel resolve to make me quite miserable."

"I should lament, were I the cause of misery to any one," replied Henry; "but think, madam, how your reputation would suffer, were you to be seen in your present situation: what in particular would your husband Mr. Montgomery say?"

"Why he, tender hearted soul as he is, he would say your heart was harder than iron. Mr. Montgomery has sense, and is never so pleased and happy as when his friends oblige me; he considers it a kindness done to himself. But lord, I don't want to talk about my husband, I have one still nearer my heart than him I assure you; but do, my dear Mr. Mortimer, I beseech you, do me this favour, only make me happy in this one wish, and you shall always find me the kindest, fondest – I will seek continual opportunities to – "

"This is too much, madam," said Henry, breaking from her grasp, "I am not formed of stone, and surely I must be more or less than man to stand this."

In a moment Mrs. Montgomery was on her knees before him: "Can you," said she weeping violently, "can you *seduce* me to this *perdigiously* disagreeable situation? can you refuse my request, will you have the heart to deny me?" Henry would have fled, but she held by the skirts of his coat." "Oh!" said she, continuing to weep, "that it should ever be my hard *fortin* to ask a favour of a man and be refused. Comply with my wishes, and Mr. Montgomery's wealth, all he has in the world, shall be at your command."

"How mean, how contemptible must you think me," said Henry, disdainfully endeavouring to disengage himself from her hold. "I beseech you, madam, spare yourself the trouble, and me the disgrace of listening to such degrading proposals."

"Mighty fine! mighty pretty, truly!" said the disappointed Mrs. Montgomery; "I admire you *perdigiously* for your lofty airs and *ideas*! A vastly fine joke indeed, for a man without nothing at all to *partend* to call it a disgrace to be offered a fine handsome woman, and a thumping large *fortin* into the bargain. But my dear Mr. Mortimer, you will I know consent, you will not be so hard-hearted, so amazingly unkind, as to disappoint my hopes, when I came here for no other purpose in the world than to gratify you and myself, and to make us both happy: only say the word, and I will open my arms to receive you."

"He must first strike through my heart," said Hugh Montgomery, rushing between them, with a face inflamed with rage, and limbs trembling with passion: "rise, unhappy woman, whom I blush to call mother; are you lost to all shame, quite dead to honour, entirely forgetful of your sex's delicacy? Rise from that degrading posture, and feel a little, if you have any except infamous sensations, for the disgrace you have brought upon your family."

"Disgrace! a fiddlestick's end," said Mrs. Montgomery, rising from her knees, "it is a most *perdigiously* amazing thing, Hugh Montgomery, that you must always be interfering and meddling, and putting in your oar, and *discomfronting* my schemes. Dear Mr. Mortimer, will you comply with my desires, will you do me the favour?"

"Gracious providence!" exclaimed Hugh Montgomery, blushing, and turning pale alternately, "I heard enough to make me miserable for ever before I entered....but are you indeed so infamous, so absolutely shameless, as to renew your solicitations even before my face?"

"Leave the place, sir," replied Mrs. Montgomery, darting on him a look of anger; "leave the place this instant – before your face indeed! the world is come to a fine pass truly, if children are to learn their parents what is proper and what is not. I see nothing so infamous, not I, in trying to persuade a man to his own good."

"My good!" exclaimed Henry, "my good!"

"Yes, sir, your good," rejoined Mrs. Montgomery; "though the affair would give me much pleasure, I think, would you consent, yours would certainly be the greatest."

"Mother! Mother!" cried Hugh Montgomery, "do not make me curse my existence: you are certainly mad."

"Then boy I wish you were tame," replied she; "I know well enough what I am saying, and I beg you will be gone, or hold your tongue. But, indeed, Mr. Mortimer, had you made me happy by consenting to receive the hand of my sweet lovely Lucretia, I think, sir, it could not but have conferred happiness on you; and if it had not been for this impertinent boy, I have no doubt but you would have seen your own interest: as soon as I had explained to you what I meant, you would have yielded to my wishes."

Hugh Montgomery, though relieved from a load of anguish by this explanation, yet felt hurt and mortified at his mother's ignorance and indelicacy, while Henry, scarcely able to keep his countenance, as he reflected on the way in which he had interpreted her agitation, and urgent solicitude, could only reply, "Me marry Miss Montgomery!"

"Yes, sir, my poor girl is quite miserable on your account," replied Mrs. Montgomery; "and her misery is my misery, Mr. Mortimer, for how in the world, sir, can I feel a moment's happiness while I see the beautiful bloom fading from her cheeks, and see her, as the poet says, *sitting like Mrs. Patience on emolument, and smiling at grief*? How can I know, I say, that love for you will soon make her as white as horseradish, and not feel for her sufferings? My darling girl, she does nothing but weep and lament; and how is it possible for her fond doting mother to see her in this deplorable situation, and not plead for her – is not her happiness my happiness?"

"Absurd and ridiculous," said Hugh Montgomery, "I am ashamed, hurt to the soul to hear your folly. Go, madam, go, return to the lovesick Lucretia, who I will venture to prophesy will not break her heart at Mr. Mortimer's refusal; tell her when women condescend to woo men always are insensible. Pshaw! It is inverting the order of nature. Come, Mortimer, will you walk?"

"Not till he gives me a consoling answer to carry to poor Lucretia," said Mrs. Montgomery, placing herself before the entrance; "not till he sends by me some words of comfort to raise her drooping spirits."

"I am grieved, madam," replied Henry, modestly, "that it is out of my power to accede to your wishes. I feel honoured, grateful for the distinction with which Miss Montgomery flatters me, but the affections are not to be influenced or commanded. I most sincerely lament that gratitude is all I can offer in return for her, and your generous intentions in my favour."

"And so you refuse Miss Montgomery, the daughter of an East-India nabob, with a *fortin* large enough to buy all Wales?"

"I beg, madam, you will allow me to pass," said Henry, perceiving by her voice and manner that she was much enraged. Hugh Montgomery took her hand, and would have led her from the temple, but advancing up to Henry, who stood near the window, she continued: "You, I say refuse, you who are living here, as it were, on Sir Owen Llewellyn's charity."

"Madam!" said Henry, his cheek crimsoned with indignation.

"Monstrous!" interrupted Hugh Montgomery, hurrying Henry down the steps of the temple, "for shame, for shame! I blush to call you mother."

"Blush, or not blush," bawled the incorrigible Mrs. Montgomery, "he I am sure ought to be ashamed to eat other people's bread, and refuse the means when they are offered him of buying it for himself."

Mortified at her ill success, and loudly railing against Henry's prodigious obstinacy, she returned to her daughter, who received the intelligence of her disappointment with the coarsest expressions of ill-humour, declaring that she would not stay another week at that hateful, gloomy hole, Dolgelly Castle: that she knew well enough that Miss Llewellyn, that tall, ugly, awkward maypole, had contrived by her arts to inveigle the affections of Henry Mortimer, fool as he was, and that for her sake he overlooked her superior charms. Instigated by her daughter, Mrs. Montgomery hired servants immediately, and had Glenwyn Priory put in order to receive them. As their presence was in spite of all endeavours at concealment evidently unpleasant to Henry, who spent the largest portion of every day in wandering along the sea-shore, or among the mountains, Sir Owen and Adeline did not oppose their departure, but received their parting adieus with much satisfaction, in the hope that being released from the tender importunities of Miss Montgomery, and the irksome solicitations of her mother, Henry would again be the life of their parties, and that Dolgelly Castle would have charms to win him from pondering over meandering streams, and sitting under the shade of melancholy boughs.

In furnishing and ornamenting Glenwyn Priory, Mrs. and Miss Montgomery forgot their recent mortifying disappointments; while Hugh, though he rejoiced that they were removed from a scene where their follies had appeared but too conspicuous, and happy to find that employment had detached his sister's mind from dwelling on a fanciful passion, which had rendered both her own and her mother's conduct not only highly ridiculous, but actually shameful, was yet fated to undergo the mortification of seeing the noble and beautiful structure they inhabited converted by the strange whims and out of the way fancies of his mother and sister into a residence neither fit for Christian, Pagan, nor Turk to inhabit.

In one apartment, heavy Egyptian furniture, with light fanciful Grecian adornments, exhibited a superfluity of wealth, and a poverty of taste; while the strange and ill-judged assemblage of colours, the confused jumble of metal and marble, of painting, glass, and statuary, seemed as if the fertile brain of invention had been racked and tortured to produce a ridiculous display of unmeaning profusion and tawdry affluence.

Within half a mile of the Priory lived a Mr. Jenkins with his maiden sister and niece. Mr. Jenkins had amassed a good fortune, and retired from the labours of trade to enjoy the comforts of ease and independence: a younger sister of his, caught by a handsome exterior, had privately united herself to the son of a baronet, whose dread of his family had obliged him to keep it a secret.

Mr. Percival was of a gay turn, and on the death of his wife, which happened a few weeks after his daughter was born, he entirely dropped all correspondence with his brother-in-law Mr. Jenkins, though he was mean enough to leave his child to the care of, and entirely dependent on that trader, whose situation in life his pride despised.

Rosa Percival was not beautiful, but there was an expression in her features, a gentleness in her manners, a melody in her voice, that won upon the heart of feeling: there was also a diffidence, a tender melancholy about her, not so much the impression or character of nature, as the depression of conscious dependence, that made her interesting to the soul of sensibility.

Miss Jenkins was a maiden of forty, who wished to pass for five and twenty; she was tall, had good teeth, a sharp nose, and dark bold-looking eyes; she possessed a great deal of confidence, together with a wonderful good opinion of herself, was deeply learned in the private history of every family in the neighbourhood, delighted in retailing scandalous anecdotes, though in the early part of her life she had not escaped censure; and some stories were yet remembered, and repeated by those to whom her haughty airs and unbounded licence of speech had rendered her obnoxious, that flatly contradicted her asseverations of maiden modesty, and virgin innocence. Miss Jenkins made a proud boast of the many suitors she had rejected, the thousands of love-letters she had returned unopened; and always concluded these recitals with her determination of spending her days in happy celibacy, though she was at indefatigable pains by the rolling of her large eyes, and her marked attentions and flirtations with all the young men whom chance threw in her way, to secure to herself an adorer; but alas! the only one who had any serious intentions towards her was a person nearly twenty years older than herself, a quiet plain meaning man, who had also retired from trade with a handsome income, and who, in consideration of her property, was turning it over in his mind, whether he should not make her his wife, notwithstanding he was perfectly well acquainted with her malevolent heart, and tyrannical temper, which he knew had from her very earliest years made her the terror and detestation of all who had the misfortune to be acquainted with her.

Mr. Thomas Williams was a widower, who had for many years successfully followed the occupation of a shoe-maker, from which he had retired with a good fortune. He had two sons, whom he had placed out in the world in situations to get their own living.

The family of the Jenkins and Mr. Williams were among the first to pay their respects at Glenwyn Priory, where Miss Jenkins no sooner saw Hugh Montgomery, than she thought he would be a much more desirable match than Mr. Williams; but Hugh saw enough in the mild interesting Rosa to render him totally insensible to the bold advances of her aunt, whose age he thought made her a more proper companion for his mother.

Eliza Tudor, whose passion for the ridiculous, and whose fondness for mischief had induced her to accept an invitation from Miss Montgomery, was at Glenwyn Priory when the Jenkins were first introduced, and beheld with delight the gaping wonder and vulgar astonishment they expressed, while viewing and handling the ill-chosen adornments and tasteless magnificence that crowding upon each other encumbered every apartment; but above all she anticipated the pleasure of becoming Miss Jenkins's rival, by shaking the allegiance of Mr. Williams, whom his termagant mistress seemed happy to announce to everybody, as the willing captive to her charms and graces.

Eliza would have felt happy, could she have prevailed on Hugh Montgomery to aid her in her design of tormenting the old maid; but he was of a temper too amiable, a disposition too grave to enter into the spirit of mischief; she was therefore obliged though unwillingly to plan and execute herself, nor was it long before she commenced her operations. Having witnessed some high airs played off about nothing by Miss Jenkins upon her admirer, who appeared not a little disconcerted at her conduct, she began by taking up his side of the argument, protesting to Miss Jenkins that she thought she exacted far too much when she expected an implicit acquiescence in all her requisitions.

"I expect," said Miss Jenkins, drawing up her scraggy neck, "I expect most certainly, Miss Tudor, to have my own way on every occasion, and never to meet opposition or contradiction; for if a man takes the liberty of presuming to have an opinion of his own before marriage, and while he pretends to sue for favour, why what can a woman hope for, if she is silly enough to tie herself to such a person she must be assured that he will not only command, but expect his will to be absolute law afterwards."

"Oh! Lord," replied Mr. Williams, plucking up his spirits, "I should expect to be comfortable to be certain, and if a woman is to be always disputing and thwarting and contradicting, why no such thing in the world could be the case you know, and if a man is to submit to all a woman's freaks and fancies, why he would have no sort of quiet, and would be made uncomfortable in bed and up."

"A-bed!" exclaimed Miss Jenkins affecting a blush, and hiding her face behind her fan, "I wonder, sir, you dare take such unwarrantable liberties; I am really shocked, sir, at your indelicate expressions."

"Indelicate expressions!" rejoined he, "unwarrantable liberties! why I never laid a finger upon you; and as to expressions, I will be judged by Miss Tudor here if I said a word that bordered upon indelicacy?"

"Indeed," replied Eliza "I was not sensible."

"Perhaps not, Miss, perhaps not," said Miss Jenkins violently flirting her fan, "but I absolutely blush at his gross allusion."

"Lord have mercy! I find I must take care and look at my words before I speak them," resumed Mr. Williams, "but I am determined never to be such a ninny as to give up altogether to a woman – no, no, she in her place, me in mine; hey, Miss Tudor?" winking at Eliza.

"Very right, sir, in my opinion," rejoined she, smiling kindly on him.

"Aye, aye, Miss Tudor, you are a very sensible good tempered young lady, and seems to understand the way that would make matrimony quite comfortable."

"Comfortable! contemptible," said Miss Jenkins, tossing her head, and colouring like scarlet, "comfortable! I despise the low vulgar idea. As to you, Mr. Williams, you are a poor quiet soul, you have no passion, no fire, and have no notion of what love means: so you can be quiet and comfortable, that is all the bliss you are ambitious of."

"And enough in all conscience for a honest man to wish for I think," replied he: "what did I toil, and moil, and slave, and bow, and cringe, and wait upon other folks for so many long years do you think, if it was not to be quiet, and enjoy myself and be quite comfortable at last; but lord, lord, if I was married, and got up in a morning and fetched a walk to get me an appetite, and sat down by a clean hearth, with my hot pot of strong coffee, my thick sweet cream, and my plate of nice light well-buttered rolls, what I say would become of my comfortable breakfast, if my wife was to din her ill humours in my ears, and take into her head to be cross grained, and out of temper, and find fault with me or the servants, and make herself and us quite uncomfortable?"

"Absurd and ridiculous," rejoined Miss Jenkins; "so in swilling down a pail full of strong hot coffee, and devouring a pile of well-buttered rolls without interruption, seems in your idea to comprise all the comfort of life."

"No, no, you are mistaken there I assure you," replied he, "I like to take a lunch about twelve o'clock; a nice slice of well cured, fine flavoured, smoked ham, as red as a cherry, or a cut of a fine fat round of beef, and a glass of bottled porter, smiling and mantling, and foaming and looking like a cauliflower head; and if I had a partner, for her to take a snack with me – that now would be what a body might call a comfortable thing; would it not? hey, Miss Tudor."

"Yes indeed it would," said Eliza.

"Ham!" cried Miss Jenkins turning up her sharp nose, "I detest swine's flesh, and wonder how people can have appetites gross enough to eat it."

"See the difference now of people's likes and dislikes," said Mr. Williams. "I am fond of pigmeat, a couple of full grown barn door fowls, and a delicate loin of pork roasted; or a leg boiled, with a pease pudding – famous dishes for my thinking. Do you dislike pork, Miss?" addressing himself to Eliza.

"Quite the contrary, sir," replied she.

"Yes, yes," said Miss Jenkins with an air of pique, "Miss Tudor seems determined to agree in all your comfortable tastes and notions."

"I think, madam," replied Eliza, "That Mr. Williams's notions and sentiments are so just and proper, that a woman must be unreasonable indeed who could not make herself quite comfortable with him."

Mr. Williams said he was thankful for her good opinion, and hoped she would honour him with taking a bit of dinner at his cottage the next day with a few friends, and then she should judge whether he did not live in a snug comfortable way.

"I beg leave to observe, sir, that it will not be in my power to make one of your party; and I mention it now, because you shall not," continued Miss Jenkins, "say hereafter that I disappointed you, and made you uncomfortable by spoiling your arrangements."

"Why sure, Miss Jenkins," said Eliza, "you would not be so cruel as to deprive Mr. Williams of the felicity of your company?"

"Lord bless me, Miss," replied he, "I should have been very

happy for certain to see Miss Jenkins at my cottage, to eat a bit of mutton, but then you know if she cannot make it agreeable why what in the world can be said? But perhaps she will turn it over, and by tomorrow morning she may alter her mind, and resolve to favour me with her company and be comfortable."

"You are mistaken, sir," replied she, "and I can see very plainly that you can make yourself very comfortable without me; so, sir, I leave you to enjoy yourself, as it is by no means my intention to infringe upon your comforts by obtruding my company where it is not desired; no, sir, I assure you I have always been considered a person of the first consequence wherever I have condescended to visit, and I am not yet inclined to be pushed into the background, I that have been so courted and admired, I that have refused such offers."

"Dear me, madam," said Eliza stifling a laugh, "it cannot be supposed but that a person of your time of life will always meet every proper attention and respect."

"My time of life!" screamed Miss Jenkins, her face flaming, and her eyes darting angry fires, "my time of life! really, Miss Tudor, you astonish me. Good gracious! I wonder how old you think I am: a mere girl as I am to be talked to in this affronting way! but I see which way the cat jumps. I understand your meaning, miss – you may proceed however; I shall be no impediment in your way I promise you; I never yet was without two strings to my bow: but thank heaven neither my person nor my fortune are so despicable as to leave me in the apprehension of dying in celibacy, unless it is my own will and pleasure." Saying this she flounced out of the room.

Poor Williams looked quite disconcerted; but Eliza, laughing heartily, flew to the Piano Forté, and began to play a lively air, which, acting like a charm, soon composed his irritated nerves. In a few moments he declared that Eliza played and sung like an angel, and that he felt himself quite comfortable; and that he wished he was a few years younger for her sake, as he would try to the utmost of his power to make himself agreeable to her.

CHAPTER V

The cloud capt towers, the gorgeous palaces,
The solemn temples, the great globe itself,
Yea, all which it inherits shall dissolve;
And, like the baseless fabric of a vision,
Leave not a wreck behind.

Shakespeare

Love reigns a tyrant if he reigns at all.

Barbauld

Deep in the heart Love's rankling arrow lies,
And tears of anguish dew his burning throne;
The tyrant joys to hear his victim's sighs,
Insulting mocks the woe-extorted groan.

Love, guilt, and sad remorse, divide the soul.

A. J. H.

THE happy party from Raven-hill Castle reached the classic and highly picturesque shores of Italy, after a short and delightful voyage, in perfect safety. Lady Isabella Lonsdale's delicate constitution quickly felt the renovating effect of a cloudless atmosphere, and a mild salubrious climate: her attentive and adoring husband had soon the happiness of seeing her become more blooming, more lovely than ever, while the domestic calamities which had pressed heavily on her young mind gradually yielded to Time's meliorating hand, which, stealing from sorrow its sombre garb, presents the future in brilliant hues and gay adornments. Her spirits as her health amended assumed a cheerful animated tone, and her ladyship, during her short stay at Naples, was declared the life of the Reilotto, and the spirit of the conversations; nor did the natural vivacity of Miss Lonsdale experience the least abatement; she laughed, coquetted, and sung with even more spirit than when in England; while Horatio Delamere, with all the enthusiasm congenial to his character, felt a sacred melancholy, an inspired awe steal upon his senses, as he trod the ground consecrated in his idea from having been the birthplace and residence of his most admired heroes and favourite poets. From Naples they made frequent excursions to the coast round the bay, and examined with mingled astonishment and pleasure all the rich remains of Grecian skill and Roman magnificence. To Horatio Delamere, versed in the poetic genius of the country, and deeply read in ancient history, with an enthusiastic taste for antiquity, Herculaneum and Pompeia afforded perpetual subjects for curiosity, discussion, and admiration. One moment he rapturously extolled the beautiful disposition of parts, the exquisite architecture still conspicuous in the superb though fallen monuments of grandeur, that loaded with rubbish, and half buried in the earth, everywhere met the eye, and the next deplored the shocking devastations made by war, ambition, and the convulsions of nature. While wandering near Puzzoli, Cuma, Micenum, and Baia, he lamented with feeling and energy that time should have so barbarously destroyed, should have tumbled down and crushed into ruins such stately productions of taste and invention. He grieved to see the rich and romantic coast, once the Eden of Italy, and inhabited by the warlike, the ambitious, and the wealthy, now deserted and abandoned to the poorest and most abject of God's creatures. He philosophised on the vanity of human grandeur, while he remembered those very walls that were once the pompous abodes of Cæsar, Lucilius, and Anthony, the wealthiest and most voluptuous of mankind, now the residence of a few wretched fishermen, who had constructed miserable huts, amidst the splendid ruins of what was once their country's ornament and proudest boast. He sighed as he saw the solitary fishermen sit mending their nets under the mutilated remains of marble columns and magnificent arches, that had been erected to perpetuate some deed of private virtue or public fame, that had once echoed with the choral songs of applauding thousands, and witnessed the triumphal entry of a conqueror. He moralized too on the mutability of human affairs, as he beheld the half-naked wretches devouring their scanty morsel on the very spot that had once been sprinkled with copious libations of rich wine, and sustained the weight of tables, groaning with luxurious banquets. He shuddered as he beheld the desolation of palazzos, that had once exhibited scenes of the most refined voluptuousness and wanton profusion.

From Naples they made an interesting tour to Palermo, where they soon formed such agreeable society, and found in the place itself so much to entertain and attract, that many months stole away, and they had still no idea of quitting Sicily. The character of the Sicilians, as portrayed by the poets, is soft and amorous, nor had Horatio Delamere been long among them, before he received many specimens of their aptitude to love. His handsome person and elegant address had rendered him so great a favourite with the ladies, that his time was absolutely occupied in pleasurable adventures; none of which, however, had interest enough to make an impression beyond the moment in which he was engaged in them, till one night on the Marine he was introduced to the Marchesa della Rosalvo: he had been listening to music of the most melting tender composition; and his mind, full of thrilling sensibility, was softened to receive the impressions she was so well calculated to make.

It was clear moonlight; a soft balmy gale wafted aside the transparent veil that partially concealed her beautiful face: her figure was tall and graceful, but her voice, her melodious voice, in silver tones found its way to his heart. As they walked, she leaned upon his arm: her touch had the power of electricity; he felt it violently throbbing in his bosom, and rushing with velocity through his veins. When they reached the end of the walk, and lingered near the temple where the musicians assembled, a symphony was played, so entrancingly melodious, that their feet became rooted as it were to the spot, and this was succeeded by a full toned mellifluous voice, that sung with feeling and taste: –

In vain thy power, O, love, I brave,
    And boast the freedom of my heart;
Sunk at thy shrine a fetter'd slave,
    Abject I kiss thy burning dart.

By all my tears, my silent woe,
    My sighs that load the midnight air,
O, make my bosom's tyrant know
    Some portion of my wild despair.

O, make the eyes whose sunny beam
Can tender tales of feeling speak,
Like mine with tears of passion stream,
Like mine repose that flies them seek.

As the strain died away, the marchesa heaved a sigh, and Delamere saw a tear glitter on her cheek. His bosom responded the sigh, and he would gladly have dried the tear with his lips. Presently with a sweet smile she said: –

"This kind of music always makes me melancholy: we Sicilians are passionately attached to the melody of sweet sounds, and give up ourselves to its enchantments, till we are hurried beyond the precincts of reason, and suffer imagination to soar into ideal regions. You think it silly and ridiculous to see me so moved."

"No," replied Delamere, "quite the contrary: I am myself an enthusiast in all that relates to music, and reverence the effect it has upon you, as the sure indication of sensibility and tenderness."

From music the subject imperceptibly changed to love; the rnarchesa confessed that she believed the softness of the climate, together with the tender and impassioned language of their poets, rendered the Sicilians but too susceptible of the passion bred in the very region of romance: their hearts imbibed tender sensations before reason was sufficiently matured to resist the dangerous invader.

"No people on earth," added she, "paint or feel love like the Sicilians; none so well know the anguish of falsehood and disappointment."

"Oh," said Horatio, fixing his eyes on the marchesa, "why cannot love be mutual and lasting."

"Because," replied the marchesa, "man is prone to inconstancy: possession of the beloved object, in the bosom of a female, increases affection, while in that of a man it produces satiety: the beauty of an angel, once become familiar to his eye, loses its attraction, and she who was once worshipped as a goddess in a short time becomes even less than mortal woman."

"Is this not too severe a censure?" asked Horatio.

"No," replied the marchesa; "unhappily it is but too just; man assails the credulous ear of woman with adulation and professions, talks of his sufferings, and vows eternal constancy; but no sooner does she yield to his seductions, than he becomes cold and indifferent, while every passing hour adds to her affection, her adoration; he flies to seek pleasure in variety, and she becomes a prey to grief and disappointed love. Such is man," continued the marchesa, "here in Sicily, and, however the character of his countenance may alter in other countries, that of his heart and disposition are nearly the same I believe all over the world."

"And are women entirely exempt from the vice of inconstancy?" said Horatio.

"No, not entirely," replied the marchesa; "among a thousand instances to the contrary you may perhaps find one woman inclined to change, but this is from example: woman is exactly what man makes her; if ever she is unfaithful, it is from the wish of being revenged on him who has tortured her with his infidelities."

Horatio smiled, and pressing her hand said: –

"Sure no man could be so senseless, so ungrateful, as to be false to you, for where could he hope to meet – "

"Hold," cried the marchesa; "I find you don't know that I

have a husband, who can find charms in any female face, so it be not mine."

"Married!" exclaimed Horatio, in a tone of disappointment and surprise.

"Even so," replied the marchesa, "but we will if you please change the subject, to me the most unpleasant one in nature; yet, if you are at all interested in my history, unfortunately every inhabitant of Palermo can relate it."

At the end of the walk some ladies joined them, and after a few more turns Horatio put the marchesa into her carriage, and obtained permission to inquire after her health in the morning. Before he left the Marine he informed himself of her history, and lamented to find that a woman so beautiful, so interesting, had in reality so much reason to accuse man of inconstancy. He went home in a state of unusual agitation; and when he threw himself into bed, her soft voice still vibrated on his ear, and her person, radiant in beauty, floated on his imagination.

"False to such a creature!" continually burst from his lips: "sure she was created to be adored! to fix the wavering mind of man, and teach him fidelity."

Sleep never visited his weary eye-lids, and he waited with restless impatience for the hour to arrive when he might with propriety visit her. If he had been charmed with her on the preceding night, how much more lovely did she appear when introduced to her boudoir. He found her wrapped in a simple robe of muslin, her glossy brown tresses unadorned, and straying in wanton ringlets over a forehead and neck of snowy whiteness: her drawing materials were before her; she had been finishing a ruin near Palermo; and Horatio discovered that to personal beauty she combined the most exquisite accomplishments. He was so enchanted with her manners, so delighted with her conversation, found in her so much to admire, that in spite of his efforts to the contrary (remembering she was married) he found himself irresistibly attracted, and fascinated by the thousand charms and graces diffused over her person and beaming from her mind. Every morning, though he resolved to deny himself the dangerous pleasure of gazing upon and listening to her, he found himself in her boudoir. Every evening, without intending it, he was beside her at the Opera, wandering with her on the Marine, or leaning over her harp, and listening to her syren warblings, or drinking from her dark melting eyes deep draughts of intoxicating delirious passion.

Horatio Delamere had taste to admire beauty meet it where he might; and a variety of opportunities had occurred since his residence in Palermo to convince him that the voluptuous air of the climate diffused its warmth and softness to the dispositions of the fair Sicilians; but the gaudy fluttering ephemera, the pretty smiling, insipid nothings, that hovered round and lisped, and lolled, and languished, and displayed their various beauties and graces to attract his notice and enslave his affections, failed in their attempts: his ideas were too refined, too delicate, his mind far too exaltedly organized to be attracted by common attainments, or interested by common forms: he was disgusted by boldness and levity, he despised affectation and frivolity, and though his passions were sometimes awakened and inflamed, yet his heart, absolutely unmoved, remained perfectly calm and at ease. The Marchesa della Rosalvo's superior attainments, her highly cultivated mind, her elegant manners, her refined conversation, but above all the witchery of her smiles, and the melting expression that floated in her lucid eyes, had spoken a language his could not fail to understand. Sparkling with animation when their bright rays rested on his face, or languishing with swimming tenderness, when their averted glance seemed to retire from his impassioned gaze, they seemed to penetrate his soul; they were not to be resisted: and to render her still more seducingly attractive, she united to a fine and graceful person all the charms and fascinations of genius and highly cultivated talents; and though a few years older than Horatio, her beauty, her sensibility, her enchanting smiles, that disclosed to view teeth of unrivalled whiteness, the voluptuous air that breathed over her whole person, were too powerful assailants to be withstood by a young man of ardent feelings, scarcely twenty-two, an age when head-strong passion amidst the overwhelming storm of inclination neither hears nor regards the admonitions of reason and prudence.

The Marchese della Rosalvo had been a remarkably handsome man; his figure was tall and commanding; and though a life of dissipation and irregularity had taken much from the beauty of his features, yet he still retained an eye of fire and an air of dignity. The marchese had married a rich heiress of the Duke Campeli, because he had fancied himself in love with her; nor was it without much repugnance he brought his mind to submit to matrimonial trammels; but Celestina's proud relatives, her high rank in life, left him without hope of obtaining her on easier terms; he therefore sighed and vowed, wooed her, and was accepted. Their marriage was celebrated with pomp and magnificence, while all Palermo prophesied that the handsome Marchese Rosalvo, though he had been a great rake, would now become a convert to the charms and virtues of his beautiful bride. But alas! how were they mistaken! for a few months indeed her beauty, her captivating manners, her talents, had made him all her own; but the calm of matrimony, undisturbed possession, was not suited to the wild capricious disposition of the marchese; he existed but in intrigue and adventure, and the lovely, the interesting, the all accomplished Celestina had soon the misery of finding herself neglected by the man on whom she had bestowed her virgin affections, and to whom she had brought immense wealth. In the sight of the marchese every woman possessed more charms than his wife; and in less than two years after their marriage, though they inhabited the same palazzo, they had separate apartments, a separate establishment, and very seldom met except at places of public entertainment, or in large parties. He was rich, and indulged to excess in every pleasure that luxury could invent or wealth procure, leaving the marchesa to console herself in any way most agreeable to her own fancy, seldom obtruding in her parties, and exhibiting on all occasions the most fashionable indifference to her pursuits, her company, and her conduct.

For a length of time the young and deserted marchesa shut herself up from the world, received no company, never went abroad, and spent her lonely hours in lamenting the loss of those affections that constituted the bliss of her existence. At length, urged by the repeated remonstrances of her family and friends, she again mixed in society, but the "arrow was in her heart;" she often smiled with a tear in her eye, and frequently retired from gay scenes of mirth and revelry, to vent the anguished complaints of disappointment and regret, while her gay dissipated husband, pursuing his career of profligacy, neither felt for the misery he occasioned, nor condescended even to endeavour to conceal his infidelities, At length wounded pride triumphed over tenderness; the marchesa began with assuming indifference, and in the end actually felt it; she sometimes indeed heaved a sigh as she remembered past happiness, but it was no longer a sigh of anguish – no, it was a respiration of pity for the man who had dashed real felicity from his lips, to indulge in licentiousness and vice. The terms on which the marchesa lived with her husband were well known to all Palermo; and many were the sighing adorers that, hovering round Celestina, would have persuaded her to love and revenge; but the object had not yet appeared that was again to awaken in her bosom the flame of love. She listened indeed to the ardent speeches that were poured into her ear by sighing lovers; she suffered them to attend her to public places, and her vanity (for what woman is without a portion of vanity) was pleased to discover that other men adored and extolled the charms her husband disregarded. The marchesa's heart was good, her temper sweet, and her disposition amiable; but unfortunately she had sensibility: the fondness she had once felt for her husband, the tenderness he might have possessed, scorned and thrown back upon herself, her exquisite talents, the luxurious style in which she lived, the adulation she continually heard, inflamed passions naturally warm, and in Horatio Delamere she found an object to fill the aching vacuity in her bosom that her unkind husband had made. Yielding to the pleasure his society afforded her, she felt not, thought not, of her danger, till the uneasiness she experienced in every little absence told her that he had established an empire in her bosom, too strong, too powerful, for the control of reason.

"And why," said the marchesa, "should I tremble at the discovery of my passion? Is he not formed by the partial hand of nature to captivate the eye? Has not heaven given to his mind every excellent endowment? Is he not worthy to be loved? Oh, yes! in his society my talents will be improved, and my virtue strengthened, for he will never make me blush while I remember the fond regard he has inspired."

So thought, so spoke the marchesa. Seated at an open lattice with Horatio, she was one evening watching the moon's course over the glittering vault of Heaven, when her cheek accidentally touching his, thrown off his guard, he suddenly pressed his lips to it: the marchesa started from her seat, and flying to her harp, began running her fingers over the strings. At first the air was imperfect and disordered, but by degrees she regained composure, and began singing a little plaintive ballad, expressive of the dangers of love. Horatio had sunk on his knees before her: as her eyes encountered his beseeching glance, her voice ceased: she held out her hand to him; he pressed it to his heart, to his lips – the marchesa fell on his neck.

"Horatio, dearest Horatio!" murmured from her lips.

"Thine, adored Celestina, thine for ever," replied he as he strained her yielding form in his arms, as he pressed his glowing lips to hers. Every day seemed to add fresh strength to their passion; each seemed to find in the other a congenial soul; the same wishes, the same tastes, the same sentiments, seemed to actuate them, and in this delightful intercourse weeks and months stole away unheeded; the lapse of time was unthought of, while the fascinations of love, of poetry, music, and painting, held their enchanted senses in a delirium of pleasure.

Captain Lonsdale beheld this attachment with much secret uneasiness; he wished to dissolve so dangerous a connection;

he knew that had the marchesa been at liberty, Lord Narbeth would not have approved Horatio uniting himself to a foreigner, and he foresaw much trouble would result from the power, the unbounded influence so lovely a woman had over his heart. Whenever their return to England was mentioned, Horatio always said that he could not leave Sicily; that as yet he had not collected half the information he wanted, nor seen half the curiosities of the country; that he had not yet visited Mount Ætna, nor measured the gigantic chestnut trees described by modern travellers, nor – "

"Yet," interrupted Miss Lonsdale, laughing, "felt weary in the company of the Marchesa della Rosalvo."

"You say right," replied he: "possessed of so many exquisite accomplishments, mistress of such various powers to please, in her society weariness can never enter; but you are mistaken in supposing – "

"I suppose," resumed Miss Lonsdale, "that what are called the rosy bands of love, are in reality – strong iron chains; and these I suspect the marchesa has so wound round your heart that you cannot escape."

Horatio looked serious.

"Come, come," continued she, patting his shoulder with her fan, "if you are in love at last I am sorry for you, and glad too now I think of it, for I smiled and simpered, and did all I could to touch your heart, but somehow you contrived to shield it so effectually that I could never find a vulnerable spot for the life of me."

"Heaven forbid," said Lady Isabella, "that our dear Horatio should be so unfortunate as to love a married woman: what must be the consequence of so hopeless a passion? – Youth spent in despair, health destroyed, and perhaps death."

"What a melancholy retrospection," said Horatio kissing her hand; "but you are too apprehensive, my lovely cousin; fear not for me."

"Death indeed!" exclaimed Miss Lonsdale, "no, no – men never die for love! what Shakespeare says is strictly true, men have died, and worms have eaten them, but not for love."

"Perhaps they may not actually die for love," replied Captain Lonsdale; "but, my volatile sister, be assured many a man, and woman's life too, has been made miserable through indiscreetly placing the affections on improper or unworthy objects; many a noble heart has been tortured by disappointment, and many a highly gifted mind been fated to experience misery, from the tyranny and caprice of love."

"Good heaven! the souls of all my tribe defend from love," said Miss Lonsdale, throwing herself into a theatrical attitude; "but I pray very ill," added she, "for here are you and Lady Isabella, a pair of fond lovers, whose affection I hope will never know diminution; I therefore only pray for Horatio and myself."

"You need not trouble heaven on my account," rejoined he: "rather than not feel the passion, I am content to suffer all its agonies."

"More simpleton you then," rejoined she; "would it not be far better to have your heart at ease, to be able to take your dinner with a good appetite, and pass your nights in undisturbed repose, than be suffering under all the tricks and mischief that little blind urchin, Master Cupid, may please to play upon you?"

"But if you are never in love, of course you will never marry," said Lady Isabella.

"Pardon me there," replied she, "it is by no means my intention to die an old maid, I assure you."

"What, marry without love!" exclaimed Lady Isabella.

"Yes," said Miss Lonsdale, "and I consider it far the wisest way: lord, lord, if I were to love a man, I should never be able to manage him. Don't lift up your eyes, child, nor your hands, brother; I repeat manage him! – if a woman is silly enough to love her husband, why she yields up even her own wishes to his, submits to all his opinions, and his will becomes her law."

"And ought it not to be so?" asked Lady Isabella. "Oh! my dear Edward," said she, turning to her husband, "so may I ever love you; may your opinions ever govern mine, and your will be my law." Captain Lonsdale threw his arms round her, and affectionately kissed her. – Miss Lonsdale called them silly, soft souls.

"I fancy," said Horatio, "you would not have much objection to be in a similar situation: come," continued he, "my pretty cousin," taking her hands, "look in my face, and answer truly to the questions I shall ask."

"What impertinence!" cried she, struggling.

"Nay, nay," said he, "resistance will avail you nothing: hold up your head, my dear, and reply with sincerity: I know the Count Respino is your declared admirer: what do you think of him?"

"That he has but little wealth, less wit, and admires his own person too much to feel any very particular regard for mine."

"Very well," replied Horatio.

"Then the Marchese Salerno is far too learned for me; I should have Greek for breakfast, Latin for dinner, and Hebrew for supper, if I were to marry him." Horatio laughed.

"Well, what do you think of the Duke Medina?"

"Why I think that he looks like a man anatomised; but yet I think, if he would give me the key of his iron chest, though he is a notorious miser, I would venture to take him for better for worse, in the hope of being able to circulate those enormous piles of gold of his, that have never seen sun or moon since they came into his possession. But as this is rather a hopeless matter, old habits being inveterate, what say you to the young handsome gay Count di Valdia?"

"No, no," replied Miss Lonsdale, "I protest against him most seriously; he is too much of my own disposition for me to have the smallest chance for happiness; our wits would be for ever jangling, our spirits mounting into flame, and the vivacity which if enjoyed only by one would form the harmony of our lives, possessed by both, instead of enlivening us, would create jars and discord; each would be striving to outdo the other in smartness and repartee, and in less than a year our spirits would be worn out, and one or both of us become hypochondriac."

Lady Isabella and Captain Lonsdale laughed heartily, while she, assuming an humble air, curtsied low, and prayed, having gone so well through her examination, to be released.

"Not yet, my dear; not yet," replied Horatio. "I confess you have hitherto answered like an ingenuous good girl, but I have yet another gentleman to propose, and having replied to him, you shall be restored to liberty. What, if the old Duke of Leonti was to offer himself?"

"Why I would not sacrifice myself to his gout, phthisics, and palsy, even to be made a dutchess."

"But if his grandson," said Horatio, looking archly in her face, which was dyed with crimson blushes, "if his grandson was to say lovely Emily, I offer you my heart and hand."

"Why I really believe," replied she, "I should accept them: to be the Countess Miraldi at present, with the expectation of being a dutchess in future, would be no bad establishment I assure you."

Horatio caught her in his arms, and in spite of her struggles obtained two or three kisses, which he told her he bestowed upon her as a reward for her sincerity.

"I would not have you believe though that his aquiline nose and fine shaped legs have won my heart; no such thing, believe me," said Miss Lonsdale; "but as one must marry some time or other; and if I was obliged to take a Sicilian husband, and all those were to offer that you have mentioned, I believe I should choose him as the least exceptionable."

"I admire your discernment and discretion," rejoined Horatio, "and have some idea that the Count Miraldi, though rather grave himself, has no dislike to your vivacity."

"Ah, dissembler!" said Lady Isabella, "you are caught at last, are you? you that have so much and so often derided love."

"Aye," replied Miss Lonsdale, "and deride it still, when carried to that romantic excess as to make those under its influence deport themselves like Bedlamites, Admitting that I do feel some preference for the count, whom I confess I consider a man of merit, believe me I am not sufficiently in love to turn poet, and make miserable rhymes in praise of his arched eyebrows, to shun the comforts of sleep, and waste the hours of night in the melancholy occupation of watching the moon. I shall not grow pale with loss of appetite, nor sink my spirits with ideal fears and jealous apprehensions, I shall not lose my relish for dancing, though the Count Miraldi may chance to choose another partner. I shall not relinquish the desire of showing my wit, nor omit any occasion that may occur of exercising it upon him in particular."

"Bravo!" said Captain Lonsdale.

"Bravissimo" exclaimed Horatio; "this is being happily in love, and absolutely reverses Othello's declaration, for 'tis loving wisely, and not too well; it deserves to be recorded, that posterity may learn a woman once loved rationally."

"And I wish," replied Miss Lonsdale, "that my sentiments could be recorded, as a check upon men's vanity, that they might know it was not in their power to make all women fools."

When Horatio retired to his apartment, he felt that love was with him a tumultuous passion, pervading his frame at times with the most rapturous feelings of bliss, at others torturing him to agony. He dared not think, because the monitor within told him that he, indulging in guilty pleasures, had no right to expect the peace of virtue, yet, could he abandon her who had sacrificed her richest possession to him, her honour, who loved him beyond fame? Oh! no, and if at some moments reason, assuming her power over his mind, made him resolve to break the dangerous connection he had formed, no sooner did he see the marchesa, than relapsing into fondness, he became more devoted, more enchanted with her beauty than before, and found her spells wound more closely round his heart. Every letter he wrote to his friend, Henry Mortimer, was filled with praises of the fascinating marchesa, expressed his adoration of her charms, and the strength of his attachment: the replies of Henry to these letters were not calculated to please Horatio, or calm his perturbed spirits; for Henry in strong terms represented the crime of loving a married woman, let her situation be what it might; bade him beware of seducing her affections and plunging her in guilt, unless he wished to devote himself to perpetual remorse. He conjured him to return to England, and in the midst of friends who loved him forget an attachment which promised nothing short of wretchedness.

"Oh!" cried Horatio, as he read the advice and remonstrances of his friend, "oh! that it was in my power to obey the friendly injunction! – Abandon Celestina! – impossible! Henry, Henry, I wanted thy fortitude, thy forbearance: I have already plunged her in guilt. She loves me, exists but for me; and can I resolve to tear myself from her, who, confiding in my truth and honour, has yielded all to me? No, divine Celestina! my wishes, my soul are governed by thee; thou art the arbitress of my fate. Leave Sicily! – no, no, it is impossible. Every deviation from virtue is followed by remorse. – Even in the magic circle of pleasure, the upbraiding voice of conscience will be heard; and 'midst the roses fierce repentance rears its snaky crest."

In vain did the marchesa seek to extenuate her own dereliction of virtue, by reflecting on the atrocious conduct of her husband: it would not do; remorse pursued her even in her most rapturous moments. She loved Horatio Delamere with the truest, most ardent affection; yet she blushed in his presence, and found that "what is in its nature wrong, no words can palliate, no plea can alter." – The void in her bosom was indeed filled, but not by happiness; the love she sighed for had destroyed her honour, and every criminal indulgence crimsoned her cheek with shame, and suffused her eyes with tears of bitter though unavailing remorse.

CHAPTER VI

Joined, not matched,
Some sullen influence, a foe to both,
Has wrought this fatal marriage to undo
Us: mark but the very frame and temper
Of our minds, how very much we differ.
E'en this day, that fills thee with such ecstasy
And transport, to me brings nothing that should
Make me bless it, or think it better than
The day before, or any other that
In the course of time has duly ta'en
Its turn and is forgotten.

Rowe

SIR OWEN LLEWELLYN saw with infinite concern the sunk eyes, the altered mien, and pale dejected countenance of Henry Mortimer; that countenance which only a few months before exhibited the bright and ruddy glow of health, those eyes that had sparkled with cheerful animation. To all his anxious and affectionate inquiries Henry constantly answered that he was well; but the solicitude of Sir Owen Llewellyn was not to be so answered or so satisfied. He saw him hourly looking worse, and growing more melancholy; he plainly perceived there was an hidden malady, a something that seemed to tremble and shrink from inquiry; but of what nature it was he could not even guess, though he saw it lay with an oppressive weight upon his mind.

Sometimes he fancied that Henry's disappointed hopes

relative to his grandfather, Lord Dungarvon, pressed upon his spirits and undermined his health; but so well was the secret guarded, so closely locked within the foldings of his bosom, so much and so constantly did he labour to conceal his feelings, that it was utterly impossible even for the solicitous eye of friendship to discover that love was sinking him to the grave.

After a variety of expedients had been proposed for relieving his melancholy, Sir Owen mentioned a change of scene, and they began to make hasty preparations for a tour through South Wales, when the frame of Henry, unequal to the agonizing conflicts of his mind, became suddenly so languid, that it was impossible to think of pursuing their intended excursion.

The faculty Sir Owen Llewellyn called in pronounced his disorder an affection of the nerves, and wisely attributed his illness and sufferings to his long and disagreeable confinement in Raven-hill Castle.

Adeline's tender and compassionate disposition evinced itself in a thousand nameless attentions to the invalid; but this was only pouring oil upon flames; her tenderness increased his passion, and redoubled pangs already past endurance.

One morning during his confinement (for he was now unable to stir abroad) Sir Owen softly entered his apartment, and finding he slept, sat silently down on a chair by the side of his couch, to watch his slumbers. – He seemed restless and uneasy, and his sleep far from tranquil and refreshing. After some time Henry started, and drawing a deep and heavy sigh, said, "How much longer shall I linger in this state of misery? – How much longer live only to feel regret? Adeline," continued he, "dear angelic Adeline! you may marry, yes, you certainly will marry, but long before you become a bride my miserable existence will have terminated. Generous, worthy Sir Owen Llewellyn!" resumed he, after a pause of a few moments, "he little guesses the state of this rebellious heart – he thinks not that I adore his angelic daughter, that I am dying for her. No, no, no, never be my aspiring passion revealed – hid, for ever hid in the closest recesses of my bosom, let the secret be buried with me. Adeline shall have a wealthy husband, shall be great and happy, when this heart shall have ceased to throb, these pulses to beat – when the miserable Henry sleeps in the humble grave of his mother. Oh that mother! – she too was the victim of love, – and so, alas! shall her devoted offspring be!"

Astonished at this discovery, and inexpressibly shocked at his despondency, Sir Owen, without speaking, softly stole from the room, and after remaining for some moments with his hand pressed upon his forehead in meditation, he exclaimed, "Ah! how blind must I have been not to have seen this! – Oh! why did he not confide his secret to me? – He ought to have understood my principles, and above all, my true affection for him. Wealth! greatness! high-sounding words indeed, but not always the purchasers of happiness. But sure it is not yet too late to save him. – He must not, shall not die. Adeline will restore my Henry. Rank! splendour! be these the objects of Lord Dungarvon's pursuit; my ideas of happiness are not, I thank heaven, modelled according to the grovelling maxims of the world, and in uniting my child to a man of honour, of principle, and of real worth, I shall ensure her that felicity so seldom found with titles, or annexed to greatness: but I will consult the feelings of Adeline."

Sir Owen went immediately in search of his daughter, to whom, in the most delicate and pathetic terms, he disclosed the important discovery he had just made; he expatiated on the great merit of Henry's honourable concealment of his passion, a concealment that had nearly destroyed his life, and spoke in high terms of his virtues and his merits.

Adeline's beautiful countenance underwent many changes while she listened to her father's recital of Henry's sufferings, and eulogium on his virtues, to which her heart bore testimony; while to the affecting description of his long concealed love, and its fatal consequences, she gave many tears. Her father drew hope from her tears, which he wiped away, and tenderly pressed her in his arms, while he conjured her to give Henry's passion a serious consideration; to remember his worth, the brilliant attainments of his mind, and the graces of his person, and if her heart really felt no preference in favour of another, which she had so often and so seriously assured him, to bestow it generously on Henry, so very worthy the possession – on him scarce less dear to his affections than herself.

Adeline was silent: she hid her face in her father's bosom, and wept bitterly.

"Adeline, my beloved child!" said Sir Owen, alarmed at her extreme agitation, "what means these tears, this excessive disorder? Surely you can have no concealments with your father, your friend. You cannot sure have deceived me in saying your affections are disengaged? Speak to me ingenuously, my child: relieve me from the tortures of suspense, and decide on the fate of poor Henry, whose life is in your power."

Thus entreated, Adeline raised her head from her father's shoulder. She smiled through her tears, and fervently pressing his hand to her lips said –

"No, my dear sir, I have never yet deceived you in any instance. My heart is indeed disengaged, entirely free – so free – but you shall hear its most secret sentiments. I love Henry Mortimer with the affection of a sister: brought up from my earliest remembrance together, I have never taught myself to look upon him in any other light than that of a brother. I am sensible of his worth; I justly appreciate his talents: but ought not the heart to feel warmer emotions than those I profess towards the object selected for a partner for life? I could be pleased to see Henry the husband of any amiable woman who was worthy of him; I should rejoice in his felicity; but indeed, my dear, dear father, it never once entered my imagination that I was at all necessary to his happiness, or that he was formed to constitute mine; for nothing that I feel for Henry bears the slightest comparison with what I have heard or read of love."

"I see, my dear artless Adeline," replied Sir Owen, smiling and pressing her hand, "I see you have borrowed your ideas of love from the fanciful and inflated descriptions of romance, ideas, my child, never realised, except in the fevered brain of the poet or the visionary; for heaven be praised, there are but few fated to feel the exquisite misery they undergo, or fancy that they undergo. In persons of uncontrolled habits, who have shook off the wise rule of reason, who yield themselves unresistingly to the dominion of strong and vehement feeling, love is most certainly a feverish, delirious, and despotic power: sweeping propriety and discretion before it, like an overwhelming torrent; but in well regulated virtuous minds it assumes a gentler rule, and divested of all its fiercer attributes, becomes a more refined a tenderer sort of friendship. Such love as this I think you feel for Henry, and such a mild and temperate passion I trust will ensure you far greater happiness, more permanent felicity, than if you were to have your heart lacerated, and your feelings agonized with excess of sensibility. But tell me, Adeline, are you stoic enough to see him die? Can you know that a noble feeling heart is breaking for you, and not wish to preserve a being so dear, so valuable?"

"My father! my dear father! do not break my heart also," said Adeline, violently weeping.

"Heaven forbid, my child," replied Sir Owen, "that I should wound your feelings in the slightest degree, or make a request which it would give you pain to comply with; but the more I consider this young man's inestimable qualities, the more I become attached to him. His brave unfortunate father was my earliest, dearest friend, and to his dying mother, the loveliest, gentlest, most amiable of women, I solemnly promised to be a father to Henry Mortimer. – Was your heart attached to another, never would I urge the suit of Henry; but as you declare its affections are actually unbiassed, I would wish, dear Adeline, child of my affection, to direct them where they may rest in full and perfect security of happiness, in the bosom of truth, generosity, and honour."

Their conversation was here interrupted by a servant hastily summoning Sir Owen Llewellyn to the chamber of Henry, who had fainted during his absence.

Adeline, left alone to her reflections, began minutely to scrutinize her heart, to consider what her father had said concerning the effect of love on different minds, yet in spite of all her reasonings, she was as still perplexed and undecided as at first. She remained unconvinced, nor could she bring herself to believe that her sentiments for Henry Mortimer amounted to anything beyond esteem, or that his graces, his merits, and accomplishments, his acknowledged virtues, had inspired a warmer feeling than friendship. Yet she felt it her duty to obey her father, and she thought too that loving no other she might indeed be happy with Henry Mortimer; nay, she believed she must, for Heaven would bless the motives that induced her to bestow her hand according to the wishes of a parent, whose every moment had been spent in fond indulgences of her, and whose every thought had been employed in forming schemes for her interest or her pleasure. Was it possible that so good, so wise a father could err? Could he, so experienced, be deceived in the paths which he assured her led to future felicity? Oh! no, no, whatever he determined must be right. Thinking thus, she resolved that he should guide her opinions and actions, that she would yield implicit obedience to his wishes. Fixed in these determinations, Adeline followed her father to Henry's chamber: as she approached, he met and led her towards Henry, who in a faltering hesitating voice said,

"Your father, dearest Adeline, has accidentally discovered the secret woe that preys upon my life. – Ah! how was it possible to be in the daily, hourly contemplation of so much beauty, to be a witness of such transcendent perfections, and not adore them? Yet I never breathed in mortal ear my presumptuous passion: a passion nourished without hope, for I never for a moment believed that I could influence you in my favour; I never wished it; I considered you above my humble fortunes: I wished not to connect you with a being, deserted and abandoned by his proud family. Say then you pity, and forgive me: and soon, very soon, this heart shall forget its tumultuous throbbings, soon shall the long sleep of death peacefully close these weary eyes, and the turf hide the wretched Henry and his obtrusive sorrows."

Henry shed no tears, but Sir Owen and Adeline both wept.

"Forbear, dear Henry," said she, bending over him, "forbear to speak thus despondingly; my father cannot part with his son, nor I with my brother – you must not talk of dying."

"Alas!" said Henry, pressing her hand to his pale lips, and sighing heavily. "Alas! the happy tranquil days are past: when in believing Adeline my sister, my mind felt placid, and satisfied, nor thought nor wished for bliss beyond the joy of that relationship – that peaceful period has long been at an end: it has given place to doubts, to fears, to restless jealousies. I am no longer contented with being distinguished as the brother of Adeline. – O! no, most worshipped! most adored! a warmer, tenderer sentiment succeeds; but I see I distress you; tears are in your eyes: nay, weep not, Adeline. I would not create an uneasy thought, give a pang to that gentle bosom to be master of the universe. Go, dearest, loveliest of women, leave this melancholy couch."

"Nay, Henry, send her not away," said Sir Owen.

"Why, sir, should she stay," replied he, "to be made miserable by my complaints? My sufferings find no alleviation by creating unavailing sorrow in the bosom of another: every tear she sheds falls like burning lead upon my heart. O God!" cried he, raising his eyes to Heaven, and clasping his hands with fervour, "make her happy; grant that she may never feel as I do, never experience the torturing agony of unrequited passion – but let her days glide away undisturbed by care or sorrow, and her nights, calm and peaceful, be blest with repose soft as her own innocence."

Adeline stood motionless; her blood chilled; her cheeks

became pale, and a heavy shuddering pain at her heart told her his prayer would never be realised.

"Look at her, sir," said Henry, as she stood with her arms crossed upon her bosom. "See how much I have affected her."

"No, Henry: no, I am not much affected," replied she, and a gush of tears relieved her overcharged heart.

She had entered the chamber with an intention of giving herself to Henry, but still she wanted resolution; and when she would have encouraged him with hope, the unformed sentence died away upon her lips.

"I feel, sir," said Henry, "a presentiment that I have not much longer to linger – not much longer will your feeling heart be wrung with witnessing the sufferings of this wretched frame: permit me, while I am yet able, to thank you for all your care and tenderness, to assure you of my gratitude, and to pledge you my word that your advice has ever been the guide and support of my actions. At this awful moment I feel the consolation of a mind free from the burthen of actual sin and guilt, and I humbly trust that he who wove the inexplicable texture of our passions will forgive the errors they sometimes lead us into."

Adeline sobbed aloud: her father took her hand, and would have led her from the room, but in a voice scarcely articulate she begged to remain.

"I trust, my dear Henry," said Sir Owen, while Adeline sunk into a chair, "I trust you have yet many years to live, and that a youth so well begun will finish in old age after a bright succession of good and virtuous actions."

Henry sighed –

"Why, my dear sir," said he, "should you wish a life prolonged that has lost its chief charm? O! no, better for me to sink into oblivion – better that the forgetfulness of the grave should cover me, than that I should live to drag on a life of misery: for never, were my days to be lengthened to the end of time, never can I forget my love – no, it is entwined in my being."

Adeline again approached the couch; she essayed to speak, but could not utter a sentence.

"What means my child?" said Sir Owen. – "What would you say, my Adeline?"

She fixed her eyes mournfully on Henry, and her tears rolled in large drops down her cheeks.

"Why, dearest Adeline," said Henry, "why are you thus affected? My sufferings will soon be over, and you I trust will forget I ever gave you pain. Leave me, dearest of women, and let me expiate by death – "

A faintness seized him: Sir Owen caught him in his arms, but unable to utter a word, he cast on his daughter a look so full of meaning of tender entreaty, she sunk on her knees beside the couch, and fervidly pressing Henry's cold hand to her lips, with extreme agitation said,

"Live, Henry, live for Adeline."

Henry's languid eyes again unclosed; a faint colour hurried across his pale cheek as feeble and trembling he pronounced: – "Great God! did I hear right! For thee, Adeline – live for thee?"

"Yes, dearest Henry, for me," said Adeline, "for me, my brother – my friend. I am thine."

Sir Owen clasped his kneeling daughter to his bosom, and fondly kissed her, while Henry, overcome by joy and gratitude, sunk back on the couch unable to articulate a single syllable, and fainted. When restored to animation, he would have spoke, but Sir Owen, fearful of agitating spirits so deplorably weakened, imposed silence, and leading Adeline from the room, left him to tranquillize his spirits, by seeking that repose his mind stood so much in need of.

"You have now, my child," said Sir Owen, with an approving smile, as he accompanied her to her apartment, "you have now acted up to my fondest hope, you have made me completely happy; and when it shall please the great disposer of events to call me to those realms where your beatified mother enjoys the rich reward of goodness and superior virtue, we shall I trust be permitted to look down from on high, and behold the felicity of our children."

Adeline burst into an agony of tears.

"My mother!" exclaimed she, sobbing, "my dear sainted mother! would to God you were alive to assure, to direct your child, who now more than ever feels your loss – who now more than ever needs your maternal advice and indulgence. Oh, that I could hear your voice directing the paths I ought to pursue."

"Believe," said Sir Owen solemnly; "believe, Adeline, that her voice speaks in mine, that I utter her sentiments, her wishes. And, oh! my child, believe also," added he, "that the doubts that waver in your mind proceed only from the natural timidity and delicacy of your character; be assured with Henry Mortimer you cannot fail of happiness."

Adeline, left to herself, begun to reflect on the momentous change that a few hours had effected; an event so sudden, so unexpected, confused her brain: she seemed in a dream: had she really promised to be the wife of Henry Mortimer should he recover – was her heart quite easy, perfectly satisfied with the promise she had given. She tried to persuade herself that it was; she remembered she was acting in unison with the wishes of a respected and most beloved parent, and though the tears streamed in torrents from her eyes, she continually said to herself; –

"I am happy! I must be happy, for has not my father said so."

She sat down to write to Eliza Tudor, to request her presence, for she needed some person whose spirits were more lively than her own to prevent her sinking into absolute dejection. Meanwhile Henry's health every hour amended: suffered to speak of his hidden love, a concealment no longer necessary, blest with the smile of Adeline, he again grew cheerful, and looked forward with delighted hope to the period when he should make her his, a period to be no longer procrastinated than till his health, as yet delicate, was thoroughly established.

Miss Tudor did not leave Glenwyn Priory without regret, for amongst the various characters that visited the Montgomerys, she found so much to employ her sportive talents, that she had never been at a loss for a mischievous adventure. After having congratulated Adeline on her future prospects, she archly said: –

"Did I not tell you that your brother Henry would ultimately marry his sister Adeline; but how is this, Adeline, you look so grave, so dismal? Lord! One would suppose you were going to be buried, instead of being married."

"I confess, my dear Eliza," replied Miss Llewellyn, "my spirits are not good: I have ever taught myself to think seriously on the subject of matrimony; and when I consider how happy, how extremely happy I have been in a single state, I may well dread a diminution of that happiness, when every day's experience proves to us the mutability of human affairs."

"But from Henry, whose disposition you know as well as you do your own, from him," rejoined Miss Tudor, "you can certainly have nothing to apprehend: his affection is too firmly fixed ever to lessen, or to alter."

"Heaven grant it," replied Adeline; "but I fear not for Henry's conduct; it is on my own account I am apprehensive, lest I should not perform the duties of my situation as I ought."

"Duties of your situation!" echoed Miss Tudor, in a tone of amazement; "why, what duties, child, will you then have to perform more than now?"

"I shall then have the opinions of my husband to attend to," replied Adeline, "his will to obey."

Eliza laughed.

"Hold your tongue, Adeline," said she, "for heaven's sake! such notions as these might do very well for the primitive woman; but now I fancy every married woman consults her own opinion, and obeys her own will; not but what as you have ever been a saintly daughter, I suppose you will make full as saintly a wife. Heigho!" continued she, affecting a sigh, "while if ever Eliza Tudor marries, she will continue as great a madcap as when single, laughing at a husband's authority, as she has at her father's, delighting in all that is whimsical and extravagant, never obeying any power but that Almighty one caprice, and turning propriety and decorum out of doors. Heaven help poor Seymour. I confess, much as I love him, I fear the man will have a hard bargain of me; even weighed in the scale against all my possessions, actual and possible."

Adeline smiled, and shook her head; yet she secretly wished that she had Eliza's spirits, her happy heart of getting rid of sorrow, her utter inaptitude to anticipate evil. While Adeline was thus thinking, Eliza suddenly turned round, and with a look of much drollery, said: –

"I have just hit upon your matrimonial duties, Adeline. I suppose you intend to mend and make your husband's shirts, small pleat his frills, knit his stockings, and when you have children nurse the squalling brats yourself; now, by the bye, if this is your intention, your duties will pretty well occupy your time and your thoughts."

"As to the mending and making of shirts, the knitting of stockings, and pleating of frills, I shall leave these matters," rejoined Adelina, "to those who better understand them; but if it should please heaven to bless me with children, I shall most certainly nurse them myself. I should be sorry to leave my children to the care of hirelings, whose want of attention might contort their forms, or fail to administer to their little wants."

"And you would suckle your children yourself?"

"Undoubtedly," replied Adeline. "I have often heard that a child imbibes with its milk the humours, vices, and infirmities of its nurse."

"Well, but Adeline, consider for a moment, how much acting in the capacity of a wet nurse," said Eliza, "must always keep the person in dishabille."

"I don't altogether see that," answered her friend; "but I should easily dispense with the glitter of full dress, when I considered that the health and future happiness of my children depended on my performing those tender offices myself, which heaven intended a mother should fulfil."

"I fear I should never fulfil them," replied Eliza. "Lord! my dear, to have an elegant lace tucker torn to atoms, or one's hair lugged about one's ears, or one's head stupefied with singing lullaby to a cross child; all this may do for your pretty demure saintship, but for me, lord, lord! I am only a poor mortal woman, and have not the presumption to aspire to these perfections: no, no, if I have children I will take care to provide proper nurses, who may feed, sing to and jump little master or miss about, while I am skipping away in a cotillion, or dancing a reel."

Sir Owen Llewellyn and Henry interrupted Eliza's speech. Sir Owen had not long entered the room, before Adeline noticed that he looked ill: she was just replying to a tender inquiry of Henry's when he uttered a groan and fell to the ground. Adeline in distraction perceived that he was quite motionless, and with a frantic scream cried – "He is dead, my father is dead!" Henry with the assistance of Eliza Tudor raised him to a chair, but he gave no signs of life. Adeline increased the distress of the scene, by throwing her arms round his neck, and fainting on his bosom. A surgeon was immediately sent for, who opened a vein, and to the inexpressible joy of the whole household, Sir Owen Llewellyn recovered to motion and speech; the surgeon declared it was an apoplectic fit, and ordered such medicines and treatment as he considered proper for the case. Sir Owen did not long continue ill, but he conceived this fit to be a warning of approaching dissolution; he thought his final end was not far distant; and under this idea, he conjured Adeline to name an early day for her nuptials. Adeline wept, and hung about his neck. "Why this weakness, my Adeline?" said he, "since death our necessary end must come; nor will your marriage, my child, either hasten or retard his approach; but should he arrive unexpectedly, I shall not die lamenting your unprotected state. I shall see you the wife of the being I love best on earth, next to yourself; consent then, my dear Adeline, to name the day, and by this acquiescence set my mind at rest."

Henry tenderly solicited, and Eliza Tudor laughed, rallied, and scolded, till urged on every side, Adeline with blushes and hesitation named that day fortnight. Her father embraced and blessed her; while Henry, joy sparkling in his eyes, and animating all his gestures, devoured her hand with kisses. The news soon reached Glenwyn Priory, where Miss Montgomery, almost choking with rage, raved and abused Adeline most unmercifully; while her brother, though his heart had not yet forgot her charms, sincerely wished them happiness; and did justice with a manly generosity to the merits of Henry Mortimer, who, though a successful rival, he confessed deserving even of Miss Llewellyn.

"Deserving!" repeated Miss Montgomery; "he deserves to be ridiculed for a fool; he might have had a much superior match in every particular." Hugh Montgomery cast on his sister a glance of mingled anger and contempt, while Mr. Williams, who was present with the Jenkins when the news arrived, caught up her words, and wondered how a man could be so blind to his own interest, as to let a larger fortune slip by, and take a less, when he might have had which he would. Miss Jenkins drew herself up in a more stately posture than usual, and told Mr. Williams that he was the most mercenary man she ever was acquainted with; that money seemed with him to comprise all good.

"Why, as to that I believe," replied Mr. Williams, "folks who know anything of the world will I fancy agree with me that there is no such thing in life as being the least bit comfortable without it. A man is a downright fool, knowing what a vexatious kind of a state wedlock is, who offers to marry without his wife brings something with her to make the pot boil."

"Dear me, that is a *perdigiously* vulgar notion," said Mrs. Montgomery; "men in India never are so amazingly rude as to ask after a lady's *fortin*."

"No," said Mr. Williams, staring, "why then I am sure I would advise all the portionless girls in this country to ship themselves for the East Indies, for they may stay here till they are as withered and ugly as the witch of Endor; they will never get husbands without having a little of the rhino to make things comfortable."

During this conversation, Mr. Jenkins was standing by a bow window that commanded the high road.

"Gad!" exclaimed he suddenly, "why, Rosa, my girl; there goes your father in that there stylish tandum."

"My father!" said Rosa, trembling, and turning pale.

"Why what ails the girl?" said Miss Jenkins, "what is your father to you, miss? If your mother's relations had not been kinder than him, you might have been sent to the work-house, to be brought up by the parish."

Rosa burst into tears. Hugh Montgomery took her hand, and attempted to sooth her.

"Pooh! d – m it, Rosa, don't snivel," said Mr. Jenkins; "never mind, my girl, you want nothing of him; but what the devil brings him into these parts I wonder, and in mourning too?"

"In mourning!" exclaimed Miss Jenkins; "lord, I should not wonder if his father, old Sir Henry Percival, was dead, and he was come to take possession of the Rhydderdwyn estates: and if the old baronet is laid under ground he shall do something for Rosa – an unnatural wretch to neglect his own child in the way he has."

While this conversation was passing a servant arrived on a foaming horse from Mr. Jenkins's house, to request that his master would return home immediately.

"Gad!" said Mr. Jenkins, "I must be off. Mrs. Montgomery, ma'am, you will have the goodness to excuse me, business must be minded."

"Business!" echoed Miss Jenkins, "I wonder what business Rosa's father can have with you? However, I shall go, and give him a little of my mind. Come, Rosa, come along; now your longing, miss, will be satisfied; you have often wished to see your father."

"And was it not a natural wish, madam?" replied the gentle Rosa.

"I am sure he has been unnatural enough to you," said Miss Jenkins: "you might have wanted bread to eat, and a garment to wear, for anything he knew or cared."

"Gad!" replied her brother, "how you stand prating; come along." They then bustled away, and left Mrs. Montgomery and her daughter commenting on the rudeness and vulgarity of their behaviour, and debating whether they should, or should not, pay a visit to the bride at Dolgelly Castle.

"By all means, Lucretia, let us go," said Mrs. Montgomery, "or they may be silly enough to think that you are *perdigiously* vexed and mortified at the marriage."

"Then," replied Miss Montgomery, "they will be vastly mistaken I assure them. Me mortified! not I truly, I only pity the poor fellow's bad taste: no, no, I own I was a little taken with the fellow's person; but as he chose to prefer that dowdy Adeline Llewellyn to me, my pride will keep me from feeling mortification, madam, I promise you."

"I rejoice to hear it I am sure," said Mrs. Montgomery:

"indeed it was a *perdigiously* amazing thing that the man should have been so ridiculous, and out of the way, as to prefer her to you, Lucretia: but there is no accounting for people's taste."

"Taste!" rejoined Miss Montgomery, "he has I think displayed very little taste; and only to think of his almost dying about her: taste truly!" surveying her person with much complacency in an opposite mirror. "I think there is no comparison to be drawn between the daughter of a rich East Indian nabob and that of a little Welch baronet; but perhaps I have had a lucky escape. I no doubt shall marry a title if I marry at all."

"Most likely, my dear, most likely," said her mother; "with your beauty, and your *fortin* you have certainly a right to expect a title. Your father intends to spend the winter in *Lunnun*, and then you will have an opportunity of picking and choosing; and then when you are married to some great lord, what a *perdigious* pleasure it will be to come down into these parts to astonish them with your grandeur and happiness, and to be called your ladyship at every word, while she is only plain Mrs. Mortimer."

"Delightful it would be to be sure," said Lucretia, "and there is nothing would give me greater pleasure than to mortify her."

"Why, what has she done to offend you?" said the nabob, who very seldom interfered, or put in a word, though pretty well acquainted with the spiteful temper of his daughter, and the equally blameable indulgence of her mother.

"Done to me! sir," said Lucretia, "I am very sorry my own father feels so little for my insulted pride and wounded peace as to find it necessary to ask that question."

"As to your pride," replied the nabob, "having so large a portion of it, Lucretia, you must not wonder that it gets hurt a little now and then; but I had no conception that your peace was affected, because as far as I am able to judge, you seem to enjoy yourself as much as ever."

"Yes, sir," rejoined Miss Montgomery, "and perhaps I have to thank my pride that 1 am able to appear to enjoy myself, for it may well be imagined that I have not with calm indifference seen myself overlooked for a person who does not possess half my perfections."

"Different people see with different eyes," said the nabob: "now for my part, I think Miss Llewellyn – "

"Nobody wants to hear what you think about her, Mr. Montgomery, I promise you, and I beg you won't distress Lucretia with mentioning her. I think it is *perdigiously* odd," added Mrs. Montgomery, "that you should take her part against your own child."

The nabob loved quietness, so he took up his hat and walked out of the room. "Did you ever see the like?" said Lucretia, reddening like scarlet. "I think the creature has bewitched every body; but it is her turn now: mine will come by and bye."

"Yes, yes," replied Mrs. Montgomery, "we will see what a winter in *Lunnun* will do. A rich East Indian nabob's daughter will have some *detraction* I warrant."

"I shall think it odd if she has not," whispered Hugh Montgomery, who with a book in his hand, reclining on a sofa, had seemed to take no notice of their conversation.

"For my part," continued Mrs. Montgomery, "for my part I should not in the least wonder if you were to be a dutchess at last."

"I will be content to be a Countess," said Lucretia, "for then when I come down into the country I shall have the pleasure of taking place of her at the balls. Brushing past her, whom I perhaps may honour with a slight nod, or how do you do, I shall be led to the upper end of the room, creating a most charming noise, bustle, and confusion, among the little gentle-women who had fancied themselves somebody before I appeared."

"O dear, dear! this will be charming," exclaimed Mrs. Montgomery: "well, Lucretia, well, my dear, go on; your description is *perdigiously* entertaining."

"Yes, yes, mamma," replied Lucretia, "and I shall be gratified, as well as entertained, to see myself worshipped like a goddess, while she, plain Mrs. Mortimer, remains perfectly unregarded and unnoticed in the ball-room, as quiet and humdrum as if she were seated by the hall fire at Dolgelly Castle."

Hugh Montgomery, who had listened till his patience were exhausted, now started from the sofa, and closing the book he had affected to read, answered,

"Wherever Miss Llewellyn moves she will assuredly be noticed, not for ill-nature, affectation, pride, or presumption, but for pre-eminence in beauty, for grace, for elegance of manners, and for every feminine charm and virtue that should adorn and dignify a woman."

"So!" said Mrs. Montgomery; "now Hugh has made his speech!"

"Oh! madam," replied Lucretia, "you need not be surprised at his eloquence on this occasion, when you recollect that Mr. Hugh Montgomery could always find perfections in every woman except the females of his own family."

"Aye, child, it is very true indeed," rejoined Mrs. Montgomery. "Hugh was always *perdigiously* ready to discover perfections in other folks, though he was as blind as a mole to those of his own nearest relations."

"I most sincerely wish," replied Hugh, "that the females of my own family would allow me to find out their perfections; I should rejoice from the bottom of my soul to acknowledge them; but while I see them perpetually employed in scandalizing those they call their friends, finding their highest delight in pulling to pieces every woman of their acquaintance, allowing neither merit nor goodness to any, however deserving, I confess, though it gives me pain to make the acknowledgment, I can only find in them the very worst of propensities, envy, ill-nature, and all uncharitableness."

"Mighty pretty indeed," said Mrs. Montgomery; "so Lucretia, my dear, you and me are made up of envy, hatred, and all uncharitableness; however, it don't signify much what he thinks about us."

"No, no," exclaimed Miss Montgomery spitefully, "Hugh thinks he hides the spleen of his heart by venting his vexation and ill-humours upon us: but though he does not choose to own it, I can see plain enough that Miss Llewellyn's refusal of him has mortified his pride, and that he wishes Henry Mortimer at the devil, though he thinks he shews himself a philosopher, by sounding the praises of those who have disappointed his hopes and wishes: however, I am not Christian enough when I have met with an injury not to resent it. I am not hypocrite enough to appear pleased when I am downright angry."

"Nor shall I be deceitful enough to say I do not regret Miss Llewellyn's refusal of me," replied Hugh; "yet, though, she could not find her happiness with me, I shall still do justice to her perfections, personal as well as mental, and shall never to cease to wish her that felicity I was not fated to constitute."

Lucretia smiled contemptuously. "I am not mean spirited enough to wish happiness to those who have paid no sort of regard to mine," rejoined she, "and I sincerely pray – "

"I shall not stay to hear your prayer," said Hugh, abruptly rising and quitting the room.

"There now – that is Hugh's politeness," exclaimed Mrs. Montgomery; "the men are *perdigiously* odd creatures. I hope he won't *partend* to set down good breeding among his own perfections."

The appointed day at length arrived that gave to the impatient wishes of Henry Mortimer his beautiful and long-adored Adeline; he received her from the hand of her father, amidst the blessings and prayers of assembled hundreds, who had crowded in and round the village church to witness the marriage of a couple whose amiable manners and acknowledged virtues had rendered them objects of universal admiration and esteem.

Adeline went through the ceremony with apparent composure; she received the congratulations of her friends with a smiling and seemingly happy countenance; but no sooner had she retired with Eliza Tudor to dress for dinner, than turning paler than the white robe she wore, she sank upon the neck of her friend, and fainted.

Eliza with the assistance of her maid soon recovered her, and would have had her father and husband summoned.

"No, as you love me – " said Adeline, in great agitation: "my spirits have been much hurried, but I am now better, infinitely better: do not let them know that I have been ill: this day seems to give them so much pleasure, that I would on no account offer the slightest interruption. I was only a little weak and nervous, but I am now quite well."

While she spoke the tears were chasing each other down her cheeks, and a universal tremor shook her frame.

Eliza Tudor, pretending she wanted something from below, dismissed the maid from the room, and affectionately taking the hand of Adeline, said, "And quite happy too, I hope, my dearest Adeline."

"I hope I am," replied she, with a heavy sigh.

After a few moment's pause, she asked Eliza if she could recollect the name of a romance she had once read a part of to her, previous to the review of the Scotch Greys at Carnarvon.

"A romance! why I have dipped into so many, my dear," rejoined Eliza; "let me recollect; – was it not called Fatal Obedience, or the Victim of Principle?"

"The same, the same," said Adeline, in a hurried voice; "step down to the library, Eliza, and bring me that book."

"Why sure you forget yourself; you never read romances you know; and, besides, you have not yet begun to dress."

"I have sufficient time," replied Adeline; "oblige me so far as to fetch me the first volume."

Eliza obeyed, and presenting the book, said, "Really, Adeline, I never saw you in so strange a way before; you absolutely alarm me."

Adeline affectionately pressed her lips to her cheek, but answering nothing, turned quickly over the leaves of the book, till she found the passage she was in search of, which she read aloud:

"When imperious love takes possession of the heart all its gaiety departs: to nights of calm repose and dreams of happiness succeed visions of terror and despair; the bosom, once the mansion of peace and tranquillity, is tortured with an agonizing train of doubts, fears, and jealousies; restless and dissatisfied, the mind busies itself with hopes that can never be realized, or in conjuring up misfortunes it may never encounter. Time ever passes too swift or too slow; the meridian sun is darker than the noon of night in the absence of the adored one, and every passing hour is devoted to trembling expectation and harassing suspense."

Adeline let the book fall from her hand, which she raised towards heaven, while she fervently exclaimed, "Thank God! thank God!"

Eliza, who had stood looking at her with silent wonder, now asked what she was so piously thanking God for.

"That I am not devoted to all this misery – that I am not the slave of imperious passion – that I am not in love."

Eliza, whose feelings had been so worked upon that she was on the point of weeping, now gladly dismissed the unwelcome tears from her eyes, and burst into a fit of laughter.

"Laugh on, my dear Eliza," said Adeline, "and I will endeavour to laugh too. Half an hour ago I thought myself the most wretched of beings, because the quiescent state of my heart reproached me with not being in love with Henry Mortimer. I now most sincerely thank God that my mind does not feel the miseries this book declares attendant on the passion; for how would it be possible to act rationally, to submit to the forms of life, to fulfil the duties of one's station, if the mind, the soul was so filled, so occupied, so tortured? – I esteem, I respect my husband; and with these sentiments I trust we shall be happy."

A tear trembled in her eye while she spoke.

"Happy!" echoed Eliza; "if two such exalted beings as Henry and Adeline Mortimer are not happy, alas! poor mortality, who shall pretend to say they deserve, who shall dare to expect felicity?"

"I will never despise romances again," said Adeline; "for this I am sure has given me a consolation I scarcely hoped for."

"I never had patience to read one through," replied Eliza. "I love to laugh, not to cry; I detest scenes of horror, to have my feelings worked upon with fictitious distress: besides, when one comes to reflect, it is highly ridiculous to suppose a delicate, timid, fragile sylph-like lady (such as an author invariably describes his heroine to be) should be able to encounter perils, horrors, and dangers enough to appal the fortitude of a hero, and fatigue the strong frame of a Colossus; not to say a word about their minds, which are always hung upon tenter-hooks and stretched upon wheels of torture. There is misery enough to be met with in the world," continued she, "without seeking it in books; and you know I hate scenes of sorrow, and always run away as fast as my legs will carry me from every thing that wears the appearance of melancholy and distress."

"Yes," rejoined Adeline, "but your heart does not forget to afford it every relief in your power."

"Come, bustle, bustle," said Eliza, gaily, and ringing the bell for her maid; "you forget that we are expected below. Lord! Lord! what would poor Seymour give if he were this day performing the part of bridegroom to that wild rantipole, Eliza Tudor! Come, come, Adeline, you forget to dress – you appear to forget every thing."

"No," replied Adeline, mournfully, "I do not forget that this is my wedding-day."

CHAPTER VII

Who shall go about
To cozen fortune, and be honourable
Without the stamp of merit. Let none presume
To wear an undeserved dignity.
O! that estates, degrees, and offices
Were not derived corruptly; that clear honour
Were purchased by the merit of the wearer!
How many then should cover that stand bare;
How many be commanded that command.

Shakespeare

THE character of Gabriel Jenkins was diametrically opposite to that of his sister: he abounded in the milk of human kindness; he felt compassion for human frailties, and forgave them: his heart melted at distress, and his hand relieved it whenever it fell in his way, without stopping to inquire whether the object was deserving or not.

His temper, though hasty, was generous; his disposition tender and humane; and the bright drop that twinkled in his little grey eyes often contradicted the coarse speech that issued from his lips.

His understanding was tolerably good but education had lent no aid for its expansion or improvement. Placed by Providence in a Welch village, behind the counter of a large shop chiefly frequented by miners and colliers, he had no opportunity of polishing his manners or cultivating his mind.

The clerk of the parish had taught him to read, write, and cast accounts; and his father had instructed him very successfully in the art and mystery of getting money.

His sister, to whom at an early age a legacy of a few hundred pounds had been left by a distant relation, was sent to a boarding-school at Carnarvon, where, if she did not become altogether as clever and accomplished in French and music as her teachers wished, no one could deny her pre-eminence in pride, falsehood, envy, and deceit.

The motherless, deserted Rosa Percival was most affectionately beloved by her uncle. Having in the early part of his life met a disappointment of the heart, he had resolved never to marry; and being more tenderly attached to his niece than to any other creature in the world, he secretly determined upon making her his heiress. From the tyranny of his sister he often rescued her; combated for her Miss Jenkins's meanness and parsimony; and while he inveighed against the unfeeling conduct of her father, who had left her upon his hands to maintain, he took scrupulous care that she should be well educated, and that neither her wardrobe nor her purse should ever be sensible of deficiencies.

Mr. Gabriel Jenkins was in person a short thick-set man, with a face as broad and round as a harvest moon, and carried before him a protuberance of sufficient bulk to entitle him to perform, in point of rotundity, Shakespeare's celebrated and facetious knight, Sir John Falstaff, without stuffing. Yet, notwithstanding the disadvantages attendant on excessive corpulency, when they left Glenwyn Priory he had bustled on at so prodigious a rate as to leave his sister, his niece, and Mr. Williams at least a mile behind him on the road.

The weather being extremely warm, in the course of his

walk he had unbuttoned his white dimity waistcoat from top to bottom, untied his cravat, and pulled off his hat and wig.

In this situation, puffing, blowing, sweating, and covered with dust, he rushed into his house, blundered up the staircase, and bounced into the drawing room, where he found two gentlemen impatiently waiting his arrival.

"Gad!" said he, as one of them advanced to meet him with extended hand, "gad! it is Edward Percival sure enough! – But no, I shan't shake hands; no, d – n me, if ever I grip a fellow by the fist whose neck I should be glad to see stretched upon a gallows."

The gentleman looked displeased, and in no very gentle tone of voice said, "Sir, I don't understand – "

"Yes, you do well enough," replied Jenkins; "and you must have had even more brass than I thought you had, if you expected a friendly reception here: for who the devil and all his little black imps would have thought of your coming here, after being away so many years? – Servant, sir," blowing his nose, and making a side scrape to the other gentleman. – "I surely supposed," addressing himself again to Mr. Percival, "I surely supposed you had quite and clean forgot there was ever such a country in the universal world as North Wales, or such a place as Birch Park; though indeed, all things considered, I don't much wonder you should wish to forget it."

"You find, sir, you are mistaken then," replied the person to whom he had spoken; "I have neither forgot, nor does it appear I wished to forget; though I must confess that Birch Park is so much altered, so wonderfully improved in every particular, that it is with difficulty I recognize it for the place where in my boyish days I spent so many happy hours – where I used to come a wooing."

"Perhaps not, perhaps not: we have made money, Mr. Percival, since those times, a good deal of money; and, gad! sir, we have made it honestly and fairly – not at gaming-tables."

"No, no, Gabriel, we know you made it across the counter; it came every shilling of it from the dirty, unsophisticated paws of colliers; it was never contaminated by the touch of a gentleman."

"Gentlemen!" retorted Mr. Jenkins; "pickpockets! – We are rich, and by our own industry, by the earnings of labour; and as Birch Park is not now the property of a paltry dirty shop-keeper, you may, perhaps, think it worth visiting; and, perhaps, too, your pride may no longer think it necessary to forget that Gabriel Jenkins is your brother-in-law."

"Really you talk very oddly, Mr. Jenkins – my pride!"

"Aye, sir, your pride; that is plain English I believe. What but your pride prevented you acknowledging my poor sister Rosa for your wife? – what but your cursed unfeeling pride killed her?"

Nature would have its way: the tears swelled in his eyes; but, as if ashamed of his weakness, he dashed them from him, and continued:

"Ah! poor girl, if she had taken the advice of those who wished her well, she would have married an honest tradesman; she might now have been alive and merry, and not obliged to her relations for keeping her poor innocent child from starving. But pray, sir, after never once inquiring after your daughter, nor letting us hear from you nor set eyes upon you for seventeen years, may I be so bold as to ask what brings you into these long-forgotten and forsaken parts now?"

"In spite of your extreme impoliteness, Mr. Jenkins, I have

much pleasure in informing you that I have at last buried my father."

"Gad! that is mighty affectionate now," said Jenkins, "mighty affectionate indeed! Only see the difference betwixt little folks and great ones: I remember I was so sadly grieved at the death of my father, that so far from thinking the laying of him under ground a pleasure, I looked upon it as the dismalest, heartbreaking thing in the whole world; but then to be sure my father was but a poor man, and had nothing but a little small bit of a farm to leave behind him. But, gad! I had quite and clean forgot my manners: – I wish you joy, sir, of the pleasure of burying your father."

He now raised his hand to his head to take off his hat, but feeling his bare skull, he hastily snatched his wig from the seat of the window, where he had thrown it on entering the room, and drawing his fingers through the curls, added, "You are now Sir Edward Percival?"

The baronet bowed.

"Allow me to introduce my friend, Lord Clavering."

Mr. Jenkins wiped his head, clapped on his wig, and returned the bow of the peer.

"Being now uncontrolled master of my own actions," continued Sir Edward Percival, "I follow the wishes of my heart – I come to visit you, Jenkins, and to introduce myself and friend to Miss Percival."

"Well, Mr. Percival – gad! I ask pardon – Sir Edward I mean; but one cannot bring one's tongue to remember things all at once; it will be a little awkward at first; one cannot learn to speak new titles all in a minute. But I hear my sister, and Rosa, and Mr. Williams. Here, come along; walk upstairs all of you," bawling from the drawing-room door: "come along,

Rosa, my girl, come along; here is your father; and, gad! you are as like him as if he had spit you out of his mouth."

In an instant in stalked Miss Jenkins into the drawing-room, followed by Rosa and Mr. Williams.

"Well, Mr. Percival," said Miss Jenkins, affecting state and dignity, "here, sir, is your daughter; and considering, sir, that she owes nothing to the great family of the proud Percivals, considering, I say, sir, that she has been clothed and fed by the bounty and charity of the poor Jenkins, she does not look so very bad, does not cut so despicable a figure altogether as might be expected."

Rosa, apprehending a scene of violence, had timidly shrunk behind her aunt, and stood trembling, leaning on the back of a chair, nearly fainting.

Lord Clavering politely advanced, and taking her hand, led her towards her father.

Pale and weeping, she sank at his feet, while he with an unabashed eye surveyed her interesting figure through the glass that hung from his neck, coldly kissed her cheek, shrugged his shoulders, said she made him look d – d old, this was the consequence of marrying so young, but that, faith, she was a tolerable fineish sort of a girl, might be made to look stylish.

"Rise from your knees, Rosa," said Mr. Jenkins; "I guess this father of yours is sorry to see you grown up a young woman; but I suppose that is because he had not the pleasure of nursing you when you was a child; but if he has any luck he may have that pleasure when you make him a grandfather. I don't know what the devil he would have, nor what he means; but I think he has every reason to be content. – He gets a child, and leaves other people to maintain it; and when it is grown up to his hands without trouble or expense, he is not pleased."

"You are mistaken, sir," replied the baronet, "I am very much pleased, much better pleased than I expected to be; for considering the girl has been brought up among the mountains, she is not so much amiss – she is not above half as rustic as I thought I should find her."

"Rustic!" screamed Miss Jenkins, reddening like a turkey-cock, "rustic! was ever the like heard? – Rustic, indeed! – Though you, unnatural wretch as you are, never bestowed a single shilling upon her, we have taken care of her education, and let her keep none but the very best company in the country."

"The best company!" replied the baronet,with a sneer; "that is the parson of the parish, the village apothecary, and the exciseman."

"What impertinence!" replied the enraged Miss Jenkins; "I would have you to know that the parson of the parish is more of a gentleman by half than you are, and as to the apothecary –"

"Oh! d – n it, dismiss the shop," said the baronet, laughing, "and proceed to her education. –What does she know? – what can she do?"

"Why she can dance," said Miss Jenkins.

"Good," replied the baronet.

"And she can play upon the piano forte."

"Better still," rejoined Sir Edward.

"And she can talk French."

"Charmont! bien allons!" said the baronet.

"And she can embroider, and cut paper, and make artificial flowers."

"Pshaw!" cried the baronet.

"Rustic! indeed," resumed Miss Jenkins. "I don't know how she was likely to have a rustic appearance, when I always have the very first fashions that arrive at Carnarvon; and as to her behaviour, I formed her manners myself, and I have been pretty generally allowed to be as well-bred and as much the gentlewoman as any in all North Wales. I have been at the greatest of pains, morning, noon, and night, to make her genteel, besides having taught her myself to spin, and net, and knot, and knit, and pickle, and preserve, and brew, and bake, and distil."

"Too many accomplishments by half," interrupted Sir Edward, "too many by one half."

"Aye, that is your thanks, your gratitude," resumed Miss Jenkins; "but I would have you to know that Rosa Percival is considered one of the most clever managing notable house-wives in all the country."

"And to be so considered was certainly every way desirable," replied Sir Edward, "while she was only known and acknowledged as the niece of Mr. Jenkins; but in Miss Percival, the daughter of Sir Edward Percival, the envied celebrity of being the very best netter, knotter, spinner, brewer, baker, pickler, preserver, and distiller, may very readily, and without any sort of regret, be dispensed with: but come, my dear Miss Jenkins, don't be out of humour; I know we shall yet be very good friends: you mentioned the piano forte; can she sing?"

"Yes she can," said Mr. Jenkins, "and sweetly too. I am sure she warbled 'Ar hyd y nos' last night till she made me cry."

"Welsh! barbarous!" exclaimed Sir Edward: can she sing Italian?"

He attempted to take Miss Jenkins's hand, but snatching it from him, she threw herself into a chair, and disdaining to afford him a reply, sat reddening with passion, and fanning herself with so much violence, as to threaten destruction to the delicate ivory sticks and painted crepe she held in her hand. Rosa, confused and blushing, had taken a seat on a sofa at a distant part of the room.

"Come this way, child," said Sir Edward, drawing her towards the window. "Come and answer for yourself – what do you blush for, you little fool? Why don't you speak – have you got no tongue – can you talk?"

"Oh! lord! sir," said Mr. Williams, laughing, and longing for an opportunity to speak, "I have heard Miss Rosa's tongue go nineteen to the dozen."

"Gad! you are wrong there neighbour, quite out, begging your pardon for the boldness of contradicting you," replied Mr. Jenkins; "Rosa never was any great things of a talker."

"So much the better," said Mr. Williams, "for when she is married, if she gives her husband the length of her tongue too often, why you know it will make things quite uncomfortable."

The baronet darted on poor Williams a look of haughty contempt, and said, as they were then upon family business, the company of an uninterested person was by no means necessary, or agreeable.

"Very true, sir, quite right," said Williams bowing very low. "I was just turning it over in my mind whether it would not be properest for me to go home."

"Certainly it would sir," replied the baronet, turning on him a contemptuous glance.

"Well, good folks," resumed Williams, "I shall take my

leave, and as to you, sir, as I have always been a wellwisher of Miss Rosa's, and have a very great regard for her, having always thought her a mighty quiet good sort of a girl, I shall be very glad to see you at my little cottage, where I will do my best to make you comfortable."

"Really you are too condescending, mister – what is your name?" said the baronet sneeringly; "you do me infinitely too much honour."

"No, not at all; not in the least I assure you," rejoined Mr. Williams, "I wish to show all possible respect to Miss Rosa's father, and as to this other strange gentleman (turning to Lord Clavering who stood silent, wholly occupied with gazing on the pensive downcast countenance of Rosa), Mr. – – I don't know what his name is, because nobody introduced me to him, but I shall be very glad to see him too, to take a bit of mutton, and smoke a pipe, and be comfortable."

His lordship laughed aloud, while the baronet assuming a tone of command bade him begone.

"The gentleman you have just now taken the liberty of addressing with so much familiarity is Lord Clavering; and I fancy it is not very customary for persons of his rank and fashion to condescend to visit men in your station."

"But it is though, and they are glad to do it, and to stand bowing down to the ground, with their hats in their hands," said Mr. Jenkins: "at election times they will cringe and scrape enough when they want votes."

"Very true, Mr. Jenkins, very true," rejoined Williams: "it is not above two years since I saw a lord arm in arm with a chimney-sweeper cheek by jowl, as thick as incle weavers: and as for the matter of that, one man is as good as another as far as I can see: we are all made of dirt and clay, and must all be relations, if we believe what is set down in the bible – for that says plain enough that we are all children of Adam, and in that case I don't see but what I am to the full as good as any lord that ever wore a head; for I am a honest man, and pay my way, and the king, God bless him, his rates and taxes: and I have always done it: no man can come to me and say I owe him a farthing: and as to my little cottage, why to be sure it is not very grand, not so fine I suppose as a lord's palace: but what of that, it is snug and clean: and if a friend drops in, why I have always a good bed at his service, and I always keep a fine Cheshire cheese, and a barrel of strong ale to make him comfortable."

"So you do, Mr. Williams, so you do," replied Miss Jenkins, "and for my part I don't see but what you are to the full as good as those who hold their heads much higher; and I have no notion of the airs and pride of Sir Edward Percival. – After having left his daughter upon our hands for so many years, to take the liberty of turning up his nose, and affronting our friends, and telling them to leave our house; I don't understand such rude behaviour."

"Gad! nor I neither," said Mr. Jenkins, "nor I won't suffer nobody to affront Williams before my face, and in my house – as honest a good kind of a man, though I speak it before his face, as ever broke the world's bread, a man that has been my friend for so many years, and so fond of Rosa."

"Fond of Miss Percival!" said Lord Clavering, viewing Williams from head to foot.

"Fond of Rosa!" repeated Sir Edward, "he! that man fond of Miss Percival! speak, child – you are not fond of him are you? Why does not the statue speak – you certainly can never have been induced to encourage – "

"Yes but she has though," said Mr. Jenkins; "she is very fond of neighbour Williams; has always been very fond of him, ever since she could walk and talk; have you not, Rosa? Speak the truth and shame the devil: and why the pepper should not she! her uncle's old friend and intimate acquaintance, one that has always – "

"Say no more, sir, say no more, I beseech you upon the subject," interrupted the baronet: "the silly girl has I find been suffered to imbibe precious vulgar notions, and to form fine attachments."

"I hope, sincerely hope, Miss Percival," said Lord Clavering, "that you are not attached to this man? You cannot I trust, you cannot be partial to him."

"Indeed, sir," replied Rosa, "I have every reason in the world to be partial to Mr. Williams; he has been always so good, so particularly kind to me, that was I not to be attached to him I should be the most ungrateful creature in nature."

"Silence, girl," cried the baronet; "your amiable gratitude can be spared in this instance."

"Begone, fellow," said he to Williams in a voice of fury, "instantly begone, before I break your bones."

"Break my bones," said Williams, staring at him with astonishment – "break my bones! what for pray? Why this is talking in the wildest oddest way I ever heard in my life. Break my bones! I don't know what to make of it. Why what in the world – break my bones! no man ever talked to me in this uncomfortable manner before: threaten to break my bones, only because when your daughter came a visiting to my cottage I always gave her the very best my pantry, and my cellar, and my garden, would afford: break my bones! a very pretty sort of civil return that would be to me, for having on all occasions been kind to her, and trying to make her comfortable: besides, I don't understand any man, if I may be so bold as to speak my thoughts, taking the freedom of threatening to break my bones; it would be but a very uncomfortable sort of a business I assure you; and though I am of a very quiet peaceable temper, and not at all given to quarrelling and making words about nothing; yes, sir, I say, though I am but a plain sort of a man, yet I shall not put up with an affront without resenting it."

"Oh! for Heaven's sake!" said the terrified Rosa, "say no more: indeed you frighten me beyond measure; pray, dear, dear Mr. Williams, for my sake, say no more."

"Well, well, Miss Rosa, don't be alarmed," replied he: "I should be sorry to kick up a riot in your uncle's house, and very sorry indeed to say or to do anything in the world to make you in the least bit uncomfortable; but I don't know what I have done or said, that I should be threatened like a little schoolboy, with having my bones broke. I am not used, Miss Rosa, to hear such uncomfortable words."

"What have you done!" said the baronet, "have not you presumed to make love to Miss Percival?"

"He make love to little Rosa!" said Mr. Jenkins, laughing till his fat sides shook again.

"Me make love to Miss Rosa!" exclaimed Mr. Williams, staring round him with astonishment.

"A man, at Mr. Williams's time of life to make love to a mere child!" cried Miss Jenkins, drawing up her scraggy neck, and nodding her head; "that would be too ridiculous; I believe the man has more discernment. Lord! lord! what a strange out of the way notion! No, no," continued she, "I must do Mr. Williams the justice," at the same time bridling, and looking on him with a great deal of complacency, "to say that he knows better how to distinguish than that comes to; he knows too well what will conduce to his future comfort."

"Well to be sure," rejoined Mr. Williams, "this is a funny kind of a joke sure enough. I have certainly always loved Miss Rosa from a baby, when I used to nurse her, and carry her about in my arms, and I never went from home but I used to bring her cakes, and sugar plumbs, and oranges, and them sort of niceties to please children with, and the little good tempered thing would sit upon my knee, and kiss me, and be quite comfortable; but as to making love to her in the way of matrimony, that is quite and clean a different sort of a matter: why I believe I am nearly old enough to be her grandfather."

Miss Jenkins bit her lips.

"And it would, as everybody must think, be the foolishest thing in all the world for a man at my time of life to think of such a young thing for a wife. Lord bless us! an old man that takes a young wife can never expect to be comfortable. But good night, gentlefolks; no offence I hope: I shall go quietly home, smoke my pipe, drink my glass of ale, and make myself comfortable."

Miss Jenkins went to see him out. – The baronet pushed the door after him with violence, called him an execrable boor, protested the fellow's vulgarity had quite exhausted him, and that if he had stayed much longer he would certainly have annihilated him.

"Gad! sir," said Mr. Jenkins, "I must be so free as to say I think you take unaccountable freedoms on another person's premises – here have you, nobody knows why, or wherefore, affronted my very worthy friend Thomas Williams, and ordered him out of my house, with as much insolence as if it had been your own. I never saw nobody take such liberties: I never saw such rude behaviour since my mother bore me, not I."

"All owing to your vegetating among the mountains, Jenkins," said the baronet yawning; "you might have seen it every day in the week in Pall Mall, St. James's, or any of the squares at the west end of the town. If you had spent your time among the fashionable people you would have known, that consulting your own inclination, using your own pleasure on every occasion, was the only way to be easy and comfortable, as your friend Thomas – Morgan – Powel, what is the fellow's infernal name – has it – But come, Jenkins," continued the baronet, " d – m it, my fine fellow, don't be sulky, for we have not met you know for many years."

"And if we had not met at all," said Mr. Jenkins, "I don't know where would have been the loss, or the harm."

"The loss would have been mine," resumed the baronet; "I should not have had the happiness of seeing you look so well, nor you the pleasure of congratulating me on my accession to my father's title and estates: nor would you have known my intentions with respect to your niece, the demure looking little Rosa there."

The gentle, sensible Rosa started; she wondered what were his intentions: the tears trembled in her mild eyes, as she heard herself named by her father, who at this, their very first interview, seemed to regard her with perfect apathy, neither in his look or manner discovering the slightest emotion of tenderness, and who seemed to be too gay and fashionable a man to be troubled either with delicacy or feeling. Mr. Jenkins took off his wig, and stood for some moments very deliberately scratching his bald pate.

"Truly I have been thinking," said he, "that it is but a sort of comical, unnatural thing, to wish a man joy because his father has kicked the bucket, and got a wooden surtout: and gad! Sir Edward," blowing his nose till the room echoed again, "it is time you did think and intend something for poor Rosa, it is high time you did provide for her."

"Why you have provided for her, have not you, my buck?" rejoined the baronet; "you intend leaving her all your fortune, don't you?"

"I don't know that I am obliged to give you an account of how or which way I mean to dispose of my property," said Mr. Jenkins: "I earned it by the sweat of my brow; I toiled early and late for it; and I have a right to build a hospital with it if I like."

"A right you most undoubtedly have, my fine fellow," answered the baronet; "but I hope to heaven you won't have such nonsensical likings, for d – m it, man, the money that people are silly enough to leave to public charities too frequently serves the perverted purpose of supporting private extravagancies; of pampering those who don't want charity; and starving the poor devils that do."

"Bravo, Percival!" exclaimed the peer, who had vainly been trying to draw Rosa into a conversation; "public charities are notoriously abused."

"No matter, no matter," said Jenkins; "cheats in all trades, and as long as a great good is produced, we must not mind a little of the money going into the left instead of the right hand pocket; however, Sir Edward, it is nothing at all to nobody what I do with my own; nor, as what we have been saying, any thing in the world to do with Rosa. Ever since she was born, you have taken no notice of her, no more than if you had not known she was your child. She is now turned of seventeen years of age, and I must be bold to say you have most surely taken no small spell in intending – "

"Say no more, Jenkins, say no more, my good fellow; you shall very shortly be obliged to acknowledge the generosity and goodness of my intentions; you know during Sir Henry's life how I was situated; you know I could not command a single guinea."

"Yes," replied Jenkins; "and I know that many a bright shining one you used to get from my poor sister during her life-time; though you was ashamed to own for your wife the daughter of a shop-keeper, you were never too proud to spend the money that was taken from the dirty hands of the colliers."

"Jenkins," said the baronet, "I wonder among all the good things with which your memory is stored that you have not given King Charles's rules a place."

"My memory perhaps is like yours, Sir Edward, convenient."

"I know that; repeat no old grievances is your meaning? But this does not suit my fancy just now; I want to know – "

"So do I, what you intend giving us for supper?"

"Supper!" repeated Jenkins, "I was not thinking about supper."

"But I was though," replied Sir Edward: "I am devilish hungry; the air off your mountains is as keen as your wit; the one creates envy, the other appetite. You no doubt have ducks fat as ortolans."

"And chickens delicate as your behaviour," answered Jenkins, thoroughly provoked at his unparalleled assurance.

"Witty, egad!" retorted the baronet; "but delicacy with relations! Pooh! d – m it! that is quite out of the question."

"Gad! so it appears," replied Jenkins, "for yours has not much stood in your way since I have known you; and truly, if I may be so bold as to speak my mind, there is not over much of that same delicacy to be seen in a man's conduct who never came near, or owned his wife's family, when he thought their calling and sphere in life beneath him; but is ready to eat, and drink, and shake them by the hand, as soon as ever he finds out that they have money enough to place them above caring whether they have his notice or not."

"True Welsh to the bottom!" said Sir Edward; "right Cambrian blood, hey! Jenkins?"

"I hope so," rejoined he, "and though you, Sir Edward, are ashamed to know yourself a Welshman, I hope I never shall; and if I am hot and resentful, like the rest of the natives, as you are pleased to call us, I hope I shall not disgrace the character of the ancient Cambrians, by wanting either gratitude or generosity."

"That is an excellent speech," replied Sir Edward; "a very excellent speech upon my soul! Why, Jenkins, there is nothing about Birch Park half so much improved as yourself; why you are quite an orator. But when you were sounding the praise of our countrymen (if you will have it so), you forgot to mention one trait for which their characters have ever been conspicuous, I mean hospitality. – I hope my friend Lord Clavering and myself shall not have reason to deny you this excellence in common with other Cambrians. You have never yet asked us to eat or drink: but come, exert yourself, my good fellow, for we intend doing ourselves the pleasure of taking up our abode with you while we remain among the mountains."

"The devil you do!" rejoined Jenkins.

"Yes, yes, we do," said the baronet. "I thought you would be offended if we went to an inn; and, besides, the distance to Rhydderdwyn being considered, the mansion-house is so out of repair, that I could not accommodate a friend at all to my satisfaction; and, finding that you have convenient stables and coach-house, I have ordered the servants to bring the carriages and horses here."

Jenkins turned up his eyes in astonishment.

"Aye," continued the baronet, "I thought I should surprise you. I am I was always ready to acknowledge the family connection."

"Whenever it answered your purpose," interrupted Jenkins.

"How is your wine – have you any of the right sort?" resumed the baronet, not appearing to notice Jenkins's interruption: "Clavering drinks Vidonia and Champagne – pink Champagne. Have you got any, my boy? For my part, I take Madeira with my dinner, and Burgundy afterwards. You used to have famous beds: no luxurious Eider down beds in Wales, Clavering; but the natives are notorious for feathering their geese, and goose feathers make a tolerable good bed. Tell us what we can have for supper, hey, my buck."

Jenkins was so new to this *sans ceremonie* treatment, so much a novice in this fashionable style of behaviour, that he stood like a statue, almost petrified with astonishment. He saw with inconceivable wonder that Sir Edward Percival at near forty years of age was to the full as wild, inconsiderate, and presuming as Edward Percival was at twenty-one, when he won the gentle, susceptible heart of Rosa Jenkins, and persuaded her to a clandestine marriage; nor, considering the gay, dissipated life he had led, was his person materially altered for the worse, for he might be still called remarkably handsome, and with a graceful figure, and fashionable dress and manners, preserved the appearance of a man whose age did not exceed thirty.

While honest Jenkins stood gaping and wondering at his consummate effrontery, divided between his affection for Rosa and dislike to her father, irresolute for her sake which way to act, whether to show him the door at once, or to treat him in his own way, with dissimulation, his sister returned to the drawing-room, satisfied with her absolute dominion over poor Williams, and proud and excessively flattered with the important idea of entertaining a peer and a baronet.

She soon appeared perfectly reconciled, and grew into perfect good-humour, as Lord Clavering quickly discovering the weakness and vanity of her character, began pouring upon her a profusion of compliments, alike empty and insincere on his part, as undeserved on hers.

Miss Jenkins in the pride of her heart had often thought herself infinitely superior in attraction to her deceased sister, and had constantly cherished the belief that she needed only to be seen to be admired; and as she stood contemplating her charms at the looking-glass would pensively repeat:

> "Full many a gem of purest ray serene
> The dark unfathom'd caves of ocean bear;
> Full many a flow'r is born to blush unseen,
> And waste its sweetness on the desert air."

And in order to obviate this, had made frequent excursions to all the wells and bathing-places in the vicinity. For years every man that had looked at her she had fancied smitten with her charms; every man that had said a civil word to her she had set down as her declared admirer; and when tired of her caprice, or disgusted with her malevolent disposition (which she could never sufficiently disguise), they were engaged in different pursuits, or attached themselves to objects more amiable, she never failed to reproach them with breach of vows, and represent them as perjured monsters; or affecting to pity their disappointment, declared that having made a vow of celibacy, she had made them miserable by a rejection of their addresses. But now for the first time in her life particularly noticed by a peer, she seriously imagined her lucky hour was arrived, and that she was undoubtedly born to be a titled lady.

Full of this exhilarating notion, she assumed such youthful behaviour, and made such use of her large eyes, that Lord Clavering, highly diverted, took every pains, by returning her glances, and pressing her hand whenever accident brought hers in contact with his, as made her believe he would assuredly declare himself the devoted slave of her beauty the very first moment she would allow him an opportunity, and grant him permission.

At supper she had profusely spread before them every delicacy that the country afforded; and when the cloth was removed, contrived, by an inundation of questions, to put off the period of separation for the night, till Gabriel Jenkins, unused to be out of his bed after the sober hour of eleven, had fallen back in his chair, and with his mouth wide open was loudly snoring, to the extreme annoyance of his sister, who took infinite pains to apologize for his excessive rudeness.

In the course of their conversation at table the family at Glenwyn Priory were mentioned, and on Sir Edward Percival expressing a wish to be introduced to the nabob, Miss Jenkins offered to take them there the next morning, provided Lord Clavering would undertake to drive her and Rosa.

His lordship easily assented to this proposal, and Miss Jenkins retired to bed, exulting with the thought of making the proud Miss Montgomery almost die with envy when she saw the brilliant conquest she had made – when she saw her mistress of the heart of a peer, and in the road to become not only a wife, but to attain the envied rank of a countess.

Rosa Percival had long been the admiration of all the young men in her vicinity, and two or three sons of gentlemen farmers in the neighbourhood of Birch Park had offered themselves to her acceptance; but their suits had been modestly rejected, for the heart of Rosa remained totally insensible to tender declarations, and continued entirely unmoved, till on her introduction to Hugh Montgomery. She found that she did not listen to him even on common topics with the same easy happy indifference that she did to the conversation of other young men of her acquaintance.

She now found that when a visit to Glenwyn Priory was proposed she dressed herself with more than usual care; that she counted every moment till they set off; and that after having passed a few hours happily with Hugh Montgomery, she regretted their separation, and lingered behind to repeat "good night" again and again.

Yet the innocent Rosa never once suspected that she was in love, nor on such a subject had Hugh Montgomery ever spoken; he had scarcely ever paid her a mere passing compliment, yet there was a something in his look, in his manner, that had captivated her young fancy, that had won her innocent heart.

When Hugh Montgomery first met Rosa Percival he was

smarting under recent disappointment, he was suffering the pangs of despised love; his lacerated heart was filled, was engrossed by the divine image of Adeline Llewellyn, to whom indeed Rosa was much inferior in personal charms; but her timidity, her gentleness, the sweetness of her temper, her unaffected simplicity, her unassuming manners, soon attracted his attention, and won him from the melancholy that was spreading its sombre colouring upon his mind.

In her society he forgot the bitter pangs of disappointed hope; he became easy and satisfied, without being sensible of from whence or what proceeded the charm: her voice had the soothing power of tranquillizing his disturbed and agitated feelings, and while listening to her artless observations, and answering her inquiries, his heart ceased to regret Adeline; while conversing with her he forgot all seasons and their change, and found that though cruelly disappointed in the first warm wishes he had encouraged, that it was possible to admit a second; in short, his heart, his feelings, his understanding, all spoke in favour of Rosa Percival's unobtrusive merits, her mild, retiring delicacy of character.

Present or absent he found that he indeed fondly loved her, but determined not to expose himself to the mortification of another refusal, the bitterness of another disappointment – he determined to restrain his looks, to put a seal upon his lips, and patiently wait till time and accidental circumstance should develop to him unequivocally her real and decided sentiment for or against him.

Lord Clavering had seen Rosa Percival at Carnarvon some months previous to his present excursion into North Wales. His lordship had in his way from Ireland, where he had large possessions, taken Carnarvon in his tour, and had encountered her at a circulating library, where he had by way of lounge been tumbling over books he never intended to read, and making inquiries, in the answers to which he was no ways interested. With true fashionable impudence he had applied his glass to the face of the blushing Rosa: he had stared her out of countenance, and made two or three fruitless attempts to draw her into conversation. There was but little to attract observation in the face or person of the peer; he had one of those common looking countenances, which, encountered every day, makes no sort of impression on the mind or memory.

Rosa, though much hurt and disconcerted by his free manners at the time, had long since ceased to recollect either his person or his behaviour; it had passed away and was altogether forgotten. Not so his lordship: native beauty and pure unsophisticated mind, were phenomena that never crossed his vision in the gay circles of the great world: he was therefore particularly struck with the genuine manners, the playful simplicity of the modest Rosa; and in consequence of the deep impression she made, he took much trouble to inform himself of her residence, her name, and connections. It so happened that the person who kept the library, and to whom Lord Clavering addressed his inquiries, was a distant relation of Rosa's, a branch of the extensive family of the Jenkins, consequently perfectly qualified in every particular to give his lordship's curiosity ample satisfaction in the history he required: but it answered not his expectations; it threw a damp on the ardency of his hopes: he was greatly disappointed to find she was the daughter of his intimate friend Edward Percival.

That important discovery put an end at once to certain libertine wishes he had encouraged, certain licentious projects his prolific brain had half formed, for he found it would not do to transplant her from her native shades into a richer soil, unless as Lady Clavering.

Notwithstanding he fully understood the extensive latitude allowed to fashionable engagements, and the indulgent liberties permitted in modern friendships, yet he felt he dared not take advantage of the simplicity of a little mountaineer, whose father, notwithstanding the levity of his own principles, would not fail to resent the seduction, and seek revenge on the violater of his house's honour.

Lord Clavering left Carnarvon, and made a tour of the principality, in the hope of forgetting the charming little rustic: he returned to London, frequented every place of public entertainment, and plunged with greater avidity than ever into the vortex of dissipated pleasure: but even there the image of the modest, the interesting Rosa pursued him.

Lord Clavering, the gallant gay Lothario, after having fallen in love an hundred different times with an hundred different women, at last found that Rosa Percival, little more than a child, had made so deep, so lasting an impression on his memory, that in spite of reason and remonstrance he found she was really and absolutely necessary to his peace; he resolved, after much debate between prudence and passion, to mention the strange occurrence to her father, whom he accidentally met at a coffee-house a few days after his accession to his hereditary title.

Sir Edward Percival, who knew the true character of the man, smiled at his declaration of love, which he treated as a mere transitory fit, the whim of the moment: but obliged by his earnest and vehement protestations to give him serious attention; he said he was sorry, devilish sorry indeed, that he had not been favoured with his confidence a few days sooner.

"And why sorry, dear Percival, why sorry?" said the impatient peer; "sure it is not too late for you to prove your friendship."

"You shall hear," replied Sir Edward: "having lost a confounded large sum of money to that inexorable dog Harry Osterly, I was obliged to mortgage the reversion of the Rhydderdwyn estate, and not being able through other losses to make the necessary payments good, the mortgagee threatens to foreclose."

"Well, go on," said the peer.

"Now you must know," continued Sir Edward, "I have raised money upon everything that would fetch a guinea."

"Proceed," cried Lord Clavering, impatiently.

"Nay, I am almost at the conclusion," said the baronet; "the rest will be told in a few words. Sir Walter ap Rice – "

"What of him? Speak, dear Percival, what of him?" said Lord Clavering.

"Why," resumed the baronet, "he offers to pay off this confounded mortgage, and supply me with five thousand pounds for present exigencies provided he shall be allowed – "

"What, Sir Edward, what?" demanded the enraged peer in extreme agitation.

"To marry Rosa," replied Sir Edward.

"Hell! and ten thousand furies!" exclaimed Lord Clavering, starting from his seat, and pacing the floor: "does Miss Percival approve him?"

"Not that I know of," said the baronet. "I don't trouble myself on that score: he has frequently seen and conversed with her it seems: his estate lies contiguous to Birch Park, where she resides with her uncle, honest Gabriel Jenkins."

"Break with him instantly," said the enamored peer, "break with Sir Walter instantly. Rosa Percival shall be Countess of

Clavering. I will redeem the Rhydderdwyn estates from the claw of the cursed mortgagee: instead of five I will present you with ten thousand pounds: and on Rosa I will settle Alberlay Castle and all the surrounding demesne, which is at least worth twelve thousand a year," said the delighted baronet.

"Bravo! my lord, you are certainly in love; there cannot be a loop to hang a doubt on, when a man resigns so much money to prove his sincerity. Rosa is yours, and as to poor Sir Walter Ap Rice, why he must console himself under his disappointment as well as he can. The man can't be such an egregious ass as to be angry, hey! my lord, when he hears how much the scale was heavier in your favour than his."

The baronet immediately sent for his attorney: an agreement was drawn up on the spot between Lord Clavering and himself, signed, sealed, and delivered, according to the established forms of law; and two days after the Earl of Clavering and Sir Edward Percival, with a splendid equipage, set off for North Wales to visit Birch Park, the seat of honest Gabriel Jenkins, and sacrifice the innocent Rosa on the altar of selfishness and profligacy.

CHAPTER VIII

When we shall meet at Compt,
That look of thine will hurl my soul from heaven,
And fiends will snatch at it.

Shakespeare

"Such is the end of guilt!"

Love and misery are closely allied,
Inseparable companions. Oh!
Beware how you give love a place within
Your bosom: once admitted, he introduces
Sorrow, anguish, pain, well if not despair.
The suicide! the self-destroyer! where
Shall he go?

A. J. H.

THE pangs, the bitter excruciating pangs, the indifference, and at last total neglect of her once adoring and adored husband, gave to the tender and susceptible bosom of the beautiful Marchess della Rosalvo, had yielded their poignancy to time and reflection; they had ceased to agonise and lacerate: reason, conscious rectitude, pride, had each exerted their influence to restore her to that tranquillity which his unprincipled, his profligate, his unfeeling conduct had for years deprived her of. To painful regrets, to tormenting remembrances, and torturing tumultuous jealousies, had succeeded resignation; a pensive calm, which though sometimes disturbed by a sign of retrospective sorrow, was always to be restored, to be wooed back by the fascination of books, of music, or the exercise of the pencil.

In the first months of their separation the innocent marchesa flattered herself that her patient endurance, her silent uncomplaining submission, her utter seclusion from the gay world, where she had constantly moved, and had ever been considered and courted "as the fairest of the fair," would have a due effect and influence the mind and feelings of the marchese to do justice to her merits. She hoped that a proper sense of her injuries would touch his heart, which she still believed, though weakly led astray by unthinking youth and impetuous passion, was not vicious, not absolutely and irreclaimably depraved; and that satiated with wild and dissolute pursuits, and convinced of the impossibility of meeting happiness in scenes of riot and licentiousness, he would yet return a proselyte to her and virtue.

Unhappily for Celestina love had rendered her blind to the real character of her abandoned husband, he had no mind constituted by nature: devoted by habit to gross and intemperate pursuits, he understood not the charm of cultivated talent: he felt not the bliss of sentiment: delighted not in intellectual beauty: but impelled by strong inclination along the stream of vice and folly, panted only for fresh victims, was eager only for untried enjoyments.

At length, painfully convinced that she had nothing to hope or expect from the justice or humanity of the marchese; compelled, though unwillingly, to notice the enormities of his conduct, she ceased to lament his dereliction, and began to wonder how a heart formed like hers could ever have been attached to a being conspicuous only for low intrigues and disgraceful propensities.

Young, beautiful, and deserted, Celestina's situation was

soon known in Palermo, and while some lamented her injuries and execrated her husband, others secretly blest his inconstancy, that gave them an opportunity of offering consolation to the fair marchesa, who no sooner re-entered the gay circle than she was surrounded by lovers; her ears were assailed with adulation, and her heart besieged with vows and protestations of everlasting felicity. Guarded by the deceits and disappointments she had met, shielded by scorn for the injuries she had sustained, if Celestina did not absolutely despise mankind, she certainly listened to them with suspicion and reserve: as a woman her vanity was pleased with adulation and attention, but on her heart they made no impression.

Sleep, sweet and refreshing, again hovered over her couch; her dreams were no longer visions of perjury and dismay – "My heart," she would say, "no longer throbs with the misery of slighted passion. Man! thy empire is at an end; my bosom, now the mansion of blessed tranquillity, shall never exchange the peace of indifference for the tumults of love."

In this happy state of mind the marchesa first encountered Horatio Delamere at a ball given by the Prince Notali a few miles from Palermo. The party she was with were not acquainted with him, and they continued strangers the whole of the evening, but she saw him gracefully wind the mazes of the dance; she heard him speak, she remarked his intelligent countenance and his fine form, and a wish to be known to the charming Englishman mingled with the enchantments of the scene: frequently she saw him pass her residence, without even suspecting that she was interested in the inquiries she made. She learned his name, his quality, his family, and that with his relations he occupied a palazzo belonging to the Count Lionti, on the other side of Monti Liloni.

Fortune at last favoured her wishes, and she was introduced to him on the Marino; nor had he paid her many visits before she found that his society gave life to her conversation; his selection soul and spirit to her music; and that her paintings without his praise were mere inanimate daubs. Alarmed at the emotions his presence occasioned, and the regret his absence produced, Celestina began examining the state of her heart, asking her emotions what they meant.

TELL ME WHAT IS LOVE?

Oh! if when ev'ry mortal slept,
And only silence vigils kept;
Oh! if when Morpheus o'er my head
The softest dreams of pleasure shed;
If midst the starry noon of night
I wake from visions of delight,
To gaze and think, my eyes are blest
To see each planet sink to rest,
To watch the east till early day
Pours her first doubtful trembling ray;
To mark her fingers dropping dew,
Tinge the light clouds with saffron hue;
While many a wishing tender sigh
Will 'cross yon lofty mountain fly,
Which dimly gleaming meets my sight,
Its blue top streak'd with new-born light;
O! if my pulses nimbly beat,
If then my fancy soar to meet
That form, which hov'ring in my dreams,

To me all grace and beauty seems;
O! if imperious in my heart
        One passion wild and lofty move;
O! if it bliss and grief impart,
        Say, is that lordly passion love?

Say, if at mention of a name
My cheek with crimson blushes flame;
If at a voice my throbbing breast
Be with such strong emotion pressed,
That in confusion sunk and lost,
Breath and reflection both are tossed;
O! if when gazing on an eye
My fainting senses almost die;
If when effusing heav'nly rays,
I on those sunny eye-beams gaze;
Their radiance pouring floods of light,
Dazzle my reason and my sight;
If at a touch keen subtle fire
Shoot through my frame and I expire;
In sweet deliriums, raptur'd bliss,
Tell me, O! tell me, what is this?
        It is not friendship's holy glow,
That thus with transport fills my soul,
That bids my blood impetuous roll,
That rushing through my beating heart,
Can such ecstatic joy impart,
        As bids soft tears delicious flow,
Friendship could ne'er thus wildly move –
Tell me, O! tell me, is it love?

When evening's banner dusky gray
Waves o'er the sun's departing ray;
When she with dew-bespangled feet,
Glides slowly through each green retreat,
And as her deep'ning shades prevail,
Draws o'er each sleeping flower her veil;
If then alive to feeling's pow'r,
I court the soft the shadowy hour;
If then enthusiastic hail
The sighing spirit of the gale,
That loves his flutt'ring wing to lave
In the clear ocean's emerald wave,
That wave, which shook with storms no more,
Soft murmuring woos the distant shore;
If then emotions sad and sweet
In my thrill'd bosom wildly beat;
If then my eyes, suffus'd with tears;
If then a thousand hopes and fears,
Should in my wilder'd fancy stray,
And chase tranquillity away;
Ye that these mingled feelings know,
    Ye that from sad experience prove,
Tell me, what means this joy and woe;
    O! say, are these sensations love.

Celestina was fated to discover what she would fain have hid from all the world, but most of all from herself: and that in spite of the resolves she had formed, and the woe she had suffered, she loved again, and with a passion more tender and more violent than before: in a moment of weakness she became the victim of her sensibility: yet though subdued, her virtue was not extinguished: she still felt the upbraidings of conscience, still felt the stings of humiliating pride.

Unable to conquer the strong and vehement passion that possessed her soul, she yielded all her hours to love and Horatio Delamere, while even genius and talent became subservient to the predominant sensations that absorbed all the better qualities of her mind.

Though she knew and felt herself the sovereign mistress of his heart, the sole and undivided possessor of all his hopes and wishes, yet she was far from satisfied, very far from happy: her mind, naturally good and amiable, felt with poignant sorrow the lapse she had made from virtue, and even at the moment when his expressive eyes beamed on her the warmest emanations of adoration, when his arms enfolded her with passionate fondness, torrents of tears would burst from her eyes, and hiding her burning blushes in his bosom, she would exclaim, "Lost as I am to virtue, do not, do not hate me."

It was after an affecting appeal of this nature that Horatio, kneeling before her, her arms entwining his neck, was endeavouring to soothe the agonies of her mind by the tenderest assurances of unabating passion, of everlasting respect, and undeviating constancy, that the Marchese della Rosalvo burst suddenly into the apartment, his hair erect on his head, his face of the ashy paleness of death, his eyes wild, his dress spotted with blood, and in his clenched hand a loaded pistol.

For some moments he regarded them in silence, while the guilty and astonished pair waited in horrible suspense an explanation of his intrusion and disordered appearance.

"See," cried he, pointing to his wife, "see another victim of my monstrous guilt. Celestina! ruined angel! if I dared hope my other crimes might meet with pardon, that look of thine, when we shall meet to render up accounts above, that look of thine would damn me! Guilt is in thy face and I, wretch that I am! I was the cause; for thou wert good, wert innocent, till I abandoned thee – left thee to seek in other bosoms the tenderness you ought to have found in mine."

Celestina had approached. – "Good God" cried she, "you are covered with blood!"

"Yes, with Ruperto's blood – the blood of my friend – the man whose purse and heart were open to me."

"Ruperto," said Celestina, shuddering, "sure you have not killed him!"

"Yes, I have," replied he: "Ruperto waits for me in the regions of the damned! Hark! they come to seek me: the officers of the inquisition are after me. But this," continued he, elevating the pistol, "this shall disappoint them. Yet, Celestina, I would fain be forgiven by you before I die. I would beg you not to curse my memory. Though what does it matter? – the curses of suffering wretches cannot penetrate the grave; they cannot reach the ears of those who led them into guilt, who brought calamity upon them. No, no, their maledictions disturb not those who sleep in death."

Celestina had sunk exhausted upon a sofa, while Horatio vainly persuaded the marchese to retire to bed, and endeavour by repose to quiet the perturbation of his mind.

"Celestina," said the marchese, advancing to the sofa on which she reclined, "Celestina, speak to me: promise me that when death shall have sealed my eyes you will retire to a monastery."

"And why," said Horatio, "why wish to extort such a

promise? Because you have made life no longer desirable to yourself, why selfishly desire to bind her to seclude herself from that world she is formed to adorn, to quit those scenes she may yet enjoy."

"Peace!" exclaimed the marchese, "peace, I charge you. Do I not know you have dishonoured her? But abject, fallen as I am, I dare not vindicate a husband's rights. Vice and a consciousness of crime make my arm nerveless. Celestina, thou art not to blame; none shall accuse thee; on me, on me falls all the guilt: on my head retribution shall be asked for thy frailty. I have seduced the wife of Ruperto; he upbraided me with my crime; we fought – this is his blood. Celestina, to my black catalogue of crimes add murder. Ruperto and myself were engaged in a conspiracy against the Prince Oscari: before this his papers are seized, and ere long the inquisition will demand me: but never," cried he, "never shall Della Rosalvo's body glut their vengeance."

Celestina gazed with terrified looks on the distorted features of her husband; while Horatio, losing in the distracted scene before him the remembrance of his own unpleasant situation, proposed to the marchese to seek some place of security where he might tranquillize his harassed mind, and elude the vengeance of the dreaded inquisition.

"And where," cried he, with a look of horror and in a tone of despondency, "in what secret untrodden cavern, buried beneath what inaccessible rock, shall I escape the retributive vengeance of heaven? Where stifle the upbraidings of a conscience stained with crimes – where lose the harrowing remembrance of youth wasted in infamy? Never till this accursed night were my hands dipped in blood; yet many are the victims that I with cold unfeeling barbarity have torn from fame, from innocence, and left to perish in vice and want. Yes, I have wantonly ruined reputations, have broken hearts: and, oh! Celestina," said he, with a deep groan, while he gazed with remorse on her pale countenance, "you, yes, you, whom heaven designed an angel, my crimes have made – but it is not yet too late for you. Yours, Celestina, is a venial trespass. Fly, I charge thee, fly the world."

The marchesa turned on him a look of unutterable anguish.

"Poor deluded wretch," continued he, "has destiny marked thee for the dupe of man? Do I not know thy mind too exquisitely organized to be happy. When the grave covers me, which will soon be the case, should thy undoer marry thee, will that act restore the blissful consciousness of undeviating innocence – would it shield thee from thy own reproach? No, Celestina, his fondest attentions would still fail to convince you that she who had forfeited her own respect could ever possess his."

The marchesa sank back, and covered her face with her hands.

"Peace, barbarian!" exclaimed Horatio, clasping the almost lifeless marchesa in his arms, "peace! do not commit another murder; do not deprive her of the only consolation your crimes and vices have left her – a confidence in my unshaken honour and my ardent love. Yes, I adore her; to make her mine by every sacred ceremony is the first warm wish of my heart; but be assured whenever she becomes my wife, never can Celestina be more loved, more respected, never can she hold a higher place in my esteem than at present."

"Thou dost hear him," said the marchese, grasping the hand of his wife; "thou dost hear this man, and thou hast heard fervent vows of love before; thou hast believed them too, and been deceived, deserted, left in the bloom of youth, in the proud boast of beauty. You must remember I so vowed, so promised; yet I was perjured; I, thy husband, the envy of Palermo. Nay, at the very instant I protested most affection, I ridiculed the weak credulity that could so listen, that could be so deceived. Hope not for constancy in man; possession palls the appetite, indulgence brings satiety, while woman fondly dotes on him to whom she yields her charms, and every fresh enjoyment twines him round her heart with closer, tenderer affection: hence the mutability of man – hence his passion for variety, and hence the pangs that woman feels from desertion, from disappointed hope, from extinguished love."

"But all men are not so ungrateful, are not such villains," said Horatio.

"Their natures are but too much alike," resumed the marchese, "and Celestina may again be fated to a renewal of the sorrows she has already experienced. We know not our own hearts: slaves of imperious circumstance, our passions are our masters, and as they direct, we plunge ourselves in gulphs of guilt, and with our enormities lacerate the bosoms that confide in us; introduce into the pure peaceful mansions of innocence the destroying fiend, revenge, who with murderous sophistry persuades us to plunge a dagger in our own hearts with the fallacious hope of wounding those who have injured us. Celestina, I conjure you," added he, "by your hopes of future happiness, I conjure you to listen to me."

"No," said Horatio, "no, most adored of women, hear not his arguments, believe not man the monster he would paint him: all are not fiends: listen not to his advice, which would tear you from the arms of him who will ever love, will ever protect you. Attend not to the ebullitions of frenzy, which would lead you to the cheerless gloom of a monastery, where all the tender ties of love must be dissolved, all the warm feelings of the heart be sacrificed on the dark altar of superstition and bigotry."

Celestina pressed the fevered, bloodstained hand of her husband between both hers, and turning her tear-swollen eyes towards heaven, faintly uttered, "I forgive you from my soul all that I have endured, all the sorrows I may yet have to endure: but if you dread pursuit why do you not fly from danger? Oh! begone, and in repentant solitude solicit pardon for your crimes: for me I am convinced this world has indeed no happiness, and I solemnly promise – "

"Oh! Celestina," exclaimed Horatio, interrupting her, "make no promise I conjure you; enter into no engagements with this man. In what instance has he ever shown himself your friend, that he should arrogate a right to dictate? Why then should his wishes, his advice actuate you to devote yourself yet in the bloom of life to seclusion and penitence? What crime loads your conscience that demands the sacrifice of your happiness and mine? Whose rights have we infringed? – not his, who abandoned them, Whose feelings have we outraged that we should be condemned to the misery of an eternal separation? Have you not a thousand times vowed to me an eternal love? What act of mine has forfeited my claim on Celestina's justice and her truth?"

"Remember, Celestina," said the marchese, sternly, "remember you are a married woman, and that no guilt of mine, however deep, will do away, although it may palliate in some degree, your failings."

"Reproach her not," cried Horatio. "O God! what crime has she committed?"

"Adultery," said the marchese, in a hollow voice. "Is it not a damning sin, Celestina? You have broken the vow pledged at the altar in the house of God; you have committed adultery, and that one crime shall weigh against your thousand virtues. Haste from the scenes that have witnessed your guilty pleasures; expiate by tears and contritions, by penances your sin."

Celestina shuddered; a more deadly white settled on her face as the marchese fixing on her a frenzied gaze, continued: –

"Oh! add not to the tortures I am doomed to undergo in that world to which I am hastening, the horror of meeting thee amidst exulting devils, who in triumphant malice shall point to thy writhing form, and shrieking in my burning ears, bid me behold my work, the fruit of damned Rosalvo's crimes."

An agonizing shriek burst from Celestina: the picture was too horrible. –

"Surely," said she, "if I am not so lost, heaven cannot so have abandoned me." – Horatio would have led her from the room, but the marchese placing himself before the entrance, said: "Heaven abandons none but those who are self-abandoned: for me, I am devoted, lost, sold to destruction; the gates of mercy are for ever closed against me: but you, heaven may yet be merciful to you. Fly instantly; I charge you fly to some religious sanctuary. Deplore your sin, supplicate heaven before it is too late. Save yourself, Celestina, from that hell to which I am destined."

"Oh! Delamere!" exclaimed the terrified marchesa, "has love done this? am I indeed reduced to such extremity? Am I a wretch whose crime almost excludes her from heaven's grace? Is there no alternative? – must I separate from thee, adored of my soul, or risk eternal reprobation?"

"Is he not a heretic?" asked the marchese. "Deluded woman! What happiness could you expect with him whose faith so widely differs from your own?"

"With what fallacies," cried Horatio, "would you bewilder her? Celestina! angel! our merciful creator will not ask, among all the various religions promulgated through the vast extended universe, which he professed who performs his duties like a Christian. Confide in me, my Celestina, nor doubt that God, who delights in the happiness, not in the misery of his creatures, will bless and smile upon a union grafted on the pure basis of true affection: let me lead you from this man, whose crimes have unsettled reason."

Horatio would again have led Celestina from the apartment, but the marchese forcibly detaining her: said, "One word more: there is yet a woe you dream not of. Celestina, in every way you are undone: owing to a mistake in your settlements, I have had the power, aye and used it too, to sell the whole of your possessions; the rich vineyards of Luscario, the flower enamelled meadows of Poentia, the grove embosomed palazzo of Mervani, all are gone."

"It cannot be; it is impossible; you are deceiving me," cried the gasping marchesa.

"No," resumed the marchese, "these are facts. You have nothing left, no not even this palazzo; all is gone. I have played, gambled deep for some time, Ruperto has supplied the means of concealing from the world the ruined state of my affairs: I have murdered him, and now nothing remains for me but self-destruction: for you, Celestina, what but the refuge of a convent?"

"What indeed!" sighed the marchesa. "Where now can the every way ruined Celestina hide her woes, but in the deep solitude of conventual gloom? where expect a friend, unless won by penitence and prayer offended heaven compassionates her sorrows?"

"Unkind and cruel!" said Horatio: "would you fly from him who lives but to adore you: whose heart, whose arms, are open to receive and shield you from each impending evil! – Let your possessions pass away; Celestina's heart, her mind, are treasures richer than empires. Never more will we separate; one fate, one fortune, henceforth shall bind us: I am thine, my adored; I swear, solemnly swear, no power shall ever force me to abandon thee."

"Horatio! dearest, best beloved! It cannot, must not be; the ruined beggared Celestina, undone in fortune and in fame, will not consent to blight thy future prospects: I feel it right as I have erred that I alone should suffer; heaven knows I love thee – fondly love thee, but we must part now, and for ever."

"Part!" exclaimed Horatio, "part! you cannot mean it! what power, whose voice, shall dare to pronounce our separation?"

"Mine," cried the marchese, "mine, her husband's!"

"Her destroyer's!" said Horatio disdainfully.

"True, most true," resumed the marchese. "Well, be it so; I confess myself a wretch most guilty. Yet, Celestina, I would, cruel as I have been, I would if possible prevent your future suffering. A moment, a little moment only stands between me and eternity: I would employ that awful interval in bidding you beware how you again confide in man; – trust not to his promises; remember he can smile, and smile, and be a villain! – take advantage of the present hour: collect your jewels; gather together what is most valuable to you, and while you are yet unimplicated in my crimes fly to the safety of some convent."

"What has her innocence to fear?" asked Horatio.

"Innocence! every thing," replied the marchese: "if once brought within the labyrinth of the infernal inquisition, she may be tortured to confess what she has never even heard of. Innocence is ever the dupe and victim of the designing and the wicked: successful villany lords it over the artless and unsuspecting. In the bloodstained chambers of the inquisition many an innocent has suffered for the crimes of others."

A noise in the outer apartment was now heard: the marchese stood opposite the door, holding the pistol pointed to his temple: "They come," said he, "the blood-hounds come: they think to drag Della Rosalvo before their high tribunal, by their accursed tortures to force his lips to criminate himself."

"O! why," said the trembling Celestina, leaning for support against Horatio, "why would you not escape while it was in your power?"

"No," replied he, "I designed to die. My fortune dissipated, my hands steeped in blood, I meant not to drag on a miserable existence, till destiny should deign to send me to the grave; no, I meant to seize on time, to burst asunder the links of being, to become whenever occasion prompted my own destroyer: the hour has arrived; one other moment and then, ye devils, snatch your devoted prey."

As he spoke the door was thrown open: a number of men bearing the insignia of the inquisition rushed in: but before they could seize the marchese he had fired: the pistol dropped from his slackened hold, but the ball had penetrated his temple. He staggered towards Celestina, and fell upon her robe.

Celestina sunk on her knees beside him.

"Now," cried he, struggling for utterance, "now promise me

to fly the world to seek for peace and forgiveness in religious retirement. I know my doom – it is in the burning caverns of hell, to dwell with fiends in everlasting tortures: but you – you may be an inhabitant of heaven. Swear to me while yet my soul is sensible of the consoling promise; swear to me that you will quit the world and devote yourself to God."

"Yes," said Celestina, overcome with the horror of the scene, "yes, I swear I will fly the world. I will in religious seclusion seek the pardon of the God I have offended; I will cast all earthly passions from my soul, and from this hour devote myself to heaven."

Horatio heard no more, a faintness seized him; he sunk beside the body of the expiring marchese, who, pressing the hand of the marchesa to his ashy lips murmured, "I thank you, I die content. Celestina, you will keep your word: forgive the wretch who has undone you."

His voice was lost in a deep rattling groan: the blood rushed in torrents from his wound: his eyes closed, and life was extinguished for ever.

In the first moments of recollection Horatio found himself in his own bed; he attempted to rise, but he found himself weak and ill; a confused remembrance of scenes of terrible import floated in his imagination, and Celestina, the adored of his heart, but lost to him for ever, appeared arrayed in fascinating beauty, making those vows that were to separate them eternally.

Captain Lonsdale sat beside his bed, and from him he would have inquired where he had been, how he had been conveyed home, and what had become of her dearer to him than light or existence, the Marchesa Della Rosalvo; but an opiate had been administered to him; and before his understanding could take in the answers given to his interrogations, he was sunk in a profound sleep. Many days past before he was thought able to hear and bear an account of what had happened. During the suspension of his reason, he had been taken before the inquisition, had been threatened with the torture, had witnessed the examination of the injured Celestina, had heard his own acquittal and hers, had seen her tear herself from his embraces, and, faithful to the promise she had made the suicide her husband, devote the remainder of her days to that living tomb, a convent. Lady Isabella and her husband saw his constitution get the better of the shocks it had sustained, and hoped everything from time and absence; they sincerely pitied the injuries and ruined fortunes of the unhappy Marchesa della Rosalvo, but at the same time secretly rejoiced that she had abjured the world, because they knew that Horatio's honour, independent of his love, would have induced him to make her reparation by marriage for the stigma he had brought upon her character; they also knew that Lord Narbeth would never have forgiven his son allying himself to a foreigner, and by that connection breaking the line of Britons, which he for ages unnumbered had with national pride beheld sustain the honours of his house and name, a house much more famous for its dignity and worth than wealth. The health of Horatio was in part restored, but his mind still languished with an incurable disease, love for Celestina: in vain were his unceasing inquiries; she was hid from his indefatigable search, fled from his ardent wishes. He had added to entreaties large bribes, but no convent in Palermo owned the Marchesa della Rosalvo for its inmate.

Walking one morning in despair along the aloe groves that beautify the entrance of Palermo, Horatio, to his infinite joy, beheld the marchesa's favourite woman pursuing the path before him: hope again animated his bosom: he at last overtook her.

"Tell me," he cried, in a voice scarcely articulate: "tell me, Olivia, where is your lady?"

For many moments the girl stood silent and irresolute, but pitying his impatience and extreme agitation, she at last said: –

"And is it now, signor, that you inquire after the marchesa?"

"I have been ill, deprived of reason, for I know not how long," replied Horatio, "but with the first beam of intellect came the remembrance of Celestina, and I have never since ceased to inquire, to seek her; but where, answer me, I conjure you, Oliva – where shall I find her? Direct me to her."

"I know not whether she will see you," replied Olivia. "She believes you false, and under this idea has wept and suffered; has entered on her novitiate, has vowed to be a nun."

"Oh, let me fly, to convince her she has wronged me! to justify myself, to snatch her from the sombre haunts of superstition, to life and love. Come," continued Horatio, "name the convent that holds the beloved of my soul."

"There, signor," said Olivia, pointing, "there are the moss covered turrets, the spires, and the grey walls of the Convent of the Sisters of Penitence. There the Marchesa della Rosalvo has vowed to devote her remaining days to remorse and heaven."

"It must not, shall not be!" exclaimed the almost frantic Horatio. "Her heart is mine! heaven will not accept divided vows."

He was rushing forward, and had nearly reached the mossy iron gate of the convent, when Olivia caught his arm.

"Hold, signor," said she, "let me go first, and prepare the marchesa, for your visit. She too has been ill, her health is yet delicate; your sudden appearance would have fatal consequences."

"Go then," cried Horatio, "go plead for me; tell my adored Celestina that never for a moment have I ceased to think of her – tell her I wait to restore her to liberty, to love, and happiness."

Horatio seated himself under the feathery branches of a cork tree, to wait the return of Olivia; he endeavoured to reason his tumultuous feelings to a calm, but every added moment increased his agitation. The splendours of an unclouded sky; the rich odour wafted from a thousand plants and flowers; the situation of the convent, rearing its ponderous sides upon a bold aspiring eminence, that commanded a view of the whole magnificent city of Palermo, and many leagues round its romantic coast; all failed either to command his attention, or still the convulsive throbbings of his heart. Suspense! expectation! agonizing situation! If there are moments in which the soul endures excruciating pangs, for which language has no description, it is when elevated with hope, sinking with despair, it trembles, glows, and writhes in dire suspense. Certainty, be it what it may, even though it annihilates our fondest hopes, our cherished wishes, is heaven compared with such a state of torture.

At length, after a tedious interval, Olivia appeared and beckoned him towards her.

"The marchesa at first," said she, "was inflexible, and peremptorily refused to admit you to her presence; but when I described the illness from which you were but just recovering, the anxiety you expressed on her account, your impatience to behold her, she wept and bade me lead you to her."

"Bless her! bless her!" said Horatio, as he followed his conductor through the heavy gates of the convent, into a parlour wainscoted with dark oak, carved into horrible figures of grinning fiends, gigantic crucifixes, and expiring saints, across the floor of which was fixed a double iron grating, that enclosed another part of the room, entirely concealed from inspection by a black cloth curtain which hung in thick folds over the grating. "And is this the retreat of Celestina?" said Horatio, as his eye wandered over the gloomy apartment; "is it in this haunt of superstition that the beloved of my soul seeks peace?"

The black curtain was slowly drawn aside, and Horatio beheld the Marchesa della Rosalvo, not as he was wont to meet her – her eyes, once so brilliant, were sunk and heavy; the rich carnation bloom of her cheek was succeeded by a deadly paleness; the luxuriant ringlets that used to wave in glossy beauty over her ivory forehead were hid under the long black veil, and instead of the light transparent drapery that used to grace her fine form, she was closely folded in the coarse grey habit of the order of the sisters of penitence.

"Father of mercies!" exclaimed Horatio, as his raised eyes encountered the figure before him, "can this be Celestina?"

"Yes," replied she with a faint smile extending her hand through the grating, "all that grief has left of her; but seeing you, Horatio, knowing that you have not forgot, deserted me, will remove a load of anguish from my heart: to know that I am not despised by him who caused my errors will console me in the hour when renouncing the world I shall devote myself to penitence."

"Celestina! you cannot mean," said Horatio, "you do not intend to renounce the world, to devote me to misery?"

"No," replied the marchesa, "I mean to restore thee to happiness, to dissolve those ties that would only wound thy fame, and entail disgrace upon thee. No, never, dear Horatio; the fallen degraded Celestina will not put thy future peace in hazard, having weakly erred, how could I hope thy confidence!"

"Oh! you have never loved me," exclaimed Horatio, "if you had, now, when each obstacle is removed, when not a barrier rises to oppose our happiness; would you thus wound my heart? Oh! Celestina, quit this gloomy monastery, leave these haunts of despair and let me lead you to felicity."

"Felicity!" sighed the marchesa, "felicity is not for me! Have you forgot the fatal night when I swore to my dying husband to fly the world, to spend the wretched remnant of my life kneeling and weeping at the altar of an offended God! Did he not in his last hour accuse me of a damning sin? Oh! seek not, dearest most loved of men, seek not to plunge me deeper in guilt, but here receive my last adieu."

"Never," cried Horatio, "never; that oath, Celestina, was extorted in a moment of terror; it is not binding in the sight of heaven."

"My purpose is unchangeably fixed," resumed the marchesa: "never will I break another oath. In the deep silence of the night I hear my husband's groans; his pale bleeding form flits before my distempered fancy, and in every hollow gust that sweeps along the solitary cloisters I hear his voice; it sounds in my affrighted ear: – 'Kneel, Celestina, pray for mercy!' "

"Sweet visionary," said Horatio; "these imaginations are

the offspring of gloomy seclusion, of monastic solitude. Consent, my Celestina, to quit these abodes of superstitious terror; return with me to that world which without you will be a desert. In my arms forget the sorrows that are past, in my tenderness hope with confidence for happiness: why those tears, that heavy sigh, that averted look? Remember how we have loved."

"Oh! spare me, spare me the remembrance," replied the marchesa: "was our love now to begin, Celestina might indeed look forward to days of happiness, but never now, oh, never – yet why pursue a subject that rends our hearts. Heaven forbids our union; an oath, a solemn oath has past my lips, I dare not break it, I dare not be again forsworn. Horatio, fare thee well; in this world we meet no more, in the next our souls, purified from sin, may claim affinity with each other."

Horatio pressed her hand to his heart, to his lips – he dashed his head against the iron grating, and exclaimed:

"I will never quit you. Obdurate, you shall witness my death, for never in life will I resign you."

"Be calm, Horatio, and listen to me. Never can I quit this sanctuary; my oath of seclusion has past before the high tribunal of the inquisition; it is registered in their tremendous archives, and it is recorded on adamantine tablets in the eternal courts of heaven. No, dearest, most beloved of men, I never can be yours. In a few days I pronounce the irrevocable vow that shuts me from the world for ever. I shall become a nun."

"O God!" cried Horatio, "will such a sacrifice be acceptable?"

"Yes," resumed the marchesa, "Heaven will accept the sacrifice of unfeigned contrition of broken heart. Consider me as dead: mourn for me a little while, Horatio; for at the solemn hour of midnight, when my trembling knees press the cold marble shrine, it will be consolation to my heart to think that thy eyes perhaps are filled with tears proceeding from the same cause that calls forth mine; that thy bosom heaves the same sigh of sad regret. Remember me as one who but for love might have been respected, might have been most happy." And now pressing his hand to her lips – "Farewell for ever."

"Yet stay," cried he: "stay, cruel as you are, and tell me why did you admit me if it were only to say that we must part for ever."

"I have indeed done wrong," said the marchesa, "and I deserve reproach, but oh! Horatio, forgive me. I wished before our eternal separation to hear thy voice, to bless my eyes with a last look: and I wished if possible to convince you that it was right that we should meet no more: here then let us separate: be happy, dearest Horatio; be happy, adored of my soul! nay, relieve me: in a few moments I shall be summoned to chapel: suffer me to employ that short interval in composing my mind, in fitting my thoughts for addressing the Most High."

Amidst the tears and ravings of Horatio Celestina tore herself away; she fixed on him a look of unutterable love and anguish, and was lost to his sight for ever.

At the appointed time the Marchesa della Rosalvo, in the presence of almost all the nobility of Palermo, pronounced the irrevocable vow that detached her from the world and Horatio Delamere; that separated her from the allurements of love, and devoted her for ever to penitence and religion.

CHAPTER IX

Alas! at what age comes prudence?

At the shrine of interest men will sacrifice their principles,
Forget even honour and humanity.

How many victims, Love, dost thou demand,
How few allow to taste thy blessings? Better
Pleased to have thy altar bathed with tears
Than to see thy votaries deck'd with smiles.

A. J. H.

WHEN the company separated, Miss Jenkins sat a long time in her chamber, delighting herself with the possibility of becoming a countess; in binding her brows with an ideal coronet; and when at last she went to bed, the remainder of the night was past in projecting schemes of future grandeur; in considering how she should the next day adorn and decorate her person so as to render it more irresistible, more captivatingly handsome in the eyes of Lord Clavering, whose heart she positively believed had yielded itself a slave to her wit and beauty; in picturing to herself the astonishment of all her acquaintance, and the mortification of Miss Montgomery and Miss Tudor, whom she supposed her elevation, which she doubted not would very soon take place, would almost kill with spite, envy, and vexation. She thought too of the disappointment she should occasion her admirer poor Williams, who had deliberated and turned the matter over in his mind, till he had worn out her patience, and who she supposed would certainly hang himself, when he heard of her marriage with Lord Clavering.

The gentle, innocent Rosa Percival was also restless and uneasy; her spirits almost sunk to despondency, but from far different causes; no visionary schemes of proud ambition, no wild hopes of rank or elevation, were rioting in her bosom; no mean malicious desire of inspiring others with envy or vexation; she was wounded, deeply wounded, by the gay free manners of her father, and still more so by his chilling indifference towards her: she had hoped to be so blest in his tenderness; she had so exulted in the hope of parental confidence and endearments; that the absolute coldness with which he received her at their first meeting had occasioned her so painful a disappointment, that her pillow was for the first time in her life wet with tears of heart-felt sorrow. She thought too of Hugh Montgomery; she recalled with saddened pleasure the soft soothing tones of his voice; her memory reverted to his generous mind, his liberal feeling heart, which she had seen evince itself in frequent instances. She recollected his elegant impressive manners, entirely divested of those ridiculous airs of foppery denominated fashion, and the warm tears of tender sensibility mingled with the bitter ones she shed for the apathy of her father.

At breakfast the next morning Lord Clavering declared that he had never past so delightful a night, that he had reposed on roses and lavender; he extolled the coffee, praised the butter, and protested that North Wales was the garden of Eden, and that he was determined to pass a part of every ensuing year of his life in exploring its beauties.

Sir Edward Percival devoured the ham and new laid eggs with an appetite that told the keen air from the mountains had given him at last a relish for the productions of Wales; a country he so generally despised, and thought so extremely savage, that he seldom allowed any thing to be good that was to be met with in the principality.

During breakfast much skirmishing took place between Mr. Gabriel Jenkins and Sir Edward, whose fashionable inanity the honest Cambrian with much humour imitated and ridiculed, and whose unfeeling negligence and indifference to his daughter he resented with feeling and indignation. After the breakfast things were removed, Sir Edward sat sometime lolling in his chair, picking his teeth, humming a tune, and examining Rosa from head to foot through his eye-glass, whom he at last asked if she was dressed after the costume of Noah's wife.

"Not but the antique is now quite the thing: though egad, child, your drapery has nothing of the Grecian about it; it is as absolutely destitute of all pretention to taste and elegance, as if you had copied from a Hottentot at the Cape of Good Hope."

Rosa's eyes filled with tears.

"Pshaw, girl," continued he, "prithee don't snivel. I hate abominably your pathetics – I detest and execrate a weeping beauty; besides, if you only knew how much smiles and vivacity were to be preferred to blubbered cheeks and red swollen eyes, you would take care how you gave way to weak nerves, and excessive sensibility: the die away sentimental has been out a long time, is utterly exploded. The gay, the frolic, the spirited, the vivacious is now the very height of fashion. A female in high life would actually expire at the bare idea of being caught in the dismals. Oh! no – a woman of breeding and fashion never sheds tears on any occasion."

"No," replied Lord Clavering, with a smile, "for she dreads to wash the Circassian bloom from her cheeks, or to have it imagined that she has feelings in common with other people. But when once Miss Percival becomes acquainted with the haut ton, she no doubt will soon get rid of the sensibility you think so ridiculous and unbecoming."

"I fear not," replied Rosa, "if I am fated, my lord, to become an inhabitant of the great world, to mix in fashionable society. I apprehend that I shall continually be meeting incidents that will be grating to my feelings, and keep sensibility alive."

"I fancy, child," said Sir Edward, yawning, "among the rest of your accomplishments, Miss Jenkins has not forgot romance reading; but faith, you will find the high flown notions and sickly sentimentality that you meet with in books only existed in the poor devil of an author's brain, whose secluded situation, empty pockets, and thin diet, made him full of chimerical notions, and flighty imaginations, not a single iota of which will accord with the rules and usage of real life."

"What! Sir Edward," said Miss Jenkins, "do you mean to assert that feeling and sensibility are quite out of fashion?"

"With all but old women," replied Sir Edward, pointedly; "they may indulge in cant and whine as much as they choose; but the young ones have better business to attend to – the Opera, the assembly: no dismal faces there; each emulous to banish care and thought, and resign their feelings to be subdued or excited according to the pleasure of the magician whim. But come, my little Celia, or Delia," addressing himself to Rosa, "will you indulge me with a private interview? Why, what now (seeing a kind of hesitation in her looks), surely your prudery cannot see the shadow of an impropriety in a tête-a-tête with me?"

"Certainly not," said Miss Jenkins, "there can be no objection."

Rosa dreaded she knew not what, but she tied on her straw hat, and followed her father to the lawn.

"A very vulgar plebeian sort of an exercise this same walking," said Sir Edward, throwing himself at full length on a rustic bench, "and fit only for the robust herculean limbs of a native savage. I suppose," continued he, gazing round him, "the mountaineers call this a fine prospect, those cloud capped hills, and that expanded ocean? Egad, people's tastes differ strangely; for my part, I think Billingsgate or Saint Giles's a more desirable prospect by half. Heaven defend me from vegetating in these mountains, among these sublime views. But I beg pardon, Miss Percival: admiring the mountain scenery, I had really forgot you." Rosa curtsied. "That won't do, child: bending the knees is not fashionable: a graceful inclination of the body has taken place of that sort of thing; but now as we have happily escaped the gogglers of Aunt Nanny, and the quite and clean gad of Uncle Gabriel, come here my little wood nymph, and make true answers to the questions I am going to propose."

Rosa's heart beat violently.

"How many lovers, my sweet rural deity, have you in this neighbourhood?"

Rosa stood silent, and abashed.

"Powers of fashion!" continued Sir Edward, "how the simpleton blushes; tell me, child, ingenuously, how many of the natives do you hold in your chains? Speak, I command you; how many do you set down in the list of your admirers?"

"Not one," replied Rosa.

"What! has not Sir Walter Ap Rice whispered soft nonsense in your ear? Take care, Rosa, no prevarication; I expect sincerity."

"Well then, sir, to be sincere," said Rosa, "I confess he has said soft things to me, so very soft, that I can without the smallest regret dispense with his admiration. My vanity soars above Sir Walter Ap Rice."

"Some spice of spirit in that, faith," rejoined Sir Edward, starting up; "that speech egad had nothing of the Jenkins in it; that was true and genuine Percival. Well then, as you reject a baronet it appears quite unnecessary to question you any further respecting the noble descendants of Saint Taffy. Will any thing under a ducal dignity content you? What think you of being a countess?"

"Really, sir," replied Rosa, "I have never yet had such ambitious thoughts."

"No! why, when you considered that you were a daughter of the noble house of Percival, such an ambition would not have been so very extravagant."

"True, sir," replied Rosa, timidly, "but having been left so many years, my whole life, unclaimed, totally unnoticed by that noble family, I never dared to suffer myself to remember that I was at all allied to them. My uncle and aunt were so kind, so very good and affectionate, that I only imagined I belonged to them. And when you reflect, sir, how far removed from scenes of grandeur I have always lived, you will scarcely wonder that my ideas have dwelt on the hope of future happiness rather than grandeur."

"Love in a cottage, I suppose," said Sir Edward, with a sneer; "for the peaceful, happy days of Arcadia to be renewed; a flock of snow-white sheep, and a crook bound with wreaths of flowers by the beloved hand of Corydon, sitting by a meandering stream, listening enraptured to the melody of his oaten reed; moonlight nights, and the warbling of nightingales."

"Ah!" thought Rosa, "with Hugh Montgomery how delightful would all this be!"

"But," continued Sir Edward, "allow me to inform you, Miss Percival, that your destiny points a different road. I came into Wales on purpose to claim and notice you, which family reasons had before prevented, to prove to you that you are allied to the Percivals, and to expect that for ever spurning the contemptible, mean, narrow notions of the Jenkins, you will act in a way becoming of your origin."

"Indeed, sir," said Rosa, "you entirely mistake the characters of my uncle and aunt, indeed you do; they have ever taught me to despise meanness; my uncle in particular has one of the most liberal generous hearts in the world; they have ever assiduously inculcated the best principles, the purest morals."

"Oh! no doubt they taught you to say your prayers night and morning, and not to pilfer, and not to tell untruths," said Sir Edward; "but did they teach you the duty of obedience – did they instruct you to honour your father?"

Rosa stood silent and embarrassed.

"I see how it is," resumed Sir Edward; "these kind, affectionate relations of yours have taught you to hate me."

"No," replied Rosa, "no, indeed; they have taught me to feel sorrow for being so long unknown to my father, so long a stranger to his affection and tenderness; but to hate you, merciful heaven! to hate my father! – Oh! no. And most happy should I consider myself, would you permit me to evince my love and my obedience."

"You promise well," rejoined Sir Edward, "we shall see. But to the subject that brought us here. – I have a particular friend that is much attracted by your person and simplicity, who wishes to marry you."

"Me, sir!" said Rosa, trembling and changing colour, "marry me!"

"Aye, you!" answered Sir Edward: "and pray have the goodness to inform me is there any thing so extremely terrible in the idea of matrimony, that you should turn as pale as a ghost at the bare mention of it."

"Indeed, sir, I don't know – I really cannot tell," stammered Rosa.

"Nobody supposes that you do know, or that you can tell," resumed Sir Edward, "but remember, Miss Percival, I informed you before that it was not fashionable to betray emotions on any subject whatever, particularly on one of so little importance as matrimony."

"Little importance!" replied Rosa; "I should suppose it the most important, most momentous event that could possibly take place in a person's whole lifetime."

"All owing to the prejudice of education," said Sir Edward; "entirely owing to your having been brought up among the mountains. With people of enlightened understandings in the fashionable world marriage is considered as a mere matter of convenience; they agree to unite their estates, and that is I believe, generally speaking, the only union that is thought of."

"Amazing!" exclaimed Rosa.

Sir Edward laughed aloud. "What you, my little sentimentalist, you supposed that like the heroine in your favourite romance, everybody married for downright love."

"And what other motive," asked Rosa, "can be sufficiently

weighty to induce people to pronounce vows that bind them together for life?"

"Interest, child, interest," rejoined Sir Edward, "or convenience; in either case people who know the world make no scruple of pronouncing vows which they break with as little scruple whenever they find them a bar in the way either of their pleasure or promotion."

"Good God!" said Rosa, "how profligate!"

"Very true, my little puritan," replied Sir Edward; "but yet this wickedness against which you complain is not without its opposite good. What would become of Doctor's Commons if there were no divorces? – a general evil is after all of general utility, like a pestilential disease, that while it sweeps hundreds to the grave enriches the families of the whole tribe of Galen and Hippocrates. Love, child, is a very capricious deity, and seldom interferes in matrimonial ceremonies; he spreads his light wings, and leaves Master Plutus with his heavy bags of gold to settle the preliminaries between the affianced pair, who care as little for each other as you do for the pope."

"I am sure," said Rosa, "no motive of interest would ever induce me to promise to love where my heart felt no preference."

"Have a care, Rosa," rejoined Sir Edward: "a splendid match now offers, an alliance desirable in every particular; you would not be so mad, so blind to your own good, so cruel to me, as to reject it, and deny yourself the power to extricate me from embarrassments of a very unpleasant nature. From various causes, too tedious to enter upon now, my estates are all deeply mortgaged. I scarcely know how or where to raise a single guinea; and now, Rosa, now is the time for you to prove the love and the obedience you have promised. My friend Lord Clavering loves you."

"Loves me!" exclaimed Rosa, almost breathless, "loves me! – Lord Clavering!"

"Aye, Lord Clavering," resumed Sir Edward, affecting not to notice her agitation. "Lord Clavering generously offers to take you without a shilling, and to remove all my difficulties."

"Indeed, sir, I am extremely sorry," said Rosa.

"Sorry! for what?" interrupted Sir Edward – "sorry that I have a friend who will assist me in my embarrassments – sorry that a brilliant opportunity occurs of removing you from a situation where your life must have drawled out in one continued round of sameness, where the chief of your pleasures must have been comprised in playing at hunt the slipper or blindman's buff at Christmas, or the sober delight of a game at whist or Pope Joan; now you may, if you don't mar your own fortune, be translated to scenes of gaiety and splendour, to all the luxuries and joys of fashionable life; dress, routs, balls, masquerades, place, precedence, noise, admiration, bustle."

"I fear, sir," said Rosa, "I am not calculated by nature to support the character of a fine lady. My habits and inclinations, like my education, are all simple. Rosa Percival among her native mountains may be able to sustain her part with propriety, but in the circles of fashion, in the giddy routine of pleasures and amusements you have mentioned I should be lost, bewildered, and by my ignorance and inaptitude only reflect disgrace on those who introduced me."

"Never fear, my little timidity," said Sir Edward, "my Lord Clavering will see to have you properly documented; in fact no man on earth is better calculated than himself to give the last polish to high breeding; his rank in life, the company he keeps, among which he is the decider on all fashionable points

– his notice I say is quite sufficient to stamp elegance, to give the lustre of the diamond even to a rough pebble. He is all impatience to have the marriage concluded; he will then take you to one of his seats, where during the honeymoon he will instruct you in the arcanum of *bon ton*, and then in winter the Countess of Clavering will burst upon the world in all the dazzling blaze of elegance and fashion. Your settlement will be a noble mansion and twelve thousand pounds a year. But to let you into a trifling secret, he is so deeply enamoured of you, my sweet blushing Hamadryad, that you may bring him to what conditions you please, you may have what settlement you think proper."

"Me make conditions! Good God! – Me talk about settlements!" said Rosa.

"And why not?" rejoined Sir Edward: "when once you commence a woman of the world you will have occasions for cash that at present don't enter that silly brain of thine. Take my word, who am more experienced in these matters, that you will find the felicity of having a handsome allowance of pin-money, and the supreme blessing of a good fat jointure. At present, my little novice, you do not seem to understand the value of money; but once entered into the amusements of fashionable people, if you should be led to play high, to gamble – "

"Gamble!" interrupted Rosa; "surely, my dear sir, no person who gambles can possibly be said to understand the value of money; if they did, certainly they would never hazard its loss on the turning up of a card, or the rattle of dice. – Besides, sir, a female gamester – the very idea in my opinion is horrible; that one vice I should imagine is the introduction to many more."

"I have nothing to say in its favour or its defence," replied Sir Edward, shrugging his shoulders; "but this I know, it is utterly impossible to live in the great world without conforming in some measure with the habits and wishes of those you associate with, consequently money is the grand desideratum; for though you may for a time stop the mouths of your impertinent troublesome tradespeople with promises, you will find that there are certain fashionable expenses and demands which your purse must always answer with prompt payment. However, as I said before, Lord Clavering is a most generous liberal character, and as his wife I dare say you will never experience the chagrin of pecuniary difficulties."

"Pardon me, sir," said Rosa, "but I never can be the wife of Lord Clavering."

"Not the wife of Lord Clavering!" repeated Sir Edward, in a tone of astonishment and displeasure: "and pray, Miss Percival, may I take the liberty of requesting to be informed why not?"

"A variety of reasons might be adduced," replied Rosa, "but two may serve for sufficient objections: in the first place, he is more than old enough to be my father; in the next, I feel no sort of preference for him."

"As to his age, child," said Sir Edward, "that cannot possibly be an objection, *tout au contraire*, it is a matter quite in your favour."

"In my favour!" rejoined Rosa.

"Undoubtedly," continued Sir Edward; "you have the happy prospect of being a widow much sooner than if you married a younger man; and let me tell you, a rich young widow is a situation the most enviable, the most desirable of any in life; egad, I know many wives at this moment who would consider no possible event so felicitous as that of putting on weeds, and placing a hatchment over their doors."

"I hope to Heaven, whenever I marry," replied Rosa, "that I shall never have occasion to wish myself a widow."

"As to your wishes, or those of any other romantic girl of seventeen," said Sir Edward, "it would be folly in the extreme to attempt at guessing them: but if you have any real notion of prudence and propriety, you will allow your wishes to be regulated and directed by those whose experience and knowledge of life renders them the properest guides for ignorant youth; and as to your not feeling a preference for the Earl of Clavering, pray may I presume to ask, have you any tender wishes; do you feel a preference for any other?"

Rosa cast down her eyes, and blushed scarlet deep.

"Egad, child," continued Sir Edward, regarding her with an eye of scrutiny, "your pure and eloquent blood speaks plainly; those deep blushes tell tales. I fear some Adonis of the woods has put thy little heart in a state of requisition: but if this is really the lamentable case, your reddening must have supplied you with sufficient examples of disappointments in first love; it is quite in the romance style. I think some one of our poets says that the course of true love never did run smooth: but I have no brain for these matters. I shall only observe, that marrying with a preference is quite obsolete, not the order of the day, as much out of date as the wide hoop and sugar loaf tete of your grandmother; an old fashioned principle that the disciples of the new school turn their backs upon as gothic and unenlightened. Nothing in nature could be more conspicuously silly, or would be more ridiculed among people of a certain rank than the folly of marrying for love."

"Then pray, sir," asked Rosa, "what is to excuse the folly

of Lord Clavering wishing to become my husband, as you have just now informed me he has nothing to expect on the score of fortune?"

"He is immensely rich," replied Sir Edward, "and can afford to indulge his fancies; besides he wants an heir to his title and possessions; however, his folly, if you have so little vanity as to give his love for you so harsh a name, is quite apropos for me, who have a pressing occasion for his money; it does not signify a straw whether you like him or not: all I request is that you will marry him. I am not such a Turk as to insist upon your loving him. He only asks permission to evince his adoration of you, by bestowing his title and a large portion of his possessions on you and me: and surely, Rosa, you will not be such an idiot as to decline such advantages; refuse being a countess, because you are not foolishly in love with the man."

Rosa attempted to speak, but could not utter a syllable; she sat down on the bench, and burst into tears.

"Miss Percival," said Sir Edward, "this childish behaviour displeases me. Once again I assure you I detest weeping and wailing: nothing can be more annoying and disagreeable: don't be so extravagant as to throw away your liquid pearls upon me, on whom they have not the smallest effect: what! I suppose you have exchanged mutual vows – sworn eternal constancy to some swain of these Alpine heights, some Welsh booby; but if you have, child, break them, break them. Jove laughs at lover's perjuries: throw all the sin on my shoulders, I am content to bear it all – attribute your change of sentiment to my inflexibility: say fathers have flinty hearts, no prayers can move them. Say you are the victim of my peremptory commands; represent me in any way you like, only oblige me by marrying Lord Clavering."

"Thank Heaven! there is no occasion for me to represent my father as a monster," said Rosa. "Indeed, sir, you are mistaken, I have given no promise, exchanged no vows."

"I am glad of it with all my soul; but here comes aunt Nanny, full of curiosity, longing to know the purport of our long conference. At present let the subject drop; only remember that it is my particular request and command that you give Lord Clavering's addresses such a hearing and acceptance as becomes the promise you just now volunteered to me of love and obedience."

During the absence of Sir Edward and Rosa, Gabriel Jenkins had strayed to Woodland Cottage, to visit and talk over the strange conduct of his brother-in-law with his friend Williams, and to apologize for Sir Edward's rude behaviour on the preceding night; and Miss Jenkins had to her very great delight been left alone with Lord Clavering, who she anxiously hoped, and indeed supposed would take advantage of the present favourable opportunity, and declare himself, what she wished, her ardent lover.

His lordship, however, to her infinite disappointment seemed not to think of love, and only talked of the fineness of the weather, of the beautiful situation of Birch Park, and what families of rank and consequence resided in the neighbourhood; to all which Miss Jenkins had constrained herself to answer with politeness, though with no small degree of internal vexation and impatience.

At last his lordship observed, if any estate within a few miles of Carnarvon was to be disposed of he should like to become a purchaser.

Miss Jenkins's hopes revived, while she asked, "Why has your lordship any notion of residing in Wales?"

"No, madam, not absolutely of residing," replied his lordship; "but there is plenty of game in the country, and as I am a sportsman, I should like to have a hunting-lodge; besides it is my intention to take a Welsh wife, and she perhaps may have a wish now and then to visit her native mountains, and the companions of her youth."

Miss Jenkins now certainly supposed herself near the point. She affected to blush and look confused, while with a faltering voice she replied: "I am sure, quite certain, that whoever your lordship does the honour of selecting for a wife will be extremely happy."

"I hope so," rejoined Lord Clavering; "I would wish to do all in my power to make her so."

"Your lordship is so good, so considerate, so extremely liberal, there can be no doubt of her felicity; and then your lordship's figure – so noble – "

His lordship bowed to the compliment.

"So very handsome a man."

Lord Clavering bowed still lower.

"In manner so extremely fascinating and elegant."

The peer stared Miss Jenkins full in the face, while she continued to say, with a half-smothered sigh, "For my part I know no woman whose heart could possibly be proof against your lordship's solicitations."

Their eyes met. His lordship took the passive hand of Miss Jenkins, and led her to the sofa.

"Now," thought she, "now comes the moment of eclaircissement, the declaration of his love."

Her colour was heightened; expectation gave fiercer fire to her large dark eyes, and her frame shook with a tremor which his lordship instantly mistook the meaning of.

He was a man of intrigue, and thought that in so remote a part of the country, where good-natured females are not so easy of access as in London, that hers was an invitation not to be refused, and the present an opportunity not to be neglected.

With these ideas he made pretty free with the lips of Miss Jenkins, whose struggles his lordship set down to the score of affectation, and impressed with this notion would have proceeded to greater freedoms.

To allow these was not, however, Miss Jenkins's plan. She remembered former errors and former disappointments, and she resolved never to let the warmth of her constitution condemn her to single blessedness. Her intention was to be Countess of Clavering; and in order to give him an exalted opinion of her immaculate purity, she repulsed his liberties with all the indignation of insulted virtue.

His lordship was not prepared for a behaviour of this sort. Her conduct at the supper-table the preceding-night, and her remaining alone with him that morning, had been construed by him into pretty plain indications of her wish to engage him in an affair of gallantry.

"I declare, my lord," cried Miss Jenkins, affecting to shed tears, "I declare I am astonished at your rude behaviour. What on earth do you take me for?"

"A woman, certainly," replied Lord Clavering; "and I hoped a woman of feeling."

"Yes, my lord, I would wish to be thought a woman of feeling, but feeling may carry people beyond discretion. I hope you don't suspect my virtue."

"Virtue! nonsense!" replied Lord Clavering.

"No, my lord," resumed Miss Jenkins, "virtue is not nonsense; it is the greatest treasure a woman can possess; and a gentleman sometimes wishes to make himself certain that a lady really possesses it, before he makes her his wife, and to be sure she is not worthy the honour of being elevated to superior rank, if she is not capable of resisting attempts against her honour, however much she may be in love with his person who puts her chastity to the trial."

A very small portion of this eloquent speech had met his lordship's ear, who had moved from the sofa to the window which faced the lawn, where he stood observing a horse, a new purchase, which was for the first time to run in the barouche, and his attention was entirely occupied by him; turning to Miss Jenkins, without at all adverting to the scene that had just passed, he merely said:

"I think I last night promised to take you and Miss Percival an airing this morning; pray, madam, will you do me the favour to let some of your people inform her that the carriage waits her pleasure?"

Miss Jenkins quitted the room to seek Rosa, not much satisfied with Lord Clavering's behaviour, though convinced that she had left him fully impressed with the highest respect for her unconquerable virtue, and greatly wondering that he had not offered her an apology for his rudeness, and declared his honourable intentions towards her. His lordship also wondered what she could mean, for it never once entered his imagination that she had intended him the honour of her fair hand.

"Mercy on us!" said he, reverting to her strange behaviour; "have we coquets among the mountains, and at her age too?"

Sir Edward Percival attended Miss Jenkins and Rosa to the house, so that had her thoughts been less occupied with the scene she had just borne so considerable a part in, she would have found no opportunity of questioning her niece on the subject of her conference with her father. Lord Clavering, as he handed Rosa into the barouche, observed that she looked serious, and expressed his wishes that nothing unpleasant had occurred. Sir Edward prevented her reply, by saying that he had been proposing a subject to her consideration, which young ladies always affected to receive seriously.

"What is that," asked Miss Jenkins, "if it is not a secret?"

"No, not a secret," replied Sir Edward, "but I dare say you can guess. What is it you most wish for, yet dread you will never obtain?"

"O! Sir," replied she, "I am not good at solving riddles, besides I don't know that I am particularly anxious after anything."

"Yes you are," said Sir Edward, "you pray for it on your bare knees every night and morning – a husband."

"A husband!" replied Miss Jenkins, tossing her head; "I need not have rejected so many good offers if I had wished to change my condition."

"Well, as you decline matrimony on your own account, what think you of dancing at Rosa's wedding, hey, my old maid."

"Old maid! old maid!" repeated Miss Jenkins, darting on him a glance of spite and fury. "Old maid! really, Sir Edward, I should never have supposed a man of your politeness would have thought of addressing me in that rude manner: old, indeed!"

"Egad, I beg pardon," rejoined Sir Edward, "sure enough we have no old women now; this is the roseate age of youth and beauty; not of wrinkles, but of smiles and dimples. A woman at forty now a days contrives to have all the bloom and elasticity of a Hebe."

"I hope, Sir Edward, you don't mean to insinuate that I am forty?" said Miss Jenkins, vexed to the soul to have her age canvassed before Lord Clavering.

"Why no," replied he, "I do not intend an insinuation at all; I know that you are a few years above forty, though I again entreat pardon for the extreme rudeness of contradicting a lady; but I am such a worshipper of truth, that I am obliged to speak my real sentiments, even if I risque the incurring her displeasure."

"I suppose it is the fashion to be quite a brute," rejoined the enraged Miss Jenkins; "I protest, my lord, I protest on the word of a woman of honour, I have never yet seen thirty. I forty years of age, indeed! do I look like a woman of forty?"

"Certainly not, madam," replied the polite Lord Clavering. "O, fie! Sir Edward, a lady's age ought never to be touched upon."

"No faith," said Sir Edward, laughing; "they are even more tenacious of that than they are of their reputations."

While this conversation passed, Rosa had sat silent, buried in thought of her father's principles; his late conversation had given her no very exalted opinion. In Lord Clavering she fancied she discovered an air of libertinism, that the purity of her mind shrunk from, and she sincerely wished that he had conferred the honour of his preference on some other rather than her, whose affections, already engaged, had not even esteem to bestow upon him. For the rank to which he could raise her, she had not a wish – not the smallest inclination to be distinguished among the fashionable flatterers, who seek notoriety at the expense of nature, feeling, and principle. She thought that were she possessed of Hugh Montgomery's love, she could combat any difficulties that her refusal of Lord Clavering's splendid offers might involve her in; but of his regard she had not the shadow of a hope, so carefully had he concealed his views and sentiments. Her only chance of escaping being sacrificed on the altar of splendid misery was the reliance she placed on the affection of her Uncle Gabriel, to whom she determined to take the first opportunity of declaring her utter repugnance to becoming Countess of Clavering.

"And so these Montgomerys have made sacks of gold, and bushels of diamonds, in the East Indies?" said Sir Edward, addressing himself to Rosa.

"I have been told they are immensely rich, sir," answered she.

"And Miss Montgomery," continued Sir Edward, "she has fifty thousand pounds at her own disposal?"

"So I have heard her say, sir," replied Rosa.

"Just the thing, egad!" said Sir Edward; "I shall make love to her immediately; she I understand wants a title and I want – not exactly a wife, but cash. Is she handsome?"

"No, truly," answered Miss Jenkins; "if beauty is a sin, she has none to answer for."

"So much the better," said Sir Edward, "a handsome woman expects so much adoration, and being obliged to ransack one's brains for compliments is very wearisome. For my part, I often wonder how the women can swallow all the cursed flummery that is crammed down their throats."

"And for my part, I wonder how men can be such hypocrites as to pay compliments, when they do not mean them," said Lord Clavering, looking tenderly at Rosa. "Why are you so silent, Miss Percival; why not honour us with your opinion on this subject?"

"Your lordship must excuse me," replied Rosa, "it is a subject on which I am incompetent to speak, never having been in the habit of receiving compliments from gentlemen."

"Then you must certainly have concealed yourself from their observation," said Lord Clavering, "for to be seen must have been to excite admiration."

Rosa blushed, while Miss Jenkins found her seat uneasy, and began considering that his lordship had never addressed a compliment to her person.

"Is Miss Montgomery of age?" asked Sir Edward.

"I fancy so," said Miss Jenkins.

"I shall marry her immediately," resumed he.

"What! without obtaining her consent?" said Miss Jenkins.

"To obtain that," continued Sir Edward, "l presume will be no very arduous undertaking."

"But she has lately been in love, and met with a disappointment," said Miss Jenkins.

"Even that circumstance is in my favour," replied he; "her heart will more easily receive another impression: her wounded pride will readily accept the consolation offered by another lover more sensible of her charms. I have no doubt of success: in less than a month Miss Montgomery shall be Lady Percival, and then for another dash upon the world, with a plentiful stock of experience. Up to all, duped by none; neither to be jockeyed on the turf, or pigeoned at the green cloth."

"Well," said Miss Jenkins, "I hope no person after this will accuse our sex of vanity, or building castles in the air, when Sir Edward Percival, the father of Rosa, at his age, when he ought to be grave and steady, not only marries himself to a person he has never seen, but even proceeds to dispose of her fortune."

Sir Edward laughed, and asked if she would bet anything worth taking up on the affair.

Miss Jenkins said she never laid wagers.

"My life on my success," continued he: "I know the heart

of woman tolerably well; there are many avenues to their affections. I shall try them all."

"Success attend the undertaking," said Lord Clavering, "I shall be happy among the first to offer my congratulations."

This conversation brought them to Glenwyn Priory, at the gates of which stood the tawdry equipage of Mrs. Montgomery, who with her daughter was going to pay a bridal visit to Mrs. Mortimer.

Hugh Montgomery was just mounting his horse to accompany them, but seeing the barouche enter the gates, he ordered his groom to take him back to the stable, while he ushered the visitors to the presence of his mother and sister.

After the usual compliments of introduction had passed, Mrs. Montgomery proposed that they should all go to Dolgelly Castle, which being warmly seconded by Sir Edward Percival, was acceded to by the rest of the party; and Hugh Montgomery being invited to take Sir Edward Percival's place in the barouche, who had contrived to express his wish of occupying a seat in Mrs. Montgomery's carriage, they proceeded to pay their compliments to the new married pair.

While on the road, Sir Edward Percival, by compliments to the mother, and flattery to the daughter, had so ingratiated himself with both, that they were unanimous in the opinion that he was the handsomest, most sensible, most well-bred man they had ever met with since their arrival in North Wales.

Sir Edward was not backward in perceiving the impression he had made, and resolved to pursue what he considered the road to good fortune, not doubting but he could persuade Miss Montgomery, who he discovered was vain, ignorant, and presuming, to accept his hand, and the title of Lady Percival, whenever he pleased.

VOLUME III

CHAPTER I

DURING their ride to Dolgelly Castle, the particular assiduities of the Earl of Clavering, and the extreme dejection of Miss Percival, did not escape the penetration of Hugh Montgomery: a thousand vague ideas chased each other in rapid succession through his mind: his own unacknowledged love, uneasy suspicions relative to Lord Clavering's pointed attentions to Rosa, the motive of her father's visit at that time to North Wales, after an absence of so many years, served to render his imagination an absolute chaos. Was he again fated to encounter disappointment? Were all the delightful hopes he had so long and fondly cherished of attaching the gentle innocent heart of Rosa to himself destined to be blighted? Again he thought, were even his surmises accurate respecting Lord Clavering's wishes and intentions, the pensive countenance of Miss Percival spoke no pleasure, betrayed no triumph, evinced no proud exultation, but rather wore the impression of regret and uneasiness: once too as their eyes accidentally encountered each other, he remarked that hers were full of tears. "Precious drops!" thought he, "how supremely blest should I be were I permitted to kiss them away, and with attentive fondness remove every uneasy reflection." But little conversation had taken place, and Miss Jenkins felt rather offended at the very small share of notice his lordship took of her, and at his directing all the remarks he made on the surrounding prospects to her niece.

When the party arrived at Dolgelly Castle, they were

welcomed with all that gentlemanly affability and politeness that characterized Sir Owen Llewellyn and his interesting family. Mrs. Mortimer received their united congratulations with a blushing modesty that heightened her beauty, and diffused additional graces over her lovely person; while Mr. Mortimer returned their compliments with that air of happiness, that evident pleasure, which told how proud he was of his charming bride, how superlatively blest in her possession. Lord Clavering and Sir Edward, ever perfectly at their ease, understood, and entered at once into the separate characters of Sir Griffith Tudor, his lady and daughter, who happened to be present at their introduction, and joined with avidity in the pleasantry of Eliza Tudor, who could not let slip the opportunity of rallying Miss Jenkins about her admirer Mr. Williams, with whom she said she shortly intended to take a breakfast, she so much longed to have a cup of his strong hot coffee, and to regale plentifully on his nice well-buttered rolls, and to enjoy his rich thick cream comfortably.

Miss Jenkins, with undisguised displeasure, told Miss Tudor that no doubt she would be a very welcome guest at Woodland Cottage, as she appeared to be a prodigious favourite with Mr. Williams; that for her part she had quite done with the quiet deliberating creature; and that any lady who had an inclination for the man had her free permission to visit him; that he was nothing at all to her, nor ever would be, let people take the liberty of talking as they pleased; they were mighty ready to marry her, but it was necessary to ask her consent first; and indeed her pride led her to look for something above Mr. Williams; it was easy enough to stoop and pick up nothing.

"Why what on earth," asked Miss Tudor, "is the matter

between these true lovers now? Why it was but the other day Miss Jenkins, nay, don't attempt to deny it, that you were ready to strangle me because you thought the poor dear good-natured soul paid me a little attention."

"I am sure he is at perfect liberty," rejoined Miss Jenkins, "to pay attention to any one he pleases; but indeed, Miss Tudor, I must confess you talk in a very odd way, just as if you wished people to believe that I cared about a man who is old enough to be my father."

"Oh! pray," said Eliza laughing, "don't mention his age: consider, my dear Miss Jenkins, this is wartime, and men are very scarce, so scarce, that heaven help us poor maidens, there is at this present juncture a most plentiful want of men: think of this, Miss Jenkins, and learn to speak with more reverence. A man is a man, be he young or old, and not to be talked of contemptuously; besides, all this is a mere copy of your countenance, for you cannot pretend to deny that you were downright jealous."

"Jealous! me jealous!" screamed Miss Jenkins, "no indeed, not I truly: no man was ever of consequence enough to me to make me jealous. Mr. Williams, I assure you, Miss Tudor, is nothing at all to me, he never was anything more than a neighbour, and an old friend of my brother's."

"I hope, Miss Jenkins," said Lord Clavering, "if you marry while I remain in the country that I shall have the honour of giving you away, an office that will afford me much pleasure."

Miss Jenkins frowned. Lord Clavering's offer of giving her away was quite disagreeable; she neither liked his speech nor his manner, which she thought was not very expressive of tenderness for her. Sir Edward, twirling his eye-glass, inquired if they were speaking of the queer old quiz who had so graciously honoured Lord Clavering and himself with an invitation to smoke tobacco and drink strong ale, and eat Cheshire cheese at his comfortable cottage. Eliza Tudor laughed, and said she was sure it was Mr. Williams.

"Upon my soul," resumed Sir Edward, "I believe I affronted the odd animal last night; but I beg pardon, Miss Jenkins," added he: "if I had possessed the knowledge of his being your favoured admirer, I would have treated him with more ceremony out of respect to your tender feelings."

Miss Jenkins thanked him with a sneer for his humane consideration, and endeavoured to change the subject, by asking Mrs. Mortimer if she intended honouring the next assembly at Carnarvon with her presence. Before Adeline could reply, Miss Montgomery said it was her mother's intention to give a masked ball at Glenwyn Priory in the course of the month.

"A masked ball," replied Sir Edward, "is the only amusement worth going to. Mrs. Montgomery has certainly the ideas of a woman of fashion."

Mrs. Montgomery bowed, simpered, and looked delighted with Sir Edward's approbation.

"And this entertainment will give you, madam," said he, with an insinuating air to Miss Montgomery, "an opportunity of displaying to great advantage that exquisite taste for which you are so very conspicuous. A masquerade," continued he, "is quite a stylish amusement, it gives to genius and fancy so wide a field to display their unlimited powers; puts into the hands of wealth a magical wand, that creates a fanciful world, and astonishes the eyes of the vulgar with splendour and expense, which they view with gaping wonder and admiration. A masquerade I suppose was never heard of in Wales, it will be so novel."

"Yes," said Miss Jenkins, "it certainly will be novel, for I fancy, Sir Edward, few of the natives, as you are pleased to call us, have ever witnessed an entertainment of that sort; they know nothing of masquerades but what they have gathered from books."

Mrs. Mortimer, Eliza Tudor, and Rosa Percival, had never been at a masquerade.

"I felicitate you on the pleasure you will enjoy," said Lord Clavering; "the novelty, ladies, will give the amusement double charms."

"I remember," said Lady Tudor, "when I was quite a girl Lord Evershaw gave a masked ball at Northglen Abbey. I went in the character of a sylph, and Sir Griffith Tudor represented Alexander the Great."

It was with difficulty that a general laugh was suppressed, as all present turned their eyes on the embonpoint figure of Lady Tudor and the diminutive height of her helpmate.

"All the company said we looked and supported our characters to admiration; but in that day," continued her ladyship, "I was an everlasting dancer, was all life and gaiety."

"True, my love," rejoined Sir Griffith, "you had not then imbibed a partiality for quack doctors; you knew nothing of the exhilarating vapour of burnt feathers, was ignorant of the virtues of valerian; you had not discovered that you had weak nerves."

"No, Sir Griffith," replied Lady Tudor sarcastically, "I was not married."

"Bless me," said Miss Jenkins, playing with her fan, and affecting to look youthful, "does matrimony lower the spirits and weaken the nerves? If this is the case, I think we girls had far better remain single."

"I am determined to try, however," rejoined Miss Montgomery, "and I think it will be wonderful if I don't contrive to keep up my spirits in spite of the frolics of a husband."

"And what a brute a husband must be," said Sir Edward, assuming a tender air, "who would wish to diminish in the smallest particular what is so exquisitely delightful; for my part, I dote on vivacity; I idolize spirit; I would not, to obtain an empire, be tied to a half dead, half alive soul, one of your good kind of skim-milk, water-gruel without salt folks; no, no, give me a wife who has sense enough to form opinions of her own, and soul and spirit enough to insist upon and defend them."

Sir Edward Percival had taken the hand of Miss Montgomery, which he was tenderly pressing, during this speech, and which she, nothing loath, suffered him to retain.

Eliza Tudor had frequently mentioned Miss Percival to her friend Mrs. Mortimer in terms of high praise. Adeline was much pleased with her interesting face and figure, but more with her gentle unassuming manners. Nor was Rosa less attracted by the graceful elegant person of the fair bride, or less charmed with her affability. Mrs. Mortimer at parting took Rosa affectionately by the hand, and entreated she might often be favoured with her company at Dolgelly Castle.

Lord Clavering as yet had found no favourable opportunity of declaring his sentiments to Miss Percival, but he supposed her father had instructed her in the purport of his visit; and his vanity was not a little piqued at the air of reserve with which she treated his attentions, and the smile of pleasure that illumined her features, whenever Hugh Montgomery addressed her on the most indifferent subject. The Earl of Clavering was, however, not of a disposition to feel much misery on account of female indifference; he had been constantly in the habit of consoling himself for the frowns of one fair one by basking in the smiles of another. The smart little person of Eliza Tudor had not escaped his observation; he was pleased with her countenance, and thought that her arch playful manner had peculiar charms; she was also heiress to very large estates; and while he considered how much more advantageous a match she would have been, he more than half repented the engagement he had bound himself in with Sir Edward Percival.

When the Montgomerys rose to take leave, Sir Edward took the hands of Mrs. Montgomery and her daughter, whom he placed in their carriage, and was by them invited to occupy his former seat, a permission he gladly accepted, not being inclined to lose a single moment in the prosecution of his design upon Miss Montgomery, in whose favour he perceived he had already made no small progress, and to obtain the possession of whose hand he determined to leave no art or flattery untried; no stratagem unattempted.

Miss Montgomery had said she would be a countess, and when Lord Clavering was introduced, her heart had bounded with the hope of possessing his title; but Lord Clavering was by no means so handsome a man as Sir Edward Percival, neither had he his easy manners, or insinuating address. Miss Montgomery was self-conceited and assuming, Sir Edward applied himself to her weak side, and was soon established in her opinion, as the most fascinating, charming creature in nature. Lucretia was again over head and ears in love, and she settled it in her own mind that Sir Edward Percival was so much superior in figure, understanding, and address, to the peer, that she would rather be a baronet's lady than a countess.

Lord Clavering handed Rosa into the barouche, and then returned to speak to Mr. Mortimer, who was kindly shaking Hugh Montgomery by the hand, and wishing him as happy in a matrimonial alliance as he was himself. Miss Jenkins, to her infinite mortification, had been left entirely unnoticed, though standing by the side of his lordship; and as she ascended the vehicle unassisted, she muttered her dissatisfaction aloud, protested she thought there was something in the air that turned the heads of the men, and made them forget everything they ought to remember.

Rosa, whose thoughts had been differently employed, innocently asked what was the matter.

"Matter enough, I think, Miss Percival," replied her aunt, in a tone of vexation, "pretty rude behaviour in a person of Lord Clavering's rank, to suffer a lady in whose family he is visiting to get into her carriage without offering her his hand; but lords I perceive can be as rude as commoners, and ruder too for the matter of that. I know plenty of commoners who would not have been guilty of the *impoliteness* of placing such a mere chit as you in a carriage before me."

"Indeed, madam," said the astonished and abashed Rosa, "I am extremely sorry; I am sure I had not the most remote intention – "

"Oh, miss," replied her aunt, "you need not take the trouble of attempting an apology, I can see how it is, without being a witch; you are trying to inveigle and ensnare the heart of Lord Clavering, but you will find he is not so soon caught."

Rosa was ready to faint; the servants were listening and tittering; but Miss Jenkins, unmoved by that circumstance, proceeding to vent her spite and discontent, said, "I think for my part the world is turned topsy-turvy – nothing but rudeness, ill manners, and the basest ingratitude, to be met; mere babies nowadays absolutely pushing themselves upon the notice of the men, languishing and leering; and the men are so idiotish, and infatuated, and stupefied, as to prefer them and their childish nonsense to a woman of sterling understanding."

"I hope, madam," said Rosa diffidently, "that there has been no impropriety in my behaviour, to provoke you to address this very severe speech to me?"

"Nothing in your behaviour indeed!" retorted Miss Jenkins, with increased acrimony; "your behaviour, and Miss Montgomery's behaviour, and Miss Tudor's behaviour, are all equally indecorous and intolerable; but as to you, Miss Percival, I can give your vanity a bitter pill; I assure you, and I speak upon pretty good authority too, my Lord Clavering has more true taste than to be attracted by your baby face."

"I hope so most sincerely," said Rosa.

"I know so," replied Miss Jenkins, "so, child, you may set your heart at rest; you will never be Countess of Clavering I promise you."

"I am sure," said Rosa, almost expiring with confusion, "I am sure I never had the most distant wish, the remotest intention –"

The conversation was here interrupted by the gentlemen, at the sight of whom Miss Jenkins bade Rosa hold her tongue, and not expose herself. It was with the utmost difficulty Miss Percival could command her tears, while the inflamed cheeks and wide extended eyes of Miss Jenkins declared evidently that some incident had occurred to disconcert and ruffle her placidity.

Lord Clavering expatiated largely on the beauty of Mrs.

Mortimer, protested he had scarcely met a finer figure either in England or abroad, though he confessed the penserosa cast of her countenance was not altogether of a description to please his taste; he preferred the arch lively expression that played upon Miss Tudor's.

Miss Jenkins scornfully tossed her head, and said she thought either of them well enough, but nothing so extraordinary as to make a fuss about – no, truly, nothing very particularly handsome.

Rosa replied, she not only thought Mrs. Mortimer beautiful and elegant, but there was something in her smile, and the tone of her voice, absolutely angelic (another toss of the head from Miss Jenkins); and though Miss Tudor was not so handsome as Mrs. Mortimer, her person and manner were extremely pleasing.

Miss Jenkins told Rosa she was vastly polite to contradict her opinion, but for her part she hated such baby faces, and wondered what the men could see in them. Hugh Montgomery observed that ladies were incompetent to judge of each other's beauty.

"And why so, sir?" asked Miss Jenkins sharply; "you I suppose imagine they are envious of each other's charms; but suffer me for one to assure you, sir," continued she, drawing up her scraggy neck, "that I am perfectly satisfied with my own person and face, indifferent as they are; and I dare say I have attracted as much notice, and had as many admirers too as Mrs. Mortimer, with her languishing looks; or Miss Tudor with her bold ones."

Rosa was ready to sink with confusion. Hugh Montgomery stared with astonishment at this specimen of the old maid's indelicacy, spite, and vanity. – Lord Clavering smiled, and that smile Miss Jenkins construed into approbation, though it was in reality the effect and expression of ridicule and contempt.

When they reached Glenwyn Priory, Mrs. Montgomery, who had arrived before them, pressed them to stay dinner, but this Miss Jenkins decidedly declined, offering as a reason, her brother being quite alone and expecting them home; but in reality hoping in the course of the day to be left again alone with Lord Clavering, and to bring him to explain his intentions, of which she yet encouraged favourable hopes. Rosa was anxious to escape observation, and in the privacy of her own chamber to think over the occurrences of the day, to meditate on him so loved, Hugh Montgomery, and fix on some plan to evade the addresses of the earl, whom she hoped, and indeed expected, would remain the rest of the day at Glenwyn Priory. His lordship however cruelly disappointed her wishes, by declining, to the great joy of Miss Jenkins, Mrs. Montgomery's polite and pressing invitation: he determined that very day to explain himself to Miss Percival, and by her refusal or acceptance of his addresses to regulate his future proceedings.

Lord Clavering had fancied himself violently in love, but a few hours had made a revolution in his feelings and sentiments. Yet, though he certainly gave Miss Percival the preference, he discovered that he was not so far gone, so madly infatuated, so entirely and devotedly attached to her; but he believed he could console himself for her rejection of him with Miss Tudor, whose spirit and animation he thought would grace and adorn his coronet nearly as well as the simplicity and mild innocence of Rosa Percival.

Hugh Montgomery had strolled into the woods with Sir Edward Percival and his father, while the ladies performed the necessary ceremonies of the toilet before dinner. Mrs. Montgomery thought Sir Edward Percival a most *perdigiously* handsome man, and amazingly polite and well bred. Lucretia said nothing in nature could have happened more exactly fortunate for her, than his coming into the country at that particular time, as he would assuredly help her to some useful hints, respecting conducting the projected masquerade; and certainly no man had more taste, or was more perfectly qualified to instruct.

Mrs. Montgomery smiled, while she replied, that perhaps Sir Edward Percival was the person appointed to instruct her in the road to matrimony, and if he was heaven bless them together, for they would make a *perdigiously* fine dashing couple. "He appears," continued she, "my darling Lucretia, to be quite smitten with your charms, and for my part I don't see what you can do better than take him, that is, my dear, if you have quite done grieving yourself about that silly, stupid fellow, that would not accept of nothing for his own advantage, that oafish Mortimer."

"Pray, madam," rejoined Miss Montgomery, "don't wound my feelings by mentioning the savage: his ridiculous fulsome fondness of that tall, awkward maypole, his wife, this morning, was actually quite sickening; he is a creature without a single atom of taste; but Sir Edward Percival is quite a different sort of character; he has sense, feeling, and discernment; to be sure I did say that nothing under a coronet should content me, but this love oversets our very firmest resolves. I really believe, if Sir Edward offers, out of pure compassion to the divine man, I must condescend to be Lady Percival."

At dinner the nabob was so much entertained with Sir Edward's droll anecdotes that he pronounced him the most facetious and best companion he had met for many years, and he so enraptured Mrs. and Miss Montgomery with his fine speeches, and still finer compliments, that when the hour of separation arrived, it was with evident reluctance on their part, as well as his, that he was suffered to depart, with a promise of being again at Glenwyn Priory the next day. Hugh Montgomery had been an attentive observer of Sir Edward Percival all day: he was the father of Rosa, of her on whom his future happiness depended, and he wished, if possible, to acquaint himself with his character: the investigation by no means either pleased or satisfied him. Hugh Montgomery's heart was the seat of honour; his principles were founded on truth and integrity, and his penetration pointed Sir Edward Percival of superficial rather than solid attainments, calculated indeed for a bon vivant, but not for a friend, of free morals, of frivolous behaviour; he thought him designing also, and he saw with real concern that this man was ingratiating himself with his father, and winding himself into the favour of his mother and sister, and he knew that to offer advice on the subject, or warnings of so dangerous an acquaintance, would only be received with contempt and resentment. When the trio returned to Birch Park, Miss Jenkins beheld Williams stationed on the lawn, on the lookout, and as soon as the carriage stopped he was ready to hand her out, which politeness she was not in a humour to receive graciously, or be gratified with: she only answered his – "How do you? I am very glad to see you look so well this morning," with "Bless me, Mr. Williams, who would have thought of seeing you here."

Now it was certain that Miss Jenkins did not wish to see her old admirer, or she would not have expressed surprise at a circumstance that happened once in every day in the week. Mr. Williams, to her infinite chagrin, answered, "that he supposed she had expected him, as his brother would take no denial, but would have him home with him to dinner."

Gabriel Jenkins, who thought he had been insulted the preceding night, and took some little blame to himself for having so tamely witnessed it, had indeed warmly insisted on his accompanying him home, and spending the day at Birch Park, swearing at the same time that all the lords and baronets in the nation should never make him meet an old friend with a new face, or oblige him to forget for one instant that what he had honestly earned was his own lawful property, and that he was king in his own castle.

Miss Jenkins most cordially wished Williams in the infernal regions: she began to discover that he was a mean looking little man, that his legs were too short, that he had an insignificant nose, that he had nothing to say for himself, in short that he was like a chip in porridge, neither good nor harm; and though he was well enough when no one else was to be had, that compared with Lord Clavering, he was a mere nobody, a quiz, a bore, a nothing at all, and she was astonished at her own patience, that had so long suffered a person who was for ever deliberating and turning things over in his mind, to dangle after her for such a length of time.

Rosa had scarcely completed her toilet, when her uncle very unceremoniously entered her room, puffing and blowing with a face full of importance.

"So, niece, I come to ask you if you know that this same Lord Clavering is come all the way from London to marry you? Gad, this is quite nice and clean, the most oddest affair I ever heard of in all the course of my business." He now seated himself, took off his wig, and wiped his head. "I say, Rosa, my girl, and so you are to be a fine lady," continued he, "and I suppose will soon forget your uncle, and that you ever knew Birch Park."

Rosa's tears would not be restrained.

"Forget my dear uncle!" said she, "no, never."

"Why look you, niece," replied he, "I believe you are as good a girl now as need to be, but when you are married to a lord it will be quite and clean another guess matter; your father was always ashamed of our family, except when he wanted money, and then he was never ashamed to mention his wants, and have them supplied from the till of the shopkeeper – and gad, child, when you are married to a lord, and go to live in London, Lord help us in Wales, we shall be quite and clean drove out of your head by fresh acquaintances, all great and grand like yourself and your husband – Well, well," said he, wiping his eyes with the end of his cravat, "I was in hopes that your father would never have claimed you. I was in hopes he would have left you where you was born and bred. I pleased myself with the fancy that he would have quite and clean forgot to remember that he had a daughter at all, as he was so many years coming to his recollection."

Rosa's heart told her she would have been full as happy if he had.

"But here now," continued Gabriel Jenkins, "here now, this Lord Clavering, he may be clever enough too for anything I know or can tell; he has really quite and clean put me in a downright *flurteration*, as I may call it, with saying that he came here with your father, on purpose to marry you, and that the bargain was made, signed, sealed, and delivered."

"What!" said Rosa, "without consulting me?"

"Aye, Rosa, without even asking you whether or not you

liked the man, or chose to marry him; but gad, I am talking just like a fool, for what young girl would refuse to be made your ladyship of, and what young girl would refuse a husband. – Bless me, Rosa, for my part, I don't like this lord at all, he carries his head so high in the air, and when he laughs, why, my girl, it seems just for all the world as if he were only making believe. Oh, dear, dear, I was in hopes you would never have left Wales, but now you must live in London, and spend your days in dressing and visiting, and coaching and carding, and running here, and flying there, telling lies, and pretending to like people to their faces, and cursing them behind their backs. Bless me, bless me, Rosa, I have heard that great people in London are nothing in the world but bags of deceit; and how, my girl, will you be able to do otherwise; why you must quite and clean forget all your sincerity; and in order to be able to pay the great folks in their own coin, gad, you must be as wicked to the full as themselves."

"I hope not, uncle," replied Rosa; "I hope I shall always respect truth, and never cease to remember the good lessons you have taught me."

"Poor child, poor child," said Gabriel Jenkins, kissing her cheek, "you are so good, and so innocent now, that it would be quite and clean a sin to take you to that wicked place London; but there it does not signify; you will have a lord for your husband."

"Indeed, my dear uncle," said Rosa, "I will not if I can help it."

"What," said Gabriel Jenkins, his face brightening, "what, why, Rosa, you would not; hey! why, gad, you would not pretend to be rebellious, and dispute the authority of Sir Edward Percival?"

Rosa looked in her uncle's face, with an affirmative on her countenance, but was silent, while he continued:

"Now, if Mr. Hugh Montgomery (Rosa's colour grew more vivid at that name); I say, niece, if Mr. Hugh Montgomery had fancied you, and you had fancied him, why I should not much have minded giving you a few thousand pounds as a marriage portion, because that would have been quite and clean a match to my mind; then I might have hoped to nurse your little ones on my knee, as I used to nurse you, Rosa, and carry you about in my arms before you could go alone, when your poor dear mother was dying by inches, all for love of your father. I won't curse him, Rosa, because he is your father; but his neglect killed my sister, as sweet a creature as ever drew the breath of life: gad, girl, you are the very image of her; I thought I should have broke my heart when she died, and I am sure if you marry this Lord Clavering I shall soon rest in the same grave with your poor mother."

"I will never marry him," sobbed Rosa, "I hate him."

"Do you, upon your soul?" said Gabriel Jenkins, dashing the tears from his eyes.

"Yes I do most sincerely," replied Rosa.

"Then I wish I may be d – d," rejoined he, jumping up, "if he shall have you; no, no, my girl, we live in a free country; no marrying here against inclination; no force in a land of liberty. Gad, but is it true though, all honour bright and shining, that you don't like this Lord Clavering – are you quite and clean sure you are not deceiving yourself and me?"

"Quite certain," said Rosa: "Lord Clavering is my aversion."

"Tol der lol,"' sung Gabriel Jenkins, capering about the room, and kicking his wig before him "gad, but this is nuts for me to crack; a mountaineer, as your father calls you, to have spirit enough to refuse a lord; but come along, Rosa, I long to let them see a bit of Cambrian blood, pure and honest, neither ashamed nor afraid to refuse the gingerbread gilding of title, when the heart does not approve the man. Rosa, kiss me, you slut; gad, I am so happy!"

"But my father, sir! I understand his affairs are embarrassed," rejoined Rosa, "and Lord Clavering was to advance money – "

"Upon you," said Gabriel Jenkins, with indignation; "your father would have sold you without pity, just as if you had been timber on his estate, to this Lord Clavering, and this noble lord would have bought you: very decent proceedings truly, just as bad to the full as if you had been a negro slave in a West-India plantation. But I shall take care to put a spoke in this wheel; I shall quite and clean alter this matter: come along, Rosa: gad, I am all agog for you to deny this lord – and as to your father, d – no, no, I won't d – n him, because he is your father, Rosa, but let him get out of his embarrassments as he got into them; let him go to the gaming table, and win somebody else's estates, as they have his."

"Gaming tables!" echoed Rosa, "my father lose his estates by gambling!"

"Quite and clean as bad," replied Gabriel Jenkins, "the Rhydderdwyn estate was mortgaged for a gambling debt, and now he would have turned you over to this Lord Clavering to redeem it; but we shall learn him that we natives are sharper than he expects."

Gabriel Jenkins led his niece to the drawing-room, where sat his lordship trimming his nails, and waiting with no little impatience the appearance of Miss Percival, whom her uncle had promised should presently give him his answer, for he had no notion of shilly shally, putting folks off to another time, when it was quite and clean as easy a matter to speak their minds honestly and fairly at once. His lordship rose on the entrance of Rosa, and leading her to a seat, said, he hoped Mr. Jenkins, who was informed of his very great partiality in her favour, had prepared her to receive his addresses, and to give him such an answer as would be favourable to his wishes.

Rosa was confused and silent, but Gabriel Jenkins pushing himself between his niece and the peer, said: "Look you, my lord, few words are the best, and plain dealing is my maxim. My niece don't wish to be made a ladyship of – nor I don't choose she should be trafficked away like a bale of goods, which it quite and clean appears was to be the case. I have maintained her to this time, my lord, and I am not tired of it yet. Rosa Percival is the child of my dearly loved sister, and while I have a bit of bread, or a guinea, she shall never be forced to give her hand where her heart is not gone before. She shall never be forced I say."

Lord Clavering had never been talked to in this way, and in a tone of disappointment he repeated the word forced.

"Aye, forced," said Jenkins; "what do you call it but force? Here comes her father, who never saw her since she was the height of six pennyworth of halfpence, and tells her a long rigmarole tale about his embarrassments; gad, if the devil had his right, he would have had him long ago."

Rosa burst into tears. – Gabriel Jenkins stopped short to ask her pardon, and console her – then resuming his discourse to Lord Clavering, said, "Well, as I was telling you, he tried to work upon the poor girl's feelings, by talking about his distresses, and no doubt tried to dazzle her eyes with the notion of all the fine silver and gold gowns and petticoats she was to wear, because the weak brains of women are apt to hanker and run after such tinsel and gewgaws. – But the truth is, my lord, she thinks you a very disagreeable sort of person."

Lord Clavering looked in an opposite mirror, bowed, and said he was much obliged to Miss Percival's opinion. Rosa would have spoke, but her uncle proceeded to say, "And you are her aversion: she don't like you the least bit."

His lordship expressed his admiration of her sincerity.

"Gad, my lord," replied Gabriel Jenkins, "our family, I mean the Jenkins, were always famous for speaking their minds freely and honestly, and that is as far as I see the best plan: what signifies being fair teeth outward and hollow within. Rosa Percival loves her old uncle, and her own Welsh hills, and prefers staying with us to marrying your lordship."

"She shows her taste and her discernment," replied Lord Clavering, not a little piqued.

"Why as to taste, my lord, you know what is one man's meat is another man's poison, and she perhaps would rather prefer a man whose face is something fresher than yours, without puckers about the eyes. I beg pardon, my lord, for mentioning it, but time will quite and clean rob a body of his youth: only see, (taking off his wig, and pushing his bald pate in his lordship's face); only see, it has made me bald headed."

"Really, sir," said Lord Clavering, "I don't understand – "

"Don't you," replied Gabriel Jenkins; "gad, that is very odd too, for I thought I spoke pretty plain. Well, I will try again; I would speak Welsh to you, but I suppose you are not learned enough for that – it is a pity you do not understand Welsh, for I am more at home in that than English; however, to make short of a long story, my niece, Rosa Percival, does not like you; do you understand that, my lord?"

"Why yes," replied the peer, "it is pretty plain English."

"And she will never marry you – is that understandable, my lord?"

"Perfectly so, Mr. Jenkins, but I wish to be certain that you are really speaking – Miss Percival's sentiments."

"Speak for yourself, Rosa," said Gabriel Jenkins, turning to his niece, "tell this Lord Clavering that you will never tell a lie in the church, above all other places, and promise to love with your lips, when your heart won't bear witness to the agreement."

"Miss Percival, what am I to believe?" asked his lordship.

"That I am sorry," faltered Rosa, "extremely sorry to disappoint the wishes of my father, but it is quite impossible for me to accept your generous offers."

"Offers! generous offers!" interrupted Gabriel Jenkins, "I see nothing so generous in his offer of taking you, as pretty a girl as any in Wales, in the lieu of a little dirty cash."

"Perhaps, sir," rejoined his lordship "you are not aware of the settlements I offered."

"A fig's end for settlements," said Gabriel Jenkins: "gad, my lord, I am glad with all my heart she does not like you; I don't want any more great men in the family; they bring nothing but pride along with them, to kick affection out of doors – and as to settlements, Rosa Percival has never yet known what want means, in any shape, and it is quite and clean out of the question that she ever should; my will is made, and she is my heiress, provided she does not marry a title, or the heir to one; if she does, not a shilling of my money, all got in trade, goes to increase the pride of those who would spend my earnings, and despise the earner."

The peer looked contemptuously, while Rosa, placing her hand in her uncle's, said, "My more than father, how shall your Rosa, the child of your bounty, ever sufficiently evince her gratitude, her affection?"

"By never marrying with lords or baronets," replied he.

"Then, Miss Percival," said his lordship, "I am to consider your uncle's refusal decisive."

"Exactly so, my lord," replied Rosa, "and I can only lament that it is out of my power to make a grateful return for your lordship's generous intentions in my favour; permit me to wish you that happiness with another which I feel incompetent to bestow."

His lordship bowed, and affected to smile, but his chagrin was too powerfully obvious for concealment.

Gabriel Jenkins observed, that he did not know why coming to a right understanding should make them enemies; for his part, he wished every man breathing well, and would do anything in reason to serve a fellow creature; so he hoped his lordship had no objection to shake hands, for it was quite and clean the most distant thing in the wide world to his intention to offend him, and that as a friend he should be glad of his company at Birch Park, as long as he pleased to stay, only that he was to remember that Rosa Percival was not to marry a lord nor a baronet.

His lordship did not refuse the offered hand of Gabriel Jenkins; but now Rosa had absolutely refused him, he felt himself madly in love with her again, and determined, if possible, still to obtain her, if it was only to plague and mortify the purse proud trader, who had dared to refuse and despise his rank and consequence, and decline the honour of his alliance.

At dinner Gabriel Jenkins was all life and gaiety. Rosa said but little; her thoughts were full of what her uncle had expressed concerning Hugh Montgomery, and she sighed to think how little prospect there was of her wishes in that quarter being realized.

Lord Clavering tried to look pensive: his behaviour to Rosa was attentively polite, but on Miss Jenkins he scarcely bestowed a glance, though she was at infinite pains to draw him into conversation. Mr. Williams appeared to have committed some high offence, for to him, whenever obliged to speak, her behaviour was stately and distant.

After dinner his lordship ordered his carriage, and left Miss Jenkins almost mad with disappointment, as her eyes followed him down the green lane leading towards Carnarvon.

It was in the midst of Gabriel Jenkins's triumph at having beat his friend Williams out of several games at cribbage, that Sir Edward Percival entered the room, and casting his eyes with careless indifference over the rest of the company, inquired for his friend Lord Clavering. Miss Jenkins said he was gone out, but he had not thought anybody there of consequence enough to tell where he was going.

"I suppose, Miss Percival," whispered Sir Edward, "he has declared himself to you on the subject I mentioned this morning?"

"Yes sir, he has."

"And you have received him according to my wishes?"

His last question was overheard by Gabriel Jenkins; who answered for her.

"No she has not." Sir Edward frowned.

"Gad," resumed Gabriel Jenkins, "I was not born so near a wood to be frightened at an owl – angry or pleased, you shall have the truth: Rosa don't like him; she shall not marry him; indeed, it is quite and clean out of all question, that she could ever like a man old enough to be her father. Lord, lord, it is quite a *perposterous* matter to suppose that Lord Clavering could ever be the husband of my little Rosa."

"What," said Miss Jenkins, stretching herself a yard taller than usual – "what did you say, brother Gabriel, that Lord Clavering had offered to marry Rosa?"

"Yes, madam," replied Sir Edward, "and what is so wonderful in all that."

"Wonderful! Oh, I shall faint," said Miss Jenkins: "the cruel, base, ungrateful man."

"Why, what now, Nanny," asked Gabriel Jenkins; "what has he said or done to you that you should call him such hard names?"

"Offered himself to Rosa!" repeated Miss Jenkins, "is it possible, to that child! offered to make her a countess!"

"Yes," said Gabriel Jenkins, "and gad, sister, you will be more surprised when you hear that he is so much in love with her, that he has offered to pay off the mortgage from the Rhydderdwyn estate, and give her worthy father ten thousand pounds, if she will consent to be Countess of Clavering."

"And you have dared to refuse?" said Sir Edward sternly to Rosa.

"Yes she has, and she did right," replied Gabriel Jenkins, "for 'tis quite and clean, as plain as the nose on your face, that the poor thing did not like such a long yellow visaged, meagre looking rushlight, though he is a lord."

Miss Jenkins fanned herself, pushed her fingers through an elegant lace veil, and trod with her high heeled shoes upon her brother's gouty toes.

"Why, what the devil, Nanny, is the matter? I don't know which looks most out of temper, you or Sir Edward," said Gabriel; "however, you may as well both of you content yourselves, for Rosa shall never be the wife of any man she does not like."

"And so, sir, you encourage children to rebel against their parents?" said Sir Edward.

"Yes, and he does right," said Miss Jenkins, rage flashing from her eyes, and flaming on her cheeks; "he does right, you ought to have been ashamed to want such a mere child, an infant as one may say, to marry; you ought to have been ashamed to listen, and that vile brute, that unfeeling monster Lord Clavering, to make proposals."

Mr. Williams asked why she was so enraged. – Rosa saw there was likely to be a general disturbance, and she left the room, glad to escape contention. Miss Jenkins told Mr. Williams not to ask questions that did not concern him.

Sir Edward said he should take measures to enforce his daughter's obedience.

"And I shall take measures to prevent it," retorted Gabriel Jenkins.

"I shall remove Miss Percival tomorrow," said the baronet, "to some situation where she may learn duty to her parent."

"Remove her at your peril," replied Gabriel Jenkins: "remember I can come upon you for the expense I have been at on her account for upwards of seventeen years; it will amount, Sir Edward, to a pretty round sum, so have a care which way you go to work. I do not mind money more than that (snapping his fingers), and if you can raise any for them sharks the lawyers, why I fancy I can come down guinea for guinea with you at any hour."

The baronet did not like this menace: in rather a low tone he said he might have expected opposition, but he trusted Miss Percival had sense enough to know her own interest, and sufficient of the Percival blood in her to despise their vulgar notions, and to act in conformity with his wishes.

"Gad, Sir Edward," rejoined Gabriel Jenkins, "I believe you are just now reckoning without your host. Rosa is a girl of upright conscience, and I am sure will never be led to promise what she can never pretend to perform. No, no, she has not Percival enough in her for that, for it is quite and clean clear as noon day that she cannot abide this Lord Clavering, and she has spoke her mind plainly to him, and I will be d – d," said the honest Cambrian, growing warm – "I will be d – d if she shall have him."

"Not have him!" echoed Sir Edward Percival, "not marry my friend Lord Clavering, I shall see to that affair."

"No, she never shall be Countess of Clavering," screamed Miss Jenkins, so loud that Mr. Williams, who had been a silent auditor of the dispute, and was just raising a bumper of port to his mouth, fairly started from his chair and let fall the glass, the contents of which were emptied into her lap, and ran in meandering streams over a richly worked muslin robe; if she was before enraged, she was now absolutely furious, and stamped and raved like a maniac.

Sir Edward, in spite of his vexation, laughed immoderately, while poor Williams stood terrified, vainly endeavouring at an apology. In the midst of this confusion Lord Clavering's carriage stopped at the door; and Sir Edward Percival, fearing to commit himself farther, hastened out of the room to learn with what temper his lordship bore his rejection. Gabriel Jenkins vainly strove to mediate between his friend and his sister. Poor Williams declared he never felt more uncomfortable in his life, but he did not mind treating Miss Jenkins with a new gown, if she would only look good natured and be quiet, and make herself agreeable, for it was quite unpleasant to him to hear such a noise kicked up about an accident, which might have happened to the most genteelest person as well as to him.

"Accident," replied Miss Jenkins; "you are the most awkward, ill-bred – but don't suppose, sir, that I mind the spoiling of my dress, though it cost five guineas. No, sir, I am above such paltry considerations, I have matters of far more consequence upon my mind. Lord Clavering offering himself to that child Rosa! – I am actually petrified at the idea."

"Aye, and well you may," said Gabriel Jenkins; "but thank God the child has more love and respect for us than to listen to such an outlandish proposal; she knows better than to introduce another great man into the family. Gad, this Sir Edward beats all my acquaintance hollow for impudence; expects to rule the roost here; wants to tie such a sweet rosebud to that long shanked ugly yellow faced lord; why it is quite and clean out of nature to think about such a match; not but that you are out in one thing, sister Nanny; and I am surprised you don't remember about five and twenty years ago, when you was Rosa's age – "

"I Rosa's age five and twenty years ago!" exclaimed Miss Jenkins; "why, brother, you are mad – you are in your dotage; why I was an infant in my cradle five and twenty years ago."

"The devil you was," said Gabriel, "you was a pretty forward infant then, for I remember you was all cock-a-hoop to marry that fellow Ross; you was dying for him, and though he was not worth sixpence, you would have had him if he would have married you; but you know you had – "

Williams was all ear, and Miss Jenkins, dreading any further bringing up old stories, begged her brother to hold his tongue, for that he sadly misplaced dates, and misrepresented circumstances.

"Well, well, Nanny," said Gabriel, "I won't make you blush with repeating old grievances; but as to Rosa I think she is old enough to marry if she can get a good husband, and I have one for her in my eye."

"You have; and pray who may he be?" asked Miss Jenkins.

"One of the best, aye and the finest young man too in the principality," replied Gabriel Jenkins; "and I am quite out in my judgment if she makes the smallest objection to my choice."

"Objection!" said Miss Jenkins, lifting up her hands and eyes; "objection! I am thunderstruck, the world will certainly soon be at an end. But pray, brother Gabriel, inform me who may this choice of yours be?"

"Why, Nanny; but gad, mum is the word yet awhile. No matter who he is or what he is; I like him, and I think Rosa likes him, and that is enough, for she shall not marry anybody she does not like, I will take good care of that I warrant; but," said Gabriel Jenkins, winking at Williams, "I shall be careful how I trust a secret to a woman's keeping; gad, that would be quite and clean what a person might call downright folly and nonsense."

Mr. Williams laughed, and applauded his friend's notion, for the only way to be agreeable and comfortable was to trust nothing to a woman. Miss Jenkins flounced out of the room, casting glances of scorn and indignation on them both, and without deigning to bestow the compliment of good night on Mr. Williams.

"Well," said he, as the door closed after her, "I don't understand the least in the world what has put your sister into such a tantrum. God bless us, when one sees the ways of the female sex, a man that wishes to pass his life quiet and comfortable will have nothing at all to do with them."

"Gad you speak like a sensible man," said Gabriel Jenkins, shaking him by the hand; you are quite right in what you say, neighbour, and as to my sister, more is the pity for her poor thing, she is quite and clean anything in the world besides agreeable."

"I have been turning it over in my mind for a long time," replied Mr. Williams, "whether it would be best to marry or let it alone; but dear bless me, I think from this time I shall never trouble my head about women: I could never bear to hear their tongues scolding and raving about nothing at all; I am for a quiet life – I love to smoke my pipe and enjoy a friend's company in my little bit of a cottage; but lord if I was to take a wife I might soon be made quite uncomfortable."

Gabriel Jenkins could not in conscience disapprove his friend's notion; he had indeed looked forward to a match between him and his sister, and had felicitated himself on the prospect of being released from her ill tempers, which seemed to increase with her years. Yet he could not wish poor Williams, for whom he had a most sincere and cordial regard, burthened with a load he himself thought at times intolerable and unbearable; he therefore consoled his mind with remembering that he had always been told there must be one old maid in everybody's family, that old maids were fractious cross-grained animals, always fretful and dissatisfied, and that man was born to trouble, even as the sparks fly upwards.

CHAPTER II

Lord, lord, there is mad work at these same masquerades;
I would not wonder if some hot-brained spark
Should, like another Paris, bear our Helen off.

He that hath the steerage of my course
Direct my suit.

If I profane with my unworthy hand
This holy shrine, the gentle fine be this—
My lips two blushing pilgrims stand,
To smooth that rough touch with a tender kiss.
Romeo and Juliet

Sir Edward Percival and his friend, the Earl of Clavering, had a long conference, the result of which was, that, notwithstanding Rosa had contumaciously and peremptorily refused his lordship's addresses, and declined the high honour of his alliance, he not only advanced the sum necessary for the redemption of the mortgage on the Rhydderdwyn estates, but moreover and above money to repair the old mansion-house, and put all things in proper state and order for the reception of his intended bride; and a circumstance still more worthy of remark, they parted better friends than ever.

Lord Clavering, as if she had never rejected him, still preserved towards Rosa the polite attention of a lover, as much to her annoyance as to the inexpressible chagrin of her aunt, whose sarcastic hints and invidious remarks, while they wounded the delicacy of Miss Percival, passed entirely unnoticed by Lord Clavering; however, to her great joy she was now no longer constrained by politeness to pass nearly the whole of the day in his society, as he, with Sir Edward Percival, had removed to Glenwyn Priory, at the pressing instance of the nabob and his lady, where they joined their united efforts to flatter Miss Montgomery, till she was become even more affected, more presuming, and more silly than ever.

Though Montgomery witnessed their arrangements with much secret displeasure, the earl and the baronet were persons whom, notwithstanding their rank, he could neither esteem nor admire; and he saw with infinite regret the unbounded influence Sir Edward Percival's opinions acquired with all the family; he knew that he was in reality a needy man, and perceived that his sister's large fortune, unfortunately at her own absolute disposal, was the sole incentive to his unwearied assiduities.

To his friend, Mr. Mortimer, in his visits to Dolgelly Castle, he had unreservedly disclosed his own passion for Miss Percival, and had also as freely expressed his dislike of her father, his suspicions of the distressed situation of his circumstances, and his intention of bettering them by the wealth of his sister.

All that related to Sir Edward Percival's ruined affairs, and his design on the Montgomery wealth, Mr. Mortimer had heard reported from many quarters, and it was with great surprise they now learned as a fact that Sir Edward had actually cleared all the encumbrances on his Welsh estates, and was getting all things in order for his immediate marriage. Cards of invitation had for some time been issued to all the people of consequence for many miles round the country, and all the beds in the village and neighbourhood put in requisition; nothing was talked of but the magnificent masked ball to be given at Glenwyn Priory.

Sir Edward Percival had undoubtedly mixed with what is commonly called the higher orders of people – that is, with titled sharpers, who ran long bills with tradesmen they never intended to pay; who made bets and rode their own horses at Newmarket; who gamed deeply, and made love to their friends' wives and corrupted their daughters; with ladies of rank, who rouged high, gambled, and intrigued; who sought notoriety at the expense of decency and principle, and who were in all things in the very extreme of fashion; if, therefore, he had in reality no taste nor invention of his own, he had certainly very successfully borrowed something that partook of both from the various amusements of which he had participated with his gay friends. Under his direction Glenwyn Priory had assumed the appearance of an enchanted palace, all the merit of which he, with the most delicate flattery, gave to Miss Montgomery.

Two large saloons were thrown into one to allow space for the dancing, and were tastefully hung with alternate draperies of scarlet and white satin, interspersed with large wreaths of poppy, cornflowers, and convolvulas. The floor was elegantly painted in watercolours, with a triumph of Venus and dancing figures. Under the canopied orchestra were two magnificent arches erected, splendidly illuminated with variegated lamps, disposed to represent the arms of the Montgomery family; beneath which were entrances to an apartment fancifully decorated with temporary pillars of green frost work, entwined with chains of red and white roses, orange flowers and jessamine, between which were spread tables covered with green velvet, and loaded with gilt baskets full of every delicious fruit that could be procured, among which appeared a rich profusion of pine-apples, melons, grapes, and pomegranates, diversified with jellies, ices, wines, liquers, and all the endless variety of cakes and biscuits, on highly burnished gold stands, interspersed with curious Indian vases bearing highly scented exotics.

Another apartment was fitted up to represent a Turkish harem – here the walls were panelled with looking glass, and low sofas supported by silver swans, and canopied with pale blue silk richly fringed with silver, and drawn back with superb cords and tassels of the same material, gave an air of voluptuousness, which the magnificent and expensive carpet, the eider down cushions spread on the floor, the flowers in vases of silver fretwork, the foreign birds in gilt cages, and the sandalwood burning in silver censers, contributed to heighten.

A large grotto at the end of a shrubbery was transformed into an Egyptian temple, and exhibited in its adornments all the monsters of the Nile. The entrance was guarded by two formidable figures of the sphinx; and the interior had on each side its altar colossean statues of Iris and Apis.

The long avenue leading to the grand entrance, the extensive gardens, the shrubberies, and plantations, poured a radiant flood of light, reflected from innumerable lamps formed into a variety of figures and trophies, and of a thousand different colours, exhibiting a spectacle of uncommon brilliancy and elegance.

On the appointed night Miss Montgomery, habited as a sultana, was literally a shining character, for the silver gauze that composed her turban, robe, and cimar, were covered with diamonds: her mother, drawn forth with peacock's feathers, jewels, and transparent clouds, looked everything but the grace and dignity of the goddess Juno. The nabob had his head wreathed with ivy and grapes, and personated Bacchus, to which character his long yellow face and tall lank figure were a flat contradiction. Hugh Montgomery had not been seen during the evening, and it was not known what character he intended to assume. Sir Edward Percival was a Turk, and Lord Clavering a friar.

At an early hour the rooms were nearly filled, and the goddess Juno hoped that the company would be all *perdigiously* entertained, as no sort of trouble or expense had been spared to render the amusements of the night amazingly pleasant.

While she was thus haranguing her guests, a very grotesque figure, designed to represent Sterne's Maria, with her hair twisted into a silk net, and leading a tame goat by a green ribband, attracted general observation; somebody facetiously observed that, like Shakespeare's Falstaff, 'sighing and grief had blown her up;' another that a goat was a filthy animal to introduce into genteel company; while a third, still more witty than the rest, remarked that goats were admitted into the most fashionable parties. The mirth this mask occasioned found a fresh subject in a May-day chimney sweeper, who with much address knocked his shovel and brush to the annoyance of some and the infinite diversion of others. A male gipsy proposed to the sultana to point out her future destiny: the sultana held out her hand.

"Here are crooked lines," said the gipsy, "that denote you will become the dupe and prey of fortune-hunters; have a care of listening to flattery – beware of men."

The sultana drew away her hand, and said in a peevish tone she did not want advice, but to be told what would happen to her.

"Disappointment will happen," replied the gipsy, "and a life of misery, if you are not very particular with whom you marry."

"How impertinent!" said the sultana.

"Yet how true," rejoined the gipsy.

The sultana affected to look stately, and passed on, while the gipsy addressed himself to a nun, who appeared devoutly telling her beads.

"Sweet saint," said he, "drop not with those beads too soft a tear. Alas! that love should heave a bosom wrapped in the sacred garb of religion. What pity that devotion cannot shield from passion!"

"What has a recluse like me to do with love?" replied the nun; "at matins I beseech heaven to guard me from its infatuation, and at vespers – "

"You pray for Hugh Montgomery," rejoined the gipsy.

The nun started.

"And from whence have you this knowledge?" said the nun.

"I read it in the stars," answered the gipsy, "and they have told me, that though you are too amiable and innocent to heave the sigh of penitence, that you are destined to heave the sighs of love."

"And who are you who seem so well acquainted with my thoughts?" asked the nun.

"One who not only seems, but really is acquainted with your thoughts," replied the gipsy; "and I will venture to pronounce that whenever Hugh Montgomery can prevail upon himself to lay aside his diffidence, and say 'I love,' Miss Percival will not be very averse to the declaration."

A tall shepherdess, with a crook in her hand, and an artificial lamb under her arm, now joined the nun.

"Well, I protest," said she, "I never saw any thing so out of character in my life, as a nun to stand talking with a gipsy."

"Sweet arcadian," replied he, "be not severe; the fair recluse was only promising me to remember my sins in her orisons."

"Raisins," said a little punch looking Cardinal Wolsey, pushing in between them, "there is plenty of raisins and almonds too in the next room; gad there is no want of anything, it is quite and clean plain to be seen that no sort of expense has been spared either to please the eye or fill the belly."

The shepherdess declared she was shocked at his gross expressions, took the nun by the arm, and walked away. The gipsy next addressed himself to a smart little figure, habited in a light blue rich jacket and petticoat, with a tartan plaid thrown in elegant draperies across her shoulder, and asked her what she would give for news from Sandy gone to the wars.

"Gude troth aw the siller I can cull mine aine," replied she.

"If you would give so much only to hear of him," rejoined he, "what would you give to see him?"

"Dinna tempt me," said the Scotch lassie, "I canna tull what I would giaw the siller I may expect to ha fra the coffers of my father and my mither."

"Thou art a brave lass," replied the gipsy; "trust yourself to my guidance and I promise to lead you to Captain Seymour."

"To Captain Seymour! but who are you that makes this promise," said she; "how do I know that I may trust myself with you?"

The gipsy took off his mask; the Scotch lassie passed her arm under his; they left the rooms, crossed the gardens, and entered a pavilion, the door of which was no sooner thrown open than she was clasped in the arms of the long absent but still constant Seymour.

"Eliza, dear Eliza," said he, as he pressed her to his heart.

She had just time to learn that he had received a slight wound, and had been sent to England with dispatches; that not daring to proceed to Tudor Hall, he had availed himself of some letters entrusted to his care by Colonel Effingham, for his friends at Dolgelly Castle, and that from Mr. Mortimer he had obtained intelligence of the masquerade, and the certainty of meeting her.

"And now, dearest but beloved Eliza," said Seymour, "prevent the possibility of another separation."

"And how, friend?" asked she.

"By eloping with me tonight."

Eliza shook her head.

"Don't you know, friend," said she, "that if I marry before I am twenty, I lose fourteen hundred pounds a year. None of your imploring looks: I love you, most sincerely love you; but yet not well enough to relinquish so much money; besides I know, were you weak enough to persuade me, and were I silly enough to be persuaded, in less than a month you would repent, and blame me for yielding to your wishes."

"Dearest Eliza," said he.

"Aye, and dearest Seymour, wait with patience till I am twenty, and then hey for a journey to Gretna Green, and a Scotch parson."

Seymour snatched her to his arms; she struggled, but let him obtain a kiss or two.

"Haud mon," said she, "I dinna kin what you mean by sic rude behaviour: gin you woll clap a mask a top on your bonny face, and gang wi me tull the ball-room, I wull dance a highland lilt wi you, and that wull be far better than aw this kissing."

The gipsy advised his retreat as soon as possible, adding that he would return with him to Dolgelly Castle, for that Sir Owen Llewellyn being rather indisposed, Mrs. Mortimer, unwilling to leave him, had declined coming to the masquerade.

By this it will be understood that Mr. Mortimer was the gipsy. Half an hour was soon passed in questions and endearments. Captain Seymour obtained, in the presence of Mr. Mortimer, Eliza's solemn promise to be his, as soon as she had attained the age of twenty. Fearful of being missed, she tore herself from his arms, and was conducted by the gipsy to the ball-room, where she immediately joined a group of dancers, and the gipsy departed with Captain Seymour for Dolgelly Castle.

The sultana in proud triumph was parading round the rooms, hanging on the arm of the Turk; and the goddess Juno descending from her high state, was entertaining everyone who would listen, with an account that her dear Lucretia had planned all the decorations out of her own head, and declaring that she was *perdigiously* gratified at seeing such a *conquest* of company *dissembled* together.

The signal being given for a grand display of fire-works in the gardens, the company hurried out in such crowds that the tall shepherdess got her crook broke and her lamb crushed to pieces.

"Now I shall cut a fine figure," cried she; "a very pretty sort of a forlorn shepherdess I shall look now, with my crook broke in two and my lamb crushed to atoms; dear me, sure never anything was half so unfortunate, when everyone said how appropriate I was dressed, and how well I supported my character."

"What disagreeable thing has happened – what in the world is the matter, Miss Jenkins?" asked a Justice Shallow.

"There now! there is fine nonsense," replied the shepherdess, "was ever such a thing known as calling people by their own proper names at a masquerade."

"Well, well, I ask pardon, Mrs. Shepherdess," said the justice; "I did not understand that these masquerades were for all the world the same as drawing for king and queen on a twelfth night, when if you happen to fix on Dolly Dishclout, you are obligated to go by that name all night."

"There!" screamed the shepherdess, "there, that Jew pedlar has carried away on the end of his box the wreath of flowers off my crook, that cost me seven shillings."

"Have him before the justice," said the chimney-sweeper, clapping her on the back with his shovel.

"Well," continued she, "this night will be a pretty expense to me; what with my lamb being squeezed to pieces, my crook broke, and my flowers lost, I have made a sweet night of it."

"I am sure I am ready to say good night," said the justice; "I begin to be heartily tired. What time will they sup I wonder? I want to sit down and be comfortable."

The crowd pressing upon them, the nun and the shepherdess were separated. The nun looked anxiously among the motley group that surrounded her, but the tall singular figure of the shepherdess was nowhere to be seen. The fair nun hoped she had returned to the ball-room, and took a path that she thought led to the priory; but after having pursued it some time, she found she was wrong, and turning into another, in a few moments found herself close by the Egyptian temple; attracted by its singular appearance, she entered and stood contemplating its monstrous adornments and colossean statues. She heard the distant hum of voices, and shouts of mirth, and recollecting her lonely situation, was about to quit the temple, when she beheld a figure habited as a pilgrim leaning against the entrance, and seemingly observing her. A faint scream burst from the lips of the nun, and she clung trembling to one of the statues.

"Of what are you afraid, fair nun?" said the pilgrim advancing, "not surely of a poor way-worn pilgrim, who journeying to the shrine of his saint, lingers here to breathe a prayer and rest his weary steps."

The voice was familiar to the ear of the nun, but with tottering steps, and in hurried accents, she entreated to be allowed to pass.

"And where," said the pilgrim, "would you go? and why, fair nun, are you here alone? Alas! I fear me that habit, which speaks a person resigned to religion, covers a heart devoted to love, else why seek this mysterious temple, why this retirement from observation? Say, charming nun, wait you here to receive the vows of some enraptured lover? but yet beware, be cautious how you exchange the simple habit, the peace of innocence for splendour."

"You wrong me, indeed you do; I came here to meet no lover, to listen to no vows; accident," continued the nun bursting into tears, "accident separated me from my company; in the attempt to regain the priory, I took a wrong direction, and chance alone conducted me to this spot."

"And will Miss Percival forgive the impertinence that has caused those tears; will she pardon one deeply interested for her happiness, who presumes to ask whether the rank Lord Clavering offers does not engage her attention, meet her wishes?"

"Whoever you are," replied the nun, "to this question I can without the smallest hesitation answer no."

"What," said the pilgrim, "so young, so lovely, and yet not ambitious, not experience the proud desire of shining amidst admiring throngs, of removing from these wild bleak mountains to a sunny spot, where your beauty, brought into observation, shall command the adulation of the multitude, where splendour, rank, amusements, shall spread their glittering fascinations round you."

"Good pilgrim," replied the nun, "these scenes which you delineate in such glowing colours have no attraction for me; I prefer the sweet healthful air of my native mountains, their sublime views, and romantic objects, to all the glare of midnight revelry, all the magic of pomp and grandeur: a title has no music for my ear, I have no vanity to shine in crowds, and attract the gaze of multitudes; I am not ambitious of admiration, and the adoration of one worthy heart would be sufficient for my desires."

The nun stopped suddenly, she feared she had said too much.

"Proceed," said the pilgrim, "proceed; I could listen for ever to that voice which so sweetly speaks the sentiments of unsophisticated nature, blest shall he live, whose happy destiny marks him the object of Miss Percival's affection, whose fate it is to dwell with her on her native mountains."

The nun believed she was acting imprudently in listening

so long on such a subject, and to a stranger too, and again she entreated to pass.

"One moment, one little moment more, loveliest Miss Percival, indulge me," said the pilgrim: "have you, I beseech you condescend to tell me, have you really rejected Lord Clavering?"

"I fear," replied the nun, "I do wrong to answer these interrogations; what right have you, a stranger, to question me?"

"None, most surely," answered the pilgrim, "none, but a most sincere interest I feel in all that concerns your future welfare, mingled I must confess with a desire to serve a friend, who is anxious to declare himself your lover."

The nun felt her cheeks glow; she thought of the gipsy, and the idea of Hugh Montgomery mingled with the soft sigh that heaved her bosom.

"Yes, Miss Percival," resumed the pilgrim, "I have a friend who has long loved you, but diffidence, the fear of offending, the dread of rejection, has put a seal upon his lips; though sure his looks, his manner, must have betrayed his secret."

The nun sank on the pedestal of the statue, the voice she was now certain was Hugh Montgomery's, and overcome by pleasure and surprise, she fainted. When she opened her eyes, she encountered those of her lover fixed on her with the tenderest solicitude; her mask had fallen off, and he had laid aside his, and now in the softest accents said:

"I shall never forgive myself for having occasioned you this alarm." Rosa's tears now happily came to her relief, while he continued to ask, "to interpret these tears? – to aversion, has the declaration of my long smothered secret offended you? I fear you hate me."

Rosa extended her white hand, and softly whispered: – "Oh, no!"

Hugh Montgomery's face brightened with hope and pleasure, as he pressed it to his lips, to his heart.

"Lead me," said she, deeply blushing, "lead me to the company: my aunt and uncle no doubt are distracted on my account; and this place, so distant, so remote from the house – "

"With me," replied Hugh Montgomery, "every place is a sanctuary that Miss Percival consecrates with her presence; but answer me – may I hope, will you listen to my vows? will you promise – "

"Nothing here," said Rosa, "tonight I will promise nothing."

"Tomorrow then – nay,"' continued Hugh kissing her hand, "I will not let you go without your promise."

"But recollect," said Rosa, "compulsatory promises are not binding."

"Nay then," said Hugh letting go her hand, "be every action of Miss Percival's life the voluntary impulse of her own ingenuous mind."

Rosa rested her arm on the statue of Iris; she murmured a few indistinct words, and unable to proceed was again silent. Hugh Montgomery had retreated a few paces from her, but perceiving her extreme agitation, he advanced and said:

"Fondly as I love you, I wish to extort no promises: if Miss Percival's pure ingenuous feelings tell her that her heart is mine, to me that heart will be a treasure invaluable, but if I am doomed to meet indifference, to find her affections point another way – "

"And would you not hate me," said Rosa timidly interrupting him, "would you not despise the weak heart that was so easily won, so soon subdued?"

"No," replied Hugh, "on the contrary I would worship the

noble disposition, adore the ingenuous mind that scorned to take advantage of the power it might assume, that relieved from the misery of incertitude the heart that idolized her."

Rosa stood silent a moment, as if uncertain how to act, then turning her mild eyes with modest diffidence upon him, said:

"I know not how to answer you, particularly in this place, but at Birch Park perhaps I might feel more confidence."

"Tomorrow then," said Hugh.

"Yes," replied Rosa, "tomorrow."

The enraptured Hugh sunk on his knees before her, and for the first time his lips met hers, for the first time Rosa received the chaste kiss of pure affection: while his arms enfolded her, he exclaimed:

"I have never known happiness till this moment."

"You have reached the shrine of your saint at last then," said a voice behind him, and a loud laugh and a confused murmur of voices met the ear of the affrighted and abashed Rosa; the friar, foremost in the throng, looking round the temple, said with a sneer:

"A very appropriate temple for worshipping so fair a saint, but rather unlucky you were caught in the act."

"What act?" said a shrill voice in the crowd that now rushed into the temple, "what act?" and the tall shepherdess, her hair all out of curl, and the trimmings of her green muslin jacket hanging in tatters, stood before the speechless and terrified Rosa.

"Why, the act of praying at the feet of Miss Percival, and twining his arms round her waist," said the friar.

"Gad, is that all," said the little fat cardinal, "I thought by the noise you all made; I supposed, I say, something quite and clean wrong, and out of the way, had happened."

"Avast, my hearty," said a sailor, "don't run the little cock-boat down in such a cowardly manner; she does not seem able to weather such a tempest; bring to, father," addressing the friar; "if you will give absolution, all will be well again."

The friar turned away, and said to give absolution in such a case would be improper.

"Improper!" echoed the tall shepherdess, "I say improper, indeed! I am sure no person of our family ever did anything improper."

"Improper," repeated the sultana, with a sneering laugh, improper, "no, certainly there can be nothing improper in a young lady making a private assignation with a gentleman in so retired a spot."

"Dare not," said Hugh Montgomery, sternly, "dare not breathe so vile, so false an insinuation; presume not to sully the purity you know not how to imitate. Miss Percival had been separated from her friends in the crowd that rushed out to witness the exhibition of the fireworks; I met her by accident at this spot, and I detained her, unwillingly on her part, to hear me declare a passion which I am proud to proclaim to the whole world."

"Gad, you are a very fine fellow," said the fat little cardinal, "and as far as my consent will go, you have it with all my heart and soul; and Rosa, my girl, don't be ashamed, there is no harm in the world done. I dare say many of these ladies here, for all they seem so shy and prudish, would be quite and clean glad to be in your situation."

"Well observed, my knowing one," said a mountebank, "you have more wit by half than my merry Andrew. In what pope's reign were you presented with your hat?"

"Gad," said the cardinal, "I never found anybody so

generous as to present me with a hat; no, no, I bought it of David Griffiths, at Carnarvon, in the reign of his present majesty our most gracious sovereign George the Third. I know nothing at all about popes."

"So I thought," said the mountebank.

"But Rosa, your aunt and I have been seeking you up hill and down dale, but we might as well have looked for a dog in a fair. Gad, I was afraid you had been quite and clean carried off."

"Yes," replied the shepherdess, "I have walked about till my feet are all blisters, looking after you, and the damp has taken out all my ringlets; and look at my petticoat, catching upon one thing, and hooking up another, it is torn to fritters; then my crook is utterly ruined, my flowers lost, and my pretty fat lamb crushed to pieces. Oh, this has been a blessed night of entertainment for me."

"I am sure," said the goddess Juno, making her a low obeisance, "I am *perdigiously* glad to hear you say so, I am sure it gives me an amazing great deal of pleasure."

"Bless me, madam, sure you don't mean to say that you are pleased that my crook, that cost six shillings, and the wreath of flowers that dressed it, which came to seven shillings more, are lost and destroyed; besides the ripping of my green muslin all to tatters, that stands me in a matter of thirty shillings; and my nice fat lamb, which I paid a guinea for, is entirely demolished, his head off, his forefeet gone, and his body squeezed double."

"Why, he has been most barbarously butchered," said the chimney-sweeper, "and all that I can advise now he is cut up, is that you should sell him in quarters."

"Oh, mercy deliver us," said the sultana, "here comes the

unwieldy Maria, and her nasty stinking goat; I am surprised, quite surprised, how anybody in their senses could think of introducing such a filthy animal into a fashionable society."

"You forget," said a Don Quixote, "that the fair Maria, unhappy maiden, had lost her peerless wits."

"Lord ma'am," replied Justice Shallow, "she looks upon this place to be like Noah's ark, and thinks that beasts, clean and unclean, may enter; for my part, I love always to do things that are agreeable, and would not for all the world bring any sort of odd out of the way animal, to make folks uncomfortable."

The friar observed that he was an odd animal enough himself, but the more ridiculous the more conspicuous, and that was the life of a masquerade.

Maria and her goat now made a terrible confusion, for the poor animal, tired of confinement, refused to be led about any longer; the chimney-sweeper began swearing, and insisting upon her letting the animal go, but Maria pertinaciously insisted on retaining him, till the chimney-sweeper growing outrageous at her obstinacy, lit a piece of paper at a lamp, and set fire to the green ribband by which he was held; away scampered the goat, upsetting some, and rushing against others, till in the midst of execrations, complaints, and loud bursts of laughter, he made his escape.

Maria, shocked at the behaviour of the chimney-sweeper, and the confusion his frolic had occasioned, fell into strong hysterics. The chimney-sweeper elbowing one, and shoving another, asked everybody for snuff, but not being able to procure any, he flew up to the majestic Juno, and snatching a plume of peacock's feathers from her head, which nodded over a brilliant tiara, he instantly set fire to them, and crammed them burning up Maria's nose, who no sooner felt the heat, than she jumped up, tore off her half mask, and forgetting her assumed character, screamed out: – "Sir Griffith Tudor, you have ruined my nose for ever; sure such another brute was never sent into the world to plague a woman."

"Brute, Lady Tudor!" said he, laughing; "instead of calling names, you ought to be much obliged to me for recovering you so soon; why, my dove, you might have screamed and kicked for an hour, if I had not seen those feathers in the head of the thunderer's wife."

"The most *perdgiously* rude thing I ever met with," replied the goddess, "to take the feathers from my head, without even asking my leave; amazingly *impolite* behaviour indeed."

"Pooh! d – n it," said Sir Griffith, "don't make a fuss about a few peacock's feathers; send to Tudor Hall, you may have a bundle as big as yourself; and as to Maria here, she looks her character now better than ever; her eyes are quite wild; that is as it should be, for Maria you know was touched in the upper story, her attics were deranged."

"I am sure," replied she, "you are enough to derange anybody whose nerves are as strong – "

"Oh! d – n it," said Sir Griffith, "if you are getting upon the nervous system, I wish your auditors patience, mine you have worn threadbare long ago."

The company now repaired to the hall, where the supper tables were spread under white silk awnings, elegantly painted with borders of fruit and flowers, and lit with variegated lamps: every delicacy that nature or art could furnish, was there in profusion, while hams and the famed sirloin made up the banquet.

The fair nun was seated between the pilgrim and the Scotch lassie; the tall shepherdess had the little fat cardinal and

Justice Shallow on each side her; Maria had disappeared but the chimney-sweeper with the tinsel trimmings hanging loose from his coat was a conspicuous figure at the table; next the cardinal sat Bacchus, who appeared to have swallowed copious libations to the honour of his own divinity; the justice got the wing of a turkey and a slice of ham on his plate, and declared he was as happy, notwithstanding he had not been out of his bed at such hours for years, full as happy as if he were at Woodland Cottage, and quite as comfortable too as if he were eating a slice of his own Cheshire cheese; "And what is life," continued he, looking round, "what is life, good folks, nothing at all you know, if one is not to enjoy it, and be comfortable."

"Gad," said the little fat cardinal, "you are right, neighbour; I shall make a famous hearty supper; and to tell you a little bit of a secret, my stomach wanted lining, it felt as hollow and empty as a tub, for as to your sweet things, and your ice, and your fruit, I can make no sort of hand at all of them gimcracks: I am for something solid," helping himself to a slice of roast beef an inch thick, "and as to your jellies and syllabubs, lord they are nothing but mere froth, and quite and clean fit for nothing in the world but to give one the cholic."

Rosa now thought the time passed delightfully, and she smiled upon, and listened to Hugh Montgomery, with attentive pleasure, in spite of the frowns and sneers of her aunt, who was again fated to be mortified by her niece taking another heart from her, which she had unsuccessfully angled for.

Eliza Tudor too was all life and spirits; she had seen her Seymour, was assured of his unaltered affection, and she joyously anticipated the period that would unite their destinies.

At length the little fat cardinal, having satisfied the cravings of his appetite, and drank more freely than usual, began to grow sleepy, and made a motion for departure.

Rosa reluctantly rose at the instigation of her aunt. Justice Shallow was also on his feet to escort them to their carriage, but the jolly god insisted that he should help him to empty another flask. Justice Shallow made excuses: Bacchus, determined not to lose a votary, endeavoured to push him again into his chair: the foot of the justice slipped, and in the fear of falling he caught hold of the white silk awning; down it came, lamps, girandoles, and all in wild confusion, and with a horrible crash – out flew the company in various directions, fancying the roof had fallen in.

Rosa had, however, contrived to hold by the arm of her aunt, and in their fright they had ran almost to the bottom of the avenue before they stopped. Here they were met by two men in liveries, who civilly asked what was the matter?

"Oh," replied Miss Jenkins, "the roof of the Priory has fallen in, and crushed hundreds to death; we have narrowly escaped with our lives; good charitable men, assist us to find our carriage."

This they promised to do, and having passed several, one of the men suddenly lifted Rosa from the ground, and threw her into a chaise, the door of which stood open. She shrieked, but her mouth was instantly stopped by a man, who was seated ready to receive her. The blinds were already drawn up, and the chaise drove off as fast as four horses could gallop. Meantime Miss Jenkins, who had entered into discourse with the man respecting the accident, did not immediately miss her niece; but on the man saying "here is your carriage", she put her foot on the step, and then turning her head round, and not seeing her, cried: –

"Rosa, child, where are you?"

The man pushed her into the carriage, and got in after her; and in spite of her loud remonstrances and struggles, it drove off.

"Where is my niece, where is Miss Percival?" screamed Miss Jenkins.

"On the road to be married," replied the man.

"And where pray are you taking me?" rejoined she.

"The same road, if you can persuade anybody to be plagued with you," answered the man.

"And you!" said she, "I should not have thought of your assurance, to seat yourself in the carriage with me. I think behind might have suited you as well."

The man only laughed, while she continued: –

"Oh, what a terrible night this has been for me: if these are masquerades, I hope I shall never have the misfortune to be invited to one again."

"Why you need not accept the invitation, you know," said the man, "if you don't like it."

"First," resumed she, "to get my crook broke, then to lose my flowers; next to have my nice fat lamb crushed all to pieces. Oh, dear! Oh, dear!" said she, weeping bitterly; "it is too shocking to think of; besides having my new green muslin torn to rags, then to be run away with like poor Miss Byron, in Sir Charles Grandison, and by a man in livery; but I suppose some gentleman has bribed you to commit this outrage on my person, for I hope it is not your own audacity; you don't intend to marry me whether I will or not; I am sure if you are so unfortunate as to be in love with me, it is no fault of mine; I never wish my charms – "

"Charms! where are they to be found. Hey! old girl!" asked

the man, laughing; "in your long purse, I suppose; for as to any other that you might have had, they have bid you good bye so long ago that folks have quite forgot you ever had any; and as to my wanting to marry you, bless your frosty face, I have got a wife already."

"Well then," said Miss Jenkins, "perhaps you intend to rob me, but there you will be disappointed; I have not a single shilling about me; I never wear pockets, nor carry money."

"Aye," replied the man, "that is for fear a poor person should ask charity from you; but I am no robber, so your having no pockets on don't concern me."

"Oh! my poor niece," raved Miss Jenkins; "what will become of her?"

"Why, she will get a husband, I tell you, if she is not a fool," replied the man.

"Surely no woman's troubles and disappointments ever equalled mine," said Miss Jenkins; "here I promised myself so much pleasure at this masquerade."

"After sweetmeat, comes sour sauce," said the man: "you have plagued many a poor soul in your time, now comes your turn to be punished."

"To be sure I have been very cruel to the men; I have certainly treated my lovers with slight and scorn; I have indeed made them feel a vast deal of pain."

"The devil a bit," said her companion; "no man ever cared a brass button for that frosty face of yours. Your niece is a pretty girl enough, and worth a man's giving himself a little trouble about, but as to you, old girl, you are not worth hauling out of a ditch, if you were to tumble in."

The carriage now stopped at a mean looking hut on a common, and it was with difficulty the man and two women could force her out; she kicked, fought, and screamed, and insisted on being drove without further delay to Birch Park. The people only laughed, and at last dragged her up a ladder into a cock-loft, where a miserable bed was spread on a dirty floor.

The man pointed to the bed, and told her she might go to rest as soon as she would.

"Rest!" said she, "rest in such a dismal hole as this, and on such a filthy bed as that."

One of the women replied: –

"Hur was mighty dainty; it was the best room and the best bed hur had."

"Oh, dear! oh, dear!" cried Miss Jenkins; "after all my troubles and disappointments, I suppose I am brought here to be ravished and murdered at last."

The man laughed till he shouted. The woman said hur might sleep in peace, for please got, no harm would come to hur while hur was in hur house. When the man could speak for laughing, he told her nobody would take the trouble of ravishing her, she was too ugly; and as for murdering her, she was not worth being hanged for; so she might lie down and sleep till night, for nobody would offer to come near her. They then left her alone, and after screaming, knocking, crying, enumerating her losses and disappointments, she found herself so weary, that she was glad to throw herself upon the bed, filthy as it was, where she slept soundly till it was dark night.

The woman came at last to wake her, and to her great surprise she found her nap had lasted all the day; being very hungry she gladly partook of some milk and oat cake; the man then told her he would conduct her home: she joyfully started up, and asked if the carriage was ready.

"Carriage," replied the man, "no, no – you must make use of your legs, old girl."

"Walk!" cried Miss Jenkins; "I can't walk, I shall die on the road."

"Then die and be – if you will," said the man; "but come along, I have no time to waste in prating."

The night was dark as pitch, and a drizzling rain fell. As the man led her through ploughed fields, her shoes stuck to the clayey ground, and it was with difficulty she was able to proceed. After various lamentations on her part, and rude replies on that of her companion, lights were seen at a distance.

"That light," said the man, "comes from Birch Park; keep to your right hand and you will presently arrive at the green lane opposite the lawn."

In vain Miss Jenkins entreated him to see her safe home. The man jumped over the hedge, and she saw him no more. Before she reached the green lane she had lost both her shoes; she was wet to her skin, lame, covered with dirt; her green muslin jacket hanging in tatters, her long black hair streaming down her back. She limped into the parlour to her brother, whose grief Mr. Williams was vainly endeavouring to console.

As soon as he saw her, his first question was: –

"Where is Rosa?"

He listened to her strange story with the utmost rage and impatience; and finding she could give no account of his niece, his sorrows became almost frenzy; while Miss Jenkins's losses, disappointments, frights, and fatigues had such an "effect" upon her, that she was many days confined to her bed, so extremely ill that her life was despaired of.

CHAPTER III

But their hearts wounded, like the wounded air
Soon close; where past the shaft no trace is found,
As from the wing no scar the sky retains;
The parted wave no furrow from the keel;
So dies in human hearts the pangs of love.

Lets talk of graves, and worms, and epitaphs,
Make dust our paper, and with rainy eyes
Write sorrow on the bosom of the earth.

But not to thee,
Meek spirit, not to thee, the morn is fair,
Nor glow the sun beams cheerily: alas!
The early carols of the woodland choir,
Echoing so sweetly in the dewy fields,
Thou hearest not: wrapp'd in the arms of death,
Thou can'st not feel the rising sun's warm ray,
Thou can'st not mark the beauty of the morn,
For dark and silent is thy narrow cell.

I'll give thee this plague for thy dowry.
Be thou as chaste as ice, as pure as snow,
Thou shall not escape calumny.

Shakespeare

THE young, the sensitive, and the romantic, erroneously persuade themselves that first impressions are indelible, and that a disappointment in love leaves on the heart and imagination an incurable malady, which no new object can alleviate, no time extirpate.

When the Marchesa della Rosalvo pronounced the solemn vows which annihilated his hopes, and separated her from his arms for ever, the constitution of Horatio Delamere was unequal to the shock; he raved for many days in actual delirium, and when his senses were again restored, he considered the world as a blank, incapable of producing an object or an event to interest his mind, or blunt the poignancy of his feelings.

For many weeks he continued gloomy, cheerless, a prey to anguish, regret, and melancholy; but absence, time, a change of scene, the various amusements at which his friends compelled him to be present, insensibly diverted his attention, by degrees weaned him from dwelling on irremediable sorrow, and a few months restored him, if not to actual happiness, to a state of tranquillity.

He thought indeed of Celestina frequently and tenderly; but his reason, unclouded by passion, was now convinced that her retirement from the world was the only step she could possibly have taken, which honour and propriety could approve. Cool and unimpassioned, he had now leisure to reflect that a marriage with her would have been highly displeasing to his father, and would have been a source of uneasiness to the tenderest and best of mothers; and while he heaved a sigh of fond melancholy regret to the beauties and fascinations of the Marchesa della Rosalvo, he yet rejoiced that he had escaped the misery of giving pain to parents so very worthy of his affection and respect.

Lord Narbeth, though proudly tenacious of preserving the male line of his family purely British, extended not his prejudice or partiality to the female branches, but cheerfully awarded his consent to his niece, Miss Lonsdale, becoming the wife of the Count Miraldi, though a foreigner.

Miss Lonsdale really liked the count, yet she did not bestow her hand upon him without experiencing a sort of reluctance. She knew that separated from her own family and connections, the greatest part of her life must be passed in Italy; she also feared that a husband might attempt to exert those prerogatives, against which her spirit would revolt: however, her reasons for appearing far weightier than those against, Miss Lonsdale became a bride.

Their marriage was celebrated at the church of St. Rosolia at Palermo, with the utmost publicity and magnificence; and at this ceremony Horatio Delamere assisted, and afterwards retired with the happy pair to a palazzo of the count's a few miles from Palermo, where balls, ridottos, and various amusements gave the fair Sicilians an opportunity of endeavouring to remove the melancholy of Horatio Delamere, and of displaying their own graces and attractions.

Lady Isabella Lonsdale being in the way that women wish to be who love their lords, Captain Lonsdale became anxious to have his child born in England, they therefore took an affectionate leave of their Sicilian friends, and, accompanied by the Count and Countess Miraldi and Horatio Delamere, bade adieu to the luxuriant and delightful shores of Italy, and soon hailed the white cliffs of their native land.

At Narbeth Lodge they were received with the warmest demonstrations of pleasure. Horatio was paler and thinner than when he left England, and the glance that shot through the thick fringes of his intelligent eye had lost much of its spirit and lustre.

Lady Narbeth beheld the ravages grief and disappointment had made in his fine person with apprehensive solicitude, and rejoiced that he was returned again to his native air, and under the maternal eye, where she could watch his health, and with her own hand administer such restoratives as she thought he required.

After remaining a month at Narbeth Lodge, Lady Isabella and Captain Lonsdale, with the Count and Countess Miraldi, took their leave, and by easy stages arrived at Raven-hill Castle, where Lady Isabella intended to wait the period of her accouchement. Horatio had promised to visit his friend Henry Mortimer, but while preparations were making for his journey, Lord Narbeth was seized with an alarming illness, which set aside for the present his intended tour through North Wales.

On the first news of Miss Percival and her aunt being missing, Hugh Montgomery, in the utmost distress of mind, rode all over the country, but without obtaining the slightest intimation of the objects of his search. Sir Edward Percival also and Lord Clavering offered great rewards, and threatened punishments, and explored the country round for many miles without success: no kind of intelligence was to be obtained.

On Miss Jenkins's return their efforts were renewed, but without effect, and the fate of the amiable lovely Rosa remained concealed from the inquiries of her anxious and lamenting friends.

Sir Edward Percival made a great noise, and appeared to be very unhappy; the Earl of Clavering declared himself absolutely miserable; and Hugh Montgomery, resigning himself to grief, became in a short time the shadow of his former self.

Miss Jenkins recovered her health, while her ill temper became if possible more intolerable than ever, so sore had her mind been made by disappointment, and hearing truth delivered in plain English; and to add to her mortifications, Mr. Williams had hired a plump good-looking dairy-maid, of whom he took more notice than Miss Jenkins approved, and she vehemently protested she would never again set her foot in Woodland Cottage, unless he discharged that pert, bold hussy, whose very looks told she was not a bit better than she should be.

Mr. Williams, however, was not so subservient as Miss Jenkins expected; he peremptorily refused to discharge the girl, alleging as a reason that she was a very good and useful servant, and suited his purpose extremely well.

"No doubt," answered Miss Jenkins, "no doubt she suits your purpose: she looks like one of that sort."

Finding she could not prevail to have the girl turned away, her jealousy became more and more inflamed, so that actually afraid of her tongue, to which she gave unlimited freedom, Mr. Williams's visits to Birch Park became less frequent, a circumstance that gave him great concern, as Gabriel Jenkins pined so much after his niece, that he stood in actual want of the consolations of friendship, having lost his appetite and his spirits, and become moped and melancholy, confining himself entirely to the house; though Williams wrote him a very kind letter, inviting him to Woodland Cottage, and stating his reasons for not venturing to Birch Park; endeavouring to demonstrate that it was the most foolishest thing in all the world for a man to give himself up to sorrow and refuse to take comfort, seeing that things that must be will be; because for a person to sit all day in the house to do nothing but groan and lament, only made him quite disagreeable and uncomfortable.

Sir Owen Llewellyn had the felicity to see his daughter in ten months after her marriage the mother of a beautiful boy: he witnessed with grateful and heart-felt pleasure the increasing fondness of Henry Mortimer; and in Adeline's tender attention to her infant he beheld the maternal softness and solicitude of Lady Llewellyn, his beloved and ever-lamented wife, renewed.

At Dolgelly Castle all was refined elegance, calm, rational, and dignified happiness. Books, music, and enlightened conversation diversified their hours, and time flew rapidly away without leaving them a desire beyond their own happy circle.

The affection of Adeline towards her child was warm and animated; she nursed him herself, while a new feeling, a rapturous sensation, such as mothers only can experience, filled her heart.

Sir Owen Llewellyn doted on his grandson, and spent a large portion of his time in the nursery. He had one morning as usual been fondling the little smiling urchin, and had but just returned him to his mother, when he was seized with the third apoplectic fit, and fell senseless into Henry Mortimer's arms.

Assistance was instantly summoned: they tried the lancet, but in vain; no blood followed the incision; the just, the upright, the worthy Sir Owen Llewellyn slept to wake no more; his spirit had flown to heaven to receive the reward of a life spent in acts of benevolence and virtue.

Adeline was now an orphan, and as she wept on the bosom of Eliza Tudor, she would turn her eyes towards Heaven and say: –

"Oh! that I too were dead. Oh! that I were quietly reposing in the grave of my mother."

Henry Mortimer, though scarcely less affected, silently mourned the loss of his father, his friend, and benefactor; he confined his grief to his own bosom: and tenderly endeavoured to comfort his distressed wife. He brought their lovely child, and gently placing it in her arms, besought her to remember how much injury the violence of her grief might occasion him, as on her health depended that of the child, who drew his sustenance from her bosom.

Adeline clasped the infant to her heart with one arm, while she extended the other hand to Henry, who prest it to his lips, while in a voice choked with grief she cried: –

"Dearest Henry! forgive me. I must weep. Oh! my father, my dear, dear father!"

The remains of Sir Owen Llewellyn, were by torch-light deposited in the same tomb with his wife's.

Henry Mortimer attended as chief mourner.

The funeral was followed, according to the custom of the country, by a numerous concourse of people of all ranks, whose tears and lamentations plainly evinced that the poor had lost a father and benefactor, whose heart had always felt for their necessities while his liberal hand had relieved. The higher sort mourned a worthy man and a valued friend.

Ned Ratlin's tears had mingled with the dust that covered the hallowed remains of his honoured patron: when he returned to the castle, he looked mournfully at the sable band that waved in his hat, and at the crape that bound his arm; the domestics had assembled round him, and he began harranguing them in such terms of simple and pathetic grief that there was not a dry eye among them.

"Death! my friends and messmates, Death," said Ned, "is an enemy we cannot fire upon and obligate to sheer off. No, he sticks close to our quarters; we cannot, let us try ever so hard, slip our cables and run away, whenever we find he bears too hard upon us. No, no, if once he claps his grappling iron aboard us, we must strike whether we like it or not, messmates. Sir Owen Llewellyn – " at this name, honest Ned's tears gushed out, and for a few seconds prevented his proceeding; at last, after coughing and wiping his eyes, he continued: –

"Sir Owen Llewellyn, messmates, was a worthy and a noble commander: but he never could have had promotion equal to his deservings here, so he has been called off to a far better station. – Yes," said Ned, elevating his voice, and flourishing his wooden leg, "at the great day of judgment, when the boatswain pipes all hands, then will be read the certificate of his services, and he will have a flag, and will sail in seas without danger of a lee-shore; no tempests, no rocks, no quicksands."

Ned wiped his eyes again, and looking kindly around him, continued: –

"And I hope, messmates, we shall all one day get upon the like station; in the mean time let every one keep a true reckoning – stick firm to their duty – never sleep upon watch, but obey the noble Captain Mortimer, who has the command now, in the hope of getting promotion too, after their topsails have been lowered by death."

On the eventful night of the masquerade, when Miss Percival was separated from her aunt, the chaise in spite of her screams flew rapidly along: her companion would answer no questions; but after having proceeded a few miles, offered her some wine and biscuits, with which he was amply provided: but too much alarmed and distressed in mind to eat, she declined accepting any refreshment; the man with perfect indifference said: – "Oh! very well, miss, just as you please for that; I shan't force you to eat against your will, but if you choose to starve, that is no reason why I should do the like just to keep you company." He then fell to, and ate and drank heartily, while poor Rosa wept, and thought in agony of the anxiety that the inhabitants of Birch Park would feel on her account.

She reverted to the hour of exquisite delight in which she had listened to the soft tender pleadings of Hugh Montgomery, to the years of bliss, of happiness, she had anticipated in becoming his wife; and her tears streamed faster as she saw herself torn from him, and all the fairy visions of her imagination melt into air. Again with pathetic energy she conjured her companion to inform her where he was conveying her, and who was his employer; but all she could obtain in reply from him was: –

"Have a bit of patience, miss, you will know all about it by and bye; make yourself easy, and don't spoil your pretty face with crying; you was born with a silver spoon in your mouth. I warrant you will be glad enough one day that what you think such a mortal trouble now did happen to you."

"No," replied Rosa, "I can never have reason to be glad that I was torn in this clandestine way from my friends, from all that love me, to know that they must suffer the most poignant grief on my account."

The man shut his eyes and slept, or pretended to sleep: while finding she could make no impression on him, she silently recommended herself to the protection of Heaven, and endeavoured to compose and fortify her mind, and to wait patiently the development of what appeared a complication of mystery, and villainous outrage.

Towards evening they reached the ancient city of Aberconway, where the beautiful river from whence it takes its name empties itself into the Irish sea; here the man rousing himself, and letting down the window, gave the driver directions, then turning to Rosa, said:

"Our journey is at an end, miss."

The chaise left the town about half a mile to the right, and struck into a road near the riverside, which terminated in an old fashioned farm-house, into which Rosa had no sooner entered, than her spirits, subdued by grief and fatigue, entirely forsook her, and she fell into the arms of a woman, whom her companion saluted with – "Here, Peg, shew miss into the parlour."

The parlour was a large room with white-washed walls, a nicely sanded floor, an enormous wide chimney-piece over which were placed three japan waiters, and half-a-dozen wine glasses, interspersed with a few broken China teacups by way of ornaments: a large casement window that looked into a yard where a quantity of poultry were feeding, and a huge sow and a parcel of little pigs wallowing on a dunghill.

The first words Rosa heard when she recovered recollection were: "Peg, where is Mrs. Howels, where is your mistress, hey, Peg?"

"Mistress is a-bed," replied the girl.

"A-bed" said the man: "is she in the old way, napsy I suppose, Peg?"

The girl laughed, or more properly grinned, and said: – "Yes, yes, you have guessed it sure enough, master."

Rosa felt sick, her head turned round, and she requested the girl to show her where she was to sleep.

The man said: –

"Why, miss, you have tasted nothing all day, I am sure you must be hungry: – you had better have some supper, it will soon be ready. What have you got, Peg?"

The girl answered: –

"Boiled fowls and ham."

Rosa said she preferred a little gruel, but before it could be got ready she again fainted, and was by the man carried up stairs into a large chamber, in which stood a small tent bed, having no adornments of any kind to boast, nor any recommendation except that of cleanliness. The girl assisted her to take off her masquerade habit, on which she now looked with disgust and terror, and being dismissed, Rosa heard her lock the door: a bolt being on the inside, she drew it, and examining a closet that communicated with the room, and finding she had no interruption to apprehend, threw herself on the bed, recommended herself to the protection of heaven, and soon fell into a deep sleep, which lasted till past eight the next morning, when the girl terrified her by thundering at the door, and telling her she had brought her some clothes to put on in place of them papery ones, and that mistress was down stairs and wanting her breakfast. Rosa opened the door: the girl put down a bundle and was quitting the room, when Rosa desired her to stay a few minutes.

"If you wants anything make haste," said the girl, "for mistress is mortal crabbed this morning; Moggy Jones has disappointed her of her drops."

"Tell me, my good young woman," said Rosa, "do you know who has employed your master to force me from my friends, and bring me to this place?"

"No, bless your heart, master never tells nobody about his

consarnments," replied the girl, "for as to mistress, hur can never keep nothing at all – for hur gets so – "

"Here you Peg," bawled a coarse voice from the bottom of the stairs. "What the devil are you clacking about hey? – Come down stairs this minute."

The girl shook her hand at Rosa, and said, "Hush," then creeping up another pair of stairs made no reply, till the same voice in a more angry tone called again, "Peg, you slut, what the plague are you doing?"

"Making your bed, mistress," answered Peg.

"Confound the bed," said her mistress. "See, you devil, if miss be a coming to breakfast."

Rosa hastened down stairs, and on entering the parlour, found a great coarse looking woman with a broad red face, and large squinting eyes, seated at the breakfast table, who saluted her with, "So, miss, you be comed down at last; you be used to quality hours I sees. Well to be sure, what a thin little bit of a shrimp you looks. – Lord! I expected to see a different sort of a body to you: but there, I suppose, you be tightened up into a Miss Bailis, to make you look just the same as two deal boards nailed together."

Rosa was astonished: she blushed, felt disconcerted; the tears rushed to her eyes, while Mrs. Howels, unnoticing her agitation, asked her husband if he would have any tea. John Howels was soon seated by Rosa, who was so terrified by the bold looks and vulgar manners of her hostess, that she was happy when the meal was ended. As she rose to quit the room, Mrs. Howels desired her to sit still where she was, for she had not time to go out with her then: and she had orders not to let her go anywhere at all by herself.

"What! am I a prisoner?" asked Rosa.

"I must keep you all the while in my sight," answered Mrs. Howels, "unless you choose to stay above stairs, and then the door can be locked to be sure, but that will be very dull for you."

"Dull indeed!" said Rosa, with a heavy sigh. "I beg to know by whose authority you presume to confine me."

"O, Lord a mighty!" replied Mrs. Howels, "by whose authority? Why by John Howels's to be sure; he takes care to let me know he is master. God help me! if I was unmarried again I should sing another tune, but them that is bound must obey: and them as is free may run away."

Oh! thought Rosa that I could run away. She looked into the yard, and saw it was surrounded by walls; and in a corner near the door, that opened on a lane, was an enormous large mastiff, chained up, who snarled and barked at every thing that approached him. Mrs. Howels told Rosa if she had a mind for a bit of work she could give her a few of John Howels's shirts to mend, or some stockings to darn. Rosa answered that she did not feel disposed to work, but would thank her if she could supply her with some books.

"Books!" said Mrs. Howels; "Oh, what you be a reader, be you, I thought by your fingers you did not use the needle overmuch; well, if you be fond of reading, here," throwing open a corner cupboard, "here be very nice books as I hears John Howels tell; for I never troubles my head about such things."

Rosa beheld two or three tattered volumes, which having examined, she found they were the Newgate Calender, God's Revenge Against Murder, and the Farmer's Assistant. Having read their titles, she was turning in disappointment from the cupboard; when her eye accidentally rested on a box of paints, and a roll of drawing paper.

"If I may make use of these," said she, addressing Mrs. Howels, "I may possibly find some amusement."

"Aye, them things belonged to my nephew, who was killed at the battle of the Nile," replied Mrs. Howels. "He must needs go aboard of a king's ship; his head was shot off, miss, and the sharks had the picking of his bones, for he was thrown overboard. If the fool had staid here – but what signifies, he is dead as mutton, and there is an end of Walter Owens – But, miss, can you paint pictures, can you make houses and trees?"

Rosa replied in the affirmative.

"And maybe, miss, you can draw folks' faces," resumed Mrs Howels: "lord I wish you would paint my little girl, a sweet pretty *hinfint* as ever eyes was clapped on."

Rosa said she would try what she could do to oblige her. Mrs. Howels looked pleased, said she would have it put into a gilt frame, and hung over the mantle-piece. Rosa asked to see the child.

"Then you must go to heaven to fetch her," replied Mrs. Howels, trying to squeeze out a tear; "for Kitty has been in her grave now above five years."

"And how on earth," said Rosa, "am I to take the likeness of a child I never saw, and who has been dead above five years?"

"Lord, it is the easiest thing in the world, if you have only a mind to set about it," replied Mrs. Howels, seating herself opposite to her; "only look at me, miss; the pretty creature was the very spit of me, just such a nose, and just such eyes; only draw my face, and it will be sure to be mightily like."

Rosa smiled, and said she feared she had not abilities equal to the painting a likeness of a person she never saw.

"I never heard nothing so foolish in my life," rejoined Mrs.

Howels, pettishly, "why there is Morgan Davids, he never saw the king in his born days, for he never was five miles from Aberconway since he first came into the world; yet he has made the most beautifulest, heligantist likeness of his royal majesty's head as ever was seen; it has brought plenty of custom to the house I assure you. It was a lucky day for Mrs. Cadwallader when Morgan Davids persuaded her to pull down the old worn out Goat, and set up the King's Head. Lord keep us all from pride and the devil. It was nothing but a little pot-house then, where any poor fellow might call for a dobbin of ale; but now it is one of the first *hinds* in Aberconway, with a bunch of grapes over the door, and wine and spirits wrote in big gold letters under it. Then Mrs. Cadwallader is grown so proud she don't know nobody as she used to be quite intimate with. There she sits in her bar, who but she, with her hair plaited like a horse's mane, and her fine dress cap all *aisidun*, just as if she had got a drop in her head; and her Miss Bailis is laced so tight about her, that she looks just like a *notomy*; indeed for that matter, I don't think hur has an ounce of flesh to cover her bare bones, yet hur fancies herself quite the genteel thing. Lord, for my part I hate to see such wizen half-starved skeletons; give me something crummy, as my poor dear first husband William Owens used to say, something to feel."

Rosa perceiving that Mrs. Cadwallader would be an ever-lasting theme, promised to try what she could do to oblige her; and obtained permission to take the paints and pencils to her own chamber, from the window of which she had a fine view of the bold scenery of the surrounding country, of the magnificent ruins of the castle, and the beautiful river Conway, rolling its broad waves to mingle with the distant sea. She soon produced a drawing of a child, after her own fancy, which so pleased Mrs. Howels, that she said it wanted nothing in the world but red cheeks, sandy hair, green shoes, and a yellow sash, to be the very spit of her poor, dear, sweet, little Kitty. Rosa, good naturedly, coloured it after the taste of Mrs. Howels. It was placed in a tawdry gilt frame, and hung over the chimney-piece, and that very evening exhibited to Doctor Powell and his wife, who had come on a visit from Aberconway to their cousin Mrs. Howels. Rosa fancied she saw in Doctor Powell's face the lines of feeling and humanity; and during the first half hour she frequently and earnestly wished for an opportunity of relating her situation, and interesting him to acquaint her friends where and how she was detained; but to accomplish this desire was rendered impossible by the watchfulness of John Howels and his rib, who took care to seat the doctor and his wife at too great a distance for her to have any private conversation. For some time indeed, the whole discourse was engrossed by the two female cousins, and ran solely on the upstart pride of Mrs. Cadwallader, the landlady of the King's Head, who was sprung from nobody, and never would have been nothing, if Morgan Davids the painter, with a lucky stroke of his brush, had not made somebody of her. Mrs. Cadwallader at length was forgot in Doctor Powell's complaints of the poorness of his practice.

"I protest, cousin," said he, addressing John Howels, "Aberconway is a starving hole for a medical man – why it is the healthiest spot in the world."

"Very true," replied John Howels; "I enjoy good health always; I am never sick, never has nothing the matter with me."

"Sick!" echoed the doctor; "no, worse luck for me; I can't

hear of any one that is: my drugs get mouldy on the shelves – there is no want of physic at Aberconway; no fevers, no distempers of any kind: and as for accidents, nothing of that sort ever happens; no broken legs or arms to set; I have not had a fractured limb this month – nothing at all to do in the surgical line. And as to any persons cutting their throats," continued the doctor, "they are far too contented and happy to throw a job of that kind in my way."

"Good heaven!" thought Rosa, "I am but a bad physiognomist, for in this man's countenance I fancied I read the lines of goodness and philanthropy."

"Let me consider," resumed the doctor, placing his forefinger on his forehead: "the last case of that kind that I attended was about two years ago; I was called in to sew up the throat of a madbrained Irish officer, who had divided his windpipe with his own sword."

"Lord a mercy! what did he do it for, cousin?" asked Mrs. Howels.

"Some people say for love," replied the doctor, "others for debt. I knew the man was past recovery," continued he, "the moment I looked at him, but the fools about him would insist on my sewing up the wound; so I did, and was well paid for my trouble; but now I am quite out of luck's way, nothing of the sort happens; ecod, I believe, Mary," addressing his wife, "I must cut Pompey's throat and sew it up again, just by way of keeping myself in practice."

"Aye do, Mr. Powell," replied his feeling compassionate helpmate; "do you, my dear, cut the dog's throat as soon as ever you go home; indeed it will be great pities for your hand to get out for want of practice."

Rosa shuddered, while she heard one of her own sex so

unfeelingly persuade another to commit so barbarous an act, and sincerely pitied the innocent animal who was devoted to suffer under such wanton and cruel experiments; and an additional weight hung upon her spirits, as she saw the hope she had only a few moments before encouraged recede as the sordid dispositions of Powell and his wife unfolded. Many days past in melancholy regrets, in torturing suspense, in expectation of evil, to which her imagination could neither give form nor name; and to add still more to the disagreeable irksomeness of her situation, Rosa discovered that the woman allotted her for a companion was not only grossly illiterate and vulgar, but also incurably addicted to the degrading vice of inebriety, in which state she was frequently carried to bed unable to assist herself, at which periods Rosa was regularly locked in her bed-chamber by the vigilant John Howels, who having become from ploughboy to be master of the farm, from his marriage with the rich widow Owens, contented himself with hoarding money, while she swallowed gallons of smuggled liquor, which she procured of her neighbour Moggy Jones, and with which she regularly before dinner got what her husband called napsy, and before bed time hunkumstary; nor did he attempt to restrain her, as he hoped that a free indulgence would soon release him from trammels into which he had entered merely from motives of gain, love of money being the sole passion of John Howels; and to gratify which he would have undertaken any act, however nefarious, that did not amount to murder. Before Rosa became convinced of Mrs. Howels's infirmity, her innocent unsuspicious mind was at a loss to comprehend what took her to bed every day about twelve o'clock, though she continually heard John Howels tell his maid that her mistress was getting napsy. One evening, being called down to tea, she found Mrs. Howels leaning her head against the wall; and on asking if she was ill, found her incapable of articulating a word; having called the girl, she told her to procure assistance, for her mistress was very ill. The girl to Rosa's astonishment only laughed, while her mistress, squinting more horribly than ever she had seen her, dropped her head first on one shoulder, then on the other, unable to keep it in an upright position. Peg placed the tea chest before Rosa, and begged her not to mind mistress, who was only in the old way, but to make the tea herself, for mistress never drank no tea when she was hunkumstary. Rosa could not comprehend the meaning of this strange word, which, however, to her disgust and terror, was soon explained by John Howels, who coming in, and looking at her, said: –

"So you have took your drops, I see? Peg, get her to bed, girl; and do you see, and put on her night cap."

"The devil!" stammered Mrs. Howels, "the devil may make a nutting bag of it – the devil himself may ride a hunting with my night cap! What do I care about night caps; give me a pint of gin."

Rosa was so frightened, that when asked by John Howels to make the tea, she poured it into the sugar canister, and the cream into the slop bason.

"Bless my heart, miss," said John Howels, "why one would think you was got hunkumstary as well as my wife, to see your actions. Why you are as white as a sheet, and your hand shakes as bad as hers does in a morning, before hur has had her qualifying drops, as hur calls em. You have made a fine piece of work among the grocery."

"Why, what have I done, Mr. Howels?" asked Rosa, with a tremulous voice.

"Nothing, only poured the tea among all the *shuggar*, and the *crame* into the slop bowl, miss," answered John Howels, "that is all."

"Pray excuse me, Mr. Howels," said Rosa, "I am unused to spectacles of this sort, and they frighten me beyond measure."

Peg grinned, while her master replied: –

"Lord love you, miss, there is nothing at all to be frightful at; this a bin hur custom for many a long year: as soon as hur gets to bed, hur will fall fast asleep and snoring, and never know nothing at all about the matter in the morning – Peg, fetch hur a little more gin. When hur has had hur quantam hur will be as quiet as a lamb."

Rosa begged for heaven's sake that they would not allow her to drink any more. Peg tried to coax her up stairs, while she, scarcely able to get out a word, declared she would not go to bed without another pint of gin; and in her fury to obtain it she tore off her cap, threw it behind the fire, and kicked her shoes into the middle of the room. Rosa made a precipitate retreat to her own chamber, where she was as usual locked in: her mind was in a state of distraction, her feelings were agonized; and as her clasped hands were raised to heaven, she exclaimed: –

"To what scenes of humiliation am I condemned! For what new sufferings am I destined?"

Many times she opened her window with an intention of escaping; but it looked into the yard, where every night the huge mastiff was let loose to range, after having been chained up all day to make him savage: and added to this, she had no money, nor any thing valuable about her, and was besides entirely strange to the road that led to her home; thus hopeless and forlorn, all that remained for her was to weep and pray.

On this night Mrs. Howels was not quiet as a lamb, on the contrary she was extremely riotous; and it was late the next day before Rosa was released from confinement, and summoned to breakfast. She found Mrs. Howels more dressed than usual. Rosa knew not how to meet her, but for her part, she neither by look nor manner seemed sensible that any thing had been improper in her conduct.

Rosa's cheeks were crimsoned with blushes, she felt ashamed for her, and lamented that any woman should so shamefully forget the delicacy of her sex: she looked upon her with abhorrence, and would have gladly evaded her invitation to walk, but Mrs. Howels would admit no excuses, would take no denial; but taking Rosa's white arm under her brawny red one, she forcibly led her for some time along the high road, which at that time was extremely dusty. Rosa said the fields would have been much more pleasant, or the sands by the riverside.

"No matter for that, miss," replied Mrs. Howels, "I choose to walk this way, I be not quite so delicate as you, besides I be gwain after a person who owes me a trifle of money, and these be not times, miss, to lose nothing; and John Howels, a stingy fellow, is so close-fisted, I can never get a farthing out of him, though he was only but my servant, and I married him for love: I believe on my soul I was witched to do such a foolish action. Aye, aye, I was mistress then; but I knows to my sorrow who is master now. He never lets me have the handling of nothing. Lord! only see, miss, what a fine coach is a coming along yonders."

Rosa looked up, and beheld the livery of the Earl of Clavering: with a sudden jerk she drew her arm from under Mrs. Howels, and ran screaming towards the carriage. Lord

Clavering saw her, she was lifted in, and overcome with joy fainted in his arms; when she recovered, to her extreme disappointment she again found herself within sight of the detested farm-house. Lord Clavering appeared surprised and rejoiced to see her, while she in transports pressed his hand to her lips, related her story, and entreated him to convey her to her friends: this he faithfully promised to do, but notwithstanding her supplications to the contrary, persisted on calling at the farm-house to interrogate the people, to oblige John Howels to confess who had employed him to carry her off. To Rosa's thousand questions and inquiries after her friends his lordship answered they were all well, and that Miss Montgomery was now Lady Percival, having been married to her father above a week. Rosa felt a pang at her heart, on the conviction that her fate, be it what it might, was of so little consequence to her father, that he had married while she was lost, conveyed he knew not whither, nor appeared to care. Her tears would not be restrained, and again she begged that she might be allowed to proceed immediately to Birch Park, the home of her infancy, where she knew she had friends that loved her, in whom her fate created the most lively interest and feeling.

It was with extreme reluctance she was prevailed upon to enter the farm-house again, where Lord Clavering, in a voice of authority, demanded to see John Howels, who quickly appeared, bowing and scraping, but refused to give any account of his employer, unless alone with his lordship, as he had taken his bible oath, he said, not to let miss know nothing about it. Upon this Lord Clavering requested Rosa to retire for a short time, while he examined the fellow.

Rosa obeyed, though not without considering it very

strange, that she, the injured person, and most concerned in the business, was not to know by whose order and contrivance she had been made a prisoner, and condemned to suffer, and for what intent. In less than an hour Lord Clavering requested her company: as she entered the parlour he took her hand, and seating her, said: "You will no doubt, my dear Miss Percival, be much surprised to hear that the man of whose character and principles you had the highest opinion is the person who has occasioned you so much suffering, and your friends so much anxiety."

Rosa's heart throbbed with painful apprehension; it was with difficulty she could ask of whom his lordship spoke.

"Of that most consummate hypocrite, Hugh Montgomery," replied his lordship, "who conceals the vilest principles, and most atrocious acts, under the saintly mask of goodness and virtue. He is the person who employed this John Howels, and with what intent requires no further explanation."

Rosa's cheek was alternately the brightest crimson and the palest white, as she faintly repeated, "Hugh Montgomery! Oh! no, it cannot be possible. I will never believe that he is capable – "

"He professed himself your lover I believe," resumed Lord Clavering, "but at the same time I understand was under engagements, and on the point of marriage, with a rich East Indian, who is every hour expected at Glenwyn Priory. He knew, Miss Percival, that surrounded by your friends, he stood no chance of bringing you to his terms; but at a distance, deprived of their supporting affection, experiencing the privation of those indulgencies and accommodations you had been accustomed to enjoy, he hoped to be more successful. Next week I find he is expected here."

Rosa listened with agonized attention. "I believe," continued his lordship, "I believe, Miss Percival, partiality for this unworthy man made you averse to my honourable proposals; you blush, and that blush declares you love Mr. Montgomery yet, deceitful and villainous as he has behaved towards you."

"No," replied Rosa, rallying her spirits, "I detest him, I despise his principles, I abhor from my soul his conduct."

"Now then, perhaps," said his lordship, "you may be inclined to lend a favourable ear to my passion; offended pride may perhaps induce you to show Mr. Montgomery his power over your affections is not so confirmed, so certain as is generally believed."

"I know not from what such a belief should have arisen," replied Rosa, "not from any confession of mine."

"Recollect yourself, Miss Percival," rejoined his lordship: "have you forgot the Egyptian temple, and the kneeling pilgrim, whose happy arms encircled you, and from whose embrace you made no effort to escape?" Rosa blushed deeply, while he continued: "Surely this was a declaration sufficient, and a man must have been more senseless than an idiot who would not so have understood it."

Rosa burst into tears, and entreated Lord Clavering to spare her the remembrance of that humiliating scene, as she had been sufficiently punished for any weakness she might then have felt or yielded to. His lordship again took her hand, and pressing it respectfully to his lips, assured her it was far, very far from his intention to give her pain, or wound her delicacy, but that he was obliged in honest sincerity to tell her, that many reports were in circulation highly injurious to her reputation. Rosa's countenance was instantly animated with conscious innocence; an air of pride gave dignity to her figure, while she replied:

"My lord, no thought or action of mine has hitherto sullied the purity of my character; I shall yet make my defamers blush for having dared to associate the name of Rosa Percival with dishonour."

His lordship answered – that for himself he felt so convinced of her innocence, so assured of her honour, that he again repeated his offer of making her his wife, and advised her both as lover and friend, to suffer him to present her on their return to Birch Park as Countess of Clavering, "the only effectual method," continued his lordship, "of stopping the viperous tongues of scandal, and crushing the infamous designs of Mr. Montgomery. You are silent, Miss Percival; will you not honour me with a reply?"

"Take me from this place," said Rosa, "from the society of this hateful woman; restore me to my friends, and give me time for consideration."

"I am now," replied Lord Clavering, "obliged to proceed a few miles beyond the town of Aberconway, on business of the utmost importance; if you will at once resolve to give me your hand, I can, as my wife, take you with me, otherwise you must remain till my return."

"Remain!" cried Rosa, "remain here! you will not surely leave me? you cannot be so cruel."

"I offer you," replied he, "rank, wealth, the honourable title of my wife, can you, Miss Percival, be so cruel to yourself and me as to refuse?"

"Oh! heaven direct me," cried Rosa, clasping her hands, on which her tears fell in large drops: "my friends, my uncle, where are you in this moment of trial? Oh! little do you think on what a precipice I am driven; but no, I cannot, must not, will not marry. No, my lord, I will not impose upon your generosity. I am grateful, truly grateful for your goodness, but I can never be your wife."

Lord Clavering rose, and coldly bowing, said, "I shall not neglect, Miss Percival, informing your friends of your situation, and where you are."

"Sure, my lord," exclaimed the agitated Rosa, "surely, for the sake of my father, whose friend you profess yourself, you will not leave me here exposed to the designs of a profligate."

"I fear, Miss Percival," replied his lordship, "that profligate has but too much influence in your bosom; I am indeed sorry to leave you so situated, but I am really an absolute stranger in this country; I know no person in whose care I could leave you while I transact the business I am come upon; and regard for your character makes me unwilling you should travel with me, without a female companion. I will write immediately to my friend Sir Edward; in the meantime make yourself as easy as you can, with the assurance that you will soon be liberated from your unpleasant situation."

Again he bowed, and laid his hand on the lock of the door. Rosa hung herself on her knee before him, and besought him not to leave her there, but to take her instantly to Aberconway.

"I can procure a chaise there," said the weeping Rosa, "and I am not afraid to travel alone; but do not, I beseech you, do not leave me in the power of these wicked, unprincipled people."

His lordship raised her from the floor and stood musing for a moment. "I have just recollected," said he, "that I have a friend within a mile of Aberconway, who has sisters: make yourself content till tomorrow, and I promise you on my honour I will remove you from this place: under the protection of two respectable females, you may return with safety and credit to Birch Park."

Rosa, unwilling as she was to remain another night under so detested a roof, was obliged to accede to this arrangement; she saw Lord Clavering depart, after having again received his assurance that he would the next day place her under safe and honourable protection.

As soon as his carriage drove from the house, dreading to encounter the vile Howels, and his still more abominable wife, she retired to her chamber, to weep over the perfidy and dissimulation of Hugh Montgomery, to hurl from the proud pinnacle on which her fervid imagination had raised it, the worshipped idol of her affections; to teach her agonizing heart the hard lesson of despising the man she had adored; to banish his idea from her remembrance, and to indulge the hope of being restored to her beloved relatives at Birch Park.

Mrs. Howels had again got in the old way, and Peg was deputed to guard miss. Rosa had not long indulged her sorrowful reflections, before she bounced into the room, with "Lord, miss, I be mortal glad you be here; I was sad frightful you had a gin us the go bye, as master calls it; marcy on us, we an all bin in such a flusteration today, that nobody has not thought anything about dinner: what shall I get you to eat, miss?"

Rosa, scarcely knowing what she said, asked where Mrs. Howels was. "On the bed, as napsy as ever," replied the girl, grinning and shewing her broad yellow teeth; "and where," inquired Rosa, "is your master?"

"Master! oh master is taking his pleasure. A is gone in a coach with that great lord as was here just nows."

"You must be mistaken, child," replied Rosa, "your master cannot be gone with Lord Clavering."

"A is though," said the girl, insisting on the point; "a is, for I seed him get in with my own eyes. Coach stopped aside the old barn, where I was a feeding the pigs; footman opened the door, and stood we his hat in his hand, just for all the world as if master had bin a great parson too; well, he let down a little ting black looking sort of a ladder; up mounts master, who but he, and the great lord shook him by the fist, and smiled upon him just like as if a had bin his sweetheart. Oh! dear, miss, how I should love a bit of a ride in that fine coach."

Rosa's head turned round; she sunk into a chair, and became pale as death; the girl was frightened at her altered looks, and pouring out some water, bade her drink. "Why Lord! miss," said she, "you looks sure as if you had a mind to sound clean away."

Rosa swallowed a little of the water, and having wept plentifully, felt much relieved. She dismissed the girl, saying she was too unwell to eat, and would endeavour to sleep, as she had enjoyed but little rest all night. Peg left the room, and locked her in.

"All this story then is false," said Rosa, hope again throbbing wildly in her bosom. "Hugh Montgomery's character has been vilified and traduced, and I am the dupe of Lord Clavering's schemes. Dear, ever-loved Montgomery, forgive me for having listened to such a degrading tale, for having for a moment believed you capable of such vile duplicity, such infamous conduct. But what is to be done; how am I to avoid this man? To-morrow he returns, to carry me heaven knows where, not to my home, not to Birch Park; no, no, having proceeded thus far, I suppose he thinks to terrify me into becoming his wife.

But I will die first; Montgomery, my heart is thine, and never shall any consideration prevail on Rosa Percival to bestow her hand unaccompanied by affection."

Towards evening Mrs. Howels met Rosa at the tea table, where she affected in her vulgar way to wonder what had become of John Howels. Rosa, unwilling as she was to enter into conversation with a woman she so much detested and despised, rallied her spirits sufficiently to tell her she might spare any farther attempts to impose on her, as she was perfectly acquainted with all their schemes, and that her friends would assuredly bring them to severe account, for having been the agents of Lord Clavering's nefarious designs."

"As to me, miss," replied Mrs. Howels, "as I am a sinful woman, I am as hinnicint as a new born baby about Lord Clavering: to be sure one of his kept misses is John Howels's sister, and a was down here last summer; but Lord our house was not good enough for madam; no sure, hur had grand lodgings tother side Aberconway, and quite turned up her nose at me, that am a honest decent woman; and as for John Howels, his mouth was as close as the poor's box, he never let a word drop to me consarning nothing, only as I was to be sure not to let you run away; and a said too that Lord Clavering wanted to make you his lady in earnest, and not a kept mistress."

"But my friends," replied Rosa, "will reward you handsomely if you will supply me with the means of escaping. I don't like Lord Clavering – I never will marry him."

"No," said Mrs. Howels, staring at her; "well, I never heard nothing so downright foolish in my life afore. Why, miss, he is very rich and grand, and keeps sitch fine coaches."

"But suppose it was your own case, Mrs. Howels," replied Rosa, "and you did not like the man."

"Oh! lord, miss, I am sure I should like him mightily," said Mrs. Howels: "I should know trap better, as John Howels says, than to refuse such an offer. No, no, miss, I should never be such a witched fool as not to like a man as keeps sitch a lot of flashy servants, and sitch a fine coach."

Rosa endeavoured to convince her of the wickedness of marrying for wealth only, and asked her if she would assist her with a little money, and allow her to escape, promising her an ample reward.

"Aye, aye, miss, promises and pie-crust is made to be broke," said Mrs. Howels; "but, as my poor dear first man, William Owens, used to say, fine words butter no parsnips; and as to money, John Howels tells me it is the root of all evil, so he never allows me the handling of none: and as for letting you go, Lord have mercy! he would play up Mag's diversion with me; I should have the devil and all of a to do with him – why he would beat me black and blue. No, no, I never can go to think of such a project; he would knock me a head like a door nail."

Rosa, finding she could make no impression on the unfeeling hearted wretch, retired again to her chamber to solicit the protection of that Being who never forsakes those who confide in him; to pray for fortitude to resist oppression, and power to sustain the afflictive conflicts she feared the next day would necessitate her to undergo, as she now felt the conviction that she was entangled in the net wove for her by Lord Clavering, who no doubt was preparing for her fresh trials and further persecutions.

CHAPTER IV

Lace and furr'd gowns hide all.
Clothe vice in rags a pigmy's straw will pierce it.

Rowe

Eye me, bless'd Providence, and square my trial
To my proportioned strength.
Beauty, like the fair Hesperian tree,
Laden with blooming gold, had need the guard
Of dragon-watch, with unenchanted eye,
To save her blossoms and defend her fruit
From the rash hand of bold incontinence.

Milton

Now the grave old alarm the softer young,
And all my fame's abhorr'd contagion flee;
Trembles each lip and falters every tongue
That bids the morn propitious smile on me.

Shenstone

Man! monster of ingratitude! behold
Thy work! – the yawning grave receives the wretch
Thy perfidy destroys!

A. J. H.

A NOBLEMAN proudly supposes he may commit any outrages on society with impunity; may defame characters, may oppress innocence, and ostentatiously oppose his rank as a shield against public abhorrence and condemnation. Thus thought Rosa, as she indignantly reflected on Clavering's behaviour; on the infamous tale he had so contemptibly forged with the diabolic design of depreciating Hugh Montgomery in her esteem, which fabrication indeed would have proved but too successful, had not the ignorant servant undesignedly opened her eyes and given her an insight into the plot.

Her distress of mind became agonizing as she considered her forlorn situation – far from all assistance, in the house of mercenary, unprincipled people, the devoted tool of a man who she too plainly perceived would spare no efforts to accomplish his design, which, if it respected her honour, would eventually destroy the peace of her future life.

The higher her detestation of Lord Clavering's character arose, as she remembered his artful speeches, his deep dissimulation, and the necessity of immediate escape pressed with additional energy on her bewildered brain; but how, or where to go without money, without being acquainted with a step of the way, she knew not, yet felt the urgency of attempting it, as the coming morrow might involve her in misery beyond all she had hitherto encountered. Busied with these torturing, these perplexing reflections, she paced the room with disordered steps: she paused before the door; she tried it, but, alas! it resisted her efforts; yet as she gazed upon it, she thought it might be possible to remove the screws that held the lock, as the wood that surrounded it appeared to be in a perishable state, and promised but little difficulty in the undertaking.

Elated with the idea of obtaining her liberty, she sank upon her knees, and fervently prayed for fortitude and protection, resolving as soon as the family were buried in repose to attempt escape. With impatient emotion she counted the tedious hours, and waited till all was quiet in the house, which did not happen till the night was at odds with morning, Mrs. Howels being as usual hunkumstary, and, contrary to her husband's asseveration, extremely riotous and unmanageable.

After listening in breathless suspense, and at last finding all still, Rosa, with a palpitating heart, and in the utmost trepidation, proceeded to turn the screws with a penknife, which at length, to her infinite joy, after much trouble and labour she effected. As she drew the last screw the lock slipped from her hand and fell to the ground. For some moments she stood in trembling apprehension lest the noise should awaken Peg or the plough-boy, who slept in the house; all, however, remaining quiet, she softly opened the door and ventured into the passage. Mrs. Howels was loudly snoring as she descended the stairs, which harshly creaked under her light foot. When she reached the front door it was bolted, and as she expected, locked also; but the key, which used to hang on a hook behind it, was to her grief and disappointment taken away.

"What am I now to do?" said Rosa, desponding, as she turned into the parlour, "here, alas! end my hopes. I am now compelled to wait my destiny – I must now bear whatever Lord Clavering chooses to inflict." She wept bitterly as her eyes followed the course of a waning moon, which every now and then, emerging from clouds of snowy whiteness, illumined the darkness of the room.

She approached the window, and beheld the terrific mastiff stretched at his length in the yard. "Oh!" exclaimed she, regarding the huge animal with despairing looks, "Oh! but for thee I might escape." After an agonizing pause – "What, if I were to venture! – most likely I should be the victim of my temerity – I should perhaps be torn in pieces by this savage creature. Well, better to perish at once by his fangs than live the lingering prey of that detested, hated Lord Clavering." Again she wept, and thought of the happy years she had passed at Birch Park, considered now more happy than ever as viewed through the medium of her present distressful situation. "If I pass unhurt by thee," continued Rosa, still gazing on the dog, his rough coat silvering in the rays of the moon, "if thou wouldst suffer me to pass, before morning I might be far distant, many, many miles from this abominable place." Again the remembrance that she had no money threw a damp upon her spirits. "But no matter," resumed she, "surely I should meet with some compassionate persons, who when acquainted with my story would humanely assist me to reach my home. Oh! my friends, most likely at this hour of night you are enjoying the blessings of repose, while I, wretched and encompassed with danger, wake to weep, to think over happiness that may never more be mine."

Again she looked at the dog with sensations of terror; then raising her tearful eyes to heaven, continued: "Oh! thou who art the protector and supporter of the unfortunate and afflicted, graciously defend and direct me – release me, if it is thy good pleasure, from this house of bondage, from this den of wickedness."

As she prayed she felt inspired with courage, and instantly repairing to the back door, exerted all her strength to remove a massy iron bar that lay across it. Finding her utmost efforts unequal to the undertaking, she returned to the parlour, and having stood a few moments irresolute, unclosed the casement, and boldly sprang into the yard. The mastiff growled horribly, and instantly quitting his recumbent posture, darted forward open mouthed to intercept her. – Rosa shrieked, and giving up herself for lost, fell nearly fainting against the wall. The dog reared his huge paws against her. She beheld his extended jaws, his large white teeth, and with sensations of indescribable horror expected them to fasten in her flesh; but having regarded her for a moment as he kept her pinned against the wall, with his broad tongue he gently licked her neck and hands, as if to reassure her.

This action of his in some measure restored Rosa to herself. Recovering a little from her fright, in a faint voice she whispered, "Tiger, poor Tiger," and at last ventured to stroke his neck and head, as he stood wagging his tail before her. As soon as terror would permit she moved forward, while the mastiff peaceably followed her to a door leading to a lane, which he suffered her to open. – Hastily passing through it, she closed it after her, and flew across the yard with the rapidity of lightning, and in a few minutes the house and mastiff were far behind her. Unknowing which way to proceed, when she reached the end of the lane she struck into the first path that presented itself, returning heaven thanks most fervently for her miraculous escape from the fangs of an animal whose temper and disposition she had always been taught to believe were fierce and savage, and who she had observed would never allow a stranger to touch him.

The sun had just risen when she entered a village, and feeling rather tired, she sat down on a stone stile near the churchyard to rest herself, with the hope too of seeing some person pass who might direct her in the road to Carnarvon. In a few moments a smart looking young man came whistling along. Rosa got up, supposing he would pass over the stile, but she was faint and weary, and, unable to support herself, reeled against a tree.

"What," said the young man, "are you light-headed, my dear, so early in the morning?" Finding she made no reply, he stood for a moment staring at her; when perceiving her pale and in tears, he gently took her hand, and in a soothing tone asked, "Where do you come from, my dear? – you don't belong to this village. Who are you? – Do you wait for anybody?" –

"Oh! for heaven's sake" at length said Rosa, "have compassion on me. I have fled from danger, from oppression – lead me I beseech you to the shelter of some hospitable, virtuous roof – I have relations who have the power, who will be most happy to reward your goodness."

The agitation, the innocence of her look, and above all the energy of her request, affected the young man. "I feel a something here," said he, laying his hand on his heart, "that always repays me when I do a service to a fellow-creature in distress; and sure I am doubly bound to help a pretty girl when she is in trouble without thinking about reward. I have got a mother living close by the green yonder," pointing with his finger to a cluster of houses at a short distance, "as kind a soul as ever broke bread; she will I am sure take care of you, and make you very welcome. Come along with me, I will see you safely lodged in a few moments."

Rosa felt grateful, but could make no reply! she suffered the young man to pass her arm through his, and he led her to a neat cottage in the middle of the village.

"Here, mother," said he, as he entered, "take care of this young woman, give her something to eat, and put her to bed, for she wants both food and rest."

"Bless thee, Johnny Wilkins," replied the old woman,

placing Rosa on a chair near the fire, and clapping on her spectacles, "who has thee brought me here, boy?"

"She will tell you all about that herself, mother," said the young man; "all I know is that she seems in trouble, and in want, and I thought you would assist her."

"Aye, by my truly, that I will, please God, as sure as my name is Ruth Wilkins," said she, going close up to Rosa, who was leaning back in the chair, totally unconscious of what they were saying. Dame Wilkins having examined her face, uttered a loud cry, threw her spectacles upon the table, and clapping her hands together, said, "where in the name of the Lord did you come from! Johnny, my son, where did you find this sweet young creature?" Johnny, astonished at his mother's strange emotion, explained where he had met Rosa.

"God preserve my wits," replied she; "I don't know who or what she is, but I feel I love her dearly, for she is the very image of my sweet Rosa Jenkins, who married that sad rake, Edward Percival."

At this name Rosa opened her eyes, gazed for a moment on the old woman, threw her arms round her neck, and fainted; when they had recovered her, she learned that Ruth Wilkins had been her mother's nurse, and had lived in her family more than twenty years, and was perfectly well acquainted with all the country and inhabitants round Birch Park. To these worthy people Rosa related without the smallest reserve who she was, and all that had befallen her, while the old woman and her son, at the name of Lord Clavering, mutually exclaimed:

"What! has not the vile monster left off his wicked ways yet?" and threw up their eyes in wonder, while she related her adventure with, and miraculous escape from, the formidable mastiff.

Dame Wilkins tied on a clean apron, and was almost wild with joy to think her poor little cottage was so honoured as to afford shelter to the child of her own dear Rosa Jenkins; and hugged her son, for having had the good luck to pass by the stone stile so early. Rosa on inquiry found she had walked twelve miles, but entirely in a contrary road to Carnarvon, a circumstance she now rather rejoiced at, as she thought it most probable when she was missed that they would seek her on the road that led to her home. John Wilkins said he would lose no time in acquainting his master that Miss Percival was there, as he intended the next day to set off for Dolgelly Castle.

"And that, Johnny," said his mother, "is only five miles from this child's home, from Birch Park. Well a day, well a day, I was a lusty young girl when I lived there; Johnny, Johnny, it was there I married thy poor father; and God help me I came here to bury him."

Dame Wilkins wept, while her son affectionately kissing her said, "He is happy, be content, mother; God has spared me to comfort you."

"Bless thee! bless thee, my boy!" replied she, wiping her eyes with the corner of her apron, "if I was to lose thee, all would soon be over with Ruth Wilkins; my poor old heart would soon break."

He shook her hand cheeringly, while he said that he was sure the Honourable Mr. Delamere, his master, would take Miss Percival under his protection, and convey her safe to her friends, if she would go with him. Rosa was pleased with the honest open countenance of John Wilkins; but she remembered how much mistaken she had been in reading the lines of Doctor Powell's face, and hesitated on the propriety of trusting herself alone with a stranger. John Wilkins understood her feelings and perplexity, he spoke in the warmest terms of the goodness of his master's character, said he had the best, the most honourable, the most humane heart that ever was lodged in a human breast.

"Aye, by my truly," rejoined his mother, "and you might, Johnny, without telling a word of a lie, have said the most tender and charitable one too, for only to think now of his staying here, and giving up his own pleasure, for no one thing in the *vassal* world, but just to bury the old blind harper, that he met by accident about a mile from the village. Aye, he was the merciful Samaritan that poured the wine and oil upon the stranger by the way side: God will bless him for his goodness to the old and poor; well-a-day, well-a-day, poor Herbert Jones, there is nothing in this world for certain but ups and downs, rich and grand families coming to the dogs, and them that was born upon a dunghill as one may say rising up, and in a few years riding about in their own coaches. Well-a-day, well-a-day! poor Herbert Jones! to think after his being so well brought up, and of such a creditable family, to come at last to know such poverty, and to be obliged to a stranger for a little earth to cover him."

"I must go, mother," said the young man, "my master will want me, but you shall see me again by and by."

He bowed respectfully to Rosa. Dame Wilkins looked after him. "Go thy way, Johnny," said she, "or a better son never blest the old age of a mother."

Rosa thought herself in Heaven, as she listened to Dame Wilkins, who soon made her some coffee, and while they were at breakfast, her daughter, a nice clean wholesome looking young woman, who was married, and lived a few doors off, came in, and prepared a little chamber, to which the old woman conducted her as soon as their meal was ended, and where she was easily persuaded to go to bed, for having been up all night, she felt sleepy as well as fatigued.

Towards evening Dame Wilkins, who while she slept had got her cloths nicely washed, came to see if she was awake and to tell her that she had got a fine roasted pullet for dinner. Rosa gratefully thanked her kind hostess, and feeling much refreshed, rose up with a heart infinitely lighter and spirits more animated than they had been since the disastrous night of the masquerade. – When she came down stairs, Dame Wilkins threw open the door of a snug little parlour, whose neat oak chairs and tables shone like looking glass, where a cheerful fire, a clean hearth, and a cloth laid in a style much superior to what she expected to meet, welcomed her; with the fowl her kind hostess placed a tart and wine on the table. Rosa expressed surprise, and also declared herself extremely sorry that she should have occasioned her so very unnecessary an expense, as wine was an indulgence she could very well have dispensed with.

"My dear child," replied Dame Wilkins, "make yourself quite easy; it is no use to tell lies about the matter; it is no expense at all to me, so eat, drink, and be merry as you can, for I am sure you are most heartily welcome; it was Johnny brought the dinner and the wine from the inn, with the Hon. Mr. Delamere's best respects; and if quite agreeable he will wait upon you, and pay his compliments himself in the evening."

Rosa said she was indeed infinitely obliged and indebted to Mr. Delamere's polite attention, but she felt awkward in accepting favours from a gentleman, particularly a stranger: her situation was very delicate.

"Aye, I see," said Dame Wilkins, looking fondly on her,

"you are a sensible good child, and know what is proper; but as to accepting favours, is not Mr. Delamere going close to your own home, and your uncle Mr. Gabriel Jenkins, my worthy master, must be mainly altered from the noble spirit he used to be, if he lets anybody that serves his family be a loser by their generousness; and lord love thee, my child, Johnny's master is so good, that he is never content nor happy but when he is doing some kind thing or other. Do you know, Miss Rosa, he came God only knows how many long miles out of his road only just on purpose for Johnny Wilkins to see his old mother, and his native village. Well, well! I believe on me truly, there is not such another pitiful, kind hearted gentleman to be met with in the wide world, and what is more, bless his proper looks, he is as handsome to the full as he is good."

Rosa smiled. "Do, my dear child," continued she, "do drink a glass of wine to his honourable health." She poured out a glass and presented it.

"Not," said Rosa, "unless you drink with me." Dame Wilkins looked pleased, and filling out a glass for herself, drank to the health of the Honourable Mr. Delamere. Rosa repeated the health.

"Aye, may God preserve him," continued Dame Wilkins, placing the breast of the fowl on Rosa's plate. "As he and my Johnny were coming along within two miles of this place, they met with poor Herbert Jones; he was lying at full length on the cold earth, with his harp under his head for a pillow; the old man tried hard to reach his native place, but he was so tired he could go no further; so he laid his poor weary bones down by the road side; and his little grandson that led him, seeing him unable to move, stood crying over him."

Rosa was all attention, as the old woman, proceeding with

her tale, said, "My Johnny saw him first, and rode up to the chaise and told his master; and would you believe it, Miss Rosa, he got out and helped Johnny to place the old man and his grandson in the carriage with his own honourable self, and my boy carried the harp."

"I am really charmed with this Mr. Delamere," said Rosa.

"Aye," replied the old woman, "some folks would have thought they had done enough to send to the overseers of the parish; but he brought him along with himself: by my truly, I believe there are not many like him to be met with. But come, my dear child, you are doing nothing at all," attempting to help her a second time to the tart. Rosa protested she could eat no more. Dame Wilkins soon removed the cloth; and Rosa, when she was again seated, begged to hear the rest of Herbert Jenkins's story.

"The rest! why by my truly, Miss Rosa," said the old woman, "you have heard none of it yet. You must know," said she, drawing her chair closer to the fire, "you must know that Herbert Jones was the only son of the vicar of —; and he brought him up to all sorts of learning, and wanted to make a parson of him too: but no thank you, my young spark had no stomach for preaching and praying. He loved music, dancing, and gaiety: and besides all this, he fancied he should look well in a scarlet coat, and he wanted his father to buy him a commission in the army: the vicar however would hear of no such thing, and many were the quarrels they had about a scarlet coat and a black one. Herbert would settle to nothing serious; for he spent all his time in making verses, for he was a great poet even from his cradle, and playing on the harp. It is a long story," said Dame Wilkins; "I am afraid you will be tired of it."

Rosa assured her to the contrary, and begged her to go on.

"Well, at last Herbert Jones fell in love with a farmer's daughter in the neighbourhood, and married her unbeknown to anybody; and this so enraged the vicar, that he swore – Yes, Miss Rosa, the man of God swore a bitter oath, that he would cut him off with a shilling; and by my truly so he did, for he died soon after, and left all his property to his daughters."

"Alas! poor Herbert Jones," said Rosa, with a sigh.

"Aye, poor Herbert Jones indeed!" repeated Dame Wilkins, "for the worst part is all to come: his hardhearted sisters turned their backs upon him, married rich husbands, and left the country; and he with all his fine learning had nothing at all to live on but what his father-in-law the farmer gave him. Well, he wrote God knows how many books; but for want of money and friends he never could get them printed, though many folks that understood such things said they were mighty clever."

"Alas, for genius!" thought Rosa, "its brightest blossoms too often wither beneath the blights of poverty."

"But then all he wrote," resumed Dame Wilkins, "were verses about love and such nonsense; and people used to say it was downright wasting of time, pen, ink, and paper; for if he had wrote sermons and godly books, or something against Bonnyparty, why he might have made a good penny: but then he was quite angry when folks pretended to direct him, and he used to say he could not follow a path that was pointed out to him. To be sure, poor Herbert Jones was always high spirited, and a little oddish as one may say, and would never listen to advice: for when the vicar wanted him to be a parson, he said he did not feel himself called to the sacred office: and that it would he profanation in him to attempt to preach the gospel."

"Then it was really conscience," asked Rosa, "that prevented his entering into holy orders?"

"Aye, by my truly was it," replied Dame Wilkins, "though his father said it was because he loved the girls too much. After the vicar's death he kept a school, but some how he did not succeed: for though everybody knew he was scholar enough for anything, yet they said he spent all his time playing on the harp instead of teaching the children, and in making verses, and composing tunes, and singing them himself; so his scholars all left him one by one, and at last he got the name of the mad poet."

"How much," said Rosa, "I should like to see some of his verses."

"Oh, please God," replied the old woman, "you shall have that pleasure directly: here," said she, opening a little buffet, "here is something my Johnny bade me take great care of, for it was in the hand-writing of Herbert Jones, and of his own making, and mighty fine; but for my part I don't pretend to understand such like things."

Rosa opened the paper, the writing was little inferior to copper-plate: on the top was wrote: –

ANACREONTIQUE

Come, Aura, and weave me the chaplet divine,
Compos'd of the myrtle, the rose, and the vine;
Haste, bind round my temples the wreath of delight,
Ere my forehead grow wrinkled, my tresses turn white;

For time ev'ry instant steals something away,
The bloom from my cheek, from my eyes the bright ray,
Kiss, kiss me, and fold me again in thine arms,
While my eyes can admire, my heart feel thy charms.

Boy, bring here the flaggon, and fill up my bowl,
I'll drink to my girl and the friend of my soul,
With summer's bright roses my goblet entwine;
Come, Aura, with kisses perfume the rich wine;

For see slyly creeping old age steals along,
To extinguish my fire, and deaden my song;
But while in my bosom one spark shall remain,
Love, friendship, and wine shall enliven my strain.

Beneath the tall vine rear my grave when I'm dead,
That its branches may shadow, its clusters o'erspread;
And dropping the tears of the night on my urn,
It may seem in the vision of fancy to mourn.

Plant the rose and the myrtle to shed their balms round,
Entwining their sweets let them ever be found,
For they shall this truth emblematic impart,
Love, friendship, and wine have divided my heart.

"Good heaven," said Rosa as she restored the paper to Dame Wilkins, "and was this man with such talents fated to die in want?"

"Aye, by my truly was he," replied she; "his wife was very sickly, and bore children so fast: to be sure Farmer Watkins her father was very good to them, and the children all died young, except one girl, and if she had died too, God willing, it would have been a great blessing; but as I was a saying, Miss Rosa, lyings-in, and christenings, and burials, run away with a main sight of money, and things went very hard with Herbert Jones, so hard that at last he was obliged for all his pride to turn harper in earnest to keep his family from starving; and though he was sometimes sent for to the houses of the gentry round about, and made much of, yet I believe there was not a much poorer hut in the village than his, though he was a great scholar and had been brought up a gentleman: however, to make short of it, for I hate long stories, his father-in-law was ruined by a fire that destroyed all his property, and after having lived well in the world, Watkin Watkins died in the poor-house."

Dame Wilkins wept at the remembrance; Rosa wiped the tears from her own cheeks, and said: – "What a dreadful misfortune!"

"Well-a-day! well-a-day!" continued Dame Wilkins, taking off her spectacles to dry her eyes, "I never see the spot where that farm-house stood but it makes my heart ache, because I remember when I was a little strip of a girl, I used to go there to play with Patty Watkins, aye, and the day she married Herbert Jones there was not a prettier girl in the parish; no, the sun did not shine upon a prettier maid. Who could have thought what sorrow she was born to; but poor thing her troubles are all over and past; she sleeps quiet enough in a corner of the churchyard, close by the stone stile, Miss Rosa, and a large elm tree waves its mournful branches over her grave. Poor soul, poor soul! but, my dear child, I fear you are tired of my prate."

Rosa assured her she was much interested, and begged her to proceed, "I mortally hate long stories," resumed Dame Wilkins, "so I shall tell this in as few words as I can. Well you must know, that Herbert Jones's wife was sick and confined to her bed when the fire happened at her father's and she was so frightened that she quite lost her wits: everybody thought her husband would have gone raving mad too, for a very short time after she was drowned in a pond close by the farmhouse."

"And did not his sisters visit nor do anything for him in the midst of such calamities?" asked Rosa.

"No, by my truly," said Dame Wilkins. "They, barbarous wretches! said his troubles were all of his own seeking, and nothing but a judgment upon him because he would not be a parson, and keep the vicarage in the family. Well, for some time Herbert Jones went about like one that was moped, and took no notice of his harp, nor making of verses, but used to sit all the while by his wife's grave, fetching such deep sighs, and looking so mournful. His daughter Jessy was grown up almost a woman, and she was very handsome, and two or three farmers in the neighbourhood made her offers, but she chose to remain and take care of her father, and she used to sew for a living, and was very good and industrious, and all the young people in the village loved Jessy Jones. Poor child! I shall never forget her falling into fits the evening her father was struck blind with lightning as he sat on his wife's grave."

Rosa turned pale.

Dame Wilkins begged her to take another glass of wine, or she would never be able to bear the rest of poor Herbert Jones's story. Rosa suffered herself to be persuaded, and her hostess pursued the tale, saying:

"As I hate long stories, I will make this as short as I can. I believe I mentioned before that Jessy Jones could handle her needle very well, and was very clever and handy in making up things for the ladies; so she was sent for to Sir Watkin Meredith's to make some new things for the family, who were going abroad, and there, Miss Rosa, there she met that wicked villain Lord Clavering."

"Lord Clavering!" repeated Rosa.

"Yes, my dear child, that vile monster, Lord Clavering; and there with pretences of love, and fine promises of making her his wife, he got the better of the poor girl's virtue."

Rosa wept.

"Well-a-day! well-a-day!" said the old woman, weeping too; "Jessy Jones was an innocent good girl as ever lived, till that vile lord turned her head with his artful speeches, full of lies and deceit: the poor thing was content to earn her bread honestly till he persuaded her she was too handsome, forsooth, to work, and that he would make a lady of her. – At last, however, his lordship grew tired of Jessy Jones, who I supposed teased him to keep his word and make an honest woman of her; so he set off for England, and left her in the way to be a mother before she was a wife."

"Unhappy Jessy!" said Rosa.

"Unhappy enough, for certain," replied Dame Wilkins. "Poor Jessy till this was a favourite with everybody; but when she happened of that mishap, why the old folks shut their doors against her, and the young ones were ashamed to speak to or be seen with her, and some were so cruel as to scoff and jeer her. – At last someone told Herbert Jones that his daughter was with child. He said but little to Jessy, but set off in the middle of one stormy night, and blind as he was, walked all the way to London after Lord Clavering."

"Blind, and walk from this to London!" said Rosa, astonished.

"Aye, by my truly, did he," replied Dame Wilkins; "he found out Cavendish Square, and in spite of all opposition from the servants, he rushed into a grand apartment, where his lordship was entertaining a deal of company at dinner. –

Herbert Jones, almost frantic with grief and shame, demanded justice for the disgrace he had brought upon an honest family, and insisted that his lordship should keep his promise and marry his daughter."

"Well!" said Rosa.

"No," replied Dame Wilkins, "no, my dear child, it was not well; for the unfeeling monster only laughed and spoke in a shocking way of poor Jessy; wondered at the old man's impudence, and ordered the servants to push him out of doors. Some of his wicked companions asked if the girl was pretty, and wondered why the devil he had not brought her with him, that some of them would have taken care of her; others said he was a d – d fool to have a handsome daughter and to be poor. It was in vain he attempted to move their pity by telling his troubles and misfortunes; he was only laughed at and treated with contempt; while Lord Clavering bade him begone; saying, the bastard might or might not be his, he could not say; if it was a boy, why perhaps he might do something for it, provided he was not pestered about it; but if ever he, Herbert Jones, presumed to force himself into his house or presence again, he would have him severely punished."

"One gentleman, who had sat silent all the while Herbert Jones was telling his story, followed the poor blind heart-broken creature into the street, and putting a purse with twenty guineas in it into his hand, told him he pitied him from the bottom of his soul, but that it was in vain for him to hope for justice or redress from a man of Lord Clavering's character; bade him make the best of his way home to comfort his daughter, and that he should shortly hear from him again. Poor soul, he did return; but when Jessy was convinced she had nothing to expect from Lord Clavering, and heard of his brutal usage of her father, she fell into strong convulsions, and died bringing her child into the world. She was buried beside her mother; and from that time poor Herbert Jones became quite unsettled, wandering about from place to place all over the country, but constantly returning once a year to visit the grave of his wife and daughter."

"But the child," said Rosa, "what became of the child?"

"It was a boy," replied Dame Wilkins, "a beautiful boy too; and the gentleman that promised Herbert Jones that he should hear from him, sure enough was better than his word, for he came down here, and stood godfather to the child, and had him christened Edwin Derrington, after himself. This good gentleman paid for the child's nursing and schooling, till he was nine years old, and then it seems he died suddenly, or else no doubt, as everybody says, he would have done something for poor little Edwin."

"What a misfortune for the child," said Rosa, "that this worthy gentleman died!"

"Well-a-day, well-a-day! by my truly," rejoined Dame Wilkins; "Herbert Jones was born to be unlucky; it was a sad evil star that reigned at his birth; however, to make an end of the story, and nobody hates long stories more than I do. He grew very fond of his grandson at last, though for a long time he could not bear to hear him named; but some of the neighbours happening to say he was the image of his grandmother, the old man had him brought to him, and feeling his face all over, he said the boy had his wife's features. The child put his little arms about his neck, and fondled him, upon which the old man took him on his knee, and stroking his curly head, kissed him, and said: – "Jessy, Jessy, you have broke my heart; but the poor child could not help your folly, nor his father's villainy." Well, from this time he was never happy but when Edwin was with him; and he would take him of moonlight nights to the church-yard, and play and sing such mournful songs, all of his own making. The boy grew delighted with the harp, and in a very short time could play several tunes; and at last as his grandfather grew poorer, and could not afford to pay for his keep with the woman that nursed him, why poor Edwin took the boy's place that used to lead him about, and for near three years they have wandered about the country together, lodging and faring hard enough: they had been away from the village near upon a year, when my Johnny's master met with them. Mr. Delamere put the old man into comfortable lodgings, gave him all sorts of nourishing things, and sent for a doctor to him: but all would not do: Herbert Jones said he was going to his wife and Jessy, and sure he spoke the truth, for by my truly, he died yesterday morning."

"And his grandson," asked Rosa, "where is he?"

"Oh!" replied Dame Wilkins, "little Edwin is with Mr. Delamere, who promised his poor old grandfather to take care of him."

"What an exalted character is this Mr. Delamere," said Rosa, "and what an abominable wretch Lord Clavering; surely the remembrance of the innocent Jessy Jones must continually haunt him; and the consciousness of having destroyed her poison all his enjoyments: unnatural wretch, to take no notice of his child."

"As handsome a boy too as ever you clapped your eyes upon," rejoined Dame Wilkins; "he looks like the son of a lord, so noble and so comely; but hark, the bell tolls for poor Herbert Jones; I hope his poor soul will rest in the grave. Well-a-day! well-a-day – there is a family gone like chaff before a barn door. It seems only like yesterday since we were children together; his wife and I were just like two sisters, first she died, then Jessy was cut down like a fine flower in a summer's morning, and now Herbert Jones himself; he made verses about many that died, and called them *celagies*, I think. Well-a-day! well-a-day – who will write Herbert Jones's *celagy*?"

Dame Wilkins was deeply affected.

"Well," continued she, "what, Miss Rosa, signifies all the wit and learning in the world; it don't seem to me to make folks a bit more beloved, or happier, or wiser, for he was what they call a great genius; but for all that, he was never out of trouble; one sorrow followed upon another all the while."

"Sure there is another and a better world than this," said Rosa.

"To be sure there is, my dear child," replied Dame Wilkins, wiping her eyes; "if it was not for that comfort, how could people bear the trials and troubles of this. Herbert Jones had nothing but sorrow in this life; now he is gone where the wicked cease from troubling."

The funeral passed by as she spoke; it was decently attended by the villagers; and as chief mourner, Rosa saw an elegant young man in black leading by the hand a very fine boy.

"That," said Dame Wilkins, pointing, "is Mr. Delamere; he has got Edwin by the hand; and there, bless his kind, heart, is my Johnny. Well, God rest the soul of Herbert Jones, and forever bless and prosper the honourable Mr. Delamere, and make him as happy as he deserves to be."

She began stirring the fire, and sweeping up the hearth.

"They will call I am certain as they come from the funeral," said she, "for every day his honour, who has not the least bit of pride, comes here to chat with me, and to tell me some story about Johnny; who is a great favourite with his master."

As Dame Wilkins expected, the Honourable Mr. Delamere called at the cottage on his way from the church-yard; he introduced himself to Rosa with the polite elegance of a finished gentleman. He informed her of his intended visit to Dolgelly Castle, and assured her that he should feel most happy if she would honour him so far as to accept his protection to her friends. Rosa expressed her thanks in the most grateful terms, while he considerately added, that if Mrs. Wilkins wished to see Birch Park again, that she should accompany Miss Percival and Edwin in the chaise; while himself and John would escort them on horseback, Rosa looked pleased at this delicate arrangement: Dame Wilkins said: – Aye, by her truly, if Miss Rosa had no objection, she should like the journey above all things in life, that she knew her old master, Mr. Gabriel Jenkins, would be mighty glad to see Ruth Wilkins; and for her part, she should be to the full as natural, and as happy at Birch Park as at her own cottage, for there was not a tree or a stile but what was her old acquaintance.

Mr. Delamere then asked at what hour she would like to set out; and this point being arranged, Dame Wilkins went to get her things in readiness, and Mr. Delamere introduced his protégé to Rosa: Edwin was indeed a beautiful boy; his bright auburn hair clustered in rich curls upon his open forehead, and his dark hazel eyes shining in tears, seemed to bespeak favour from all they rested on; he was near twelve years of age, tall and well formed, with an air of grandeur that distinguished him above the common class. Of music he spoke in raptures, and of his grandfather with enthusiastic affection. Having committed Edwin to the care of John Wilkins, who was to go with him to take leave of the woman who had nursed him, Mr. Delamere spoke of Herbert Jones as of a man who had possessed a first-rate genius.

"I have met," said he, "among his papers a poem of his writing, suggested no doubt by his own situation, which has affected and pleased me beyond anything I have lately met with; perhaps it may not deserve the praise of a perfect composition, but certainly it is a lay of the heart, and speaks a language infinitely more interesting than the elaborate productions of learning: it is called 'Hoel's Harp;' and if you are partial to poetry, I think, Miss Percival, you will have great pleasure in its perusal."

Rosa said she was particularly fond of poetry, and should no doubt be highly gratified, having already seen some lines of his, which had infinitely pleased her. Mr. Delamare said it was his intention to collect the poems of Mr. Jones, and print them.

"The author when living," continued he, "obtained by his talents only empty praise; perhaps now his head rests on the lap of earth, his grandson may reap some emolument from the genius that has been universally acknowledged, though suffered to live in penury, and wander indigent and friendless."

"Good heaven!" replied Rosa, "how many persons of talent have had the hard fate to pine all their lives in poverty, and die in absolute want: it seems as if genius was ordained to sustain more hardships, to encounter more afflictions, than fall to the lot of minds of a common stamp."

"The observation," returned Mr. Delamere, "unhappily is but too just; genius has but few friends; the rich and great who ought to support and encourage talent are too much engrossed by frivolous and unworthy pursuits to become the patrons of merit; frequently they are envious of talents, with which they are not enriched; they fear to have their own poverty of intellect discovered, and hate the highly gifted mind, because they cannot understand or attain its excellence: from this cause, so many persons of genius have lingered out their days in obscurity, have perished without a friend to soothe the parting pang; however, when once the head of genius reposes on a turfy pillow, envy also expires, and those who suffered the poet to want bread, will honour his memory by giving a large price for those effusions which, when the author lived, they disregarded and despised."

"Of the poems of Herbert Jones," continued Mr. Delamere, "I have in my possession a collection sufficient for an octavo volume, and prefaced with a few of the striking incidents of his life, I think they will attract the public notice."

When Mr. Delamere took his leave he left Rosa charmed with his character, and delighted with his manners and conversation. Dame Wilkins had collected together her holiday cloths: she spread before Rosa a rich flowered chintz of a pattern large enough for bed hangings, and told her that was the gown she had on the day her mother was christened; "And by my truly, Miss Rosa," said she, "it shall go again to Birch Park, and my quilted pompadore petticoat along with it. Aye, I remember, when I was a young woman I was vastly admired in that dress."

Rosa helped her to place her very best things in a little trunk, while she every now and then stopped to tell her that she knew every foot of ground for miles round Birch Park: "And only to think," said she, smoothing her apron, and smiling, "and only to think of Ruth Williams going in such a grand way to visit her master and Miss Nanny; but bless us," continued Dame Wilkins, "Miss Nanny must be getting old now, for she was many years older than my sweet Rosa."

"Whatever you do," replied Miss Percival, "do not speak of age before my aunt: you will lose her favour forever; she cannot bear to be thought elderly."

"What vanity!" said Dame Wilkins, putting on her spectacles. "Well-a-day! well-a-day! why old age is honourable; and I don't see what Miss Nanny should want to be thought young for."

Rosa knew very well her aunt's reasons and motives, but on this point she did not choose to be communicative; she therefore changed the subject. At an early hour she wished Dame Wilkins a good night, and retired to bed, to sleep, to dream of dear Birch Park; of the kind affectionate congratulations, the joyful surprise of her uncle and aunt; to indulge in delightful happiness with Hugh Montgomery; to fancy herself his wife enjoying with him the bliss of elegant retirement, the murmur of streams, the charms of music, the moonlight walks her father had so ridiculed. "Oh!" said Rosa, as she laid her head on the pillow, "Oh, that it may be my happy fate to be the wife of Hugh Montgomery; to live with him in peace and innocence, far from the giddy scenes of dissipated pleasure, of fashionable vice."

CHAPTER V

– So it falls out
That what we have we prize not to the worth
While we enjoy it; but being luck'd and lost,
Why then we wreak the value; then we find
The virtue that possession would not shew us
Whilst it was ours.

Shakespeare

O, happy they! the happiest of their kind!
Whom gentler stars unite, and in one fate
Their hearts, their fortune, and their beings blend.

Thomson

THE first beams of the morning found Rosa up and prepared for the journey; her extreme impatience to reach Birch Park had chased sleep from her eyelids long before the dawn of day, hours too before her usual time of rising. She thought Dame Wilkins lay very late, and when at last the good old soul came down and bustled to get breakfast, her anxiety was too great to allow her to eat; every now and then she rose from the table, opened the casement, and looked out, and inquired what o'clock it was: and thought every moment an hour till Mr. Delamere arrived. At length, seated in the chaise with Dame Wilkins and Edwin, they joyfully pursued their way, and had reached within three miles of Birch Park without stop or impediment, when on ascending a part of a road cut along the top of a remarkably steep hill, they discovered a carriage shattered to pieces, lying in a hollow at the bottom, which appeared from its situation to have been precipitated over the side. Having gained the top of the hill, their attention was arrested by seeing a crowd of people assembled round the door of a mean little hut by the road side. Mr. Delamere rode up to ask what had happened: but as the language was all Welsh, he could obtain no information respecting the accident; 'till having beckoned to John Wilkins, they found that the horses of Lord Clavering's carriage had taken fright on the hill, and had dashed the carriage with his Lordship down the side: that the coachman and the horses were killed, and his lordship had so many bones broke, and was otherwise so cut and bruised, that it was thought he had not long to live. Mr. Delamere and John left their horses to the care of the people, and pushed into the hut, where they found his lordship extended on the ground, with a leg and an arm broke, and his face so bruised and mangled, that it scarce retained a vestige of a human countenance; he was entirely surrounded by ignorant people, who crowded round with gaping curiosity. His servants rode off to Glenwyn Priory, as the nearest place to give information of the accident and obtain assistance. Mr. Delamere instantly acquainted Rosa with his lordship's situation, who being so very near home, proposed placing him in the chaise, and walking with Dame Wilkins to Birch Park. Mr. Delamere admired the amiable disposition that could forget such recent injuries and inconveniences, and so readily wish to alleviate and administer to the sufferings of an enemy. He bestowed on her generosity the praise she deserved, but thought it would be exposing her to unnecessary fatigue, as Lord Clavering's servant had been from what he could gather absent a sufficient time to authorize the expectation of his immediate return.

Rosa however, considering that every moment's delay in his lordship's present state might be fatal, had already sprung from the chaise, and was waiting while Dame Wilkins gave some charges respecting the little black trunk that held her best flowered chintz gown to her son Johnny, when the Montgomery equipage drove up to the door of the hut, with Hugh Montgomery and a surgeon in it: his eyes soon caught the form of his worshipped Rosa. Those only who have experienced the misery of a separation from the object of their tenderest wishes, who have felt the extinction of every cherished hope, they alone can justly appreciate the unutterable transport of Hugh Montgomery when he beheld Rosa Percival, while he again pressed to his beating heart, to his quivering lips, the hand he had believed lost to him for ever; when he beheld in her blushes, in the tender glances that shot from her mild eyes; when he heard in her soft tremulous accents the dear assurance that their unexpected meeting had communicated mutual pleasure, reciprocal delight.

A very few moments served to introduce Mr. Delamere and Hugh Montgomery to each other's character to conciliate esteem.

While the surgeon was binding up Lord Clavering's broken limbs, Mr. Delamere explained at large to the deeply interested Hugh Montgomery the occasion of his meeting Miss Percival on that spot, and under his protection. He also related as briefly and delicately as possible Edwin's claims upon the earl, who, utterly unconscious of his affinity, was busily employed in rolling the bandages and supporting the head of his father. During the recital resentment flashed in the eyes of

Hugh Montgomery, and flamed across his glowing cheek; but when he beheld the miserable mangled wretch, indignation was lost in confusion for his sufferings.

Rosa was safe, had escaped from his machinations, and stifling every angry emotion, he afforded all the help in his power to place him in the coach as easily as possible, on pillows brought for that purpose, and assisted Mr. Delamere, the surgeon, and Edwin, with the utmost humanity to support him steadily, while the carriage moved slowly on towards Glenwyn Priory.

Rosa and Dame Wilkins pursued their way to Birch Park, where her return was no sooner known, than the servants crowded round her with joyful acclamations: her presence instantly restored health, gaiety, and happiness to her uncle Gabriel Jenkins, who no sooner held her in his arms, than he burst into tears, and swore she was as dear to him as his own soul; he then dashed his nightcap upon the ground, tore off his gown, and whistling Saxoni's hornpipe, soon danced the slippers from his feet: being out of breath, he kissed Dame Wilkins, told her again and again he always liked her, but now he was downright in love with her, and that if she preferred Birch Park to her own village, he would keep her there like a lady all the days of her life; that as for him, he had been just for all the world like a sick turkey, but the sight of Rosa's sweet face had made him well; nothing was the matter now, he was quite and clean stout and hearty, but as for that long shanked, yellow visaged Lord Clavering, though it never was his custom to wish ill to no living soul, yet he should not have been sorry to hear that every bone in his cursed skin was broke. Miss Jenkins was glad to see Rosa, for her brother's lamentations and confinements had made the house like a dungeon: she as certainly rejoiced to find her unmarried, though she thought the girl was bewitched to refuse being a countess; and vexation and fury raged in her heart on the discovery that she had been carried off by a ruffian of a fellow, insulted with gross language, made to undergo the fatigue of dragging her limbs through ploughed fields, been wet to her skin, and her life actually endangered, for no other purpose but the forwarding Lord Clavering's design upon a chit of a girl, and that chit her own niece, which made the outrage still more galling: these were affronts her philosophy could by no means support with anything like patience or composure: she raved with acrimonious violence against men in general, called them monsters of deceit and ingratitude, but against Lord Clavering in particular her anger rose to a most ungovernable pitch, and of him and his character she spoke in terms of absolute scurrility, protesting for her part that so far from being sorry for the accident he had met with, she should have rejoiced most sincerely to hear that his vile neck had been broke. Rosa had often witnessed her aunt's violent temper, but it was now wrought up to a height that was quite terrific. Dame Wilkins said the miserable sinful creature was sorely punished for his evil doings, and the scripture told folks that they must forgive if they expected to be forgiven. Rosa retired to dress, and Miss Jenkins having become something calmer, and hearing that the Honourable Mr. Delamere, a handsome young man, was expected, after viewing herself in the glass, said she must go and dress too, for she looked dreadful ill. Dame Wilkins had placed her spectacles on her nose, and was surveying her as she made this speech, and said in reply, that by her truly considering how very fretful Miss Nanny had been from a child, she thought she looked surprisingly well at five and forty, especially as she had never got a husband. Miss Jenkins frowned, but the old woman continued:

"Every body says that old maids are apt to be discontented and fractious, and peevish, which makes their faces purse up and wrinkle, and by my truly, wrinkles don't add much to beauty. Lord bless me I remember when the men used to call me a good looking girl, but now, well-a-day, my face looks like the pleated chiterlin of Johnny's shirt."

Miss Jenkins darted a look of fury at her, called her an old fool, and said she did not know how much matrimony had mended her looks, but certainly it had not much improved her manners. Gabriel Jenkins laughed heartily, shook Dame Wilkins kindly by the hand, who looked a little disconcerted: he good-naturedly told her not to mind Nanny's tantrums, who hated nothing half so much as to be reminded of her age, for that having but a shortish kind of memory, she had quite and clean forgot sixteen or eighteen years of her life.

In the afternoon Mr. Hugh Montgomery introduced the honourable Horatio Delamere at Birch Park, where Gabriel Jenkins, with the honest warmth of a Cambrian, thanked him for his care and attention to his niece, protested that he wished he knew in what way to return his kindness; and that as for that worthy fellow John Wilkins, he would be sure to reward him in such a manner as should make him joyfully remember the stone stile and Rosa Percival as long as he lived.

Rosa compassionately inquired after Lord Clavering, and was told that great fears were entertained for his life.

"Confound the rascal; let him die then," said Gabriel Jenkins; "the world can very well spare such a scoundrel; it is well for him that he has met with this accident, or I would have let him see that a Welshman puts up with no insults: a pitiful hound to force away a girl that had been honest enough to tell him she did not fancy his lantern jaws. Gad, gentlemen, it was quite and clean the most dirty unhandsomest thing I ever heard of. – What the devil and all his little black imps! force a girl to love him, whether she would or not. He deserves a halter as well as any highwayman that ever swung."

Mr. Delamere said that he was deputed to offer Lord Clavering's apologies to Miss Percival, and to express his sincere penitence.

"Aye, aye, now he can do no more harm," said Gabriel Jenkins, "he is sorry. Gad, I honour him for that; now his sins have him, he fancies he runs away from them."

Miss Jenkins thought it would be indelicate to express what she felt and wished before strangers, she therefore threw all the placidity she could command into her countenance, and contented herself with observing, that her brother had but too much cause for indignation, when it was considered how much the family had been insulted, for certainly Lord Clavering's conduct had been so very abominable that it almost precluded pity for his sufferings.

Hugh Montgomery said, that in addition to his leg and arm, nearly all his ribs were broken, and that it was feared a mortification would ensue, unless he allowed the amputation of his leg, to which operation he was at present extremely averse.

Rosa shuddered, and asked if he had yet seen Edwin.

"You will be pleased, Miss Percival," replied Mr. Delamere, "to be informed that he has not only seen but acknowledged him; the scene was affecting beyond description. An attorney at this moment is making ample provision for Edwin, and Mr. Montgomery and myself are appointed his guardians in case of his father's decease."

"Heaven be praised," said Rosa, "the sweet boy will now move in a sphere congenial to his talents."

"His lordship," resumed Mr. Delamere, "was so much moved at the sight of Edwin, who it seems strongly resembles his mother, that he lamented he had not married her, and given this charming child a right to his hereditary honours; to the innocence of the unfortunate Jessy Jones he now does ample justice, and confesses with shame and horror the arts he used to seduce her."

Miss Jenkins was all curiosity respecting Jessy Jones, and they were under the necessity of going through her father's mournful history.

Gabriel Jenkins wiped his eyes several times during the recital, wished he had known Herbert Jones; he should not have wandered without a friend, or a home; "And as to the vicar, his father," said he, "gad, he was nothing at all in the world but an unfeeling sort of a person, with a heart as hard as a rock; why nobody can pretend to say that he was anything but a wicked Christian, quite and clean unfit for a parson, for while he was preaching charity and forgiveness from the pulpit, mercy upon us, he was acting as one may say by the rule of contrary, and was altogether unmerciful and unforgiving."

Miss Jenkins drew up her scraggy neck, and observed that Jessy Jones had only met the reward of her fault, and exactly what she might have expected; "For if young women," continued she, "will be weak and vain enough to listen to the deceitful flatteries of artful men, sorrow and disgrace will always be the consequence."

"Hold your tongue, Nanny," replied her brother; "hold your tongue, it is not always the consequence; and that you very well know; it is better," said he, nodding his head significantly, "for one body to steal a horse, than for another only to peep at him over the hedge. Some have the good luck not to be found out in their tricks, and then they pass for quite and clean honest women in the eyes of the world. Gad, I wonder if their consciences never give them a comical sort of a twitch when they are railing against a poor stray sheep that has not been so lucky as themselves."

Miss Jenkins's face became the colour of scarlet, her seat grew uneasy, and she suddenly left the room.

Mr. Delamere approached Rosa, and said, that having made Lord Clavering's apologies to Miss Percival, he was yet further commissioned, but that he feared to give her pain; yet it was necessary on many accounts, as well as for some trifling extenuation of the earl's conduct, that she should be informed that she had been carried off with the entire concurrence of Sir Edward Percival. Gabriel Jenkins started from his chair, and swore if that was true he was the biggest scoundrel in all the world, and that he should like to break every bone in his unnatural carcass.

Rosa, pale and trembling, begged her uncle to be calm, but Gabriel's Welsh blood was up, and it was with difficulty they prevented his going that instant to Rhydderdwyn, in search of Sir Edward Percival, of whom he vowed he would have satisfaction.

"Lord Clavering," continued Mr. Delamere, "considered all stratagems fair in love concerns, and perceiving that Mr. Hugh Montgomery's pretensions to Miss Percival's favour were encouraged – " Rosa blushed, and in confusion rose up, and would have left the room, but Hugh Montgomery took her hand, and gently detained her, while Mr. Delamere proceeded to state, that Sir Edward Percival had supposed that when removed from her relations, in a strange place, surrounded by difficulties and disagreeables, and above all, persuaded that Mr. Montgomery had carried her off with a dishonourable design, Miss Percival would gladly accept liberation on the terms of becoming Countess of Clavering.

"And if she had," said Gabriel Jenkins, "I never would have owned her for my niece."

"To obtain Sir Edward Percival's acquiescence to this hopeful scheme," continued Mr. Delamere, "his lordship advanced thirty thousand pounds, which had enabled Sir Edward to pay off the mortgage on the Rhydderdwyn estate, and marry Miss Montgomery."

Rosa shed tears at this discovery of her father's unfeeling indifference to her happiness, at the undeniable conviction of his unprincipled selfishness.

Hugh Montgomery said that he suspected the marriage between his sister and Sir Edward Percival would be productive of but little felicity on either side, and foresaw they would be mutual torments to each other; he also feared, that should Lord Clavering recover, of which indeed at present there appeared but little hope, yet still was in the chapter of possibilities, Miss Percival would again be exposed to his solicitations.

"Rosa," said Gabriel Jenkins, "come here, my little girl." Rosa left her seat, and stood beside her uncle. "Now," said he, tell the honest truth, "do you love me?" Rosa threw her arm round his neck, and affectionately kissed his cheek. "Do I love you, yes, most sincerely, most dearly," said she; "have you not been my protector, my friend, my father?"

"Well, well, I believe you, my girl," replied he, pressing her to him; "but will you do a little trifling matter, just to please my whim, Rosa?" said he, smiling on her.

"Yes, most certainly," replied she, "or I must be a most ungrateful creature, after all you have done for me."

"Come then," resumed he, "throw aside all nonsensicalness and shyness, and show at once fairly and honestly that you are quite and clean above all sort of hypocriteship and disguise."

Mr. Delamere's eyes were bent on the varying cheeks of Rosa, while Hugh Montgomery, breathless and agitated, wondered how this speech would end.

"If you love Mr. Hugh Montgomery," continued Gabriel Jenkins, "which I have long had a notion of, give your hand to him now frankly and generously, and by consenting to marry him, make me the happiest old man in North Wales, aye, gad, Rosa, in the whole world; but take notice, not unless you do love him, and like him above all other men, for I would not have you believe that I am such a monster as to wish you to tie yourself to anybody in the world, unless you quite and clean made the man your own choice; for gad, all the riches in life is nothing at last but dirt, as a body may call it, without happiness, and there can be nothing at all of that sort where folks marry just for the lucre of gain."

Mr. Delamere felt his heart attached to Gabriel Jenkins, he honoured his sentiments, and waited with almost as much impatience as Hugh Montgomery for Miss Percival's reply; but taken by surprise, overcome by confusion, her head sunk on the shoulder of her uncle, while his arm encircled her waist. Hugh Montgomery took her passive hand, and gently pressing it, softly whispered to Rosa, "Beloved Rosa, speak; this eventful moment decides my fate, for happiness or misery must be mine, as you accept or reject my vows."

Rosa raised her face, covered with the bashful blushes of modesty, from the shoulder of her uncle, and in a voice scarcely articulate said, "Be happy, if Rosa Percival can make you so."

Hugh Montgomery caught her in his arms, "Thus then," said he, "I receive my lovely bride, my adored Rosa."

Mr. Delamere congratulated them, and Gabriel Jenkins snatching off his wig, threw it up to the ceiling, kissed his niece, shook the gentlemen by the hand, whistled Saxoni's hornpipe, capered about the room till he was quite out of breath, then seating himself, he told Hugh Montgomery he was the only man in the principality he thought worthy of his niece, and that it quite and clean rejoiced the very cockles of his heart to think that his choice had been hers – that he would give her twenty thousand pounds for a marriage portion, and all he possessed at his death, provided they did not give their first boy any fine names, but christened him plain Gabriel, after him.

As Rosa wanted some years of being of age, and they also feared that Sir Edward Percival would oppose his authority to prevent the marriage, it was concluded that the following Tuesday herself, her uncle, and Miss Jenkins, if she chose to be of the party, should be met by Mr. Hugh Montgomery on the north road, when they were to proceed as expeditiously as possible to the first town in Scotland, there be made one, and after their return to have their marriage again publicly solemnized in the village church.

With this arrangement Gabriel Jenkins was quite pleased. To out-do Sir Edward Percival in a scheme delighted him beyond measure. He was charmed with the idea of disappointing any future project he might form of uniting his daughter to one of his right honourable acquaintance. He expressed his utter abhorrence in the plainest language of men of fashion, saying that one of the crew was quite and clean too many in a honest family; and persisted that high life was only another term for all sorts of debauchery and wickedness.

Miss Jenkins, when made acquainted with the intended marriage, felt very much against it; but Gabriel was determined; therefore, though she was far from satisfied that such a mere child as Rosa Percival should get a husband while she continued single, a circumstance that considerably ruffled her heavenly meekness; yet when she reflected that the wife of Hugh Montgomery could not possibly be the Countess of Clavering (should the earl recover), and also most cordially hating Sir Edward Percival, whose wishes and intentions she rejoiced to circumvent, she concealed as well as she could the chagrin of seeing her young and lovely niece preferred to herself, and consented to figure in her suit as bridemaid, though Rosa's matrimonial expedition was not acceded to on her part without many expressions of surprise that her brother, Gabriel Jenkins, should wish to hurry such an inexperienced child as Rosa into marriage, at an age when she could not be supposed to understand the nature of the situation she was going to embrace, when she could not be sufficiently mistress of her own mind to be certain of what she did or did not like.

Gabriel Jenkins thought Nanny's speech would never be at an end; but when finished, he told her he had set his heart upon the match, and she might as well hold her tongue; that she had been ill-tempered enough about not having a husband, and, gad, he believed would be quite and clean ready to jump at any man that would offer; but he was determined Rosa should not be an old maid; she was as good-tempered a little soul as ever drew the breath of life now; but if she lived single to her age, why no doubt she would be equally cross and ill-natured – "So, Nanny," continued he, "be you content to pass for a virgin, and please yourself if you can with your own vagaries, and let Rosa please herself and me by taking a husband."

Miss Montgomery had languished for the title of Lady Percival, and so great had been her impatience to obtain it, that she had married the divine man without having even a part of her own fortune settled upon herself. She was in love – he was all adoring tenderness – and herself and her mother thought all might be trusted to his generosity who seemed only anxious to possess her – who had never once mentioned money. But no sooner had he become possessed of her fortune than his behaviour changed from the attentive lover to the cold polite husband. – Before the first week had elapsed she found out that Sir Edward was many years older than herself, and that Lady Percival was fated to endure contradictions that Miss Montgomery had never even dreamed of.

It had been settled previous to their marriage that they were to spend the ensuing winter in London, but the various alterations and improvements it was necessary Rhydderdwyn mansion house should undergo demanded the actual presence of Sir Edward, and he determined to remain in Wales. It was in vain her ladyship wept, scolded, and condescended to entreat; her lord and master continued inflexible, and obstinately determined to keep her true to her vow of obedience.

Her ladyship complained to her mother, who undertook to talk to Sir Edward. – He listened with perfect indifference, while she expressed her astonishment that he should be so *perdigiously* altered in his behaviour in so very short a time. "I *partest*," continued Mrs. Montgomery, "I think it amazing rude indeed, Sir Edward, that you should *partend* to contradict Lucretia's wishes in this manner. I thought you was so very fond of her that you would have let her have her own way in everything."

"Not, madam," replied Sir Edward, "when her way would be to expose herself and me. Your daughter will do very well as Lady Percival in North Wales; but in Saint James's Square – *pardonnez moi*," bowing with provoking assurance.

"Was ever the like heard?" said Mrs. Montgomery. "What! Sir Edward, has my daughter brought you a *fortin* of almost an hundred thousand pounds in money and valuables to be spoken of in this *perdigiously* odd way? But she shall not be used in this shocking manner – she shall go to *Lunnun* if she likes."

"And you," rejoined Sir Edward, "may go with her if you like; but you will have the superlative goodness to excuse my attendance, and to provide lodgings for yourselves, as my house in St. James's Square is let."

Mrs. Montgomery was speechless with rage. – The town-house let, in which she had planned to receive so much gay company, and exhibit her own and her daughter's finery, was too much to bear – she absolutely cried with vexation. Sir Edward trimmed his nails, examined a picture through his eye-glass, and hummed a tune without taking the least notice of her.

At this juncture Lady Percival walked in, and seeing her mother in tears, asked what was the matter. Mrs. Montgomery said she was *perdigiously* sorry that she was obliged to shock her with saying that Sir Edward was a most monstrous deceitful man.

"Why, my dear Lucretia, only to think that after having promised to take us to *Lunnun*, and to present you to their majesties, that he says he won't go to town, and that his house in St. James's Square is let. Was there ever such barbarous usage? – and to a wife that has brought him such a *fortin*, not to say a word about her beauty."

"As to her beauty, madam," said Sir Edward, "you may take it back to Glenwyn Priory if you please. I am a reasonable man, and her fortune alone, without any other addition, will content me."

"Why sure I don't hear right," said Mrs. Montgomery; "why you are not such a *perdigious* brute as to wish to part with your wife?"

"Anything, madam, for a quiet life," said Sir Edward: "her ladyship wanted a title, I wanted cash; we are both supplied with the article needful; so far all is right. She concealed her bad temper and put on her most amiable looks to get a husband, I flattered and promised in order to secure a wife: our ends obtained, the curtain drops, and the farce concludes – deception is no longer necessary. I shall not present Lady Percival at court, and for this reason – the late Lady Percival, my mother, was not only extremely beautiful but was also a finished gentlewoman: the present Lady Percival I fear would lose by the comparison."

Mrs. Montgomery sat for a moment astonished, while her ladyship walked up and down the room too much enraged to speak; at length turning to Sir Edward: "So then, all your raptures, all your praises of my person, and my accomplishments were deception?"

"Nothing more I assure you, child," replied he: "as to your person, it is hardly tolerable, there is not a single line of grace or beauty in it; your eyes are too round, your nose is too short, your mouth is too wide, and your teeth too large."

"Mighty well, sir, mighty well," said her ladyship, "pray go on."

"Well, certainly to oblige you," rejoined Sir Edward, "or else egad I hate to say shocking things. Your neck is too thick, your shoulders too high, your waist too square, and your hands and feet," continued he shrugging his shoulders, "every thing in the world but handsome; to be sure you have what our polite neighbours the French call the devil's beauty, youth, and that is the only recommendation you can possibly boast."

"Yes, sir," screamed her ladyship, "I can boast another, money, sir, money, and I now perceive, though too late, that men are such contemptible, selfish, mean wretches, that they will marry anything, yes, even their aversion, provided they can enrich themselves by it."

"Very true, very sensibly observed," replied Sir Edward; "money is really so extremely essential to a man's ease, that he will make some sacrifices to obtain it. However, having been obliged to tell a few white lies to secure your ladyship's fortune, I shall endeavour to prevent its dissipation, having, I assure you, suffered much privation and inconvenience for want of cash. My affairs at present are a good deal embarrassed, and I have prudently resolved to lead an economical life, till I can again figure in the world in the style I have done; in the meantime your ladyship has the choice either to content yourself with showing off at the Carnarvon assembly once a month, and displaying your consequence among such of the natives as will visit you at Rhydderdwyn Mansion House, or to fret yourself into a consumption as quickly as you can."

"Vastly obliging and polite, and generous too on your part," said her ladyship, "to allow me such liberal alternatives."

"Oh, child," resumed Sir Edward picking his teeth, and lolling against the wall, "I assure you it is not in my nature to be otherwise than polite: fondness between married people has been exploded long ago, nothing in nature can be so tiresome and disgusting as matrimonial love scenes: but though any woman, and every woman, is in general more attractive than a wife, yet nevertheless she is entitled to politeness."

"Well I never heard the like before," said Mrs. Montgomery: "I should think it *perdigiously* odd indeed, and not polite neither, if Mr. Montgomery was to talk in this way to me."

"Very likely, madam," replied Sir Edward. "Mr. Montgomery I think I have heard was attracted by your beauty, and married you for love, it is therefore by no means a case in point."

"You polite!" said her ladyship, "you!"

"Don't call names, child, it is very unladylike."

"Oh," resumed she, "that I had been sick in my bed before I had consented to be Lady Percival, before I had united myself to such a brute."

"Very true, Lucretia," said her mother, "and bestowed your *fortin* on such an unthankful – "

"There you are mistaken," said Sir Edward; "I am extremely grateful on that score, I assure you; but as I always love to see the female countenance beaming smiles, and to hear the lips breathing gentleness and good humour, I shall wish you a good morning, ladies, and hope to meet you on my return more reconciled."

"Reconciled!" echoed her ladyship, "no, never: I shall never be reconciled to such a hypocrite."

"It must be my endeavour, then," resumed Sir Edward, "to reconcile you to your duty, for though in general I detest old systems and customs as much as I do old fashions, yet in one or two particulars they are worthy observance, namely, obedience in a wife."

"Obedience! lord!" said Mrs. Montgomery; "I never heard a man boast of his politeness, and yet be so *perdigiously* rude as to mention obedience. Why Mr. Montgomery never said a word of the sort to me in all his life."

"And if he had, madam," said Lady Percival; "I suppose you would not have been such a fool as to have attended to it. I tell you, Sir Edward – "

"Good morning, Lady Percival," said he bowing. His groom was waiting at the door with his horse; he vaulted into the saddle and rode off.

"I wonder what I saw in the ugly wretch," said her ladyship, "to induce me to marry him; but I will let him see he shall do as I please: I will pass the winter in London: a pretty thing indeed to bring a man such a fortune, and be denied the pleasure of spending part of it."

"Very true, Lucretia," replied her mother; "but he seems so determined."

"Yes, madam, and I am determined too; what did I marry a man so much older than myself for," said her ladyship; "only because I supposed I could more easily manage him: how that mawkish thing Mrs. Mortimer will exult to hear that I am obliged to submit to a husband, and to give up all my own desires to his. No, no – he shall neither have his way, nor throw me into a consumption; I will let him see that I will do as I please, and go where I please, and spend what money I please. His impudence to pull my person to pieces! me that brought him such a fortune! to have the impertinence to say I shall spend the winter in this dismal hole, after promising I should go to court, and give routs, and balls, and masquerades, myself!"

Having raved herself out of breath, she threw herself into a chair, while her mother said: – "Oh, that you had but listened to Hugh, he had sense enough to see through this man; he would have persuaded you to secure your fortune on yourself, he advised you not to marry. Oh, it was most *perdigiously* wrong not to listen to Hugh."

"I am astonished to hear you," replied Lady Percival; "you advised me to marry Sir Edward Percival, and now blame me for not attending to Hugh. I suppose in a short time you will be for recommending me to be obedient to my lord and master, and sit down contentedly and thank him humbly for the humdrum life he is pleased to allot me."

"I protest, Lucretia," resumed Mrs. Montgomery, "I am so amazingly astonished at what I see and hear, that I am most *perdigiously* puzzled to know what sort of advice to give. The man before marriage seemed such an angel, that nobody could never have thought of his turning out such a devil in scarlet: why he is as bad as the man in the play, that calls his wife his ox, and his ass, and his kitchen stuff. However, as he is such a strange out of the way temper, you had better try to coax him. Everybody as knows anything will tell you there is no making a silk purse out of a sow's ear; so if you can't make nothing of him by shewing a spirit, why you must try what you can do by being gentle and good humoured."

The conscience of Lord Clavering told him that he was not in a state to die; and as the surgeons who attended him held out the flattering hope of recovery if mortification was prevented, he suffered the amputation of his leg, and, contrary to the expectation of all about him, in a short time began to gather strength. He had earnestly prayed to live, being content to bear the ills he had, rather than fly to those he knew not of; for to the loss of his leg were added dreadful seams across his cheeks and forehead, that made his face horrible to look on. Thus entirely spoilt for love-making, his lordship began seriously to reflect on his ill spent life, and determined on devoting the remaining part of his days to the education of Edwin, in whose affection and duty he found more real happiness than he had ever experienced in his most brilliant moments of youthful enjoyment, the only alloy to which was the reflection that though blessed with every personal grace, and intellectual endowment, his vices had deprived this amiable, this deserving son, of the honours of his ancestors, and that his title must descend to a distant branch of the family, for whom he felt not even esteem, while the youth whose mind and manners would have reflected dignity on the most elevated rank was condemned to blush for the crime of others, to bear the stigma of illegitimacy.

Sir Edward Percival having accomplished his purpose in securing the fortune of Miss Montgomery, felt but little concern respecting his daughter's establishment in life; he hoped when he heard of Lord Clavering's dreadful accident that he would die, remembering that death cancelled all obligations; and he was not a little vexed to find that his lordship was recovering, but in a state so mutilated and disfigured, as to render it impossible to hope that Rosa would ever be brought to accept him. While her father was thus occupied by disagreeable reflections, Rosa became the happy wife of the adoring Hugh Montgomery. Sir Edward Percival had been paying his lordship a visit, when on his return to Rhydderdwyn he met two carriages, whose horses and drivers were ornamented with bridal favours: he had scarcely time to wonder who or what they should be, when Gabriel Jenkins popping his head out of the window, saluted him with: –

"Gad! Sir Edward, I wish you joy."

"I thank you, sir," replied Sir Edward; "though you are rather late in your congratulations."

"Late!" said Gabriel Jenkins; "early you mean; you are quite and clean mistaken if you suppose I was giving you joy on your own marriage; nothing in the world was farther from my thoughts, I promise you, because I hate to make game of a serious concern. No, no – I was giving you joy of your son-in-law."

"My son-in-law!" repeated Sir Edward, gazing after the carriage, which at that moment passed him.

"Aye," continued Gabriel Jenkins, "Mr. Hugh Montgomery, who is now the husband of Rosa. Gad! what a long face you make, Sir Edward; I told you she did not like Lord Yellow Phiz, and that we would have no more great people in the family. You see some folks are quite and clean as clever at schemes and plots as other folks: what have you nothing in the world to say on this business, Sir Edward?"

"I have only to say she has acted like a fool," replied Sir Edward, "to content herself with marrying a private gentleman, when she might have been a countess; but it is all owing to her education."

"No reflections upon that," said Miss Jenkins, thrusting her head forward; "if she had waited till you bestowed an education upon her, I wonder what accomplishments she would have excelled in."

"Not in knitting, knotting, spinning, brewing, or distilling, I suppose," replied Sir Edward; "but as the girl prefers Welsh mountains, and the native savages to more brilliant scenes, and more enlightened society, why her attainments and education may render her the lady bountiful of these parts. I confess she has rather disappointed me."

"True," said Gabriel Jenkins, "I suppose she has, for now Lord Lantern Jaws must have his thirty thousand pounds again. It was quite and clean for all the world like buying a pig in a poke, his lordship advancing that large sum upon such a wild sort of a speculation; but fools and their money are soon parted. Hark, the bells are ringing: gad, I never was half so happy in my life. Drive on, coachman, I long to get home that I may have a dance."

Sir Edward Percival went home also, not a little puzzled to know in what way he was to raise thirty thousand pounds, which he supposed Lord Clavering would expect to be reimbursed as soon as he heard of Rosa's marriage. Edwin had expressed a wish to visit Mrs. Hugh Montgomery, to whom he felt particularly attached; and as Lord Clavering's conscience and better feelings told him he owed her some reparation, he enclosed Sir Edward's bond for the thirty thousand pounds in a letter, dictated by real contrition, in which he begged her acceptance of that sum, as a peace-offering, assuring her that it by no means injured his fortune, and that he should consider her refusal of it as a proof that she had not pardoned him, but still retained resentment in her heart. To the wealthy Montgomerys thirty thousand pounds was by no means an object of consideration. Rosa felt uneasy at the embarrassments of her father, notwithstanding his conduct to her had displayed an utter indifference to all that concerned her further than as she was in any way conducive to his interest. Hugh Montgomery therefore advised her returning the bond to her father, as an obligation to Lord Clavering was repugnant to his pride and feelings: he waited on his lordship to express her gratitude for his intended generosity, but to insist on adding the thirty thousand pounds to Edwin's fortune. Rosa threw herself into the arms of her husband; she knew he did not love or respect her father, and she doubly felt the value of an arrangement prompted solely by affection for herself. When Sir Edward Percival received his bond, and read the respectful and tender envelope, which did not breathe a syllable of resentment, or a line of reproach, he said it was a handsome sum for the peer to pay for a frolic; and how the devil when he looked at his rueful visage, scarred worse than the fore finger of a seamstress, and contemplated his cork leg, he had brought himself to pay thirty thousand pounds for such extraordinary benefits he could not understand – "However," continued he, deliberately tearing the bond, and throwing it piece by piece into the fire, "what concern is it of mine; I gain by the business, let who will lose; the girl has disposed of herself tolerably well, and has behaved on this occasion very properly; and Montgomery too, if the fellow had only been a peer, and was divested of a few of his old fashioned notions, and prejudices, why he would certainly be more endurable." He then rang the bell, and told the servant to inform his lady that he wished to speak with her. Lady Percival was then informed that it was his wish that she should accompany him to Birch Park: her ladyship refused, observing that she had a right to expect the compliment from them of a first visit. Sir Edward ordered the carriage, arranged his hair and cravat, then examining her ladyship through his eye glass, said: –

"Upon my soul, Lady Percival, your morning dress has an air of style; you are certainly devilishly improved, child, since you have been honoured with my alliance. Hold, hold – that is not a graceful toss of the head; it was too quick, and had more of the knowing jerk of a chambermaid in it than the scorn of a woman of fashion: besides, that drawing down of the corners of the mouth does not convey half contempt enough; you should elevate your eye-brows, and having darted from your eyes a glance full of derisive meaning, suddenly let the eye-lids fall, and turn with a stately step to some other object. However, under my instruction I think you will do, that is if you pay proper attention, for at present you have an infinitude of awkwardness to get rid of; a variety of vulgarities to correct. Study expression," continued he, turning to a mirror; "practise attitude, for on these depend all the attraction of woman. A plain face may be mended by pearl powder and Circassian bloom – but expression and attitude give to the person all the graces of the Grecian."

Sir Edward perceived he was talking to himself, as her ladyship had retired. "Well," said he, laughing, "if Lady Percival had been educated in the first circles, she could not have displayed a more perfect knowledge of fashionable rudeness. Egad, if she continues to improve as rapidly as she has begun, she will shortly be able to vie with any of the high bred dames of quality with whom I have the honour to be acquainted."

Sir Edward was received at Birch Park with more respect and affection than he expected. From Gabriel Jenkins indeed he got some severe rubs, but these he parried in his usual lively careless way; protested that he had lived a very gay life, and dissipated his fortune among those who wisely lived upon the folly of others – but now he was resolved to reform, to nurse his estates, and grow rich. "Aye," said Gabriel Jenkins, "out of the frying pan into the fire. Gad, after having spent your money like an ass, you will begin to hoard it like a mule; the one is quite and clean as bad as the other; I should not wonder, as you were always upon the extremes, if you was to turn miser in your old age; and even grudged yourself the morsel you put into your maw, and the rags that covered your carcass."

Sir Edward escaped the severity of Miss Jenkins: she had began to consider that even the quiet deliberating Williams was, in the present scarcity of men, better than having no dangler at all, and in the hope of meeting him, she had taken a walk towards Woodland Cottage, resolving to make one more effort to have the cherry-cheeked dairy maid dismissed, whose influence over his heart she feared, if not put a stop to, would soon exceed hers. Mr. Williams saw and invited her into the house, nay, he accompanied her home, and stayed dinner, for he had a sincere friendship for Gabriel Jenkins, and a real affection for Rosa, in whose happiness he warmly participated. But after having turned the matter over in his mind, and given it due consideration, he resolved to remain a widower the rest of his life, because when a man had a pretty maid, whom he contrived to make useful, if he grew tired of her, or she grew neglectful, or took greater liberties than he liked, he could pay her her wages and discharge her; but a wife was a log about a man's neck that he could by no means get rid of, and the very best were not at all times agreeable. He therefore remained quite insensible to all Miss Jenkins's advances, though she smiled, and helped him to all the nice bits at table: he knew his own love of quiet, and her turbulent temper; and as he had money enough for all his purposes, he determined to have his pot of hot coffee and his nice buttered rolls in peace, and to smoke his pipe and drink his glass of ale, without being made disagreeable and uncomfortable by the ill humours of a wife.

Miss Jenkins finding he would not return to his allegiance, grew more inveterate than ever against the dairy maid, professed herself absolutely scandalized at the shameful way in which Mr. Williams lived, thanked her stars that she had found him out, not that it had ever been her intention to marry him, though it was well known to every body that he had proposed it to her; but no, she hated men, the deceitful, perfidious ungrateful wretches, and had made a vow which she never would be tempted to break of leading a life of celibacy.

CHAPTER VI

> Of all our passions love is the least subject to control; strong and impetuous, born of sentiment, it establishes an empire in our hearts, even before we perceive it. Caution may dispute with, and guard against other passions, but love is a rapid fire which seizes and inflames us in a moment; it neither weighs nor reflects, but creating a world for itself, shuts out every idea, every object but the one adored.
>
> EXTRACT FROM A LETTER

> And said I that my limbs were old,
> And said I that my blood was cold,
> And that my kindly fire was fled,
> And my poor wither'd heart was dead,
> And that I might not sing of love?
> How could I to the dearest theme,
> That ever warm'd a minstrel's dream,
> So false, so foul a recreant prove!
> How could I name love's very name,
> Nor wake my harp to notes of flame.
>
> *Lay of the Last Minstrel*

In being united to Adeline Llewellyn, her so idolized, so adored, the young and sanguine Henry Mortimer fondly supposed he had gained the summit of sublunary felicity; nor had any thing happened to obscure the bright prospect that imagination, aided by hope, had coloured with the gayest tints, till the good Sir Owen died, for his days, unclouded by care or disappointment, had rolled on in a blissful succession of prosperity and content, and even the sorrow introduced by that event might have yielded its poignancy to time and resignation, had not the too sensitive mind of Mrs. Mortimer sunk into an oppressive melancholy, which not all the tender assiduities of her husband could remove: when with weeping remembrance she recalled her buried father's look, his smile, his affection, she seemed as if all her earthly good had forsaken her; she felt a mournful presage that the halcyon years of her childhood, which had all been diverted by fond parental solicitude and indulgence, of every thorn that could disturb her enjoyments, or create uneasiness, were most assuredly succeeded by hurricanes, that would eventually wreck her peace, and desolate the frail remains of happiness his death had left her.

Mr. Mortimer, whose passion for Adeline seemed to augment with every added hour, anticipated the arrival of Horatio Delamere, as the epoch that would again restore her to the domestic circle, to cheerfulness and animation; he knew that his friend "was formed by nature's partial hand," was blessed with every grace "that wins the friend, or that enchants the fair." He was sensible that Mr. Delamere was endowed with talents of the richest stamp; he knew also that he used to possess an imagination lively and playful as brilliant; and he hoped, from the spirited contests between him and Miss Tudor, who spent the chief of her time at Dolgelly Castle, that Mrs. Mortimer would find such amusement as would insensibly beguile her mind from scenes of sorrow, detach it from dwelling on the grave of her father, and bring it back to that delightful cheerfulness which had once shone in streams of radiance from her bright eyes, and played in bewitching dimples round her lovely mouth. At present her child was the only object that appeared to interest the feelings of Mrs. Mortimer, or rouse her to animation; on her lovely boy she gazed with sensations of melancholy rapture; over him she shed the delicious tears of regret and affection, for he resembled her sainted father; and while straining the little rosy smiling cherub to her bosom, she would mentally pray that he might also resemble him in goodness and virtue; that like him he might behold the errors of his fellow creatures with mercy and charity; like him be excellent in understanding and generous in disposition.

When the Hon. Mr. Delamere, who had been some days expected, arrived at Dolgelly Castle, he was ushered at once, without any previous announcing, into a saloon where on a sofa sat Mrs. Mortimer, with her beautiful boy standing up behind her, endeavouring to place an artificial white rose among the shining ringlets which his playful exertions had drawn in profusion over her neck and forehead; Eliza Tudor was busily employed in netting a purse for Captain Seymour; and Henry Mortimer, leaning against a window, was reading in ecstasies the Lay of the Last Minstrel. Such were the interesting group that presented themselves to Mr. Delamere as he entered. When introduced by her husband to Mrs. Mortimer, her blushing confusion considerably heightened her beauty: to him she appeared beyond comparison the most lovely, the most attractive woman he had ever beheld; even the fair and interesting Sicilian, the Marchesa della Rosalva, whose beauty yet sometimes obtruded on his dreams, and hovered in his imagination, was now exceeded; the symmetry of her graceful form, the soft-melting enchantment of her voice, yielded to the superior loveliness of Mrs. Mortimer. He viewed her with delighted wonder, while the fascinating assemblage of charms, spread over her whole person, filled his bosom with sensations such as he had before experienced when his senses were enslaved by Celestina; sensations which he now determined to suppress, because dishonourable to encourage.

With the sprightliness of Miss Tudor Mr. Delamere was diverted; he honoured the goodness of her disposition, while he smiled at her mischievous frolics; her lively sallies called forth the innocent retorted jest, the elegant repartee; but Eliza Tudor had nothing either in her person or manner to touch his heart, or interest his feelings, while if even Adeline's voice, on the most unimportant subject, met his ear, its entrancing melody ran in thrilling currents through his frame, and shook with impassioned tremblings its minutest fibres; the glance of her eye shot a flame that penetrated the inmost recesses of his heart, and in spite of his utmost efforts to subdue the passion, in spite of the united arguments suggested by reason and honour, he found that if he had before loved Celestina, he now adored Mrs. Mortimer; he shuddered at the impetuosity of his feelings, the wildness of his wishes, while he remembered she was the idolized wife of Henry Mortimer, the companion, the dearly loved friend of his childhood, the worshipped of him, for whose sake he would have thought no effort too much, to serve whom he would have sacrificed even his existence.

At the first sight of Horatio Delamere Adeline started as from a dream: she awoke to a new existence, as his dark expressive eye flashed on her soul: at the fatal conviction that the calm happiness, the unruffled tranquillity of her life was dissolved, like the baseless fabric of a vision, to leave not a wreck behind, she viewed his elegant person, the expression of his fine intelligent countenance, with emotions till then unknown and unfelt. When they retired for the night, as Henry spoke of his friend with all the enthusiasm of regard, Adeline felt her face burn with blushes: the name of Horatio Delamere seemed formed of necromantic characters; it awakened a new pulse in her soul: and when her husband fondly demanded her opinion of the companion of his youth, she dreaded to give utterance to the warm praise that hovered her lips, lest her husband should conceive it too glowing, lest it should rouse suspicion in his bosom. Suspicion! The idea made her blush, suspicion of what? Mrs. Mortimer, terrified and abashed, shrank from the task of investigating her own feelings; she feared to inquire the cause of the tumultuous throbbings of her heart, of the new sensations that hurried in vivid flashes across her cheek, that one moment chilled the current of her blood, and the next seemed to scorch her frame with fever. Observing the coldness of her encomiums, Henry Mortimer said he felt disappointed in her not expressing for Horatio Delamere the same warmth of friendship that he did: "But when, my love," continued he, "you are more acquainted with him, your esteem, your admiration will increase; for to a mind highly cultivated, adorned with the richest, most valuable stores of ancient as well as modern literature, he unites the noblest, bravest, most liberal mind, and a disposition replete with generosity, tenderness, and humanity. I have studied him for years, and I have ever found him such as warrants my wearing him in my heart's core, even in my heart of hearts."

Adeline could with delight have echoed the praises of Horatio Delamere, but for the first time in her life she threw the veil of hypocrisy over her real thoughts and opinions, and merely answered, that it was probable she might in future think as highly of Mr. Delamere as her husband did. At present he was a stranger, though she confessed she thought his person extremely elegant, his manners prepossessing, and his conversation entertaining and instructive.

"I rejoice that he is arrived," continued Mr. Mortimer: "your harp, my beloved, has long been silent and neglected. Horatio Delamere is a master of music; I trust that his taste will allure you to what was once a favourite study. I flatter myself that I shall again have the felicity to see you return to your accustomed amusements, and that the various talents of my friend will recall my Adeline from the unavailing melancholy which she has suffered so long to envelope her, will restore to me the sweet smiles that used to enrapture my heart, and whose deprivation I have so unceasingly lamented."

Adeline endeavoured to stifle a sigh, but it escaped not the attentive Henry, who fondly pressing her to his bosom, said, "To lament with such bitter and continued grief a blessing heaven has been pleased to deprive us of, is, dearest Adeline, to appear insensible to those we possess" –

"No," replied she, "no, dearest Henry, believe me not so ungrateful to heaven, so insensible to thy worth, to thy affection, so deficient in tenderness to our darling child."

"Adored of my soul," said Henry, "I meant not to reproach you; let me but see you restored to cheerfulness, let me again hear your voice warbling its enchanting strains, let me again behold your lovely mouth dimpled with smiles, and I shall be happy, supremely happy."

Mrs. Mortimer was soon conscious that the arrival of Mr. Delamere had dissipated much of the gloom that had hung upon her spirits. It was true she yet lamented her father, but her grief had lost much of its poignancy; it had assumed a softer character. Her thoughts had a new object to rest on, too attractive, too fascinating for her peace. In order to escape the spell whose witcheries were winding round her heart, she again sought the relief of music – again her fingers glided over the keys of the piano forte, and her hand swept the strings of her harp. But here was, alas! a fresh enchantment. The taste and skill of Horatio Delamere were exquisite, and in duets and glees his voice accompanied hers, while his whole impassioned soul breathing in the notes conveyed to hers in melting cadences and entrancing swells a language delightfully, though dangerously, expressive of tender feeling. – For a short time Adeline believed herself completely happy. To see, to walk with, to converse with Mr. Delamere seemed all that was necessary to constitute felicity, and the doting Henry Mortimer again saw her eyes beam with animation, again transported beheld the smiles of pleasure dimple her cheek.

But it was not possible for a mind like Adeline's to remain long in the delusive maze of passion: at once she awoke to reflection and anguish, to deplore the guilt of having for a moment thought of Mr. Delamere with other sentiments than those of friendship: for now, alas! love, vehement and uncontrollable, had taken possession of her bosom. Her nights no longer acknowledged the balmy influence of sweet and refreshing sleep; the image of Horatio Delamere pursued her even in dreams, and the seductive harmony of his voice vibrated on her disordered fancy in the deep silence of the night.

Frequently Mr. Mortimer would in jest tell Eliza Tudor that her heart was no longer true to the Scottish lad; that it had strayed from Captain Seymour, who was now almost forgotten, and that the Honourable Horatio Delamere had superseded him in her affection: to which she would laughingly answer – "You are egregiously mistaken; I should equally as soon think of falling in love with Lamban Libræ, or any other bright star in the heavens. I am not so vain as to aspire to such perfection. I would not have him for all the world, unless I might (as Beatrice says in Much Ado about Nothing) have another for working days. – He would be too costly to wear every day. Mr. Delamere is far too transcendent for me. No, no, Archibald Seymour and Eliza Tudor are better suited. With minds and abilities nearly upon a par, they may pursue the matrimonial path with a tolerable chance for happiness, because being of congenial minds, my nonsensical prattle and monkey tricks would have charms for him, who can cut as many capers and be to the full as frolicsome as myself; but with such a husband as Mr. Delamere – mercy on my little mad head! why I should always be in fear of saying or doing something to outrage sense or propriety – I should be thrown at an awful distance, only appearing like a little attendant satellite receiving partial splendour from the radiance such a comet would elicit."

Sir Griffith Tudor, whose resentment against Captain Seymour had not yet subsided, would have been happy to see the Honourable Mr. Delamere distinguish his daughter, who he often swore was one of the finest fellows he had ever seen, and infinitely superior in every respect to that hot-headed fellow, Seymour, who had been such a d – d ass to prefer the fatigues of a military life and all the hardships of a camp to ease, content, and a fine girl with a handsome fortune. He would then say Seymour had a devilish strange taste, for he preferred the sulphurous smell of gunpowder to the more savoury one of roast beef.

An intimacy had been cultivated with much satisfaction on both sides between Mr. and Mrs. Hugh Montgomery and the family at Dolgelly Castle. Mr. Delamere had discovered so much in the mind and conduct of Mr. Hugh Montgomery to esteem and admire, that next to Henry Mortimer he considered him the most perfect character he had met among all the men of different nations with whom either chance or inclination had associated him. For Rosa he felt a kind regard, which both Mr. and Mrs. Montgomery were assiduous to increase and retain, feeling proud of possessing the esteem of a man whose virtues they conceived entitled him to their respect, and whose superior talents did credit and honour to their warmest eulogium. The delicate timid reserve and gentleness of Rosa was a beautiful contrast to the unwearied vivacity of Eliza Tudor; while Sir Griffith's eccentric sallies and Lady Tudor's affected complaints, with Miss Jenkins's phillippics against the men, and her brother Gabriel's honest though ludicrous remarks upon fashionable people and fashionable manners, afforded a diversified scene and variety of argument, which at the same time that it was highly amusive was not devoid of instruction; for certainly the follies and imperfections of others hold up a mirror to the thinking mind, which while it exposes the deformity of vice, produces compassion for the frailties of human nature.

It was at one of these parties that Mr. Delamere mentioned Lord Clavering's desire to engage a tutor for his son; one who was learned without pedantry, and united the graces and elegancies of a gentleman with the more brilliant acquirements of the scholar. Mr. Delamere observed, that Lord Clavering wished to have Edwin's education completed under his own eye, as he particularly disliked the idea of sending him to a public school, where in proportion to the knowledge boys in general gained, they contracted habits and imbibed vices, which only direful necessity, and imperious circumstance, could correct or extirpate. The mention of Edwin, who was a general favourite, recalled the remembrance of his grandfather, and Mr. Delamere was reluctantly obliged to listen to his own praises, as Rosa related his humane and feeling conduct to the poor blind harper, whose last moments he had soothed with the voice of compassion, and whose last pangs he had softened with tenderness and generosity. Mr. Delamere was embarrassed at his own praise, which he told his friends he did not deserve; what he had done for Herbert Jones was only an act of common humanity, and not worthy to be rated so highly; he then related the old man's history: they said 'twas pitiful, 'twas wondrous pitiful, and gave him for his pains a world of sighs. Mr. Delamere had retained the harp of Herbert Jones in his possession, intending to present it to Edwin, whose grief as yet was not sufficiently subdued to bear the sight of an instrument so loved and valued by his grandfather. At the request of the company the harp was introduced. Mrs. Mortimer played several tender and affecting ballads on her own instrument, but in passing her fingers lightly over that of Herbert Jones the tears started into her eyes: his mournful story, the fate of the unfortunate Jessy, rushed on her fancy, and in visible emotion she resigned the harp to Mr. Delamere, who played with much skill many popular English as well as Italian airs, for which he received the applause of his delighted auditors.

"It is presumption in me," said Mr. Delamere, "to wake the strings that Herbert Jones swept with so bold and masterly an hand. – Only a few hours before he died, he played that sweet and affecting Welsh air, "Ar hyd y nos," with such taste, feeling, and expression, as told me plainly that the fingers then trembling with age, nay actually at the moment in the chill grasp of death, had once charmed the soul with strains of richest melody, had once called from the quivering strings *notes of flame*. Herbert Jones's harp, like that of Ossian, cannot indeed hang in the hall of his fathers, but no doubt the affectionate heart of Edwin will thank me for preserving the precious relic, and years hence, when the melancholy fate of his mother, when the misfortunes of his grandfather, cross his memory, he who is an enthusiast in music, will wake the sleeping strings to many a pensive strain, congenial to his own feelings, and breathing tender requiems for those over whom the dark grass waves."

Rosa reminded Mr. Delamere of the poem he had promised to lend her, written by Herbert Jones.

"His talents," replied Horatio, "are not confined to music; he was enamoured of poetry, and to the last continued to evince his devotion by composing verses which if they add nothing to his fame, will always be testimonials of a liberal mind, and a feeling heart. We are all I believe admirers of the muses, and with your permission I will read as well as I am able what I think you will consider, if not the brilliant coruscations of superior genius, the effusions of a good and tender disposition."

Lady Tudor ordered her carriage, protesting her nerves were not equal to hearing anything more concerning the ill-fated Herbert Jones. Sir Griffith departed with his lady, saying, that if he had wrote hunting songs why he could have listened to tallyho and tantivy with pleasure but he had no taste for pathetics. The company being re-seated, at their request Mr. Delamere produced the manuscript, and read it to his attentive auditors.

HOEL'S HARP

O'er the chill moon the clouds had roll'd,
The path was wild, the wind blew cold,
In many a hollow gust it past,
While round the scatter'd leaves were cast:

No star was seen, no sound was heard,
Save of the distant ocean's roar,
Or harsh note of the screaming bird,
That loves to wing the rocky shore;

Or rushing blast whose mournful tone
O'er death and shipwrecks seem'd to moan;
While dark and cloudy was the hour,
And thickly fell the drizzling show'r.

A wandering harper, old and poor,
And sightless too, came slowly on;
A stripling led him o'er the shore,
Whose eye was sank, whose cheek was wan.

The old man seem'd to woe resigned,
His grey locks scattering in the wind,
As deep he sigh'd with troubled thought,
As sad his steps the village sought.

Plaintive he said, "Heaven help the blind,
Compel'd to seek precarious bread,
Who knows not where a hut to find
To shelter his unfriended head."

His harp, of other days the pride,
Was feebly borne against his side,
A load too weighty to sustain,
Now dragg'd along with toil and pain.

Full oft the stripling's arms were rais'd;
        Earnest he begg'd the harp to bear;
Oft too its airy form he prais'd,
        Yet ne'er obtain'd his urgent pray'r.

"No, no," the old man would reply,
"Why should'st thou wish the load to try?
Thy voice no strength of nerve doth speak,
Thy arm feels like a woman's, weak.

"This harp in many a noble hall
        Has spread delight and mirth around;
And many a castle's moated wall
        Has echoed its melodious sound.

And oft the chieftain's greedy ear
        Has drank its martial sounding lays,
And many a high-born maiden's tear
        Bestow'd on me delicious praise.

But age has damp'd my bosom's fire,
Genius and strength at once expire;
My hand now feebly sweeps the string,
From which no strains of rapture spring:

Yet still to memory 'twill impart,
        When 'midst its chords my fingers move,
Events recorded on my heart
        When I was young and sang of love.

Oh! days of bliss for ever fled,
Near eighty winters snow my head,
Nor morn nor evening bless my sight,
I wander now in rayless night.

My eyes no more with raptur'd gaze
        Behold creation's lovely form,
Mark with delight the noontide blaze,
        Or midnight's desolating storm.

Yet time has been my voice could charm;
Once vig'rous was my flexile arm;
And I with grace my hand could fling,
Waking to melting sounds the string.

And in the days of youth, now fled,
        The power of beauty too I felt,
Though now my wonted fires are fled,
        My soul has known with love to melt.

My proudest song was beauty's praise,
        Still pour'd at Love's almighty shrine;
But gone, for ever gone the days
        When this warm heart, O Love, was thine,

Return again in dreams of joy,
 Hours of my youth, around me roll;
Oh! once again in bliss employ
 The chill'd sensations of my soul.

Revive again this faded frame,
Give to my breast thy fiercest flame;
Lend to my long and dreary night
One glowing vision of delight.

In vain I ask; yet Love's dear theme,
 From which my strains shall ne'er depart,
Gilds with a soft and tender gleam
 The fibres of my wither'd heart.

And while my touch can wake a note,
Love ever o'er my harp shall float.
Still thrilling from my wasted veins
Shall trembling start the cherish'd strains.

Decrepit now, and dark, and weak,
 Winter's rough tempests round me rave;
A few short days, and I shall seek
 The quiet refuge of the grave.

Boy, why that sob? – Youth still is thine,
Hope bids thy future prospects shine;
Fortune on thee may blessings pour,
When Hoel's harp resounds no more."

And now they stop, intent to find
Some cottage taper glimmering near,
Or hope, in pauses of the wind,
The village watch-dog's bark to hear.

Now driv'n across the morbid sky,
The fleeting clouds divided fly;
The misty moon with sickly gleam
Sheds o'er their path a wat'ry beam;

And now, faint streaming o'er a rill,
A distant light the stripling spies;
Soon, safely shelter'd by a hill,
A cottage met his anxious eyes.

And soon within the wish'd retreat
The weary harper found a seat;
And soon was spread the homely board
With best the cottage could afford.

And hearty welcome banish'd care
As brisk the foaming cwrw past;
The aged harper prais'd his fare,
And all his griefs behind him cast.

But sad and silent sat the boy,
Unheeding all their social joy;
The starting tear bedew'd his eye,
And his breast heav'd with many a sigh.

"Reach me my harp," old Hoel said,
"The cwrw warms my aged veins;
Not yet my kindling soul is dead,
Not yet expire its jocund strains."

His cheek assumes a crimson glow,
As sweet his tuneful numbers flow;
Bright as he swept the sounding wire,
His features beam'd with youthful fire;

PRAISE OF CWRW

O'er many a desert wild and bare,
The drooping son of want and care,
If faint the way-worn pilgrim stray
From dewy morn to closing day;
Oh! when his cheek with toil is pale,
When his exhausted spirits fail,
Bring, bring the nut-brown beverage near,
With cwrw then his sunk heart cheer.

If lost in woe the lover sighs,
If sleep forsake his weary eyes,
If hopeless still his pulses beat,
If his breast burn with feverish heat;
Oh! bid him drink, and growing wise,
Love's pointless arrows he'll despise:
Bring, bring the foaming beverage near,
With cwrw the forlorn one cheer.

The soldier who from battle bore
The foe's dread standard steep'd in gore,
Whose body, seam'd with many a scar,
Declares how he sustain'd the war;
When sad he thinks of kindred slain,
Whose limbs have strew'd the hostile plain,
To him the nut-brown beverage bear,
With cwrw his sank spirit cheer,

Bright cwrw from thy stream of old,
Cambria's sons grew stout and bold;
And even I, whose functions fail,
Whose hand is weak, whose cheek is pale.
Thou giv'st this feeble frame of mine
A lingering spark of fire divine:
Place, place the sparkling beverage near;
With cwrw still my spirits cheer.

He ceas'd; enamor'd of the sound:
        They praise his song, applaud his skill;
And still the rustics shouting round
        The foaming cwrw brimming fill.

The boy alone retir'd and sad,
Express'd no mirth while all were glad;
Regardless of the tuneful strain,
He heard alone the pelting rain;
And listen'd to the stormy blast,
And thought of home and pleasures past,
While many a lost joy through his mind,
Shot swifter than the eddying wind.

And now a horn was shrilly blown,
The cottage door wide open thrown,
Two strangers came of courtly form,
To ask a shelter from the storm.

The first a young and graceful knight,
    With checks like summer roses red,
Whose locks of richest chestnut bright,
    Cluster'd in curls around his head.

Tall and erect his stately mien,
Studded with gems his vest of green;
But brighter than the diamond's blaze,
His hazel eyes translucent rays.

The other knight a soldier seem'd,
All bright his shining falchion gleam'd;
And as he firmly march'd along,
His port claim'd homage from the throng.

The blazing hearth, the cwrw's power,
    Gave to the strangers welcome rest;
For they had long endur'd the shower,
    Been by the midnight storm oppress'd.

And soon the harp engag'd each eye:
The young knight's fingers o'er it fly;
But not a tone could he command
To equal Howel's matchless hand.

"Give me the harp," the master cried,
"For me it speaks, by me 'twas strung;"
His bosom swell'd with conscious pride,
As o'er its quiv'ring strings he hung.

And soon with inspiration fill'd,
As bolder thoughts his bosom thrill'd,
The swelling note from soft and low,
Burst forth in proud and lofty flow.

THE SOLDIER

When angry gleams the sanguine star,
And fiercely burns the rage of war;
When loud and shrill the trumpets sound,
Prepar'd the valiant soldier's found.
His straining nerves feel tenfold might,
As rushing on he joins the fight;
Now engag'd in hottest battle,
Hark the thundering cannons rattle.
Trumpets, drums, together sounding,
Clang and din of arms resounding.

And thus he thinks – dear friends at home,
As o'er the bloody field I roam,
Put up a prayer, if doom'd to death,
With glory I may yield my breath.
If thus I fall, oh happy state,
May valorous friends avenge my fate;
And higher bliss upon my bier,

My grateful country drop a tear.
No fear his dauntless bosom knows,
But for the battle throbs and glows;
Routed foes disorder'd flying,
Trampling o'er the dead and dying;
All his soul with ardour burning,
Ev'ry thought of danger spurning.
The soldier then with martial pride,
Hews down ranks from side to side;
Groans and shouts, and shrieks arise,
Conquest! conquest! rends the skies.
Valour's rays around him streaming,
Glory o'er him brightly beaming,
Laurel wreaths his brows entwining,
Spoils and trophies round him shining.
Then he rears the standard high,
Weeping o'er his victory;
Bids Fame her clarion sound,
        To the listening world proclaim,
Throughout all its ample bound,
        Britain's great unrivall'd name;
Then let humanity celestial glow,
Shewing soft mercy to the vanquish'd foe.

The ardent soldier caught his hand,
        And warmly prais'd his matchless power;
"Oh, thou that thus can'st sound command,
        Why dost thou wander friendless, poor?
Can Genius nowhere find a home,
That sightless, old, thou'rt doom'd to roam;
Blest should I be thy strains to hear,

If I thy wasting lamp could cheer;
But robb'd of all, save noble birth,
The hostile sword must carve my bread,
Midst noisy camps on damp cold earth,
Compell'd to seek a flinty bed."

"Well hast thou sung," the other said,
"And given to glory ample praise;
Come now, by softer passions sway'd,
To love awake thy tuneful lays.

Bid from thy harp love's humid sighs
In sweet pathetic notes complain;
Yes, bid some mournful ditty rise,
That tells of love's disastrous reign.

"Oh, once my harp in tender strains
Could sing of love's ecstatic pains;
But lost," said Hoel, "is the hour,
When my heart's throbs confess'd his power,
But yet the theme delights my soul;
Once more the worshipp'd tones I'll try;
Still o'er my harp the sounds shall roll,
That swell with love's delicious sigh."

THE ROSE OF COEDHELEN

The flow'r of the summer late blooming and gay,
Now scatter'd and whirl'd in the wandering gale,
It blushes no more, like the dawning of day;
The rose of Coedhelen is wither'd pale.

Divided alas! from the fostering stem,
Where it flourish'd the pride of the vale,
Its lustre is faded, sweet odorous gem,
The rose of Coedhelen is wither'd and pale.

No dew drop of eve shall ere bid it resume
The fresh breathing perfume it us'd to exhale;
The canker worm preys on its beautiful bloom;
The rose of Coedhelen is wither'd and pale.

'Twas love stole the bloom from Gwynida's cheek,
The enchantments of passion prevail;
Betray'd and forsaken, the narrow grove seek,
Where the rose of Coedhelen lies wither'd and pale.

The song had ceas'd, but yet a note
Would lingering still harmonious float;
Sweet plaintive low it seem'd to sigh,
And then in soft vibrations die.

To ev'ry breast the strain was dear,
'Twas form'd the sternest heart to melt;
From ev'ry eye the starting tear,
Declar'd the song was deeply felt.

And ghastly grew the stripling's face;
Tottering he rose to quit the place;
A murmur'd groan a passage found;
Fainting, he sunk upon the ground.

"Raise up the boy, and give him air,"
        The young knight said, and aid bestow'd;
His hat was lost, and down his hair
        In mazy ringlets loosely flow'd.

And pale the young knight's cheeks became,
His eyes with wildest passion flame,
As nearer to the boy he drew,
As features once belov'd he knew.

And now the snowy breast display'd,
The female wanderer betray'd;
As to his face she rais'd her eyes,
As Tudor's name escap'd in sighs.

"For this alone did I implore,
        I only pray'd to see thy face,
My bosom's pangs will soon be o'er,
        I shall not long survive disgrace.

My days of happiness are past,
I'm scatter'd in misfortunes blast;
Wandering I seek some distant shore,
Coedhelen views its rose no more.

Yet Tudor by the love you vow'd,
When swift the hours of transport flew
When I, of vaunted beauty proud,
Too fondly gave those charms to you.

Ah, when the heart shall cease to beat,
Convey me to my native seat;
My parents then may cease to blame,
May weep my fate, forget my shame.

Though now bereft of all my charms,
Victim of love I sink to death;
Yet, Tudor, fold me in thine arms,
And catch Gwynida's parting breath.

Dying for him I love too well,
To silly maids my fate make known;
But at the weeping marble tell,
This breaking heart was thine alone."

"Live, live Gwynida, live for bliss,
Thy Tudor swears, by this chaste kiss,
Tomorrow's sun if he has life,
Shall hail Coedhelen's rose a wife,

Llanbeblig's towers and ancient walls
Shall hear the harper's jocund song,
And thou within its sumptuous halls
Shall strive his moments to prolong.

And when at last he yields to death,
Swept by the south wind's gentle breath,
His harp though lost to "notes of flame,"
Shall whisper Hoel's matchless fame,

Rouse, Hoel! rouse the sleeping string,
Of Love and Beauty's triumphs ring;
Awake the notes thou know'st so well,
The thrilling cadence melting swell.

Yes, yes, my harp, thy master's hand,
Thy proudest notes shall now command;
Love breathes upon the dulcet strings,
And o'er my soul his fervour flings.

And hope to Hoel's mental sight,
Dispels misfortune's chilly gloom;
Effusing rays of heavenly light,
To gild his passage to the tomb.

TRIUMPH OF LOVE

Love, to thee the song I raise,
  God of the unerring dart
Thou shalt have my proudest lays,
  Sovereign of the human heart.

Ambition, Glory, Avarice, see,
  Submissive bend the prostrate knee;
Adoring at thy burning shrine,
  All declare thy power divine.

Wing'd with many a tender sigh,
That from breast of ivory stole;
Tipp'd with flame from Beauty's eye,
Love, thy arrows pierce the soul.

Yet to fond idea dear,
Rich in Love's voluptuous tear;
Sweet is Love's ecstatic sigh,
Breath'd in "blissful agony."

Love to thee shall virgins bring,
Trembling at thy awful power,
Offerings of the early spring,
Wreaths of ev'ry odorous flower.

Timid glances, fragrant sighs,
As incense at thy altar rise;
Still their steps will linger there,
Breathing warm the votive prayer,

God of the resistless bow,
Cities, deserts own thy sway,
All thy rapturous blessings know,
All thy potent will obey.

Now when life is near expiring,
Thoughts of former joys inspiring;
Love, as thy Almighty name,
Glows my breast with sacred flame.

Brightly gleaming on my soul,
Visions of the future roll;
Love, for thee I wake the string,
Love, thy triumphs proudly sing.

Dimpled smiles, and young desires,
        Ardent wishes, all are thine;
Hopes and joys, and blissful fires,
        Round thy votaries' hearts entwine.

Tudor, take the lovely treasure,
Thy delights thou can'st not measure;
Coedhelen's rose again shall bloom,
Again exhale its rich perfume.

And many a blossom from the tree
        Shall round thy manly trunk arise;
Love this blessing gives to thee,
        Coedhelen's rose is Tudor's prize.

Thus Hoel's harp in days of yore,
Could thrilling tones of rapture pour;
His genius then, with matchless skill,
Could melt the soul, could rule the will
Could by the charm of tuneful lays,
Compassion, honour, justice raise.

Music and love, oh sounds divine!
        Still sweetly floating murmur near;
When fate demands this heart of mine,
        To my last moments bless mine ear.

When ev'ry other record flies,
Let me with harmony impress'd,
While love awakes my latest sighs,
"Fading in music" sink to rest.

CHAPTER VII

A woman mov'd is like a fountain troubled,
Muddy, ill-seeming, thick, bereft of beauty;
And while it is so, none so dry or thirsty
Will deign to sip, or touch a drop of it.
Shakespeare

What is the world to them,
Its pomp, its pleasure, and its nonsense all,
Who in each other clasp whatever fair,
High fancy forms and lavish hearts can wish.
Thomson

SOME months had now elapsed, and Horatio Delamere, tortured with a concealed and utterly hopeless passion, began seriously to think of tearing himself from the fascinations of Adeline, of flying from the indulgence of the destructive pleasure her society afforded; a pleasure that he every moment found more dangerous to his honour, which, no longer able to combat against the passion that consumed his peace, now unresistingly consigned him to the impetuous and overwhelming power of love. Hitherto he had guarded with watchful vigilance his looks, his words, and actions, while in the presence of Mrs. Mortimer; but the restraint was terrible, and he every hour dreaded lest some unforeseen circumstance should shock his friend with the discovery of his fatal secret. Every night he determined on leaving Dolgelly Castle the following day, but morning still found him irresolute, and unable to resign the bliss of gazing on her; though if he saw her husband touch her hand, or receive from her attention, he suffered all the excruciating pangs, all the hell of jealousy; in vain would reason tell him that Henry Mortimer was worthy of Adeline, beautiful, amiable, and accomplished as she was; that he was her husband, entitled to her tenderness by the most sacred of rights, and that he, loving the wife of his friend, was actually sinning against every precept, moral and divine. After passing a sleepless and agitated night, best part of which he had wandered along the sea shore, listening to the melancholy dashing of the waves, Horatio Delamere, at an early hour of the morning, strolled into a wood, through which serpentine walks had been cut to a gothic temple; a spot which had been particularly admired by Sir Owen Llewellyn, who in an elegant arched recess had placed a fine toned organ; its walls were tastefully decorated with romantic drawings of the surrounding scenery, by the correct and elegant pencil of Mrs. Mortimer, who to this secluded spot was in the habit of bringing her work or a book, and passing a portion of the morning either in reading, or apostrophising the spirits of her ever-lamented parents, while her child, the little Owen, gambolled with sportive innocence along the winding walks, gaily chased the fluttering butterflies, or gathered the flowers that grew in profusion round the temple. Horatio Delamere had wandered, so lost in uneasy reflection, that he had gained the portico of the temple, without even an intention to visit it. It was now the latter end of autumn; the trees had lost their emerald liveries, part of their boughs waved in naked melancholy grandeur; while others partially, yet "richly dight" in various shades of brown, olive, and yellow, still glittered with the beams of the sun, as it feebly darted through a thick mist: their leaves lay in scattered heaps before him, or were whirled in distant eddies by the hollow gale, that whistled through the bending branches.

"Just so," said he, with a heavy sigh, "just so my happiness is blighted; just so the gay promise of my youth is scattered, the winter of despair freezes the hopes of joy: spring shall return to these woods, they shall bloom again with renovated beauty, but my peace shall revive no more." He took out his pencil and wrote on a marble tablet: –

> Autumn's rich tints, torn by the sickly gale;
> Bids on remembrance joys departed roll,
> When hope around me wav'd her glowing veil,
> When her gay visions floated on my soul.
>
> Now dark misfortunes damp each youthful fire.
> And love, and hope, and friendship all expire.

He now entered the temple, and drawing from his bosom the white rose, which on the night of his arrival the playful Owen had been trying to place in his mother's hair, and which she in compliance with his request had alternately kissed, as he offered that and his own rosy mouth to her lips.

"Here," said he, fervently kissing the flower, "here, safe from prying observation, I may give ease to my burning heart, I may breathe her idolized name, I may whisper – Adeline, I adore you. Happy rose," again kissing it, "thou hast felt her beauteous lips; her balmy breath has touched thee; thus embalmed I will treasure thee for ever: happy emblem of her unspotted innocence, rest in my bosom the only witness of the stifled sighs that murmur Adeline, I adore you."

The astonishment and confusion of Mrs. Mortimer, who at that moment entered the temple, is not to be described, when she beheld in the hand of Horatio Delamere the identical white rose which she remembered to have given the little Owen some months before to play with, and which she had kissed to please the smiling prattler. Mr. Delamere hastily concealed the rose in his bosom, and in evident embarrassment stammered out the compliments of the morning. Mrs. Mortimer's confusion more than equalled his; she would have beckoned the nurse and Owen, but they were no longer in sight: trembling and agitated, she sat down: for a few moments they were both silent, at last Adeline, almost unconscious of what she was requesting, proposed that he should sing, and accompany his voice upon the organ. Never less inclined for music, he seated himself before the instrument, while she rejoiced that she had found an expedient to divert his attention from her; to relieve her from the investigation of his penetrating eyes. Unfortunately a music book was open at the song – "We must not love." He began to play, while Adeline, all ear, listened to the song: –

Why, tyrant love, the hearts enslave
Stern fate forbids to meet,
Why wilder than the ocean's wave,
Bid hapless wishes fleet?
Oh, why bid fancy idle rove,
Where reason says we must not love?

To other bosoms, tyrant, bear
Thy deeply wounding dart,
For what, alas! but sad despair,

Can fill the trembling heart,
When doom'd thy fatal power to prove,
And reason says we must not love.

The notes were in perfect unison with their feelings, soft and tremulous; the words were expressive of their situation. A deep sigh in defiance of her efforts to suppress it burst from the bosom of Adeline, as the last cadence died on the organ: it was a sigh full of agonized feeling; it reached the ear of Horatio; it sunk impressively on his soul; his fingers became motionless on the key of the instrument; the blood retreated from his heart; his face assumed the ashy paleness of death; his eyes closed, and overcome by the perturbation of his senses, he sank back without motion; his head fell on the knees of Adeline, who loudly shrieked for help; no one, however, come to her assistance; at length recollecting their distance from the castle, she applied her smelling bottle to his nose, while her tears plentifully bedewed his face. After a few moments of insensibility, the colour began to mantle on his pale cheek, his languid eyes unclosed; he threw himself at her feet, and snatching her hand, with a frenzied look exclaimed: –

"Why did you not let me die? Too lovely woman, you have destroyed my peace! you have embittered my days! you have devoted my youth to hopeless wishes, to unavailing regrets."

"Alas!" said Adeline, "have I done this: wretch that I am! but if peace is fled from your bosom, oh, Delamere, it inhabits not with the miserable Adeline; if your youth is devoted to wretchedness, mine too is blighted, and only in the grave can I hope to regain happiness."

Surprise had impelled this incautious speech, and with

recollection came the consciousness of impropriety: she started from her seat, her face dyed with a blush of the deepest crimson, and hastily quitting the place, when Delamere gently detaining her, begged her to listen to him one instant.

"I must not, dare not hear you," said the trembling Adeline; "I have already too long, too fatally listened; duty, virtue, every good, every honourable sentiment forbids me – Do not, I beseech you, do not detain me; every moment that I remain is an offence to delicacy, and an injury to Mr. Mortimer."

"Forgive me, loveliest of women," replied Delamere, "and be persuaded that the suffering wretch before you would not for the wide world's wealth offend your purity, nor harbour a thought injurious to the honour of Henry Mortimer. Yet, sure it is not, cannot be criminal to love the fairest of her sex. Oh, frown not, Adeline, loveliest of women, while I confess that I adore you; but it is with an affection pure and holy angels feel. Yes, I solemnly swear, thus tortured, thus hopeless as I am, I have not a wish injurious to Henry Mortimer; he is my honoured, valued friend, worthy even of thee. No, Adeline, worshipped, adored Adeline, I do not ask you, do not wish you to return my passion."

Mrs. Mortimer sunk into a chair and wept bitterly.

"Oh! why," resumed he, "why did not destiny keep us for ever unknown to each other; why did we ever meet, since we have met only to be miserable!"

"Oh! why, indeed," sighed Adeline.

"Forget me," continued he, pressing her cold and trembling hand between both his, "forget the earth contains so miserable a wretch as Horatio Delamere. I will quit this place immediately; in absence I will expiate my unpremeditated, my involuntary guilt; I will go abroad again: on foreign shores I will sigh the name of Adeline. I will pray for her felicity, though my own is lost for ever."

"No," replied Adeline, "say not so, say not for ever. Time, absence will restore you to peace; some other object of happier destiny shall obliterate me from your remembrance, shall receive your vows, shall constitute your happiness."

"Never," said he, emphatically; "my fate is now decided: once, Adeline, once before in the inexperienced effervescence of youth, I fancied that I loved: but oh! how different were my feelings, how unlike my present passion; thou art my fate; thy image is interwoven with my existence, and the last convulsive throb of my heart will be for Adeline; whether I freeze in arctic glooms, or scorch beneath the tropics, thy idea will fill my mind. Adeline, worshipped Adeline! I quit England for ever: it is a sacrifice, however painful, that honour demands. I owe it to myself, my friend, and you." He pressed his lips upon her hand, and rushed from the temple.

Mrs. Mortimer stood for some time without motion or recollection; the impassioned declaration of love that she had just heard from Delamere, the consciousness of her own unhappy passion, all operated so powerfully on her spirits, that she remained many minutes in a state of stupefaction. At length her situation burst upon her mind; her temples throbbed with violence: as pressing her cold hand on her forehead, she exclaimed, "Merciful Heaven! to what have I been listening? Am I a wife, a mother: oh! recollection of anguish – my husband, my child! am I fated to give sorrow to your hearts, to tinge your cheeks with the burning blush of shame." Sinking on her knees, her hands clasped, and her fine eyes streaming with tears, raised to Heaven, she prayed in an agony of passion: "Spirits of my sainted parents, hover round me;

tear this fatal infatuation from my bosom; fortify my weak, my erring heart, with that undeviating virtue that so conspicuously adorned your own pure lives; teach me the duty I owe my husband and my child."

Becoming more composed she rose from her knees, dried her eyes, and seeing the nurse with the child at a short distance, she joined them: the little Owen clinging round her neck said he had made her a nosegay: "But all the nice flowers," continued he, "are withered; nurse says the roses are all dead, mother."

Adeline blushed, as she remembered the white rose she had discovered in the hand of Horatio Delamere. Suppressing a sigh: "The roses," replied she, tenderly kissing Owen, "the roses, my cherub, will bloom again; summer will return, and your favourite flowers will again flourish in fragrance and beauty."

As she spoke, a tear to the remembrance of her peace for ever faded, for ever dead, started in her eye. Owen gambolled before her, as sad and musing she pursued her way to the castle, where perceiving Mr. Mortimer busily writing in the library, she consigned the child to the care of the nurse, and passed on to her dressing room. Sir Griffith Tudor being seized with the gout had sent for Eliza home, a summons not altogether agreeable to her, who declared, that nothing could possibly be more downright spiteful than her father being seized with a fit of the gout just then; "For," continued she, "in a very few days I expect Captain Seymour, and there shall I be confined to Sir Griffith's apartment, employed in warming flannels, shaking up pillows, and trying to soothe his ill-tempers, while it will require all the philosophy I can boast, and Heaven be praised for all its gifts, that is but little, to keep my own from flaming out into rage and impatience, when I know the poor Archibald will be blowing his fingers, and kicking his heels in the cold, and waiting with equal temper and patience to catch a sight of me; but bless me, now I think of it, if he should persuade me to be so undutiful as to run away, and I should be naughty enough to attend to his persuasions, why to be sure Sir Griffith is not in a condition to run after us. Well, well, I find I am much more clever than I suspected, and a moralizer too, for I find I can extract good out of evil."

The gout had seized Sir Griffith in both his feet, the pain of which was not a little augmented by the irritating recollection that his daughter would in a very few days be twenty years of age, at which period she came into possession of a fortune, left to her by a deceased aunt, which would enable her to marry Captain Seymour, without the fear of embarrassing his circumstances; and this reflection it was that had induced him to send for Eliza in such haste from Dolgelly Castle, as he conceived, that having her under his own eye, he should undoubtedly be able, though tied by the legs, to counteract any scheme she might form of eloping, and by marriage free herself from the restrictions of parental authority. In this mode of reasoning Sir Griffith evidently proved that he only argued as he wished: he deceived himself, for so much did all the servants at Tudor Hall love and respect Captain Seymour, that it was their unanimous opinion that he had been shamefully used, and scandalously ill-treated by Sir Griffith; and so much did they pity Miss Tudor, and admire the spirit she had shown, that not one of them would have betrayed the lovers, had they been admitted to their confidence.

The Earl of Clavering, now tolerably recovered, prepared

for quitting Glenwyn Priory, and returning to London; and so sincere a penitent was he become, and so different a turn had his hitherto profligate mind taken, that he rather rejoiced at than lamented the accident that had so deformed his face, and made him a cripple. In the fearful and tremendous minutes when trembling on the verge of eternity he had become thoroughly sensible of the enormities of his former life, and with true humility, with unfeigned gratitude, returned Heaven thanks for having preserved his being, for having allowed him time to make by his future good actions some trifling atonement for his past misdeeds, for waste of years spent in levity, extravagance, and licentiousness. After having made every proper acknowledgment and apology to all by whom he had been obliged, or whom he had offended, he left North Wales, seriously admonishing the gay Sir Edward Percival to profit by his disaster, to be grateful to Providence for the fortune he had so unexpectedly attained, and by a far different course to that he had invariably pursued, evince that the understanding with which he was gifted was not thrown away. Sir Edward yawned, shrugged his shoulders, and looking at his watch, said the enemy had gained an hour upon him, for 'pon his soul he did not think it was so late; he thanked his stars for the release from such tiresome prosing. As the earl, supported by the attentive and affectionate Edwin, ascended his carriage, and as it turned down the avenue of Glenwyn Priory, he surveyed his own figure; and obsequiously bowing before a mirror, he said: –

"To kind Madam Nature for all her gifts I am truly grateful, and am her obliged humble servant. Upon my soul, madam," turning to Mrs. Montgomery, "I have not the smallest doubt but my ci-devant friend, the Right Honourable Earl of

Clavering, will very shortly turn methodist, and appropriate a portion of his vast wealth to the pious purpose of building conventicles, in which he will sanctimoniously hold forth against the sinfulness of the times. Egad, when a man by accident or infirmity, is incapacitated for enjoying the pleasures of this life, why he may as well make a virtue of necessity and have the credit of reformation."

Lady Percival said she was glad the old fright was gone; for it was really disgusting to view his face all over with seams: and it quite tired her to see his limping about with his cork leg.

"I am *perdigiously* amazed," said Mrs. Montgomery, "after all the trouble he has given us, Lucretia, that he had not the politeness to invite us to *Lunnon*, particularly as he knew how much you wish to spend the winter there, and that Sir Edward had let his own house."

"His lordship, madam, perhaps thought as you are a stranger in England, you might be at a loss for a beau to escort you to public places."

"Why dear me," continued Mrs. Montgomery, "could not he have gone about with us himself?"

"His lordship," replied Sir Edward, "would probably feel reluctant to appear in public now his appearance is so considerably altered for the worse. Poor Clavering's person never boasted much to recommend it, but now, upon my soul, I don't understand how he survives under such misfortunes. Consider, madam, the rueful scarifications of his countenance, never very handsome, now hideous; why the poor devil looks as if he had been engaged in a war with the Saracens, not to say a word about his unhappy cork leg, which certainly adds nothing either to the dignity or elegance of his gait."

"Nonsense about his person, and his face, and his gait," replied Mrs. Montgomery, "all that signifies nothing at all, Sir Edward; pray is not he a lord? And the accident he has met with takes nothing at all from the dignity of his title; though your daughter thought proper to choose my son, who, to speak the truth of him, is a *perdigiously* fine handsome young man, and said to be very like me, yet I warrant there are plenty of young women without no *fortins* who would not mind his saracen's head nor his cork leg, so they might be made a countess."

"Very possibly," said Sir Edward, carelessly.

"All I have to say," continued Mrs. Montgomery, "is, that I think it was *perdigiously* uncivil, aye and ungrateful too in him, not to pay me and Lady Percival the compliment of asking us to go to *Lunnon* and spend a few months at his house, after putting us to so much trouble on his account, and making Glenwyn Priory just like an hospital for sick and wounded."

"He thought," said the nabob, who sat silent for a long time, "that you could not leave Wales now Hugh's wife is so near bringing an addition to the family; he thought you would be too much occupied in the pleasure of nursing your grandson, to think of the gaieties of London."

"He was *perdigiously* mistaken then," said Mrs. Montgomery, bridling; "me nurse indeed! no, no, Hugh must get nurses for his children that have more experience than I have; besides, indeed, I think it amazingly odd to be made a grandmother at my age; I declare it is a most *perdigiously* wrong thing of Hugh to have made a grandmother of me already."

Sir Edward Percival picked his teeth, looked through his eye-glass, and seemed as if he had no sort of wish to attend to the conversation passing between the nabob and his lady; but Mrs. Montgomery, displeased herself, determined that he should come in for his share of the vexation, maliciously asked him how he should like to be called grandpapa.

"The very idea," said Sir Edward, "is completely horrifying. Plague on it, this comes of boyish attachments – this is the consequence of marrying young; however, madam, we have yet a chance," continued he, "the brat may die; at all events I shall instruct Mrs. Hugh Montgomery never to let her children address me by any other title than that of Sir Edward Percival."

"And what end will that answer," said her ladyship, "for every body of course will know that they are your grandchildren; and for my own part, Sir Edward, I can't see why you should be averse to the venerable distinction of grandsire, when every living soul that takes the trouble to examine your face may see, without the help of glasses, that you are very far from a young man."

"Not near so far from youth as your ladyship is from good manners," retorted he.

"Lord, Lucretia," said her mother, "I am sure Sir Edward is a most *perdigiously* fine looking man for his time of life."

Sir Edward bit his lip.

"And if it was not for the crow's feet at the corner of his eyes – "

"Crow's feet!" said Sir Edward.

"Yes," continued Mrs. Montgomery, "the crow's feet, or in plain English, since you won't seem to understand, the wrinkles I mean, Sir Edward."

"Wrinkles!" echoed he, in a tone of surprise and vexation; "wrinkles! – really you astonish me; I did not know, madam – I never perceived I had wrinkles in my face."

"None so blind as them that don't wish to see," said Mrs. Montgomery.

"O dear, madam," replied Lady Percival, "he has to the full as much vanity as the youngest of his sex, and I dare say perceives no defects in his own charming person; but when it is remembered, Sir Edward Percival, that you are more than old enough to be my father, that furrow in your forehead, as well as those wrinkles my mother spoke of at the corner of your eyes, may very easily be accounted for. Time is too sincere a remembrancer to be studious of politeness and generally scores age very accurately on the countenance."

"An attempt to blend the witty and severe," said Sir Edward, trying to laugh, though far from pleased with the conversation, as he had always flattered himself with the belief that the youthfulness of his looks hid at least fifteen years of his real age; but Lady Percival, who was well acquainted with his foible, chose to pursue the subject, by saying: – "Every body was astonished at me, with such a fortune marrying a man so many years older than myself, I that might have picked and chose where I pleased, and really I wonder myself how it come about."

The nabob detested disputes; he saw spite in his daughter's countenance, and a frown gathering on Sir Edward's, so leaving them to amuse themselves in their own way, he quitted the room, while Mrs. Montgomery, whose disappointment of a journey to London lay rankling at her heart, endeavoured to blow the coals, by observing: –

"Why, dear me, Lady Percival, you married Sir Edward you know because you was in love with him."

"Pardon me, madam," rejoined Sir Edward, "it was because she was smitten with my title, but having become familiar to her ear, it may probably have lost more than half its charms."

"No, on my honour, you are mistaken there: I still dote on the title," said her ladyship, "and if you had been as tender and affectionate after marriage as you promised, and as I expected, why possibly I might still have been in love with you, Sir Edward, notwithstanding the difference of age; but I find courtship is honey, and matrimony vinegar and gall."

"How often, Lady Percival, am I to remind you of the extreme vulgarity of matrimonial fondness," replied Sir Edward: "a poor miserable mechanic, who labours hard all day to maintain a wife and squalling brats, may return at night, and for want of more refined ideas, or the means of procuring higher gratification, indulge in the plebeian pleasure of caressing them, because fate has placed him in a sphere where other enjoyments are unattainable; but a man of fashion, heaven and earth! he is a creature of another nature, as distinct from this in his disposition and wishes, as he is in appearance; he carefully avoids the disgrace of being said to love his wife."

"And is at no pains to conceal he has low intrigues elsewhere," said Lady Percival, taking him up abruptly; "witness your frequent visits to the woodman's daughter, at the end of Dwynny's lane, Sir Edward."

"Jealous! absolutely jealous, by all that is fascinating," replied Sir Edward, laughing.

"Do not deceive yourself with that flattering idea, I beseech you," retorted her ladyship, "believe me I feel a fashionable indifference as well to your person as your amours; I only supposed that a man of your vaunted taste, who affects to be such a connoisseur in beauty, might have selected a more lovely object for his amusement."

"What do you mean, Lucretia?" asked Mrs. Montgomery.

"Only that Sir Edward's present charmer, madam, is a great fat blowzy red armed wench."

"Variety," said Sir Edward, with provoking indifference, "variety is the charm of life; the girl you speak of is ripe, glowing, and luxuriant: you, child," looking at Lady Percival through his eye-glass, "you are raw and bony, thin as a cane chair, consequently no banquet for a voluptuary; to be sure in a hot summer's day it would be highly advantageous to have you walk before one, for if a breath of air was stirring, your sharp edges would divide it, and one should have two gales instead of one."

"Lord, Sir Edward," rejoined Mrs. Montgomery, "I never heard nobody so amazingly rude before; I am sure Lucretia is a *perdigiously* fashionable figure."

"At Glenwyn Priory, madam," replied he, with a sarcastic smile, "perhaps she may."

"Yes, or anywhere else, sir," said her ladyship, reddening with passion, "and in any other eyes than yours; and far superior to the dirty trollop you visit so frequently."

"I am downright astonished," exclaimed Mrs. Montgomery lifting up her hands and eyes. "Lord bless me, Sir Edward, this can never be true sure: is it possible that you can be so *perdigiously* wicked?"

"It would be the height of unpoliteness to contradict a lady," replied Sir Edward, bowing.

"Yes, madam, he does visit the audacious slut," resumed Lady Percival; "he was seen go in there yesterday morning, though what attraction he can find in the great blowzy, heaven only knows."

"It is that very plenitude, Lady Percival, against which you are exclaiming, that is the alluring charm, for, as a certain gay modern author says, 'I dote on the flesh, though I never was partial to bones.'"

"Well, for my part I never heard nothing to fellow this for ill-manners," observed Mrs. Montgomery; "and if all men of fashion are like you, Sir Edward, I must needs say they are *perdigiously* rude. Why one would have thought that you would have taken the trouble to deny the matter, but here are you as bold as Turpin, and so amazingly confident, that you acknowledge having an intrigue at once, just as if it was something to be proud of."

"Why so it is, madam," rejoined her ladyship: "a man according to Sir Edward's account can make no pretensions to high breeding, unless he sets decency at defiance, and is only accounted fashionable according to the magnitude of his vices, and the assurance with which he defends them."

"Bravo!" said Sir Edward; "upon my soul that had point; you really have some talent for the satirical, but you are crowning me with a wreath that I have not deserved; I have merely said that the girl Lady Percival alludes to is plump, has the rosy glow of health, and is in many particulars a desirable object, but I did not confess that I either had, or intended, to make her other than I believe she is at present, honest, ignorant, and industrious." – Her ladyship smiled incredulously. "When your ladyship is better acquainted with my character," continued he, "you will know that I am too indolent to commence seducer. Oh, lord no," yawning, "one need not be at any kind of trouble in these affairs, when there are so many kind creatures who are willing to spare one the fatigue of solicitation. At present, child," addressing his wife, "I have no *affaire de cœur*, I assure you on my word of honour, but have a care that you don't if you continue prying and jealous find out some real cause for complaint."

"Complain," replied her ladyship scornfully, "no, sir, I have too much pride for that; the loss of your person would be a matter of perfect indifference, I assure you; but don't imagine I should be so destitute of spirit, as to sit down tamely and contentedly under injuries; no, no, revenge is sweet; retaliation, Sir Edward, retaliation, do you understand the value of that word?"

"Dear me, Lucretia, child, don't talk in this odd fashion," said her mother; "only consider what a *perdigious* scandal and disgrace you would bring upon the family."

"And what a large sum of money you would put into my pocket," rejoined Sir Edward gaily; "you would be too good, too kind, too generous, by such a conduct, for you would not only free me from the burthen of a wife, but enable me to sue for such damages as would authorize me to keep a mistress in the first style of fashionable expense."

Mrs. Montgomery hoped that he would never drive her dear Lucretia to take such a *perdigiously* wicked step. "What would Hugh say?"

"Hugh say!" retorted her ladyship contemptuously: "what Hugh might please to say on such an occasion would weigh very little in the scale of my intentions."

"But dear me, Lady Percival, what would all the world think and say?" asked her mother.

"The world, madam," replied Sir Edward, "would think that her ladyship was not gifted with more virtue than many of the rest of her sex. The world would very easily reconcile itself to so common an event, it would furnish a few impertinent paragraphs for the public prints, a few whispering conversations for the idlers and loungers of fashion, among whom those who call themselves my friends would affect concern for my dishonour; it would afford scandalous debates for the tea tables of malicious disappointed old maids, and antiquated dowagers, who having had the supreme good fortune never to be found out, pass for chaste and virtuous, and in a short time the *faux pas* of Lady Percival would give way to something of a newer date."

"Well," said Mrs. Montgomery, "I never heard nobody settle things with so much ease in my life; why you speak of such a terrible affair, Sir Edward, with as much carelessness as if it was a matter of no kind of consequence; why should not you be amazingly hurt, *perdigiously* shocked if such a scandalous business was to happen?"

"I should most certainly do all in my power, madam, to bear my misfortune with Christian patience," replied he, "and happily I should have many brothers in adversity to keep me in countenance: and now I recollect, I have a distant relation, a learned limb of the law, who has made himself very conspicuous in setting forth in a most pathetic style the injuries of the forsaken husband in crim con cases, and no doubt on such an occasion he would exert all his oratorical powers to procure me thumping damages; and when I weighed my gain against my loss, I think my philosophy would not have much difficulty in resigning me to my disgrace."

"What then," asked Lady Percival, "you would not fight a duel on the occasion?"

"A duel!" echoed Sir Edward, "no, upon my soul I would not; I have far too great a relish for life, to place it in any kind of hazard for the sake of a woman who could be capable of shewing so little respect for herself. It is not uncustomary to hear of challenges being given and accepted in cases of dogs and mistresses, but never in any affairs relative to wives; oh, no, that would be antediluvian indeed; that would be a solecism that a man of fashion could never hope to have overlooked or be forgiven."

Such and similar scenes were every day acted between Sir Edward Percival and his lady, who hoped by continual disputes and ill temper to oblige him to carry her to London; but here she was doomed to meet disappointment, for the prophecy of Gabriel Jenkins was rapidly fulfilling: from being wantonly improvident and extravagant, even to profuseness, Sir Edward was falling with miserly habits, growing penurious, and felt pleasure in hoarding money; and her ladyship had soon the added mortification of seeing her daily expenses curtailed, of being called to strict account, as to the how, and in what, she continued to expend the small sums he at long intervals gave her with a niggardly hand. Quarrels and discontent filled Rhydderdwyn Mansion-house. Lady Percival with a high spirit, and in high tones, protested against her husband's meanness and barbarity, while he with inflexible indifference listened to her remonstrances; but so far from altering his plan of parsimony, seldom let a week pass without retrenching something at his own table, which he denominated either useless or superfluous, or curtailing the kitchen of some of its immunities. Lady Percival, in whose ears her mother often sounded "Oh, that you had been so *perdigiously fortinit* as to listen to Hugh's advice, when he told you that to marry in haste was to repent at leisure," now secretly wished that she had been more attentive to her brother's admonition; for thwarted by Sir Edward in all her wishes, and opposed in all her opinions, besides being treated with the most fashionable negligence, she found that she had purchased her title at too high a rate, the expense of nearly one hundred thousand pounds and her happiness. As Lady Percival, she expected to have been uncontrolled mistress of her own actions, and on the contrary she found herself infinitely more restricted than when Miss Montgomery: her temper, naturally imperious and spiteful, had lost nothing of its original violence from the weak indulgence of her mother, and the early knowledge that a large fortune had been left her, of which she was to have the entire disposal at the early age of eighteen. The constitutional indolence of the nabob, averse to all kinds of exertion, except that of pushing the bottle about, had consigned his daughter entirely to the management of his wife, who, totally uneducated herself, and unfortunately rather weak in intellect, supposed that wealth was an equivalent for higher attainments, and while she saw her daughter flattered by mercenary dependants, and crouching menials, ignorantly believed that her darling Lucretia was a model of elegance and beauty. Having by sullenness, tears, or violence, invariably subjugated her mother's inclinations to her own, and equally ruled the domestics, her ladyship supposed that a husband was to be managed after the same methods; but here she was fated to meet a disappointment, mortifying as it was unexpected: not all her virulence could provoke Sir Edward from the calm easy indifference under which he entrenched himself, never for a moment suffering passion to overcome his politeness, or shake his resolutions, which having once formed, the united remonstrances of mother and daughter had no power to alter in the slightest degree.

Lady Percival beheld the serene happiness of her brother and his gentle amiable Rosa with the malignant and jaundiced eye of envy; her being likely also to give an heir to Sir Edward's title and estates not a little increased her vexation and discontent, particularly as there appeared no likelihood of herself having a child, she having in a moment of anger separated herself from his bed, to which he had never invited her return, and to which her pride determined her never to discover an inclination. After every visit to Birch Park her ill temper and discontent augmented, till at last disputes ran so high between her ladyship and Sir Edward, and gained so irreconcilable a pitch, that she declared to her mother she could no longer endure the ill usage of Sir Edward, who had curtailed her of numerous indulgences, all of which she detailed with exaggerations suitable to her purpose, and the weak understanding to which they were addressed; and these charges against her husband concluded with his having meanly and tyrannically threatened to put down her carriage, as one would do very well for both. Her mother would have mediated between them, but this Lady Percival would neither hear of or allow, violently protesting that she would reside under the same roof with such a barbarian no longer. The nabob was roused into oratory on this momentous occasion, and made a long speech to prove the impropriety of a woman flying from a husband's protection, and quitting his house, to which it was entirely at his option whether she should ever return. With all the energy he could exert, he opposed the intention of his daughter separating from Sir Edward, a measure he considered disgraceful and impolitic: he would have sent for his son, to endeavour at bringing about an accommodation between the contending parties, or if he failed in this, to prevail on Sir Edward Percival to make some settlement on his wife, of the folly of whose marriage without such a provision he was now thoroughly sensible, and most severely censured himself for not having, according to the advice of his son, resolutely opposed. Lady Percival obstinately refused the interposition of her brother, for judging by the malignancy of her own heart, she supposed he would rejoice at the accomplishment of his predictions; and the tears and representations of Mrs. Montgomery, which he was too imbecile to resist, soon wrung from the nabob a reluctant consent to his daughter's returning to reside at Glenwyn Priory. Early the following morning Mrs. Montgomery entered the breakfast parlour at Rhydderdwyn Mansion-house, and without much ceremony informed her ladyship she was come to fetch her to that home where she had never known contradiction or opposition to her wishes. Sir Edward smiled contemptuously, but continued sipping his coffee with his usual careless indifference, while Mrs. Montgomery, in no very gentle terms, upbraided him with his shocking ill usage of her darling Lucretia, whose bed he had quitted, she supposed to share his own with some trumpery abandoned slut. Sir Edward laughed, but made no answer to this charge, false as it was indelicate; while Mrs. Montgomery continued to enumerate all his omissions and remissions, which she concluded with saying his barbarous treatment had ruined the health, and nearly broke the heart of her poor dear child. Sir Edward merely replied, "Women they say have tender hearts; he must strain hard that breaks them."

"Aye," said Mrs. Montgomery, "that is what hump-backed Othello says in the play. Other folks have read a little too, and have perhaps to the full as good a memory as you have, Sir Edward, with all your sneers."

"Oh! no doubt, madam," said the baronet, pouring cream into his coffee.

"Yes sir," continued Mrs. Montgomery, anxious to shew her

reading, "I recollect perfectly well that the crook-backed Black Prince Othello – "

"Prince!" repeated Sir Edward, "I understood Othello was only a general."

"Well, prince or general, that is of no consequence," said Mrs. Montgomery: "he sees the apparition of his father, and he smothers his mother in her bed with a pillow, and has his *fortin* told by witches, and tears out his nephew's eyes, and poisons his wife, and promises a Jew a pound of his own heart, and ravishes his sister-in-law, and – "

"Mercy on us what a terrible Turk," said Sir Edward, leaning back in his chair convulsed with laughter; while Lady Percival, astonished at her mother's erudition, scalded her fingers while staring at her, and attempting to reach the sugar basin.

"Aye, aye, you may laugh, Sir Edward," said she, with a triumphant toss of her head, "but you see I have not read to no purpose, any more than yourself."

"No one can presume to disbelieve that, madam," replied Sir Edward, "who has the honour to converse with you, and to hear your very accurate association of persons and incidents."

"Very well," said Mrs. Montgomery, taking his speech for a compliment, "I am glad you will allow that however – but I must say, Sir Edward, with all your vast politeness, you have not discovered any very great *speciment* of good manners, to speak in such an indecent way about women, before me and your wife."

"I protest, madam," rejoined Sir Edward.

"Oh, pray don't want to stop my mouth with a sugar plum, Sir Edward, for fine words won't butter no parsnips; and I say again, it was not over polite in you to introduce stuff out of plays at such a time as this, when I come on purpose to say – "

"Pray proceed, madam," said Sir Edward, ringing the bell, and ordering the breakfast things to be removed, "but have the goodness to be as expeditious as you possibly can, for I have an engagement at eleven o'clock," taking out his watch and placing it before him on the table – "the enemy warns me; it only wants twenty minutes."

"Well, I never heard anything so *perdigiously* rude since I was first created," said Mrs. Montgomery, "but you shall not stop my tongue I promise you; I will force you to hear that you ought to be ashamed of yourself after having such an immense *fortin* with your wife, to be so mean and grudging as to want to bring her to account for every guinea she lays out, and almost starving her, because poor dear she has a delicate appetite and can't eat the coarse dishes that are set before her."

"I shall not attempt," replied the baronet, "to confute these absurd charges. Lady Percival is too extravagant to have the uncontrolled possession of money; if I was as little provident as her, we might soon expect to be reduced to a state of absolute poverty."

"I am determined to put up with no more of your prudent restrictions, however," said Lady Percival; "no more of your economical one dish dinners for me. I shall leave you munificent sovereign of this splendid mansion, where, if ever the voice of hospitality was heard, it is buried in the grave of your right noble and illustrious ancestors. I shall return with my mother to Glenwyn Priory, and I beg to know what allowance your generosity will allot me out of the wealth with which I purchased myself a mean avaricious tyrant."

Sir Edward looked at his watch, while Mrs. Montgomery finding he made no reply to her daughter, repeated the question, "Aye, Sir Edward, what allowance do you mean to make my poor dear deluded Lucretia out of her own *fortin*?"

"Not a shilling, madam," replied the baronet rising: "if Lady Percival chooses to expose her character to public animadversion by quitting her own house, and the protection of her husband, she must make up her mind to consequent inconveniences; not a shilling I repeat will I allow; those who abet her in rebellion against her duty, who advise her to such indiscreet procedure, must maintain her in her contumacy and folly."

"O! mighty well, sir; you carry things at present with a high hand," said Lady Percival, "but we shall see – "

"Yes, Lucretia," rejoined Mrs. Montgomery, "I have seen many a tumble out of the saddle into the mud. Sir Edward talks *perdigiously* grand and large: but we shall try if the law won't learn him another guess sort of a lesson. I never knew nothing to fellow such amazing rude behaviour in my life; refuse to maintain his own wife! I think nobody can say nothing in defence of such shabby mean ways: he polite indeed! a hog knows as much of manners; but I shall employ counsel on this business, I shall see –"

"You will see, madam," replied Sir Edward, "that the law will not encourage the subject against her liege lord; but my time is expired," putting up his watch. "I lament that an indispensable engagement prevents my attending any longer to your edifying and elegant conversation. Ladies, I leave my character behind me, and you are welcome to treat it in what way you think proper. I have the honour to wish you a good morning."

He took up his hat, made them a graceful bow and left the room. Lady Percival declared that his apathy made her mad, and nothing provoked her half so much as not being able to put him in a passion. Mrs. Montgomery proposed calling at Birch Park, but to this her ladyship objected, declaring her spirits were too much exhausted, and her mind too much irritated, to listen with any degree of patience to Hugh's long speeches about thoughtlessness and impropriety; and then added she: "The sight of his wife, that poor milk and water thing with her increased size, will only add to my present vexation, to think that my money is gone to redeem and improve estates that her squalling brat will inherit."

The happiness of Hugh Montgomery, who resided at Birch Park in compliance of the wish of Gabriel Jenkins, had no other allay than what the domestic broils of his sister occasioned. In the gentleness and affection of his amiable Rosa he found all the impassioned hopes of his heart realized: mild, tender, and delicate, she seemed to look up to him for that support which his manly appearance promised, and her feminine fragility demanded. Gabriel Jenkins declared that Rosa's marriage had made quite and clean a new man of him: that, gad he never was half so happy in his life as now he was superintending the workmen employed to erect a new wing to the house designed for a nursery; and he whistled Saxoni's hornpipe in a tone of higher glee as he gazed on his niece, now near the time of becoming a mother, and on that account the object of his fondest solicitude.

"Here," said he to the blushing Rosa, as he pointed out the convenience of the building, "here you and I will spend many hours in the day. Gad, I am one of the best nurses in all the world: but, Rosa, let me beg of you not to bring us a muling puling girl. What say you," slapping Hugh on the shoulder, "had not you rather have a sturdy boy?"

Hugh Montgomery, kissing the cheek of Rosa, said it was equal to him which, so his beloved did well.

"You are right," said Gabriel Jenkins, "since you must have what God pleases to send. Girls though are quite and clean troublesome bargains; but gad, if you have a boy, Rosa, why in two or three years I shall be able to teach him to play at marbles, spin a top, and trundle a hoop."

"No doubt," said Miss Jenkins, "no doubt you would soon teach him to turn the house out of the windows, and make him as rude as a bear; now I hope for the sake of peace and quietness that Mrs. Montgomery may have a girl, for I am sure if it should be a boy it will be totally spoilt." –

"And if it should be a girl," replied her brother, "and Rosa is so silly as to let you interfere in its management – "

"No, by my truly," said Dame Wilkins, who happened to be present, "Miss Nanny must have nothing to do with it."

"And why, pray?" asked Miss Jenkins, in no very gentle tone.

"Because," replied the old woman, "old maids are too fretful and peevish to be good nurses." –

Gabriel Jenkins laughed. Miss Jenkins muttered something about impertinence, and turned into the house.

"I wish," said Rosa.

"What, my love?" said Hugh Montgomery, anxiously.

"Aye, Rosa, what do you wish?" said her Uncle, "is it for anything to eat or drink? Gad, only say the word, it shall be had if North Wales produces it."

"That the child," answered Rosa, "may be a boy, because I fear my uncle would not be fond of a girl."

"No fear of that," replied Gabriel Jenkins. "Gad, I loved you, and nursed you long before you could speak: and the first time your little tongue lisped uncle, the sound made me feel quite and clean like a fool, because, Rosa, you had no mother, and as good as no father. Gad, my girl, do not put on that sorrowful look, for your child when it comes into the world will have father, mother, uncles, and aunts; and I promise you I shall love it, quite and clean as much as I do you, whether it is a boy or a girl."

CHAPTER VIII

What is this sentimental love,
This spell of the romantic mind,
Whose flimsy texture fancy wove
Too weak, th' impassioned heart to bind?
Taylor

In the undisturbed solitude of her dressing-room, Mrs. Mortimer remained a considerable time sunk in the very depth of woe. She had convulsively shuddered at what she thought criminal feelings; she had wept the frailty of her heart with bitter tears of shame and compunction. A reflective calm succeeded the tumultuous transports of grief, and her mind, tortured and agitated almost beyond human sufferance, at last yielded itself to the dangerous and seductive sophistry of Platonic love. She caught with avidity at the palliating, though fallacious idea, that her passion for Horatio Delamere was distinct and independent of his person, a person adorned by the partial hand of nature with every attractive grace, and had its origin and rapid progress in the virtues of his mind, a mind the rich repository of every elegant accomplishment, the sacred temple of every perfection.

"Why then," said Adeline, "is my passion criminal, since to love virtue and Horatio Delamere is the same?" Such were the ideas, such the arguments of Mrs. Mortimer, when she received a summons to attend her husband in the library. A sensation of terror, such as she had never before experienced, seized the frame of Adeline, as she rose to follow the servant;

a blush of the deepest dye suffused her cheek; her pulses throbbed even to agony: as she descended the stairs, she dreaded lest Delamere, equally agitated by honour and passion, might in the delirium of the moment have betrayed to Mr. Mortimer a secret she wished to remain unknown, to all the world, but most of all to her husband. Possessed with the fearful idea that some fatal disclosure had been made, she reached the library with unsteady steps and a palpitating heart. Mr. Mortimer was pacing the room with folded arms: his appearance was disordered, his face was flushed, and his manner agitated.

"Adeline," said he, as she entered, "an event so unexpected – " he sunk on a chair, and unable to proceed, gave to the apprehensive imagination of his wife time to conjure up all the terrifying consequences that would attend the discovery of Delamere's passion. Her mind full of the occurrences of the morning, she faintly exclaimed: –

"Oh, God! for what more of wretchedness am I reserved?" Her exclamation recalled her husband to recollection; he flew to her, and tenderly folding his arms about her, entreated her to be composed, to forgive him the alarm he had occasioned her, an alarm which the excessive agitation of his own spirits had prevented his foreseeing and guarding against. Reassured in some measure by the tenderness of her husband, Adeline ventured to ask what event he had alluded to, which had so powerfully affected him.

"Oh, never," said Henry "never let man in the sunny zenith of prosperity proudly suppose himself beyond the power of misfortune; never let him arrogantly boast he is a mark too exalted for misery to reach. Adeline, the mighty are fallen; the haughty Lord Dungarvon waters the earth with tears, mourns in hopeless agonies the deaths of those he haughtily looked up to as the props of his illustrious house; the transmitters of his title and his wealth to posterity. Two months ago the wife of Richard Mortimer expired in giving birth to a dead child; and to complete the catalogue of his woes, last week his idolized son Richard Mortimer, by a fall from his horse in the sight of his distracted parents, fractured his skull. – Lady Dungarvon fell into convulsions, out of which she never recovered, but with her son waits to be laid in the mausoleum of their ancestors. Oh, Adeline! who shall say that the hard of heart are not punished in this life; who shall say that pride meets not retributive mortification." Adeline gasped for breath.

"You then are now the indisputable heir to the proud dignities of Lord Dungarvon," replied Henry Mortimer. "My mother, my sainted mother, now let thy injured spirit be appeased, for thy dying prediction is fulfilled, the abandoned neglected son of the despised Louisa Beresford heaven has ordained the heir of Lord Dungarvon; to him he looks up for consolation; sues to him for pity and forgiveness; humbled by repeated strokes of chastising affliction, writes in terms of pathetic contrition to him he has scorned, and denied affinity with, to come and receive his sighs of penitence, to accept his blessing, and close his eyes. Oh, if I had ever wished revenge – but heaven can witness for me I never prayed even for vengeance for my mother's injuries. What must his haughty spirit have suffered before it could be brought to this humility!"

"You go then to England?" said Adeline.

"Immediately to London," replied Mr. Mortimer. "Lord Dungarvon, from the account of his messenger, is confined to the bed of sickness, perhaps death; in that letter," putting one into her hand, "you will see, my love, how earnestly he desires to see me; he says he cannot leave the world in peace, unless he hears my voice pronounce his pardon. Can I refuse the request of a dying man, and that man my grandfather? By the late melancholy events I am the heir to his title and estates; for your sake, for the sake of our darling boy, it is necessary I go."

"How wondrous," said Adeline, "are the ways of heaven!"

"Wondrous indeed," replied Henry. "How different is the style of this letter to the haughty contemptuous language I last heard from Lord Dungarvon. Why do you weep, my love: if his lordship dies, and from his letter, to which his physician has affixed a few lines, there appears but small hopes of his recovery, my beloved Adeline will be enabled to move in that elevated rank which she is formed to dignify and adorn. Title and splendour will receive new brilliancy from her graces and beauty."

"Let me go with you," said Mrs. Mortimer.

"It is utterly impossible, my love: the speed with which I must travel would be too great a fatigue for you; besides, the house of sickness, nay, perhaps at this moment of death, would only again serve to revive scenes of melancholy, which I would wish you to forget. My friend, Mr. Delamere, will be the protector of my beloved till my return, and I dare say Sir Griffith Tudor, when he is acquainted with the important circumstances that call me to England, will allow Eliza to remain with you. Let a messenger be dispatched to Tudor Hall immediately; her vivacity will support your drooping spirits."

As he spoke, Horatio Delamere entered the library in a travelling dress. "Hey day," said Mr. Mortimer, "accoutred for a journey! where, my dear fellow, are you posting?" "Business of some importance," replied he, "recalls me to Italy; I merely go to Narbeth Lodge, to apprise my parents of my intention, which is to leave England as expeditiously as possible."

"Some love affair, I suppose," said Mr. Mortimer; "but I have no time to bring you to confession."

The varying cheek of Adeline, from the deepest flush of crimson, to the ashy hue of death, evidently told the interest she felt, as he answered with a heavy sigh, "You have guessed alas, too truly."

Mrs. Mortimer turned to the window to hide her emotions, while her husband, who had not heard Mr. Delamere's reply, affecting a gaiety his heart did not acknowledge, said, "Come, come, no demurs against my sovereign will, pleasure, and command; order your horses immediately from the carriage; for the present you must remain a prisoner at Dolgelly Castle, impressed into the service of friendship."

Horatio Delamere, supposing his friend had no particular motive for wishing his stay, would have excused himself, and persisted in setting off instantly, saying that he had hoped to have escaped the painful ceremony of taking leave, when Henry Mortimer, advancing to his wife, took her hand, and bade her tell Horatio that she could not spare him, that he must stay to play with Owen, and that the lovely signora must wait a longer period before she was blest with a sight of his divine person.

Adeline, confused and trembling, saw the dark, penetrating eye of Horatio seek hers, as if to read her wishes: hers fell beneath the scrutinizing glance.

"My Adeline," continued Mr. Mortimer, "is too much agitated to repeat my request, but I am convinced she desires your stay as much as I do. Here," added he, tossing the letter he had just received from Lord Dungarvon over to his friend, "read that, and you will perceive the necessity of my departing immediately for England; and surely you will not think of leaving Mrs. Mortimer without a protector in my absence; and with whom," affectionately pressing his hand, "with whom could I so securely confide this treasure of my soul as with thee, the approved of my reason, on whose honour and friendship I can confidently rely to cheer her spirits, and divert the melancholy hours till my return."

Adeline would have objected to Delamere's remaining; she had a secret foreboding of evil, but she feared to oppose her husband's wish, without giving a reason for her conduct; and to do that she found impossible.

"Besides," resumed Henry, "Mrs. Mortimer will send for her friend Eliza Tudor; she like an enchantress will enliven the scene, and with the spell of sprightliness charm you to forget the languishing beauties of Italy."

"Dispose of me, dear Henry, as you please," replied Delamere: "if my remaining will in the least contribute to your content, or Mrs. Mortimer's security, I resign my own intention with pleasure."

Mr. Mortimer warmly thanked him, while Horatio added, "Rely on my friendship and attention to Mrs. Mortimer."

"I thank you from my soul," said Henry Mortimer: "I know your honour, and in confiding my Adeline to your care, I depart with a mind lightened of half its sorrow."

His chaise was now at the door; he shook Delamere's hand, kissed his little Owen again and again, and folded the weeping Adeline with passionate fondness to his heart; bade her be careful of her health, tenderly chid her tears, while the big drops started in his own eyes: ashamed of his weakness, he tried to smile, to speak cheerily.

"Farewell, my love," said he, "expect to hear from me the moment I arrive in London; remember I exist but for you and our little darling." Again he kissed the tears from her cheek, again he pressed her to his heart, while Delamere stood a statue of woe, almost unconscious of the passing scene, till roused to recollection by Henry's repeated charges to keep up the spirits of his wife.

"Horatio, my friend, comfort this worshipped of my soul," said he. "Adeline, if you love me, be careful of yourself."

He sprang into the chaise, which in a few moments whirled him out of sight. The moist eyes of Mrs. Mortimer followed the chaise, till the intervening woods shut it from her sight. Turning from the window, she beheld Delamere with a countenance pale as monumental marble, but her head and heart were too full of recent events to enter into conversation on any subject; and dreading a repetition of the temple scene, she hastily left the library, faltering out as she passed him, "We shall meet at dinner."

She flew to indulge alone and unobserved the mournful luxury of shedding tears, a luxury unknown to beings who have never felt the misery of disappointed passion, that have agonized with hopeless love. Delamere stood the personification of despair; his looks were wild, and his thoughts delirious: it was some time before reason pointed out the propriety of ordering his horses again to the stable.

Mrs. Mortimer's delicacy soon suggested to her the awkwardness, as well as danger of being without a female companion, she therefore exerted herself to write to Eliza Tudor, to whom she gave a circumstantial account of the important change likely to take place in Mr. Mortimer's affairs, and entreated her immediate company at Dolgelly Castle, where her lonely situation demanded the society and consolations of friendship. Having sealed her letter, she instantly dispatched a messenger to Tudor Hall, and then hastened to make some trifling reform in her dress; while occupied at her toilet, the dinner bell rung, and again put her weakened spirits into flurries, again caused her blood to rush with painful rapidity through its channels, for at table she must meet, and alone, Horatio Delamere, the adored, yet dreaded Horatio Delamere; the Platonic system, according to the calm, temperate wishes – of which, a few hours before she thought she had regulated her passion, of the innocency of which she had endeavoured to convince herself, seemed at that moment to dissolve before the fascination of his form, the seductive enchantments of his conversation; and the second bell hurried her to the dining parlour, in a state of agitation equal to his, who languished for, yet also feared her presence, who trembled lest her transcendent beauty, the soft tones of her mellifluous voice, should seduce his mind from honour, should render him a traitor to his friend.

Their conversation turned on the absence of Mr. Mortimer, and the haughty inflexible character of Lord Dungarvon, now so humbled; and the little chance of his surviving, to prove how worthy of his fondest love, how calculated to add lustre to his honour, and dignity to his rank, that grandson was, whom he had so unfeelingly neglected, and only noticed now, when heaven to punish his arrogance and hardness of heart had deprived him of those whom he, with overweening pride, had believed were to inherit his title and his wealth.

"Heaven," said Horatio, "suffers man, inflated with his own ideal consequence, to exercise for a time his fancied superiority over those beneath him, a little rule, a little sway; to form schemes of proud futurity, never to be accomplished, for at these eternal justice mocks, and in the triumphant hour of security arrogates to itself the power of terrible retribution, of crumbing to dust the lofty fabrics of ambition, and proving on the heart of him, who never felt for other's woe, that he alike is vulnerable to adversity with the meanest of his fellows. Of this the haughty Lord Dungarvon is a living proof: how inhuman, how relentless was his conduct to the parents of my friend, how despicable his behaviour to Henry himself; but he is now so humbled, that humanity forgives his vices, while it weeps their punishment."

The return of the servant from Tudor Hall interrupted the conversation; he brought a reply from Lady Tudor, congratulatory on Mr. Mortimer's prospects, and promising that Eliza should be at Dolgelly Castle on the following morning, being then absent with her father on an airing, he being something better. The evening set in dark and tempestuous. Confined to the house, Adeline attempted to divert her thoughts by joining in the little sports of Owen, who often increased her confusion by addressing Mr. Delamere with the tender appellation of father. Often too her thoughts reverted to her husband; she considered the brilliant change likely to take place, and sickened at the sad conviction of the inability of grandeur to insure or purchase happiness. The hours wore away in reserve and melancholy on both sides, for it was equally as impracticable for Horatio to be entertaining, as it was impossible for Adeline to be entertained: on other evenings when they separated Horatio had been accustomed to kiss Mrs. Mortimer's hand, but she departed without extending it, with only a cold formal good night. Horatio retired immediately to his chamber, murmuring at being denied the pleasure of touching her hand.

"She hates me," said he, as his head leaned against the wall, "she fears the touch of my lips will contaminate her."

He listened till the profound stillness told him the domestics were safe in their apartments; he then stole down a back staircase, and gaining the lawn, stood for some time with his eyes intent on Mrs. Mortimer's window: the light still burned in her apartment. The curtains were of thin muslin; but though closely drawn, he could plainly discern the shadow of some person pass and re-pass, as if walking with a quick step.

"Adeline," whispered he; "Adeline sleeps not; she wakes to think of her happy husband, to pray for his safety, to regret his absence. Wretch that I am! and dare I repine at this? dare I envy him the possession of her heart – a treasure only he is worthy of?"

Again he stood buried in reflection. The rain fell in heavy sheets, and a sudden gust of wind carried his hat to a distance beyond his ability or will to regain it: unheedful of this circumstance, he continued to watch the passing shadow of Adeline, till he saw her white hand unclose the curtain; in the next instant she threw up the window, and looking out, said: –

"What a dreary night! – heaven preserve my husband!"

The wind rushing through the open window extinguished her taper, and Adeline, as she looked through the thick gloom, which almost precluded view of exterior objects, fancied she saw the figure of a man; starting with alarm, she suddenly closed the window and retired to bed – not to sleep, but to revolve the strange circumstance of a man under her window, and in such a night. Strange to her no doubt it was, but not to Delamere, who, "used to bide the pelting of the pityless storm," night after night wandered beneath her window, when every eye except his own was visited by the sweet pressure of repose; and every heart except his found in refreshing sleep an oblivion of care. Fearful that he had been seen, and that Adeline, mistaking him for a robber, might alarm the servants, he flew to the shelter of the woods, that now, nearly stripped of their leaves, groaned as the boisterous wind rudely rushed amid their quivering branches; as the rain poured on his uncovered head, he found that when the mind's free the body's delicate.

"Oh!" exclaimed Horatio, "the tempest in my mind doth from my senses take all feeling else save what beats there. Pour on, I will endure."

Horatio listened to the hoarse blast as it rushed impetuously along, till his heated imagination was wrought to believe, 'thick thronging fancies,' that he heard in the rustling of the agitated branches, prophetic whispers of his own approaching dissolution.

"For what," said he, stretching himself along the wet earth, his head resting on the fantastic root of an old withered elm; "what have I to do with life, denied its joys, cut off from its enjoyments? – All evil constellations joined their malignant influences at my birth – I was from the first decreed for misery. Love, the origin of blessings, the rich source of joy to other bosoms, only inflames mine to curse me. Celestina, thou didst pray that at the still midnight hour our tears might fall together; perhaps at this moment thy eyes – . Oh! not for me, I trust thou dost not weep for me; thy image, once thought peerless, fades before a brighter form. Oh! may thy prayers ascend to heaven, unsullied with a thought of me. Another, Celestina, sways the heart no longer thine; may peace with angel wings shadow thy bosom, and obliterate every trace of him who prays to be forgotten. Henry Mortimer, avenge my treachery; I, the approved of thy reason, the distinguished companion of thy youth, I adore thy wife. Honour, friendship; futile are your admonitions, unavailing your opposition against the gigantic power of love – that way madness lies. Oh! that the rain which pours upon my head could quench the fever of my brain. Oh! that the winds that chill my shuddering frame, could sweep away upon their stormy wings remembrance of my tortures, destroy the fatal record that I am doomed never to love but where irrevocable vows have bound the object of my wishes to another."

This was the first night since her marriage that Mrs. Mortimer had passed alone – it was a night of horror. In vain she endeavoured to banish the idea of Delamere: if for a moment her wearied senses sank into slumber, fancy immediately united her to him; but as her arms expanded to embrace him, she would find she enfolded the pale lifeless corpse of Henry Mortimer. From these dreams of terror she would start in agony, and, afraid to close her eyes, exclaim: –

"Oh, heaven! can I not tear from my bosom this guilty, this disgraceful passion? Henry, dear injured Henry, thou art the best of men, and I the most criminal, the most ungrateful of women: this fatal flame preys upon my health; I feel I am going to the grave: forget me, Henry, forget the wretched Adeline; seek some other worthier object, who, feeling for thee a reciprocal tenderness, may reward thy truth and goodness."

In such exclamations the long hours of night rolled cheerlessly away. With the first dawn of light Adeline arose, and throwing on a loose wrapper, descended to the library, to seek that volume from which on the day of her marriage she had selected a passage from whence she had then drawn comfort, but alas! now appeared to have been written as the particular description of her feelings. With trembling fingers she turned over the leaves till she came to the page herself had folded down: – When imperious love takes possession of the heart, all its gaiety departs, to nights of calm repose, and dreams of happiness, succeed visions of terror and despair: the bosom, once the mansion of peace and tranquillity, is tortured with an agonizing train of doubts, fears, and jealousies: restless and dissatisfied, the mind busies itself with hopes that can never be realized, or in conjuring up misfortunes it may never encounter. Time ever passes too swift or too slow, the meridian sun is dark and gloomy as the noon of night in the absence of the adored one.

"Too fatally," said Adeline, as the book fell from her nerveless fingers, "too fatally do I experience the truth of what I once thought chimerical, of what I once considered the effervescence of a wild imagination."

At that moment footsteps in the hall disturbed her; she caught up the volume, and hastened again to her chamber, but too much disturbed to read; her eye only rested on the title page. All that her understanding could take in, was, "Fatal obedience," "Fatal indeed," sighed Adeline, as her cold hands, pressed on her bosom, seemed to wish to suppress its tumultuous throbbings. "Gracious Heaven! thou who in the fibres of our hearts amongst its nicest chords hast wove these passions, teach us, in mercy teach us to subdue them."

Lonely, weeping and dejected, Mrs. Mortimer passed the hours till breakfast in her dressing room, and when she descended to the parlour, she found Mr. Delamere already there, his fine eyes sunk and heavy, and his whole appearance denoting that he had passed the night in a state of inquietude equal to her own. The first salutations were scarcely over, before a messenger arrived from Tudor Hall, with the intelligence that Miss Tudor had the preceding night eloped with Captain Seymour, and that the family were all in the utmost confusion; that Sir Griffith in spite of the gout was gone in pursuit of his daughter, swearing that if she did marry Captain Seymour that he would never forgive her, and that Lady Tudor, after being for a long time in fits, was at last gone to bed, so ill that a physician was sent for from Carnarvon, and that Tudor Hall was the seat of uproar and disturbance.

"Fortunate Eliza," said Mrs. Mortimer, as the servant left the room, "thou wilt now be united to the man of thy choice, and the exertion of that very spirit which I have so often condemned, will be the means of securing thy future happiness. Captain Seymour was once received and favoured by the family as Miss Tudor's lover, but some difference of opinion arising between him and the baronet respecting his continuing in the army, a measure Eliza warmly approved, Sir Griffith, in a paroxysm of rage, not only forbade him his house, but also forbade him to think of his daughter, who he swore should never be the wife of a soldier. In vain have the friends on both sides endeavoured to effect a reconciliation: Sir Griffith has remained inflexible. I knew Eliza expected Captain Seymour, but she concealed from me her intended elopement; and since she has taken this step, I trust they will outstrip Sir Griffith, whose rage, should they be overtaken, will I know be ungovernable."

"May they be happy!" said Delamere in a tone of fervour. – "Amen!" responded Adeline. Again they were silent, and Adeline was seeking a pretence to quit the room, when Horatio, after a pause of some moments, in which he appeared to labour for utterance, broke the silence by saying, "I have been thinking that matrimony must be a state of most exquisite felicity where the parties whose fates are linked together love each other, but when there is no union of soul it must be misery in the extreme."

"Misery indeed!" echoed Adeline, not considering what she said. The eyes of Horatio Delamere were in a moment fixed on her face, the variations of which explained too evidently that her unguarded exclamation was the true expression of tortured feelings.

"Oh God!" continued Delamere, "what state can equal theirs whom happy destiny unites in the soft bond of reciprocal love. In a lone cottage on a bleak mountain's side a more than paradise would be theirs: obliged even to labour for subsistence, the homely board would be decked with epicurean luxuries, for love would preside at it: the clear beverage drawn from the running stream would be delicious as the nectarean bowl, for love would sweeten it: the hours allotted to rest how delicious, for the frame fatigued with toil would be entwined in the embrace of affection, and the wearied would repose on the bosom of love."

"Oh! had heaven been pleased so to dispose of me," thought Adeline, as the picture he had drawn swam in her imagination, as her own marriage, to which she had felt even more than indifference, pressed upon her mind. "My father, my sainted father, how little when you urged me to marry Henry Mortimer, how little did you foresee that the calm mind of Adeline was to undergo all those tortures you ridiculed as the poet's idle dream! Oh! why did your persuasive arguments enforce my obedience – my fatal obedience?"

"To beings thus happy," continued Delamere, "thus living

amidst the grand sublimity of nature, how insignificant must appear the pomp of wealth: while possessing in each other invaluable treasures, they feel their utmost wish accomplished, and thank their great Creator that gave them the riches of love."

As he spoke an hysterical sob burst from Mrs. Mortimer. She was standing near a window, in which her tremulous fingers were endeavouring to arrange some exotics. Delamere approached her; he would have spoke, but Adeline was not in a situation to hear; she had fainted, and would have fell to the ground but for the supporting arms of Delamere, which extended themselves to receive her. The character of death was on her countenance, and her ivory neck hung over his arm as he bore her to the sofa. For a moment he stood in indescribable terror, irresolute how to proceed for her recovery; he dreaded to summon assistance lest any unguarded expression should expose them to the animadversions of the servants. At length his eye fell on the water that had been brought for the plants: he hastened to sprinkle her temples and her hand: she slowly unclosed her eyes while kneeling before her; he was in the act of pressing his lips to her cold hand.

"Forbear," said Adeline, the warm blood glowing in carnation tints upon her neck and face, "forbear! In pity spare me, Delamere; take not advantage of the wretch you have subdued. Strengthen with manly virtue the weakness of my mind – assist me to extirpate the guilty passion you have inspired."

"Never," replied Horatio. "I call heaven to attest that I receive this confession of your love with rapture – it is my pride, my glory, the only solace this agonized heart can know. Here, Adeline, you reign."

The face of Adeline sank on the sofa.

"Adored of my soul, why those blushes, this alarm? On my knees I solemnly swear I will never breathe a wish offensive to virtue – from you I will never solicit an indulgence incompatible with my friendship for Henry Mortimer. Yes, Adeline, I will love thee with a passion chaste and holy – I will ever respect your vows, made to the best the worthiest of men. He shall have your duty, but I," his eyes lift up with tenderest expression, "I will have your heart."

What mind of sensibility has not at some period listened to the sophistry of love? – what heart has not on some occasion or other deluded itself into a belief that what it wished was true? Delamere argued with persuasive eloquence, that a Platonic passion was not criminal; that as long as they respected chastity their love was innocent. Alas! poor Adeline, she listened and believed. It was now that softened by his passionate expressions, that lulled into confidence by his promises, Adeline told every circumstance relative to her marriage, confessed that she had given her hand to Henry Mortimer in compliance with the wishes of her father, lamented her inability to love him, upbraided herself with repaying his fervid affection with cold esteem, and at length, won by tender entreaty, acknowledged that her heart had never felt a preference for man till he inspired it. – This explanation having taken place, they were both calmer, their hearts were more at ease, and as they resolved never to carry the passion to criminal lengths, they perceived not the dangerous consequences of indulging it.

In a few days an express arrived from Henry Mortimer, now Lord Dungarvon, bringing intelligence of his own health and the death of his grandfather, who had expired in his arms a few hours after his arrival in London. His letter to Adeline spoke the tenderest impatience to be with her and his boy, his extreme regret at being obliged to attend the funerals of his relations to the family vault at Mortimer Abbey, and afterwards to wait the arrangement of his affairs, he having succeeded to the wealth of Richard Mortimer as well as to the title and estates of Lord Dungarvon. The express also brought letters for Horatio Delamere full of affectionate charges and affecting requests to be informed how Adeline bore his absence, whether he succeeded in making her cheerful; of expressions of unabating regard for himself, and reliance on his honourable friendship. The heart of Horatio smote him as he read, but he stifled the upbraiding monitor by saying, "We have outraged no law, human or divine; we injure no one; we commit no sin in loving each other, for we ask no higher indulgence than that of expressing our adoration, of deploring together that unhappy destiny that denies a union of persons where the souls are indissolubly cemented."

The express, among many elegant presents, brought books: with these came the Sorrows of Werter, a novel, which however elegantly written, ought not to escape the censure of the moralist. The title struck Adeline; her mind sought to lose its own sorrows in attending to fictitious ones, and placing it in the hands of Delamere, she requested him to read it. He complied; but the story was too similar to their own situations not to excite sensations of the most painful nature. – Adeline wept for, and trembled with the anguish of Charlotte, like herself united to an amiable deserving man, yet not the choice of her affections. Delamere's bosom throbbed with the pangs of Werter; like him, he felt the agonies of a passion never to be rewarded. His mind, too sensitive, too highly wrought, entered into all the anguish of the hero of the tale, till his inflamed imagination, no longer amenable to reason burst into wild and passionate complaints. He dashed the book to the floor, and traversing the room with frantic gestures exclaimed: – "Of what value is life to me? – the desolating hand of despair crushes my youth, while fevers fierce and excruciating drink the current of my blood. Adeline, worshipped of my soul, think of the tortures I endure. To view those lovely eyes, where every luxuriant pleasure beams, yet know their voluptuous rays must never bend one on me; to see that form, where beauty and symmetry fashion every limb devoted to the embraces of another – "

"Is it thus, Delamere," replied Adeline, terrified at his demeanour, "is it thus you observe your solemn promise? Sure you are mad."

"Mad!" echoed he; "oh! would to God I were mad! I should then forget my miseries; but reason lives with me to torture, to make me sensible that to the last moment of my existence I shall bear the burning arrow in my heart, that honour, friendship, philosophy fail to extract."

Adeline took up the letter of her husband that lay beside her; she would have persuaded Delamere to read it, but with a frenzied look he said: "Tell me not of the virtues of Henry Mortimer; calm and temperate by nature, he cannot love as I do: he feels not the harrowing sensation, the delirious torture of hopeless, incurable passion: his soul cannot worship you as mine does; to him, as to me, in the deep gloom of midnight your image cannot be present; your voice sounds not on his ear, vibrates not on his heart: he wakes not from dreams of bliss to agonize with disappointment. No, no, he wakes from visions of delight, to an ecstatic certainty – to clasp a heaven of bliss, while I, condemned to misery, wander through the dark woods, groan to the sighing winds, which as they sweep across my fevered breast, in hollow gusts murmur, 'Lost, wretched, hopeless Delamere.'"

"Heaven," said Adeline, weeping bitterly, "heaven ordains we should be miserable; our part is resignation."

"And will you, Adeline, pretend you love me, yet calmly talk of resignation. Heaven, my adored, rejoices not at our tortures, it formed us for each other; the union of our hearts, the similarity of our tastes, all proclaim it. Oh, Adeline," continued he, advancing to the sofa on which she sat, every feature in his fine face animated with passionate fondness, "this snowy hand was formed for me; those balmy lips, whose touch is bliss unutterable, for me to press."

Adeline sunk on his shoulder; their hearts distinctly throbbed against each other; reason and virtue fled, duty was forgot, and love triumphed. Adeline first recovered from the delirium of guilty pleasure, and starting from the arms of Delamere, that fondly circled her, her bosom heaving, her face the semblance of despair, in a voice of tremulous agony exclaimed, "What have I done? where shall I fly to hide my shame! Oh, that the earth would gape and swallow me."

Opposite to her hung the portraits of her parents and her husband: her eye as it rolled in frenzy round the room fixed on them. "See," she cried, "see how they frown upon me; save me, Horatio, save me from the just fury of a dishonoured parent and an injured husband."

"Father of mercies," said Delamere, who had stood immovable gazing on her, "forgive me for this deed, Adeline; lovely adored Adeline, I have undone thy peace. Oh! Mortimer, my honoured, injured friend, what compensation shall be made to thee? Villain that I am! he, generous and confiding, reposed with me in fond security the treasure of his soul, and I have basely plundered the rich casket of his joys; have treacherously left him destitute of all, save shame and sorrow."

"Will he not kill me?" said Adeline: "alas! he need not; soon, very soon, shall this guilty head be bowed to dust. Fly, Delamere, fly this fatal spot, the tomb of peace and virtue."

"We will fly together," said Delamere; "I will hush thy griefs with tenderest assiduity every moment of my life shall be devoted to thee; in my fond impassioned bosom thou shalt forget the name of Mortimer."

"My child!" said Adeline, shuddering, "my angel little one, shall I abandon him! Oh! never, never."

"He shall go with us, and he shall be mine, the inheritor of my fortune. Is he not a part of thee, my Adeline?" said Horatio. –

"Yes, but shall not inherit his mother's infamy," rejoined she. "Is he not Mortimer's heir? Inhuman as thou art, hast thou not fascinated me, lured me from innocence, seduced me from my duty, robbed the confiding Henry of his idol, and wouldst thou deprive him of his next dear treasure, of his child?"

"Be calm, my Adeline," replied Delamere, "believe this event as deeply wounds my heart as thine; I would give worlds did I possess them, to live again the last hour; but since it cannot be recalled, let us concert some plan for future happiness." Adeline cast on him a look of such despondency, as for a moment took from him the power of utterance. "Thou now art mine; this deed of ours separates thee eternally from Mortimer. Let us leave this place immediately; let us fly to Italy."

"Am I so sunk in your esteem already," said Adeline, indignantly, "that you can suppose I would consent to such a plan of shame and infamy? No, Delamere, I confess I love you; fatal has been the proof; you are dearer to this bursting heart than is the light of heaven; but yet I will not fly with you; I will not bring a public disgrace on him I have already injured beyond the power of reparation. No, thus degraded, thus fallen from virtue as I am; I will still prove my soul reveres, though I have sullied its brightness; I will confess my guilt to Henry Mortimer, implore his pity and forgiveness, then haste to some obscure retreat, and hide my opprobrious head for ever."

"Then here I swear," said Delamere, violently dashing his body on the floor, "here I swear to end my days; I will on this spot wait the return of Mortimer. Adeline, cruel Adeline, I will not, cannot live without you: I will provoke his rage: you shall see the blood that feeds the heart, which dotes upon you, shed in your presence. Yes, Adeline, my life shall expiate the injury I have done to Mortimer."

"Forbear, rash man," replied she: "Oh, that my ear had never drank the magic of that voice, that I had never seen those wizard smiles, I had then been innocent and happy; but let me fly thee, fly for ever thy persuasions. Under this roof was I born: here in an ill-fated hour I became the wife of Henry Mortimer, and here," continued she, "here will I die. Oh, my distracted brain! it seems on fire. Delamere, adored of my soul, dear unhappy Delamere, we meet no more."

As she spoke, she rushed with frantic speed from the room. Horatio Delamere lay a length of time stretched on the floor without reflection; the violence of his feelings had exhausted him, and when memory began again to exercise its functions, the whole seemed like a disjointed dream. But the darkness of the room, and his finding himself on the ground, soon brought him to a sense of his misery; he rang the bell; of the servant who entered he inquired for Mrs. Mortimer, and was answered that she was retired to bed, very unwell.

"Ill," said Delamere, "did I understand you? ill! – Fly for a physician, lose not a moment." –

"My mistress has forbade our calling in assistance; she says, sir, that she merely wants repose." With this answer, having brought lights, the servant left the room.

"What a night of horror is this!" said Horatio, as he listened to the loud wind that shook the windows; "everything that stirs alarms me, and seems the presage of some impending evil. Even my own shadow startles me. Oh! Henry, Henry, how have I abused thy confidence! thy soul was bound in Adeline, yet you must meet no more; *I*, the destroying fiend, the murderer of happiness, decree your eternal separation. Angels of peace hover round her, calm her dear bosom; sleep fall gently on her beauteous eyelids, and steep them in your sweetest slumbers. Oh, abandoned wretch!" cried he, striking his forehead with his clenched hand, "thou hast frighted peace from this once happy mansion; thou hast violated the sacred rights of a husband, poisoned the cup of thy most dear friend; but, Adeline, more than ever loved, we must begone. I will write to her."

Seating himself at the table, he took up a pen. "In vain, Adeline, you tell me to forget you, and to fly – my fate, my soul are yours; I cannot, will not separate myself from you, consent to fly with me. I know thy exalted mind too well to suppose you will ever again consider yourself the wife of Henry Mortimer; let us then forget and despise the world, and blest in each other, haste to some clime where this unhappy deed of ours may remain unknown. Come, as you are mistress of my destiny, be my wife, by the holy thrice blessed rite of divine affection. Love shall strew his own roses on our couch, and every new day shall wake us to new joys. Consent to this plan, my Adeline, and we may yet be happy."

A burning tear fell on the last word and blotted it, as if to tell him that guilt and happiness were incompatible, never to be associated. Horatio felt the conviction, but to soothe the agonies of Mrs. Mortimer was his chief aim; he therefore sealed his billet, and retired to his chamber; he threw himself on the bed, but his brain on fire, his senses whirling with the past event, sleep was chased from his pillow; while his passion for Adeline acquiring every moment new force, mingling with the sense of injury heaped on his friend, gave to the darkness of a tempestuous night more than natural gloom, and the long dreary, heavy hours, passed in misery inconceivable, except to those who have writhed with the accumulated tortures of love, horror, and remorse. At early morning, Horatio Delamere left his bed, his heart all anguish, and his body in a fever; and gladly would he have exchanged conditions with the meanest labourer that he saw in the adjoining grounds. All the agonies of hopeless passion appeared now blissful ease, compared with the scorpion stings of guilt, that darting through his heart and brain, sounded in his ears *thou art a villain*. A thousand times was he on the point of ending his miseries with his own desperate hand, but the pale weeping form of Adeline intervened; and saved him from the additional crime of self-murder. At an early hour he got the letter he had written overnight conveyed to Mrs. Mortimer, and waited gasping on the rack of breathless expectation and suspense, fearing she would refuse to comply with his wishes. After a tedious interval, he received this reply.

"I conjure you by the love you profess for me, leave Dolgelly Castle immediately, unless you wish to hear that with a desperate hand I have put a period to those miseries which are almost too great for human constancy to support. Go, I beseech you, leave this place, no longer proper for you to inhabit. When I have reasoned my distracted senses to a calm, you shall hear again from Adeline."

The grief of Delamere on reading this was frenzy. Again he wrote: again with all the vehemence of sorrow, with all the energetic eloquence of love, entreated for an interview; said all that passion and desperation could suggest to persuade her to fly her paternal home, to become the partner of his future fate: but vainly he entreated. Mrs. Mortimer peremptorily refused to admit him to her presence, or to accompany his flight; but again fervently and pathetically repeated her request that he would immediately quit Dolgelly Castle. As Delamere found the utter impossibility of bringing her to acquiesce with his desires, and saw how earnestly she requested his absence, he took an affecting and tender leave of Owen, who fondly and innocently twined his little arms round his neck, and said he would go with him, told the servants that particular business obliged him to follow their master to London, and with a bursting heart left the house, having secretly deputed John Wilkins to procure him lodgings in the neighbourhood. Mrs. Mortimer had now confined herself to her chamber near a fortnight; she scarcely ate anything; she spoke to no one but her own maid and her child; became so pale and emaciated, that she looked only the beautiful spectre of her former self: yet her mind felt more at ease when she found that Delamere was actually gone. The idea of her husband's return, which she every day expected, had terrified her beyond measure; for she was well acquainted with his nice sense of honour, and foresaw with anguish inexpressible that the death of one, perhaps both must have been the dreadful result, when the unhappy affair came to his knowledge; and she had brought her mind to the desperate resolution of concealing no part of her own indiscretion. Another express arrived from Lord Dungarvon: it was wrote in a gay style, in high spirits; it detailed at large the particulars relative to the arrangement of the affairs that gave him possession of the title and vast estates of his ancestors, as well as the wealth of Richard Mortimer. His letter breathed all the impatient fondness of a lover, told her he expected to find Lady Dungarvon more beautiful than ever, and concluding with bidding her on the following Monday evening expect her adoring husband. The letter, on which her tears had fallen in heavy drops, fell from the nerveless fingers of Adeline; a sorrowful smile hovered on her lips, a blush of the deepest tint flamed across her cheek; she clasped her hands on her bosom; her eyes with a mournful expression turned towards Heaven, while in a voice of woe she said: "before then – yes, I trust Heaven will spare me the shame, the anguish of such a meeting! – Yes, I trust before then my miseries will know cessation. Oh, my parents! before then the erring heart-broken Adeline will rest with you."

The domestics of Dolgelly Castle, most of whom had grown old in the service of the family, were bewildered with unpleasant surmises, and actually feared to ask each other the meaning of their ladyship's strange indisposition, for which she had peremptorily refused medical advice and assistance; this, however, and the Honourable Mr. Delamere's sudden departure, who had been seen by the servants night after night wandering about the castle, after having said he was setting off for London, awakened suspicions, and gave birth to conjectures that furnished continual conversations in the hall and the kitchen. One hoary-headed old man, the butler, shaking his old white locks, said he had lived from childhood in the family, and had never found cause for sorrow, till his dear and honoured lady and Sir Owen Llewellyn died: "But now," continued he, his eyes filling with tears, "I shall soon follow them. My sweet young mistress will never enjoy her new title. No, no: she is fading away, like a rose new blown and scorched by the morning sun. I saw her yesterday from her window so pale, so thin, she can't live long, and I, unhappy old man, shall break my heart. How often when she was an infant have I carried her in my arms, while her brother, as she used to call him, my Lord Dungarvon, skipped beside us. With what pleasure I have listened to her innocent prattle while her pretty arms were clasped round my neck. Blessing on her, she is as good as she is beautiful. Would to God," said he, his voice choked with sobs, "would to God Mr. Delamere had never set his foot in Dolgelly Castle." Ned Ratlin had not been an unobserving spectator of the passing scenes: he said that the gale which had blown Mr. Delamere into North Wales was a foul wind indeed, and he wished with all his soul that it had blown him another course, as he feared that he would run foul of the Mortimer, and damage her beyond repair: "And shiver my timbers," said Ned, "I would sooner be froze in an island of ice for six months, with only Greenland bears for my messmates, than a cockboat belonging to the noble Mortimer should founder."

Sir Griffith Tudor's speed did not keep pace with that of the lovers, who had besides the advantage of some hours before their elopement was discovered; and the ritual of a Scotch and

English marriage had confirmed Eliza Tudor the wife of Captain Seymour, while yet her father was at the distance of many miles. The conviction that he had not the power to separate them enraged the temper of Sir Griffith Tudor to so violent a degree, that by extravagant ravings, joined with the great fatigue he had undergone in travelling, the gout seized his stomach, and he lay at an inn on the north road seemingly at the last extremity. Fortunately the physician who was called was a man of sense and humanity, as well as skill, and succeeded in allaying the disorder of the patient's mind, as well as removing the gout from his stomach to his feet. Being informed of the motives of Sir Griffith's journey, and perceiving that he was neither prepared nor willing to die, he took some trouble to persuade him that he was in danger: after every mortal symptom had disappeared, and under the influence of impending dissolution, to write to Captain Seymour in terms of reconciliation, entreating to see him and his wife, before it was too late for him to bless or be blest by them. This summons was instantly obeyed: Captain Seymour and his lovely Eliza hastened in extreme terror to the town where Sir Griffith Tudor lay again tied by the legs; but previous to an interview with him saw the kind physician, who instantly removed the fears Mrs. Seymour had entertained for her father's life, whom her heart affectionately loved, notwithstanding the delight she had ever found in contradicting him.

The terror of approaching death had certainly damped much of the fire of Sir Griffith's temper; yet when he saw Eliza enter his apartment leaning on Captain Seymour; when he beheld on her finger the badge of matrimony, he could not forbear flaming out, and calling her a little damned disobedient minx; but at last yielding to the remonstrances of his medical friend, who had pointed out the dangerous consequences of giving way to rage in his case, and softened by the pleadings of Eliza and her husband, he pardoned them, swearing that all the sin of his broken oaths would fall on them. From this hour he recovered health and spirits: tenderly nursed and attended by Eliza, and amused by Captain Seymour, in a few days the gout entirely left him, and he stood firm on his legs again; and persuaded that travelling would be serviceable to him, and that he could not be happy without the company of his daughter, he sat down to inform Lady Tudor that he had forgiven that little mad devil Eliza the d – d trick she had played him, and that he expected she would do the same; that he had kicked the gout out of doors, and that he was now able to dance a reel, which he hoped soon to do to the music of the bagpipe; that he was on the way to visit the lairds of the Seymour clan, and designed to accompany his son and daughter to make a tour of Scotland, when they designed to return and spend the ensuing summer at Tudor Hall. He concluded with observing that her ladyship would now have undisturbed opportunity of indulging all her nervous affections and hysterical complaints, and that she might assure herself that he would not fail to lay in a good stock of Scotch snuff, which he had no doubt would be equally efficacious with Irish blackguard. – Mrs. Seymour wrote a letter of respect and duty to her mother, and another of affectionate explanation to Lady Dungarvon, excusing herself for not acquainting her with her intended elopement, knowing that her timidity and delicacy would have revolted from and advised against so bold a step. "A step which I trust," added the lively Eliza, "I shall never be forced to repent, as Archibald promises to love me for ever: if he keeps his word all will be well; if he does not, tit for tat you know."

Adeline washed the letter of her friend with bitter tears, remembered how often she had censured the wild sallies of the playful Eliza, and blushed at the mortifying conviction that it is easier to teach twenty what were good to be done, than be one of the twenty to follow one's own teaching. When Mrs. Seymour's letter reached Tudor Hall, her ladyship's imaginary complaints were forgotten in a real illness, which prevented her attending Lady Dungarvon, for whom she felt a natural affection, and whose indisposition not a little added to her own sickness, and increased the melancholy of Tudor Hall, which no longer sounding with the boisterous lungs of Sir Griffith or the sprightly voice of Eliza, had become dull and gloomy.

CHAPTER IX

There is a destiny in this strange world?
Which oft decrees an undeserved doom.
Let schoolmen tell us why.

Hume

THE loud ringing of the village bells, and cavalcades of joyous peasantry dressed out in their holiday clothes, prepared to meet and welcome their beloved and respected lord, ushered in the earliest dawn of this eventful Monday, so ardently wished, so anxiously expected by Lord Dungarvon, so dreaded by Adeline. Henry drew near to Dolgelly Castle, the seat of his dearest hopes and wishes, with the tumultuous sensations of a lover, the impatience of a doting husband, the tenderness of a fond father.

Lady Dungarvon was evidently hastening to that bourn where grief forgets to groan, and love to weep. Her features were sunk and altered, and her fragile form appeared but as the airy shadow of an immortal being; yet though hourly declining, she had constantly and peremptorily evaded calling in medical assistance; ever silencing the dutiful remonstrances of her weeping attendant, by declaring that she was not sensible of bodily indisposition; that her malady was of the mind, and mocked all earthly power; for who can minister to minds diseased,

"Pluck from the memory a rooted sorrow,
Raze out the written sorrows of the brain;

> And with some sweet oblivious antidote,
> Cleanse the full bosom of that perilous stuff
> Which weighs upon the heart?"

Evening was already arrived; the moon's chilly crescent was slowly ascending over the woods that surrounded Dolgelly Castle; the village bells yet rang a merry peal, sounding on the apprehensive ear of Adeline like the deep and awful knell of death, when having long listened for the approach of her husband's carriage, she desired that her son might be brought to her apartment: as he entered with her nurse, she waved her hand for the servants to withdraw, and being left alone with Owen, she pressed him in agony to her bosom; in tones of pathetic supplication she besought him not to hate the memory of his mother. As his rosy lips kissed hers, he told her repeatedly that he loved mamma better than any body, dearly to his heart. The big tears fell in heavy drops from her eyes and bedewed his innocent face; while he, though ever accustomed to her caresses, felt uneasy at their unusual vehemence, and wiping her tears away with his little soft hand, told her papa was coming home, and that nurse said he would punish the naughty people that had made her cry.

Lady Dungarvon felt a cold shuddering creep through her veins, as she thought of the possibility of her words being verified, and with a look of anguish, accompanied by a harrowing groan, exclaimed: "Murder! occasion murder! no, God forbid!" While she was thus mournfully employed. Lord Dungarvon's carriage, drawn by his delighted tenants, who had taken out the horses, entered the gates; but his heart partook not of the joy of his people. The day had been beautifully mild and fine, yet neither Adeline nor Horatio

Delamere were on the road to meet him: their voices, most dear to his heart, were not mingled with the congratulatory shouts of the peasants. A thousand undefinable apprehensions, to which he could give neither form nor name, crowded his imagination, which was heightened even to agony, when he beheld no wife, no friend to welcome him. As he descended from his carriage, "Where," demanded he from the domestics, who had joyfully crowded around, each anxious to catch the honour of his first notice; "where is Lady Dungarvon? – where is Mr. Delamere?" A pause of hesitation succeeded these questions, which none were willing to answer; and Ned Ratlin, who had crowded among the foremost to the hall to welcome the return of Henry, now slunk behind the crowd, fearful of its becoming his task to reply to these painful interrogations.

Lord Dungarvon repeated them with breathless anxiety, and was at last answered: "Her ladyship is confined to her room, and Mr. Delamere is gone to England." Henry heard only what concerned Adeline: he sprang with the velocity of lightning up the grand staircase; he threw open the door of her dressing room, but what was his unutterable anguish, to behold her pale and emaciated on her knees, invoking heaven to bless him and her child, who, kneeling beside her, was holding up his little innocent unconscious hands in imitation of her action. As Lord Dungarvon entered, Adeline turned her heavy eyes towards him, uttered a faint scream, clasped her hands together in the gesture of supplication, murmured out some inarticulate sentences, fell into his arms, and breathed no more.

At first Henry supposed his sudden appearance had overcome her spirits weakened by illness, and occasioned fainting: he gently laid her on a couch, and rang for assistance;

but when he found that every effort to recover her was unavailing, and that she was really dead, his grief was little short of madness; he tore his hair from his head, dashed his body with frantic violence on the floor, accused the attendants of want of duty and affection in not sending for physicians, in not informing him of her illness. "My absence," exclaimed he, "has murdered her." He would then press her in his arms, talk to her as if she were alive, and utter such wild extravagancies, that the terrified and afflicted servants trembled for his intellects, nor could their persuasions or united efforts detach him from the corpse. "Oh! beauteous lily," said the distracted Lord Dungarvon, gazing on the pale inanimate form of her he had so worshipped, "thou art cut down before thy sweets had gained perfection. What now, alas! are titles, rank to me, the world and its fallacious pleasures? hateful, hateful all. – Is it thus the gay visions of hope are realized – are these my expected enjoyments, my promised joys. – If I ever desired the proud distinctions of rank it was for thy sake, my Adeline; thou art gone to realms of bliss, to join thy sister angels in the sky; and the forlorn, the wretched, widowed Henry shall never more behold thy beauteous countenance emanating smiles of love and goodness. Thou art lost to me, and nothing now in this wide world can give a joy to my sad heart. Oh Adeline, my life, my love, my Adeline."

In this state of distraction Lord Dungarvon passed the greatest part of the night; at length throwing himself beside the remains of his wife, overcome by fatigue and sorrow, his aching weary eyes closed, and he sunk into a profound slumber, which lasted till day-light. Sleep refreshed and calmed his spirits, and though his bosom was wrung with the bitterest affliction, he behaved and spoke with rationality. It was now that he wept the tender tears of paternal affection over his lovely motherless Owen, who, delighted at the return of his father, and encouraged by his endearments, innocently asked questions that were daggers to the heart of the sorrowing Lord Dungarvon, who now made particular inquiries after Mr. Delamere. The answers he received were by no means consolatory or satisfactory. His friend, to whom he had left the care of his adored wife, quitting the place on her being taken ill, was an enigma so obscure, so inexplicable, that his tired imagination turned from the impossibility of its solution; but the greater woe absorbed the less; his sensibility was wounded at what he considered Mr. Delamere's unfeeling conduct. But the lifeless Adeline engrossed his faculties, filled every sense with sorrow; her loss was an affliction so sudden, so unexpected, that it prevented reflection dwelling on any other circumstance.

The breathless form of Lady Dungarvon, arrayed in a robe of vestal white, had lain above a week, to keep alive the poignant sufferings of her husband. In vain had Hugh Montgomery and his gentle Rosa represented the necessity of interment; deaf to their representations, he had every day persisted in decorating the couch on which she lay with fresh flowers; and every day found him more averse to their final separation. But a change now visibly took place, and it was with anguish unutterable that Henry was convinced of the danger he incurred to himself and household by keeping her longer from that earth to which she was so evidently returning.

As Lord Dungarvon consented to consign her so dear to her last dreary resting place, his grief knew no bounds; the tears chased each other down his pallid cheeks, and kissing her icy lips, he exclaimed:

"Must I then part with thee, my Adeline; must that angelic form become a prey to corruption; are then thy melting eyes closed for ever? Shall thy tuneful voice bless my ears no more? Oh, anguish insupportable, must I consign thee to the dark cold grave; must the damp earth rest on that lovely bosom, and divide thee from thy husband? Oh, my child," continued he, grasping the hand of Owen, who stood in silent wonder beside the coffin, "your mother, who idolized you, shall see you no more; she is gone for ever, and with her is fled all joy, all comfort, from the desolated heart of your father."

The child, who had no conception of death, and imagined his mother only slept, gently shook her, and holding up his finger, innocently said: – "Hush! mamma is asleep." "Oh, God, she will never more wake in this world," said Lord Dungarvon. Again Owen touched her, and whispered, "Speak to me, mamma;" but when he saw her eyes still closed, and found she did not answer, he hung upon the knees of Lord Dungarvon, and looking piteously in his face, mournfully repeated: "Mamma will not awake, she will not speak to Owen."

"No," said Henry, shuddering, "no, my child, she will speak no more; the melody of her voice shall never again dissipate my sorrows, nor will she awake, till angels like herself welcome her to the abodes of heaven. Creator of the universe," added he, sinking on his knees beside the coffin, "thou who hast thought fit to steep me in affliction to the very lips, teach me to bear this worst of calamities as becomes a Christian and a man."

Before the lid of the coffin was screwed down, Lord Dungarvon came to take his last leave of all his soul held dear;

he dismissed the attendants, and removing the covering from her face, which was now much discoloured, he stood for some moments horror struck at the change which even a few short hours had effected; but the still adoring Henry was not withheld by this circumstance from repeatedly pressing his lips to hers, her forehead, and her cheek. "How thou art altered, my adored one," said he, with a heavy sigh, "how has the rude and desolating hand of death defaced thy beauteous countenance; but, perhaps, at this moment thou shinest in heaven, arrayed in the unfading bloom of immortal beauty. Look down, bright cherub, from the realms of bliss, and inspire my fainting soul with fortitude."

His bosom heaved, he covered his face with his hands, and wept the enanguished tears of blighted hope and disappointed love. "Oh!" added he, with a deep and laboured groan, "oh, that the chords that strain with agony about my heart would burst, then would I follow thee; but I must live: the tender pledge of our affection demands the protection of his father. Forever, my Adeline, we part forever. Yet, surely no – not forever. In heaven, my adored one, we shall meet again."

Hugh Montgomery, with the affectionate solicitude of friendship, came to lead him from the room; nor were his eyes dry, nor was his heart unaffected, as he pressed his lips on the damp cold hand; as he took a last farewell of her once so loved and lovely. Many times had Hugh Montgomery motioned to depart, but Henry still bending over the corpse, continued to press the icy lips; and when at last, with gentle violence, he was forced from the apartment, his gaze was fixed on her, till the closing door shut her from his view for ever.

Again the chapel belonging to Dolgelly Castle was hung with black, and the remains of the once beautiful Lady

Dungarvon was borne through its dusky aisle, and deposited by torch-light in the vault of her ancestors. In the recess of an elegantly painted window her husband caused to be erected a magnificent cenotaph of white marble, on which was exquisitely sculptured figures emblematic of her beauty, her virtues, and his incurable sorrow. Many weeks wore away: the friends of Lord Dungarvon had been unremitting in their attentions and endeavours to amuse him, but their efforts were unavailing; melancholy had marked him for her own; and never for a moment was the idea of Adeline absent from his mind, never for a moment did he cease to bewail her loss; nor were his regrets for her unmingled with painful sensations as he reflected on the cruel dereliction of Horatio Delamere, to whose broken friendship and strange conduct he could find no clue, never having once heard from him since his accession to his title, while he recollected their boyish attachment, which had seemed to strengthen with their strength; he felt new pangs, and he would sigh heavily and despondingly as he thought of the specious virtues by which his esteem had been won, as he sorrowfully exclaimed: – "Such are the friendships of the world."

The only consolation Lord Dungarvon found in the midst of cherished woe was to gaze on a miniature picture he wore of his wife, and in the instruction of his little Owen, whose warm remembrance of his mother, and fond inquiries after her, made him more interesting, still dearer to the heart of his father. Six months had now past, and never had the foot of Henry ventured into the dressing-room where he had taken his everlasting leave of Adeline.

One morning he had stolen from his friends and wandering along the corridor, his hand rested on the lock of that door through which the form of his adored had passed to the house of death. A faint sensation seized him: twice he retreated; but irresistibly propelled, he at last made a desperate effort and entered the room. The tasteful adornments disposed around, the inventions of her genius, and the work of her elegant hand, brought her with added grief and tenderness to his imagination. Her harp stood in a corner of the room: Lord Dungarvon raised the white silk veil that covered it, and gently passing his fingers across the strings, it uttered a sound so plaintive, so full of woe, that he sank upon the seat she used to occupy, and for many minutes remained lost to himself and the world. A curious inlaid cabinet stood on the toilet table; it used to contain materials for drawing. "Here," said Lord Dungarvon, opening the spring with a trembling hand, "here I shall find the productions of my Adeline's pencil, the blended proofs of her unrivalled taste and matchless fancy." Among some beautiful views of mountain scenery he found a portrait of himself, and an exquisitely finished likeness of Horatio Delamere. – "What a resemblance!" said Henry, as his eyes wandered over the features; "who to see those eyes, to look on that countenance, could believe it belonged to a bosom heartless and unfeeling." At the bottom of the cabinet lay a letter addressed to himself. He broke the seal with painful trepidation; but what language has words sufficiently expressive to describe his tortured feelings at the disclosure that followed as he read:

"Unhappy Henry!

"At this very moment, while I, giddy and trembling, hover on the awful verge of eternity, thou art amusing thy unconscious mind with gay visions of happiness to come: thou, kind and generous, art busied in contriving pleasures for the wretched Adeline. – Perhaps even now thou art on thy way to what thou fondly callest thy home, thy cheek flushed with joy thy bosom throbbing with expected transport, thy soul elevated with the fond idea of introducing to rank and grandeur, to the diversions of a fashionable world, her who is hastening with rapid pace to the cold and dreary confines of the grave. Yes, Henry, I am gliding out of life, and the only consolation I am capable of feeling is the certainty that I shall not exist to see thy frowns, to hear thy reproaches. – Oh! Henry, fortify thy heart; make it strong to hear that Adeline, the daughter of Sir Owen Llewellyn, the wife of Lord Dungarvon, has long nourished in her bosom a criminal passion. Ungrateful to thy unceasing tenderness, spite of the sacred vows I plighted to thee at the altar of my God, I have dared to love another. Hate me, scorn me, lose all remembrance of me, Henry; for, oh agony! I have dishonoured thee. Yet listen to the story of my heart. Brought up together from our earliest infancy, I ever regarded you as my brother; you had my friendship, my esteem, all that an affectionate sister could be supposed to feel for an amiable brother, I felt for you, nor did I dream a passion of a warmer nature existed in the human mind. Ill-fated Henry! This fatal form in yours inspired a warmer one: you loved me. My father beheld with pleasure your growing attachment – to unite his child with the son of him who had been his dearest friend, was the first, most darling wish of his heart. I described to Sir Owen Llewellyn the state of my feelings: unhappily blinded by his wishes, he misinterpreted them; he deluded himself with the belief that esteem was love. I listened to the arguments of my parent as to the unerring Voice of heaven; I thought it impiety to dispute his wishes. Fatal obedience! I gave you my hand, Henry, and I ignorantly supposed I had given you my heart. Oh that I had never been undeceived! My days were tranquil, and my nights were undisturbed by care or sorrow. I fancied I was happy. Dear hours of felicity you fled too fast; quickly you vanished, never, no never to return. Peace fled my bosom the moment that (how shall my trembling fingers trace the guilty name?) Horatio Delamere arrived; his presence was as the electric stroke of heaven, it shot at once into my soul, and I felt the full force of that imperious passion I had ever ridiculed as ideal. In vain I tried to extinguish the guilty fire: I invoked the spirits of my parents, but they heard me not. I thought of you; I brought to my remembrance your unceasing adoration of me; I saw my own ingratitude; I trembled at the criminality of my passion; I blushed when I remembered I was a wife, I shuddered when I recollected I was a mother. But, alas! I was also a woman too sensitive, too weak to struggle against the dominion of love. – At last in an evil hour I completed my own and thy dishonour. Now then let rage, contempt, disgust, possess thy soul – hate, abhor the memory of Adeline – yet I beseech you abandon not my child, my cherub Owen; pour not your vengeance on his innocent head; let not your wrath extend to him; though he is mine, remember, Henry, he is also yours, and while you feel the just indignation of an injured husband, forget not you are a father. This I know is a needless injunction for thou whose mind is generosity, whose soul is humanity and honour; thou wilt not confound the unoffending with the guilty. My father loved you; my mother was to you a parent when death deprived you of your own – remember and respect their virtues. For their sakes seek no revenge on the miserable Delamere; his mind sufficiently punishes him for all the woes which he has heaped on you. Let not the daughter of Sir Owen Llewellyn, of him whose life was one pure stream of unsullied honour, become a subject of sport for vulgar tongues. By the memory of my virtuous mother I conjure you spare my reputation; for the sake of our dear, our precious little one, let not my fame be blasted, but let my infamy be buried with me in the grave. My fall from virtue will give you many pangs – but me – Oh! Henry, could you read my soul, behold the torturing anguish that rends the chords of life, the deep repentance and unceasing tears that fall to wash away the stains of my pollution, you, injured as you are – yes, you would pity me. – The flame that feeds my life is nearly quenched; my eyes grow dim, my pulses stop, these are my last pangs. Oh! Henry, dear betrayed and injured Henry, forgive me!"

The frame of Lord Dungarvon shook with convulsive shudderings; a cold spasm like the cold damp of death seemed to crush his heart; discordant noises rang in his ears, and his bosom laboured for respiration. "The dreadful mystery of Delamere's absence is now explained," murmured from his lips as his head sank against the table; "her supplicating attitude, her dying scream all accounted for. Wretched, ruined woman! villain Delamere!" After a pause of speechless misery he started up, and pacing the room with maniac steps, his burning brain seemed no longer to own the government of reason; he laughed convulsively, gnashed his teeth, and struck his head with violence against the wall. – From his nose gushed out a torrent of blood, and this fortunate hæmorrhage happily restored his faculties, but with returning sense came the remembrance of his injuries. "Oh misery!" exclaimed he, "she never loved me. Delamere, the happy treacherous Delamere, was the object of her wishes: even in my arms her soul was filled with his idea; accursed was the hour in which I invited him hither, but doubly damned the hour in which I left her to his protection. – His life shall answer for his crime."

Then musing. "Yet, what consolation will that afford – plundered of all I loved, despoiled of all that rendered life desirable, will his blood restore my Adeline? Will it give back the days when content led the hours, and peace shed its smiles ineffable around us? – Will it resuscitate from the grave her whom even my infant heart idolized; will it restore her innocence, her unspotted fame? – No – it will do none of these. Let me then drive from my soul this spirit of revenge, let me obey the wish of her, adored even in her death. Live, treacherous, faithless Delamere. Live, and, if thou canst, repent. It is well that she is dead. Father of mercies, thou who hast laid thy chastising hand upon me, thy will be done: let me not murmur at my destiny, hard as it is. My soul doted on her, she was my hope, my joy, my comfort. Yet, was she living, and dishonoured. Oh! it is too much; anguish too great to think of. It is better she is dead." He sighed as if his heart was breaking.

From the window he walked to the balcony, where the plants were placed that Lady Dungarvon's hand had reared: he fancied they drooped and looked sickly. "They sympathize with me," said Henry, as he regarded them. "No longer cheered by the sun-beam of her eye they wither like my heart." Again he read the letter, and considered it attentively.

"Unhappy Adeline," said he, "thy acute sense of honour has destroyed thee; – yet thou wert not to blame. Our affections are involuntary, for who would be wretched were they free to choose? The Being who traced upon our hearts their glowing characters, will, I trust, forgive their accidental weaknesses, their unpremeditated errors. Oh yes, the power who wove the passions of our souls, he will pity, will forgive them. Adeline, thou hast expiated thine offence; be all remembrance of thine error buried with thee. I commiserate, I forgive thee from my soul; yet it is better thou art dead – though here," added he, pressing his hands on his heart, "here, while I inhabit this breathing world, thou wilt reign spite of all. Abandon thy child, the beauteous image of thee. Oh! never, never. This act of thine has fatally deprived him of his mother, but in my tenderness he shall find both his parents. Creator of the universe, enable me to form his mind to virtue; for me I will lowly bend before thy throne; I will adore thy hand, that has thus crushed my proud hopes to dust; I will supplicate thy aid to vanquish my unavailing sorrows, to enable me unmurmuring to submit to thy decrees." With these resolutions Lord Dungarvon joined his friends; he no longer shunned society, or refused its consolations, but became every day more composed; a sigh of regret would indeed frequently heave his bosom, and a tear drop glisten in his eye as he thought on past events; but the summer, which was now nearly at a close, beheld him resigned though pensive. It was the custom of Lord Dungarvon every night to visit the cenotaph erected in memory of Adeline: his heart still adored her, and he had a melancholy delight in pouring out the impassioned effusions of love and grief before her tomb.

A severe cold had confined him for some time, but

believing himself better he again repaired to the chapel. It was near midnight; the full-moon wandered in unclouded majesty over a clear blue sky thickly studded with stars; a soft breeze sighed through a long avenue of yew and cypress through which he had to pass, whose waving branches were partially silvered by the moon-beams that chequered his path. The spirits of Lord Dungarvon were languid; he felt not the extravagance of grief, but his mind was heavy with presaging melancholy, not the superstition of his nature, but the gloomy offspring of afflictive occurrence. He entered the chapel, and the sound of his steps ran in murmuring echoes along the aisles. Once he started as he fancied a groan met his ear. "It is the moaning of the wind," said Henry, and he knelt beside the cenotaph. The moon poured a flood of light through the painted window: in the fervour of devotion he raised his eyes towards heaven, and perceived the form of a man stretched on the marble.

"What wretch art thou," said Lord Dungarvon rising; "that liest here exposed to the unwholesome night?"

"A wretch indeed," answered a hollow voice; "one who has done with life, and waits here the hour when he shall be released from mortal suffering: whomsoever thou art, be gone, disturb not the last moments of a woe-devoted being who hates the world; who execrates the light. In mercy begone, and let me die."

"Surely," said Lord Dungarvon, gasping with emotion, "surely that voice is known to me, – Oh, bitter recollection! Oh God! thou art Delamere."

"Yes, thy treacherous friend," said he, leaping from the tomb, "the selected of thy choice, the approved of thy reason, the miserable guilty Delamere. Here," added he, throwing himself at the feet of Lord Dungarvon, and baring his bosom, "strike here, be speedy, and revenge my crime and thy injuries. I have tinged thy cheek, with the disgraceful blush of shame, (Henry uttered a groan of anguish) I have murdered thy angel wife. (Henry reeled against an opposite pillar) I have destroyed thy happiness for ever. I, thy friend. What could thy most inveterate enemy have effected worse against thee?"

The moonbeams (as in the agitation of his utterance he shifted his position) fell full on the face of Horatio Delamere; and Lord Dungarvon, spite of the indignation of his spirit, could not help shuddering at its altered character. His fine hair was matted and neglected, his dark eyes had lost their effulgence, his cheeks were sunk and ghastly pale; and his wasted form seemed but the shadow of his former self.

"Behold," said Henry, as he gazed upon him, "behold the sad effects of guilt. Rise, Delamere, from the earth. Heaven has punished thy crime severely. Unhappy man, how thou art altered. Where is the vivacity that sparkled in thine eye, the healthful bloom that glowed upon thy cheek?"

"Buried," replied Delamere, with a harrowing groan that seemed to rend his heart; "buried in the grave with Adeline."

"Thou hast destroyed for ever the peace of my mind; thou hast betrayed, deceived me, injured me beyond the power of reparation, devoted me to wretchedness," said Lord Dungarvon; "yet if to know that I forgive thee, will it in any measure speak comfort to thy lacerated bosom, hear me now before the tomb of Adeline solemnly swear I do sincerely pardon thee."

Horatio Delamere fell senseless on the marble pavement at the feet of Henry, who hearing distant footsteps called to know who was approaching: in the answer he recognized the voice of John Wilkins, who knowing that his master was in the habit of paying midnight visits to the chapel, had followed with the intent of persuading him home. He was an athletic young man, and raising the lifeless form in his arms, pushed open a low arched door, and admitted the air, which blowing freshly on the face of Delamere, restored him to sense and misery. His eyes with a look of unutterable woe rested on Lord Dungarvon, and in a voice scarcely articulate he said, "now then I may die in peace."

"Talk not of dying," replied Lord Dungarvon, "live and be happy."

"Happy!" sighed Delamere, shivering as he accidentally placed his hand on the tomb of Adeline.

"Go to thy bed," continued Henry, "and may the refreshing balms of sleep restore thee to health and blest serenity; farewell. Oh! Delamere, disturb not the prayers I nightly pay before this tomb: you robbed me of her love, deprive not my aching heart of this last sad consolation."

"Not for the wealth of worlds," said Delamere; "farewell, may peace attend your orations; for myself, I dare not supplicate. Oh, Henry! if thy exalted soul can so far soar above humanity, when you bend the pious knee, beseech forgiveness for the guilty Delamere."

He departed leaning on John Wilkins, who had waited at a respectful distance to attend him. Lord Dungarvon, who this unexpected interview had much agitated, remained in the chapel, earnest in devotion till morning. On his return home he was seized with cold shiverings; a fever succeeded, which with alarming violence threatened to settle on his brain: he got the better of this, but was rapidly advancing in a decline; his physicians recommended a warmer climate, and advised the south of France. Henry was unwilling to quit Dolgelly Castle, but every day growing weaker, for the sake of his darling Owen began to arrange his affairs, and make preparations for his departure; but alas! it was too late, he was seized with symptoms that told his final dissolution too near to admit unnecessary trouble and unavailing fatigue: he saw his end approaching with evident satisfaction; he bore his pains with manly unmurmuring fortitude; his son was all that raised an uneasy thought, or pressed with heaviness upon his heart. With respect to his fate one wish was predominant in his mind, and in his last hours he sent for Horatio Delamere, who obeyed his summons with pangs like those that separate the soul and body.

When he arrived at Dolgelly Castle, he was unfortunately shown into the very saloon where the fatal act had been committed which had deprived Lady Dungarvon of life, and made him the most miserable of created beings. His sensations whirled his brain almost to frenzy, as he beheld a portrait of Adeline suspended over the sofa, in the very dress in which he had last seen her; the expression of the countenance was mournful; and as he gazed upon it, he fancied the lips moved, and the eyes reproached him; he turned away from the picture with horror; shuddering, he sunk upon the sofa, but from this resting place torturing remembrance instantly drove him; he started up, while cold drops of perspiration hung upon his forehead.

"Here," exclaimed he, "here I enjoyed the most exquisite bliss; for a little moment I enfolded in my arms the loveliest of women; I felt the delicious throbbings of her heart – that heart how inestimable: too soon was I roused from the dream of rapture, too hastily the vision of delight faded, to renew no more. Oh! what since then have I endured – and yet I live, grief cannot break a heart so hard as mine. The reproaches of Adeline still sound in my ears, they press upon my memory with accumulating anguish; I see her despairing look. Oh! misery, she is dead – the virtuous Adeline, though for a moment subdued by love, could not survive dishonour. Oh! she was chaste, was pure; thy soul, dear angelic Adeline, was the unpolluted temple of honour, spite of thy single error. My friend too, the generous confiding Henry, here on this very spot despoiled him of that peace which in this world shall never again be his; my crime deprives the cherub Owen of his father. I shorten the thread of his existence; but he is hastening to Adeline, to the abodes of everlasting happiness, while I, having made their child an orphan, shall, like the first murderer, wander despised of men, abhorred of myself. Oh! that the Everlasting had not fixed his canon against self-slaughter, then might my own hand free me from the accuser within, silence the upbraidings of conscience, and in the oblivious darkness of the grave bury my guilt and misery."

The entrance of a servant to summon him to the presence of Lord Dungarvon interrupted and put an end to his ravings; he cast a despairing look on the portrait of Adeline, and followed in silence. Henry was seated on a couch, supported by pillows, in Adeline's dressing room. A hectic flush had given to his cheek a more than mortal bloom, and his eyes shone with uncommon brilliancy. Lady Dungarvon's favourite plants and flowers were ranged near him, many in full blossom seemed as if expanding their glowing beauties ready to strew his corpse.

Pale, trembling, and covered with confusion, he approached the invalid, who said in a low tremulous voice, "Delamere, heaven has listened to my ceaseless supplications; I am going to Adeline." Horatio covered his face with his hands, and sunk on his knees before him.

"Kneel only to thy God," said Henry solemnly, "rise, be calm, and listen to me; I sent not to reproach you, no, all earthly resentments are subdued in me; I sent for you to restore peace to your bosom, to reconcile you to yourself – to repeat to you the assurance that the past is all forgiven."

"Generous noble-minded Henry," replied Delamere, "thou mayest with more than mortal goodness pardon, but while memory lives, never, no never, can I forgive myself."

"Thou wert," said Lord Dungarvon, "the friend of my early youth, valued and preferred before a train of gay companions. I loved you, Horatio. I confided in you – "

"And I became a villain. Oh! God," exclaimed he, "I basely, treacherously betrayed that confidence. I became a fiend."

"Forbear thy self accusations," continued Henry, "and listen to me. – Absolute perfection poor mortality can never reach. In all but that one point thou hast been all that man should be; noble, generous, liberal, and sincere. In thy situation, seduced by resistless beauty, ensnared by imperious love, I might have been deaf to the voice of honour, I might have forgot my friend: in the grave all sense of injuries will moulder, and in according mercy to thy offence, I trust I shall obtain it, when this mortal evil is shuffled off, and I am judged, even to the death and forehead of my sins." Horatio Delamere sobbed audibly.

"Nay spare thy grief," resumed Henry, "and rather rejoice that my sufferings are nearly at a close. I sent for thee to give thee an opportunity of repairing the wrong thou hast done me; to prove if thy affection for Adeline was perishable as her beauty, or whether it survives the triumph of the grave."

"Go on," said Delamere. "What is it you can ask that I shall not gladly, willingly perform?"

"Horatio," said Lord Dungarvon, raising himself up from the pillows on which he had reclined, "as thou art a man, answer me sincerely. Remember it is a dying friend that questions thee, one who in a few short hours will bear thy words to an eternal record; answer me truly, dost thou love me?"

"Yes," said Horatio, firmly; "yes, most truly – so may heaven remit or punish my offences."

"Then," continued Lord Dungarvon, "attend my last request: – My child, Delamere, Adeline's boy, my little cherub Owen, the lovely infant, image of her so much adored, when his unfortunate parents moulder into dust, wilt thou protect him; wilt thou be the guardian of his youth; wilt thou be a father to the son of thy friend, of her who died, Horatio, with a mind unsullied by a crime, save that alone of loving thee too well? Say, wilt thou accept this dear, this sacred trust?"

"I will," replied Delamere, fervently raising his eyes to heaven, "and as I faithfully perform it, may I be punished or rewarded in the world to come."

"Enough," said Lord Dungarvon. "I am satisfied. Thou art again my friend, come to my arms while I have strength to fold thee."

Horatio Delamere rushed to his embrace; they wept, they hung upon each other, but the mortal powers of Henry, already nearly exhausted, were unequal to this transport; his eyes grew filmy, his nerves slackened, and the numbing hand of death pressed heavily on his heart. Owen was brought to take his last farewell of his expiring father; he repeatedly blessed him; many times he kissed his rosy cheek, and at length consigned him to the care of Horatio Delamere.

Almost in his last moments Lord Dungarvon spoke the cheering words of consolation to his disconsolate domestics, whom he told he had in his will provided for; "And for you, my good friend," said he, addressing Ned Ratlin, "I have taken care for your comfort; while you live, Dolgelly Castle will be your harbour."

Ned tried to speak with a steady tone, but it was an unsuccessful effort, and he at last blubbered out, "One sail, your honour, will serve to wind us both up in. You was my sheet anchor: when your cable is coiled up, why the same signal that commands you to steer for a better world will find me ready to sail in company." Lord Dungarvon was visibly affected at the honest expression of his attachment, and when the servants were dismissed, he particularly recommended the old disabled seaman to Horatio: growing faint, he requested to be removed to the balcony. Here, as his languid eyes followed the moon over the blue arch of heaven, he said, his voice growing every moment fainter, and his respiration more difficult: "Ever in the open air, as my wandering eyes viewed the magnificent structure above us, and the millions of gems that glitter in the stupendous concave, my mind has thought of the littleness of human grandeur, the insignificance of all sublunary greatness, and my heart has glowed with more gratitude, more elevated devotion towards the omnipotent creator of this brilliant arch, as I have thought, if so much splendour and beauty is permitted to human vision, what must be the glory of the heaven of heavens." As he spoke, his head gently declined on the shoulder of Horatio Delamere, and he appeared as if he had fallen into a sweet sleep.

"Thou art gone to enjoy, to prove the glory of that heaven," said Delamere; for Lord Dungarvon had expired, without a groan, or a convulsive struggle; his soul gently released itself from its mortal tenement, and flew to 'realms unsullied with a tear.'

Ned Ratlin, silent and heart-broken, followed his youthful patron to the grave: his looks were mournful, but he uttered no lamentations, he shed no tears. In the hall, after the funeral, as he listened to the exclamations of sorrow vented by the weeping domestics, he said his pumps were choked, though his heart had sprung a leak. "Farewell, messmates," said he, shaking them severally by the hand, "I am going a long cruise, and I have hopes that I shall be promoted to a birth in the same frigate with Lord Dungarvon." Ned Ratlin spoke truth, he was going a long cruise; he died in three days after the interment of Henry. Sir Owen Llewellyn's death was a severe shock to the honest tar; but the loss of Lord and Lady Dungarvon was too much for his affectionate heart to bear: old and infirm, he, who had bravely fought the battles of his country, and stood undaunted the appalling strife of elements, no longer strong to contend with sorrow, was obliged to strike, and the domestics of Dolgelly Castle, as they followed him to his last station, bore weeping testimony to the honest unoffending simplicity of his manners, and the goodness of his heart. Sir Griffith Tudor, accompanied by Captain and Mrs. Seymour, returned home a few days after the funeral of Lord Dungarvon. The lively high-spirited Eliza was so much shocked at the melancholy changes which had in so short a time taken place, and so deeply lamented the disastrous fortunes of her early friends, that it appeared to her sick fancy as if she had returned to a spot

"Where nothing,
But who knows nothing, is once seen to smile:
Where sighs and groans, and shrieks that rend the air,
Are made, not mark'd; where violent sorrow seems
A modern ecstasy; the dead man's knell
Is there scarce ask'd, for whom? and good men's lives
Expire before the flowers in their caps,
Dying, or e'er they sicken."

Eliza had suffered hope to plan such scenes of felicity in the society of Lord and Lady Dungarvon that she was unequal to their annihilation; she fell into a nervous complaint, that nearly baffled the skill of the most eminent of the faculty, united with the attention of her fond husband and disconsolate family: it was long before she recovered health, and though she tried change of scene, and the amusements of a variety of fashionable watering places, her spirits never regained their former hilarity. The names of Henry or Adeline were never mentioned without tears; her affection for Owen was of the tenderest character, for all the love she had felt for his lamented parents seemed to centre in him.

The sight of Dolgelly Castle threw her into agonies, and for a length of time her carriage was driven to Carnarvon by a circuitous road, for her mind tremblingly alive to all the tender remembrances of friendship so fatally dissolved, could not bear to pass a spot where she had enjoyed so much felicity with those dear friends who now inhabited the narrow house. Lady Tudor's real illness, from which she had slowly recovered, considerably lessened the *en bon point* of her person in the terrors of actual indisposition; she began to consider the sinfulness of affecting complaints she did not feel, and she made a serious resolution never on any occasion, however favourable to the display of female delicacy and timidity, to counterfeit another hysteric fit; and this resolution was confirmed by the malady of Mrs. Seymour; for Lady Tudor by nature weak in intellect, and grossly superstitious, when she beheld the trembling frame and distressed state of her daughter, considered it as the visitation of Heaven, and that her sins were being punished in her child. Impressed with this idea, her dressing room was cleared of physical herbs and quack medicines; and Sir Griffith Tudor had the pleasure of seeing surfeit-water, sal volatile, valerian-water, hartshorn, and asafœtida, mingled with the waters of an adjoining stream.

The late melancholy occurrences at Dolgelly Castle that so rapidly followed each other were not without their salutary effects on the temper of Sir Griffith; he became far less boisterous in his manners, and more patient of contradiction, impressed with the awful reflection that his friends were only departed a little time before him to that world where he also would be obliged to render up a true account of how he had conducted himself in this. Mrs. Hugh Montgomery obliged the wishes of her uncle by presenting her husband with a fine boy, who was, agreeable to his request, named after him plain Gabriel, as he protested he should never be able to remember fine quality names. On this joyful occasion an ox was roasted whole, and several hogsheads of ale distributed to the neighbouring peasantry, while the village bells rang merrily; and bonfires, and various useful presents made to the poor cottagers round, spoke the goodness and joy of Gabriel Jenkins's heart, who insisted in being at the whole of the expense for the christening of his godson. Lady Percival and her mother were the only persons whose congratulations came from the lips unprompted by sincerity of heart. Lady Percival felt envy, rage, and mortification, while she reflected that her brother's son would in all human probability inherit her husband's title, and be also enriched by the wealth she had so improvidently thrown away on a worthless unfeeling man, who had not only by the assumption of specious manners and insinuating arts, wheedled her into trusting him with the whole of her fortune, but had disappointed all her expectations, and thwarted all her wishes. Mrs. Montgomery underwent her full share of vexation; because not feeling old, and still looking handsome, her son Hugh had, contrary to her desire, been so *perdigiously* rude, so amazingly unthinking and undutiful, as to make her in her forty-sixth year a grandmother. Mr. and Mrs. Hugh Montgomery,

"Attun'd to happy unison of soul,
To whose exalting eyes a fairer world
Of which the vulgar never had a glimpse
Displays its charms; whose minds are richly fraught
With philosophic stores, superior light,
And in whose breasts enthusiastic burns
Love which the sons of interest deem romance."

They, happy in themselves, content with all around them, rejoiced to think that the sex of their child so little important, was a source of felicity to the loved and respected Gabriel Jenkins, who frequently told Rosa that the boy had quite and clean twisted her nose on one side, for that he should make his godson heir to every farthing he was worth in the world; this declaration by no means delighted the ears of Miss Jenkins, who though amply gifted with the goods of fortune, thought her brother might have made some reserve in her favour in case she should outlive him; and she began now more bitterly than ever to repent that she had not taken the trouble to rein in her imperious temper, and restrain her clamorous tongue before her late admirer Mr. Williams, who in spite of his little nose, short legs, and cool deliberating manners, was not so very despicable a person, particularly when the war and the scarcity of men were considered, and to have been mistress of Woodland Cottage, nothing higher to be obtained, would certainly have been a state infinitely better than that of perpetual celibacy of single blessedness; but her reflections came alas too late. Mr. Williams overlooked her superior charms and attainments; the pert saucy rosy-cheeked dairy maid had so wound herself into her master's good graces, had obtained such influence, had made herself so useful, that he often in her hearing, to the total extinction of her hopes, declared there was nothing in the world so desirable as for a man to make himself agreeable and comfortable, and he was sure that never could be the case when a poor fellow had the misfortune to be tied to a wife, who had a fiery tyrannical temper, and a brawling tongue.

In Sir Edward Percival the prophecy of Gabriel Jenkins was literally fulfilled, exactly as he predicted: from being a man of style and fashion, a buck, a spendthrift, a prodigal, and a libertine, he had become mean, parsimonious, an absolute miser; his *aura sacra fames* swallowed up every other passion, and he, who had but a very few years before considered gold as dirt, had only valued wealth as it enabled him to gratify his licentious inclinations, and pursue the career of folly: he who with a wanton hand had profusely wasted thousands, now absolutely trembled to part with a guinea to purchase the common necessaries of life. With the most abstemious and rigid parsimony, he enabled himself to clear all the mortgages from his several English estates, that the unbounded extravagance of his youth had heavily encumbered, and was hoarding money, which Gabriel Jenkins would laughingly say his godson would enjoy.

Frequently the melancholy Delamere leads his youthful charge to the monument of his ill-fated parents, and while he sheds the tears of mingled love and friendship, of grief and repentance, he enlarges on their virtues, and tells the attentive Owen as much of their sad history as he can confide to him without injury to the reputation of his mother, and rendering himself a monster in his eyes. To the end that Owen may not be unacquainted with the manners of the world, the Honourable Mr. Delamere sometimes mixes with the gay and fashionable part of mankind, but even to the circles of pleasure the pale phantoms of Lord and Lady Dungarvon pursue him; and from the noisy scenes of bustle and dissipation he hurries to the sublime mountains of North Wales, to vent in the dark woods that surround Dolgelly Castle the anguish of his heart; there hurrying along the winding paths he endeavours to fly from retrospection, from himself; or stretched beneath an o'er shadowing cypress, watches the wind wave its melancholy branches, or sweep in mystic whispering o'er the dark green grass, while with disordered imagination he sees the thin forms of Adeline and Henry flit before him, and vows to devote his days to Owen.

In the meridian of his days, eminently gifted by nature and fortune, Horatio Delamere is a living proof that even in this life Heaven punishes the indulgence of criminal inclinations; of the wide devastation the slightest deviation from the path of rectitude may spread around, and that the contagious influence of a single error may involve the health, the peace, the happiness of the innocent: his waking hours are devoted to sad regret; his sleep is harrassed with distressing visions, his conscience loaded with the dreadful reflection that his ungoverned passions had destroyed the two persons he loved best on earth; his woe-worn countenance evincing that only the truly virtuous can be truly happy.

Lady, throw not down the volume in disgust, deny not to the frailty of Adeline thy commiseration and thy tears; be merciful, and say not in the proud security of unassailed chastity, I would not have acted thus. Be doubtful of thyself, examine thine heart, explore its secret recesses; perhaps thou wilt find some tender woman's weaknesses; confide not therefore in thine own strength, depend not on thine own fortitude, but remember with humility that *Every one has Errors*. Bend then the suppliant knee humbly before thy Maker, pray never to be placed in such a situation, never to be so tempted. Guard well each avenue to your heart, stifle the first symptoms of a lawless inclination, so shall your days glide pleasantly away, the pitiless taunt of scorn shall not wound your ear, the consciousness of error shall not lacerate your bosom, but you shall surely feel that innocence is happiness.

ABOUT HONNO

Honno Welsh Women's Press was set up in 1986 by a group of women who felt strongly that women in Wales needed wider opportunities to see their writing in print and to become involved in the publishing process. Our aim is to develop the writing talents of women in Wales, give them new and exciting opportunities to see their work published and often to give them their first 'break' as a writer. Honno is registered as a community co-operative. Any profit that Honno makes is invested in the publishing programme. Women from Wales and around the world have expressed their support for Honno. Each supporter has a vote at the Annual General Meeting. For more information and to buy our publications, please write to Honno at the address below, or visit our website: www.honno.co.uk

Honno, D41, Hugh Owen Building,
Aberystwyth University,
Aberystwyth, Ceredigion, SY23 3DY

Honno Friends

We are very grateful for the support
of all our Honno Friends.

For more information on how you can
become a Honno Friend, see:
https://www.honno.co.uk/about/support-honno/